Jewel Sowers
A Novel

by

Edith Allonby

Double 9
BOOKS

Jewel Sowers
A Novel
by Edith Allonby

Copyright © 2024

All Rights reserved.

ISBN: 978-93-62206-30-5

Published by

DOUBLE 9 BOOKS

2/13-B, Ansari Road
Daryaganj, New Delhi – 110002
info@double9books.com
www.double9books.com
Tel. 011-40042856

ABOUT THE AUTHOR

Edith Allonby was an English writer and teacher. (Her surname was occasionally spelled Allanby or Allenby.) She created two novels set on a fictional planet before committing suicide in an attempt to draw attention to her third work. Allonby was born in Cark as the daughter of Joshua Allonby and Jane Deborah Orr Allonby. Her mother died while she was a little child. She attended Whitelands College. Allonby worked as a teacher and schoolmistress at St. Anne's National School in Lancaster. She wrote three novels, Jewell Sowers (1903), Marigold (1905), and The Fulfillment (1905). Frustrated by editors' requests for modifications and the lack of attention her prior novels received, she committed herself by consuming carbolic acid in Lancaster in 1905, at the age of 29. She had obtained three bottles of the poison by sending an aide to buy each one, claiming that it was required for a school lesson. Her suicide note, which concluded with the phrase "I have died to give God's gift to the world with as few stumbling blocks as possible," was extensively circulated, notably in The London Standard and The New York Times. Within months of her death, The Fulfilment was published, with minor editing and annotations added.

CONTENTS

CHAPTER I
AN INTRODUCTION TO LUCIFRAM

In the little planet Lucifram, that spun a brilliant and solitary course among the stars, exchanging annual salutations with them as the waxing and waning of the solar laws brought them out of the void and within hail, the people each and all walked upside down. The trees were upside down, the houses, the churches with their steeples, the palaces, the oceans, rivers, lakes, mountains, animals, and fishes, each and all, reversed our own conception of mundane propriety. Cultivate a patience with the seeming strangeness of this extraordinary planet, even to the reading of this simple book, and let that virtue lead you nearer to another sphere, more to your liking.

There were a few, indeed, upon this sphere who did their best to stand upon their feet. Sometimes they succeeded; but others were bowled down in the struggle and ended by standing once again upon their heads, or lying crushed, paying the debt they owed to Outraged Custom.

The circumference of this sphere was something like two thousand miles. It bulged out towards the north and south, with giant hollows to the east and west. And because *everything* that existed was contrary to our idea of things, all things looked normal.

When Nature and architecture combine to alter things, making them contrariwise, as people call it, what wonder if morality and all ethics blend with the custom?

To begin with governments and kingships. Unlike those upon a two-legged basis, a king was never chosen for his worth, but for his frailties. He was chosen to strew the path of his subjects with flowers which all might pick like little children out at play, and then would quarrel over.

Alas! To be a king in the planet Lucifram! That little planet topsy-turvy. Here, though a ruler might have the will of a Hercules to turn a somersalt and land upon his feet, some diviner instinct calling him to that, the pigmies around him pinned him with millions of tiny threads, an anchorage whereby to hold his head safe to the ground. Threads worked in gold! Held for the wonder of the multitude.

So for the kings. The Gods of all the stars looked down on them. They heard those faint sighs of weakness—those breathings after higher things—and pitied some, and smiled at others. And though in the topsy-turvy synagogues and churches the people prayed for them, no prayers reached heaven except those simple few the kings themselves breathed in solitude. Prayers that must travel very, very far, as all prayers must, and which needed the giant strength of great simplicity to bring them to the end of their weary journey.

So for the kings and princes. An arduous task is theirs—bound thus with chains—God only knows how hard! As each insidious little link might whisper, telling its own small share in the universal tale.

In our world we always speak of "Church and State"—a correct and steady way of speaking—but in Lucifram 'tis always "State and Church," and that is why the palaces and kings claimed our attention first.

The Church, composed of temples, synagogues, and priests, jumbled together in luxurious profusion, was dressed and bedecked so finely that the God the people worshipped fell almost out of sight. In their chief temple, in the greatest city, was a three-tailed golden Serpent, coiled around a golden pole above a table decked in red, and set with incense vessels. Dim and mysterious was that holy place, where priests, all flowing and bedecked in golden garments, came each day to bow before the Snake. Its three tails, the gold of them burnished like fire, spread out like fans on high, against a background of mosaic. Below, resting on the altar, was the great head, lying quite still; the genius of ages worked in its cruel fangs and awful eyes. Eyes never closing, jewel-glinting, green and fiery, all-surveying, all-watching. Those terrible eyes lit up the gloom, and compelled men to stand upon their heads as it itself was forced to do. For by the grim and dreadful fascination of those never-closing eyes, unconsciously the worshippers changed to position like to it, tails up, heads down, blinded by their religion.

In this temple the people sat in the big gloomy aisles, each on a little chair with a ledge in front for kneeling, and heard the priest from the pulpit, and the reader from his desk. Awed by the grandeur and the solemn dimness, they bowed and salaamed before the triune tails, hidden from the vulgar gaze by a red silk curtain blazoned in gold. And when the mighty organ rolled and rumbled, and the angel voices of the choir boys rang through the gold-washed rafters, their senses were stirred by some far hidden mystery, and their eyes would dim or kindle as they felt it; only the gleaming eyes within the veil remained unchanged.

Now it was customary for the priests who waited on the Serpent to fast a day each month and marry only once. A layman in Lucifram might wed twice. No priests could marry under forty. For laymen, the age was twenty-five for the first attempt, and forty for the second; that is, for the few who preferred company in their latter years to peace. But though the women, by Act of Parliament, enjoyed the privilege of marrying twice, just as the men did, there were certain things clearly beyond them, they being in Lucifram, as here, the weaker vessels. On those great days whereon the priest drew back the silken curtain and displayed the Serpent, all women were debarred from entering the temple.

And so enough for an explanation and a prologue. Take my hand, descend, and tread on Lucifram!

CHAPTER II
FRIEND AND EXECUTOR

In the capital of Lucifram there is a great park—a city park—planted with trees sown centuries since by the restless winds, when all was peaceful country. To the right stretches the city—work and pleasure, laughter and tears, and perpetual hurry-scurry. All round the park sounds and sights of human life, condensed within a curiously small circle, were in evidence. Silent streets, tall and shadowy, lit by occasional gas lamps, fringed on a brilliant thoroughfare, with omnibuses, cabs, and people hurrying everywhere. Most spacious squares, with fountains and statues, backed by huge buildings, erected both for grace and durability, lay on all sides. The mansions on this side of the park were in many cases of plain exterior. This gave the lie to the magnificence within. On the right side of the park, facing it and running along its entire length, was built the famous Greensward Avenue.

In the centre of the avenue, standing back under the shadow of the high walls of two palace gardens rising on either side, stood a large square house built of black marble. It was built in black, and the blinds were of deep red, the only colour to relieve it. Those were not visible till night came. Thirteen imposing-looking steps lead up to an imposing door, in black polished oak, rarely carved. Two narrow windows in the wall reached down on each side of it. The house consisted of three storeys and a basement, and to the back were pretty and extensive gardens protected by high walls.

The owner of this house was a certain Camille Barringcourt, who had but lately come there, within the last three years. With the exception of servants, he lived quite alone—a bachelor in the land of double marriages.

Now the house in which he lived was very appropriately called "Marble House." It had been built by a millionaire quite recently, despite its old appearance. The reason why it had such an appearance of age was because it had been erected from a spoiled cathedral in the remotest corner of Lucifram, where instead of worshipping the Serpent they worshipped the Toad. It had cost a vast amount of money to cart the marble and oak right over from east to west, but it was done right royally, and the house itself,

from this point of view at least, was very interesting. No sooner was the great mansion completed, and royalty entertained on one single occasion, than the millionaire died. Men and women agreed on this, that his death was at least mysterious. He was found dead in bed. So far as the doctors could tell he suffered from nothing, and had come by no foul play. He had died painlessly, in the big plain bed-chamber containing little else but the desecrated altar of the Toad, with a fac-simile of the Serpent rising above it—a shrine which all good people in Lucifram kept in their private rooms. And so he was buried, and the ladies mourned. He had been generous. And then his will was read.

All his vast wealth was given to charities; all went to charity except the house. That was left "To my friend, Camille Barringcourt, as a slight token of esteem, and in remembrance of the past." That was all. No one had ever heard or seen anything of this friend, and no one knew anything of the past. But lawyers, like detectives, have a way of hunting people up. In a little time it was spread abroad that Camille Barringcourt lived in Fairysky, or at least was staying there, a country which much resembled Italy on the Earth.

It may also be mentioned here that Camille Barringcourt and the lawyer were left executors of those vast charities.

The first thing about the new-comer's arrival that excited general interest was the advent of six horses. All were black as night, with long tails, fiery eyes, shining coats, and tossing, untamed heads.

Nearly all the little boys in that aristocratic neighbourhood were late for school that morning; or better, never went. Accustomed as they were to beautiful horses, they had never even in their experience seen anything to equal these. The six black horses travelled through the crowded thoroughfares singly led, each by a groom. Their trappings were of a deep red, and no unnecessary weight was placed upon them. The men who led the animals were men who understood their business, and had great patience with their coquettish, curvetting ways. Just as the journey was drawing to a close the traffic in the streets was for the minute stopped. Five of the six horses had passed the crossing, and the last was drawn up close to Lady Flamington's carriage. Whether it was her ladyship's hat (she was one of the best dressed and most beautiful women of the day), or whether her two thoroughbreds were ready to enter into the fun of the thing, and dance a lively impromptu pirouette with the new arrival, it would be hard to say. However, the black steed began a dance, anything but safe in the state of the crowded thoroughfare, and the bays in harness did their best to follow suit. It was a spirited attempt; then the groom for once lost his temper.

"Get up, you devil!" said he. The horse took him literally and reared up, despite his efforts to keep it down, dragging him with it, in its wild, untamable fury. The trampling forepaws struck on the cushions of my lady's brougham. What might have been the result it is impossible to say, for her escape on the other side was cut off by a huge lorry drawn up against her like a wall, but just at that moment a voice fell on the hubbub and the consternation, and the "voice that breathed o'er Eden" on the day of her marriage had never been so welcome to Lady Flamington as that one now. At the same time a hand, the whitest, the most beautiful she had ever seen (so she told her friends after), grasped at the bridle.

"Waugh-o, Starlight—Starlight! Come, then."

The words, the tone, the caressing hand on one side, the firm hand on the bridle, were too much for the four-legged beauty. Won over by more words, more pressure on the hateful bit (even though silver), and more caressing patting on her glossy neck, she came gracefully down to earth once more.

It seemed to Lady Flamington that the stranger had sprung up from nowhere. As a matter of fact, he had sprung from the hansom behind, in which he was following, at almost walking pace, these six prancing treasures. Then just as the traffic was starting again he looked across at her.

"You are not hurt," said he. "I should have been bitterly sorry if that had happened."

For once her ladyship could find no words. She bowed, he raised his hat, the procession moved along. Then she knitted her brows thoughtfully.

"He should have been sorry in either case," she thought, and fell to studying his face in her memory.

Meanwhile the six black horses had turned into Greensward Avenue, where likewise at a quicker rate her ladyship's carriage was progressing.

All the way to the spacious private stables at the rear of the private grounds, Mr. Barringcourt, for it was he, led that most spoiled of all spoilt animals, Starlight. The little boys followed admiringly, till the big doors of the stable-yard closed cruelly upon them.

"That looks like a dook turned undertaker," said one.

Rumour had spread a report that Camille Barringcourt was a twice married gentleman, with a large family.

"How unlike poor Geoffrey Todbrook," said the ladies, and sighed.

But rumour for once was entirely wrong. One bachelor was dead; another succeeded him.

The new arrival settled quickly into his new home. Seeing it was already furnished, that was but natural. His servants were all foreigners, dark, tall, all very unlike the people on this side of Lucifram. Yet there was an inexpressible charm, dignity, and quiet repose about them that delighted and mystified everyone. Among them were some women, parlourmaids, sewing-maids, and housemaids apparently.

Each one of these servants, men and women, dressed in black, faced with deep red. It was a kind of uniform.

Now, a few words are needed as to the personal appearance of the Master himself. In figure he was tall, athletic, graceful, broad-shouldered. His hair was black and short, crisp at the ends, as Lady Flamington noticed when he removed his hat. People called his face "odd." It was dark and swarthy, with a strong forehead, and black eyes which were gloomy and deeply set. The nose was straight, bearing in its lines more sensitive refinement than any other feature of his face.

When he smiled he showed, though not obtrusively, a sparkle of white and even teeth. When Lady Flamington admired the beauty of his hands she was within the right. For strength and suppleness they would be hard to beat, and for whiteness also. This then, in short, was the figure of Camille Barringcourt, come to dispense the charity of his friend of the past; come to settle in Marble House, of Greensward Avenue.

Lady Flamington, some dozen houses off, persuaded her first and only husband to call there, soon after the arrival. He did so, hoping to see the fine black horses she had spoken of. Horseflesh was his hobby. He saw the gentleman, but nothing else in the way of interest, took a sudden fancy to him, and invited him over to dinner on Friday night. The invitation was as suddenly accepted. Sir James went home with some misgivings. He didn't know whether his wife liked swarthy men; she was fastidious. His wife had no objection to them. She was delighted to welcome any of his friends, except turf acquaintances and bookmakers.

On Friday night Mr. Barringcourt came. It was a little formal affair, one or two of the family circle and an intimate friend. The stranger sat beside his hostess for dinner, and they talked commonplaces. At last she turned to him with a pretty grace.

"You have not yet demanded my thanks," said she.

"For what?" he asked.

"You know for what."

"Your thanks would necessitate my apologies."

"I am surprised you never offered them."

"It was unnecessary."

"There I must confess to some curiosity. Do you remember you said to me, 'You are not hurt.'"

"Well?" said he, and smiled—a smile all the more charming as he bent his head to hers.

"Well!" she retorted. "I was hurt; your horse frightened me. To be frightened is to be hurt. Can you dispute it?"

"I never saw anyone stand pain better. Your face was a vision of—of—"

"Of what?" she asked.

"I do not understand your language very well, as yet. I shall improve in it; you must be patient. In a week or two I shall have found the word I need."

"And till then?"

"Learn to be gracious to a poor speaker."

"Ah! But I do not intend to let you off so easily. After telling me I was not hurt, you next proceeded to say, 'In that case you would have been deeply sorry'—you see my memory is good. Now, am I to understand that under the circumstances you felt no sorrow?"

"Most certainly."

"Now we shall quarrel, unless you can explain yourself."

"Is it necessary?"

"You shall discover how much so if you do not explain your meaning instantly."

"Then do not blame me if I sink still deeper into the mire. Under the circumstances, I was not sorry. I had been told on coming to this country I should find all the women forward—most of them ugly—the remainder plain. After three days' looking round me I had come to the same conclusion. Suddenly by the merest chance my eyes lighted on you. Can you wonder I should feel no sorrow?"

She frowned, then laughed, and looked at him.

"Where did you learn this grossest form of flattery?"

"I see your ladyship has no education to appreciate the truth."

"Talk to my husband about horses. I have no more to say to you."

"Is he a lover of horses?"

"Yes. He attends every Race Meet in the county."

Mr. Barringcourt smiled. "That speaks for itself," he said.

CHAPTER III
ROSALIE

Let us pay a call on Cinderella.

Alas! not a Cinderella with a prince and gorgeous clothing, but one without a tongue, or rather, tongue-tied.

Rosalie Paleaf, for that was her name, lived alone with an aunt and uncle. Both her parents were dead. She was pretty, of that fair delicate type called "picturesque." Her hair was of a palish yellow tint, glossy, but straight; her skin was fair and delicate. The eyes were grey, with dark curling lashes, and delicately marked brows. Her nose turned up just the least little bit, the most charming upward, delicate little curve in the wrong direction it would be possible to meet. The corners of her mouth, however, turned down with the saddest, most wistful droop imaginable. In fact, there was only one feature in her face that kept it from becoming most woefully pathetic, and that was the little, inquisitive, life-enjoying nose. To come back to her eyes for finishing touches. Their greyness was very pale. The pupils generally were large, with an equally black rim along the edge of the iris. Inside this rim the colour gradually paled to the pupil, which gave her eyes a curiously bright appearance. And then being tongue-tied! She had nothing she could talk with but her eyes, and so she used them.

Uncle and aunt were very kind to her. Who indeed could help being that? She was the gentlest, kindest creature, harmless and very helpless, with the sweetest face, the happiest manner, and sunniest smile upon occasions.

They were people of moderate circumstances in a very quiet way, and if Rosalie had not the hardest work of the house to do, it was because her aunt always insisted on doing it, with the help of an occasional charwoman. And so, when very young, she learnt to hem, and dust, and do the toasting. Later she got promoted to wiping tea-things, then dinner dishes, and ended as a fully-fledged young housekeeper, ready to bake and cook, darn, and make and mend, to sweep and dust, and do all work that is useful.

Beyond this her education had not progressed. She could read and write, 'tis certain, but very little more. Accomplishments were beyond the means of her relations, and had they not been it would never have struck them a child apparently quite dumb should need such things. So she stayed at home and was happy, except in the company of strangers, when her sad defect made itself felt under their pitying glances of surprise, however well they might try to conceal them.

But a child's happiness often constitutes a woman's misery. As the years passed by Rosalie began to feel her loneliness, her utter incapacity for the work of the world. She felt also something deeper, stronger, more unwordable. It was more real than anything else in her life, yet, because unseen, it was unsympathised with as having no existence. And so, although her happiness was gradually becoming overshadowed, she never fully recognised it till one October evening when she had turned twenty.

To look at Rosalie the spectator would never have taken her for that age. All her life had been spent in one long silent dream—the privilege of childhood.

It was the kind of autumn evening made for thought and sadness. The sky was very clear, with a suspicion of purple in it, and the gold of ages was in the west. As she stood by her bedroom window looking out at it, there came that terrible foreboding of sadness and sorrow that seems to do its best to crush young hearts, though perhaps it only moulds them.

And along with it came a longing for expansion, a weariness of the endless routine, the companionless silence and that nameless thirst after something, she knew not what. How could Rosalie, walking in the mist, having no speech or utterance, explain it even to herself? She wanted something, the purple of the sky suggested something—suggested, nothing more. And from that day forward the nameless longing grew, settling itself within her heart, finding no happier outside quarters. I do not know that she looked thinner or more frail, her physical strength was too great for that. No one beyond herself knew of the longing, and she attributed it all to discontent, and tried to stifle it.

At last one evening she understood. The inordinate longing for speech rushed over her.

But how to manage it? It is all very well to find out what you want to do—but how to do it? There was only one way—only one way, at any rate, that suggested itself to her, and that way was prayer.

Now, her religious education had not been exactly neglected, but Rosalie was one of those heedless creatures who hear a little and invent a great deal.

She had been told with great piety by her aunt of the great golden Serpent, its wonderful power, its relentless cruelty to those who crossed or vexed it, its generosity to those who did as they were told, and from those few rudimentary remarks she had built up a little golden temple of her own, quite an unseen spiritual affair, in which to worship the Supreme Being of Lucifram. She certainly gave to the gorgeous Serpent many qualifications she had never been told it possessed, but what of that? She was but a poor, helpless creature at best. But with a reverent, far-away love she had always worshipped the Serpent, although as a sex she had been given to understand he reckoned her somewhat inferior.

But now, sitting up in bed, there came to her one of those terrible convictions, never to be misplaced, that are in themselves the sheerest madness or the sheerest sanity, that she must get her tongue untied. And the Serpent, being the strongest of all powers on Lucifram, was the likeliest to do it.

Next afternoon at five o'clock saw Rosalie kneeling in the famous temple, her head buried in her hands, praying in the silence as only sincerity and helplessness can pray.

"Oh, Serpent, give me my tongue! Let me talk," said she, a most natural request when coming from a woman.

Then she went home quite comforted, as only the simple can be.

"One does not pray for nothing," she thought "I feel the Serpent heard me."

And that night she was so happy, she did not notice her uncle's troubled look and silent way. She did not mean to be selfish, she was thinking purely of her prayer.

Some weeks went by, and every day she walked to the temple and prayed:

"Oh, Serpent, give me my tongue! Let me talk."

But no answer came to her prayer, and at last she got tired of kneeling down among the empty pews. The building was so big that she felt quite far away, so she picked up her courage and went up the big aisle, right up through the choir stalls to the steps rising towards the altar, hidden by the curtains. It was legitimate for any woman to go so far. She was perfectly within her right. So she went up the steps and knelt down quietly beside the golden railing.

And there she prayed to the unseen Serpent—prayed, and believed it heard her. Then she went home. How near she had been to that Unseen Power! How fervently she had prayed! The Serpent always answered prayer, always looked after the helpless.

On going home her ring at the door was answered by a neighbour with a white face and swollen eyes.

What was the matter?

An hour ago, soon after she went out, her uncle had been brought home after a stroke. Since then he had died, just after the arrival of the doctor.

Rosalie sank back against the lobby wall, her hands by her sides, her eyes filled with horror.

"Your aunt is upstairs in the back bedroom," said the neighbour, who had told the story as quietly as she could, as gently as its tragedy allowed.

Rosalie pulled herself together and went upstairs, trying the bedroom door at the back. It opened, and she was thankful. Her aunt sat in a chair, her head buried in the pillow of the one spare bed. Rosalie went to her and touched her shoulder. The elder woman moved slowly, and then sat up, smoothing her grey hair.

"I've been here long enough," she said dully. "I must go and see to things. Sit here, Rosalie. It isn't for you to be about."

Her dull grief repelled all sad advances. From the time that Rosalie found her lying there cramped against the bed she showed no further signs of weakness, no further signs of giving in, till the funeral was over.

Then when the blinds were drawn up once more, and the November light had flooded the room, she took her foster daughter in her arms and wept as only a broken-hearted woman growing old can weep.

"We went to school together," she said at last, twisting her wet soiled handkerchief around her fingers. After that she scarcely mentioned her husband again.

But now time showed a great difference in the little household, in addition to its greatest loss. Money troubles and worry, of late months thickening ominously, had helped to bring about the sudden end. There were no more happy meals at tea-time, no bread to toast, nothing but the barest, rude necessities of life. For they were poor, so poor that they scarcely knew how to look the future in the face. Both were very helpless.

The elder woman in a few short months had grown old, shrunken, and thin. She tried at times to smile bravely, to take interest in life and neighbours, but life and interest had gone for her in the old playfellow and life love. And more and more each day since her uncle's death Rosalie felt the want of speech. She could give none of that bright assistance that was needed. No better than a living shadow she was bound to go about the house. Yet still she went to the temple to pray in humility and faithfulness.

And then, as the spring came round, she heard vague, disquieting rumours of the little house being shut up. Her aunt was going to live with a married brother, whose wife had little in common with her, and she herself, Rosalie, was to be sent to a Home for the Deaf and Dumb and Blind, a large charitable institution, greatly enlarged and improved upon by the munificence of a dead millionaire, one Geoffrey Todbrook by name. Insufferable thought! To separate her from the only human being she had learnt to love, shutting them each within a dungeon of strangers! "O God! O Serpent!" What of the prayer of months, to give one atom in the multitude the powers of speech? Prayer of presumption! Its punishment the taking away of everything that makes some lives worth living, the precious gift of freedom.

And yet Rosalie set her lips hard, there was no drooping, and went once more, with faith supremely high, but heart all wrong and tortured, to kneel and pray to God within the temple.

CHAPTER IV
THE GOLDEN SERPENT

The afternoon was cold and gloomy, and by the time Rosalie reached the temple the little light that ever came there had quite died away. There were no Americans in Lucifram, no English tourists either, consequently the sacred building from morn to eve was silent as the grave except for matins and for evensong. But evensong was held at seven, and now it was but four.

Rosalie's heart was in that terrible state of aching which approaches physical pain. Speechless, she knew herself quite helpless.

For lack of speech she must be separated from one who had suddenly grown more helpless than herself, one whom she could not bear to part with, one who had grown accustomed to her great defect, and had never labelled on the door those words: "Home for the Blind—the Deaf—the Dumb—Incurables."

"Once I get inside there I am dumb for ever," she cried to herself, as she stumbled up the darkening aisle. "Oh, I cannot go—I cannot! I want to live like other people. To be free—free—free!"

And so she knelt down beside the altar railings, and buried her face in her hands against its golden bars.

"Oh, Serpent, let me speak! Give me a tongue like other people have. I cannot go to that asylum—I cannot really. I cannot live without my aunt. We are all in all to each other. What good am I if I remain a speechless log? I might as well be dead."

No answer. Darkness and silence. That was all. The impenetrable hardness of it sank to Rosalie's heart. Suddenly she got up and looked round cautiously, with pale face and dark-rimmed eyes. There was no noise. Nothing moved in the empty building save herself. Silent and trembling, she took a step forward inside the railing, then another, and her hand touched the crimson curtain. Again she looked around, assured herself again that she was quite alone, silently drew back the heavy fold and stepped within. The lights upon the altar, burning by day and night, changed the dull gloom to brightness. Her wandering, awe-struck gaze fell full upon the Serpent, its head and jewelled eyes all shining underneath the slowly swinging lights.

Here, then, was the hidden God that all things worshipped. This was the God who punished some, rewarded others, and wore the creeds of ages on its three-pronged tail. Her eyes were dazzled by the brilliancy, but the Serpent's wisdom gleaming from those curious eyes attracted her.

"Give me what I want! Give me what I want!" she whispered, and stretched out her white arms till her hands had clasped behind the Serpent's head. Then she leant forward and pressed her lips against the cruel, hardened, lifeless fangs, and whispered yet again:

"Give me what I want—just so that I may serve you!"

As silently she unclasped her fingers, rising to her feet. She passed down the three steps leading from the altar, and became aware, with beating heart and sudden tumultuous fear, that she had been watched.

For, stepping from the side way, came a stranger, stopping her progress outward to the other side of the veil.

"What is it that you want?" he said.

In his eyes there shone the priceless worth of wisdom's jewels, giving them in their brilliant expression something of the same impenetrable light the Serpent's had.

Rosalie became confused, and mixed the two together. How could she help it, seeing both had come together? But no words were there for utterance. She raised her hand to her mouth, her eyes to his face—eyes that had grown in sadness and in beauty throughout a lifetime—and then she shook her head.

"Dumb?" said he.

She nodded.

"Is that what you came to pray about?"

Again she nodded. She looked up at him, and her eyes sank. After all, it was the secret of a life, for none knew of these daily visits to the temple, and now a stranger had discovered it—the secret which had been guarded so jealously all these years.

"And you come in here to pray often?"

She shook her head vehemently, and pointed outside.

"I see. You stay outside?"

Again she nodded.

Then he held the curtain aside, and she passed out, he following her.

The church without was black.

Rosalie gave a muttered cry of dismay—the building was so large, its pews, and steps, and labyrinths all so intricate. But her companion produced a light that glowed like a thin taper, but burnt with a clearer and a stronger light, and plainly lit the church around them.

"Never trust to the church to give you light," said he whimsically, "unless, as now, you penetrate to the Holy of Holies!"

Rosalie smiled; she felt it was but polite, unaccustomed as she was to strangers.

Together they walked down the long aisle, and once she stole a glance up at him sideways, with great curiosity, to see what he was like. But the stranger was looking at her, and she bent her head downward again. She evidently did not possess the gift of sweet unconsciousness of self.

"I presume you wished to come away?" he said at the end of their journey, before he opened the heavy doors.

She nodded.

Then he laid his hand upon her shoulder.

"The Serpent must be very cruel and hardened if he withstand such a prayer as that you offered."

There was more amusement than pity in his voice and expression. Rosalie felt, but did not understand it. Never had anyone in her narrow life been able to put so much expression into a mere hand-touch. In gratitude she could have taken and kissed it many times.

They passed out on to the high steps leading from the temple. The rain was coming down in torrents. The street lamps glistened through it, and the passers-by were infrequent.

"How are you going home?" he said. The outside world seemed to have separated them.

She pointed to her feet.

"Walking? Well, hurry and don't get wet. It would be a pity to spoil the prayer by leaving no time for its fulfilment. Good-night!"

Then he moved away a step or two, and she stopped to put up her umbrella. Suddenly, however, he turned round, and came with quick strides toward her.

"See, here is my card. When you have made headway with the Serpent, and received an answer to your prayer, come and see me!"

And he scribbled on the back of the card "Admit Bearer," and then handed it to her, once more leaving her standing on the steps.

Then Rosalie, having succeeded in getting up the umbrella, and gathering up her skirts, turned in the direction of home. It was a walk of about twenty minutes, and all the way she thought of the stranger, of his interesting face, deep eyes and mellow voice, his hand laid so kindly on her shoulder. She remembered, also, that sudden perceptible change when outside the church, a mixture of harshness and coldness and pride, more shown in his manner than his words.

"I wonder what he was doing inside the curtain?" she thought. "Perhaps he had gone there to pray like me. I hope I did not disturb him." Then she sighed. "He looked a rich man, and he could say whatever he wanted to. There could be nothing he was wanting half so much as I."

On reaching home she was met by her aunt. As soon as they were seated at the frugal tea, the lady explained that a Mr. Ellershaw, an acquaintance of her dead husband, had called that afternoon to see her. On hearing how matters stood, and the separation that was imminent, he had told her of a post of caretaker he knew to be vacant, where the work was to look after a large building in the city let out in flats to different business men. There would be a certain amount of work to do in connection with this—and he did not know whether either of them would care for such a post; but it was there if they wished. It would ensure them living together, four rooms in the topmost storey. Rosalie looked across her tea-cup and nodded her head eagerly.

"You like such a prospect?" her aunt asked quietly.

She nodded again.

"It will be very hard work, and I am not as strong as I used to be."

Rosalie held out her hands and looked at them triumphantly. Then she pointed to herself, and smiled.

"You think you could undertake some of it?"

So together they wrote a letter accepting the post, and a week later left their old home, with all its memories and associations, to settle in a fifth storey dwelling amongst the skylights.

Rosalie felt her prayer in part was answered. They were not to be separated after all. Hard as the work might be, it meant freedom and the company she loved. She was content, went to the temple, knelt humbly and returned thanks. Then she went on praying for a voice with a faith born of simplicity and her own idea of God.

One day a priest found her praying there. He inquired the cause. Like the stranger, he was not long in finding it. He put his hand upon her head, and blessed her in the name of the Serpent's three tails. Then he went back to the priests' lodgings, and kept his story for supper. He was a jolly man, of the earth earthy, and his idea of the Serpent was that his golden coils were lucrative. The priest was not bad-hearted; he was simply mediocre. But he had a sense of humour—and who, indeed, but the soured and stupid have not?—and the idea of a girl kneeling by the altar railings (he had never seen her, as on that one unique occasion, step beyond) praying persistently to be allowed to talk when plainly she was physically beyond it tickled his sense of funniness. He laughed and shook till the tears ran down his face.

"And she believes it—*that's* the biggest joke," he cried. "Believes that if she prays long enough the Serpent will weary or turn merciful, and fulfil her prayer."

"According to our history of the past, with its wonders and miracles, that is not so impossible as it seems," said one, more thoughtfully.

"She'd best jump back a hundred year or two, and cap one miracle by another, then," remarked a third.

"What did you say to her, James Peter?" asked a fourth.

"Oh, I blessed her, and prayed to the Serpent to look serious, and the request was granted. 'Twas a miracle on a small scale, I can assure you. I could have roared right out."

"What is she like to look at?" put in a fifth.

"Pretty—sad-looking—just the sort of woman to get an idea. That is the sort we can't afford to quarrel with. They tip so handsomely on Sundays."

"Little or tall?"

"Oh, tall! Medium, at any rate. Couldn't smile if she tried. Sacred liver of the Serpent! What a sermon for one of you fellows with a love of sentiment to preach on Sunday."

"Wait till the woman is made whole, and sitting in the congregation. Then our fortunes are secured," said another drily.

And in this respect the priests of the Serpent were very different from our own. Amongst themselves they never acted the hypocrite—the heathen idolaters!

So next day, when Rosalie went to pray, one or two passed in and out silently to behold the phenomenon. After a time they grew accustomed, and took no further notice of her. After all, a woman might as well spend her time in an attitude of humble devotion. Experience generally proved those to make the best sort of wives.

Rosalie and her aunt had been established a little over six months in the new home, and the work was so hard and unaccustomed that it was beginning to tell on both of them.

The older woman was little better than a breakdown before she came, and gradually without much complaint, but growing silence, she sank into the bed of weakness more. It was a sickness from which she never rose.

She had been too old to face these sudden changes, was not made of the stuff that endures, or not enduring, fights. So then this cloud had only risen in mockery to sink the heavier. Where was Rosalie's prayer of love and thanksgiving?

The last week of her aunt's illness was very strange and unreal to Rosalie—strange and unreal when, after the second funeral within a year, she sat alone in the little empty four-roomed storey.

Her hands, roughened, though not coarsened, by hard work, were clasped between her knees. Her head had sunk forward on her breast, her open eyes saw nothing.

Vaguely she hoped that she might be the next to go, thought of her prayer for speech, and dashed the bitter tears from her dull eyes. What of her prayer? Perhaps to the Serpent it sounded nothing more than clamorous presumption and self-will.

Again she had been offered the shelter of the Home for Deaf and Dumb by those who recognised her sad position. Was she ungrateful? Many poor waifs there were, she knew, in that great city, with none to help them to the scantiest food and shelter.

"I can't believe you're either kind or just, and I won't pray to you any more!" she cried inwardly, jumping up fiercely at last. "I wasn't made to be without a tongue. I wasn't! I wasn't! You haven't the power to give me one; that's what it really is."

But no bricks and mortar fell to punish such an outburst.

"What have I done that I should be left here alone?" she continued. "I want to go along with aunt and uncle. You know I do. I can't live here alone."

But there was no answer. Gradually a calmer spirit came over her, together with a wish to find out that sphinx-like secret that wrapped itself in icy silence.

"What's the good of making me want to talk if you won't let me?" she asked.

Out of the vast silence a voice seemed to shape itself at last.

"Give up! Sacrifice!" it said.

It was such a very beautiful voice, and yet so very cold, that Rosalie shrank from it. Sacrifice was such a heathenish thing! Besides, what was there to sacrifice in the way of a tongue—she hadn't got one, not a serviceable one, at any rate.

"The Serpent's will comes first with all believers," cried the same voice out of the silence.

"I wish we could agree," said Rosalie, with no disrespect, and then fell a-thinking.

Yes. After all, it came to the old, old thing. A clashing of wills—one human, one divine—if such it could be called. And therein lay the only sacrifice that God or the Serpent ever needed. It meant the sacrifice of will.

Slowly and clearly the truth unfolded itself. If her faith were pure and unselfish, she must be willing to give up longing and praying for that which was beyond her, and still love and serve the Serpent even without reward.

And to what path did her duty point? The thankful acceptance of a shelter that was offered, a gentle surrender without bitterness into God's hands. An ending of a prayer He thought fit not to answer.

It meant a great deal to Rosalie. The priest had laughed at her simpleness in expecting the performance of a miracle. Perhaps would all else had they heard it; but to her it was a very real thing, the outcome of real belief, that left a shattered feeling of disappointment when the ending came.

"I thought the Serpent always answered prayer when it was real," she said, and felt suddenly like one moving uncertainly in unknown lands amongst a host of strangers.

The time was drawing round to autumn again, and now that her aunt had been removed, arrangements were being made for her going. Within the week, she had been told, she would go the Home. Those who had interested themselves on her behalf did not like to think of the lonely girl. The doctor who had attended the aunt and uncle had very kindly made it his business to remove all delays, such as often took place for those who were admitted.

Another woman, older and stronger, and more accustomed to the work, was engaged. She had been there for some time before her aunt's death. Rosalie, in this new and quiet mood, recognised the kindness that had been shown to her on all sides. But though she was truly thankful, she could raise no enthusiasm. The next day, when afternoon came, she dressed herself as carefully as her worn clothes would allow, and went once more towards the temple.

But with what different feelings! For two years past she had gone always with the same earnest prayer, with no doubt of its acceptance, and now she was going to give up the prayer and everything that made her life worth living.

It was just such another wet, dull day as that a year ago when, with excess of feeling, she had drawn aside the sacred curtain and stept within the Holy Place.

To-day, as usual, she went and knelt beside the railings. All was growing dark. The same silence, the same utter emptiness, pervaded the temple now, as then. Now, as then, the great longing seized her to pass within the veil. So silently she rose, drew back the curtain stealthily, and stept within. The Serpent's steadfast gaze demanded her first glance. Then she looked round, but perceived no stranger. Assured, she ascended the steps and knelt beside the gorgeous table. With tenderness and love, the outcome of simplicity and pure devotion, she clasped her hands once more about the Serpent's head, kneeling before it.

"I'm sorry," she whispered, her lips close to the terrible mouth. "I made a god of my own tongue instead of you. But now I understand. And, oh! Serpent, teach me the right way to live, and keep me from growing bitter."

Then, as before, she imprinted a light kiss, tender and loving, on the unkissable mouth, and silently bowed her head some minutes on the table.

Then on a sudden Rosalie rose, her eyes wide open, and stared at the golden god. They stared in wonderment, but growing understanding. The light of dawning wisdom was in her eyes.

One minute, two minutes, three, passed away. She turned round suddenly, emerged into the church, dark now as once before about a year ago. A light was in her hand; she cared not how she came by it, but partly knew.

A priest from one of the choir stalls was watching her, with a feeble candle in his hand.

He called out "Treason! Blasphemy!" to see a woman thus emerge from behind the sacred curtain. It was James Peter.

Rushing forward, he slipped over a footstool, and fell down heavily. His light was extinguished. Down the vast aisle, with the lightness of a spirit, Rosalie ran. Her eyes were laughing, a flush was on her once pale cheek.

James Peter, rising, followed her. He puffed and groaned at every priestly step.

But when the door was open she turned and nodded to him in the distance. The door closed. He was in darkness. He had followed solely upon her light.

Not till the lights were brought for Evensong did he extricate himself from the toils of the massive building. Then he told his tale.

"I tell you she turned round at the door and called to me 'Bon soir, monsieur! Adieu!'" he cried for the third time to his companions.

"Good Lord! What does it mean?" said one.

"Was she not dumb?" asked a second.

"As dumb as the Serpent!" replied James Peter. "She went into the Holy Place, and is cured."

"A woman in the Holy Place!"

"Yes! I called 'Blasphemy!' but the damned footstool tripped me! Had it not been for that I had caught her and brought her up before the great High Priest."

"A footstool tripped you!"

"Don't speak so sneeringly, brother Thomas John. I said a footstool tripped me."

"And you lost the woman?"

"What could I do without a light?"

"Strike matches."

"I followed her eyes till the door closed, and forgot about them. Besides, not being a smoker, I never carry any."

"Did you say you found a woman in the Holiest Place?" asked others, crowding round.

"I did not find her there, I saw her coming out."

"Coming out! And never stopped her?"

"No!"

"But we must find her. What is her address?"

"I don't know. What's the punishment when we have found her?"

"In olden times it was to have her tongue torn out by the roots."

"But the Serpent had just given her one, I tell you."

"Nowadays, I expect, the punishment will be modified. Strict silence on penalty of death, maybe."

"But if the Serpent has given her a tongue, who then dare take it away?"

"How has the Serpent given her one?"

"I tell you, before she was dumb."

"Impossible! No woman was ever so afflicted—worse luck!"

"I tell you she was dumb, and is cured. She said to me at the door, 'Bon soir, monsieur. Adieu!' Very pretty words," and he mimicked the tone and gesture.

"This is sheer madness. There is no sense in the words!" cried another.

"Is it necessary for women to speak sense?" asked James Peter.

All the others laughed. He looked dangerous. And so they talked, and all gesticulated. But the mistake was on the part of James Peter—in part, at least.

He never heard the lady speak. It was his own imagination which coined strange words without meaning

CHAPTER V
THE MASTER

Rosalie outside the temple never paused, apparently, to think. She did not take the direction of her old home, but flew on as if scarcely touching the ground towards that portion of the city where lay the mansions and the ancient park. The usually crowded streets were almost deserted, the rain kept wayfarers within doors. Nothing hindered her rapid movements onward.

Greensward Avenue was one long vista of shining pavements, dripping trees, and glistening street lamps. Here and there brighter lights shone from the entrances to houses. But on Rosalie sped till she came to the central house, which stood a little back behind high iron palings.

The door had two leaves, and opened inward from the centre. There was a vestibule beyond, and then another double door of thickest glass, polished and cut to shine like diamonds. Above the hall door a deep red lamp was burning, which cast its light well out into the street. The only furniture within the vestibule was a broad chair of oak, and a massive umbrella stand all carved with hideous faces, very ancient, no doubt, but not exactly beautiful.

Rosalie noticed these as she stood on the top step touching the bell, and because each face was very fascinating she would have continued looking at them had not the inner door opened upon the instant.

It was not a creaking door. It opened noiselessly and swiftly, and in the doorway stood a man.

He had none of the superabundant dignity generally associated with the servants in rich houses. His hair was not powdered, his dress was plain, and black.

Rosalie, so swift and impetuous until now, came to a standstill. She looked at him, and he at her. She had no voice with which to explain her errand, and suddenly remembered her only chance of admittance there was the card. For it was to Marble House she had come, the house of the man whom she had met in the temple just a year ago.

"What is it that you want?" he asked. These were the exact words with which she had been greeted by the master.

Then she remembered the card was hidden away in the bosom of her dress in a little silken bag she had made in an idle moment for it months ago. She must produce it, that was evident, and trust to Providence to do the rest. She turned round towards the many-headed umbrella stand, and began to extricate the card of introduction. The man stood there waiting, and when she turned round, flushed and flurried, holding the card, and glancing at him suspiciously to trace the smile upon his lips, she found nothing there, not even surprise. He evidently was old enough to be beyond it

Rosalie pointed to the back; he read it, then motioning her to sit in the chair facing the hydra-headed umbrella stand, went in once more behind the polished doors and closed them after him.

The door opened silently again before long.

"Come this way," said the low, serious voice.

The doors swung to behind them. They entered upon a large square hall. It was not brilliantly lighted, and the farther end was dim and scarcely discernible. But every thing was rich and massive, and highly polished. It reminded her in some indescribable way of the temple she had just left. Carved oak chairs, just as those seen in the sacred building, lined the walls, standing round in a perfect square, except where interrupted by some other article of furniture. These chairs seemed to be endless.

As Rosalie passed along she became accustomed to the dimness, and noticed from this farther end a spiral staircase ascending to the upper floor. It was built in polished oak, and went round and round in a way that reminded her of the Serpent's coils. It led to a gallery that overlooked the hall on all sides.

Three double glass doors of the same peculiar lustre as the entrance (which made the fourth) led out of this hall, one on each side, one being beyond the staircase.

Her companion passed through that door to the left, and she followed him. They came upon a corridor, and stopped before the last door on the left-hand side. Her guide knocked, then opened it. There was no name to give; Rosalie had no tongue to speak, no card to show. Then the door closed again, and she found herself in the presence of the man whom she had come to seek.

He was sitting by a table reading. A fire was burning in the hearth near by. A high shaded lamp stood on the ground beside him. The floor was thickly carpeted, the walls were lined with books from floor to ceiling, one other door led from the room.

The Master looked up as she entered, then got up, pushing the book away.

"So you have come," he said. He came forward and held out his hand.

Rosalie, trembling and uncertain, returned the hand-shake, nodding.

"What! you cannot speak yet?"

She shook her head, but as he was withdrawing his hand she clutched it eagerly, unconscious of anything but this one little sinking straw of hope.

This time he looked at her more closely. "What is it?" he asked.

She raised her other hand to her throat and mouth, then pointed to him, her eyes full on his face.

"I'm not the Serpent," he answered, and he shook his head and tried to disengage his hand.

But Rosalie's fingers tightened with a fierceness and determination altogether foreign to her. Her cheeks flushed, her eyes flashed angrily; she gave one little imperious stamp with her foot.

The Master looked at her and smiled—a smile that travelled from his eyes to the corners of his mouth.

"I see. You do not intend to go till I have performed an—an impossibility?"

Rosalie nodded in all seriousness.

"It is the gift of speech you're wanting?"

She nodded.

"It's very dangerous; leads people into all kinds of indiscretions."

She shook her head vehemently.

"You think you differ from the commonality?"

But Rosalie neither shook her head nor nodded. She only looked up at him with no other expression in her eyes except dumb entreaty.

"Come to the light," said he, "and try to look less ghostly. After all, if you can't be cured you can't. You're brave enough to stand that, aren't you?"

Again she nodded, still looking at him.

He pushed the shade of the lamp up. "Now open your mouth," he said.

Obediently Rosalie did as she was told.

"Why, you've got a tongue!" said he, bending his brows, and stooping down to her. "Can't you move it?"

But Rosalie could not. It was complete paralysis of the muscles evidently.

"Come with me, and I'll see what I can do."

He led her through the other door into another room. The walls of this place were lined with chests and cupboards with glass fronts, containing curious instruments. In the centre was a long table. The room was also fitted up with chairs such as dentists use, and a marble washing basin fitted with water pipes, hot and cold.

Yet when the light was turned on the general effect was cheerful. Rosalie found it so, at any rate, for renewed hope was springing in her heart. She sat down upon the chair he drew for her, and watched him whilst he went to the cupboard and brought out something shaped like a very long darning needle. It was thick at one end, very fine and pointed at the other. Then from another shelf containing flasks of glass polished and cut he took a liquid shining like silver, and poured some into a tiny crucible. With these he came back to her and placed them on the table. Then he looked at her, smiling.

"This will hurt you very much," he said; "but you asked for it, so you will have to go through with it."

Anyone but Rosalie would have noticed that the expression of his face was not particularly kind. But she noticed nothing. She leant back against the head-rest; he placed his hand upon her eyes. After that they were too heavy for her to open them. She opened her mouth instead.

It was a curious kind of pain, if pain it could be called. Never in the whole of her life had she ever felt anything so soothing. She could not tell how long the sensation lasted, but it ceased very suddenly. Then although her eyes were closed she felt (this was the curious part of it) a strong light shining into her mouth, right back to the roots of that so far silent tongue. It was a light that had the power to heal and strengthen, and for a long, long time it played upon every unused nerve and delicate muscle. At last all was over; the master laid his hand upon her eyes again and opened them.

"Now," said he, "the miracle has been performed. Are you satisfied?"

From long custom Rosalie nodded.

"You must speak," he answered, laughing, "if but to show your appreciation of the gift."

"Thank you," she said, quite perfectly, with just a little break in the word that took nothing from its sweetness.

"Did you find the pain very bad?"

"I nev-er felt it."

"Never felt it?" he repeated. "Give me your hand."

But her pulse was even, and he frowned.

"Where did you come from when you came to me?" he asked, bending his eyes down to hers with a keen, penetrating glance.

"I came from the temple."

"From the prayer?"

"Yes."

"Then you—" but here he stopped. "I see," he continued, but in reality he didn't.

"Did you expect I should be hurt?" she asked.

"I can hardly believe you were not."

"But I should have screamed. I made no sound."

"That was scarcely possible. For my own part, I always think it best to guard against screams, they are so unhelpful and unnecessary."

Now Rosalie looked at him, with eyes just as keen and penetrating as his had been.

"Why do you stare at me?" he asked, smiling.

"To see if you are disappointed."

Here he laughed.

"Be careful. Your tongue is getting rather out of bounds already."

"I think you would rather have enjoyed my being hurt."

"Well, what can you expect in a country where vivisection is disallowed? One must take what little pleasure one can get."

Here he led the way back into the outer room. When they were both through he turned the key and put it in his pocket.

"I rarely go in there," he said. "Few folks are fool enough to come to me. I have no ambition to become a doctor, and I shun the popularity that hangs upon the quack."

They were both standing by the table now, one on either side. Rosalie's eyes were fixed dreamily on a large glass ink-stand in the centre of the table. She was beginning to feel indescribably tired. There was nothing very wonderful in this, the operation had lasted longer than she was aware. But though tired, she was feeling remarkably light-hearted, longing to get outside and give herself two or three decided pinches to become convinced she was awake, and that this great good fortune of her prayer had at last come to her.

But over and above the tired feeling and the unreality came gratitude to her deliverer. The thought of this made her suddenly raise her eyes and look across at him.

Certainly his face was very proud, and the shadows lurking underneath his eyes and at the corners of his mouth gave it a dark, forbidding expression. It was not altogether pleasant.

"The feature I like best is his nose," thought Rosalie. "The one that frightens me most is his mouth; the one that most interests me is his eyes."

"You have been very kind to me," she said. "Is there any way in which I can pay you back?"

But he shook his head.

"I do not think you could give me anything tangible, but perhaps you yourself will be able to suggest something."

Rosalie flushed to the roots of her hair. "I haven't anything," she answered

"Not even a soul?"

"What is that?"

"That part of you which under certain conditions becomes immortal."

"That part of me belongs to the Serpent."

"The Serpent passed you on body and soul to me."

"The Serpent did nothing of the sort," she answered vehemently, if slowly. "I—I—I—"

"You what?"

"I nothing."

His eyebrows came together in a frown.

"Yes," he answered quietly, "there is one way in which you can pay me back. Speak the truth in answering my questions."

"I'll try," said Rosalie meekly.

"Then put an ending to that 'I—I—I—.'"

"I came because I thought it was time. I got a little bit tired of the Serpent."

"Why?"

"Because it never took any notice of me."

"Are you sure?"

Rosalie's curious eyes looked up innocently and met his.

"Does that surprise you very much?"

"I confess that it does."

"Do you know, I'm very tired. If you don't mind, I'll come again to-morrow and talk it over."

But he shook his head, and smiled again.

"I don't think I'll let you go," he said. "Your answers are not very satisfactory. Besides, where is there you can go?"

"Oh, with a tongue one can go anywhere and do anything."

"You think so?"

"Yes."

And here from sheer weariness and exhaustion she slipped down in the arm-chair beside her.

It had been a very hard day, and the ending had told upon her strength. She had not fainted, however, she was only sleeping.

Mr. Barringcourt crossed the room and looked at her very narrowly, even dropping on one knee to examine her features more nearly.

It was a very pale, thin, and tired face he looked at, delicate and fragile, with dark lashes, and faint blue shadows underneath the closed eyes. The backs of her hands were rough, and he took each up and examined it as though he had been a fortune-teller—back and front.

Then he began walking slowly back and forwards through the room. His face, though handsome after a kind, was certainly not of the most prepossessing; and yet in repose his expression was one of weariness and contempt.

"What shall I do with her?" he muttered. "Keep her to prevent blabbing as usual. Keep her and bring her up to talk properly. When she is old enough, or rather fit enough, I'll let her out on a lease long enough to take her to the devil. Always the same! everlastingly the same! coming and going, with nothing to give and everything to ask. Dull to the very core, chattering like magpies, smiling and aping God knows what! Rich and poor, all of them alike. And for some reason best known to myself I stand it. What an excellent patient fisherman I should make!"

Then he sat down again very deliberately in his chair, and drew the book he had been reading towards him, at the same ringing a bell. The same man who had admitted Rosalie answered it.

"Take her away, and see she doesn't get out," said he, without looking up; and the other evidently understood so well that he never asked a question.

CHAPTER VI
NEW EXPERIENCES

When Rosalie awoke next morning, it was with a pardonable sense of bewilderment and estrangement.

Instead of the little bedroom, bare of carpet, and devoid of all furniture, except the poorest and the simplest, she found herself in one that was really palatial.

The bed had deep hangings of red silk, and she was not up to date enough to tear them down as breeding microbes and all things unhealthy. Then by degrees, her eyes travelling beyond the bed, she gradually became acquainted with the other things within the room, washstand, dressing-table, sofa, chairs; and here Rosalie gave a squeal of delight, and jumped out of bed, for there opposite was a wardrobe, as respectable as carved black oak could make it. But it was not the wardrobe that attracted her attention so much as the mirror set full length in its middle door—a mirror larger than she had ever seen before or dreamt about. Rosalie was not vain, but she had always entertained a great longing to see her feet at the same time as her head, and had thought it only a luxury and privilege accorded to the rich. When she had become accustomed to this novel vision she walked over towards the windows. Here, so far as beauty was concerned, a disappointment waited on her. All three of them looked upon a high blank wall opposite. It gave a sense of extreme dulness to the place.

Just then her explorations and discoveries were cut short by a knock at the door, and on it entered a woman carrying a tray holding a cup of tea. Rosalie, who understood nothing of this sort of thing, stared at it and the bearer.

"I'm quite better now, thank you," she said, shaking her head. "I was a little tired last night. I'd rather not have my breakfast in bed, if you don't mind."

"This is not your breakfast," said the other, in a voice so well modulated that many seemingly more exalted might have envied it.

"Oh, what is it?" said Rosalie, standing still with her hands behind her looking at it.

"A cup of tea to help you to dress."

She had the sweetest voice imaginable. Rosalie thought it the saddest she had ever heard.

"I shan't be ten minutes dressing," she replied decidedly.

"Quite an hour, I should say," replied the other.

"Oh!" gasped Rosalie. Then she clapped her hands together, caught up the flowing robe and skipped across the room to the bed.

"If I'm not dressed in ten minutes, my name's not Rosalie Paleaf."

Then with a sudden change to alarm in her manner, she turned round, growing alternately hot and cold.

"I say, where are my things? I can't see them anywhere."

"I took them away last night. There are your clothes for the day." And she directed her attention to a chair on which some very pretty and expensive *lingerie* was laid.

Rosalie looked at it, then drew herself up.

"I want my own clothes," she said. "These are too good for me; the others might be poor, but they were my own."

"I am afraid you cannot have them; you must dress in these."

The tears rose in Rosalie's eyes.

"I want my own clothes," she said again. "Auntie and I cut and made them together. They were the last pair of stockings that she ever knit."

There was no answer.

"Won't you bring them back?" said Rosalie at last, the tears still standing in her eyes.

"I am afraid it is against the rules of the house."

Then Rosalie got up with a sigh, and prepared to get inside the first garment.

"There is your bath first."

"I never bath in the morning; I always leave that till night."

"I think you had better do that which is customary."

Again Rosalie sighed, and followed her tormentress to an adjoining bath-room.

And so it took her well on into the hour before she was dressed, ready to leave the bedroom.

Mariana, who stayed to help her, insisted on arranging her hair, and after all arranged it much more becomingly than Rosalie herself had ever done.

But the black robe with its red silk facings, that fitted her companion so becomingly, suited her not at all. The fit was as perfect as it could be, but otherwise she looked quite out of place in it.

Breakfast was served on the same floor as that on which her bedroom was—three rooms away.

All this portion of the house evidently looked out on to nothing better than the wall mentioned before; but the beauty of the interior compensated for outside gloom. Rosalie was charmed with everything she saw, though somewhat awe-struck, and she took her breakfast shyly from the hands of what she described to herself as the handsomest man she had ever seen. She also made a mental note that he must be brother to the man she saw downstairs.

Rosalie had not gone all this time without grateful remembrance of that ordinary gift she had come to possess; but somehow there was some vague, indescribable thing in her surroundings that took away a full appreciation. She was longing to be outside, to talk with people more like herself, not all in black with red silk facings and knee breeches, and voices modulated to a soft perfection.

Rosalie's voice was sweet, but it was not the sweetness found in theirs. Hers was the outcome of expression, theirs of classical harmony. But how was she to get away? She dare not ask Mariana, for she was getting an uncomfortable idea that Mariana, from no ill motive, always thwarted and opposed her. So, watching her opportunity, she escaped and passed down the spiral staircase.

In the big hall below all was silent as death. Evidently no one was about.

She ran across to the big doors with a palpitating heart—outside them was freedom, she scarcely knew from what.

Alas! Another hand had touched the large glass handle before her own.

"Your card, madam. Your passport out."

"I have none. I shall not be away five minutes."

"I am afraid you cannot go."

"But I must go."

There was no answer. Exasperated, Rosalie stood and faced him.

"You let me in, and you can let me out."

"The orders are that you are not to pass."

"Whose orders?"

"The master's."

"Then take me to him."

"He is engaged at present."

"I'll go myself, then."

CHAPTER VII
A DEBT OF GRATITUDE

As Rosalie passed along the corridor her sudden decision was sealed by growing annoyance and a longing, almost amounting to fear, to get away.

With scarcely a pause she knocked upon the door, that door through which she entered last night. Without stopping she opened it. Mr. Barringcourt was there alone, at a table littered with papers, writing. He was indeed busy and engrossed, for on her entrance he did not raise his head, till accosted by her voice, and then he looked up sharply enough.

"You!" said he, bringing his eyebrows together in that dark frown which Rosalie had seen last night, and seeing had never forgotten.

"Yes. I want to go out."

"Impossible!" said he, with an impatient gesture of his hand, and returned to the paper.

"I want to go out," she repeated. "And you have no right to stop me."

"In my own house I have every right. Go away, you are interrupting me."

"So are you interrupting me."

He laughed, not altogether kindly, and looked up at her again.

"That is little short of impudent."

"I don't care. I want to go out, and if you won't give me leave, I shall take it."

"Take it then, by all means."

"That man at the door won't let me."

"Knock him down. It will be one way of surmounting the difficulty."

"He is such an elephant. I disliked him the very first time I saw him," she replied with energy, and as much simplicity as the truth occasioned.

"Well, go away and fight it out with him; watch the door, and bounce out when he's not looking."

"I won't do anything so undignified. I shall make friends with the kitchen people, and creep out that way."

"The kitchen door leads into the garden, and the walls are high, and the gate is locked. I keep the key myself, to ensure no one getting to the stables."

"Then give me leave to go out at the front."

"Now, why should you want to go out at the front? You have as beautiful a home as you could possibly wish for. What more can you want?"

"Fresh air and human beings."

"You have them here."

She shook her head. The tears rose in her throat, and were very hard to choke down again.

"It's the dismallest place I ever came to; and I'm no use. The people here always contradict me."

"You are the first person who has ever complained of them; and your opinion goes for nothing, your own conduct leaves so much to be desired."

"In what way?"

"In my time I have experienced much ingratitude, but never any quite to equal yours."

"I—ungrateful?"

"Most decidedly!"

"What are you wanting from me?"

"Quiet submission."

Rosalie's eyes opened wide, her lips parted; her expression was one of unfeigned surprise.

"What's that?"

"To do what you're told quietly. Now you *know*, there is no excuse for your not complying."

"But to submit means to stay here."

"Of course!"

"But I can't. Oh, I can't really! Anything but that."

"Nothing but that. You come to me with the most unusual request, and I am fool enough to put myself out of the way for you. Then you expect to go away, or rather slip away, without any more words about repayment. And when you are brought back, all this squalling."

"Nice people are quite content with 'Thank you.'"

"I'm not nice, and 'Thank you' never appeals to me."

"But if I stay here I can do nothing."

"Yes, you can mope."

"In return for a tongue?"

"Why not? It would be the height of self-sacrifice, and the perfection of thanksgiving."

Her serious eyes met his thoughtfully. "Do you really wish me to stay here?"

"I not only wish, but am determined on it."

"Then my self-sacrifice can never be spontaneous."

"You mean you are changing your mind. You are wishful to stop?"

"Not wishful, but if you want it, I'll—I'll try to settle down more cheerfully. After all, it's only just."

"That is so."

"Shall I often see you?"

"Never. I am not fond of inflictions."

He spoke so drily, and the words were so unkind, that Rosalie's wistful face grew paler. Yet still she argued to herself it would be selfish to wish to be free, to have a tongue and everything. And after all, the stranger was so clever that he must of necessity know best.

"Will you let me out just for an hour?" she asked at length, with a voice greatly subdued from the first clamorous outburst.

"Not for an hour."

"But I have an aunt, and she is dead. I shouldn't like strangers to take what once belonged to her."

"Where is your uncle?"

"He is dead too."

"Your people?"

"I have none."

"Where then, in the name of all the devils in Lucifram, do you intend to go to?"

"I thought when people knew I had miraculously come by a tongue they would—"

"Ah! I thought as much. You want to behave with all the absurdity of a hen that has laid an egg."

"Indeed!" said Rosalie, flushing.

"You want to get out just to cackle."

She was silent.

"You admit it?"

"I admit nothing but your want of manners."

"What a waspish, vinegarish tongue yours is."

"It's the fault of the doctor, then. If one cannot produce a sweet instrument one might as well admit oneself a failure."

"How was I to tell? Your face was so deceptive."

"Maybe so is my tongue. I was only speaking in fun. Let me out for one hour. Lend me twopence, and I will return, having spoken to no one, and in the right frame for being submissive."

For a short time he was silent. At last he said:

"Promise me faithfully you will return."

"I promise you most faithfully."

"Within the hour?"

"Yes."

"You understand perfectly that my reason for bringing you back is not for any personal gratification I should derive from it. It is simply so that you may not obtain any great or particular pleasure from having a prayer perfected."

"You speak plainly enough for the dullest mind."

"I'm glad. Now you may go. And remember, come back if you have any sense of gratitude."

So Rosalie passed out again into the farther hall.

"I have permission to pass," said she at the door, and then she stood outside.

It seemed to her when she reached the parapet that she had been out of the world for years. And oh! to be back in the world again! To see and hear the sights and sounds, so commonplace and ordinary, yet to her stilled ear so sweet again. Never had that terrible silent mansion struck her as so terrible till now she stood amongst the noise of work and life once more.

One hour of freedom. One hour with the light, jogging world, and then to pass once more beneath the shadow—a silent spirit in a silent world. The 'bus rattled on, taking its own slow time towards that quarter of the city where she had lived. She found the upper storey empty, and none had missed her. Yesterday the doctor had told her his intention of coming for her at four o'clock to-day. It was not yet quite twelve.

Each of the little rooms was now quite bare, except the tiny attic called her bedroom. In it were gathered the few trivial things she prized as belonging to days that were less dark than these. There was a necklace of coral, a collar of lace, a pair of gloves, kid, backed with astrachan, the last present her uncle ever gave her; a tiny brooch of gold, left by her aunt, and always worn by her, and but little else. One other thing she found, a book that in that planet compares nearly to our Bible. Sadly and lovingly she placed them all together, and kissed them many times, her eyes blinded with tears; and then a voice whispered:

"Why go back? Go to this doctor. Tell him everything, for he is kind. None would blame you for not returning to that prison mansion, even though under a promise. It was an unfair advantage."

But Rosalie shook her head.

"I must go back, because I promised. I asked everything in return for nothing. And God, in His own good time, will make the dark path plain."

The struggle gradually died, and Right conquered.

At last she was ready to go. Glancing round for the last time, she saw upon the mantelpiece a key, a solitary one upon an iron ring.

"It belonged to uncle's safe, the one that had so little in it," she thought. She took it up. Its dull appearance suggested so much dull tragedy to her. "I'll take it with me," she thought, and slipped it in the pocket of her dress.

Then she passed down the broad stone steps out once more into the street. Her brief holiday was over. The short hour was almost passed. She clenched her hands together, and drove back the blinding tears that struggled in her eyes. Gradually she drew nearer to the Avenue—how eagerly she had rushed there on the night before! The great black marble mansion came in view, its dusky grandeur having a certain sinister lowering to her understanding eye no different from a prison.

"I wonder when I'll walk along this street again?" she thought, and ascended the marble steps, hiding all trace of past emotion.

CHAPTER VIII
A BOOK OF INSPIRATION

"The master wished to speak to you when you returned," the attendant at the door said to her when he answered it.

Rosalie crossed the hall, feeling that vague sense of satisfaction that generally accompanies honesty, and which at times appears so poor a recompense.

This time on knocking she waited for the answer. When it came she opened the door and entered.

Mr. Barringcourt was in the act of filing papers, and generally tidying up the littered table.

"You are quite punctual," said he. "And what is more, astoundingly honest."

"You did not expect I should return, then?"

"No! Honestly speaking, I thought I had seen the last of you."

She shook her head.

"Gratitude brought me back at the expense of inclination."

"You should have yielded to temptation, and run away."

"Perhaps my action in returning was not quite so commendable as you think. I was much tempted to run away, and then—"

"What?"

"I could find no place to go to."

"You have no appreciative friends?"

"Not one."

"The doctor?"

Rosalie looked up quickly, and flushed. "Why do you speak of him?"

"I'm sure I don't know," he answered drily; "I believe I was meaning myself."

"Oh—yes—of course," stammered Rosalie. "I thought you meant Dr. Kaye."

"Then you had notions of appealing to him?"

Rosalie laughed. "You are not the pleasantest of companions."

"You might as well make a confidant of me. I am the only one you will find for some time."

"Well, yes, then," she answered, looking across at him with a timid glance. "I thought of running to the doctor, informing him you intended making a prisoner of me in a free city, and asking him to give me the benefit of his protection and advice."

"And you thought better of it?"

"You told me if I was grateful I should return. I was grateful, and though there seems something very topsy-turvy about the recompense you ask for, there is something in it that appeals to my sense of justice."

"That is why you came back?"

"There is no other reason."

Mr. Barringcourt all this time had been sitting in his chair by the table. Rosalie was standing at the farther side of it. Now he got up and walked over to the fireplace, where the fire was burning brightly.

"What is your name?" he asked.

"Rosalie Paleaf."

"Brought up by an aunt and uncle?"

"Yes."

"Always dumb, and therefore very much out of the world?"

"Yes."

"Where did you learn the little bit of knowledge you possess?"

"I listened to it. I was not deaf, you know."

"Could you read?"

"Yes, I can read. That is how I used to spend most of my time."

"Travels, novels, or biography?"

"A little bit of both—all three, I mean. 'The Life of Krimjo on the Desert Island,' which was my favourite, contained a little of all, I think."

"Ally Krimjo was only make-belief," said he ruthlessly.

"Indeed he wasn't! He had gone through everything he spoke about, the shipwreck and the loneliness, the savages and everything. Make-belief! Oh, Mr. Barringcourt, have you ever really read it through?"

"Yes, at the time it was written."

Here Rosalie laughed again triumphantly.

"That shows you don't know the book I'm talking about at all. The man who wrote it lived hundreds of years ago. Quite three hundred, I should say."

"At that rate I must be mistaken. Then if you are so fond of travel and biography, I have some volumes here all on that subject, written, too, about the time you speak of. You will have a great deal of time lie heavy on your hands; perhaps you would like some?"

Rosalie looked dubious, and her eyes travelled to the imposing-looking book-shelves.

"I never found anyone quite to come up to Ally Krimjo," she replied regretfully.

"You refuse my offer?"

"Not if you give me something interesting. But as a rule I don't like biographies, because the people always die. Now, Ally Krimjo—"

"You're quite right," said Mr. Barringcourt grimly. "Ally Krimjo hasn't died, so he deserves to live. Have you the Book of Divine Inspiration?"

"Oh, yes! I don't suppose there's anyone without that?"

"Here's one with pictures; look at it."

He took down from a shelf a heavy and ponderous volume of the Book of Divine Inspiration, as written and compiled in the planet Lucifram, and carried it without the least apparent effort to the table.

"Now come and look at the pictures. I'll show you a few, and then you can take it away with you and look at the rest."

He opened it at the first page—the frontispiece. It was a picture of the Golden Serpent, so lifelike that its appearance was most startling. The book, likewise, must have possessed the property of magnifying all contained in it, for suddenly the head and coils and tails seemed to enlarge to the same gigantic size as that within the temple.

"I don't like it. Don't show me any more of that book," Rosalie said.

"But why?" he asked, with apparent surprise.

"Oh! I don't know," she answered, almost whispering. "It's the Serpent. I don't like it."

"But you are the young lady who was kissing its head, and throwing your arms around it."

"Yes, I know. That was because I did not understand."

"And now?"

"Oh, now! I think it's cruel and deceitful."

"That's nothing short of blasphemy. The Serpent is a god!"

"Do you believe that?" she asked, suddenly looking up, and fixing his eyes with a look as keen as it was serious.

Two pairs of eyes, dark and light, each encountered one another—each trying to read the other's secret—and both for once inscrutable, dark and light alike.

"Yes. I've got a pretty good mental digestion; it can take most things," he said, the corners of his mouth curving into a smile. "Look! Miss—Miss—What's your name, by the way?"

"My name is Rosalie—Rosalie Paleaf."

"Well now, Miss Paleaf, let us turn to the second picture."

Reluctantly she turned round once more, to behold a forest jungle, as fine and beautiful a scene as one could wish. Its size and realism made her put out her hand to pull a twig of feathery foliage, when suddenly she was startled to see beneath it a pair of eyes, wild and yet intelligent, gleaming out at her. It was an animal shaped and sized much like a monkey. Behind it was another of the same kind, a partner in its joys and sorrows evidently.

Rosalie sprang back.

"Look at that hideous thing!" she cried in horror, pointing to it. Then recollecting herself, she said, with an effort at more self-control and appreciation: "Are—are they extinct now?"

"I don't know, I'm sure. What would *you* say?"

"I sincerely hope so, I'm sure. Put it away. There is something uncanny about that book. That creature startled me."

"It's an acquired taste. Here we come to another."

He had turned onward to a third picture, in which was shown a woman sitting on the roots of a tree, the expression of her face long and uncompromising, full of discontent. She wore no clothing, but her long and silky hair was sufficient covering. She was of no particular beauty, and her expression of discontent, mingled with curiosity, subtly introduced, and having little intelligence to enlighten it, gave the girl a feeling of repugnance. In one hand she held a fruit of brilliant scarlet; a mouthful was being eaten, and its taste did not seem altogether to her liking.

"What do you think of this?"

"I like it very little better. The man who painted it, judging from her face, understood human nature, and had very little mercy for it."

"There you are mistaken. It is a caricature," he answered softly, "painted one day by a man, and sent to his dearest friend—a woman."

"But she is eating a tomato."

"Of course! Let us continue."

The next picture showed this same woman standing beside a man who sat upon a rock cracking nuts with his teeth. As Rosalie looked the scenes began to move and become lifelike, pretty much in the same way as a cinematograph. At first the man did not perceive his companion, but turning suddenly, in the act of taking a broken shell from his mouth, he saw her holding the scarlet fruit, from which she had taken no more than two fair mouthfuls. On seeing this his jaw dropped, his eyes expanded.

Thin, far-away voices came from the picture, aiding the illusion.

"What for did you that?" said he, in a voice devoid of beauty and expression.

"To find out," she replied, in the same manner.

"But we die—we die—if we eat fruit of blood colour!" he cried, with superstitious horror in his voice.

"We no die, we live and grow fat. I eat, I live; but I miss something."

"What?"

"I know not. Eat, and tell me." Her look was cunning.

"I dare not."

"It is the best of all kinds—but for one thing."

"And what is dat?"

"Eat, and tell me. You be my faithful love."

Gingerly he took it in his hand, applied it reluctantly to his lips, sucking the juice alone.

"It wants—"

His low forehead wrinkled. He could not formulate his thoughts.

"What?"

"It wants—"

And then all round a million voices echoed:

"*It wants but salt!*"

"Salt!" he shouted, drowning the harmonic voices in his new discovery.

Hereupon the woman fell upon her knees, and almost worshipped him, kissing his hands and feet, weeping tears of pleasure on them.

"Scrape me some up," he uttered, taking advantage of her low position.

She did it with her finger-nails.

"Now stand back whilst I eat it."

"But I—I found it."

"Stand back, goose, and watch me eat."

"I found it first," she whimpered.

"Here's a seed—that's all you're worth," he answered. "Now I go to find more," said he, jumping up valiantly. "You bake bread and get me butter for when I return."

"I come too!" she cried. "You eat the whole while I worky work."

"Fool—toad—weasel—monkey! bake me the bread, or I your neck am breaking!"

And with that they disappeared from the page. Only the picture in its first stage remained visible.

"That's not pretty at all," said Rosalie.

"Few things are in real life," he answered.

"But that was caricature."

"Not in the way you think. It was caricature, I grant, but with a difference."

"Yes. I don't think the eating of salt with tomato could make a man really superior, do you?"

"No; but it was the fact that he discovered salt."

"But he didn't. He was as ignorant as she till the voices whispered it."

"Nevertheless, he caught the first sound."

"Yes, of course," said Rosalie thoughtfully.

Here Mr. Barringcourt laughed.

"You do not appreciate its true absurdity," he said; "but that, maybe, is scarcely necessary. Now, that picture, or series of pictures, was painted by a woman, and sent to the man who had sent her the first."

"But how about the voices?"

"Oh! she was no ordinary woman, by any means."

"Was she quarrelling with the man?"

"No. They were amusing each other in wet weather."

"They paint most beautiful scenery, but I don't like their men and women."

"You are not intended to. Now, shall we go on?"

"No; I'd rather not, really. It gives me headache, and I've had it ever since yesterday afternoon, except for that little bit after you had healed me."

"You are tired of the Book of Divine Inspiration?"

"I'm tired of the pictures; they are no better than caricatures and skits. I don't think that's a good book to keep in a house at all."

"You astound me! Were you not brought up to worship the Serpent?"

"Yes; but the Serpent disappointed me."

"I see. You only worship a God who is content to spoil you?"

She shook her head.

"I don't know," she said. "Perhaps I'll settle down again before long."

"I hope so. Has it ever struck you, Miss Paleaf, how completely you are in my power?"

"No," she answered, looking at him quickly.

"Well, you know, I found you in the temple, in the Holiest Place—the place forbidden to women. Do you know what the punishment for that transgression is?"

"No."

"To have your tongue torn out by the roots."

"Impossible!"

"Not in the least. In this one interview with me you have said enough against the Serpent to set all its scales and coils bristling, and its fangs working."

"I have said nothing."

"'Cruel and deceitful,' were not those your words?"

"Yes; but to tear my tongue out would not be to prove it otherwise. The Serpent's wisdom should assert itself and prove the opposite. You were also in the Holiest Place."

"Of course; but for a man the offence is not so capital."

"Tomatoes and salt," said Rosalie, and she laughed. He laughed also.

"Your impudence is only beaten by your ignorance."

"As often as I offend solely with my tongue, you must take the blame yourself. I think you must have oiled the wheels too freely."

"It is a good thing you have no relatives, Miss Paleaf; they would have missed you, disappearing so suddenly."

"Under the circumstances, I suppose it is."

"Were you happy with them?"

"Oh, yes! As happy as the day, when we were in prosperity. But this last year has been nothing but shadow and poverty, and I don't think I ever realised how many things I had to be thankful for till they were all gone."

"The gift of speech does not compensate for all things, then?"

"I don't know. I have had it so short a time."

"You are longing for freedom, and can find nothing to compensate for the bitterness of its loss. Is not that it?"

"I don't think it is only that. My aunt was only buried the day before yesterday. I should be very callous and ungrateful if I could forget her so readily."

"Yet you cannot deny the events of the past day have put a great gulf betwixt you and her."

"Yes; I could think she had died a year ago along with uncle. Poor thing! It would have been so much better if she had done so, I think."

"How long do you think your term of imprisonment will last?"

Rosalie shook her head.

"I don't know. The future has always been a blank to me. I never built those castles in the air that many love to build."

"How about your prayer to find a tongue?"

"I don't know. I longed to speak, but never looked into a future crowned by successful prayer."

"Well, your term of imprisonment here lasts three years."

"It is a long time."

"On the contrary, reckoned justly, a very short one."

"What do you mean by 'reckoned justly'?"

He took up a bundle of filed papers from the table.

"These are accounts of long standing," he answered gravely. "It is strange how quickly a high rate of interest accumulates. What you wipe off in three years or less by ready payments, some are leaving till a future date, till it accumulates and doubles, then maybe trebles, and some day swamps them."

Rosalie's eyes opened with unfeigned surprise.

"But whom is the money owed to?"

"To me."

"Have you all those debtors?"

"These are a few—a very few. People find out the softness of my heart, and then they come to me. Women with stingy husbands and extravagant tastes, men with limited brains and boundless ambition. Each and all, with many other pleas and reasons, call upon me and win me over to their way of thinking. I am always won. No simple hearted fool within the country gives in more easily than I when I can gain security of person."

"But don't you tell them that you expect return?"

"No; I like them to think there's one generous person in the world."

"But that is scarcely fair. You ought to tell them what you want."

"The argument would be beyond them. Besides, it would come then too much like making bargains. I am no shopman. Those who seek me find me. Others stay away."

"But this is nothing short of madness. How can you make people pay without a signature or anything?"

"I never jest but when it suits my purpose. And for madness, I grant upon the surface it may appear as such. But each bill works backward—item by item, year by year. Mathematicians and philosophers looking through them would find a subject more than fascinating."

"But if when you show your bill the people refuse to pay, and say they never got the goods?"

"Why, then, one little snip and the fabric ravels out again, loop by loop, as it was knitted up. Back it goes to the fundamental working, as rigid as machinery, as true as time, and ends in nothingness."

Rosalie was silent for a time, and then she said: "Is that how it is you are such a rich man?"

But he shook his head.

"I am poorer than many people think," he answered. "And richer too— wealth is comparative. But now," he continued, with more energy, "I have come to the conclusion that your term of prison life shall not be quite so dull as you expected. You may come to me at any time, provided I have leisure. Moreover, you may borrow any book; amongst all these there will be surely some to suit you, even though it be but a uniquely pictured book of Ally Krimjo."

"But what are you expecting in return? You say you like people to esteem you generous, and are not in reality so at all. This generosity to me may end in nothing but a high percentage. It may bring me down to nothingness."

"You have the advantage of being young, you see. I might end your debtor if I tied you up in an unsympathetic prison, and let you out at last, to find I was too late, and your spirit killed by solitude."

He was looking at her with a puzzled and thoughtful expression, as if trying to weigh or settle something in his mind to his own satisfaction.

"I think you were easier to understand dumb than you are speaking," he said at last.

"Well, yes, because I would be less complex," said Rosalie wisely. "I was minus something before, now I'm not."

"Maybe. When will you come to visit me again?"

"To-morrow morning, if I may. From twelve to one?"

"Yes. We'll arrange for that hour twice a week. It will be neither too long nor too often to bore either of us. The rest of the time you'll spend as best you can within the house and gardens."

CHAPTER IX
MARIANA

Rosalie went away again, upstairs to that corridor on which the rooms in which she lived were situated. Another meal was there in readiness, for the hour was now past one. She ate with little heart, the silent attendant by her side unwittingly depressing her. When the meal was over she went to a little sitting-room which Mariana had shown her, taking her small parcel of belongings with her, and shut the door.

Here a fire was burning, the only one in that particular wing, for they seemed to be chary of fires here. The room had little of brightness about it otherwise. Its walls were panelled oak without design or ornament. An oaken table on three legs, a few high-backed chairs, a rug before the fireplace, polished boards the floor; that was all. A narrow window looked out upon the blank wall opposite, giving the room a gloomy, darkened look. Yet there was something about this simply furnished room that Rosalie liked. It was less luxurious than any other in that house which she had visited.

She drew one of the high-backed chairs toward the fire, and sat down, her feet upon the fender. She had taken her small Book of Divine Inspiration from the parcel, and sat holding it idly in her hands, staring at the flames. After all, it was comforting to be able to hold something, something familiar and not strange, something that had been handled and read by loving hands and eyes, though now they were passed away for ever.

For Rosalie, despite her behaviour downstairs, was only playing a part. Laughing or answering, there had been ever in her heart the Serpent's tooth. It gnawed and stung with almost unendurable pain. O God! to be but rid of it for five sweet minutes.

So far as Rosalie was concerned, there were no late dinners in this house of mystery. She had ordinary tea at five o'clock, and then the lights for the evening were brought in, and the red curtains drawn. About seven Mariana knocked at the door, and entered.

"This is my evening for playing," said she quietly; "would you care to come and listen to me?"

"Thank you; I should like to come very much. What do you play?"

"Play? Oh! I always play on a violin; it's my favourite amusement. It's the way I always spend my night out."

"Night out," thought Rosalie; "what an expression coming from her lips!"

Aloud she said: "I'm very fond of music. Have you learnt long?"

"I don't remember learning, but I suppose I must have done."

She led the way along the corridor, down the slippery stairs, and turned in at the glass door leading from the central hall towards Mr. Barringcourt's study; but she did not go there. Instead, she paused at a door next to it on the same side. She passed in, and held the door for Rosalie to follow. The room within was dark, but it must have overlooked the Avenue, for lights from the outside shone weirdly in through the long windows, lighting up short lines of furniture, half a grand piano, a strip of table, an ottoman, and a piece of wall.

Mariana turned on one light. It was soft and shaded, but had not strength enough to illuminate the whole room. The farther corners were entirely in the shade.

"Will you not turn on more lights?" asked Rosalie.

"No; I like the twilight best. I can think and feel better when the light is low."

Then she uncased the violin which she had brought down with her, and tried the strings, testing them by the piano, which was now a little better brought to view.

Rosalie went over to a window—it was the natural instinct of a prisoner—and looked out of it with hungry eyes.

Passing, passing, never ceasing, went the traffic, and through the closed windows came the muffled sound of horses' feet, and wheels, and voices. Feverishly she scanned each face as closely as she could in the distance; but she read nothing on them but what one reads on a hundred faces every day. Her heart beat with an aching longing to touch the pavement again with free feet. Three years! It was a lifetime. One day in a house like this contained an agony of years.

"I am impatient," she said, and closed her lips patiently and tight.

She had forgotten Mariana's music—in the testing of the chords—till suddenly, after a short pause, she began to play.

Rosalie's attention was first divided between the music and the street. What was played seemed to fit in with her mood—a simple air of sadness. But this harmonic accompaniment had its dangers, for by degrees Rosalie felt her spirits, instead of keeping pace with it, begin to follow. Then the street claimed her attention less, the music absorbing it. And at last she turned round reluctantly and looked toward the player. Mariana, never an ordinary-looking woman, was by the one pale light quite extraordinary. The long graceful robe she wore made her look more than commonly tall. Her pretty arms, white and delicate yet, full of a certain indefinable strength, and the ivory whiteness of her face, had a curious charm and fascination in the dim lights. But beside her playing, the musician herself was insignificant. From sadness her notes changed to melancholy, from melancholy on to misery, from misery to despair. Despondency, tragedy, hopeless complaint, and restless, weary wandering on those spiritual wastes where no light comes, or even narrow track to show that ever pilgrim passed before—this was her music.

Her face as she played betrayed no great emotion. The brightness in her eyes spoke more of mental activity and retrospection than of sentiment. Gradually the listener's eyes fell on the furniture around. Much of it, in conjunction with the rest of the house, was of polished oak, carved finely and curiously. Opposite there was a cabinet museum about the height of a man, and above it the carved head of some idolater's god, growing in clearness as she became accustomed to the light

But surely the music had affected it. Its ugly eyes, protruding and rid of all intelligence, altered slowly to expression almost human. For every quivering note struck from the violin found a resting-place within these staring orbs, filling them both with misery. Their dumb speech was terrible, but when Rosalie moved away, more ghastly still by reason of their persistence. She looked away. There on the floor beside her was a tiger-skin, a rug of worth and beauty, with a head and glassy eyes. Its eyes met hers. Their dumb misery told a tale beyond the power of speech. Shivering, she turned and moved away.

When would Mariana stop and take her from this wretched room? She had moved within range of the statues, those dim, misty forms of whiteness which rose like ghosts with out and upstretched arms to beckon her. Faces of cold, white, and deathly beauty, and eyes! Oh, terrible! all gazing into hers with that sad gaze and straining misery, reaching to the height and depth of agony.

It was enough. Had they but wailed, or cried, or uttered sound, the spell had broken. But here was silence—ghastly, terrible, because so secret and so unexpected.

At last the tension reached a limit. On all sides Rosalie encountered ghastly faces of long-suffering pain to which the music seemed to form a fitting background. Turning hurriedly to escape one face belonging to a child, set in a picture hung upon the wall, her glance fell by chance upon the mirror and revealed herself, strained horror in her eyes, with blanched cheeks and open lips. She scarcely recognised who stood there. It was enough. She crossed the room half running, and clutched Mariana's arm.

"How much longer?"

"The time is up. Alas! how quickly it has passed. Never again till next week, and then but two short hours. And yet you ask me, 'How much longer?'"

"Can you play like that, and never feel it?"

Mariana shook her head.

"It's the only time I ever feel, the only time I ever live."

"But it is pain and sorrow."

"Better than emptiness. Now I have lost the only thing I love. All week it lies quite mute, a thing of idleness, bursting with life. And when I take it up it utters so long a wail, so sad a sigh, that my heart returns to it, and we weep together till pain becomes an ecstasy and sadness joy."

"Oh, Mariana! what a life is yours!"

"No different from the rest. A life of grey to-morrows that come and go in endless twilight."

"Will you feel like this to-morrow?"

"No. To-morrow brings a calm existence. To-night I fill my heart with tears."

"What was it brought you here?"

"Oh! I loved not wisely, but too well, this little fiddle."

"And has it brought you to this pass?"

"Yes, if pass you call it."

"Then, Mariana, give it up!"

For her the dimness of the room had vanished, its fantasies and ghostly shadows thrown off with one great effort. She grasped the other's arms in both her hands, and stared at her, taller by her sudden force and fierceness. The other looked at her, and then recoiled.

"Give it up! The only joy of life—the only life beyond a dull existence! Why, I should die—the very thought would kill me."

"No! It would make you live!"

But Mariana only looked at her, and shook her head.

"Rosalie, can I play? Can you make anything out of it?"

"I never heard such music; but it is wrong—it's the wrong sort."

Then Mariana came close up to her, just as before she had drawn back, and, with a sudden weakness, drooped her head upon the other's shoulder, clasping her hands about her waist.

"Don't say that!" she cried, her voice little above a whisper. "I cannot bear it. I can do nothing more. There is no time. Once or twice I asked the Master would he listen, and he did. But he said there was no tune in what I played, no harmony of any sort—that all was a delusion, a fancy of my brain."

"But that was not the truth." And Rosalie held her very tight, that woman who in the morning had seemed so strong to her. "And he only said it because he knew you would be fool enough to take it all to heart."

"Hush! hush! It's treason to talk like that."

"Nothing's treason but failure. You follow my advice, and give up the fiddle. Then after a while you'll get it back again in such a way that even Mr. Barringcourt will not be able to say there's no tune in it."

Mariana looked at her, with surprise and misunderstanding on every feature.

"I can't give it up. I'm bound to play for two hours every Wednesday night, harmony or discord."

"Why bound?"

"It was the stipulation I made when first I came here. It's the kind of thing one can't break through."

"You don't want to?"

"No, I don't; but if I did I could not."

"You would rather live for two hours a week than seven times twenty-four?"

"I don't understand you."

"No, and never will."

It was Mr. Barringcourt's voice, and he spoke from the door, through which he had entered.

CHAPTER X
A CONVERSATION IN SHADOWS

When Mr. Barringcourt was in it, the great black house held its mysteries and shadows; without him they seemed aggravated fourfold. Not long after the Wednesday evening music, Rosalie stood in the centre of the hall suddenly smitten with the most chilly fear she had ever experienced in her life. No noise, no sound, not even the wind without, penetrated those walls of iron marble. Shadows and silence in endless vista met her eye. Shadows and silence like a sigh congealed, changed from nothingness into reality.

Dreading the loneliness, and her own want of nerve to go upstairs, she went to the door and accosted the keeper there.

"Does this house frighten you?" she asked.

"Not at all," he answered, most politely.

"That is strange, because I feel most frightened here. It is not haunted, is it?"

"What do you mean?"

"There are no—no ghosts?"

He smiled. "That depends upon your imagination, I should say."

"I want to go upstairs, and I dare not. You don't think me very foolish, do you?"

"Where is Mariana? Does she not look after you?"

"Yes. But she went away, nearly an hour ago."

"Shall I call her?"

"Oh, please do!"

He touched a bell, and a minute later Mariana appeared coming down the staircase. She looked as calm as ever. The short outburst of the evening had died away.

"I'm sorry to trouble you. But I really could not come upstairs alone. The house was so quiet that it frightened me."

"You will get accustomed to the silence by degrees," she answered, and led the way towards the staircase.

When they reached the little sitting-room where the fire burnt, Rosalie was pleased to find a white cloth laid there, with supper on it. It was a very plain repast, but cheerful, possibly because of the bright lamp and firelight.

"When do you have your supper?" she asked of Mariana.

"I have had mine."

"What is the time?"

"Almost ten o'clock."

"How late! That is the time I generally go to bed. What time do you go?"

"As soon as you are settled for the night I shall retire."

"Where do you sleep?"

"In the next room to yours. If you want anything in the night, you may ring or come to me."

"But then I should have to come out on to the corridor. I hate corridors."

"No. My bedroom opens into yours. Your door that opens into the passage is locked at night."

"By whom?"

"By me."

"Why do you lock it?"

"I don't know, I'm sure. You are safer with it locked, I expect."

"How long have you lived here, Mariana?"

"Three years this autumn."

"And how long has Mr. Barringcourt been here?"

"The same length of time. I came with him."

"And you are happy here?"

"I could not be happier—under the circumstances."

"Were you ever happier?"

"I think I was once. But it is a very long time ago. I don't remember how long, so that it cannot really matter."

"Where did you live before you lived here?"

She shook her head.

"I can't quite remember. I think it was a very cold and dark place, and one day Mr. Barringcourt came and asked me would I like to go away."

"And you accepted?"

"Yes. I wanted to get warm again."

"And are you warm?"

"Yes. Every Wednesday night. If it were not for that I should grow cold again."

A silence. Then:

"Who lived here before Mr. Barringcourt?"

"A man who died. His name was Geoffrey Todbrook."

"What?"

"Geoffrey Todbrook."

"Why, he's the man who started homes for incurables. There was one for the dumb and deaf and blind. I should have gone there."

"I have heard he was very charitable. He left this house to Mr. Barringcourt."

"Were they related?"

"No; I rather think myself the Master had let it to him on a lease. Then when the lease expired he died, and left a will to smooth all difficulties."

"Was Mr. Barringcourt living in the city before Mr. Todbrook's death?"

"Oh, no! I don't think he had ever been here before. He took me to the opera one Wednesday night, and he said it was only the second time he had been there."

"The opera? Did you like it?"

"Yes, I liked it; but it made my head ache. I was trying to remember something all the time."

"Do you often go out with him?"

"Oh, no; that would be to get oneself talked about. Besides, so long as we remain here, I am but a servant."

"Why does Mr. Barringcourt keep me here?"

"I expect you have some secret he wishes to discover, otherwise he would not trouble himself about you. When he took me to the opera it was to discover something."

"What?"

"I don't know."

"Then how can you tell?"

"Because, up to the time we went, and through the performance, he was very affable to me. Afterwards he took no more notice of me, and never has done."

"Don't you hate him?"

"Why should I? I had no secret. His conduct was permissible; and I had rather be left alone."

"And what secret can I have that he should be agreeable to me?"

"I cannot tell. Perhaps, like me, you have none. But if you have, rest assured you will not leave this house till it has been discovered."

"Have you ever had anyone staying here before in the same way that I am?"

"Not in my time. People with secrets worth knowing are few and far between."

"Then what can make the Master think such an insignificant person as I could hold a secret?"

"I cannot tell. I only said it might be so; there is no other reason why he should tolerate your company?"

Rosalie laughed, despite a very uneasy feeling in her mind.

"Do you ever have company here?"

"Yes. Last Christmas there was a ball, and we had two or three dinner parties and entertainments. Lady Flamington generally acts as hostess. She and Sir James are very friendly with Mr. Barringcourt."

"What is she like?"

"Very beautiful, I think, with very pleasing manners. She must be so to please the Master; he is so hard to please."

"Perhaps she has a secret?"

"Oh, no; I hardly think so. He makes a convenience of her."

"Good gracious!" and Rosalie laughed. "You don't give him an enviable character."

"I speak as truthfully as my perceptions allow me; but at times I may be wrong."

"And does she not resent being made a convenience of?"

"No; it is only self-respect that keeps her from falling in love with him."

"Is he then so agreeable to her?"

"He gives her everything that is not worth the having."

"What do you mean?"

"He gives her everything but love."

"But that, with a husband, no one would want."

Mariana's eyebrows rose. "There are double marriages on Lucifram, I'm given to understand."

"Yes; but no one thinks much of a woman who marries twice, unless she is a widow."

"Indeed," Mariana answered, and was silent.

"But is Mr. Barringcourt fond of no one?" Rosalie pursued.

"I never heard of anyone. He is cold and proud, and often takes no trouble to hide it."

"But then there are so many good and beautiful women in the world."

"They find partners, perhaps, that need them more."

After another silence Rosalie continued: "And Mr. Todbrook—what did he die of?"

"I think he went down the back staircase."

"In his own house?"

"Yes."

"What do you mean?"

"He died."

"In which room?"

"The one the Master sleeps in now. There is a portrait of him in the picture-gallery. To-morrow you shall see it."

"What did he die of?"

"He had quick ears. He heard the spirit voices calling, and he went to them."

"Painlessly?"

"Like one sailing on a sea of glass. They say his end was merciful; and I know it was. He suffered nothing—he suffers nothing now."

"Is he in heaven?"

"I doubt there was too little pain for that; but yet I cannot tell. He may have suffered previously. Men's lives are strange. And the roughest rocks are coated by smooth waters. They keep their secrets all too well."

"I'm tired, Mariana. Shall we go to bed?"

"Yes. When you wish it."

So they rose and went together to the bedroom, which had a chilly air in it after the cosy room. When at last Rosalie was in bed, Mariana smoothed the coverlet and tucked the bed-clothes in.

"Leave me a light, won't you?"

"Yes; I'll put it on this table. But there is nothing to fear. An easy conscience may sleep well here, secure from harm." She moved away, but after a few steps returned. She stooped over the bed and kissed Rosalie's brow. "Good-night, little one. Sleep peacefully till daybreak." And then she went away.

Big tears rose in Rosalie's eyes, for the words had awakened in her a terrible longing for love and companionship, stronger and more powerful than ever Mariana, in her terribly set existence, could ever know how to give. For Rosalie felt that she was even now the stronger of the two, and wept for Mariana's solitude as well as her own.

CHAPTER XI
GARDEN AND HOUSE OF SHADOWS

The next morning the sensation of waking in such fine surroundings had lost all its charm. Rosalie awoke with a dull leaden pain at her heart, that gained rather than lost power as she recalled one by one the articles of furniture in this new home. The long mirror had lost its fascination; so had the silken bed-hangings. She did not jump out of bed, but rather lay there idly, with no wish to rise; oppressed with such a heaviness that to lie still seemed the only ease from all those aches and pains that twine around a heavy heart. As the grey light of early morning brightened and broadened, she curled in among the bed-clothes, and shut her eyes.

"If only they would let me lie here, and not disturb me! I would never disturb them, I'm sure. I feel so weary that the least exertion is the biggest effort."

Then she lay very still for a long time, till at last Mariana knocked at the door and opened it, bringing the customary cup of tea.

"I feel so tired, Mariana," Rosalie said, "and there's nothing to do. Don't you think I might spend the day in bed?"

"It is against the rules."

"Who makes all the rules here?"

"The Master."

"But he has gone away till to-morrow."

"That does not excuse us."

"But he would never know unless you told. I am tired, really, Mariana. I could just lie still, and never move an inch all day."

"You must get up."

"When I get up my heart aches."

"That does not enter into the consideration of the rule. You must get up, or you will be shaken out when the bed is made."

So very reluctantly Rosalie rose, with a day of nothingness and imprisonment before her. She was dressed in about the same time as yesterday, had breakfast served in the same room in the same way, and then walked out on to the corridor aimlessly and disconsolately.

Mariana had disappeared. Although Rosalie tried every door along the corridor she could not find her. Many of these were locked, and others she discovered to be bedrooms, furnished much as her own, with the exception of the little sitting-room and the room in which she had her meals.

At last, weary of this, she passed out to the high gallery overreaching the square central hall. She walked round it, and tried various doors leading off from it, but all were locked. Below, the dim hall lay in silence. Nothing of light or life was there, though it was not yet mid-day. She looked down over the high oaken balustrade, and sighed, and the echo brought her sigh back to her. She whispered "Rosalie"; the word ran round the arching dome, and then returned—a mocking, hollow voice within the silence. So the morning crept away, with no brightness to speed its dragging hours, no companionship, no occupation. Not a sound fell on her ear. So still was everything, the house might have been a City of the Dead.

At dinner-time she ate mechanically the food they placed before her. To refuse was simply to raise up insistence. Then she withdrew to the little sitting-room, to idle away what time would go, to find after endless waiting that scarcely an hour had passed. Then she got up and went back to the bedroom to bring her hat, and with the same difficulty as the day before, reached with safety the foot of the spiral staircase.

The doorkeeper was sitting not far away from it, reading a paper. She went towards him, and as she approached him he looked up, and then rose from his seat.

"Would you mind telling me which way I should go to find the garden?" she asked.

"Certainly. If you will come this way I will take you."

Rosalie smiled sadly.

"Suppose somebody got out or in whilst you are away?"

"No one would wish to go out, and the door only opens from within," he answered.

He walked across the hall, and she followed him to the glass door behind the staircase. This door likewise entered upon a corridor with doors leading from either side of it. The house seemed all doors, but at the farther end a spacious fernery opened out, the curtains (of deep red) which shut it off being now looped and drawn back, so that much beyond was visible. Through the magnificent fern-house he led her till they came to a door of glass leading down into the garden beyond.

The doorkeeper opened it, and let her pass through, himself following.

Outside, broad flights of steps descended by terraces to a lawn of smoothest grass. The terraces were paved in large squares of black and white marble, and from the central one a huge fountain was sending up showers of sparkling water to meet the brilliant sun. Beds of flowers, all of colours resembling scarlet geraniums, were laid out bordering the side walks. One magnificent bed of what looked like crimson gladioli ran up a steep bank bordering the left-hand wall. The high walls themselves were covered with creepers, all of brilliant red, just as autumn leaves are often found, and the only relief afforded was that of the dark foliage of the trees that clustered willow fashion in the rear portion of the garden. This was a kind of wooded avenue along which a carriage drive led from the big gates in the outer wall round to those stables where the Master's favourite horses were.

"This is the garden," said her companion, when he had brought her so far; "you will return any time before five. After that the doors are locked."

When Rosalie was left alone she walked across the lawn slowly, taking in all the beauty and striking nature of the scene. The gardens were large. The avenue and shrubbery beyond were shaded, and provided with many rustic and artistic seats. Rosalie walked along the carriage drive as far as she could, and then a sudden and unaccountable gloom seemed to fall upon her and all things. Just then a sudden bend in the road brought her full in view of the stables. It seemed to her for one instant as if against the gloom surrounding her they shone out in flashing whiteness. They were flat-roofed, though high, and the strong pillars supporting and ornamenting the building were an exact fac-simile of those used in the decoration of the temple.

And standing there looking at it, Rosalie smiled.

"I wonder whose idea that was?" she thought. "A devout architect and designer would never have thought of such a thing. But perhaps I'm mistaken; this may be a private place of worship. I'll go on and see."

So she advanced as far as the building; but whether it were stable or chapel she could not tell, for it possessed no doorway. She walked around it as far as she could on either side, till prevented by a wall of great height, but found nothing to serve as a clue as to the nature of its use. No sound came from within—none of the odour that generally characterises such places, either of sanctity or horses—and for the third time Rosalie walked round with growing curiosity. Marble, marble, all was marble, cold and hard and lifeless.

"I really think granite would be a welcome change," she said, and sighed and walked away.

But it was really pleasant and enjoyable to be in the open air. To be able to look up at a sky that belonged in common to prisoners and free men, there was some little consolation in that.

As she emerged once more from the wooded avenue, her eye fell full on the house. She was surprised and startled at its beauty, viewed thus from the back. Whereas looking at it from the street it showed as nothing but a large square mansion, almost ugly in its plainness, it was from here one of the most graceful and artistic buildings she had ever seen. It was turreted and towered, with polished oriel windows, shining with a lustre all their own against the dusky background of dark marble. The windows on the basement all opened on the ground.

"I believe this is the front, and the front is the back," thought she. "A kind of topsy-turvy, like the rest of things. What a magnificent door!"

This last expression escaped her involuntarily and aloud.

The door from which she had come was a small side one leading from the conservatory of palms and ferns, but in the centre of this huge construction of glass was a double door of thick carved glass, or some substance very like it, of fine workmanship and execution.

Rosalie went up the many steps towards it, passing the silver fountain that fell with almost a merry sound into the marble basin. Both leaves of the door were shut, and the carving represented was that of a temple, the inner portion, with arched aisles and fluted pillars, and in the centre an altar, with above it the image of a toad. Below it, on the steps outside the customary railing, bowed figures knelt in bare feet, their shoes and stockings at some considerable distance. The representation was comprehensive. Each figure and detail was drawn with great exactness and clearness. The curious polish it possessed was its most striking feature, especially that brilliancy radiating from the toad. Rosalie bent her eyes closer to it, shuddered to find that there was something horribly repulsive in such an animal, and then found herself attracted by the light shining from its head. Its eyes were meaningless and staring, even in the carved picture, but from its head, and this she only discovered after steady looking, the light shone very curiously. Instead of the white light of the rest, this was almost red. Just a faint tinge of red! All the rest, carved as it were from blocks of ice, was utterly lifeless. Yet it was this tinge of colour, so subtly introduced, which made the whole great difference between an uninteresting and an interesting thing. At last she left it and looked down once more into the garden. She saw that several narrow paths led into the shrubberies at the sides. But what struck her attention most was that glorious rising bank of scarlet lilies and harebells and gladioli, that extended right down one side to the wooded avenue beyond, and reached almost to the height of the wall.

She perceived a narrow winding path led up this bank to its summit, and there a garden seat was placed. This was the highest point of vantage in the garden.

"I believe if I could only get up there I should be able to see away over the opposite wall, for it's lower!" she cried excitedly. "Oh, how glorious to be able to see the city and everything! I'll go."

But alas! from the times of Cinderella downwards, clocks have often had a knack of striking at an awkward time. And now there came the sound of chimes, the silver warning, and then the five plain strokes that told the closing hour of fettered liberty.

Rosalie re-entered the house. In the central hall she met Mariana coming from the entrance door in hat and jacket, and carrying a muff.

"Where have you been?" she cried, running across to her.

"Out for a walk."

"Oh, Mariana! What a shame never to tell me, and never to take me!" And she took hold of her hands hungrily, and kissed her on either cheek.

"Why do you kiss me?" the other asked, smiling.

"To try to get some real fresh air into my lips."

"It is not very fresh. There is quite a fog coming on."

"Ah! But it's free air. I feel all the better just for kissing you. But why do you never take me?"

"It is against the rules."

"But why can you go, and not I?"

"I'm sure I don't know. See, I have brought you some sweets," and Mariana held out a very pretty box containing a delicious assortment of chocolates.

Rosalie took it, somehow more touched than she liked to show by this simple little act of graciousness.

"Come and sit with me after tea, and let us eat them together."

"I am afraid I cannot. I am always busy in the evening."

"What are you doing?"

"Making a wedding-dress."

"Are you going to marry, then?"

"Oh, no; I'm not making it for myself. I don't know that it is a wedding-dress either. However, I am making it very beautifully, and so I am ambitious for it."

"Who is going to wear it?"

Here Mariana's brow puckered, and a puzzled, tired look came on to her face.

"I don't know," she answered. "I expect if I finish it, and no one applies for it or wants it, it will shrivel up again. For there is no wardrobe but what is overrun with moths; and the moths here eat away all colours except red and black."

"Then how can you preserve it till it's done?"

"By steeping the silk I sew it with in tears. But when the last stitch is in the effect has gone. The moths cannot perceive the bitterness afterwards. They eat it all away."

Rosalie stared at her, as well she might.

"Won't you let me see it?" she asked at length; but Mariana shook her head.

"It would be no pleasure to you."

"Indeed it would. Let me see it, Mariana, just for one minute. There can be possibly no harm in that."

"The room I sew in is very damp for such as you."

"But I'm stronger than you. I'm accustomed to hard work."

The other looked at her and smiled, with more sadness than mirth in her expression.

"What strange ideas you get about things, Rosalie. The work I do would kill you in a month."

"But you will let me come with you, will you not?"

"Yes, if you wish it very much. After tea at six o'clock I will come for you."

CHAPTER XII
AN ACT OF DISOBEDIENCE

At six o'clock Mariana knocked at the little sitting-room door, and Rosalie opened it, quite ready to accompany her, armed with the box of sweets.

"You must not bring those," said the elder woman.

"But I want you to have some."

"I'm not like you. I'm not fond of sweets, and have no intention of making my fingers sticky."

Then Rosalie put them down, and followed her in silence and obedience.

They went downstairs together, and took the door opening into the central hall to the right, the one through which Rosalie had not yet passed.

But at the threshold Rosalie stood still. It seemed to her as if a great spider's web was barring their further progress. A breath of darkness and dampness was wafted out to meet them, and inclination bade her turn back there and then. Mariana evidently noticed nothing of this hesitation; she passed through the door, and held it open for Rosalie to follow. The gigantic cobweb was nothing but delusion evidently, and melted into nothingness.

"Don't shut the door," Rosalie whispered; but it had closed silently even as she spoke.

And here was darkness and cold dampness. She heard her heart beat wildly in the stillness, and groped for Mariana's arm. It seemed cold and lifeless, having no animation.

"Can't we get a light?" she whispered, with dry lips, and her voice sounded hollow in her own hearing.

"The light is farther down the passage."

That, at least, was reassurance. It was Mariana's voice, no different from what it ever was, just as subdued and gentle.

By degrees her eyes became accustomed to the intense gloom, and when Mariana turned on the one flickering light, she recognised a length of passage similar to that in the other two wings. But here the doors were all quite low, and made of plain black wood. There was no attempt at adornment. The floor was plain wood, the walls, the ceilings, and everything was dreary, damp, and cold.

The doors, too, were numbered all in red, and it was before No. 13 that Mariana stopped. It opened to her touch, and together they entered.

"This is the room I work in," said Mariana, and again turned on one feeble light. It seemed the only one in the chamber.

The black rafters of oak hung low above their heads, and their heaviness perhaps helped to increase the gloomy aspect of the place. A long table of deal ran down the centre, with a chair at either end. This table was covered with a white cloth reaching the ground on either side.

Two chests of oak, shabby and worn, were the only articles of furniture the room possessed. The walls were whitewashed. Here and there the plaster had fallen from them, with a dispiriting effect. There was neither fireplace nor window in the room.

"Can you work in here?" Rosalie asked, looking round with an involuntary shiver.

"Yes. One becomes accustomed to surroundings. I never notice them; I'm too absorbed."

She went to the table and drew away the cloth, folding it, and placing it upon one of the vacant chairs. Below, a shimmer of satin, and gold, and silver, all strikingly in contrast to the bareness and poorness of the room, met the eye.

"How lovely!" said Rosalie, drawing her breath. "Do you know, I thought that big white cloth was the material, and it looked to my eyes more like a shroud."

"This is only the material," said Mariana. "I finished it the day you came, after being engaged on it three years. It is all hand-spun and woven, but now I've put the loom and spinning-wheel away in those big chests. One does not want too many things about."

"But who taught you?"

"Oh! it is knowledge one acquires. It needs a certain kind of brain and a given pattern, that is all."

Then she went over to one of the chests and opened it, and took from it a parcel which she untied. It contained a quantity of most lovely lace, the like of which Rosalie had never seen before.

"Did you make this?" she asked.

"No; it belongs to the Master. I found it in the lumber rooms among the attics, and asked him for it, and so he gave it to me."

"Gave it to you? It looks almost priceless."

"I know—reckoned from some standpoints. But I liked the design. It is lovers' knots, and sprays of lily of the valley. Have you noticed it?"

"Yes."

"It was that that put it in my head about the wedding-dress. When I have finished, it will be a beautiful creation."

"But do not the moths attack the lace?"

"Oh, no; you see it belongs to the Master, otherwise it would have been eaten long ago."

"But why do you not wear it yourself, if he gave it to you?"

Again the tired, puzzled look came over Mariana's face.

"I have no use for it. Besides—I don't know. I think it has something to do with sacrifice or freedom. I can't tell which."

"Will you give it to Lady Flamington, do you think?"

"I shall not give it to anyone, except the one who asks."

"But you will be besieged."

"How can that be when no one knows about it?" And she spread the lace upon the ivory satin, and drew it into graceful folds, just as an understanding artist would. As she did so, even by the meagre light Rosalie perceived its exquisite beauty.

"Who is to be fitted for it?" she asked.

"I don't know. One does not like to trouble people; I think I shall use my own discretion. After all, I scarcely hope that anyone will wear it."

"Could I be of use to you?"

"It is too cold for you to take off your dress."

"Oh, no! Let me do it, just to feel I've done something in the day."

"Thank you," said Mariana. "You are neither too tall nor short. I think it would show to advantage on a figure like yours. I'll fit it for just such a one as you."

She cut a piece from the soft piles of satin, and began to shape it to a bodice lining.

"Are you going to try it on with *satin*?" asked Rosalie, astounded at such extravagance.

"Yes; inside and out must be both alike for a perfect finish. I might use silk, but I prefer the same material."

What a marvellous fitter on she was! and yet how wonderfully patient Rosalie stood, the whole long evening through. It was no light twenty minutes—not even an hour—but dragged out into three.

Mariana forgot herself evidently in her occupation, and had no mercy on the model she was fitting. She treated her as a thing of wood and stone till she had realised the full effect in fit of bodice, skirt, and train, which, when perfected, she removed and folded into tissue papers, all labelled for the purpose near at hand. Then suddenly when all was finished she looked at her, and saw how deathly white her face had grown under the lengthened strain.

"Ah! now you are ill, and I am to blame for it," she said.

But Rosalie shook her head, though she shivered.

"It's the cold; everything is so damp down here."

"Yes. Indeed, it has been kind of you. I never hoped to get a model. We can't ask favours of each other here, and I'm sorry if I tired you; but—but—I don't know whether it may not be against the rule, so it was best to complete it before the Master came, in order to plead ignorance."

Truly this last was the most human thing Mariana had ever said to her, the only deviation from a hard, set rule of living.

"Yes," said Rosalie, smiling despite the faintness and shivering that overcame her. "When you've done a thing no one can say anything, can they? At least, they can't say much."

Mariana helped her on with her customary dress, and just then the clock outside struck nine.

"My work-time is up now," she said. "I will return with you."

Perhaps no one ever greeted fire, and light, and warmth as Rosalie did when back in the small sitting-room in the storey up above. In bed at night she remembered the moths that had flickered round the dim light, and round her also, as if claiming this work as soon as finished, and identifying her with it, so it almost seemed to her. And yet how beautiful the thing had looked, how out of place with its surroundings! Suddenly great tears of bitterness fell on the pillow for this lonely woman, so utterly without the pale of human sympathy, and yet so uncomplaining. How beautiful she was! Once during the fitting on she had thrown a piece of satin on her shoulder, too busy for the second to turn round and put it down. And how its ivory smoothness had matched the smoothness of her neck and cheek. How well it had contrasted with her dark eyes and hair. And then there was about her such a nameless grace and gentle refinement! Yet there she had worked in the cold, damp cell, and been content to work, with apparently no hope for the future, but moths and mildew and decay.

It was in the midst of these reveries on Mariana that Rosalie fell asleep, to wake many times throughout the night, shivering, to think herself alone within that gloomy room below, tried on for shrouds by ghosts with horrid grinning laughter.

It was a night in no wise likely to raise Rosalie's spirits from the curious depths of unreality and pain where they had fallen; yet towards morning she fell into a sleep so deep, that she never awoke from it till Mariana came to call and waken her.

"Mariana," she said, "you promised you would show me Mr. Todbrook's portrait yesterday, and you never did."

"It is in the picture-gallery. You could have found it for yourself."

"I don't know where the picture-gallery is."

"I had forgotten. If you wait for me in the corridor after breakfast I will show it to you."

So after breakfast Rosalie went out into the passage to wait for her.

The gallery was downstairs in that same wing, facing toward the gardens, where the conservatory was.

It was a very large gallery, longer than broad, with polished floor, and seats upholstered in red velvet stood along the walls. The light was admitted from the roof, but very beautiful electric candelabra hung from the ceiling, which was all panelled and carved in black oak.

Mariana led the way to the portrait of the late owner of the Marble House. There he stood in the correct evening dress for a man of his position, with one hand leaning on a table and the other by his side. He was slightly built and scarcely of middle height, with a refined, delicate, and quiet face, and a look of wistful melancholy in his eyes that interested and attracted Rosalie.

"Who painted it?" she asked, after studying it for some time.

"I don't know. There is no name to it. I think myself the Master may have done it. It was painted after death."

"From his corpse?" asked Rosalie, in horror.

"Oh, no! From memory, I should say."

"Does Mr. Barringcourt paint, then?"

"In his spare time, yes. I think he must have done this. I don't know who else could. Even millionaires are bad to remember when once they've passed away."

"Is it like him?"

"I don't know. But Everard says it is almost lifelike."

"Who is Everard?"

"The man who keeps the door."

"I don't like him at the door. Do you?"

Mariana looked up with almost startled eyes. "Don't like him? I like everyone."

"I don't like him," persisted Rosalie. "He's one of those men who always does what he is told. If Mr. Barringcourt told him to wring your neck round, or mine, he'd do it soon—as soon as wink."

"Of course," said Mariana, as if that were the acme of perfection.

"Well, he has neither heart nor head. Now, if Mr. Barringcourt told me to wring your neck, I'd tell him to do it himself, I'd had no practice that way."

Mariana looked at her in utter surprise, and then suddenly she sank back upon the velvet seat, and began to laugh. Unhappily, her merriment did not last, for almost as suddenly she jumped up again, her face white with pain, and her features drawn and contracted.

"Oh, for Heaven's sake don't make me laugh! The pain at my heart is something terrible," and she caught Rosalie's arm in her hand, quite unconscious of the strength of the grip she had taken.

In surprise and alarm, the unconscious offender stood still.

"What is it?" she gasped at length. "Is the pain very bad?"

Mariana looked at her and nodded.

"Talk about one's heart breaking," she said, with a wintry smile. "Every time I laugh I get that feeling."

"Let us go away," said Rosalie, noticing that the great pallor of her face did not decrease.

"Yes. It's time I was back at—at the wedding garment."

"But you're not going to that damp, dark place this morning, are you?"

"Yes."

"Then I shall come with you."

"No. I told Everard, and he does not approve."

"But he is not master here."

"No; but his advice is very good to go upon."

"Did I not tell you how heartless he was?"

"You mistake what is meant for kindness. Let us go."

In the central hall she took leave of Rosalie, and disappeared inside the gloomy eastern wing. And Rosalie made no further attempt to come with her, for her horror of the previous night was still fresh in her mind.

"I don't know how Mariana can do it," she thought, standing still in the great hall. "It's killing her. She looked like death this morning. And to go there right away, to be buried in that damp sepulchre! It's terrible, terrible! I *hate* Mr. Barringcourt! He's bad—right-down bad! The worst man I know!"

But then she knew so very few.

She was awakened from this reverie to find Everard, the doorkeeper, coming toward her.

Her first impulse was to turn away and walk toward the staircase, which she did.

"Miss Paleaf!"

His tone attracted her immediate attention. There was a certain strong gravity in it that appealed to what gravity and steadiness there was in her.

"Yes," she answered, turning round to view this wringer of necks in prospective.

"You have endeavoured to do an incredible amount of harm since coming here. Don't you think it would be advisable to practise a little self-control?"

"Yes. I think if it were practicable it would be advisable to shut myself up in a tin box, or oak, perhaps, and turn round once a week for recreation."

"You rush from one extreme to the other without any attempt at reason."

"And—and you?"

"For Mariana's sake I wish to advise you to be careful."

"Not for my own?"

"No. I know nothing about you, and you seem pretty capable of looking after yourself."

Rosalie looked at him, not knowing whether her dislike was growing or lessening.

"Do you know you're taking a great liberty?" she said, her colour rising despite her efforts to keep cool.

"Yes. And under the circumstances it is pardonable."

"What circumstances?"

"You are doing your best to destroy the happiness and peace of a working woman."

"Happiness! Happiness! Do you call it happiness to be fastened up in there the greater part of the day-time?" And she pointed to the door through which Mariana had passed a short time before.

"When she is contented it is, at least, the nearest approach to happiness. And your ignorant meddling can never have a good result."

Then Rosalie was silent, and with no heart to answer she turned away, and went upstairs to the little sitting-room.

Her own heart ached enough in all conscience. O God! to be free! away from all this coldness and hardness, and gloom and silence.

She buried her face in her hands and cried from utter dejection. When she went to wash her hands and face for dinner, she was dismayed at her own plain looks. She was very far from being ready for a meal, and made little attempt or pretence at eating what was placed before her. At last the young man who waited on her presented a red lozenge to her on a silver plate.

"What is it?" she asked, not being accustomed to this particular dish.

"The nutriment you require to keep you in health. You have eaten nothing, and this is less troublesome if you have no appetite."

She frowned in indecision, and for one minute looked at him and then at it. Then without another word she ate the contents of her plate, and afterwards a plate of plain milk pudding.

But when alone again the same weak desire to cry began to gain upon her, and it was only after a very hard fight she overcame it.

"I don't know how it is," she sighed. "They make you do things here however much you don't want to. I wonder now if the eating of my dinner was a lesson in self-control."

Then she went back to her bedroom and shut the door, and knelt down by the bed to pray, if prayer it could be called. Despite her efforts, everything was most incoherent and jumbled, broken by big sobs, and ending in no prayer at all, but silence. At last the silence must have brought its effect of soothing, for Rosalie rose from her knees with scarcely a vestige of the past emotion upon her face. She combed her hair and smoothed her dress, and then went for her hat.

"I'll go into the garden," she said, "and see if I can see the city."

It was a glorious afternoon, with just sufficient sharpness for autumn in the air. It was considerably after three by the tower clock, and she recognised with regret there was time for little more than an hour there. Her hopes were realised. From the top of the red bank of flowers she could view the city very plainly. She saw right across to the high-standing temple, with every building of note and height rising in between. Behind her she could see nothing, for the wall rose exceptionally high, but from here she could look in the direction of the old home, and to that other magnificent erection that contained all the best prayers and aspirations of her dumb life.

After all, to look on to the sights of freedom is in a measure to the prisoner freedom itself.

From the city beyond, Rosalie's eyes wandered back toward the mansion. There was something wanting in it; its magnificent outline attracted and repelled.

"What a lovely fairy story one could write about it," she sighed. "It seems to me a kind of haunted, sleeping palace; and everything looks so strong, and dark, and silent, and yet beautiful, that I don't know whether the story would have to turn out well or ill."

She sat down on the rustic seat with the arbour of trailing leaves twining above it, and dreamily contemplated the wide expanse of city.

Suddenly she heard the ominous striking of the mansion clock.

One! two! three! four! five!

Rosalie turned her eyes from the sky and looked at it. A faint pink flush from the sun was shining on it, and she clasped her hands.

"I won't go in. They can't do anything to me if I don't. Five o'clock! the very nicest time of all the day—the only time to see the city and the sun look at their best. It isn't wrong of me; I know it isn't. I haven't done anything wrong that I should be a prisoner. I haven't, really. I feel I haven't!"

The sunset deepened.

Suddenly the great gates leading from the garden flew open to admit a dog-cart and one chestnut horse driven by Mr. Barringcourt. Behind him sat a groom, and as they took the sweep of drive leading past her toward the terrace steps, her eyes fell on the horse and man in livery.

She saw that they did not belong to this place. What was there about everyone who lived here that made them different from all else? That groom was just the ordinary groom that one saw every day within the streets and parks.

As Mr. Barringcourt passed below he suddenly looked up, and catching sight of her, took off his hat and smiled. Rosalie's heart gave a leap of excitement.

The flush of evening had dyed her pale cheeks, and given lustre to her eyes. She watched the light vehicle draw up below the central steps, saw Mr. Barringcourt dismount, and the groom lead the horse away by the shorter carriage drive. Rosalie clasped her hands and watched, and made no sign of moving down.

And the sunset deepened.

For one minute Mr. Barringcourt stood on the steps looking at his boots, or maybe on the ground, in apparent thoughtfulness; then he turned round with sudden decision, and crossed the lawn to the path leading towards the bank of flowers where she stood. Yet no step downward did Rosalie take in that direction, and so he came up the narrow, winding path, and very shortly reached her.

And how different from all the others he appeared! How full of life and animation! how strong! how quick at seeing, and therefore understanding!

How weak and lifeless her hand felt in his! And suddenly she felt that intense admiration for strength which all weak things must have. Yet she searched his face narrowly for that tired and weary look that she had seen there twice before.

Her scrutiny was well returned. Out of the purity of a lonely spirit longing for some companionship her clear eyes had looked full into his, the ending of a day of weakness and tears and silent waiting. And under the deep scrutiny of those stronger eyes she had not power to look aside till every little secret not worth hiding had been read. Then having got rid of all the weakness, Rosalie came to the reserve strength.

She drew her hand out of his, and asked suddenly, with an everyday interest:

"Have you any horses of your own, Mr. Barringcourt, or do you hire them all?"

"I have my own; but they're too good for everyday work."

"But when do you exercise them?"

"Occasionally at midnight I give them a run round. They are black, so they don't show. Nor do they advertise their coming by too much noise."

This time she looked at him with puzzled incredulity.

"What do you mean?"

"What I say. Why are you waiting here?"

"To see the sun set."

"It has set."

"I'm waiting for the afterglow."

And as she spoke, the whole sky from east to west flushed to a sudden lowering crimson. It was reflected on his face, on hers, shone from the many windows—red—red—a sea of golden red and copper colour, dyeing all things.

"But you have no business out here after sunset, have you?" he said.

"I don't know. You should be judge of that."

"I'm judge of nothing except the mood I'm in, and to-day I'm not sorry to find you here; but it's rather a dangerous game to play in a place where strict discipline is observed. Don't you know it?"

"No. I couldn't imagine any punishment worse than being a prisoner."

"Could you not? Oh, there are many worse. You are a prisoner at large, you must remember."

"The reason why I stayed out is because I could think of nothing I had done wrong."

"Are you a good judge of your misdoings?"

"I don't know. A tongue makes things so complicated."

He laughed. "What have you been doing since I went away?"

"Trying to be contented, and help Mariana."

"Help Mariana?"

"Yes. I tried on a dress for her last night, but the room was so gloomy I dare not go again this morning."

"What kind of a dress were you trying on?"

"A wedding-dress that gave me the shivers. Do you know, Mr. Barringcourt, I think Mariana the most splendid woman I ever met."

"Indeed."

"Yes, and I think she's the most shamefully ill-used woman, too."

"No one is ill-used, except dogs and dumb animals in general."

Rosalie gave him one of her sidelong penetrating glances.

"Well," said she, "there are dumb animals and dumb animals; Mariana is dumb."

"Indeed!"

"What I mean is, she never complains."

"Very sensible of her. There is no one to listen."

"There is Everard! She asks his advice upon everything."

"She told you that?"

"Yes. She talks about everything but her own hard life."

"That is why you wish her to speak about it. Did she do so, you would wish her silent. The world is very contrary, Rosalie."

He stepped aside to let her pass before him down the narrow path. There was no alternative but to obey, as the sunset had now completely died away, and the dusk of night and its accompanying chilliness had wandered in, bringing a sense of desolation, of misery.

The Master did not lead the way to the side door, but approached the central one. He let himself in by touching some spring acting in the toad's head, and Rosalie followed with a creepy sense of awe as she passed between these high doors, with their magnificent workmanship all hidden in the dusk.

The darkness of the big conservatory was partly dispelled by tiny electric lights, coloured crimson, that glimmered here and there among the foliage like glow-worms in a forest. As they passed the picture-gallery, Mr. Barringcourt noticed that the door was open.

"Who has been in there?" he asked.

"Mariana and I went this morning to see Mr. Todbrook's portrait. Who painted it?"

"I did—from memory. A man's best friend should represent him most faithfully. Don't you think so?"

"But had you nothing to work from?"

"Oh, no! Nothing but memory. Memory is a very wonderful thing if one only cultivates it."

"If I died, do you think you could paint me?" asked Rosalie, turning her face up to his.

"No," he answered. "I have not known you quite long enough. I could attempt nothing better than a caricature at present."

She laughed, and said: "I must endeavour to live a little longer, then."

CHAPTER XIII
THE FOLLY OF SIMPLICITY

Together they entered the central hall, and saw Mariana standing waiting there. When she saw Rosalie she stepped towards her, but on seeing Mr. Barringcourt beyond her she stood still.

"What are you waiting for?" he asked.

"For Rosalie. It is long past her time for coming in."

"You have wonderful patience to stand here waiting. Anyone else would have gone to look for her."

"If one waits long enough one generally gets what one wants," she answered, rather irrelevantly.

"Well, don't stand there any longer. You're not needed."

"Thank you."

She turned away with grace and easy dignity, and walked toward the staircase; but when there she looked across at Rosalie.

"Tea is ready."

What a dungeon-knell there was in those three words! Tea in that little shabby sitting-room, away from everything of light, or life, or understanding. A piece of bread, a cup of tea and whatever else was going, eaten alone, and the dreariness of a long dull evening beyond. And somehow or other the thought of the evening frightened Rosalie. It was so dark. The long passages above so ghostly, dim, and silent. And below? She shivered and looked towards the door of the eastern wing, that in some unaccountable way seemed to pervade all things with its shadow and odour of graves.

So though Mariana, after she had spoken, stood still and waited a while for the effect of her words, Rosalie delayed to follow her.

The freedom and grandeur of the sunset was still running in her veins; the pleasantness of conversation and companionship had its influence on her also.

"Ought I to go?" she asked suddenly, looking up at Mr. Barringcourt.

"I don't know, I'm sure. If you admire Mariana as much as you profess I think you should go."

"It isn't a case of Mariana. It's me—myself."

"Well, what of you?"

"I'd much rather stay, and have my tea with—with you."

"I don't indulge in tea."

"Then do they insist on your eating a red lozenge instead?"

"Oh, no! They recognise that I am quite able to look after myself."

"Everard told me I was capable of doing that. And yet at dinner-time to-day I was presented with a red lozenge on a silver salver to take the place of ordinary food."

"And you accepted it?"

"No, I didn't. But if you don't have tea, I'd better leave you."

"I'll waive a point to-night. I have had so pleasant a holiday that it is somewhat distasteful to settle down again. Go and remove your hat, and come down."

But when Rosalie essayed to move towards the staircase she found Mariana gone, and suddenly she stood still.

"Why do you stop?" he asked.

"Oh, I'm frightened! I really am! I dare not go about this place at night by myself. I don't know how it is, but I dare not."

"Nothing will hurt you."

"It's the shadows and the darkness—and the silence."

"Run along. It's your imagination."

"Are you sure there's nothing to be frightened of?"

"Nothing!"

So Rosalie went, and returned like the wind. Her eyes shone with fear, and her breath came in quick pants.

"What did you see?" he asked, laughing.

"Nothing! I did not stay long enough."

So then, in the comfortable cheerfulness of Mr. Barringcourt's study, they had tea.

Rosalie sat in the big arm-chair by the fire; he in his customary one drawn from the table. Very proud she felt to pour out tea, and quite forgave the youth who waited on them for his officious behaviour of the morning. Besides, this was such delicious tea. It was not a bit like that which she had upstairs. The china was superb, with far richer colours than Crown Derby, or anything at all resembling it upon the planet Lucifram.

No wonder that, in the midst of all this luxury and comfort, with a glorious fire and sufficient light, she heaved an unconscious sigh of great contentment.

"Still discontented?" asked Mr. Barringcourt, breaking the heavenly silence.

"Oh, no! Just the opposite. I sighed because I was so happy."

"Have you any book on etiquette?" he continued, casting an eye round his own well-filled book-shelves thoughtfully.

"Etiquette? What is that?"

"Good behaviour, I think, but I'm not sure."

"No, I haven't any book on etiquette; but I remember what my aunt taught me."

"Well, what did she tell you?" he asked, leaning his head against the chair-back, and looking across at her out of half-closed eyes.

"She told me always to be polite to people, and unselfish. You see, there wasn't much else she could tell, because I couldn't talk."

"To be polite and unselfish! Umph! that's good behaviour, is it? I think I've explained etiquette wrongly to you, then." After a silence he continued: "I believe etiquette has to do with correct behaviour. Do you know anything about that?"

"Oh! I expect that is being stiff. No, I don't know anything about that. We weren't at all stiff at home. You see, there was no need to be. We had no servants nor anything, and we always said what we thought. At least, uncle and aunt did, and I listened. But why are you asking about it?"

"I'm very undecided in my mind about you."

"Yes. I get very undecided about myself sometimes. I don't think aunt would approve of me altogether now."

"In what way?"

"My tongue. It is so sharp, you know. You said it was."

"Oh! I'm not thinking about your tongue. I am trying to settle whether we are breaking the laws of etiquette in thus drinking tea together."

"Oh, no! The curates always do it, and they are more correct than anybody. They like you to offer them tea. Aunt used to say so."

"Then we are just as we should be?"

"Yes. Does Lady Flamington never come to have tea with you?"

"No; I generally go there."

"Well, it's just the same."

"Who told you of Lady Flamington?"

"Mariana. Mariana does not give you a very good character, you know?"

"And is your strength of mind great enough to withstand her libels?"

"Well, yes. I like to form my own opinions. Besides, the best fun is, Mariana does not understand she's saying anything against you. She tells me all kinds of things, taking you quite for granted."

"When do you find time for these interesting conversations?"

"At night—and sometimes in the early morning. She never neglects her work to gossip. But when she talks it's always to the point."

"Rosalie, if you wish to possess any fascination, which is another word for beauty, you must learn to keep all your thoughts, opinions, and feelings to yourself. It is not conducive to interest to be told of a person's state too freely. One must be left to find it for oneself."

"Do you find me uninteresting?"

"Very much so. I do not know another man of my acquaintance on Lucifram who would tolerate your company for half an hour."

Her eyes travelled to his with a very real and living pain in them.

"I don't know anything about men except that they're very clever. But I'd be quite content to earn the good graces of the women."

"Why either?"

"Oh, because one must be friendly somewhere. It would be awful to have no friends at all, men or women."

"How many friends would you need for happiness?"

"As many as I could get. You see, when you're poor you can't expect to have many."

"And when you're rich you have less."

"No, indeed. I'm sure you have heaps of friends, Mr. Barringcourt."

He laughed in a harsh, dry sort of way.

"You flatter me. In reality, I have no more friends than you."

"But Lady Flamington? — Why, Mariana says she is in love with you."

Mr. Barringcourt bit his lip; but the smile debarred access there travelled to his eyes.

"Well, what if she is in love with me, as you call it. That makes her one of my worst enemies."

"Oh, no! To love anybody is to be their best and biggest friend."

"I grant if the love be disinterested; but then, how often is it so?"

"What does disinterested mean?"

"I don't know, I'm sure," he answered impatiently; "you must look it out in a dictionary."

"I'm sorry," Rosalie answered meekly, "but I thought disinterested meant unselfish—and I can't understand love being anything else."

"Can't you? Then you have much to learn. Why do you love the Serpent?"

The question came with unexpected rapidity.

"I don't. I—I—I—" Another pause upon the thrice repeated unlucky vowel—and Rosalie shivered from head to foot quite coldly.

"Is this an attempt at fascination?"

The tone was so cold and cruel, and the words carried so sharp a sting, that they cut Rosalie's heart like some whip might have done.

She shook her head.

"I don't understand the Serpent," she said, rubbing her hands against the chair arm. "How, then, can I love it?"

"That implies that you *do* understand the Serpent, and therefore you are not disposed to love him."

"You aspire to understand me better than I understand myself."

"Oh, no! I take you at your own word. I asked you did you love the Serpent, and you said, 'I don't.' Surely there was not much to understand in that."

"Don't let us quarrel," pleaded Rosalie.

"Quarrel? Quarrel? Oh, no, certainly not. I had no intention of quarrelling with you. I remember your telling me the other day you had no particular affection for the god of Lucifram."

"But do *you* love the Serpent?"

"Oh! I—I—I—"

"That is unkind of you, and not polite."

"We ought to have your aunt here to act as chaperon. They say it's scarcely wise to leave a man and woman to themselves, and now I recognise it."

But Rosalie was not far behind in the argument. From cold shivers she began to experience a certain amount of heat.

"I don't know about a chaperon," she said. "I thought a chaperon was a woman who looked after a woman, and I should like to know who looks after the men? Chaperons are silly and stupid, and women, if they were honest, would say they wanted to have nothing to do with them. Besides, it was you who lost your temper then. I didn't a bit. I haven't yet, only you annoyed me by the way you spoke."

"I? lost my temper?"

"Yes, of course. You know you did. You think I've got a secret, and I haven't; so if you don't like, you needn't be nice to me any more."

And Mr. Barringcourt laughed. Under that laugh Rosalie shrivelled up like a white butterfly under the breath of ice.

"But I do like," he answered, still laughing. "You must not quote from Mariana. It is too absurd. And so you have no secret. I can scarcely imagine a woman without one, nor a man "

The merciless mocking eyes were fixed on her, so that she seemed incapable of moving. There rose within her a terrible weakness, a longing to lean on him, to be guided by his advice, to speak of all those doubts that preyed upon her mind, and state the few plain facts that raised them. Again, as before in the garden, she recognised that he was strong, and she was very, very weak. She looked across at him. There was little of sympathy on his face—much of contempt and ridicule—and Rosalie, sensitive to both, shrank from it and him.

A very awkward pause followed—to her, at least.

"I think the tea-party is ended," he said, getting up and pushing his chair back to the table. "It was very enjoyable whilst it lasted, but there is such a thing as folk outstaying their welcome."

But still she sat still, and made no effort to rise.

"What has made you angry?" she asked.

"I don't know, I'm sure. You say I'm angry, so I must be. You should be able to discover the cause when you've noticed the effect."

"I can't. But when I stumble or stammer I notice it always puts you out."

"Then don't do it."

"I'll try not. But if I sometimes said the things I thought, they'd sound so foolish that you'd laugh at them."

"They could not possibly be more foolish than the things you say."

"Are all the women of your acquaintance very sensible and clever?"

"More or less so. Of course, they have the advantage of education and upbringing; but still that does not do away with the fact that they possess many natural gifts."

"It must be very nice to possess natural gifts."

"Yes. Few women are born without them."

"Am I one of the few?"

"So far as I can judge you are. With talent and cleverness, you should be able to escape from prison."

"But I'm staying here on principle. I never thought of trying to get away."

"That shows your inherent stupidity, and a surprising lack of spirit. Cannot you find a door of escape?"

Rosalie shook her head and sighed.

"No," she answered. "I thought of the chimney once, but that was absurd."

"Can you think of no other door?"

"No. It's no good my trying to get out where every door is either locked or guarded."

"You have not wit enough to think of one, you mean?"

"Perhaps so," she answered, and looked at him with eyes full of a great and wistful longing to be told.

"Well, I'll tell you. There is the door of my heart. Any other woman would have thought of it at once."

She shook her head.

"I've had no practice that way. I shouldn't know how to go about to find it."

"No? As women go, you are intensely stupid. You possess all the disadvantages of a school-girl, without any of the attractions of youth."

"I'm not very old," said Rosalie. "I'm only twenty-three."

"There you are again. You can keep nothing to yourself."

"I only told you what my age was."

"Well, I've none of the curiosity of a census paper, and women who tell their ages are a pest."

"But why?"

"Because it is either a boast or a lie. Both are objectionable. Keep your age to yourself. No one wants to know it, and if they do, let them find out or guess."

"Is that what the clever women do?"

"I don't know. If you become a clever woman at second hand, you will become an abomination."

"What must I do then?"

"Remain stupid."

"Then I'll never get away."

"Oh, no; as soon as I pointed the way I blocked it. Had you discovered it yourself, it might have been unguarded."

"I don't believe you would have let me through, even if I had found it out."

"Of course not. One never believes that which touches one's vanity."

Rosalie sighed. What a contrary mood had suddenly seized him! She got up, with little of life or spirit in her movements.

"Then if you find me so very dull I won't come again. Three years seem a long time, but I have no doubt God will help me to live through them."

He laughed.

"God, being dumb, refuses no one, least of all religious women, they force themselves upon Him so persistently. Yes, I shall be glad to be relieved of your company for a while. And so please confine your wanderings to the upper storey where you live. And leave the garden to those who can appreciate its beauty sufficiently to be in by five o'clock."

Rosalie looked at him. Pain and fear was on her face.

"Live upstairs!"

"Yes; live upstairs. And eat red lozenges when your appetite is bad. You can't die, you know."

She turned toward the door.

"Good-night!" he said, drawing an open book toward him on the table, and sitting down.

"Good-night! I see now my fault and punishment in staying out of doors beyond the time."

For only answer he laughed. As he did so the door closed.

CHAPTER XIV
BROKEN SPIRITS

So full of pain and heaviness was Rosalie that all her childish fear had vanished. She passed up the slippery staircase into the corridor, from which her own small sitting-room was.

Never to go downstairs again for three long weary years! Never to be out of the grey, silent, ghostly shadows of those upper rooms—never to have human companionship or friendliness! A part of the meaning floated through her mind, and cast its heavy shroud on all things.

It was still early in the evening, too early for Mariana to return from the work which held her. She sat down in the high-backed chair before the fire, and listlessly looked into it. The flames burnt low. There was none of the brightness of the other day in them—no whispered message of hope.

Rosalie's spirit ached more from the cruel heartlessness of the Master's conduct than even from the thought of coming imprisonment. For this was in the present—that the future. None had ever spoken so to her before— sharply, no doubt but never with this harsh and cruel coldness. Every feeling in her simple nature seemed outraged and lacerated. Once only she moved uneasily in her chair, as one undergoes some great pain, and cried, or rather moaned:

"It's unfair—unfair! I haven't done anything that's wrong, and it was silly and stupid of me to ever think of coming back again."

At last the door opened, and Mariana entered with supper. Rosalie did not turn round till they were alone again, and scarcely even then, till Mariana came and stood beside her, and looking down, said:

"Rosalie, why did you not come in at five o'clock?"

"Don't ask me. I was foolish. There is no other reason."

"Is Mr. Barringcourt's company more agreeable than mine?"

"I thought it was, and have paid the penalty. Don't reproach me. I can't stand it to-night. Perhaps to-morrow."

"I don't wish to reproach you. Once I thought the same, for an hour or two, like you. But I got over it as you have done. You will not care for his company now?"

"No."

"That is well. I suppose you know you are not to go downstairs again?"

"Yes. What am I to do, Mariana, to pass the time away?"

"I don't know of anything. I wish you had come in by five o'clock. There are so many interesting things below."

Rosalie laughed.

"Oh, I didn't come in, so there's an end of it! I'll take supper now and go to bed."

She sipped the glass of warm milk silently, and then together they went to bed. How cold it was in the corridor. How ill lit and melancholy it appeared And Rosalie lay awake, with burning tears, which were never shed, in her eyes.

Three years! And Mr. Barringcourt had said a woman of brains or spirit would have forestalled them and have escaped.

And then it seemed as if across the silence there came that clear, pure voice that spoke to her before, after her aunt was dead: "Neither brains nor spirit, but the path directed."

And silence and sleep and comfort fell—night's gentle curtain and soft pillow for all weary heads.

Sunday, Monday, Tuesday, long or short, according to the circumstance. Each resembled some long and silent eternity of Nothingness. Here was nothing to do. Mariana said there was nothing, and she knew best.

"Bring me a little bit of sewing."

But she shook her head. "I cannot bring it from the workroom."

"Then something from above."

"There is nothing. Each has her work; for you there is none."

"Have you no books?"

"Mr. Barringcourt has the key to the library. I can ask him for one if you like."

But Rosalie shook her head. "No, thank you."

And how difficult she found meal-times, when she must force down food against all wish and inclination. Sunday and Monday it was managed fairly well, but on the Tuesday at dinner-time Rosalie recognised the task was quite beyond her.

"All this tastes of cobwebs and damp soil," she said. "If I must have one, give me one of those little lozenges you offered me the other day."

It was brought. She took it with a glass of water, then rose from her seat. When she got to the door she turned round. Her pretty eyebrows were slightly raised, and she laughed.

"That was essence of cobweb, I believe. Thank you; I feel better already for it."

All was lost upon the youth; he bowed gravely, and returned no answer, and Rosalie went away.

Up and down! Up and down the long dim corridor she walked, with nothing to do but think or mope, or grow melancholy through despair.

After tea Rosalie did not venture out beyond the sitting-room, for the old fear of the darkness had returned; and moreover, to-night a strange weariness oppressed her. At last she fell asleep. Her head rested on the table, and she slept there for nearly an hour.

A little after nine came Mariana and the supper.

"How is the dress progressing?" asked Rosalie.

"It is doing very well."

"How is Everard?"

"He is very well."

"Have you seen Mr. Barringcourt to-day?"

"No. He is away till to-morrow."

"Have you taken a walk this afternoon?"

"A short one."

"Where did you go?"

"My customary round. But you must not ask so many questions."

"But why?"

"Because," Mariana's voice sank to a whisper, "if we talk much I must leave you, and Sybilla will come. And she never speaks all the week, except on my one night out, and then in a language I never heard before."

Rosalie's pale face grew paler. Suddenly she took Mariana's hand and held it very tight.

"Are—are you making fun of me?" she asked.

The other shook her head, and thus abruptly the conversation ended.

At midnight Rosalie suddenly awoke, to hear the great clock striking—a sound which she had never heard before in that room. The ache and weariness of the evening had entirely vanished. She sat up in bed and looked round the room, lit by one meagre night-light. All was as usual, very still; the corners of the room were all shadowy. In another second Rosalie was standing on the floor looking around her in a puzzled sort of way. Understanding came with the swiftness of lightning to her brain. She stood alert, listening, listening, but there was no sound. Quickly and silently she dressed, holding her breath, fearful of being found thus dressing in the middle of the sleeping night. Then with courage screwed to desperation she went toward the door.

"If I'm found out, God only knows what will happen," she thought and turned the handle.

It had one advantage with all the rest of that big house: it was silent.

Mercifully, a few straggling moonbeams lit up the room, shining from door to door, leaving the rest in obscurity. Without glancing toward the shadowy bed, she crossed to the outer door, opened it, and stood in the corridor. The fears born of reality and action had quite killed those of imagination. She no longer started at shadows, nor trembled at the darkness, but went on quickly till she reached the stairhead. Her shoes she carried in her hand to prevent sound. She feared the slippery staircase, lest she should stumble and waken some light sleeper. But to-night it seemed scarcely so slippery as before. Perhaps it was the descent in her unshod feet. At last she stood safely at the bottom in the large hall, with its Spartan plainness and great richness. Chairs, each worth some small fortune, statues in bronze and marble, and above all the great, oppressive shadow, emanating from that eastern door of glass, polished like diamonds, all met her fearful glance.

"If—if I fail—if I'm caught, that's where I go—"

The thought flashed like lightning through her mind, and she looked round breathlessly to find a doorway.

That leading to the conservatory—it stood wide open. On! On! along the corridor, dark but for one dim electric light, such as was also shining in the hall. Then through the palm-house, and toward the central doors. A red spot gleamed upon the centre—the toad's head—for this door was carved alike inside and out. Instinctively she touched the shining knob. The door flew open. The cold damp air of night wafted toward her as she stood thus upon the threshold of the garden. Then, closing the door behind her, she moved forward to the steps. And here again Rosalie returned thanks to that light upon the ugly head. For whereas within it showed her where to touch the spring, here it shone with a direct brilliancy that lit up the entire straight path across the garden, right across and through the wooded shrubbery at the farther end, that led toward the stables. For though the faint light of night might have been strong enough to guide her to the avenue of trees, nothing could ever penetrate this heavy gloom, save only a light such as this steady red one, that lit up the whole long path, right to the stables, as clear toward the end as at the beginning. So without trouble she came to the doorless building. One gigantic slab of marble, between two pillars, was slid back into the wall, and the red light penetrated in beyond. She followed on the path it lit for her, and stood within a sumptuous building. It was certainly a stable, though at the moment it was empty.

Here she looked round, not from curiosity, but to find some means of exit. She walked round many times, but found nothing but one small door, more like a cupboard than a door, built low in the wall, and quite beyond her power to open.

She wrung her hands in despair, and a terrible sweat broke out all over her. No way of escape! Up to now all things had been so easy, as if aiding and abetting her in this wild dream and dash for freedom.

Suddenly upon the still and ghostly midnight air came a sound: the rhythmic trampling of horses, and then a neigh half-echoed by another, as the sound came nearer.

"God help me!" she said, and leant against the carved partition of two stalls, with that deathlike sweat and fear robbing her limbs of any strength of motion.

"The key! The key!"

What voice was it that rang so clearly on the night?

She fumbled in her pocket, and found the old disused one of her uncle's safe.

With nothing but desperation for a guidance she applied it to the little door, close-built to the ground. It fitted and turned. The door flew open. As it did so, from the garden came the crunching sound of horses' feet on gravel, and of wheels.

The little door closed again. Rosalie was without the precincts of Marble House, and breathed her first long sigh of freedom.

CHAPTER XV
A WAYSIDE HOUSE AND GLOOMY CELL

But what and where was this place that she had come to? Instead of coming out upon a mews or narrower street of that big city on the planet Lucifram, she stood upon the borders of a wood. Foxgloves, cowslips, and pale wood anemones bordered its shaded paths. She passed onward, conscious of a new sweetness in the air, and a certain subdued light which, though faint, was quite devoid of shadows.

And oh! to tread upon a path of velvet—velvet of Nature's making, all soft and soothing to the foot.

And though the beauties of the forest awed, they did not trouble her, for their shade was instinct with the mood that she was in—a mood which had much of quiet thankfulness, but no elation. With little feeling of fatigue she walked along the pleasant path, coming out at last upon a city all deserted. Its buildings were the most majestic she had ever seen. There was no ordinary streets of houses all in a row. The buildings had the strength and beauty of past ages. With courtyards of green, and gates with armorial bearings, the windows of the houses were narrow. During the ages, here and there a cornice or a step had crumbled, giving a certain hoary majesty to the houses, showing they had long withstood the inroads of all-conquering Time. No sound of life enlivened the scene; all was silent as the house which she had left. In the central square two churches stood, one in a state of erection, one in the middle stage of being pulled down. Truly it was very curious. All around betokened signs of recent workmanship. But as in dreams one cannot pause to reason, neither did she.

Through the silent empty streets she passed, and came once more on to a stretch of country which rose in hills not far off. These were steep and high, as Rosalie found on coming nearer to them, but the path bordered with wild flowers led her to and up them, and when at last she stood upon the summit of one that rose amongst the highest, she looked down upon a country of gentle slopes and valleys, and dark stretches of forest. A broad and glorious river rolled its even course picturesquely, curving to right and left, here disappearing in the shade of the woodlands, here glittering in the rising sun. With more heart and renewed vigour she descended from the hill-top into this pleasant country beyond it. The path led along the boundaries of a wood, and suddenly there came in sight a low white house, lying far back within a wide expanse of garden, banked with wild flowers of Nature's growing. On the sunny side it was unshaded by the forest, and deep-coloured peaches were glowing in the light. A low verandah ran along the façade, and many sweet and lovely creepers twined about its slender pillars. The big front door stood open, also the garden gate. Rosalie, with tired feet and thankful heart, went up to it and knocked.

Within was a simply-furnished hall, arranged with simplest taste. Bowls of roses stood upon the tables, and the windows, in the recesses formed by the window seats, were open, admitting straggling stems of flowers that clustered upward from below. Built in the wall was a golden fluted organ, the ivory keyboard open, and all the mystic stops clear to the view.

Rosalie knocked.

A door at the farther end of the house opened, and a youth appeared, coming toward her. He was so handsome, and walked with such grace and youthful brightness, that Rosalie's heart went out toward him on the instant. He did not wait for any word of explanation, but said:

"My father will be very pleased to see you. We have been expecting your arrival for almost a week."

"But where did I come from?" asked Rosalie, as taken with his gentle way of speaking as his appearance.

He laughed.

"I don't know; but from a hot place and a great distance, I should think, or else your wits would never have been sharpened to take so long a journey."

"I wonder how old he is?" thought she. "Fourteen at the most. He should have more respect for me than to speak so—so freely; and yet it's nice to be spoken to quite humanly again."

"Yes," she answered; "I've come a very long distance."

"Come this way. See my father, and then you may rest."

He took her to a room furnished simply, and not unlike that of Mr. Barringcourt's; and there, seated at the table, occupied much as he had been in studying, writing, and arranging papers, was the father of the boy.

His hair was very white, as white as silver, and his face was beautiful and clearly cut. He had an appearance of great age, and his tall figure was thin and muscular. In some indescribable way he reminded Rosalie of Mr. Barringcourt. A vague fear began to spring in her mind—for in his dress and manner there was something strangely reminiscent, even though he looked so very old, with his lined face and silver hair.

But he used what Mr. Barringcourt had never used, and that was a pair of glasses; and his glance was very keen as he looked up at her above them with bent brows. And whereas Mr. Barringcourt's eyes were as black as night, his were of a piercing blue, or some colour very like blue. The quality that struck Rosalie most was their intense brightness.

The youth, having admitted her, withdrew, and closed the door behind him.

"You are punctual, Rosalie, and I'm very pleased to see you."

He rose as he spoke, and drew a chair for her, and on the hearing of his kind, grave voice much peace and reassurance settled on her.

"I couldn't help myself," she answered. "I had to come. But you can't be half as pleased to see me as I am to see you!"

He looked at her. "Are you then so much in need of a friend?"

"Yes; but I think I should make better friends with your son than you."

The vestige of a smile crept into his eyes. "But why?"

"Well, I expect you will be too clever. You would soon learn how stupid I was; and then perhaps we should quarrel."

Rosalie looked up shyly as she spoke those last words. The quarrelling, she felt pretty certain, would be all on his side, as it had been with Mr. Barringcourt, for she would never have presumed so far.

"You give Billy credit for being more forbearing than I?"

"Oh, no; I think he will be less observant. I'm very stupid, you know," she continued, with her large, earnest eyes fixed on his; "and people get very soon tired of me. I thought it might be just as well to tell you now, in case you might form a wrong impression, and then be annoyed after, and blame me for it."

"Well," said he, smiling, "that will do for the present. Sleep to-night, and in the morning we will hold a longer conversation."

"But it's morning now."

"Oh, no! It's evening coming on. The sun has set. No travellers ever come to us with morning. The journey is too long for that."

"But everybody cannot come to you just at the same time."

"Well, pretty much at the same time. We live in the centre of a circle, and the distance from every direction is fairly equal."

"Do you get many travellers?"

"Not compared with many wayside inns. But we have a select few that are always very welcome, for we know that they possess some merit, or they would never reach us."

"Ah! Then I am afraid I am not equal to the rest. I have no merits. Nothing but chance and God's goodness brought me to you."

He smiled. "That is curious coupling," he answered. "Chance and God's goodness."

"Well, it was so extremely strange and unexpected."

"We will speak more about it to-morrow. But now I will come with you to see what light refreshment our house affords."

He rose from his chair and led the way into another room where lamps were lit, though there was still much light outside, and a clear fire burning.

"How stupid of me not to notice the sun was setting. I thought when first I saw it it was rising."

"That is a common mistake, much commoner than you'd think, with those coming from Lucifram. You see, it is the direct turnabout, and it is apt to muddle one at first."

"Yes, indeed. What lovely flowers!"

Rosalie was looking at the pretty supper-table and its exquisite decorations. There was something so pure and delicate and delicious about everything, from the snowy linen and flowers all white and flaxen coloured, to the china and vessels of silver and crystal glass. Moreover, there was no shadow lying here. One might eat in happiness and sweet contentment, and the thankfulness born of these.

And moreover, she did not sit down alone. Her host took his place at the head of the small square table, she to the side of him. Every dish was ready served. But first he offered her a little glass of purest sparkling water. Rosalie drank it. The intense fatigue had vanished almost on the instant. She made no effort to talk much, for he said nothing, but ate her supper in silence. Then at last he rose.

"I will show you to your room," he said. "Billy has gone home; he only stayed to welcome you."

"I thought he was your son?"

"So he is. But this is not my home. It is but a temporary lodging, conveniently situated for business purposes."

"Does no one else live here?"

"No one. You need not be afraid. I am sufficient protection."

She followed him with trust and all simplicity to the bedroom set for strangers. When she was alone, by the light of two soft lights hanging from the ceiling, she compared the pure white hangings with the crimson silks at Marble House. Here, indeed, was light-heartedness and freedom from all depression; and with her head once on the pillow, she slept the first genuine sleep of happiness for many a day.

Marble House lay swathed in the mist of early morning. The sun had not yet risen, only that just perceptible twilight that makes known the distant approach of day was at hand. But one by one various lights made their appearance in several of the upper rooms. The occupants were rising at their accustomed hour. It was close on six.

Mariana also awoke, and with the first return of consciousness came the consciousness of loss, vague and alarming. When the light was turned on she noticed the door leading to Rosalie's room wide open, and her own upon the passage standing closed but for the catching of the clasp. Hurriedly she passed into the inner room, to find, almost as she anticipated, the bed unoccupied, its inmate gone. She went to the dressing-room beyond. It also was empty. Then turning back to her own room, she dressed with a curious silent haste. A dull, murky grey sky showed through the window. It caught Mariana's eye and intruded itself upon her memory. Then when her toilette was completed she went out into the corridor. There was no sign of Rosalie either in the little sitting-room or dining-room, and the truth forced itself undeniably upon her. Rosalie had gone—escaped in the night. But where? On second thoughts it seemed impossible. Who ever yet escaped from Marble House in Greensward Avenue upon the planet Lucifram? She smiled forlornly to think of such a thing. And then a sudden fear and trembling for the unhappy girl came over her.

She had tried to escape and had been detected—must have been detected. There were many cells in the east wing, and to attempt to escape and fail in it was of all crimes most criminal.

A feeling, or the memory of a feeling, surged in her heart, so cold, and even, and restricted. Like some quick-gliding spirit she sought the staircase and descended, finding Everard arranging a large batch of papers on the table in the hall. He looked up at her approach, and seeing the slight alteration in her features and expression, said to himself, "It's Wednesday," and went on with his work. But the earnestness of her voice attracted him.

"Everard!" There was more in it than her usual simple, even tone.

He looked up again.

"Everard! Where is Rosalie? Where have you put her?"

"Rosalie? I have not seen. Is she not upstairs?"

She shook her head.

"Is she in there? You have not put her in there?" and pointed to the right-hand door.

He shook his head impatiently.

"She is nowhere of my putting or knowing. She should be upstairs yet. Eight o'clock is her hour for getting up."

"She is not there."

"Not there?" He put the papers he held in his hand down, and looked at her.

"No. And nowhere else upon the corridor."

"Have you searched well?"

"Yes. I did not like to wake the others. Do you think she can possibly have got away?"

"Impossible! The doors are barred—and double locked—and spring-locked."

"I know. But where is she."

"There must be a search instituted."

"Thank God the Master is away."

"He came home last night at midnight."

His voice was grim as his information was short.

"Come home! Come home!" repeated Mariana. "What shall I do?"

"You had best go and tell him."

"Is he up?"

"Yes. An hour ago."

"I can't go. Do this thing for me, Everard. I never asked you anything before."

He looked at her with a face half serious, half cold, then turned in the direction of the west wing.

Mariana sat down on one of the many chairs—a solitary figure in that big empty hall, with clasped hands and shrinking form, fearing vaguely.

Everard knocked at Mr. Barringcourt's door, and obeyed the summons to go in. Before Everard could speak the Master looked up, and said, with a pleasantness not always customary in him:

"Good morning, Everard! When Rosalie Paleaf has had breakfast, I want you to see her. Don't forget to tell Mariana. What is it?"

"She has disappeared in the night!"

"Who?" and the dark brows contracted slightly as he looked across at the speaker.

"Rosalie Paleaf."

"Disappeared in the night? Tell fairy stories to those that believe them."

"She is not in her bedroom, nor the corridor to which she was restricted."

"Who has told you this?" said the Master, getting up.

"Mariana."

"Confound Mariana! Go and search house and gardens, and take the search-light, and bring her back in half an hour."

Everard withdrew.

"Disappeared!" said Mr. Barringcourt, left to himself, and his brows came together blackly. "That is impossible, without the help of Mariana," and then he turned to the letter he was writing and finished it, though it was a long one, before Everard returned.

On his entrance the Master looked up.

"She is nowhere."

"You have searched in every place, likely and unlikely?"

"In every place."

Then a very cruel light leapt into his eyes, in that deep shadow that encircled them, and his lips closed one over the other grimly, as he looked across at the doorkeeper.

"Who is to thank for this?"

"It was a circumstance quite unforeseen."

"I don't doubt it. Where is that heavy-sleeping ass, whose snores swallow up footfalls and opening doors?"

"You mean—"

"I mean your first cousin for dulness of perception. Send me that brainless thing called Mariana."

Everard withdrew. He walked along the corridor as evenly as usual. Whether doubt or misgiving was in his mind, it showed nothing in his face.

There, in the outer hall, scarcely having moved during the whole time, sat Mariana. On the opening of the door she looked up.

"The Master wishes to speak to you."

"Is he very angry?"

"Nothing but what may be appeased. But you had better say no more than you can help."

She got up without a word, and went to the study.

"Where is the girl I entrusted to you?" he said, as soon as the door was closed.

"She has escaped during the night."

"At what time?"

"Between ten and six."

"The time is vague. You're a sound sleeper to be able to count eight hours of unconsciousness."

"I merit it by hard work during the day."

"Oh! you should have explained this a little earlier. If your work was too hard, others could have been set to watch. Your excuse is admirable."

"It is no excuse, it is the truth."

"You never heard a footfall, nor a door creak?"

"No. The doors, as you know, have never creaked."

"I know nothing. You will perhaps enlighten me, and not take too much for granted."

"I can say nothing but in answer to your questions."

"And you know nothing of the hour of escape?"

"I know only that I saw her safely into bed last night, looking utterly tired out. She fell asleep almost before I left the room. This morning I found the door leading from my room into hers standing open, and that leading to the corridor off the latch."

"Has she left anything behind her?"

"I found her hat and cloak in the wardrobe; I do not think she can have taken them."

"Your deduction is beyond argument. A little less sleep would stir that muddled, dreamy brain of yours into some semblance, at least, of action."

"I don't think it's the sleep that makes me stupid. It's the dull greyness of the sky."

"Maybe. What penalty are you inclined to pay for your neglect and lack of vigilance?"

"It was not neglect. I slept heavier than I have ever slept before. I believe God helped her, for she was young and good and innocent."

"You seem to entertain no sorrow for your neglect of duty."

Her puzzled eyes, tired and questioning, met his.

"No, I do not feel sorry. How can I? She could not settle to this prison life as I have done. She was of a softer and more yielding nature. What hardens me would soon have killed her altogether."

"Better be killed than get away alive without permission. And you, being the offender, must bear her punishment beside your own."

A wintry smile crept to her lips.

"Oh! I am strong enough for any punishment. I have a frame of iron buried in what seems like flesh. If I have sinned, then name the punishment. But sin at times, if sin this be, brings near an echo of happier things beyond this life to conjure."

"You are too hard-worked, you say."

"I said I slept the sounder for it."

"Sound sleeping is a thing for swine. You shall not work so hard, for you must sleep less heavily. You are intent upon a wedding-gown, I hear. Leave it unfinished."

"But I have worked at it three years; the dullest work is finished. This is the part I love, that makes some compensation for that other thing I worship."

"And for the double punishment, seeing your working hours have been reduced and cancelled, there will be no further need for that night out—excruciating torment for the all unhappy listeners."

"Rosalie loved my playing." Her dark eyes shone out from a face pale as death.

"No. She was bribing you to stop by flattery. Did she not counsel you to give it up?"

"Ah! that is impossible. I ask nothing but two little hours a week. If that goes, I might as well be dead."

"You might then, for you have done with them."

"It was the stipulation when I came here."

"You have broken the stipulation by your carelessness."

"What am I to do, then?"

"Nothing. Learn to appreciate the luxury of idleness."

"You have not weighed the fairness of such a punishment."

"You have angered me."

"Give me but one hour a week, then. Give me but one."

"No, not one! Get away out of my sight, lest I be tempted to kick you out."

"Where must I go? I have no place amongst the others now."

"There is the workroom. You had best guard what you have made from moths. That is sufficient occupation surely for one who hitherto was too hard-worked."

"It is a return to the life I led before I came here."

"The information does not interest me. You live your life according to your own making. Go; I have no more to say to you."

Mariana's eyes glittered.

"I would I could appeal to some power without against this cruel sentence."

"Oh! there is no power without. The world is too busy with its own affairs. You had best sink into silence gracefully. You have got past the age of screaming and past the age of tears. You have let go the only prisoner I set my mind on keeping, and need expect no mercy for it. Imbecile! Go!"

The words were accompanied by an action so indicative of savage irritation that Mariana, without further reply, turned to the door and left the room.

Daylight, unaccompanied by much warmth, had taken the place of twilight. The lights were out, and morning had begun.

Along the corridor into the central hall, with face all deathly white, she passed. She met Everard there. He had waited for her.

He read her untold story by her face, for she never said a word, and glided past him like a ghost in a painted picture toward the eastern wing.

The door swung open. Here no light had ever penetrated by night or day, save only the artificial glimmer and pale ghastliness.

Then at No. 13 she stopped, and opened the low-built door. She gave one hurried glance back to the big double door that shut her off from life, then passed into the damp, dark cell, and closed the door behind her.

No longer the work that filled with a certain pleasure the long hours of day. To sit there idle, without light, or companionship, or occupation— that was her doom now. And then, to give up that precious pleasure and intoxicating dream that came round once a week! She shuddered at the black thought.

Down she sat upon one wooden chair. And as she sat, the moths descended one by one about her. But when she sighed they flew far off again. The moths in flimsy clouds hovered above, and knew quite all too well their time had not come yet.

So there for the present we must leave her—stiff, rigid, and unmoving. Crushed down by pain and heaviness so great, she had no strength to move or cry.

CHAPTER XVI
THE GOVERNOR

The morning came, and Rosalie awoke, light-hearted and ready to arise. No one came here to call her except the sun and singing birds outside the window. None else were needed. When she had dressed, she passed out on the landing and down the staircase, and seeing the door open to the dining-room where she had supped last night, went there. Its open windows opened on the ground. Breakfast was laid for two, and as none else was visible she passed out into the garden, eagerly drinking in the wondrous freshness of the morning air.

At last she saw the stranger of the night coming toward her from a gate in a high yew edge that separated the garden from whatever lay beyond. He carried a basket in his hand, and as he came nearer Rosalie saw that the basket contained small seeds. Though he wore glasses when writing in the house, he evidently did not need them here. In fact, it did not seem to her that a man with eyes so blue and piercing could ever be short-sighted at all, but still it must be so. He wore no hat. The sun shone on his silver hair, a brilliant lustre. He walked with ease and gracefulness, and again the odd resemblance in appearance to Mr. Barringcourt recurred to her.

"Good morning, Rosalie! I think a spray of flowers would greatly improve that sombre dress of yours. Gather what kind you like, and come to breakfast—it is waiting for us."

He passed on as he spoke, and disappeared within the house.

Following his advice, she gathered a cluster of pale roses, and placed them in her belt. Truly, his words, though simple, had had a very good effect. She no longer felt she wore a uniform of black and red. The flowers had given the happiest relief.

After breakfast he invited her to his study, "for," said he, "I wish to have some conversation with you before eight o'clock. After that I am engaged till twelve, and rarely find much spare time till evening has closed, and to-night I cannot spare you even that."

When they were both seated there, he began the conversation by saying:

"Last night you told me you knew of no merit that could have brought you to me, but I think that, between us, we must endeavour to discover one. Perhaps, if you will repeat your story to me, I may be of use in finding it."

So on that Rosalie recounted the story of her early life, simply and truthfully, up to that last visit to the temple. Nor did she omit her meeting with Mr. Barringcourt there, and the short conversation she had held with him. But on mentioning the last visit, after her aunt's death, she came to a sudden stop, and seemed undecided and unknowing how to proceed.

"You say you went once more inside the sacred curtain. But why?"

"I felt I had given up so much that the Serpent must recognise how much I really loved him. Besides, I felt I wanted to get some real strength to go on living after every hope and aspiration had died away."

"What was it made you wish so badly for a tongue?"

"I don't know. I don't think it was me that wished; I think it was something else."

And then she flushed, for that was the style of speech Mr. Barringcourt would have ridiculed. And she herself recognised that truth at times, to the ignorant or wilfully blind, may appear silly and foolish. But this new acquaintance made no remark immediately, only his keen eyes travelled across her face, as if reading something there.

"And that something?" he asked at length.

"I don't know, I'm sure. But it never gave me any peace, and it wasn't myself, I am sure. Sometimes I used to reason that I couldn't possibly receive the gift of speech, and yet the inner voice repeated, 'Go on, go on!' so that, apart from my own great wish, I was obliged to do as I was told."

"And you received the gift at last?"

"Yes."

"On that last visit to the Serpent?"

"No, I—I—I—for that I went to Mr. Barringcourt."

"The Serpent did not heal you, then?"

"Oh, sir, could it?" Rosalie's voice was almost a remonstrance.

"Is not the Serpent the God of Lucifram?"

"Yes, and that is what has troubled me so heavily ever since; far more than imprisonment and harshness."

"What has troubled you?"

"Perhaps if I tell you, you will think me fanciful."

He smiled.

"Fancies are all put to the test here," he answered, and a certain sternness rang in the kindness of his tone that reassured Rosalie, somehow or other, when she thought it would have frightened her.

"Well, after I had resigned my will, and prayed for strength, I closed my eyes, and it seemed as if a great vision flashed before me in the darkness. The Serpent seemed to have turned round, and to show that from the back it was all hollow, and in its three tails, so black and dingy from the inside, three dwarfed jesters sat, with caps and bells, all grinning and pointing, as if to make a mock of everything. And then a fire of purest light and radiance, with a centre of unearthly brightness, more beautiful than any sight I ever saw, rolled over everything, and burnt the hollow symbol to a cinder with its all-conquering strength."

Rosalie's eyes were shining as they looked across into his.

"And in my mind the same thing must have happened. For somehow no longer I thought upon the Serpent. All was changed. Whatever humble love I had to give, and strength to ask, were given and claimed by some wise reasoning Being far above, whose faintest breath could shrivel into cinders this grinning mockery worshipped of man."

"What of the cinder?"

"Oh! I remember it never burned away. It shone like a little ball of gold within the fire, and I wondered at the time why it had never disappeared."

Then suddenly she got up and crossed the room and knelt down beside him, and clasped her hands upon the arm-chair.

"And I believe it," she said. "I could never think of going back to the Serpent after the higher thing; I loved to see the pure white light within that glorious fire. It was so peaceful, restful, strong and light-giving. I hardly think I could have spent the week that followed, with all its brilliant lights and gloomy blackness, and everything so fresh and new, had I not had that light so pure and still to think upon. It was divinest comfort to me even when the blackness tried to quite obscure it, and set such a terrible gap betwixt me and every living thing."

"And after this you left the temple and went to Mr. Barringcourt?"

"Yes; there was nothing more to stay for. And I think the same thing led me to him that has now led me to you—calling 'On! on! on!' in spite of everything."

"And when you got there?"

"Then he healed me, by a very natural process it seemed, that had little of the miracle about it. But I felt no pain, and I remember he was very much surprised at it."

"And the cure was perfect?"

"Yes, I think it was too perfect. My tongue became most glib and voluble. Words slipped out I often wished unsaid."

"You had had no practice in restraining them?"

"Well, no. But I think myself Mr. Barringcourt really did oil the wheels of my tongue too freely, because I don't think by nature I should ever be given to answering back. But when I was there that seemed the one thing in life I was capable of."

She had risen from her knees and walked towards the fireplace.

"But what reason should he have for doing so?"

Rosalie looked at him sideways. Then suddenly she laughed.

"You've got to learn some day how intensely stupid and simple I am, so perhaps you had better know soon as late. Well, I think the reason why he brought my tongue to such a pitch of volubility was because he is very keen on finding out all secrets, and he thought I should save time and trouble by being made very talkative."

"He is keen on finding out secrets?"

"Yes; it sounds silly, but it's true. He was most peculiar. If other men are like him, I pity the women that have to deal with them, and often think how fortunate my aunt was, for uncle was most quiet and peaceable."

"Your experience of people is not very great."

She sighed.

"No; I could not tell whether he was like other men or not. That's how it was I felt at such a disadvantage all the time. Anyway, he wasn't like any of my relations, the girls and women that I knew, nor even like the doctor that attended us, nor the bread baker, nor the butcher, nor any of those. But then Everard wasn't. None of them were, in fact."

"What led to your discovery of his *penchant* for secrets?"

"Mariana told me; and when she told me, I laughed to myself, it seemed so utterly ridiculous. But afterwards I came to understand it. That is why he quarrelled with me, and left me a prisoner in the upper storey."

"In so short a time?"

"Yes. He found I had no secret worth discovering."

"But had you not?"

"No. Sometimes I felt tempted to tell him the real facts of my last visit to the temple, but something always held me back. And after all, if I had told him I should have become a prisoner all the same."

"Maybe. Then in the end you quarrelled with him?"

"No, he quarrelled with me. We were getting on, as I considered, very nicely, and suddenly I could say nothing that would please him. Afterwards I understood it was because he had grown tired of me, and found me unprofitable, so far as secrets were concerned."

"And so you were consigned to shadows, and a suite of rooms in an upper storey?"

"Yes, and it was terrible. I never wish to go through such a time again. It seemed to me eternity. Even now I don't believe it was a week. It was a year of weeks."

"Did Mr. Barringcourt ever ask you any questions about the Serpent?"

"Yes; he often asked me questions."

"And you never told him what you had seen then?"

"No, I couldn't, much as I wanted to. When I got to that part I only stammered, and that used to make him angry."

"Then how can you say he discovered you had no secret worth discovering when you distinctly had one?"

"He would have simply ridiculed it, and said there was no truth in it. So what was it worth to him?"

"You used some little reason, then, in the controlling of your tongue?"

"Perhaps it was I, but I gave the credit elsewhere."

"Now we have to discover the merit that lit the path for you to here."

"Will you not put on your glasses? It will be hard to find."

"How long did you say you prayed to the Serpent for the gift of speech?"

"Over two years; and the prayer was answered in a different way from what I thought."

"By the way, you spoke a little time ago of Mariana. Who was she?"

"A kind of waiting-maid at Marble House. I do not know what else she could be called, unless a sewing-maid. But she was beautiful, and different altogether from any sewing-maid that I had ever seen. And even in a week I grew to love her, for underneath a cold and smooth exterior she had the sweetest, kindest disposition of anyone I ever knew."

"Did she derive much happiness from living there?"

"None, except two hours every Wednesday night. And then she played upon a violin. I never heard such music, though it was weirdly sad. But Mr. Barringcourt blinded my reason to believe there was no harmony in what she played."

"You do not give him an enviable character."

"That is what I said when Mariana told me of him." And suddenly Rosalie shuddered. "How can I give him an enviable character when he was cruel, hard as marble, and vindictive. He was bad, really bad, and the worst thing is I knew it all the time, yet had he been agreeable to me, really agreeable, I would have shut my eyes to everything."

And from a very real feeling of shame, her colour deepened, for Rosalie was not one of those people who are blind to their own shortcomings and weaknesses.

Then suddenly turning to her host, she said, changing the conversation:

"What must I call you? Everybody has a name, but yours I never heard."

"Well," he answered slowly, "I don't know that for the present I have any name worth going by. Some call me the Traveller's Friend, some the Physician, some the Task Master. You may call me what you will for the present. Hereafter we may find a better name."

"Well, Mr. Barringcourt was called the Master. Suppose I call you the Governor, without any abbreviation to a lesser name."

"Why that?"

"Because Mariana told me I was weak, and weak people want someone very strict with them, and I should like to have a good understanding, you know, because I'm very ignorant."

He looked at her.

"Well, you will find me strict enough. And for the rest, it's bound to follow."

Then he got up, and took down a large volume from a book-shelf, and seated once more in his chair, with the book on the table, adjusted his glasses, and opening the leaves, turned them slowly, as one looking through the pages of a dictionary to discover something.

As last he found the place he needed, and for some time read in silence; then closed the book and instantly removed his glasses as he looked across at her.

"I've been through the list of merits, Rosalie, and have decided yours is the questionable merit of clinging on. None others have had much time to develop yet. They may be there, no doubt, but have not, as it were, yet come of age."

"Clinging on! It's very questionable, isn't it?"

"Yes; but you'll have one or two stiff examinations to pass in it before you've finished."

"But—but the people who cling on are—are so insufferable." And it must be acknowledged a very real tear of disappointment stood in her eye.

"Would you have liked some higher-sounding virtue?"

"Yes; I thought you were going to say meekness and gentleness, or some of the great gifts of the spirit. I never read that 'clinging on' was counted much in the Book of Divine Inspiration. Besides, who have I been clinging on to? I deserted the Serpent just—"

"Just at the right time. There is where the virtue comes. Had you been any earlier you would have shown great fickleness. Besides, after all, I don't think you're very heavy, Rosalie. You would not be such an insufferable load to drag along."

"I don't know, I'm sure. But anyway, I'll trust to you."

"Well now, whilst you stay with me there is much work to be done. But for to-day, until you become accustomed to your new surroundings, you may take holiday. To-morrow morning be up as early as to-day. After breakfast I will show you in what direction your work will lie."

After that she went away, and saw no more of him all day. It was an ideal holiday in the sun and warmth and beauty of the outdoor life. And for the noontide meal, Billy came and sat with her, though he only drank one glass of water whilst she ate.

"Are you not hungry?" she asked.

"Well, yes. I'm getting hungry, but it isn't my meal-time yet. You'd be astonished if you saw the amount I eat compared with you," and he laughed in the gayest, happiest tone. After a while he said: "Have you made friends with the frog yet?"

"With whom?"

"The frog. My father's pet frog. It is in the garden, but is rather shy of strangers, but very talkative when once you get to know it."

"A frog? And it can talk?"

"You bet! It has a better fund of words and style of oratory than many a statesman."

"Well, then, it should be a human being."

Billy looked at her, and his brilliant sparkling eyes were laughing.

"Well, no, hardly that. It is quite contented to remain a frog—a very superior kind of frog."

"Do you come every day for lessons?" asked Rosalie, uncertain what to say.

"Three times a week. And the other days I walk over in my spare time."

"Then you have not far to come?"

"Not far, comparatively speaking. The distance lessens as one grows older, I find."

"Then it would be less to me than you?"

Again he laughed.

"Well, no; I expect I've had more practice than you. Good morning!"

And he was gone, leaving Rosalie to ponder on that odd kind of powerful beauty in his face, and that exuberant merriness that made her sigh to lose him. For that was the worst of Billy. He seemed to come and go more like some brilliant spirit, a kind of Mercury, with winged heels, to bring one ray of sunshine, and then depart.

CHAPTER XVII
A PLANTATION

The next morning after breakfast the Governor led her down the garden to the gate in the edge of yew. He carried in his hand the basket she had seen the day before, containing seeds. But whereas yesterday they had looked green, to-day they had a silvery-white appearance, toning to a liquid aspect as of water in the centre. Beyond the edge stretched a square plot of uncultivated land bordered by willow trees, and at the further side a little hut of wood, just in the shelter of the forest. But here the sun did not shine so brightly. The garden of Pleasure was left behind. This was the field of *Work*.

The Governor led the way across to the hut. It consisted of two rooms, a living- and a sleeping-room, and moreover a little cellar, where she discovered all kinds of garden implements and spades, and one large fork that looked as if it were for digging heavy soil.

He put the basket down upon the table, and then he said:

"This is your little house. These are the seeds to be sown in the strip of land you see without. You must dig and sow, and then wait for the harvest. The books upon the shelves you may study in your leisure, but you must grasp each subject thoroughly before your time of apprenticeship is over."

So saying, without any word of advice or caution he left the hut and crossed to the gate that led to the garden. Rosalie was left alone.

But though on one side lay a great and unknown forest, she experienced no fear at being left alone, even though when she looked out she noticed how uncompromisingly high the edge appeared, shutting her quite away from sight or sound of the pretty wayside house.

But just then a voice attracted her attention.

"Well! well!" said it, most harshly, "what's the first thing that a farmer does before he sows his seed?"

"I don't know, I'm sure," answered Rosalie; "I've never lived in the country," and looked round to find the speaker.

And there on the doorstep was a frog sitting, looking up at her half contemplatively, half pityingly. Its colours were beautifully striped, green and white. On its head these colours blended brilliantly, taking away some of the staring effect of the wide-open eyes.

"Don't know?" it answered. "Well! well! You'll have to dig. Get a fork and dig. Well! well! best to know nothing than to know too much."

Rosalie went as she was told, and brought the big fork she had noticed. It certainly was very big, and looked aggressive.

"Do you mean this?" she asked.

"What else should I mean? Now then, set to work. The quicker you begin, the quicker you'll finish."

"But—but what must I do with it?"

"Grasp it in both hands. Stick it in the ground, and push it in with your foot. Well! well! the sooner you learn, the sooner you'll know."

"I won't!" said Rosalie. "It's a man's work; why, it's digging. I know I was never intended to do that."

The frog, by way of showing its disgust, gave a contemptuous croak.

"Man's work? It isn't the work most men would thank you for giving them. Even as far back as the days of Divine Inspiration mankind was ashamed of it. It's woman's work! What man won't do always falls to the woman."

"But women never dig in our country," said Rosalie, still bent on the argument.

"What country's yours?"

"The biggest in the whole of Lucifram."

"It would be bigger still if the women applied themselves better," said the frog, and a short silence followed.

"Do you really think I ought to do it?" said Rosalie, at last, not being of that stubborn nature that delights in saying "no" and sticking to it.

"Well, I don't see what else is to be done," said her companion. "If you don't dig you'll never sow, and if you don't sow, you'll never reap, and if you don't reap you'll never—"

"Never what?"

"Prove you're anything but a fool."

"Really?" said Rosalie.

"Really!" said the frog; but the expression in each voice was different.

So she stuck the fork into the ground, and found it took a great deal of strength to make any impression upon the surface. But once having put her shoulder to the plough, as it were, there was nothing for it but to go on, for the old voice kept ringing "Go on! go on!" and consequently on she went.

The frog, for some considerable period, watched her from the side, but finally hopped away into the hut. At noonday it appeared again, and summoned her to dinner, which was already prepared in the little living-room.

"Who prepared my dinner?" asked Rosalie, after she had washed her hands and settled to the meal.

"I did," it replied. "It's a woman's work certainly, but if you waited for a woman to do it for you, you'd come badly off. No; I'm a frog, but when there's no one else by I can do other work besides my own. How do you like digging?"

"It makes me very tired, and the inside of my hands are quite sore."

"Are they? Well, you've got to go on again this afternoon, you know. If you don't get the seeds in before very long they'll wither."

She answered nothing, but after the customary hour of rest returned again to the hard labour.

It was slow work and very hard, and not a soul came near all the day long. In fact, during the afternoon even the frog seemed to have deserted her, and it was not till the first faint tinge of evening crossed the sky that she again heard the familiar voice calling from the wooden doorstep:

"Time's up now; tea's ready."

Rosalie let the fork drop on the ground, and turned round as eagerly as her tired body would allow.

Whilst she ate her tea, this new friend sat upon the hearth.

"I shall be as stiff as a board to-morrow," said Rosalie, laying her tired arms upon the arms of the chair.

"No; my master sent down that little bottle on the mantelpiece for you. You must take it before you go to bed, and you will be all right in the morning—so far as stiffness is concerned, anyway. We don't go in for torture here, but we believe in hard work—very hard work sometimes."

When the meal was finished the frog said:

"Now, if you will take this arm-chair by the fireplace, I will remove the table."

She did so, and was surprised to see that when the frog pulled a small knob in the wall the whole table, which, however, was not large, disappeared through an opening partition, and left the room clear.

"If you want to read or study, you must draw that writing-desk nearer," continued her instructor.

"I don't want to do anything to-night. I'm so tired, I think I'll go to bed early."

"That wouldn't be a bad plan, seeing you have only been at work one day, and find it all so strange. You'll be more accustomed to it to-morrow, and get more done."

"Yes," said Rosalie; "I'm all impatience to be finished. It is such dreary work, and I'm quite inquisitive about the seeds. I wonder whether they'll grow up roses, or lilies, or nasturtiums, or dahlias, or hyacinths, or chrysanthemums, or what?"

"Don't you know much about seeds?"

"Nothing. Uncle was very clever that way; but I never cared about seeds—they looked so very uninteresting; I only cared about the flowers."

"If I were you," said the frog, "I would rub a little of that liquid out of the bottle on my hands. If they are blistered and sore it will heal them very quickly. I've had sore hands myself, so I can sympathise. And here's a pair of gloves," it continued, drawing a pair from behind the coal-scuttle. "I made them this afternoon, instead of coming out to keep you company. I might have made them outside, but I thought it would be a little surprise for you."

"Oh, thank you," said Rosalie. "How very thoughtful of you! Where did you learn everything you know?"

"Well! well!" said the frog, with quite a sorrowful croak, "I learnt it in the school where it is most generally taught."

"Where was that?"

"In the school of experience and adversity, for the most part."

"Don't you think that people can be kind unless they've gone through a great deal of suffering?" asked Rosalie.

"Now and again, just now and again, one finds them. But they're few and far between."

"I think suffering and trouble make people bitter, or else break them up altogether."

"Not if they're made of the right stuff," said the frog. "It's the needle's eye that rich and poor men alike have to pass through. If you can't stand sorrow, you can't stand happiness, though you may think you can."

"But we were made to be happy. The Serpent—God rather, meant us to be so."

"God meant us to be happy eventually," said the frog gently. "But like all things else worth having, it takes a great deal of fighting for. Contentment and peace are the nearest approach to it one generally gets the other side of heaven."

"I don't like the word 'peace.' It reminds me of a fat woman, and a dinner of suet dumplings."

"You're prejudiced, or else you've mistaken it for lethargy."

"Well, is not contentment a state of lethargy?"

"No; when you're most contented, you're least so. The two things naturally go together, and keep up a constant flow of action that does away with torpidness."

"How long do you think it will be before my work is finished here?"

"I don't know. It's rather a foolish question to ask. No one knows. It depends upon what time the seed takes to ripen and the bent of your mind."

"And in the evenings must I study?"

"It is your only time. But what you want is plenty of hard work and plenty of deep thought."

"And that is almost everything," said Rosalie.

"I believe it is," answered the frog; and by the simple process of pulling another knob emptied a shovelful of coal on the fire out of the chimney-side.

It was not long after this when Rosalie prepared for bed. She rubbed the liquid on her hands, and found it very soon relieved them. Then she drank the contents of the bottle and retired to the inner room, first bidding the frog "Good-night."

"I sleep on the doorstep," said it, "so you may sleep doubly secure. Nothing evil can cross me, for my life is charmed."

And, somehow or other, there seemed more life, strength, and independence in this small creature than there had ever been in Mariana. Poor Mariana! Rosalie fell asleep thinking of her, wondering how she had taken the news of her escape, and whether Mr. Barringcourt indulged in anything further than a frown when the truth was told to him.

But these thoughts did not keep her long out of the land of dreams. Perhaps it was that Rosalie had enough to do thinking of her own affairs just then. It never struck her that her escape could make any material difference to Mariana. She imagined her living the same even life, with one real pleasure in the week in compensation for its darkness, and saw within her mind the wedding-dress nearing completion, and trembled in her sleep to think it soon must be finished and fade again to nothing for want of one to wear it.

And in the night she dreamt the seeds were sown, the time of harvest came, and every seed appeared as a huge and barren stone. Then in despair and disappointment she wept upon them, and they disappeared.

CHAPTER XVIII
SEEDS GROWING CONTRARIWISE

After that, life began in earnest for Rosalie. For some weeks her days were given to digging, her nights to mastering the alphabet of some unknown language. It was all dry work, and very hard.

No one came near, except the frog, and she often found herself wishing for more human companionship. But still it was not Rosalie's nature to grumble too much at circumstances. She contented herself with an occasional sigh, and for the rest learnt to love the harsh, croaking voice that had something to say about most things, and was always kind enough to revive her drooping spirits with cheering words.

At last the plot of ground was all prepared, and considering it had been digged by a woman, it was not at all badly done. No one would have known the difference if they hadn't been told, though afterwards they might have discovered the depth was not so great. However that may be, the seeds were sown in it, and began doubtless to do their own little bit of digging, and go down so far that no one could find them where they'd first been put. After the sowing came the time of waiting. There was much weeding, and more watering, for no drop of rain ever descended there, and all had to be carried from a stream near by.

Rosalie watched the ground impatiently to see when the first bright blade would appear, but though she waited one month, two, three, four, nothing at all except an occasional weed altered the surface of the ground. And her whole heart was buried in that little garden. It seemed as if it, too, must have taken root down there, away from the sunshine and the warmth.

And the waiting was far worse than the working, for after three months certainly something ought to have shown. But when it went on to four, five, nay, at last came out into six long months, and nothing yet had come to light, Rosalie went back into the little hut, and laid her head upon her arms upon the table, and cried from sheer disappointment and low spirits. For during this time of waiting and subsequent doubt no one had come to see her, no one at all, except the frog.

In this fit of depression, which was the first of its kind, the outcome of disappointment and hope deferred, the frog spoke.

"What is it, Rosalie? I've never seen you cry before."

"I can't stand it any longer, I know I can't. I've waited for six months, with never a soul to speak to but you, and nothing has come up. It's all a failure. My heart is as heavy as a stone. If it gets much worse it will break right in two. I know it will."

"Where is your heart?"

"It should be in my body, but I believe I must have sown it along with the seeds in the garden, and it's turning to stone while they're rotting."

Then the frog spoke rather shyly, as one who fears to be ridiculed, and is slightly apologetic.

"Perhaps the seeds have turned to—to—to—stone, too," and it looked hard in the fire instead of at Rosalie.

She, however, looked across at it with eyes wide open.

"Well, really! It doesn't seem unlikely, considering the time they are in coming up."

"What will you do?" said the frog.

"I'll begin to dig again," cried Rosalie.

"It's the wisest thing you've said since you came here," the frog answered, and its colours flashed quite brilliantly.

So the next morning (for it was evening when they spoke to one another) Rosalie rose with a much lighter heart than for some time past, went out into the garden with the fork, and began to dig. She dug all day, but found nothing, till just at eventide she noticed something shining in the dull, damp soil. She picked it out with her fingers very eagerly. It was a dull enough looking stone for the most part, with here and there a substance in it that shone like glass—not very brilliantly. Whatever it was, it was enough to brighten Rosalie's spirits for the time being, and as just then she heard the frog's voice calling her to tea, she made as much haste forwards as she could over the clodding soil to show her treasure.

"See what a beautiful thing I have found!" she cried, and held it up triumphantly.

"It isn't very brilliant," said the frog, looking at it critically.

"Don't you think so?"

"No. You do, because you've been looking at black soil all the day, but I've been looking at the sun."

"Well, but then the brightest thing would look dull if you compared it with the sun. How am I to find out really what it is?"

"Take it to my master."

"I can't open the gate."

"The gate will open of itself, if you've anything to take to him."

Rosalie turned about to run off at once, but the other said:

"Wait and have tea first. He is never at liberty till six, and now it's only five."

So after tea, Rosalie, having previously changed her heavy boots and generally tidied herself, set off in the direction of the house.

The gate this time responded easily enough to her hand, and soon she was walking through the garden, holding her stone the tighter, in that she was quite sure, from the fact of the gate opening so readily, it must be worth something very considerable.

The door leading into the garden was open, and after knocking she passed through, and went at once to the study.

The curious thing about the sun here was that it always set at the same time of day, and that between five and half-past, so that now twilight had fallen, and the lamps were lit, though the blinds remained undrawn.

The Governor sat as usual, and must have been expecting her, for he held out his hand as she entered, saying:

"Well, what have you brought?"

She placed it in the hand he held out, and waited whilst he looked at it. This did not take very long, for almost on the instant he looked up, and said:

"I'll send it to an expert in the city of Lucifram, and get his opinion on it."

"You think it is very valuable, then?"

"I'm afraid I don't, except in a way that doesn't count. But we'll send it to someone who is unacquainted with the digging, and watering, and heartburning it has necessitated, and therefore who will be less prejudiced than I."

"When will you send it?"

"To-night; and you will hear the decision in something like a fortnight."

So then she went away. The next two weeks were passed in waiting, and in the study of those books which Rosalie found more dry and difficult each succeeding day. For there was no one to explain them, and in some parts there seemed nothing but big full-stops and commas, with wide gaps between.

But at the end of that time the frog came to her one morning and said the Governor wished to see her.

Rosalie went in fear and expectation, and the first thing her eyes lighted on was her stone upon the table. This, she felt, was not quite as it should be.

"The decision is that it is rubbish."

That was all the Governor said.

She felt rather miserable. She thought it must be with hurrying across the garden. However, there was nothing to be said, and Rosalie withdrew. After that some very hard, frosty weather followed, and the ground was so hard that for a long time she was able to do nothing—outside, at any rate.

Then when it thawed a little she went out and digged again, and found just such another stone as the one before, only of a little lighter and brighter substance.

After tea she took it to the Governor, as last time. He promised to send it to the city, and get the opinion of an expert upon it. Rosalie withdrew to wait. At the end of a fortnight she was again sent for to the Governor's house. Her stone was on the table.

"The decision is that it is rubbish," said he.

And she felt disappointed this time, but not miserable. One is never quite so sure of things after the first time—that is, if they've miscarried. She went back again to the plantation and the hut. Again the ground had frozen, and for some time it was impossible to do anything, even had she had the inclination.

After this, every time the thaw came Rosalie set to work again, finding the work a change and relief from study. And though the disappointment always lasted out the frost, it always disappeared with the thaw. And every time she went up to the house, the particular stone she had last found lay on the table, and the words were:

"The decision is that it is rubbish."

This went on for a long while, till at last it seemed to Rosalie all the hope had been crushed out of her, and she went back to the garden and found it quite frosted over. But after a while the frost broke, and the frog, seeing Rosalie made no attempt to go to dig, said to her:

"The frost has broken."

"I know."

"Will you not go out into the garden?"

"No; I'm too impatient. I want the seeds to grow quicker than I can learn. I've been thinking about it all, and I feel that I must wait. Bright stones take longer to grow than flowers, because they fade less quickly."

Thereupon the frog let fall a tear of gratitude, but turned the other way during the odd process, so that Rosalie never noticed it.

Then followed a very long and dreary time, with no companionship; nothing but the even days and dull books, and the sympathetic frog. And this went on so long that many a time Rosalie went out to look at the ground, and sighed, but never thought of touching it, because something had said "Stand still." At last, after a very long time had gone by, she went to bed one night, feeling particularly sad.

Some hours later she awoke to find the moon shining full into the chamber. She got up and dressed, and went through into the outer room. The door was open, and the frog was sitting contemplatively upon the step, looking out on to the beauties of the night. Occasionally it gave a croak of satisfaction.

Rosalie went to the cellar and brought out the big fork, and thought she was so quiet the frog had never seen her. But then, poor thing, its eyes were so large, they stared out from every side of its head, and as she approached the door it hopped down, and moved aside to let her pass.

"Why don't you ask me what I'm going to do?" she said, laughing.

"That's plain to be seen," it answered, and hopped after her in the moonlight.

Suddenly Rosalie began to dig, just on that portion of ground where a shaft of moonlight had fallen. For some time nothing but loose soil came up, but at last the fork hit upon something hard. It did not move till a space had been cleared all round it, and then it appeared nothing but a heavy hard mass of black earth, with an irregular surface.

"Well?" said the frog.

"There are other tools in the cellar beside a fork," said she. "But we've done enough for one night. It can stay now till the morning," and she took it in both hands, and lifted it out of the deep trench dug about it.

So then once more night reigned undisturbed. But with the morning work began again, this time with finer instruments to chip away the thick layers of soil and find what lay beneath. It took a very long time, much longer than Rosalie ever anticipated, though in other ways the hours passed quickly under this keen absorption. In many places the soil seemed more like marble than rock, and required much patience to remove it, for none of the instruments were particularly sharp, nor specially adapted for that purpose. But what of that? Working, working, ever unceasingly, on went Rosalie, and one day she looked up at the frog, and half laughed, and said:

"I believe my heart is inside here, and I'll never be happy till it's free, quite free."

But the frog only turned away and sighed, and Rosalie was so intent that she never heard the sigh.

And at last!

Bit by bit a brilliant jewel unfolded itself, all flashing green-and-moonlight colour, and with one gleam of ruby red, just one bright gleam upon the middle surface.

And she pressed it to her lips and kissed it. This was no dull stone with intermittent flashes of light. No, this was *real*—a lovely thing of sparkling colour.

It was finished just at sunset. She scarcely needed any tea, so eager and impatient was she to get away.

And then she appeared before the Governor with this precious prize.

"I've found something really, at last," said she, with bright eyes and cheeks.

As of old he held his hand out for it, but said nothing.

"Why don't you speak?" she asked.

"It is not for me to speak," he answered; and so she went away.

But Rosalie was scarce content with waiting now. She doubted not that all would see the value of the stone she had so lately found, and most of all an expert. And indeed there seemed to be no time for waiting. The voice said, "Go on." Truly the harvest was beginning. Who would sit down with but one sheaf tied?

And she was justified in doing so. Another lump of hard black earth (to be chipped away slowly and surely) appeared amongst the looser soil. And after a time the under surface partly appeared, and it, too, as far as she could see, was bright and brilliant.

But as this was in process the message arrived at breakfast, the Governor wished to see her.

She did not allow herself to think, because she dare not, but whatever thought rose in her mind it was success.

She knocked at the study door and entered. There, in the same place that all the others had been in turn, lay the shining jewel, and the cold voice answered:

"The decision is that it is rubbish."

The pain within was so great that Rosalie could have screamed, and then came sickness and faintness, so that she leant against the door and looked at him.

"What does it mean?" she asked.

"It is accounted of no worth."

"Oh, but it is! it is!" she cried, and looked at him so hard that he looked back at her.

"I have told you the decision."

"But what do *you* say?"

"I say nothing."

"But what is wrong with it?"

"I believe the decision was that it was gaudy. It shone too much."

She looked at him dully, and then turned and went away.

There in the plantation was the work she was engaged on. Her eyes were too dull to see the sparkle of light, her heart too black to care. And suddenly she laughed, and picking up the fork lying near, began to dig again. The frog sat by and watched.

In furious haste, without apparent thought, she worked, and at last came upon a much smaller mound, containing one much smaller stone of transparent substance that had no lustre at all. But bitter tears were running fast from her swollen eyes, and two of them flashed on it. When she tried to rub them off upon her sleeve they seemed quite hardened, and they never moved.

"Is this gaudy?" she asked, turning suddenly to her companion.

"I don't think so," it answered meekly. And then she sighed.

"It seems to me it's hardly bright enough, except the tears."

And in the evening she went with it again to the Governor.

After that the time was very short till she was again summoned to the house.

And there the lesser jewel lay, just as she had brought it, and the decision was once more that this was rubbish also.

Then she turned to him, and cried bitterly:

"You gave me the seeds—what is wrong with them? I cannot alter them from what they are."

"Perhaps it would be best if now you left the garden," he answered slowly, "seeing it is so profitless."

But she looked at him with straining eyes, and answered:

"I can't. It's the work I have been put to do, and I must finish it. I told the frog I thought my heart was in that first hard mound, and I believe it is. But there's something else beside my heart, and that's there too, and I'll never be free till it is free. And what can I do? I am mad. I see things beautiful that others only stare at, and then pass by with scarcely one comment. And the old cruel voice keeps crying, 'Go on! go on!' and whither can I go? The path is all so black that, forward or backward, I am lost whichever way I turn."

Then because he did not answer, she said at last:

"Send it, the first I brought to you, that brilliant moonstone, to some other place. The man who called it rubbish can't have any eyes."

"Just as you like," he answered.

Then she went away.

In the plantation there had set so hard a frost that everything was white and stiff and ice-bound. There lay the half-chipped mound containing the other jewel scarce yet visible. But Rosalie had no heart to touch it, even had the frost allowed her.

And no result came from sending the moonstone to another place. One general and unanimous opinion: it had no value—that was all. And still for months the blighting frost lay dead on everything.

In vain, with burning fever under the outward chill that froze her too, did Rosalie take the fork and try with what little strength was in her arms to break the iron earth. Nothing moved. It only made her recognise the more the great impossibility, the strength of life imprisoned by the frozen hands of death.

At last (for now the gate within the edge was never fast) she went again to the Governor.

"What am I to do?" she asked. "I can't get on with anything, nor move either way. I've prayed to God a thousand times to give me peace or break the ice, or let me get the price of freedom from that jewel which I brought to you, and nothing ever answers, except in contradiction. I prayed one night the thaw might come—a hundred times and more I prayed it. In the morning a double frost had settled, petrifying hard as iron. Another night I prayed for peace and rest. I could not stand so terrible a strain. I never dreamt as that night. Ten times I dozed and woke again, covered with sweat, all shivering in the cold, to think myself alive within a coffin, buried within the ground. And most incessantly that other prayer to reap the price of freedom with the stone, and as you know, it lies here in your keeping—a useless thing, and judged devoid of worth."

"You say your heart is in the stone," he answered.

"Yes; I think it sends out shafts of brilliancy to pierce to that dull, empty place, and prick it into fearful pain. What can I do? I've prayed to God— what more can I do?"

"There is one thing more. You'd better give it up."

"Oh! but that is everything—the whole of the little garden. For the frost will never break till the stone is free, and I."

"You can give the garden back to God who gave it."

"But why give me a thing and take it back just when it's fit for using?" and then a great pain and fear came into her eyes. "I would do as you tell me, I would really, but I haven't the strength, and I'm afraid. The frost is too strong for me. It freezes my heart, and leaves my mind quite free, so that the blood courses through my brain in quickest time, and then stops suddenly. It's worse than killing me. I'm going mad, and what use am I to God, or how can I see the light of heaven, if once that heavy cloud descends, and coupled with the frost, freezes upon my eyes and lips, and eats out everything?"

"To trust in God is to be sane—have peace," he answered.

"Ah, peace!" she answered greedily. "What does it mean? I know no peace—nothing but the mocking, cruel voice that says 'Go on!' and shows no way."

"It's the stone, Rosalie, that stands in your light, and blocks the way. Can't you see it?"

"I expect I'm very blind. I'm not clever enough to understand. I haven't spirit enough to find a way out. Mr. Barringcourt told me so, and he knew best. I was handicapped from the beginning to be born without a tongue."

"But that difficulty, and still another, has been surmounted."

"Yes, but I did nothing myself."

"Fiddlesticks!" said the Governor, and he spoke so naturally that Rosalie laughed, even though not particularly brightly.

"Well, I didn't do much myself. I don't see how I could."

"You did as much as was necessary, which is never in any case very much; and now there is one little thing more to be done—give it up."

"I dare not," she said; "it would send me mad. If it would kill me I wouldn't mind." And she looked down to hide the light in her eyes.

"Give it up to God. Do you trust God and think He will forsake you?"

"No; it's myself I am not sure of."

"You should be part of God."

"Not here."

"Where else, then?"

"In heaven."

"It begins on earth for those of sufficient intelligence; and for the others, they do not count."

"I'm one of the last, then. It is so hard, so very, very hard, and I have no strength at all."

Then a very long silence followed—the terrible fight between weakness and trust, between blind ignorance and all-conquering wisdom, the spirit's humble discipline; and at last she turned to him, and said:

"I'll give it up! And if I sacrifice my heart or head, it's all the same, seeing God is the receiver, and He knows best."

And then she turned away, with the knowledge of having done some duty that now seemed extremely simple.

But the Governor rose from his chair, and came towards her, and took her in his arms, and kissed her cheek, and the caressing action reminded her somehow of that time long ago, when Mr. Barringcourt laid his hand upon her shoulder in the temple.

Bur that kiss seemed to revive her strength, and give some of that peace she had so lately craved for.

Yet this reward was so very unexpected. It never occurred to her that the Governor could possibly care whether she walked right or wrong, except, perhaps, as a spectator. But the magnetic sympathy of that kiss, and the great, but gentle, strength in his arms as he drew her to him, awoke her eyes to the fact that here was her friend, the only one she had ever known, maybe would ever meet.

But being too full of feeling for words she slipped quietly towards the door, and crossed the lawn towards the hut.

That was her little home, to be filled with contentment and happiness, in which it would be her task to dig graves for bitterness, repining, and wild craving and longing for that which was not to be. It would be a hard task. Rosalie recognised it as she looked at the frozen mounds of soil, whose digging had occasioned so much eagerness and anticipation.

And in her mind she looked below the frozen surface of the plantation to where other jewels all lay buried, and she had given them up to God, and they must lie there.

But the kiss and the strength of those strong arms had worked a miracle for her. She no longer felt the weak restlessness and alternate blackness of despair and madness. She went into the little hut bravely, with tears trembling on her eyelids, partly the outcome of the struggle she had gone through, and partly of a vague sense of happiness and satisfaction that was beginning to glow within, like some glowing light of summer. Later she said to her companion:

"There was a man who healed my tongue for me, healed it with light, and now I think my heart is being healed, and it is still Light, Light, Light, on the poisonous darkness."

"Then you have given up the moonstone. It was a dangerous stone. I like the little tear-stained one the best."

"And I love it too," said Rosalie. "It gave me work to do at the time I most needed it, and set my mind on the road it has travelled ever since."

Then she took down the lesson-books, and found to-night they were much more understandable, and it was with growing lightness of spirit that she slept that evening.

CHAPTER XIX
A HUMBLE CRUCIFIXION

The next morning sunshine and warmth had come, the frost risen and fled. The birds were singing in the forest, and the melting icicles had none of the dispiriting effect of thaw, but sparkled in the sunshine. The ground was free.

Rosalie went out and took the fork and began the old process—digging. It took a long, long time, days, and weeks, and months, to chip away the soil from the new mound.

And at last the first bright ray—uncheckered—burst through. Rosalie started up with a cry. The frog hopped up to witness. Both of them shed a tear of joy and admiration that glistened like a pearl, though dull beside this other. At last a gem of purest brightness was displayed, that shone with so soft a radiance, yet so pure and bright, that it lit up the garden like the bright sun on an early summer's morning, and seemed a dazzling emblem of light.

And Rosalie said: "This is the light which cures as well as beautifies—the talisman against all ills—the gift of God, the pearl above all price; never pearl shone like to it, or diamond, or ruby, or any stone dug from the mines or caves. I'll take it to the Governor. None can fail but to acknowledge its beauty, if but for the one central spark from the raised inner surface."

And she took it to him, but as she offered it, said nothing, and he showed no surprise, but smiled gravely, as one who might approve in silence, but said no words.

So Rosalie waited, and in a shorter time than she had ever stayed before, less than a week, was sent for by the Governor.

The flashing jewel was on the table by his side. He looked across at her, but her eyes were fixed upon the stone. So soon, and it was back! And the time it had taken to dig! and the long months of blackness before! And at last her eyes travelled slowly from it back to his face.

And he said with curious intonation: "The decision is the same as hitherto."

"But God's decision! Tell me that!" and the pain in her voice was very terrible.

"The decision of God is that it is as He has made it."

"That is sufficient. Thank you," and she moved away; strong only in the friendship of that silent man, who in so few words conveyed so much of meaning.

So once more she made her way to the little hut, where the frog as usual sat waiting; but her lips were set in a smile so stony, that she said never a word, but sat down in her chair by the fire, and forgot to try to form even a syllable.

At last her eyes lighted on the frog sitting there upon the hearth. Its big, wide, mournful mouth drooped at the corners, and its round saucer eyes were brimming with tears, yet there was something very comic in its attitude—so much so that Rosalie laughed. At this it jumped so literally that had it not borne a charmed life it would certainly have settled in the fire, but as it was, it came down inside the fender, and then hopped out.

"Ah! when you laugh in sorrow your heart must needs be broken altogether," it said.

"Oh, no! I feel nothing, nothing at all, one way or the other, only hard and empty, and sorry, not for myself, but for others, that they should be so blind."

"It's well you feel hard. It doesn't do to feel soft at times like this," said the frog, and tried to speak cheerfully, but somehow failed.

Outside a white mist was settling, so silently that they never noticed it. But just then the frog piled more coal on the fire, and soon the room looked very cheerful.

"Come and sit on my knee," said Rosalie presently; and she almost laughed again at the rapidity with which her request was granted.

Although they had lived together so long, this was, as it were, the first time she had seen the frog close.

She took one of its little feet in her fingers, and noticed it was pierced with a hole. Then in turn she looked at each foot separately, and found the same mark in each.

"How did you come by these? They look as if they must have been very painful at one time."

"It was very stupid of me," said the frog shyly. "Generally I put a jewel into each, and everyone remarks about my pretty feet, but to-day, with thinking about your affairs, I forgot. It was most negligent of me."

"Where did you get the jewels from?"

"My master said I found them by myself, but I think he really gave them to me."

"But tell me about these holes, unless you'd rather not."

"It's a short and very common story," it answered evasively; "I don't think it would interest you."

"Indeed it would; you have been so kind to me all along that I know you won't deny me this."

"Well, there was a time when I used to be a very ordinary little frog, jumping about, and eating all that I could get. And I was very vain of my appearance, for I knew that my coat was brighter than any of my neighbours, and I wished them to know it too. But I wasn't content with being admired by my own kith and kin; I thought I should like to gain the admiration of mankind as well. Instead of confining myself to the shrubs and well in the garden, I contrived to make myself plainly seen by hopping about the paths. There were no children in the house adjoining, so that I felt doubly safe, for the two servant maids used to walk in the garden often at dusk, and talk about their sweethearts, and at these times they always found a kind and flattering word for me. Meeting with such kind treatment from them, I grew doubly proud, and formed the erroneous idea that all mankind was equally kind and simple. I made no doubt that had I been taken before the Queen, my manners, colour, and deportment would have astonished her, and called forth her admiration. As discontentment had first grown toward my own people, so at last it grew towards the maid-servants. I wanted more than two admirers, and almost lost my brilliant colour pining for them. About this time, however, my old mother died, and what with the nursing of her, and seeing to her respectable removal afterwards, I had little time for thinking of myself. But when things had settled themselves again, my old longing revived. I must go out along the paths again and try to gain more admiration.

"Now, there lived in that house a man. He always wore spectacles, and whenever he walked in the garden always carried a book, and from what I could gather from the maids' conversation, was really very clever. Now, being myself very ignorant, I naturally admired clever people, and a great longing grew in my mind to gain his approbation and attention. So whenever he walked out in the garden, I watched my opportunity, and hopped along the path beside him. But for a long time he either never noticed me, or if he did do so, was never attracted by my charms. This upset me so much that my health became visibly enfeebled. I felt that if he could but see it, I might become of value in his eyes, and thus raise myself in his good graces and esteem. Still, I felt I could not give in, for I had a friend of somewhat duller coat always watching me, ready to say upon the first occasion: 'I told you so.' So I continued hopping by his side in these walks, which, of late, had become habitual. But one day, as he came down the path, he closed his book, and his eyes suddenly lighted on me. I know not what the expression in them was, but my vanity took it favourably. I sat there as still as a frog can sit, because I had heard it was a sign of good breeding to sit still, and pretended to be gazing at the sun, because I thought it would appear good taste to admire a thing so generally esteemed. And he stood still too, but I was quite content that *he* should be admiring *me*. It would have disappointed me had he turned his attention likewise to the sun. Suddenly he stooped down, and made a grab in my direction. I had almost waited for this, and being prepared, hopped quickly to one side. I felt it would not enhance my charms to be caught too quickly. He made no further attempt to catch me, but went back into the house, and I heard my friend of the duller coat laughing, as much as to say, 'I told you so.' But I pretended to consider we had made great advances. In a little while, however, he came out again. He carried in his hand a curious string thing, which is called a net, and this he laid with great ingenuity across the path where he and I had previously been walking. This I took as a great compliment; the ground was evidently not good enough for me to walk upon. Over this he spread a few crumbs. They were not, certainly, to my mind, as I liked more tasty things, but I thought he had probably noticed my fragile appearance, and was showing his sympathy with my delicacy. So to show my trust in and appreciation of him, after a little coquettish skipping on the edge, I hopped straight to the centre of the net. He was kneeling by the side, and I must admit my heart beat loudly at my own boldness, but still remembering the kindness of the maids, the only human beings that I knew, I felt no particular or definite fear. In fact, I felt like some great queen before a kneeling courtier. But the next moment I was much upset to find the net swung over me, and both of us caught roughly and inelegantly from the ground, in a manner I had never before experienced. I struggled, but only succeeded in getting one leg through the net. My position was indeed perilous. The last thing I heard in the garden was the laughter of my friend who had the duller coat. So can the frog heart be upon occasion very hard.

"I was thrown down afterwards upon a table that had neither moss nor anything else upon it, still enveloped in the hateful net, so that there was no chance of me getting away, and there I stayed for a long time, choking with fear and partial suffocation."

A tremor ran through its little body.

"I shouldn't like to speak of all that followed. As frogs go, and being cold-blooded, I can stand a fair amount. But that was neither here nor there. I don't know how long I lived there, but it was a long time, and almost every day I was put to some torture or other. Often others used to come in to see how the different inflictions affected me, and once someone remonstrated with him, and said I must suffer; but he said he was always very careful with me, and the other one seemed satisfied.

"'Besides,' he added, 'it is in the cause of science. And what little inconveniences may be suffered by this reptile may be the means of saving many lives.'

"That night as I was lying in my prison, with every limb aching and swollen, and big pains shooting through my body, I thought on his words. It was only the extreme pain that kept me from growing proud, so instead I felt a little thankful.

"But after that the times of torture were growing more frequent, or I less able to bear them, and I longed and prayed to something I couldn't understand to set me free. And one day, as he took me out of my cell, he said to someone who was with him at the time—I think he called him his assistant: 'This thing is on its last legs; I'll just try one more experiment with it, and then it can be thrown to the midden.'

"That was a little comfort to me.

"But just then he ran something through my hand that made me struggle and gasp with pain, and then the other three, and I was lying fast nailed to a board, and could not even struggle. I'll never forget it, though the worst never comes back to me. It was the last time, the last time with a vengeance, and there I died. And I think I must have looked very queer at the last, for the last thing I was conscious of was that someone laughed. But how could one compose one's features nailed to a board, and suffering agony. And when I woke up I was in this pretty garden, and I was as feeble as a baby. But my master tended me with his own hands, and before long I had grown strong and happy again, and less wishful to been seen. And though my coat is brighter now than ever it had been, I think less of it and more of other things. But even now it's sweet to hear a little praise, and never anyone has come to see my master but they have a pleasant word for me."

"Then why do you stay with me? You should be hopping in the garden, not in this dull place."

"Oh, I asked to come. I knew you'd have a deal of sorrow once you came here; it's meant to be a place of sorrow; and I remembered that period of my own life when I was all alone without companions. And I think if someone could have come to me and said, 'Cheer up, Croaker, it'll soon all be over,' I would have felt a trifle stronger for the end."

"Was your name Croaker?" asked Rosalie gently, for the story had much affected her.

"Yes; I used always to be longing to be called 'Bright Coat' or 'Slim Body,' or one of those names when I was young, but my parents had different thoughts from me, and gave me just a family name. The scientists sometimes called me 'Goggle Eyes,' and I believe my eyes did grow unnaturally big whilst I was there."

"It's very kind of you to stay with me when I'm so dull."

"You're not dull," said the frog. "No one is, unless they do nothing but nurse their sorrow, and expect other people to carry both them and it."

Rosalie laughed.

"Yes, one has a great deal to learn," she answered, and took down a book from the shelf.

And hereafter most of her time was given to learning, for the lesson-books had suddenly developed into coherent reading. They were still hard and dull, and many a time she would have given up but for the ever-ringing voice that revived her lagging spirits, and above all the remembrance of that jewel of pure light, the like that she had seen within the temple.

Outside the mist still continued heavy and white, so that it was impossible to find the way about. It hung like a heavy curtain. This continued for a long time, until one day it gradually lightened, and in a week's time the sky was clear again.

"I'm going to dig again," said Rosalie to the frog, laughing. "I feel I am intended to. The ground is soft, and though my eagerness has gone, I still can work when there is opportunity."

And so in the same way she unbedded another stone, and though it was smaller than the last, and not of the same worth by any means, it had its merits, and one pure flash in the centre to show it was related to the larger one. Having given it into the Governor's hands, she returned to her own dwelling, and waited some short time.

But one day as she was going round the plantation, holding a book and reading, with the frog hopping by her side, she was startled to hear someone calling over the gateway, "Good morning, Rosalie!" and looking, she beheld

Billy standing there, his arms folded over it, and his face all laughing, as was usual when he came.

"Good morning!" said she, and her eyes brightened at such a change in the day's programme.

"I've brought you bad news."

"Ah! then don't repeat it. I know already what it is," and Rosalie sighed.

"You know, I don't think you're ever going to get out of this little paddock," said he.

"I don't think so myself. Soon I shall be getting past breaking in."

"How do you like digging?"

"Oh, I've taken to it fairly well, thanks to my little friend Croaker here. I regard myself as a worm, and feel lowly contentment. Many a time I have thought myself dead and the sun set."

"You must be very wretched to wish yourself dead."

"Yes, the day is intensely long."

"The worm will develop."

"With a bruised head?"

"It's imagination! A second miracle, and the worm becomes a serpent."

"I would much rather remain as I am. The worm is harmless—the serpent dangerous; the one a little use—the other useless."

"And you from Lucifram!"

"Ah! your mind was fixed on one particular Serpent. Defend me from it."

"You don't look much older, Rosalie, for all your work."

"But you were tall before, and now you're taller. You actually seem older than I, and when first I saw you I reckoned you quite ten years younger."

"Well, you've been burrowing in the ground. I've been advancing. It makes all the difference. What effect has my news had upon you?" he continued.

"Oh! for a change it has made me angry."

"Has the worm turned?"

"I believe it has been so long in a state of constant wriggle that one turn more or less makes little difference."

"Suppose you leave your unprofitable trade, and come away?"

She took two steps forward with a thankful heart, and then a great stubbornness rose within her. She shook her head.

"I won't go yet," she said. "It would be giving up too early. I have pleased God, and by God's grace I'll please man, and if man is not to be pleased by God's grace, what is it that can please him?"

"That is a question for my father. I should not like to say. What do you intend to do here now?"

"Dig again. Begin to-day. There is no frost, and the ground is soft and loose."

"Is that the message I'm to return?"

"I can think of no other. It was good of you to bring the news to me."

"I thought it very ill. I never delivered an unpleasant message in my life before, and did it just for practice. I had much rather have told you the other thing."

"Your face was very expressive of sorrow when you came to me."

"I'm glad. I imagined my countenance was too smiling."

She laughed.

"Never look sad on my account. I have no wish to forfeit your company for a sad mask. Indeed, I counted it a very great kindness your coming to me at all."

"Truly, Rosalie, you are improving. I think you must be growing older."

"I've forgotten my age. It's a thing women never remember. Years were a form of imaginative punishment invented by the devil. Some folks are sensitive about them."

"When you have finished this, will you bring it to my father?"

"Most certainly; who else could I take it to?"

"He has brought you little luck."

"It's a word I should never use in connection with him."

"Well, I will leave you, and may you be prosperous. I don't know what else I can say, except that you will forgive me for the news I brought."

So saying, he turned about, and went away again.

And the old work began once more.

CHAPTER XX
A SIMPLE CONVERSATION

One day, when Rosalie had about completed the stone she was engaged upon, the Governor sent for her, by the frog.

"And I think," said Brightcoat, for Rosalie had changed its name, not liking Croaker, "that it would not be at all a bad plan for us to look and see if there are any new clothes anywhere about. This old dress you are wearing is most worn and shabby."

"There are none," said she. "I have looked many a time, and have never found anything except the coarse brown apron I wear to protect my dress from the soil."

"Well, there's a time, and not a time, for looking for things. Suppose we look in the little wardrobe together now. If you stay dinner with the Governor, you must be fairly suitably dressed for it."

And what was Rosalie's surprise, on looking in the diminutive dress-closet, to find a pretty dress of softest silk, white and apple green, just ready made to fit her figure, and everything besides to match, even to silken stockings and pretty slippers, and a cluster of red and golden leaves upon the dressing-table, as simple and pretty as the rest.

Rosalie, from feeling old as the hills, suddenly felt young as a blue-bell blowing on an early summer morning.

"Oh, Brightcoat! I never felt so happy in my life. To get rid of this old black and red thing! Why, that in itself is Paradise. But to wear these! It's past belief. Now, if you were me, how would you wear your hair—high or low? Which do you think suits me?"

"I say in that loose bundle at the back you used to wear when you first came to us."

"The way Mariana did it."

"Was it?"

"Yes. Oh, dear, dear! I'm afraid I shan't do it a bit nicely. When you try to do your hair nicely it always looks hideous; have you ever noticed that?"

"No; you see I haven't got any."

"Of course not! My dress is almost the exact colours of your skin. Have you noticed it?"

"Yes. My master said the colours were chosen out of compliment to me."

"How delightful! Frog green! It's quite an innovation in fashions, and a very pretty one."

Brightcoat's eyes sparkled with pleasure at this little bit of innocent flattery, and if it showed vanity, vanity of a sort is a very delightful thing.

So Rosalie dressed with fluttering happiness and eager haste.

"Your hair doesn't look a bit as if you'd taken pains with it," said the frog from the bed, where it was sitting.

"What do you mean?" she asked, with sudden alarm.

"It's very becoming."

"I'd rather your flattery was a little less open. I know you mean well, but it's embarrassing to have one's defects spoken of so charmingly."

By this time the dressing was completed, and in the eyes of her simple companion no one had ever looked more lovely.

"You must come too, Brightcoat. I shouldn't think of leaving you here alone. Besides, you are always welcome at the house, and I am only there on suffrage. If I behave badly I must go. It's a very terrible thing that, when you think about it. Enough to make me tremble and shake all over."

So the frog jumped lightly from the bed on to her shoulder, and made a most delightful ornament.

As they walked across the garden to the house the nightingales were singing in the soft still air of night.

The Governor, who was walking on the terrace, greeted his guests, and they passed into the house, which was all brilliantly lit to receive them.

"This is your last night with us, so I have asked you here to dine with me," said the old man.

"My last night?" Her voice was full of wonder and sadness.

"You surely will not be sorry to leave the soil?"

"Ah! but you and Brightcoat are here. I would much rather stay. Besides, my heart is in the garden yet, and here with the jewels that I brought to you.

Oh, you have been my friend; and there is none other. Where else can I go? Let me still live in the little hut, with the freedom I have bought to-night."

But he shook his head and smiled as they sat down to dinner just alone.

"You imagine you have become attached to the hut. But there are other and better places, believe me."

"And does the way back lead as I came?"

"Pretty much so, I believe."

"Into Marble House, with its shadows and cobwebs. I'm sure I daren't go."

"Perhaps it has become less shadowy since you were there. There is spring cleaning, you know, in all well-regulated houses."

"But it is not well regulated. There is one part all moths and mildew, and people live in it, or rather work there. I know, for Mariana does. How I should love to see her once again! And upstairs it is wretchedly lit. In fact, Mr. Barringcourt's private room was the only human-looking place I ever saw there. But perhaps by now he has a wife. But she'll need great strength of mind to get the necessary repairs done, I'm thinking. He seemed as if he would be very conservative, except where things affected his own comfort."

"I don't think he's got a wife yet," said the Governor.

When they had finished the meal, and the frog had had its full share of the dainties that were to its taste, the Governor led the way to his own room, and placing a chair for Rosalie near the fire, he drew his own to the other side of the fireplace and sat down.

"Do you object to smoke?" he asked.

"Oh, no! Uncle had a pipe that he had smoked for years and years and years. And the night before he died he let it fall, and it broke. I remember how sad he looked at the time—and perhaps there was more in it than just the breaking of the pipe, for he said nothing, but that he could soon get a new one. And if all things had been right I think it would have angered him."

"You were greatly attached to your uncle?"

"Oh, yes! I loved them both. No one could have been kinder to me than they."

"And now, when you go back to Lucifram, you have neither friend nor relation to go to."

"No. Must I indeed go?"

"I see no other way for it. But there are some friends of mine live there, or friends of someone that I know. They will fill, to the best of their ability, the old place."

"How do you know? They might take the utterest distaste to me on first sight, and then what would happen?"

"They are not people of prejudice."

"I wish I were not."

"You fear, then, you may take a dislike to them?"

"Oh, no! I'm always trying to get the better of my feelings, because they are so often wrong."

"Well," said he, "second thoughts are best. I give you the benefit of a second opinion upon most things."

"But there is where I fear to go back to Lucifram. It's a place where one is so terribly misjudged, and it's a place, too, where you have just the knack of saying the things you wished unsaid."

"Well, then, choose. Will you go back, or will you stay?"

But Rosalie, on second thoughts, made answer:

"You know best, and it is for you to choose. Somehow, I could not think to doubt or question what you say; and after all, why should one bother about to-morrow, if one does one's duty to-day."

"And I have promised you friends in the place of your aunt and uncle."

"Yes; but I thought Mr. Barringcourt might have a word to say about that."

"Well, we're all bound to trust the future to a certain extent. There is no telling; on second acquaintance he might prove kinder."

"When must I go?"

"To-morrow, in the early morning. The journey takes a day; it will be dark before you reach your journey's end, for autumn is far advanced with them."

Here the frog, who had so far sat quiet on the hearthrug, put in a word.

"It will be very lonely going back to Lucifram alone. My advice and companionship might be of some little help occasionally."

"Oh, yes!" cried Rosalie eagerly. "You have been such a faithful and loving friend to me, that your brightness would dispel half the gloom, I'm sure it would."

Both of them turned their eyes toward the Governor to gain his opinion.

"You bear a charmed life, little frog," said he, "so I don't see what harm or inconvenience can happen to you. In fact, I think the outing would be a pleasant trip for you, and add something to your store of knowledge."

"You don't think," said Rosalie anxiously, for second thoughts were beginning to intrude themselves, "that any harm could come of it. I remember Mr. Barringcourt saying something about vivisection once. It would be terrible if anything happened, and I was powerless to prevent it."

"I don't think anything could happen," replied the Governor. "A frog that has once jumped from Lucifram successfully to heaven could, on a pinch, repeat the process with much less inconvenience."

And soon after this the interview and evening ended.

CHAPTER XXI
A MAN WHO STOOD ON HIS HEAD,
ACCORDING TO LUCIFRAM

The two wanderers were standing once more in the cold, inhospitable streets of Lucifram. But they were not alone. A tall lady descending from her carriage had noticed the forlorn Rosalie, and pitying her tired condition had taken her within her house, promising her one night's shelter at least. It may be simply stated to whom Rosalie in this hour of need had come. In this particular house in Lime Tree Square of the chief city of Lucifram there lived a very great painter and his sister. In his early youth he had had a hard struggle, not so much because he was poor, but because he was original. Now, for a man to have his own ideas in the city of Lucifram was to set all the dogs barking, the mob stone-flinging, and the Riot Act fluttering.

It was very strange, but thousands of years of experience had taught little or nothing.

The painter, as has been said, had his own ideas, and so at first they said he was an upstart, and very justly laughed at him. But laughter never yet cured madness or stamped out the truth, and as the painter seemed to be giving surreptitious invisible spiritual bites all round him, and setting the infection flying, it was recognised at last there must be some truth in his madness, and to a certain extent they let him be.

And so from being badly abused the painter at last sprung into fame. He was a shy and reserved man, and somewhat irritable in his temper. But that was because his temperament and his work were of a kind that wear the nerves unevenly. But still when he liked he could be very charming, even Lucifram admitted that, and for the hidden virtues, they left those with a shrug to God the Serpent.

And so in comparative early middle age he found himself the recipient of a knighthood; that is, he received a title very similar to "Sir"—and for simplicity we will call it such. Some spiteful people said this was on account of his good looks, but as it was a man sovereign who gave him the title, it's hard to see what that could have to do with it. Now, Sir John himself had little belief in titles, but his sister had great belief in *him*, and though herself the simplest of plain women, she had ambitions so far as he was concerned.

"A title's an empty thing," said he, looking at her in his serious, thoughtful way.

"No one knows it better than I," she answered, in her downright one. "And if you hadn't the real thing to outshine it, I'd hate to see it offered to you. But it's a courtesy you owe to the world in return for its courtesy. If you don't accept it, you are churlish. Besides, I always think it's the greatest honour that can befal a sovereign, to confer distinction upon genius, so that, even on a royal consideration, I think you ought to accept."

And so plain John Crokerly became Sir John, and was just the same before and after—neither more or less brilliant or imposing.

From being poor he became rich. He never married, but continued happily in the society of his one unmarried sister. The affection and understanding were very mutual, and perfectly to the contentment of both.

On this particular night Miss Crokerly entered her brother's presence with some trepidation. After all, she had a reputation for common sense, though, like him, maybe a little eccentric, and the brightness of the frog and the prettiness of Rosalie's face hardly seemed pretext enough on second thoughts for inviting her into the house.

"John," said she, betraying no misgiving in her voice, as she closed the door, "I've invited a young girl from the country, who is lost, to come in and shelter for the night."

"What's her name?" and he looked up over the top of the paper which he was reading, for daylight was precious just then, and morning meals too hasty to allow of much newspaper indulgence during them.

"I don't know; she is a perfect stranger to me. I came to see if you approved."

"It won't matter to me. I shan't see her," he answered.

"Of course not." Then, after a pause: "You think I'm not running any risks by bringing her in?"

"I don't know. You can't very well turn her out again now you've done it. Small-pox is pretty prevalent, to be sure. Did you make particular inquiries if she'd been successfully vaccinated?"

"You have no objection to what I've done?"

"Not after you've done it," and he relapsed once more behind the paper.

But Miss Crokerly, after turning to the door, looked round again.

"I should like you to see her," she said, for her, very hesitatingly.

"In the morning," he answered.

"In the morning you will have less time and inclination than now."

"But what purpose should I serve in going to look at her? Is she different from the generality of country folk?"

"I don't know," she replied slowly; "but I think she is much prettier. And she has with her a frog with the most brilliant colour I ever saw."

At this he laughed. "My curiosity is not excited in the least," he answered.

"But mine *is*," she said, with a return to her decided manner; "and you really must come, if but to see the frog. It is a marvel."

"Bring it here to me, then."

"Certainly not, unless I bring her too. You are growing terribly lazy, Jack."

"Well, come along," he said impatiently. "Only please don't drag me into any more of your charitable whims, frogs or no frogs."

"Of course not. This is an exception. You might ask her her name and address. I quite forgot to do so."

So together they went into the hall where Rosalie still sat. The frog, with a wisdom born of its dead vanity, had again settled itself conspicuously to attract attention on her shoulder.

Rosalie's pale face and large bright eyes also possessed a peculiar beauty and fascination, although she was tired with the journey and sick from want of food.

Now, Sir John's heart was as kind as that of his sister, and, moreover, he had a great admiration for woman when her beauty was of that delicate yet exquisite type that approaches the ideal, and contains little of the heaviness or substantiality of flesh. As they both came toward her, Rosalie rose, and her movements were so quiet, graceful, and well-bred, that one might have thought the frog's spirit of wishing to do the correct thing for the sake of admiration had settled upon her. All his irritability, which was not of a very lasting or savage kind, vanished.

"You have a delightful little companion there," said he pleasantly, looking at the frog.

"Yes."

"It is rather an uncommon kind of pet," put in Miss Crokerly; "and how brilliant! Is it real, or some highly-polished stone?"

Rosalie laughed softly.

"Oh! it is real enough, and can jump prodigiously." And she put her hand up caressingly to its coat.

"And you," said Sir John—"you look tired. What part of the country have you come from to get lost in the city?"

"I have been walking all day. I came from a little hut and plantation beyond the forest."

At this the painter looked at his sister and she at him. For outside this city of Lucifram there was a tremendous forest full of jungles, and only the pure in spirit and those led by a light of superhuman brightness could pass through it.

"And did you pass through the forest unhurt?" he asked.

"Yes. We were pleasant company to each other. But I lost one of my garden clogs. I think that was very unfortunate, because I never missed it till it was too late to turn back."

She spoke evidently without any knowledge of the terrors of the forest. But whatever reticence she showed about her journey was from now respected by them.

"Then you have no home to return to?" said Miss Crokerly, after a pause, during which she had revolved things in her mind.

"No," said Rosalie simply, and her wistful eyes filled with anxiety and shadow.

"You must spend the night here, then, as I said before, and in the morning we will arrange things. Come with me."

Then Sir John shook hands with her in that grave, kind way of his, and wished her good-night, and then went back to his easy-chair and paper.

He himself knew something of the terrors and blackness of the forest. It had been responsible for some of his best work. But he was a man whose hair was turning grey, and this girl, whose name, by the way, he had forgotten to ask, appeared so very young. He was interested in, and felt sorry for her, and yet could scarcely credit the tale that she had come hither from the forest; on second thoughts it seemed so utterly improbable.

Yet where else anywhere upon Lucifram could that brilliant frog have come from—or Rosalie's expressive, shining eyes?

So when his sister came back later in the evening, he said:

"I think, for the present, at any rate, we must keep her. Providence has sent her to us, and converts a duty into pleasure."

"Yes, indeed. She has had supper and gone to bed. And strange to say," she continued reflectively, "although for the last twenty-five years I have been trying to cure myself of impulsiveness as one of my besetting sins, and was just thinking as I drove home to-night that at last I had quite succeeded, yet now I cannot help loving her at sight, as much," she added softly, "as if she were my own sister."

"That is fortunate for her," replied he. "She appears so destitute."

"And I don't doubt fortunate for me. It is not often one receives a traveller from the forest."

"You have ascertained, then, that she really came from there?"

"Of course! I ascertained it by attending simply to her voice and manner. One needs no other guarantees."

"Well, I can but hope your friendship stands the test of time. For myself, I can only say, as usual, I think you showed true discernment in admitting her to shelter for the night, though at first, to speak truthfully, I must admit your conduct greatly astonished me. What is her name?"

"Rosalie Paleaf."

CHAPTER XXII
A NEW LEASE OF LIFE

When Rosalie awoke next morning, it was in a comfortable modern bedroom, furnished with regard to health, and a conception of beauty thrown in.

For the first time truly in her life and experience she awoke with a light heart, and such unusual brightness of spirits that she seemed at last, for the time at least, to have realised the pleasure and joy of simply being alive. The tired sickness of the night before had entirely vanished.

The sky overhead was blue and bright, the air cold. Nothing could have been more promising for a new entry into an old world.

Brightcoat, who had spent the night on the marble washing-stand, now took recreation in the basin of water Rosalie poured for him, whilst she, being less cold-blooded, as it were, was nothing loath to accept the warm water that was brought for her.

But this part of the day's programme being finished, Rosalie turned disconsolately to her dress.

"It's so shabby and short," said she.

"Well, look amongst your luggage," said Brightcoat, who was engaged in jumping for further recreation over all the articles on the washstand.

"My luggage," said she, looking towards the little hand-bag. "It can't be in there."

"No harm in looking," said the frog, and jumped clean over the water-jug, and then sat as still as if jumping were the last thing it would ever think of doing.

Rosalie laughed, and then opened the bag and looked.

There was packed into that little leather hand-bag everything to make a perfect though not extravagant outfit. A coat and skirt that no fashionable tailor would be ashamed to turn out, a pretty, simple dress for household wear, the evening dress which she had worn the other night, slippers, gloves, and all accessories. Last but not least, there was a little box of jewellery in perfect taste and finish.

"Oh, Brightcoat, look, look!" she cried, as one after the other she drew out those new delights. "Who can have done it? I don't think it could have been the Governor. I'm sure he never bothered much about one's clothes."

And then the frog's voice fell to a reverent whisper, so it almost seemed.

"I once saw the Governor's wife pack a Christmas box for a little boy a long way off at school, and it was quite miraculous."

"Was he her son?"

"Oh, no! At least, not exactly her son. But she was very fond of him. She forgot nothing, and sent it in such little room that no one thought she was sending anything much at all."

"You have seen her, then?"

"Yes, I've seen her; and never anything more absolutely beautiful. It was she who put her tender, gentle hand upon me when first I came all dead and dull and stunned from Lucifram, and by her radiating brightness changed my poor coat to brilliancy. But have you turned out all the contents of your bag?"

"Yes. No. Here are two letters. One for me and one to Sir—John—Crokerly. Who's he, I wonder?"

"The man who lives here," said the frog, who was primitive, and believed in calling men men, and women women, with no thought of discourtesy, but from lack of education in those matters.

"The gentleman," said Rosalie. "He's sure to be a gentleman if he has a title. But how do you know his name?"

"Well, I heard someone speak of the—the lady last night as Miss Crokerly, and they said something about Sir John. And putting two and two together, I've come to the conclusion it is he who lives here."

"How strange!"

"Stranger things have happened. Have you read your letter?"

"No," and she broke open the envelope. At first she read it seriously, then burst out laughing.

"What is it?" asked Brightcoat eagerly, who, having long ago got over the seriousness of vanity, could enjoy a joke.

"Oh, this letter! It's been written in a kind of rhyme, and I'm sure I don't know what it means. It seems utter nonsense."

"If it's not very private, and you read it aloud, I might be able to help you," the frog replied courteously.

"Well, listen. There is no address. It begins:

"'The road of Life

    Is the path to my wife.
    Its struggles and turmoils ended—
    Horses so white they dazzle the sun,
    A car of dazzling glory spun,
    Driver all fearless of peril.
    From depth to height the race is run,
    The equipage right royal.
    The meet a queen come decked as a queen
    In shining garments past satin,
    With pearl-sewn tears to laughter changed
    And heart-blood drops to jewels.
    A thousand colours of rainbow light
    The trophies of many a hard-won fight,
    Before pale faith was lost in sight
    And eyes cease weeping on trial.
    A driver find,
    A purse well lined,
    A gate and road all open.
    And horses six,
    To avoid the Styx,
    Yet climb the invisible mountain.'

There now, Brightcoat, what do you think of that? Can you fathom it? I think it's a very charming puzzle."

"Who do you think wrote it?"

"Why, the Governor! And out of compliment to his wife I feel bound somehow or other to—to endeavour to accomplish the task set me."

"Horses so white they dazzle the sun, and six of them," said Brightcoat thoughtfully. "Do you think you'll ever manage it?"

"I don't know. But there's no harm in trying." And she laughed again, and was most becomingly dressed in no time.

Then together, the frog taking its accustomed place upon her shoulder, they descended the staircase.

In the hall Miss Crokerly and her brother stood talking, he in a thick overcoat ready for going out.

Rosalie approached and handed her letter to him, which he received kindly, though with some surprise.

"I found it in my bag," said she, "and had no idea it was there. I think you are Sir John?"

"Yes."

After he had read the letter enclosed, he handed it to his sister. She read it with evident interest, then returned it to him, and holding out her hand to the new-comer, said:

"We're very pleased to receive you, Rosalie. And as long as you care to stay with us you will be welcome, apart from any considerations except those of friendship."

"I'm afraid I'm too poor to accept your hospitality for a longer time than it takes me to find work."

"Poor? The letter to my brother is from the wealthiest banker of our acquaintance, the safest and surest. And his statement proves you anything but poor."

Then Rosalie remembered the jewels she had found, and remained silent. She had prized them very much and loved them, and now she understood their value, in one of those flashes of perception that occasionally comes to all of us.

After that Sir John went away, and Miss Crokerly led the way into the dining-room, where breakfast was laid for Rosalie only, as the others had long since had theirs.

And that day passed away as healthily and normally as Rosalie could wish, and a morning's shopping was quite a pleasant recreation to her, and in fact the first of its kind she had ever indulged in in her life.

For to be dumb is a great drawback, as most of us can understand, and curtails most pleasures, little or big.

And then for tea some very interesting people dropped in, or so Rosalie found them, and altogether the weary, dead, dull, lonely level of life seemed to have vanished.

CHAPTER XXIII
THE SCANDAL OF THE TEMPLE

Now it chanced one night that Miss Crokerly wrote a letter after the bag had gone to post, and Rosalie, seeing that it was dry and frosty, had offered to take it to the pillar-box, which was a few minutes' walk away at the end of the next square. It was so pleasant out of doors that she took the longest way, and having slipped the letter in the box, prepared to take the same road back.

On turning a corner, her attention was attracted by someone coming towards her, scarcely fifty yards away, reading a letter, so it seemed to her, with apparently no more trouble than if it had been daylight. But that fact, though it afterwards occurred to her, was forgotten in the shock of recognising that here was Mr. Barringcourt.

Rosalie stood still under the gas-lamp, unable to move, paralysed with fear. An instinct of safety should have made her move along, but here she stood, courting observation by standing directly in the path, with big wide eyes fixed upon his face. Just then he looked up with bent brows and eyes. They came directly in contact with Rosalie's white and terrified face. In an instant his abstracted air vanished, and a very present alertness took the place of his thoughts. Like a flash of lightning Rosalie turned and sped the near way home, reaching the safety of the doorstep in less than three minutes. She did not stop to breathe till safe within the friendly shelter of the hall, where something told her to regain a little composure, at any rate, before appearing before Miss Crokerly. She went upstairs and removed her hat and the rich evening wrap she had drawn round her, sat down for a little while to recover her breath, and then descended to the drawing-room again.

Miss Crokerly, intent upon some fine needlework, did not look up on her entrance; but Rosalie had one friend whose eyes were sharper and perceptions more acute. The frog, whom she had left sitting upon the timepiece, looked across at her. Rosalie gained assurance from that glance.

She sat down without any remark, and took up the book she had been reading, making some pretence of continuing her occupation as before.

"I've heard a rumour," said Miss Crokerly presently, "that the Great High Priest is resigning."

"Who is he?" asked Rosalie absently.

"The Great High Priest of the Serpent," continued Miss Crokerly. "I can scarcely credit it, though. He is barely seventy-two. And he can have no reason for it either. It's an office never vacated till death. Dotage doesn't count."

"Maybe he is more conscientious than most," said Rosalie, rousing herself from her own line of thought to take an interest in the conversation.

"I don't know, I'm sure. There have been whispers of it for the last three years. I think he has enemies."

"I suppose all men in prominent positions have."

"Yes; but there are enemies and enemies. Now my opinion of the Great High Priest is that he has hidden enemies, or perhaps he chances to be merely unfortunate."

"What do you mean?" asked Rosalie, beginning to be interested in the conversation.

"Well, it began with a scandal. A rumour got about that he had admitted a woman to see the Serpent, and some said such conduct was nothing short of blasphemous. But that was either hushed up or contradicted. Contradicted, I think, and then hushed up."

"Would it be such a terrible thing for a woman to see the Serpent?"

Miss Crokerly smiled.

"Well, there's a great deal of superstition and ignorance mixed up with our religion, as all simple and right-minded people can see. But it grows in suitable soil, so it's strong and holds well together."

"And did it not please the people that a woman had seen the Serpent?"

"Naturally not, after thousands of years of prejudice. Some of the best—by that I mean the *narrowest*—women I know withdrew their support (they were extremely wealthy) from the temple for some months during the scandal. They said they felt the brightness of the Serpent had been sullied."

"Absurd!" said Rosalie; and the blood began to course a little quicker through her veins from indignation.

"Well," said Miss Crokerly slowly, "one can't judge quickly. Of course you know the Great High Priest is not allowed to have a wife. She is separated from him the day he takes up office, and if he did admit a woman from idle curiosity to see the Serpent—well, judged from one point, it was very serious."

"Maybe," said Rosalie, whose tongue was itching to say much more. "But do you think there was any truth in it?"

"Well, yes. A woman's handkerchief with a red rose embroidered in the corner was found upon the altar."

"Never!" said Rosalie, with such a visible jump and accents so sharp that Miss Crokerly looked up, and the frog's eyes grew wide with warning.

"It was so, indeed. My brother had it on good authority. One of the Golden Priests went in that evening to offer the prayer at the New Moon. He found it there. And then this hushed-up scandal followed."

Again Rosalie was silent, why, she could scarcely tell. She recognised the handkerchief, which in after events she had never missed. It was her aunt's birthday gift, with a little silk-embroidered rose in the corner instead of a name.

"But why did the Golden Priest remark upon it?" asked Rosalie.

"That is what I say. And it is that which makes me think the Great High Priest has enemies."

"But such a thing as that, once died down, could not make him resign."

"Perhaps not. But I don't think it ever really did die down. And last year at the 'Feast of White Souls,' after the Fast of Black Ones, as he was coming out from between the curtains to sprinkle white confetti down the temple aisles, a most unfortunate thing occurred. The crimson curtain suddenly tore from the rings and fell, and there behind, to the view of a mixed assembly, shone out the Golden Serpent. I was there myself, having gone to hear the music, for on these occasions it is very fine, and was sitting with my brother quite near to the choir stalls."

"And what did you do?"

"Well, it was very strange, but we all instinctively did the same thing. I took one real good look at the Serpent (and I don't know any woman there who didn't, except those who screamed, and some who fainted, for what, it would be hard to tell), and then, from a sense of what was due to the male part of the congregation, we covered our eyes with our handkerchiefs, and all turning our backs upon the God we worshipped, were led solemnly out, with comparatively little confusion. The service could not continue, and that event has made him the most unpopular man on Lucifram."

"Then," said Rosalie, half laughing, half sarcastically, leaning back in her chair, and looking at the fire, "I should say it would not be a bad idea to introduce a 'Feast of Handkerchiefs' to take the place of the unfortunate White Souls. A handkerchief betrayed one woman and saved the rest. It should receive a place of honour in the temple."

"What a pity he did not take it in that way," said Miss Crokerly. "But I've heard since that the occurrence has depressed him terribly. And the last news is that he is resigning."

"And which of the Golden Priests was it who spread the first report?"

"His name is Alphonso. I know him slightly, but do not care for him. I think him ambitious, and unscrupulous, and narrow-minded. I cannot help but think myself he is the greatest enemy the High Priest has, though there are some who uphold him as the strictest and highest principled man within the Church."

"I dislike him already," said Rosalie impulsively.

The other laughed.

"Well, you will have an opportunity of meeting him to-morrow night at the Sebberens'. He is unmarried, so you may be as charming as you like to him, and no one's heart will break. But for all that he's greatly run after by the women. They regard the Golden Priests and the Great High Priest as demi-gods."

The Golden Priests were those whose rank came next to that of the Great High Priest, and when this latter died his place was always filled from this exclusive body of great men, the wealthiest and most powerful in the Church of Lucifram.

"Oh! that will make me dislike him all the more," said Rosalie. "The men who are run after by women, and the women who are run after by men, are both equally detestable. I mean, of course, in excess."

"But that is fascination."

"I prefer the fascination that is clever enough to captivate its own sex."

"Well, men admire him in an intellectual capacity."

"A general favourite? Most insipid!"

"Really, Rosalie!" said Miss Crokerly, and she laughed.

"You cannot expect me to love him. A man should always be loyal to his superior."

"Well, of course, I am only giving you my own opinion. And you must not repeat it on any account; because it is not generally believed or certain that he might be prompted by motives of ambition to make known the incident of the handkerchief."

"I hope that if the High Priest does resign someone less self-seeking takes his place."

"Than Golden Priest Alphonso? But that is scarcely likely. He has Mr. Barringcourt for his great friend, and—What is the matter, Rosalie? Your cheeks are all aflame."

"Oh! I—I—I've had springes of toothache all day, and the sudden pain makes me flush. I'm all right now. What were you saying?"

"Alphonso is sure to succeed to the High Priestship sooner or later. He has much influence on his side—the Prime Minister, and Lord High All Superior for public and official friends, and Mr. Barringcourt, whom I just mentioned, who has great influence in outside circles, and more money apparently than even poor Geoffrey Todbrook had. Now there's a man for you to dislike cordially on the grounds of general favouritism. The women idolise him, and men will hear no wrong of him."

"And what kind of a life does he lead? Is he a good man?" asked Rosalie, leaning forward and looking across at her.

"I don't know. My brother thinks greatly of him, and so do I. But it's hard to tell who's good and who's bad when you come to private life. There are so many things for and against it."

"Of course."

"Still, I think as rich men go, who are young and unfettered by anything, he must be fairly good. I don't remember ever hearing anything against him. And I know he has carried out all Geoffrey Todbrook's wishes with regard to charities to the letter."

"Is he executor?"

"Yes."

"Then it would be surprising if he fell short of his duties, would it not?"

"Perhaps so. I expect he too will be at the Sebberens' to-morrow night But if you have any conversation with Mr. Barringcourt at all, you cannot choose but like him."

"Is his temper unfailingly pleasant, then?"

"No; it isn't altogether that. I have known him very absent and off-hand. But I suppose people occasionally find that rather pleasant in a world of suavity and insincerity."

"I don't agree with you. I'd rather have people unfailingly suave. It spares a great deal of friction."

"What has upset you, Rosalie? You are most argumentative to-night."

"I expect you are spoiling me, and I've never been accustomed to it. You should treat me with stern severity, and you would find me improve wonderfully."

"And you just preaching unfailing suavity."

"Oh! I preach by the Creed of Contrary."

But Rosalie's argumentative mood sprang really from the irritation that followed on the evening's escapade.

In a cooler moment, and on reflection, she was not over and above proud of the way in which she had fled so precipitately before the enemy. And yet what was there to be done? To have stood still was to have hazarded, so Rosalie thought, far more than she had any intention of hazarding. She registered a mental vow never to go out at night alone again, and wished, oh! wished most intensely, that nothing had tempted her out that night. In her own room the frog broke the silence by saying:

"You seem very upset to-night."

"Yes. I—I met Mr. Darringcourt, and I ran away."

"What made you run?"

"I was frightened of him."

"What harm could he work you?"

"Oh! he might have persuaded me in a moment of weakness I owed him a debt of gratitude."

"And yet you have the kiss of freedom on your brow."

"Yes; but like most abstract things, it sank before the concrete."

"You'll get over it by the morning. Sleep upon it."

"I should have had you with me. You have far less fear than I. The farther off the episodes of Marble House become the more I dread them. They seemed all right, and yet they were all wrong."

"Miss Crokerly said you would probably meet Mr. Barringcourt to-morrow night."

"Yes, I know. And it was only this morning I congratulated myself he was not in her set, and that I should never be likely to meet him."

"If you meet Mr. Barringcourt to-morrow night, you won't run away—will you?"

"No; because it will be light, and there will be people about, and I shall have you. No, I won't run away in any case. But you will come with me?"

"Of course! I should have very much enjoyed the fresh air to-night; but you did not invite me."

"I'm sorry. But I've paid the penalty of my negligence; from henceforth you must never leave me."

"What dress do you intend to wear to-morrow night?"

"The one I have worn all along."

"It's as shabby as if you'd been digging in it. But the morning may bring you another."

"I hope it may not be very heavy, in case I should have to depend on my heels again."

CHAPTER XXIV
AT THE SEBBERENS'

The Sebberens were people who indulged greatly in private theatricals and other sorts of entertainment. With the amateur they included the professional, and in between the acts, songs and recitations were contributed by the latter.

Mr. Sebberen had been engaged in pork, and had made enough money thereby to make the pig respected—as an investment, anyway. He married a waitress in a restaurant, who was neither more nor less charming and handsome than most of her class. She had ambitions, and was young.

But for ten long years they had no children, and never a scrap of the pig was wasted. And those ten years were years of increase. Then to put spirit to an ambition somewhat sordid, a little daughter was born. Both parents were beside themselves with joy. It is not everyone who can manage so much, after breeding nothing but gold or pork, and so they felt. It's a common thing to be a mother after a lapse of one year, but after ten! they grew proud on the strength of it.

And another ten years had trebled the ample fortune, nay, more than trebled it, and Mr. Sebberen, a comparatively young man—scarce forty—found himself with a daughter only ten years old.

Another decade saw her twenty, he in the prime of life, her mother too. "Sebberen's Pork" was of world-wide fame. The king and the chief prince had it on their breakfast tables; the poor still bought the sausages, and doctors still evinced a weakness for onions, milk, and tripe.

No one would have known, to walk into this grand house, that its occupants once lived behind a little pork shop. For Susiebelle was handsome and clever, and had taught her mother a thing or two, and made great friends at school, not from any particular virtue, but from the glamour of outside show. She had a great deal of the outward semblance of that inward spirit that had made her father what he was. She was shallow and brilliant, and a perfect mimic of the world.

When the world wept, she wept. They called her tender-hearted.

When it laughed, she also laughed. They called her gay.

When in a mood for admiration, she, too, had time for adulation, admired arts and music, knotted her pretty brows at science, and bought rich copies of all the works of fashionable poets. And what was all this for?

Susiebelle at twenty made up her mind to marry, and marry as well as could be. Her father had just had a tremendous stroke of luck in business. She set her mind upon a duke, shooting high to reach as far as fortune favoured.

One year had passed away, and Susiebelle's ambition has not yet been granted. A poor baronet, an insipid, weak-eyed lord; not bad for a beginning, certainly.

And this brings us to to-night, the amateur theatricals, and gay company.

Sir John was under commission to paint the lovely Susiebelle, and had undertaken it with a fine courtesy that made her mother glow with pride to think the great were servants of the—the small. And Sir John would do it successfully after all, for she was pretty enough to appeal to the sense of beauty in any artist, and her parents were over and above willing to pay.

And that is why Sir John went to the party—from motives of conscientiousness. And Miss Crokerly went because she wished to give pleasure to Rosalie. She, an ideal chaperon and friend. And Rosalie went because there was no way out of it.

But Rosalie's dress was in itself that night a thing of beauty. Green, as bright and dazzling a green as the frog's coat, that fitted to her graceful figure as perfectly as the shining scales of a serpent's coils, worked with tiny seed jewels and edgings of gold.

"You look just like the mermaid," said the frog, "your hair is so pale, and your eyes so bright, and your skin so fair, and your lips are as red as coral."

And Rosalie looked in the glass just as once before when comparing herself with Mariana, and laughed again just as then, and clasped her hands.

Then, when she was ready, she went to Miss Crokerly's room, who, on seeing her, uttered an exclamation of surprise.

"What is the matter?" asked Rosalie.

"I believe your frog is a beautifier. Take care no one steals it in the crush to-night. Or perhaps I ought to take the credit to myself. I think I shall. You have improved in appearance since coming here, Rosalie, and to-night you look quite radiant."

"Thank you," and with a sudden touch of impulsiveness Rosalie kissed her. "You are so kind to me that the credit is yours."

When they reached the Sebberens' the large party was assembling in the great drawing-room, which had been changed into a theatre for the occasion. Supper was to follow, but light refreshments were being handed round, and proved very useful to take the chill off the commencement, as it were. And music not too obtrusive helped digestion. Rosalie's heart beat quicker as they entered the brilliantly-lit room, advance and retreat covered by Miss Crokerly and her brother, before and behind.

Just inside the wide doors stood Mrs. Sebberen talking to a grey-haired man; Susiebelle was busy behind the curtain, so could not be in attendance upon the guests.

She greeted Miss Crokerly effusively, stared, as is perfectly compatible with good manners, at Rosalie from head to foot, became effusive to her, and then bestowed the same greeting upon Sir John. There was no doubt about it, she was a happy and genial woman. She evidently considered them among her guests of honour or chief friendship, for in person she conducted them to a line of seats near to the front. She was dressed in rich black satin, and looked handsome enough to be imposing.

On the way she talked much to Miss Crokerly, but looked much at Rosalie, her dress, her face, the curious little animal upon her shoulder.

Beyond a certain interest, Rosalie read nothing in her glance. Then when they were seated, she passed away again, and Rosalie found time to look around. Everything and everybody were very brilliant. And she recognised some of her new acquaintances, but none more intimate. At last she whispered to Miss Crokerly—Sir John had left them for the moment:

"Where is the Golden Priest Alphonso?"

Miss Crokerly's sharp eyes travelled round the assembly.

"He is not here yet," said she. "Of course I don't know, but I expect that he will come. There is Lady Flamington and her husband. Is she not beautiful? but very sad-looking."

"Lady Flamington—Lady Flamington! Oh! where is she?" said Rosalie, in an eager voice.

But just then the lady spoken of, who was sitting some distance to the right a row in front, turned round, and seeing Miss Crokerly, rose and came toward her. Her smile was very pleasant.

"I am deserting my husband for better company," said she. "I dragged him here against his will, low be it spoken, and am paying the penalty in sulks. Your brother is easier to manage, Miss Crokerly."

"The privilege of management is not mine. I am only his sister."

The other shook her head.

"You are too modest. There was never a man yet who governed himself; he couldn't manage it. It ends in sudden death or corpulency. Both are dreadful things."

Miss Crokerly laughed.

"You will perhaps have heard what heavy responsibilities I have taken upon myself lately."

"Yes; I hear you have turned chaperon," and Lady Flamington looked across at Rosalie and smiled as pleasantly as before.

Miss Crokerly introduced them.

"Are you fond of private theatricals?" she asked.

"I've never been to any," replied Rosalie candidly.

"She was an only child, and brought up very strictly," said Miss Crokerly, at which Lady Flamington said "Oh!" and looked toward the door.

She remained sitting by them till the play began, talking with both of them. At last she said to Rosalie:

"Do you know, I have the oddest sensation that I have met you before."

"I don't think so," said Rosalie. "I have a very good memory for faces, and I have never seen you anywhere."

"Perhaps I am mistaken. People often resemble each other so curiously."

But now silence was imposed. The play had begun in earnest, and it was quite interesting enough to retain the attention. When the act was over, a song by a very well-known singer was announced; but before this came off a few late arrivals made their entrance.

"There is the Golden Priest," said Miss Crokerly.

He came in with two more gentleman. He was tall and thin, with a narrow face and black hair. His eyes were deeply set and fixed close together. His nose was long, and his lips very thin and straight. He looked clever; beyond that he was scarcely prepossessing, but he was evidently made much of in that assembly. They gave him a seat upon the very first row. And yet he never ceased to preach that the pig was unclean! It was a canon of the Church.

The play had more fine dresses in it than cleverness or substance, but it was received as warmly as the more deserving performances during the interludes.

Everybody was in high good-humour apparently, and the next day the paper said it was the most successful entertainment and supper party Mrs. Sebberen had ever given, which, coming from such good authority, must have been the truth.

When the temporary curtain had fallen for the last time upon general and good-natured applause, a movement was made toward the supper-room.

They put a little round-headed man with weak eyes to look after Rosalie. He blinked upon her critically, and then smiled. Rosalie did not like him.

However, not being dumb now, she needs must talk to him; never had anyone been more tongue-tied. The coldness of the weather, their only conversation, scarcely matched her conduct to him. The supper-room was brilliant; nothing had been spared that money could buy to please the eye or taste. He forgot her in the contemplation of his food, and she was glad; it gave her time to look about.

The table was long, and everyone apparently was seated at it. There was not a plain-looking woman among the number, so it seemed to her; and many of them were really beautiful. But Lady Flamington possessed a certain individual grace, a coldness and sadness under her exterior charm of manner, that raised her much above the ordinary plane. Sir John was sitting by her, and they were talking pleasantly to one another. She gave one the impression that she could be very fascinating.

But as Rosalie's eyes travelled up the table on the opposite side, she recognised Mr. Barringcourt for the first time that evening, and he was sitting next to Susiebelle.

Susiebelle was evidently in good feather, for everyone had been congratulating her upon her acting, and she was simple-minded enough to believe them, which gave her quite a charm. She was talking to him with great spirit and gaiety, and looked quite handsome enough to make any mother proud. Mr. Barringcourt was listening so politely that his attention seemed to lack interest. When she laughed he smiled; when she smiled he listened gravely; when her face was serious, as it rarely was, he took the opportunity to look around.

On one of those occasions his eye travelled across to where Rosalie sat. No sign of recognition was visible in them, but a little later he looked at her again.

Rosalie was annoyed to find that both times she had been looking at him, and for the future looked discreetly the other way, nay, cultivated the acquaintance of her companion, and found him scarcely as uninteresting as at first she had imagined.

But at last the evening was over, and she standing by Miss Crokerly in the hall, waiting for their carriage.

The coldness of the day had changed to snow, and the ground outside was white; a sight which somehow or other always surprises people when first they see it, however much they may have expected it. Thick white flakes were still falling rapidly. People drew their wraps round them and shivered, or pretended to.

Lady Flamington's carriage drove away as Miss Crokerly and Rosalie reached the top step. Mr. Barringcourt had seen them off, and closed the carriage door. Before moving away himself, he looked up at the steps and saw these two descending. He raised his hat, looking at Miss Crokerly.

"Sir John is not returning home with you?"

"No," she answered anxiously. "He said he preferred to walk; but I'm sure he can have no idea of the state of the night. I have not seen him since before supper-time."

"I'll seek him out and bring him to you; it's a beastly night." And he ran lightly up the steps, whilst they got as quickly under cover as possible.

He was not long away, and returned, bringing Sir John along with him.

"You surely are not walking yourself?" said Miss Crokerly, as he proceeded to close the door for them also.

"Yes. It never occurred to me to order a carriage, and I have neither wife nor sister to be concerned about my getting wet."

"Then," said she decidedly, "you must come with us. I noticed as you went up the steps your shoes are not at all suitable to the night."

It seemed almost as if he would decline, then suddenly he said "Thank you," and stepped in beside Sir John, and they were off.

Now, the frog was so bright that the carriage was quite pleasantly lit, for it had crept out from beneath Rosalie's wraps to its accustomed place.

Miss Crokerly then introduced him to Rosalie; but as he showed no signs of recognition, neither did she, but leant back in her corner and listened to the conversation.

"What did you think of the theatricals?" asked Miss Crokerly.

"I did not arrive in time for them. The secretary of Todbrook's Home for Deaf and Dumb came to see me about a Christmas treat for them. For myself, I can imagine no treat that would appeal to incurables. But he has faith in turkey, and I think he said plum-pudding."

"It must be a terrible thing to be afflicted with either defect. What else are you going to do for them?"

"I don't know, I'm sure. I said I'd call to see him in the morning."

"Oh! you should have a Christmas tree, and a cinematograph, and take them all to the Pantomime to see the transformation scenes," said Rosalie.

And she sat up again, and her eyes were very big and bright, because the subject was especially interesting to her. The other three looked at her.

"Are you a philanthropist?" asked Mr. Barringcourt, with a vein of coldness running in his words, in direct opposition to her heat.

She laughed.

"No; but I was told you were," and leant back in her seat, and evidently felt safe enough to betray no outward fear.

"I was speaking last night about your exertions on behalf of the deaf and dumb," said Miss Crokerly, in explanation, recognising, without understanding it, the tone in each of their voices.

"You were naturally prepossessed in my favour then," and he looked at Rosalie again, speaking in a voice not free from sarcasm.

"No. I simply recognised that you were doing your duty."

"Which you must admit is the hardest of all things."

"I take your word for it. From to-day I honour you as a martyr. I was not prepossessed in your favour at all. Forgive me for my stupidity."

Rosalie's voice was changed from hot to cold. Miss Crokerly heard it with surprise, and a silence must have fallen had not Sir John, whose mind ranged on different topics, put in suddenly:

"I hear that it is quite true the Great High Priest intends to resign office."

"I have heard the same thing," said Mr. Barringcourt. "It is a very unusual occurrence."

"Did you hear the reason of it?" asked Sir John.

"I believe it has something to do with the Feast of White Souls. The episode was rather unfortunate. A great many are in favour of his resignation."

"Might I ask your opinion?" said Sir John.

"Yes. I think the Great High Priest should be above scandal, and he is evidently not."

And he looked at Rosalie, and his eyes were laughing, though his face and voice were as serious as those of a judge.

The old distaste rose in her, as of some dumb thing against a cruel and powerful oppressor. But she said:

"Do you indulge in scandal, Mr. Barringcourt? I thought it was the recreation of idle women."

"Oh, no," he answered, with the coolness of rudeness. "Idle women in these parts are known by the sharpness of their tongues."

"I'm very sorry," she answered, suddenly changing in tone and manner, "but I can't help liking the Great High Priest; and as for Golden Priest Alphonso—I detest him."

"Oh, dear! dear!" said Miss Crokerly, with agitation, laying her hand on Rosalie's knee. "You must not talk like that, Rosalie, indeed, you must not. It is not usual. Remember he is Mr. Barringcourt's friend, and bears an excellent reputation."

But as the carriage drew up, she stopped speaking of necessity.

"You will drive on, will you not?" asked Sir John.

"No, thank you. I'll get out, and borrow whatever Miss Crokerly cares to lend me. I never had a cold in my life. The experience would be new to me."

So he came with them into the house, and seemed in no particular hurry to depart. Rosalie said to him:

"Will you do me a favour, Mr. Barringcourt?"

"To the best of my ability."

"Then give me one good point in the character of your friend."

"Which friend?"

"The Golden Priest."

"He is a man of great integrity."

"What's that?"

"Honour."

"What's that?"

Rosalie's questions were not contemptuous; they were put with a great desire to find out.

He shrugged his shoulders.

"There you have me," he answered. "I'm sure I don't know. The word generally speaks for itself to all but the ignorant."

"Then you cannot defend him on the strength of it?"

"No; he is clever enough to defend himself, I hope. You are wearing a very pretty and uncommon ornament, Miss Paleaf."

"It is not an ornament. It is alive, and one of my dearest friends."

"Such a friend is rather questionable on Lucifram."

"Why?"

"The Serpent has a weakness for frogs. In a natural state they form part of its food."

"My friend has powers of self-defence as well as yours."

"The Serpent has a very big mouth."

"Yes. And is ambitious enough to prefer men to frogs upon occasion."

He laughed, and the conversation changed to general topics.

CHAPTER XXV
THE GOLDEN PRIEST

That night when she and the frog were alone together, Rosalie began the conversation by saying:

"What do you think of Mr. Barringcourt?"

"I like him," said the frog, quite shortly.

"What has prepossessed you?"

"Nothing particularly. But I like him. I'm sorry you were so rude to him."

Rosalie flushed. The tone was almost grave enough for a rebuke.

"I? Rude? Oh, Brightcoat, how can you say so? I always try to be polite to him, and it always ends in failure. It is he who is rude to me."

"No," said the frog; "you take no pains to act or to speak sensibly. And to say you detest anyone is absurd, ridiculous, to say nothing of bad manners."

"You've never lived in Marble House, so you can afford to talk. Talk about vivisection! It was Mr. Barringcourt who openly deplored to me there was no such thing in our country. What do you think of that?"

"There are worse things than vivisection," replied the frog. "If it were not for that I should never have been here, or alive now."

"But—" said Rosalie, staring at it.

"Why don't you cultivate a charming manner, Rosalie?"

"I expect I'm not made that way. Are my manners so uncouth?" and her expression was doleful.

"No; but I don't see how you're to get your six horses, chariot, and all the rest, unless you try to be more charming."

"Well, Mr. Barringcourt will never help me that way. You should have seen the look he gave me last night, and then to-night, as if he'd never seen me before. Such folk give me quite a creepy feeling. Besides, talking about horses, his are black. Can't you see he is the exact opposite of what I want? He would do all he could to hinder me. If it were not that once I saw him looking very tired I should detest him too. Oh, how I hate Lucifram! Somehow or other, I never feel at home here," and she sighed.

"And you've got about all it can give you."

"Then I'm like all the rest—ungrateful."

"Rosalie, has it ever struck you you are very pretty?"

"Yes; every now and again it has. But what of that? All the women we saw to-night were pretty. It's the commonest of all things. If I'd a big hook nose now I might appear imposing. But no; even that is common enough to-day."

After a pause the frog said: "I heard someone say to-night you were the prettiest woman there."

"Please, don't! I'd so much rather you left my personal appearance alone."

But the frog continued:

"It's as well for people to think about these things at times. I know many a lovely woman who has been ruined by thinking too much of her beauty in one way, and too little in another. They know they are beautiful, and that knowledge is all-sufficient to them; their food and recreation, and all in all."

"But I'm not one of those."

"No. I think you might put yours to much more use than you do."

"You speak in puzzles."

"You are not so dull but that with a little consideration you will understand me."

So Rosalie went to bed much sat on by the frog, but maybe profiting, as most of us do, from a little compression and criticism.

Next day everything was sloppy, wet, and dismal. Rain began to fall in the afternoon, and going out, no matter of pleasure on such a day, was not indulged in.

Tea had just been brought in, and Rosalie and Miss Crokerly were preparing to enjoy it alone, when visitors were announced. They were Mr. Barringcourt and the Golden Priest Alphonso.

"I came to return the umbrella, Miss Crokerly, and met the Golden Priest on my way."

"Then you will have tea," said she. "On a wet day you are doubly welcome. No one else has ventured out."

"We are fortunate. Miss Paleaf, allow me to introduce my friend, Golden Priest Alphonso, to you."

And Rosalie, having a severe and cold critic perched upon her shoulder, rose very gracefully and bowed.

"It must have been very important business that brought you out on such a day," said she to him, as they sat down, with charming sympathy.

"Well, I was out begging, and a beggar cannot choose his weather. I was going in search of Mr. Barringcourt for a subscription for a new decorative curtain for the temple."

"In place of the old red one?"

"Exactly. It was old and shabby, despite its richness, and we think it must be rotten. There is every indication that it may give way again, and so we are making all speed with the new one."

"Then you are not superstitious enough to think it gave way before from anything but natural causes?"

He looked at her sharply and narrowly.

"Oh, no," he answered. "One can find a natural cause for everything. Therein lies the greater miracle."

"But how?" said Rosalie, subduing her tongue in deferential attention to the pillar of the Church.

He smiled, as became one of exalted intellect.

"Well, there is nothing like order—cause and effect—to work a lasting miracle. A startling thing has a short life. The rottenness of the curtain was the symbol of something still more rotten. Nothing takes place in a day."

Rosalie's eyes opened innocently, though they were very far from innocent. There is no doubt the frog must have been to blame for it.

"What is still more rotten? But perhaps my questions bore you. I am so inquisitive."

Again he smiled.

"You could never be that. But what is still more rotten is the system that lets old men continue in office after they have proved themselves unfit for it."

Rosalie's eyes betrayed a charming depth of horror at this cold-blooded statement.

"But, sir," said she, "who is to be the judge of their incapacity? And, again, it seems so cruel, and—and—doesn't it make a terrible lot of enemies for you, saying things like that?"

The Golden Priest laughed. The last remark evidently was to some point.

"In the cause of common sense one has no objection to making enemies. And I cannot for the life of me see why the highest position in the land should never be filled by a man till he's nearly in his dotage."

"Oh! it's more restful. Besides, a great and a good man should retain his intellect to his death, however old and feeble he may be."

"Granted! But feebleness is no qualification for an important post. And greatness and goodness should discern its own capacity."

"Is it true, then, that the Great High Priest is resigning?"

"Yes; in a few months."

"He has discernment, then?"

"I think his action is a little too late for that. His plea is ill-health. None of us have heard anything further—not those nearest to him in office."

"And then there will come the general election for his successor?"

(For in Lucifram they chose their highest priests that way. The clergy vote for them.)

"Yes; in a few weeks from now."

"It will be a very distracting time?"

"Scarcely more so than the last year has been."

And so the silent plot of years had worked to a fulfilment, the veil or mask at length being thrown aside. To-day was spoken openly what a month ago had been whispered and kept down.

Here the conversation was interrupted by Miss Crokerly.

"Mr. Barringcourt tells me he saw the secretary again this morning, and arranged for all the things you suggested, Rosalie."

"Yes. He has never doubted my judgment before, but I think he must have detected a foreign influence, he looked so dubious."

Rosalie laughed.

"Are they to have force-meat and sausages with the turkey, do you know?" she asked.

"It never occurred to me to ask."

"And you an executor of a will! And never to inquire about the gravy and bread-sauce. It's plain you don't attach enough importance to a Christmas dinner. But if I were you, Mr. Barringcourt, I'd countermand all orders, and give them 3s. 6d. each, and a free day to enjoy themselves anywhere and anyhow, with a night each end, to make a complete sandwich and a delightful holiday."

"You imagine them to be prisoners. On the contrary, those who have friends or relations who care to receive them may have leave from the Home once every month. And for the inmates, you must remember it is no prison that they live in, and they are very happy."

"I suppose so," said Rosalie. "But I always dread those public institutions for defects."

"You are prejudiced," put in the Golden Priest. "They are the greatest blessings in existence. I always regard them as branches of the temple."

"So do I," said Mr. Barringcourt; but the tone was questionable.

"I have the greatest longing to go through Todbrook's Home," said Miss Crokerly. "One hears so much about it. I should like to see the inmates at work."

Rosalie shivered.

"Oh! would you, Miss Crokerly? I can imagine nothing more galling to them than to be watched by strangers."

"But is it such an infliction to them?" asked that lady, turning to Mr. Barringcourt.

"I don't know, I'm sure," said he. "I hardly think so. I think myself it would be better if they had more visitors from the outside world. Lady Flamington is the only lady I have ever taken over the premises."

"I had just left there," said the Golden Priest, "before I met you to-day. I hear she caught a severe chill last night, and is confined to her room."

"Indeed," said Miss Crokerly; and Mr. Barringcourt and Rosalie looked at each other, from no apparent motive.

When tea was over the two gentlemen rose to go.

"I think," said Mr. Barringcourt, in a lower voice, to Rosalie, as the others were speaking of a special fern which both were rearing—"I think it would not be a bad plan for you to go over the Home with Miss Crokerly. The matron will willingly take you over, and you'll find there are worse things in the world than being deaf and dumb, or even blind."

Then somehow or other they looked at each other, the first time really since the Saturday night. How long ago it seemed now! And each was very curious about the other evidently, for Rosalie's eyes searched his, and his eyes hers, but what conclusion either came to it would be hard to say.

And then she shook hands with the Golden Priest, and the door closed.

"Do you think," said Miss Crokerly, "that Mr. Barringcourt told the Golden Priest your opinion of him, and brought him here to-day in consequence?"

"No, I don't think so," she replied thoughtfully. "I think Mr. Barringcourt must have recognised the Golden Priest has no sense of humour, and would resent instead of forgiving opinions."

"Your tone proves appearances are deceptive. I thought by your manner you had changed your estimate of him."

Rosalie half shuddered, and stretched her hands to the blaze.

"I was simply carrying out a lesson in obedience. And yet my estimate of him *has* changed. I find him so uninteresting."

"It is the common lot of most of us to be uninteresting."

"Oh, no, indeed. You are interesting; so is Sir John; so was—was—so have been many people I have met—Mr. Barringcourt, for instance. But this man is petrified by ambition. It is eating up his heart and head."

"Well, I am not particularly fond of him myself, as I have told you. Still, I am surprised that with your views you should find Mr. Barringcourt interesting."

Rosalie's brows knitted.

"I don't understand him. I never did understand him. Have you ever met anyone, Miss Crokerly, who at times struck you as being very, very good, and at others almost cruel? And that is how he appears to me."

"But you know so little of him."

"Yes, of course. I forgot. I spoke as if we were almost old acquaintances."

CHAPTER XXVI
CONVERSATION AND A LITTLE PIG-STUFF

After that a short time passed away, during which Rosalie saw much of Mr. Barringcourt and the Golden Priest, though not intimately.

During this time Lady Flamington, young, beautiful, much courted and admired, died. It caused a great sensation at the time, because she had only been ill a week, and the doctor had great hopes of recovery because she was strong. But it was double pneumonia, and whereas many a poor person less well attended to gets well and strong again, she, with all attention, passed away.

Rosalie, though knowing comparatively little of her, was somehow much affected by her death. Sir John went to the funeral, and she was put away in a manner that would have done many a poor person's heart good.

The next morning was bright and frosty, and Rosalie took an early walk in the Park. Walking there, she met Mr. Barringcourt, and as it was daylight, and the frog was with her, she did not beat a retreat. She expected to find him doleful, searched his face for the usual signs, but found nothing. She remembered Mariana's words, and thought there must be truth in them.

"You are out early," he said.

"Yes. I left Miss Crokerly feeding the birds and cleaning the cages. She prefers to do it alone, so I don't offer to help her."

"You are happier with her than you were with me."

"Of course. I was not at all happy with you, Mr. Barringcourt. You knew it."

"I don't think you waited long enough to find out."

"I escaped by the first open door, in case none other should present itself."

"Which door was that?"

"That is my little secret. You must be as charming as charming to me, and I will be sure never to let you know."

He laughed. "Mariana again?"

"Yes, Mariana," said Rosalie, suddenly standing still and looking up at him, for they had walked along together. "How is Mariana? I want to see her again."

"Oh, she is perfectly well, I think," he answered. "But you cannot see her. The guest of Sir John Crokerly cannot fraternise with a housemaid."

"When did you find me a snob?" asked Rosalie. "Of course I can see her. I—I should have written and asked her to call and see me, only things in your house aren't quite on the highest principle."

And Rosalie's nose went one degree higher, and she drew her skirts more severely round her, and moved quite half an inch further away as they walked along.

"What do you mean?"

"Well, the postman would do his part of the work, but I doubt whether Everard would."

"Then, if you don't trust Everard, why not call yourself?"

Rosalie's eyes opened.

"Do you mean to say if I wouldn't trust a letter I should trust myself? How you reason, Mr. Barringcourt."

"You could neither be torn up nor burned."

"No. But it is my firm intention never to enter Marble House again."

"You are the young lady who once said you never had run away, and never intended to."

Her ears began to burn.

"To recall things that are past is mean—and—and abominable."

"I am not recalling things. I merely wish to point out to you people always do the things they say they won't do."

"Do they?" she answered, and turned a pair of mermaid eyes on to his profile, and tried to recall things that he had said.

Under the scrutiny he turned his face to her again, laughing.

"Still the old trick of staring, Rosalie."

"You must be very careful how you speak to me. See, I carry my chaperon in my muff," and she tilted it up and showed the frog sitting there.

"If you had lived two hundred years ago, they'd have called that little animal your familiar spirit, and burnt you as a witch. Where did you get it from?"

"Another secret, Mr. Barringcourt. You must be still more charming, and I'll count twenty every time before I speak. But when may I see Mariana?"

"Mariana has forgotten you."

"Has she married Everard, then?"

"Oh, no! Their friendship is as pleasant as iced milk in summer. If you want to see Mariana, you must come and seek her."

Rosalie bit her lip. "I've told you I won't."

"Why?"

"Because if I came you'd never let me out again."

"You say so, so I should be very ill-mannered if I contradicted you. My road lies this way. Good morning!"

"Mr. Barringcourt."

"Yes," and he turned to find her standing there, with a puzzled and anxious look on her face.

"Would you mind giving me a little advice—telling me what to do, I mean?"

"About what?"

"It's about a handkerchief that was found in the temple, so it seems, some time ago. It belonged to me. I keep wondering ought I to tell, and I don't want to. I would have asked Miss Crokerly, only she knows nothing about it, and might not understand. What would you do if you were me?"

"I'd worry; but being myself, I'd let it pass."

"But it caused a scandal, and did the Great High Priest a great deal of harm."

"Why did you not speak about it at the time?"

"Because I wasn't in Lucifram. I—I—I—You see, I haven't got out of my old habit."

"No," he answered, and raised his hat and turned away again, and spoke with such a short kind of pride, that just the one sharp monosyllable was almost more than Rosalie could stand.

"There now," said she to the frog, as they walked home, she with a burning heart. "Do you like him now? Did I not tell you no one could be nastier?"

"Well," replied Brightcoat, "you ask advice, and only give half the information—not that."

"I see you have conspired against me. If I told him the story of the Governor, and how I met with you, he would only laugh and say I was dreaming."

"You shouldn't stammer when you're speaking. People always misconstrue it, and give it more meaning than it has."

"Because people are so stupid. Well, we've quarrelled again now, and you can blame me if you like; but I blame him. And I would so love to see Mariana again. And to think he called her a housemaid! Housemaid? I've seen no woman to compare to her in beauty or grace since I came here. The only thing she needed was life. And housemaids, as a rule, have too much of that."

It is sad to relate that a few days after this the Great High Priest died, and his death was a general relief. He was little mourned for. The public do not always forgive a man readily, even when he has the grace to die, though it's certainly a great point in his favour. But still there was a certain section still in his favour, or rather, in favour of a certain Golden Priest called Phillipus, who was the oldest of that superior gathering, and likeliest, therefore, to come soonest upon dotage. Now Phillipus, if seniority had anything to do with it, ought to have stepped into the vacant throne, and would have done, if the events of the last two years or so had not undermined public feeling.

He was a man of sixty, so well preserved, and of an intellect so keen, he appeared as one in the very middle youth of life. But when events are against a man, he may be what he will, he doesn't make much headway, from a worldly point of view.

But the death of the High Priest, so unexpected as it was, threw things forward a bit. The election for his successor must come off sooner than was expected. In lieu of this, a famous conclave was called together at a dinner-party—a party at which the dinner was not to be so important as the speeches to follow.

Whilst this was in progress of preparation, cards of invitation were issued for a great ball in Marble House on Christmas Day.

And so it was the day before the big dinner came off, and about a week after the invitations for the ball had been issued, Susiebelle rushed into the drawing-room of her great friend, Miss Groggerton.

Now, before proceeding, it may be as well to introduce this lady cautiously. She lived in Lucifram, not upon Earth. She was so shockingly and vulgarly outspoken that on our modest sphere she would never have been tolerated; but there she was.

And why? Well, the reason is a good one. She had twice been crossed in love. That on Earth makes a woman bitter. Not so on Lucifram.

Crossed once, she does become embittered; crossed twice, she becomes a scourge in the land. And Miss Groggerton had been crossed twice.

She therefore spared no one, man, woman, or child, and in consequence all persons with a spite against anyone went to her. She poured pepper and vinegar upon their wounds; then salt, and healed them.

So it was that Susiebelle rushed into her room, furnished in yellow satin.

"I think it's shameful!"

"What's shameful?" asked Miss Groggerton, laying down her yellow-backed novel.

"The way Camille Barringcourt has behaved!"

"I knew you'd never manage it," said the other.

"Manage what?"

"To get him up to the scratch."

"You've failed often enough; you needn't talk to me.

"I was talking to myself."

"It's scandalous the way that grey-haired old Agnes Crokerly gets into everything. The reason her brother's never got married is because she never lets him out of her sight."

"The reason he's never got married," said Miss Groggerton, "is because he's no morals."

"You know a good bit about people," said Susiebelle, more respectfully.

"I should think I did! People are no better than pigs; they're swine."

"Pa made his money out of pigs."

"They're one degree better than people, then."

"I wish you'd let me say what I came to say."

"Go on. No one's hindering you but yourself."

"Camille Barringcourt's a pig. He's gone and asked old Agnes Crokerly to play hostess at his big do. And I thought now Lady Flamington was gone there'd be a chance for ma and me."

"What d'ye want with *him*?" said the other sneeringly. "He's not a duke. He's plain Mr.! Bless me, you're coming down!"

"Ah! but he's got a mint of money."

"You've got enough money for two and more, if need be. What you want is a title. If you looked back into his people you'd find they kept a chip potato shop, I dare be bound."

"Never!" said Susiebelle, with emphasis, the tears rising in her eyes. "He's so real a gentleman he makes Lord Hysquint look like a twopence-halfpenny waiter in a restaurant I don't want a duke" (her voice was rising), "I won't have a duke! They're common little sniggling things that are too proud for their place. One might think they'd never tasted sausage! I'll marry who I want to, and if I don't marry who I want, I'll make everybody's life a burden to them!"

And her voice rose to a high pitch, for she was hysterical, and had never been much crossed in her life before.

Miss Groggerton was enjoying the oratory so much, she made no attempt at interruption. This would be a delightful tale for repetition. Susiebelle, once having begun to speak, had lost control over her tongue, a state with which many will readily sympathise.

"I went to the temple specially when Lady Flamington died, and thanked the Serpent, because I thought it was my turn next, and—and—and now it's old Agnes Crokerly—old cat!"

"Old Agnes Crokerly!" said Miss Groggerton, with a snort and a sneer. "Old Agnes Crokerly!"

"Well, he's asked her to do the thing for him. And he giving a big affair with Lady Flamington warm in her coffin yet! And never a crape band round his arm or his hat for her."

"Well! Women who make themselves too cheap can't expect to be respected even in their graves."

"She never made herself too cheap. Ma fought tooth and nail to get her to our place, and wouldn't have managed it then if it hadn't been for Mr. Barringcourt, who's more democratic in his views. He brought her to a charity concert when her husband was away in the land of Big Boasts and Loud Voices, and ma improved the occasion."

"And now," said the other contemptuously, "you say John Crokerly's sister has taken her place."

"Yes; it's the way with young men. Mollycoddled by women old enough to be their mothers."

Her tears began to flow again.

"He's not so very young," said Miss Groggerton impressively. "And you bet your bottom dollar it's the other one he's after."

"Which other?" and Susiebelle opened her big brown eyes.

"What's her name? Pa—Pa—Paleaf."

"What!" screamed the other. "The girl with the pug-nose, the green eyes and washed-out hair. Sprung from nowhere! A lot you know about it."

"I know plenty, because I watch. Didn't I see them walking in the Park the other morning? I'll do him the justice, though, to say she kept calling him back when he was all for getting away."

"I don't believe it. She knows how to dress, and there's an end of it."

"She's a right-down pretty woman," said Miss Groggerton spitefully, who would have been just as eager to pronounce her ugly upon another occasion.

"There's no dash, no 'go' about her. She gives one the impression she's been sleeping in a bandbox. I'd rather have Agnes for company than her."

"You would. But then you're not a man. It makes all the difference."

And then Susiebelle, being quite overwrought, put her head on the sofa pillow and cried aloud. Truly Miss Groggerton was cruel. But it was not her nature to remain so long, if justice must be done her. Suddenly she said:

"Are you very gone on Barringcourt?"

"Dead gone. If I don't marry him I'll marry no one. So pa had better look out."

"Well, it's Miss Paleaf he's gone upon now, though it may be only a passing fancy. But why not set yourself to work to do her out?"

"How?" asked Susiebelle, raising her head.

"Well, she never goes anywhere but what she takes a hideous green toad with her. These are days of extreme religion. Let's say she worships it. There would be scandal in no time, and it might end seriously for her."

"Yes; but I'm thinking of him. I don't think he's a very religious man. It might make no difference to him if he's f—f—fond of her."

Miss Groggerton laughed aloud.

"You'll never get married if you're such a greenhorn. D'ye think any man would care for a girl who worshipped a toad when he was there himself to be worshipped? On my word, Susiebelle, you don't know everything."

"Of course not," said the other humbly. "How—how shall we begin?"

"Oh! I have a great friend, a priest called James Peter. I'll speak of it to him as a serious matter and scandal. There's no one like the priests for spreading gossip."

CHAPTER XXVII
AFTER-DINNER SPEECHES

After that Susiebelle went back to her accustomed life, and behaved as a young lady who had been presented to the Emperor *should* behave.

The great night of the dinner had arrived; the following day was to be the great election, and the two most popular and powerful candidates were, to even the inexperienced eye, Golden Priest Alphonso and his brother Phillipus.

Now, since the death of the Great High Priest it was very plain the latter had come into more favour. Why, it would be hard to say. A little whisper here, a little whisper there. "He is ambitious" — deadliest sin in a path of life that fosters ambition. And Golden Priest Alphonso, with his far-reaching, numerous feelers, like the octopus, must have been conscious of it. Yet the poor were his upholders. One night a week, at his own board, they were his guests, and he was seen sitting down with them. *This* man ambitious? The people's friend Alphonso! That means so little and so much, just as in the days of our own French Revolution.

But now the night had come, and everything was a buzz of simmering excitement.

Thanks to tickets sent from Mr. Barringcourt, probably through Golden Priest Alphonso, Sir John, Miss Crokerly, and Rosalie were enabled to go. The Sebberens only got one ticket, as happened in most houses, and that at a side table, still a place of honour, where the wealthiest sat, and were content to sit.

The Golden Priests, robed in their flowing vestments of richest satin and cloth of gold, sat interspersed amongst their guests, at the two principal tables. The great hall was crowded, and so constructed that all speakers, from one end to the other, could be distinctly heard when there was silence.

It was an off-shoot of the great temple, and was called the Golden Hall because its ceiling, walls, and other adornments were overlaid with gold. Men were there in the preponderance, but there were women also from the more influential houses. People were heard lamenting the absence of Lady

Flamington. Somehow or other to-night, even in that tumultuous world, her presence was missed.

Rosalie was there. Rosalie, in shimmering grey, like frozen shining *crêpe*, only soft and clinging. She was as one in half mourning among that brilliant throng. On her shoulder was the shining frog, shining in green and white, and for some reason or other her face was very pale, and her eyes big and bright.

On the opposite side, a little farther up the table, Mr. Barringcourt sat. He wore the curious gleaming jewelled pin she had seen before, and the persistent red light it cast was nothing short of wonderful. On the side lower down sat Golden Priest Alphonso. Still farther off sat Phillipus. To-morrow the race and the fight would be decided.

Now on this great occasion the Golden Priests themselves did not speak. Naturally, a man cannot speak on his own behalf. The only thing he can speak for is a Cause.

But when dinner was over (and it was finished in a remarkably short time, being, as it were, but the trumpet sound calling to greater things), the friends and upholders of each candidate spoke in turn. No names were mentioned—views only were put forward, facts also. Each speaker was allowed fifteen minutes and no more.

The speeches began in earnest, and they revolved round the two chief men of those chosen—for and against.

Now it was plain that the unfortunate episode of the lost handkerchief, or rather *found* one, still rankled deeply in people's minds. A debt of gratitude was still due to the man who discovered and made known this scandalous piece of information. Affairs in the temple had for centuries been kept too close. A Great High Priest was needed whose actions would be as light as day, and character above reproach.

So on the speeches went, all interesting and conclusive, because they all pivoted on one concrete thing, a handkerchief with a rose in the corner. The thing itself was never mentioned, for that would scarce have been diplomacy. Like the Serpent, the handkerchief was hidden out of sight.

And so on one little lie, or piece of misunderstanding, one man was gaining a position which clearly was too good for him. So at least thought Rosalie. She studied the faces of the two candidates, and took a sudden fancy to that of Phillipus. He came from a line of uncrowned kings. The speeches were going against him; he bore it with dignity and polite attention to every speaker.

At last one speaker, bold with champagne, ran full tilt at the red rag, rose, or whatever else it can be called. He spoke of it openly, and the result was—fatal.

For suddenly the frog said to Rosalie, "Speak!" and being obedient, she spoke.

She rose to her feet with one deep spot of colour flaming into either cheek, the rest white as snow. A curious silence fell on the room, which had been silent before.

"I think there has been a little misunderstanding about the handkerchief," she said, in a voice that ceased to tremble. "It belongs to me. I never saw the Great High Priest in my life, but I did go into the most sacred place three years ago, with—with a petition, and by mistake I left it there."

Now there was a certain purity in Rosalie's voice and simplicity in the words that carried conviction.

For half a minute silence followed, then Golden Priest Alphonso broke the silent spell.

"What right had you going there? You! A woman."

"I—I was very much in earnest."

"Then," said he harshly and pitilessly, "you are to blame for all the events of the past three years." Then his voice altered, and he said: "Truth is pleasant. It is a relief to find the late High Priest was better than one thought. But you, what excuse is there for you, to keep silence so long, and let a man go to his grave misunderstood? Fear, I presume, of being found out."

"I knew nothing," said Rosalie, in a kind of self-defence, for the expression in his eyes under the hypocritical sternness was very sinister. And then someone hissed at the far end of the room, and then someone else. Truly the Serpent was alive, and no golden image either.

But hissing was contrary to the dictates of good manners in such an assembly, and the chairman called to order. Rosalie sat down trembling, all colour gone from her face, though she had sufficient strength of will to keep her from giving any further signs of the ordeal she had passed through. Her eyes travelled magnetically from the face of the Golden Priest to that of Mr. Barringcourt.

He was leaning forward, his elbow on the table, looking at her. In his eyes shone the old mocking, laughing light, that said in so many silent words, "Now you've put your foot into it." They showed no sympathy.

Then a man, seizing the opportunity, got up and spoke in favour of Phillipus; another, then another. The tide seemed turning—was turning. Rosalie sat as an icicle. Every now and again she felt the sinister eyes from below, the laughing ones from above, fixed on her.

Who would have thought the popularity of a man hung on such a little thing as a handkerchief?

Then at last Mr. Barringcourt got up. In the midst of passion and eloquence, he was passionless. In spite of his height, in spite of his deep, unfathomable eyes, in spite of his firm mouth and certain lines upon his face, he seemed to be by far the youngest who had spoken, in manner, in voice, in a certain confident easiness. People settled in their places, smiled when he smiled, and became suddenly more good-natured, for at times he had a very bewitching smile.

Rosalie looked at him. She recognised that in Lucifram she had never seen so handsome a man, or one with so much grace. A dull pain and a sharp pain struck at her heart together.

"Ladies and gentlemen," said he, for on these occasions titles were disregarded by the speaker, "the record speech of the evening has been delivered by a lady with a style and simplicity it would be impossible for us to beat." (Popular opinion fluctuated. Was Rosalie so bad as five minutes before they had imagined? The speaker spoke so easily, he made them feel more easy. Wonderful gift of oratory!) "Now I agree with my friend, the Golden Priest Alphonso, the lady should have spoken earlier, when things could have been righted. But her silence no doubt sprang from the best intentions."

"That's all very well," called a voice. "But what about going into the sacred place against orders?"

"When one is in earnest, one goes much farther than one intends. It's an unconscious action. The lady said she was in earnest; she has accounted for what she did."

"She's liable to severe punishment."

"So then are all the women who looked at the Serpent when the curtain fell. I remember hearing a conversation between two sisters who were present at that—that unfortunate service. One fainted, the other retained presence of mind. Since then they have scarcely spoken—one was enabled to see so much more than the other. It is generally acknowledged that all women worthy the name did what was natural."

Whether Mr. Barringcourt were laughing or no, there were few there who took him anything but seriously. They considered this the acme of perfection in simplicity of reasoning, for the time, at any rate.

"But," continued he, "to return to the general subject, the choice of a Great High Priest. It seems to me the greatest fault in the past has been the age of the chosen candidate. What one wants at the head of such a great organisation as the Church is younger men—younger blood—younger principles and ideas."

Dissentient voices.

"You don't agree with me. But lately I was travelling in Lucifram in a country of world-wide respect and renown. It surprised me at first to find all the places of importance filled by comparatively young men—State, Church, professions, even trades. In the centre of their chief city I saw a famous statue in marble of a man, and underneath in letters of gold was carved 'Aged sixty-five.' There was no mistaking it; the smallest child could read and understand it. On seeing this I made inquiries, and was told his history by the High Sheriff, himself a man of about fifty-five.

"His name was Hugo de Bretton, and as a lad he had been an errand boy, and in that capacity acquired an unfailing stock of good manners and alertness, the necessary adjuncts to all successful men who are not boors. From thence he travelled the ordinary roads of success till, in due course, he became a great banker. His own fortune was enormous—his power equalled it. This at fifty. At sixty his wealth was increased. At sixty-five he seemed in the very zenith of his glory—physically and mentally of astounding strength. His name a magic spell in speculations. Then suddenly he resigned from public life." Here a shrewd little smile, almost imperceptible, wrinkled Mr. Barringcourt's face.

"Now, you know," continued he, "that a man who amasses a fortune, a very great fortune, I will not say how great, does the greater part of it by stepping on other people's corns—not intentionally, but he does step all the same. And with increasing gold his feet at times become so heavy they do more than crush corns—they crush life unconsciously.

"This man was no fool. The past had been very profitable years to him; so should the future be. How great a sacrifice his self-resignation was it would be hard to say, but it was done with little ostentation.

"He lived for a period of fifteen years longer, and, I venture to say, in that time he did more practical good than any statesman or soldier of his time. He gave of the accumulated experience of life, generously and widely. He invested large sums for the aid of respected and aged poor, a thing which hitherto had been thought to be the work of the poorhouses. He spent the last years of his life a philosopher and philanthropist, respected and beloved—leaving the outward battle of life for those who had still to win their spurs. So great was the impression left by his conduct that others, lesser men or equal, followed suit. And gradually the law came in that all at sixty-five resigned their office, not as unfit for work, but as having done their full share of labour in the field—ready to give advice when sought, and ready to turn a life's experience into a profitable channel for the good of the community. And with such critics standing by, capable of judging, and unsparingly, it acted as a spur to the generation following.

"And so it is that age is there the most respected. Generation of workers follows generation in perfect order. In State, in Church, in every division of labour there is vigour and freshness. For why is the Church to be excluded? On the plea of sacred exemption? A most sacred fallacy that is so ticklish it won't bear touching, and holds together pretty much as the old crimson curtain in the temple held, till the hand of God, through the agency of moths, tore it down from the rings of gold."

"There's many a man young at sixty-five," one argued.

"Have I not given you a notable example of one who turned his mind from business to philanthropy, and gave his mind and energy and wealth to it."

"There's many a man has died soon after giving up the business of his life, if it's compulsory."

Mr. Barringcourt laughed.

"He's either narrow-minded, with no interest outside his own affairs, or he worships his work above the Serpent. He should be careful."

"Many of our finest clergy are over the age you mention."

"They push out or keep down the younger men who are just as fine. If they wish to remain in office after age, let them work for the love of the thing—for nothing."

Then he sat down. And not long afterwards the guests departed.

"What a curious speech that was of Mr. Barringcourt's," said Miss Crokerly to her brother, as they drove home.

"Yes. He'd argue black was white when in a mood to do so. But I'll call on him to-morrow. According to his verdict, there's only three years good work left in me now."

"He didn't say that," put in Rosalie from her corner, where she had been sitting mutely. "Just think, Sir John! Under certain conditions you might paint the best picture you ever did in your life after sixty-five, and what a great thing it would be if you gave the proceeds to some great scheme of general improvement, that had too much genuine good to have any of the sentimentalism of charity in it. I think it would be a splendid thing, and economise resources."

"Under the new *régime* we'll have to become Spartans," said he, not unkindly. "But tell me, Rosalie, is it true that the lost handkerchief belonged to you?"

"Yes," she answered, breathing quickly and leaning forward. "I went there one day, nay, twice, when I was in terrible distress. I never mentioned it before; I didn't quite know how to. But some day I'll tell you all, but at present I would rather not. Has it made any difference to you? I had to speak to-night. It has weighed so long on my mind. And I couldn't bear to hear them bringing that up as a blot on the late High Priest's life. If it had not been so cruel, it would have been ridiculous."

"We wish to know no more than you care to tell us," he answered kindly. "And it has made no difference. The time was awkward, certainly, but you had not been here long enough to know how things were going,"

"Oh! but it's Mr. Barringcourt," she continued quickly, with a queer ring of pain in her voice. "He knew, and has known all along, and could have spoken and set all things right. It was cruel, cruel! I can't understand that anyone who spoke as he spoke to-night could act as he has done."

"Did he know about the handkerchief?" said Miss Crokerly.

"He must have done. He—he—he was at the temple the same time as I. If only he had spoken sincerely! But it was simply to further the schemes of an ambitious man."

When they got home Miss Crokerly went up with Rosalie to bed. A fire was burning brightly in the bedroom.

"Rosalie, did you ever know Mr. Barringcourt before you met him at the Sebberens'?"

"Yes, indeed. I stayed in his house nearly a week. I met him first in the sacred place of the temple."

"Why were you staying at his house?"

Rosalie looked at her with the look of fear and pain in her eyes that had haunted them half the night.

"If I tell you, you'll never repeat it, even to your brother?"

"No."

"Well, I was born dumb, and I remained dumb till I was twenty-two, and then he cured me completely, just as I am now."

Miss Crokerly would have doubted, but Rosalie's tone carried conviction as before.

"And it took a week for the cure to be completed?"

"No. Afterwards he kept me as a prisoner. I ran away, or something led me away. I don't know which."

"It's a curious tale. Almost unbelievable."

"I know. That's why I never repeat it. I should have gone to be an inmate of Todbrook's Home, but I couldn't bear the thought of it, somehow or other."

Then Miss Crokerly went away. She saw that Rosalie was overwrought and tired, and recommended her to think about nothing till morning, and go to sleep.

When the door was closed, Rosalie flung herself down in a chair before the fire, and the frog hopped on to the mantelpiece.

"Why did you tell me to speak?" she cried. "I did no good. Only incurred cold glances and hisses and hatred."

"Flea bites," said the frog.

"Bred out of serpent's poison, anyway. If I'd followed Mr Barringcourt's advice I'd have said nothing."

"He always goes by the rule of contrary."

"It's a rule I never learnt."

"It's answerable for a great deal that happens in this world. Why do you take things so much to heart?"

"Oh, I don't know. I'm a lonely, lonely woman."

"I'm a lonely, lonely frog."

She laughed. "You make light of my misfortunes."

"I think you are much more fortunate than you think. I bear a charmed life, and yours is the next best thing. We'll struggle on together, anyhow. Remember, we're in search of six white horses and a capable driver. That's all we've got to mind."

"Of course," said Rosalie. "Life's more like a dream than reality."

Here the frog yawned, and Rosalie, much soothed, was soon asleep.

CHAPTER XXVIII
REVENGE IS SWEET

Next day this particular city of Lucifram was buzzing. The great election was coming off. Yet there was no doubt who was winning. Golden Priest Alphonso had regained his old popularity. When the poll was read at night he headed the list. The people received it with shouts of acclamation. In other circles the news was as well received. He was barely forty. A precedent was established. He was the youngest Great High Priest in the record of time.

But our history is not so much with public events as private persons, and we return once more to Susiebelle and her friend Miss Groggerton.

Neither of them had been at the great dinner, but the one had heard from her father, and the other read from the paper, the trend of general events.

"And," said Susiebelle, with pious horror, "to admit right out she'd been into the most sacred place—a place no woman has ever been in before. Such impudent boldness is enough to make one's hair stand on end. She's a disgrace to our sex. If I met her in the street with the Emperor himself I'd turn my head away."

As this was never likely to be, Susiebelle was very safe.

"Yes; but what I can't understand is Mr. Barringcourt's conduct," said Miss Groggerton. "I hear that he defended her, or the next best thing. Made everyone laugh and then serious at the same time."

Miss Groggerton was green when she said it, but Susiebelle became greener.

"Pa says no right-minded woman would care to hear her conduct made the subject of open criticism, and if she'd had a ha'porth of modesty, she'd have kept her tongue still. But I know the kind she is. Those pug-nosed women are all alike. Pushing themselves to the front if they have to pay body and soul for it. Have you seen brother James Peter yet?"

"Yes. He called the day before yesterday. And I explained to him about her. He was to be at the dinner last night, so he would see her."

Just at this moment, in accordance with the old proverb, brother James Peter made his appearance. He has been previously introduced to the reader at the beginning of this book. Once brother James Peter fell over a footstool, and got lost in the dark, was laughed at by his brother priests, and to this day heard occasional remarks made about his conduct. He remembered very well the source of his misfortunes, and had again scented the innocent cause of them all. He was the first to hiss last night, proving himself to be a true cross-breed of the Serpent. To-day he came in as one with news. He had given his vote; for him the day's work was over.

"You look pale, Sir Priest," said Miss Groggerton, who would have called up the devil to prove him another, behind his back.

"The events of last night have distracted me," he cried, sitting down. And Miss Groggerton rang for his favourite collation of whisky and ham sandwiches.

"Tell us, is it true?" they both cried, as the provisions were being prepared without.

"That woman is in the power of the Evil One," said he solemnly. "And the sooner that little squat animal is taken by the hind leg and cast into the fire—the—better."

"Yes, indeed," said Miss Groggerton, in joyful anticipation of slaughter.

"I believe it's that frog that gets her a reputation for beauty. Loathsome little thing!" and Susiebelle shivered, and then laughed.

"Listen to me," said James Peter, raising his fat finger. "Make none of your own little spiteful remarks, but listen to me."

Being a priest, he spoke as one in authority, and the women submitted.

"That woman," said he, "is a dangerous and unprincipled character. Three years ago—listen carefully—she came into our temple and pretended to be drunk—dumb, I mean. She used to come and kneel up close to the crimson curtain, and I believe she contaminated it and made it rot. She used to look up at me with her lovely eyes (she has lovely eyes, Mademoiselle Susiebelle, whatever you may think), and point to her lips, and shake her head, and I—I used to pity her. She gave me to understand she was praying for the gift of speech."

Here the women laughed shrilly, shook with laughing, as he had laughed long since.

"But that," continued he, "was all a ruse. She was waiting her opportunity to slip inside the curtain, eaten up with preternatural and unwomanly curiosity. But one afternoon, as it was getting dusk, I went into the choir stalls to get a psalter that I needed, and thought I heard a curious sound coming from out the sacred place. I could not understand it. I hid myself in the shadow of the carved screen, suspecting theft, and recognising sacrilege. A little later, out came this woman, carrying a light. I know not where she got it from. But seeing me, she ran all down the nave at quickest speed, I following."

"You caught her?"

"The devil helped her. She escaped; and at the door she turned right round and put her tongue right out at me, and said: 'Did you ever know a woman who couldn't talk if she wanted to?' You have the story in a nutshell."

"And you never reported it?"

"Three hours afterwards. I was as one imprisoned in a living grave for three long weary hours."

"But did you not tell?"

"Yes; and the Great High Priest would not believe me. He laughed. That was the beginning of all his troubles. He was too lax, they say. Under the new *régime* there will be greater strictness." And he sighed.

"Why, she's a witch, a witch—an impudent, underbred thing," said Susiebelle excitedly. "Have you told Mr. Barringcourt?"

"I am not personally acquainted with him. But last night, from the way he spoke, one might almost have thought he was excusing her. Of course, there was no putting out of tongues or giving pert answers last night; she spoke as meek and as mildly as you please."

"If it hadn't have come from the mouth of a clergyman I wouldn't have believed it of her," said Miss Groggerton, glad to have such a reliable source of information.

"But—but" continued Susiebelle, "isn't there a severe punishment for going inside the curtain, for a woman?"

"It used to be to have her tongue torn out."

"Who will do it? Who will do it?"

"No one will do it nowadays. The biggest punishment would be a fine. Pawn a few jewels; it's done in no time."

"She doesn't worship the Serpent at all; she worships that little blinking frog," said Miss Groggerton.

"Well, I've got my eye on her. And if there are any heathenish practices going on, you may be sure I will report them before long," said he, and soon afterwards got up to go.

That same night, when all the wear and tear and excitement of the day were over, and all the cabs had rattled home, and all the theatres been closed, the new Great High Priest sat in an arm-chair in Mr. Barringcourt's study, whilst the owner sat in his accustomed one beside the table.

Sacred Priest Alphonso was white and haggard, and the deep lines on his face showed the strain that he had passed through. His arms hung heavily on the arms of the chair, his eyes were fixed on the carpet. Mr. Barringcourt was writing a letter. When he had finished it, he sealed it, and tossed it on the table, then bent his eyes upon his guest as a doctor sometimes does upon an uncertain patient he treats as an experiment. Without saying anything, he got up, and went to a side-table, and poured out two glasses of red wine. One he filled, the other only half, then turned his head round and looked at the Priest. Still he sat in the same weary lethargy. A smile curved Mr. Barringcourt's lips. "Very far gone," he muttered, and filled the glass.

Then he took it across and offered it to him. He took it carelessly and drank all the contents. Mr. Barringcourt drank half his and flung the rest into the fire. It blazed up in a brilliant red light, then died away as suddenly, leaving the fire dark, as if water had been poured on it. But this beverage must have refreshed the High Priest wonderfully; for suddenly rousing himself, he looked up at Mr Barringcourt, and said, clapping his hand upon the chair arm:

"To-day has ended successfully. But the first thing I do on coming into office is to bring that woman to trial."

"Which woman?" said Mr. Barringcourt, sitting down on the opposite side of the fireplace.

"That fool who nearly spoilt everything last night by having too long a tongue."

The wine surely had had a heating effect.

"Miss Paleaf?"

"Yes. The one I took rather a fancy to at the Sebberens', and asked you to introduce me to." And he laughed cynically.

"Oh," said Mr. Barringcourt easily, "you'll let that die down. Set a constant guard of two priests to watch the curtain. Such vigilance will satisfy the people. Besides, Crokerly is doing the work of the panelling, and none can do it like him. You can't afford to quarrel with him over the mischiefmaking propensities of a woman."

"Do you mean to say you would look lightly on her conduct of last night?"

"Of course! She did you no harm. It's herself she's harmed, as she'll find out as time goes on. It's always best to be a bit forbearing with women; they're given to flying off rather unexpectedly at times."

"No excuse. No excuse at all. She did it from malicious intention and love of meddling."

"What do you propose to do, then? Tear her tongue out?"

"Imprison her for life."

"O Lord!" said Mr. Barringcourt, and he laughed. Then he laughed again, and again he said, "O Lord!"

The other frowned, and the light of anger glinted in his eye.

"You seem to rather approve of her conduct," he said. "Certainly I have to thank you for your speech, though, candidly speaking, neither I, nor I believe anyone else, could make head or tail of it" (he spoke in a genuinely puzzled voice), "and for various other things I have to thank you; but in the matter of dealing with this woman, I beg you will not interfere."

"Yes," said Mr. Barringcourt, in a low, clear voice, "I shall interfere. The Serpent is like everything else. It can't afford to get too much talked about, or its reputation's gone. If you prosecute her, you make yourself and it the laughing-stock of Lucifram."

"I uphold its sacredness and sanctity."

"Cant and tomfoolery! You say I made a speech last night you didn't understand—and I didn't take the pains to understand it myself. But if you persist in this, I'll make another before long which will appeal to everyone, and tread on no general corns at all, but that of the individual."

"You are in a quarrelsome mood to-night."

"Yes. I've been in the society of priests all day, and they weary me."

The other laughed.

"That's a hint to me. However, for the present you may have your way, but I tell you candidly, if there's any hubbub made, I bring her to trial."

Then he went away; but walking along the silent streets he said:

"Barringcourt's as spoilt as a child. Cross him in the least thing, and he's inside out in no time. Yet in some whimsical, flimsical kind of way he's been the best friend I've had, and helped on considerably the present affairs. All the same, that girl shall suffer. The thing to do in this world is to teach people to keep their tongues still. It's three parts the battle of life."

And Mr. Barringcourt, left to himself, stood a long time looking into the rekindled fire, which tells so much to those who read it properly. And his face betokened more weariness and contempt than even in the past years, and the lines of his features were finer.

"Revenge first; thanks a very doubtful second," he said at length, and then went off to the stables.

All through the blackness of the night the black steeds galloped, and some mistook their dusky forms for passing clouds, and their wild eyes for distant stars, and the rhythm of their feet for the rumbling wind.

That night, as Rosalie slept, the frog left its customary place on the washing-stand, and came close to her ear. And though all the room beyond was dark, the light round her head and pillow was very white and pure.

All the things the frog whispered it would be unfair to say, for the frog was working for its own ends, as most of us do, and therefore coloured things to its own liking.

Rosalie woke in the morning, and looked at the deceitful frog, now sitting on the washing-stand, and said:

"I've been dreaming that a tiny little angel came and sang to me and laughed. And though I can't remember one word of what it said, I know that everything was very pleasant—so that many a time I found that I was laughing too."

CHAPTER XXIX
A CONFESSION

Time flew on till it was just two days before Christmas, or, at least, the festival which in Lucifram takes the place of Christmas in our world.

On this particular afternoon Rosalie dressed with the greatest possible care, and looked three consecutive times sideways in the glass, to see if her nose was any better disposed to turn downwards; but it wasn't. Still, it detracted nothing from the general effect, and, indeed, might be said to help, if only on the side of morality, to keep her from growing conceited.

The frog, having come to that stage when one evidently regards oneself as quite perfect enough, felt no qualms as to its appearance, took not one doubtful glance into the glass.

Rosalie, when she was ready, put her head through the door to tell Miss Crokerly she was going to pay a call; she did not say where.

Miss Crokerly, busy with festival matters, simply nodded her head. It was just a little after three.

Rosalie left the house, and walked on quickly till she came to Greensward Avenue. Coming here, her steps slackened; but she continued walking till she came in sight of Marble House. Here she came to a dead stand, and looked blindly on the pavement. Her heart was beating so quickly that if the passers-by had not been walking along so heavily they must have stopped to inquire about it.

But from a full stop she ran lightly and hurriedly up the steps and rang the bell. There was no escape now, for within thirty seconds it had opened. There stood Everard, just the same as ever, as silent, as polite, no more surprised.

Rosalie took her courage in both hands. There was that hideous umbrella stand that a dowager-duchess had once exclaimed was the most charming novelty she'd ever seen.

"Is Mr. Barringcourt at home?" said she.

He looked as if he had never seen her before, but after a moment's pause he said:

"Yes. Will you come this way?" And led her through the outer vestibule into the wide and gloomy hall.

There he left her, and went in the direction of the Master's study, but soon returned.

The afternoon had quite faded now, and as he conducted her along the western corridor he turned on the lights.

Mr. Barringcourt received her almost silently. He made some remark about the weather—it was of little importance. He drew a chair for her. Rosalie sat down.

"I came to see you," she began, clasping her hands tightly inside her muff, "because—because—"

"Because," said he, in the most distant of voices, "you wished to see Mariana."

"No. I'm afraid I was too selfish to think of Mariana. I was thinking only of myself."

She did not notice the alteration in his expression, because she had not noticed the previous hardness of his voice. But she got a vague idea he was not particularly pleased to see her, yet was determined to go on.

"It has sometimes struck me," she began hurriedly, "that it was very ill-mannered of me to run away from you. I—I—I escaped by a little door in the stable wall."

A very curious silence followed this remark; then Rosalie continued:

"The country beyond was very beautiful—at least, I thought it was. It—it led me to a white house, with a low verandah and a pretty garden. It took me a whole day to go, and the sun was setting when I got there. In the house I met a youth—at least, I thought he was young; but afterwards he told me he was nearly as old as you. But he seemed to grow very quickly in the time that I was staying there. He took me to his father. At first I thought he was very old, because his hair was white. I had just one day's holiday when I was there, and then I went to live in a little hut all alone, with a plantation in front of it. I sowed a basket of seeds in the ground that the Governor (that is the name I knew him by) had given me. But first I had to dig in the soil, and I didn't like digging at all; I hated it. After that, everything went by the rule of contrary. The seeds never came up; they grew underneath, and looked to me like very beautiful jewels. But they took a great deal of digging out and freeing from the soil. I took them to the Governor, and he sent them somewhere, I think he said it was to the city, to be tested and valued. But every time they were sent back and marked as rubbish. I've never felt quite the same since. I used to feel young before, but ever since I've felt as old as old. And I do nothing but pretend all day long, in little and big things alike. I pretend least with you of anyone, and that night I ran away from you in the street (you remember it?) I felt quite surprised, and in one way just a little happy. It made me feel just a little more alive. But after a while the Governor said I had better come back again into the world. I didn't want to, because there was nowhere to go to, and I did not want to come back to this house again. I was tired of prisons. But when he told me to come back into the world I was obedient, because I knew he was much wiser than anyone that I had ever met before. He was kind to me in some ways, although he never threw kindness away. So one morning I started on the return journey, and Brightcoat came along with me for company.

"When we were in the streets, I went along scarcely knowing what I was doing, I was so tired, and at last I sat down on a doorstep. It was Sir John Crokerly's, and when his sister came home she took me in; and I have lived there ever since. There is nothing else to tell you. Now you know all, you need trouble yourself to be agreeable to me no longer. After all, I owed it to you to tell you. You gave me a greater gift than I thought it possible anyone on earth could ever give me. And you no doubt put it down to science, but I put it down to God. And—and about my coming here, when first I did come to you. I came from the sacred place of the temple. I had given up wishing to be cured of being dumb—at least, praying to be cured, because I thought God was not wishful to cure me. And I prayed to the Serpent just to help me to live the right way, because I knew that that was the only thing God really cared about And the Serpent seemed quite to disappear; in its place came the presence of God. Only one little ball of light and gold was left out of all that giant frame and jewelled head. And I don't know quite how it was I came to you, any more than now I have gone to Miss Crokerly."

With these words said, she got up and stood facing him, for he had not sat down during this monologue but stood looking at her, a thing which, after first beginning, she seemed quite unconscious of.

Her words had been simple, her sentences short and abrupt, and at times somewhat disconnected, but Rosalie's voice was so sweet that it seemed to run like a silver bell in and out the mazes of this experience.

Now she held out her hand.

"I have detained you long enough. Perhaps you'll forgive the school-girl style. Though I feel so old, I can find no other."

"Come with me to the stable," said he, "and show me the door. I don't believe there is one."

"You will be able to find it yourself."

"I had much rather you came with me. It is the only way in which I can credit your story."

So together they went through the silent house and silent grounds and silent shrubbery. The red light shone full down the middle pathway to the stable door. But Brightcoat shed a softer brilliancy round about, if not so clearly and direct. But then there was no need for it as guide to-day.

The stables shone out with a certain curious light of their own—a dusky, shadowy brightness.

At a certain touch the unseen door slipped backward, and revealed the shadowy twilight within.

And as is customary with horses, they turned their graceful heads and looked with wild eyes on the newcomers, and one in the far corner neighed. But they seemed shadowy. All were shadowy. Eyes shone like carbuncles, the only distinctive feature. And there was nothing of warmth there. Everything was cold and chilly as a vault

But Brightcoat's light was useful here. It shone in direct rays on to that little unnoticed door that was built so unobtrusively in the wall.

"There," said Rosalie, and she touched his arm. "I went through there."

"Strange," said he. "I never saw that door before. How did you open it?"

"With the key of my uncle's safe. But that has gone. I don't know what I did with it. I was in such a hurry to get through and close it after me."

"And the path led you to a low white house with a verandah?"

"Yes. Let us return. It is cold here. You'll give your horses rheumatism if you keep them in so damp a place."

"You are not acclimatised. But we will go. Strange I never noticed that door. As for the others, I suppose if they did notice it, they imagined I had done so too."

When they were back again in the house, which seemed cheerful after the intense cold without, Mr. Barringcourt said:

"Will you have tea before you go?"

"No, thank you. Our last tea together had not a very pleasant ending, though it began so charmingly. We're like most people—best friends when parted."

"Then I may not see you again till Festival night."

"Do you still renew the invitation?"

He laughed.

"If I were not very contrary, you would make me angry. You harp so constantly upon an unreasoning subject."

"Ah!" said she suddenly. "Let me see Mariana. Send for her."

"Not to-night"

"Yes, to-night. I will not keep her longer than a minute. Just to see if she is just the same."

"She has not altered. Take my word for it."

"You said if I came here I should see her."

"You must have misunderstood me. I never said so."

"I—I don't believe you ever mean me to see Mariana again," she said.

"Indeed? What makes you think so?" and he laughed again, not at all kindly.

"Because you know quite well that I should do my very best to persuade her to come away with me."

Rosalie bowed, and swept away toward the door, and when she got there she said to Everard, quite loud enough for Mr. Barringcourt to hear, who still stood in the hall:

"When next you see Mariana, please give her my love, and tell her I asked to see her, but was not successful."

He bowed solemnly and let her pass, but took no further notice than if he had been made of stone.

CHAPTER XXX
FESTIVAL

Now came Christmas night. On Lucifram Christmas Day wasn't marred by any subsequent church-going. It was nothing better than a heathen feast; the Serpent had nothing to do with it.

On that day the children went simply wild, and gave themselves incredible airs; demanded their best toys, gorged oranges and apples, made themselves ill with plum-pudding, demanded their full share of turkey, and got it, and looked with expectant eyes on the iced cake when it appeared. Just as if they'd been starving all day! The little wretches!

The grown-up world, unless it was going out to an evening party, yawned, and ate its customary Christmas fare, and drank it too. Then the old people played cards, and the young people sang, especially the young men with untrained voices, and the lovers behaved as if they really were in love with one another.

Come and watch Rosalie.

Now that day there had arrived two Christmas presents so beautiful that many an empress might have envied them. The first came early in the morning, before the postman; a curious and unusual thing. There is no doubt Santa Claus was on the war-path, for such a lovely ball and reception dress could only have been made in some magic fairyland. It was like shining silken *crêpe*, all frosted over with tiny sparkling jewels, all in white. It shone like soft pure snow in the sunlight, and fell in folds of simplest grace. It was so very simply, yet so very wonderfully made, that one wondered what it was that gave it such a beautiful effect.

"Is it not too dead white to suit me?" said she to Brightcoat, after going into raptures on its beauty.

"See here, there is a little box below," said it.

And Rosalie opened it, and uttered the most real cry of delight in her life.

"It's my stone, my first stone, that I loved so, all set in gold and ready to wear. Oh, Brightcoat, Brightcoat, look!"

And she sat down on the bed and hid her face in the pillows, and cried from different emotions. At last she wiped away the tears and looked up, her eyes falling on the shining stone again.

"I love them all as if they were my children, and that somehow the most, because it was the first. And I believe it loves me too. Look how beautiful a ray of light it sends towards me! And I never hoped to see it again."

Rosalie took it up, and kissed it, and shed tears upon it, but the light from it was never dimmed; one might have thought it was made tear-proof.

"I need no other colour. This is quite enough. And you, Brightcoat."

"Yes; of course, there's me," said the other thoughtfully.

This was the beginning of the day. But when the postman came, besides bringing letters and cards without end, some of the latter bearing halfpenny stamps after the style of circulars, he brought a parcel, also directed to Rosalie, in handwriting that the frog declared was superior to anything it had ever seen.

It was opened in public, and inside was a pair of slippers as white as snow, and worked in diamonds. And they were such a curious shape they looked as if they must really be antique, because they had little square toes, and gold straps across. They reminded one of the daintiest garden clogs, so light were they, and when Rosalie put them on she wanted to dance right away.

"They're made on the same pattern as the little wooden clog I have upstairs," cried she. "Look, Miss Crokerly, they dance of themselves," and in excess of spirits she pirouetted round the room, and kissed both those elderly people from superabundance of excessively childish glee.

Where they had come from she didn't know. She thought they had come from the same source as the first, although they came by post. So that evening she dressed for the real pleasure of the thing. And when it came to pinning the jewel into the bosom of her dress, her hands trembled just because she loved it so. It shed just the same soft shades on to her dress as the light of the moon might shed on to the snow—a passing green and golden and palest blue that melted into white. And on her shoulder the ever—present frog, and a new light in her eyes, because the ice-tears had rolled out of them.

And underneath the shining jewel her heart beat quickly. She went with Sir John, Miss Crokerly having preceded them in Mr. Barringcourt's carriage some time ago.

"Do you know," said she, "I thought at the last minute you'd change your mind and stay away."

"Oh, no," he replied. "I always go when Barringcourt throws his house open. There are so many things that interest me there."

"Yes. It's quite after the nature of a museum, is it not?"

"Yes. Unlabelled. So that it has an additional charm."

They took their turn in the long line of carriages, and after a considerable time were enabled to alight.

There was an awning from the parapet to the door, and the steps were also covered a deep red.

Rosalie looked for Everard. He was not there. Two powdered footmen instead. They were not inmates of the Marble House. Neither were any of those who personally waited upon the guests that night. There was not a waiting-maid anywhere about to compare with Mariana, and Rosalie could not have imagined her proud and delicate face amongst that throng. But how different did the wide hall look that night! Brilliantly lit, and with huge fires burning at either end. Fires fit for Festival and freezing weather. And no undue crowding of guests to do away with comfort and beauty and enjoyment. The wide doors to the southern wing, leading to the picture-gallery and conservatory, were thrown open. So also were those to the west, containing the reception rooms—no empty, echoing fireless places now, but full of life and laughter and vivacity.

A reception was held first; dancing did not begin till eleven, when a well-known princess was to lead with a gavotte. She was very proud of her instep.

At twelve supper was to be served in the large subterranean hall, a place Rosalie had never been in, nor, indeed, anyone else. And after that dancing began again, and continued till four. Then carriages and home.

On entering, Rosalie was presented with a programme that explained all this. It was book-shaped, with a mother-of-pearl back, and in the centre a perfect little garden clog with a broken string in gold, and underneath "Christmas 0039"—that being the year as reckoned in Lucifram.

"Oh, how charming!" cried one lady, who had just received hers before Rosalie. "An old clog for luck! It is delightful!"

Flowers the most gorgeous and tasteful banked every available corner; truly, the house had been completely altered from darkness into light.

Mr. Barringcourt on these occasions made an excellent host. He had none of the clumsiness of the bachelor host, being for all the world as much at home as if he'd been married and had ten children. Now, it was a dancing night, and thanks to an excellent example, there was not one smoke-absorbed, or card-absorbed, or billiard-absorbed man present. For one night everybody made a delightful martyr of themselves, and secretly enjoyed the process.

Rosalie's programme did not fill so quickly, for there were many there who took her to have religious mania, and doubted they might have something to put up with. Moreover, there were very few persons there that she really knew. At last she was suddenly accosted by Mr. Barringcourt.

"The first and last dance, Rosalie," said he, and they looked at one another. Then looking down at her programme, he said: "What an empty list!"

"It's quite right, thank you. I don't care about dancing. I'd rather watch other people, and listen to the music. Find me some quiet old lady whom I may sit by, and who does not talk too much. It is all I ask of you."

"There are not many present. They are all young and frivolous, or old and giddy. A much easier task would be to find you partners for every dance."

"I should be dead tired before supper-time; I can't talk to strangers, and I don't know every dance. And it takes rather a brave man to accost me; I perceive them mentally screwing themselves up to the pitch as they approach."

"Under those circumstances, it was very kind of you to come. Here comes the Princess. I'll return later."

The Princess smiled so condescendingly all round that everyone was charmed with her. She had a light walk, as one who treads on eggs and fears to break them, and her admirers said she glided as the spirits do.

As soon as she came—and, of course, she came rather late—the proceedings of the evening began. She danced the gavotte, and brought her own dancing-master and fiddler to play, as she was accustomed to be played up to.

When the real dancing began there was one of the best bands in Lucifram in readiness, that all the evening more or less had been playing favourite airs, and another to relieve them when occasion needed.

Mr. Barringcourt sought and found Rosalie.

"Should you not have given the first dance to the Princess?" said she.

"No. My step does not suit her, and she is sufficiently truthful to tell me of it."

"I can scarcely believe *your* step is wrong."

"No? She is easier to deal with than you. She goes greatly on credit. It's a royal failing. Come, let us begin; if this waltz is as it should be, it will be all too short."

And no seventh heaven could have surpassed, if equalled it.

"How lovely," said she suddenly, "if one could die dancing!"

"It would mean company on a lonely road," said he. "And cheat death of some of its tragedy, with well-matched partners."

"Did you—did you send me those slippers that I'm wearing?"

"What makes you think so?"

"The little clog on the back of my programme. It's the exact fac-simile of one I used to wear."

"I had a little story as near as possible to that of Ally Krimjo. For one morning there was found in the middle of my hall a little garden clog without owner or companion. It came there through barred doors and spring-barred doors, and none could make out how it came there. Not even I. I never learnt it till the night when you came to say your lesson. I proved it when you wore these little satin-covered skates to-night."

"You'll give it back to me?"

"Oh, no! I'm keeping it for luck. That is a lovely stone you're wearing."

"It's one I told you of. Dug from the garden with a great big fork and spade, just as a man digs."

"I believe I've seen it before in my father's house."

"No, indeed. Unless your father was the Governor I spoke of."

He laughed.

Then at last the dance was over.

"I've found the lady you asked me for," said he. "Miss Crokerly is my guardian angel to-night. It is she who discovered her. Here is an excellent place where you may sit and see everything, and hear the music to advantage too."

And then he took her to a seat, and introduced her to a lady sitting there. She was so charming a companion. Her silences were never awkward, and now and again she would give Rosalie information about certain people, all of a good-natured if shrewd kind, that was the highest entertainment.

At twelve punctually the company descended to supper.

The staircase down was of black marble, and spiral also, like the one above. It had none of the slippery treachery that characterised its sister staircase, though, and it seemed altogether of a much more reliable make. To a spectator the gay colours of the ladies and their sparkling jewels looked like brilliant multicoloured scales on a gigantic serpent, reared pillar-wise to support the vast chamber below.

The subterranean banquet hall of Marble House was nothing better, nothing worse than a crypt.

It had great and massive pillars of hardened, blackened marble; a fitting support for a fitting house.

Its floors were tiled in marble. Its walls of marble too. But whereas a crypt, if lit at all, is content with lamps of oil, or the feeble glimmer of electricity, this place was deluged with light. The most brilliant candelabra hung from the ceilings, sparkling in the thousand glintings of diamond glass. The tables were covered with finest snow-white cloths, and all the decorations were of silver, purest and brightest and most finely worked. And all the flowers were red.

Here, screened from view, the band was playing gently. A soft and scented air of luxury arose, as if to show that crypts upon occasion have finer possibilities than dining-rooms.

The Princess, led by Mr. Barringcourt, descended first, and half way down stopped to admire.

"Which was the pirate, you or Mr. Todbrook?" said she. "I'm sure you carted off the plan of a cathedral, and the material too."

"That is an open secret," replied he, laughing. "But his was the theft, not mine. I simply inherited what he had left. But he had gloomy taste. Now, were I building, I'd fix upon a little bungalow, a whitewashed place, with a world-wide garden for the summer-time."

The Princess was not of that simple nature that enjoys simplicity, but she delighted in anything odd, as she considered it, because it made her laugh.

"Do you really mean to say you are philosopher enough to grow accustomed to things?" she asked.

"Till I see a way of escape."

"And you see none from here?"

The Princess had not such keen eyes as Rosalie; she was not fond of studying faces, except for what animal beauty they might possess.

"None," said he. "Although 'tis said Todbrook escaped by the back door."

"He died," said she, and looked at him with a vague suspicion of horror in her eyes. She was of a superstitious nature.

But he laughed.

"You talk of death at a dance?" said he. "One might almost think, Princess, you were primitive, and scorned the guarded terms of civilisation."

The conversation had taken a turn not to her fancy. He had thrown a shadow over the brilliantly-lit supper-room. She shivered involuntarily, and looked about her petulantly, and said:

"Are you quite sure this place isn't damp?"

"Not at all! Not a rheumatic dampness, anyway. Spirits do not count; they are above it."

Then their conversation ran into a lighter channel suited to the occasion, and the feast began right royally, when the plumed peacock was carried in, to be admired in death, a lasting tribute to its vanity.

The band played, and the people laughed and feasted and talked. In the whole of Lucifram that night could not have been found a gayer or more brilliant company.

CHAPTER XXXI
MYSTERIES IN MARBLE HOUSE

But there was one person who never came down to supper—at the right time, anyway—and that was Rosalie. She had strolled off alone to the picture-gallery, led to look again on that curious representation of the former master of Marble House.

The silence as the last guest went down below made her heart beat a little faster. She listened to the last echoing laugh, and he seemed listening too. The slightly bending figure indeed betokened an attitude of close attention—almost the hidden smile of one who, listening, understands.

The long line of pictures ran either side of her, each in itself a work of beauty. She remembered that day when Mariana had gone off to the east wing from here.

To-night the east wing was closed. All this great glare of artificial light never traversed there. A heavy crimson curtain hid the polished door that led to it.

But Rosalie's spirit wandered off in that direction. A great curiosity, with a deeper feeling underneath to give the strength it needed, led her out into the central hall—led her gliding towards that gloomy fatal door.

She drew the curtain back with one white hand, white as snow against this deeper shade, and turned the handle. The door opened. Blackness, dampness, and the smell of decay and mildew met her, like a blast of foul despair.

She threw up her head, passed through, and the door slipped to behind her. And for one moment it seemed as if the parting kiss of freedom glowed on her forehead once again. And yet again the darkness was dispersed, for both the frog and jewel, and her own shining dress, that shone apparently without the aid of outer light, gave all the light it needed.

And here, within this gloomy place, at last came life and beauty, and the soft, tender light that lived in its own strength and was unborrowed.

No. 13! How well Rosalie remembered it! Mariana's workroom, a worse place than many a prisoner's cell. Yet it had about it an air of indefinable grandeur, the place of no petty criminal, or one sunk in moral disease. The rusty latch uplifted and disclosed the low-built room beyond, and the dim burner, the oaken chests, the damp, peeled walls, the shadowy corners, the tragedy of silence.

But what of these? They served but as backgrounds to a picture, and fitting backgrounds. For there, beside the long, low table, hid by the sheet, as white to-day as ever it had been three years ago, sat Mariana. But nothing there equalled the marble whiteness of her face. Her graceful figure bent forward, her hands were clasped on the table, and on her lips was that curious smile of pain, quite frozen there, as, wide open, her eyes stared at this hidden treasure on the table.

Some spider, mistaking the silent figure for a thing inanimate, had weaved a web of finest threads from head to foot, covering her silken hair and rough-spun dress. But respecting the icy chill that hung about those cold-cut features and hands, it had left them free and bare.

All about the cell fluttered the silent moths, settling and rising from the table. Yet they were powerless to canker anything. The bitter iron of living sorrow had too hard a crust.

The light that Rosalie brought with her lit up the room. She stood upon the threshold, gazing spellbound with horror on the central form. Could this be Mariana—this frozen statue, this figure nipped to the spirit with unavailing pain? Oh, never, never! For there this beautiful machine, working so fine a marvel of creation, had come upon a horrid pause, a fearful counterfeit of death, a fearful mockery of life!

Then the spell broke. With outstretched arms she hurried forward. "Mariana!"

No sound or movement came in reply. She placed her hand upon the stiffened shoulder. The cobweb broke; the spider saw, and ran away. She threw her arms around the other's neck, and kissed her stony cheek. No sound or movement in reply.

Burning tears fell from her eyes. They had no power to melt that which had been congealed so long, frozen from ice to marble.

Nothing availed—even when she fell upon her knees, and pressed her warm lips a hundred times upon the death-chilled fingers.

Powerless and weak! O God! for strength, strength, strength of some sort, to give life to the dying or the dead! What blasphemy! what heresy!

what presumption!—the ignorant tumult of a still untutored heart. Then she drew back and looked at Mariana, fighting down every emotion to make way for thought. Her eyes fired with indignant protest, and she said:

"I'd rather be a murderer out and out and hanged for it! And to think of this night, when in this very house there is no sound of anything but gaiety and laughter; and people feasting! And here there sits a prisoner and worse, and one man conscious of it. Oh, Brightcoat! How can you think well of such as he! I cannot bear to look at him again." And then she stooped and took the slippers off she wore. "I wore them happily at first, but now they're all so tight they pinch my feet I wonder what sweating or freezing system it was brought them into shape? And I so selfish as never to insist before on seeing whether she were free or no."

The slippers off, she looked at them, then at the silent figure sitting there, and turned away, half-shivering. She placed the slippers upon the table on the sheet.

The moths descending, fluttered round them, yet did not touch; for, taught by instinct, they had learnt what could and what could not return to dust.

Then with one parting call of "Mariana!" one loving kiss, one shivering glance around the dismal place, she went away, closing the door behind her, into the outer passage.

Curiosity bade her try some of those other low and numbered doors; but all were locked. This tragic wing was surely haunted. The air was condensed of sighs—an essence which hung heavy on the heart.

But before opening that crystal door, all rusted iron and cobwebs from this inner side, Rosalie stood still to think. Then she pushed it open, and emerged into the brilliant hall, still silent. From here she passed toward the staircase leading down to the supper-room, where all the guests were now assembled.

But to return to them.

There was no lack of merriment throughout the length of tables. But as the supper progressed, and people became accustomed to their surroundings, general comments were made upon a long and double-folded curtain of heavy material that hung from floor to ceiling at the lower end of the vast chamber beside the staircase.

There was present at that supper a young girl just out that season—as giddy, as merry, and full of happy spirits as one unknown to care or saddened thoughts can ever be.

And to close a spirited discussion with some as young and thoughtless as herself, just as the feast was ending, she left her place amidst a laughing silence, and ran to the farther upper end of the table, where Mr. Barringcourt sat beside the Princess. With the happy assurance of youth never rebuffed, she accosted him.

"I come," said she, still laughing, "to plead on the side of our religion. They say that dismal curtain bears a resemblance, and a very striking one, to the crimson one within the temple. Will you not contradict them?"

He looked across the room toward it "One's black and the other's red," he said, and smiled.

"Yes; but we were discussing what might be beyond," and her face was demure, though her eyes were sparkling with merriment.

"With what result?" said he.

"We all grew curious. Princess, will you be curious, too?"

"Oh, instantly. What is beyond that curtain, Mr. Barringcourt? Tell us, or show us, pray."

The silence of expectation had settled on the guests Barringcourt leaned forward toward the table, playing with the half-filled glass of wine beside him. And when he spoke his voice was low, yet perfectly distinct.

"You know," said he, "it was a foible of Mr. Todbrook's to collect as many heathen gods and false ones as lay in his power. This house was built on a system—I might say systems—of idolatry; its furniture collected from disused temples sought for all over the face of Lucifram.

"Behind that curtain stands a god, more hideous than any I have ever seen, and I've seen plenty in my time, as maybe most of you have done. The curtain came along with it from the temple where it stood, and in a state of wonderful preservation. Over one thousand years in age."

"What is beyond?" was the general question throughout the chamber.

"A death's-head of unusual size, worshipped and feared of all in the parts from where it came."

"Let us see it." A general murmur of anticipation ran round the room.

"These poor heathens!" said one lady, and her tone was patronising. "How ignorant they must have been."

"And are still in some parts, madam," said he.

"We do our best with the missionaries," she replied.

"Let us see it, please."

This was the voice of the charming youthful pioneer from the back.

"It's a death's-head," said he, and he smiled very kindly as he spoke. "They are not beautiful."

"But I've enjoyed myself so much all evening, Mr. Barringcourt, that I could not bear to be disappointed now. Besides, the Princess has commanded you. Please show us the head."

"It has never to be seen but in complete darkness. It's a clause of the will. It was the condition on which he bought it, I believe, from a few crazy priests, who had no congregation."

But they all wished to see it, light or no light. It was a little novelty to wind up supper and take the place of toasts.

So suddenly the light switched out, and left the place in total darkness. Those who were on terms familiar enough clasped one another's hands. They found the situation not unpleasant.

And then upon the instant the black curtain swung backwards and revealed a space beyond, from which gleamed out, in ashen whiteness and dusky hollows from the blackness, the skeleton head of death. It was the head of some great giant of unusual size, with yellow teeth discoloured, but all present. All looked at it with gloomy interest, and some began to wish, as darkness continued, they'd been less eager to examine it.

But suddenly and swiftly in the silence two gleaming balls of light glared red from the empty sockets, to turn their gaze at every individual round the room, and with a gleam most sinister. This was truly horrible. A room so black and dark that none could see each other. The bleached skull and skeleton of a superhuman head. And above all the terrible gleaming eyes, the only flash of light in the whole room, that had the power of penetrating, and gave each the impression the evil eye was fixed on him alone. A spell of silence had fallen. No woman cried; the laughter of ten minutes since had died; even the very sound of breathing was now quite hushed. This was the deadened, powerless load of nightmare.

Suddenly a light appeared on the spiral staircase. The gleam of snowy whiteness, the soft glow of an undying lamp, and the pure colours of a splendid moonshine. And above all a face and figure of most simple beauty, eyes pure and starlit in contrast to the red gleam. And a crown of mermaid flaxen hair, and expression sweet and thoughtful! It was a wonderful and sweet relief to the ghastly spectacle below.

And on a sudden the full lights flashed on again, and a sigh of relief burst from every heart and many lips. The black curtain had fallen. Rosalie alone remained of the weird scene, descending the spiral staircase. A little thing will often bring about reaction, and from being shunned by many, she from this opportune arrival gained a fair share of popularity.

"Where have you been?" a dozen voices cried, glad to make sound again.

"Trying to find a partner," cried she, and laughed; and others laughed as well, the search had been so long and unsuccessful.

"Supper is finished."

There was no lack of those to offer attention now, and along with this came the general bustle of those leaving the supper-table.

But by the side of Mr. Barringcourt stood the girl who, from a mixture of youthful spirits and curiosity, had asked the first the curtain might be moved.

"I am glad I had finished my supper," said she, with an attempt at laughing still. "I'm sure I could never eat anything in here again."

"It is fortunate refreshments are served upstairs," he answered. "You would not let so small a thing interfere with your evening's pleasure?"

Reassured somewhat by his tone, she said:

"After all, it was only an idol, was it?"

"That's all. They must be very brave folk to worship it, eh?"

"Yes. The Serpent is much less gruesome. Isn't it?"

He laughed. "Well, an empty skull often looks much worse than it is."

"But," said she, "it wasn't empty. I never saw such eyes. Never! Never!"

"You haven't seen the Serpent yet?"

"No; but mother did, and she said nothing about its eyes. She said it was plain to be seen we worshipped the true god, his scales were such a lovely gold. I am going to ask Miss Crokerly to introduce me to her friend. I'm sure if she had not come then I should have fainted right away. And I always laughed at Blanche for fainting. She used to do it so conveniently."

So saying, she slipped away, and to the upper regions, where, so far as she knew, there was nothing gruesome hidden away.

And soon the episode of the death's-head was forgotten, and the evening's enjoyment began again with even greater zest.

Rosalie's programme filled, but she never danced. Who could, when wearing only stockings? But she did not go home, but waited for that final dance, and no one noticed her slipperless feet.

CHAPTER XXXII
DIPLOMACY

"I have not the slightest inclination to dance, Mr. Barringcourt. I've spent one of the most delightfully lazy evenings I ever spent in my life."

"I envy you. I've been going through a species of treadmill. I've danced with every school-girl in the room."

"Myself included. You began the evening badly, you know."

He sat down beside her.

"Where were you all the supper-time?" he asked.

Rosalie looked at him. She detected the old, tired, wearily contemptuous expression on his face. She herself was far from tired. Her eyes were bright. Her cheeks had flushed a pretty pink; she had been under no unwilling exertion to please anyone.

"I stayed upstairs to see how long I'd be forgotten, and when no one remembered me, and I grew hungry, I came down."

"You should have acted the part of the jealous fairy godmother, and blasted us all."

"Well, though I be a school-girl, yet I've none of the attractions of youth, and so I've learnt toleration."

"It's hardly fair to keep repeating what I once said at random."

"Was it at random? I set a whole night apart to weep about it."

"You had nothing better to do, then?"

"The most miserable of all states, you must acknowledge. And through no fault of my own."

"Whose, then?"

"Yours. You have much to be answerable for, Mr. Barringcourt."

He laughed. "I have expiated most of my offences to-night; I have danced the polka."

"With Miss Sebberen. I saw you."

"Let us go into some quieter room. This dancing wearies me. I never was fond of it."

Rosalie's trailing dress hid her feet, and they passed into the picture-gallery. It was deserted.

She sat down under the picture of Geoffrey Todbrook.

"One day Mariana brought me here and showed me this picture. I forget what was said, but somewhere in our conversation she laughed. She said laughing always produced a pain at her heart."

"Mariana laughed? You utterly astonish me."

His face betrayed no signs of conviction of cruelty, certainly.

"Yes," said Rosalie. "It is astonishing, truly. Had I lived here as long as she, laughing would have been utterly beyond me."

"It is a good thing you escaped, then."

"You don't grudge me my freedom?"

"I grudge no man anything if he wins it, or woman either. And far from grudging you your freedom, I'm glad you won it."

"You were glad, then, when I ran away?"

"Well, no—not at the time. I do not know that I ever became thoroughly reconciled to you till you came to see me the other night."

Here a pause followed, broken only by distant strains of music.

"You have another dance on New Year's Eve, Mr. Barringcourt?"

"Yes. You will come? It is the one night in the whole year worth dancing on."

"I would come gladly; but I can find no dress to my liking."

"You have a week before you."

She clasped her hands round her knee, shook her head and looked at him.

"I won't come unless I can wear exactly what I want."

"And what is that?"

"The dress that Mariana was making long ago. But I expect she's finished it, and the moths have eaten it away. But all the same, I won't come unless I have it. It is the one thing on earth I've set my heart upon."

Mr. Barringcourt looked at her. The pretty air of reasonless determination suited her.

"It's impossible," said he.

"The moths have eaten it away, then," and without pretence or acting two big tears rose in her eyes and fell—one for sorrow at his hardness, one for the memory of Mariana in the cell.

But two tears upon occasion can be very fascinating.

"You never did reason, did you, Rosalie?" said he.

"Yes. It's the one thing I've done all my life. But the simpler you are in this world the more you're derided. Let me see Mariana to ask her about the dress?"

"Oh, hang Mariana!"

"Are you speaking broadly?"

"What do you mean?"

"You should never use abusive language towards the individual. I learnt that long ago. If you want to be profane you should generalise."

"Whose lax teaching was that?"

"I learnt it from the Governor; the gentleman whom I met when I ran away from you. But he wasn't lax, I'm sure. Perhaps I misunderstood him."

"I wouldn't put it beyond you. But give me a form of forcible language that would fit in with his exposition."

"Well, the only one that presents itself at all to me is 'Damn it.' You see 'It' means nothing in particular, is quite impersonal, and therefore no one is any the worse for it, yourself included."

"You're an advocate of that particular form?" said he.

"I'd allow it to you upon occasion, but not to myself."

"Indeed! Why?"

"Because if I were a perfect woman I'd never have any inclination to go further than the 'd.'"

"You're striving after the perfect woman?"

"Yes," sighed Rosalie; "but she's very delusive. It's so easy to overstep the bounds and become saintly."

He laughed. "I don't think you'll ever be that."

"But why?"

"The strain would be too great. You'd best remain as you are. I believe the dance is ending."

"And—and never a word settled about my dress."

"Are you so much in earnest about it?"

"Indeed, yes. I went through all the pains and penalties of trying it on, stood three weary hours as model, and it was so beautiful my heart longed for it then, and has done so ever since."

"It's nothing but imagination. You must look for something else."

They rose together, and suddenly she put her hand upon his arm, and said in just such a voice as a mermaid might, half laughing, half plaintively:

"I won't come to dance the New Year in; I've nothing fit to come in. And as for the slippers that you sent to me, you can search for them just where you like. I don't want them, and I won't wear them. I only want the dress." And she showed him her foot in its silk stocking, without slipper or other covering.

"Where are your slippers?" said he.

"I've hidden them, and you may find them."

And suddenly he looked at her quite sternly, and he said: "You've been to see Mariana."

Rosalie returned the glance as meekly as became the situation.

"The doors were all unlocked. Besides, you should have found me a partner for the supper-time. I resented it."

"And what do you think of Mariana?"

"I think that you and I are inexpressibly different in our idea of things."

"Indeed! It is because of you she's placed where she is."

"And because of me you ought to place her where she isn't."

"I am not disposed to laugh. Your constant prying is objectionable."

"I pay dearly for it: hard words and cold glances from everyone, yourself included."

"Not too high a price, it seems."

"Dear me, no! I trust to the luck that saved Red Chin's wife. I'm not in the least bit inclined to cry to-night, Mr. Barringcourt I feel happy enough to dance without slippers on." And she stooped and kissed the precious stone she wore.

He looked at it and then at her. "Give that stone to me," he said suddenly.

Her cheeks paled as quickly. "I love it too well to ever think of parting with it," she answered.

"The price of Mariana's freedom."

"No," and her voice was a mixture of a gasp and weakness.

"And yet you love Mariana! How you do misjudge the word! You don't know what love is."

"Neither do you."

"I make no professions."

"I have no right to give away this stone; it was given to me."

"Keep it, then. I simply asked for it to prove your inherent selfishness."

"You could have proved it by a much simpler test. It is one of the dragon's heads impossible to conquer. Every now and then I give it a sleeping potion, and get some rest. It's very efficacious, I can tell you."

She turned and went away, and they did not see each other again that night, or rather morning.

CHAPTER XXXIII
THE WORTH OF A JEWEL

The next morning, rather earlier than usual, Mr. Barringcourt called to see Miss Crokerly. He saw her alone; but as he was crossing the hall on going away, he was stopped by hearing Rosalie's voice from the staircase, and by seeing her coming toward him.

"I have been waiting for you," said she, raising her finger as if in warning as she came nearer, and speaking very softly. "The dragon is sleeping, completely under the influence of a powerful drug. In the interim I've brought you this. The thing you asked for last night." And she held toward him a tiny jewel-case.

He took it slowly, looking at her, and then at it. Then the contents dawned upon him, and he looked at her again and laughed, though his eyes had a piercing keenness in them that took away the effect of the laughter.

Then her manner changed, and she too laughed. She raised her lips to his ear and whispered:

"I drugged the dragon with *Reason*, think what you will," and still laughing, would have moved away.

Now it just chanced (for those who find no excuse for what followed) that there hung just above them a bunch of misletoe. Miss Crokerly was a great advocate of Christmas parties for children, had had three such since December began, and holly and other Christmas decorations were much in evidence. But neither person concerned was at the moment cognisant of this fact. One was looking down, and one was looking up, but not at the ceiling.

But all the same, in opposition to the laws of etiquette, yet quite in accordance with those of nature, Mr. Barringcourt suddenly stooped and took her hands and kissed her. It wasn't a bit like the ordinary kiss a man would give a woman. It fell as softly on her lips as a breath of snow — nothing of fire — so that she laughed again, and shook her hands free, and saying "Thank you," ran away again.

After that Mr. Barringcourt went away, looking as thoughtful and preoccupied as if he had never been frivolous in his life.

He went home, and passed at once to his own private laboratory and study. He took with him the tiny jewel-case, and going up to one of the big windows facing the front of the house, took out the stone and looked at it. He looked at it so long that a bystander would have grown impatient. Then he went to the other side of the room, and opened what seemed to be a cupboard, but was really a set of shutters opening upon a window looking on the garden at the back. The light from this window showed the jewel differently.

Before it had been softest green and pink; now a constant red ray gleamed from the centre. He noted it, and turned it many ways. The light still remained—no passing brilliancy or change of colour. Then he went into the inner room, and noted the different blendings and the texture by placing it beneath a glass, there to examine it minutely. Finally he poured out from an old flagon, worked and chased in a substance like polished silver, a liquid that flamed up in the crucible like white-flamed fire, intense and beautiful. And into this he threw a stone that matched in some respects the one he carried in his hand. Under this great strength of heat it disappeared; no tiny fragment of lustre or of substance now remained. And quite remorseless to its fate, he next flung in the stone that Rosalie had given him, and bent forward eagerly to notice the effect.

No change! A glimmering blend of colour on the surface of the flame. Then with his fingers, as if the leaping tongues had been but water, he took the jewel out, and dashed the sprays of fire away like drops of water.

A smile, incredulous and all surprised, at first played on his lips and in his eyes as he looked at the jewel. Then after some deep thought, he started as one from a dream, the light of sudden understanding in his eyes. He placed the stone once more within its case, and put it in an inner pocket, then left the room and locked the door again.

Leaving the wing, he went out into the central hall, and passed across it to the eastern side, with its brilliant door and exterior brightness, all so false to the sordid truth behind. But there he paused, and called across the high, empty, echoing space:

"Everard, what is Mariana's number? I forget."

"Thirteen." The answer was simple and distinct.

"That's a lucky number, isn't it?"

"I believe it's a significant one. Unlucky, some say."

"We go by the rule of contrary. I think myself it must be lucky." And he laughed and flung open the great doors and passed inside. They swung to after him.

Then at the door he sought for he stopped, and with the same quick movement threw it open.

Inside, the miserable cell, the scanty furniture, the covered table, the cobwebs, the thick dust, the cloud of hovering moths, the stiff and rigid figure; but to his eyes on entering, not the central figure of attraction. For there upon the table, standing daintily upon the covering cloth, he saw the little satin clogs, with their golden strings and skate-like edges, that turned up daintily, bearing an almost laughable resemblance to someone's pretty nose. For in the same way that many persons' clothes on wearing them become a part of them and look like them, so these, scarce worn, became and looked a part of Rosalie. And in the midst of all this mildew, and decay, and icy lifelessness, they stood a thing of life—an open protest against everything surrounding them.

Without looking toward Mariana, he went and took them in his hand. They were not soiled. They had only danced one short delightful dance, and stood demurely side by side, longing to start again. The moths had never touched them; they were invulnerable. Then placing them once more upon the sheet, he leaned his hand upon the table and looked at Mariana.

Neither pity, distress, cruelty, nor any other emotion played on his face. He stood and looked at her, as deep in thought as if his mind was occupied with pages of a book, a long, long time. Then throwing back the covering from the table, he revealed the thick piles of satin that she had worked at in the three years passed long since. So this was the dress that Rosalie coveted; well, it was worth asking for, or would be when finished.

For the first time on Lucifram, and here in one of its most dismal cells, a smile free from artifice, from cynicism, from pride, from cruelty or contempt, ran on his lips and centred in his eyes.

But the machine? and how to set it working? Only one way. He crossed to Mariana, laid one hand upon her head, the other in her hands, and stooping, kissed her lips.

Then very silently, as some passing from life to death have done, she, with a sigh that trembled gently into every limb, swayed back to life. And on the second breath that stirred her bosom, looked up, and her eyes came to the face of Mr. Barringcourt.

"You've slept long enough," said he. "You can't complain now of being overworked. A long spell of rest, and now comes a short one of work. Are you ready for it?"

"Yes."

She rose from the chair, no stiffness, the old slow, easy motion born of coldness; itself born, who could tell of what.

"Six days to finish this—and alone. Can you accomplish it?"

"For whom?"

"Rosalie."

"Has she asked for it?"

"Yes."

She stretched her arms, then drew them in.

"It's well, because I fitted it for her, having no other model."

"You are to make it especially beautiful."

"It is not necessary to tell me so."

"And jewels? Everard will bring them to you."

Now she raised her eyebrows slightly and looked at him, and a faint smile came to her lips.

"Is Rosalie then so strong to bear so heavy a burden of sorrows as this house affords?"

"Search all you can find from the dust hidden in this room, and he will bring the rest. Did Rosalie appear to you so weak?"

"I loved her on that account I think."

"Part of a cause that changes weakness into strength. You feel yourself strong, Mariana?"

"Oh, no! But cold. The strength of ice, not iron."

"Rosalie has suffered from your complaint, I think. But she's cured."

Her eyes rested on his. There was a thoughtful expression in them, and she said:

"Cured? Then the ice was frozen less deeply."

"Or maybe the fire was stronger. There's something in that, you know."

"Yes," said she; then suddenly: "These moths are a great hindrance. I have no time to spend in sighs if I must work hard and finish in six days."

"Then I'll remove them for six days. After that they'll come back again, but you'll have finished."

"Yes. For Rosalie. And when to wear it?"

"New Year's Eve."

"Thank you. Now you had better leave me. What of these slippers?"

"Sew them with jewels."

"And make her tired feet? Is it some practice of cruelty?"

"No. A whim of mine. To show honour to an escaped prisoner."

"I must wake. Six days to make a dress, and it is rumoured that one of the planets was made in that time! I must hasten."

So then he left her, and she worked alone. And hour by hour some fresh seam in the design became completed, and on the third day Everard came. He carried a large sack, and it was full of jewels of every known description, small and large. Standing there, he said suddenly:

"Can I help you with these? Sorting or stringing?"

"But surely it's against the rules."

"It is advisable to break them in emergency. And I doubt if this be not finished, some great calamity will rise. The Master is away. The work is out of all proportion to the time. For his sake, for yours, and for hers, I wish to help you, for this day, at least."

So Mariana gave way, and one little flame of heat passed over the icy barrier almost unconsciously. The cell, being less lonely now, lost its ghastliness.

Thus the time passed away until completion, the last day of the old year, the eve of the new.

And on that afternoon at four o'clock Mariana heaved a sigh of apparent contentment, for all was now in readiness. And Everard, having done his full share in the arrangement of jewels, and whatever else was needed, returned to the door in order to welcome Mr. Barringcourt, who just then returned.

CHAPTER XXXIV
"A GIFT, A FRIEND, A FOE, A BEAU, A JOURNEY TO GO"

To return again for a brief interval to that day following Christmas Day. Mr. Barringcourt, when he had left Mariana, went to see the Great High Priest, and afterwards attended with many others the Service of Dedication of the Curtain. Miss Crokerly was there, but not Rosalie. Afterwards Mr. Barringcourt said to the new High Priest when left alone together, and the guests departed:

"Why didn't you invite Miss Paleaf?"

"I have told you why. I am only waiting for a sufficiently good opportunity to bring forward the trial."

Mr. Barringcourt's lips set. "You make a great stir about nothing," said he.

"I don't forget the awkward time at which she spoke."

"And when do you propose to send out the summons?"

"On New Year's Day. A public trial and an ecclesiastical court."

"And you as judge?"

"Oh, no! There is Golden Priest Ferdinand. I take no further steps in the matter publicly."

"And the punishment?"

"Life-time imprisonment."

Mr. Barringcourt looked at him and laughed.

"You laugh? After all, it is worth nothing better. People must be taught a proper respect for established religion."

"In childhood, yes. I doubt when they get older it's too late. And so you contemplate lifetime imprisonment?"

"Could you suggest anything better?"

"Well, there's escape. What do you say to that?"

"Futile. Absolutely futile."

"The Devil has helped her once; he may do so again."

"The Devil! Who or what is that?"

(They were ignorant of such a person on Lucifram.)

"Ah! I had forgotten. He was never fashionable here. The Devil is a libel on virtue; the exact imitator of God."

"And she is on familiar terms with this—this atrocity?"

"I owe a general pardon. I was confounding him with a Superior Being, an error commoner than one thinks of."

"You speak in riddles," said the Great High Priest, and his tone was irritable.

"I mean to say God helped her to escape twice before—nay, three times. You are brave, to say nothing more of it, to put another spoke in the wheel."

"By God do I understand you to mean the Serpent?"

"As you will. To my certain knowledge she has kissed the Serpent. The sensation must have been a new one, almost a dangerous one. After ages spent hearing the dull praise of men coming from lips all stereotyped, one soft kiss would have its—er—its value."

The Great High Priest looked at him sternly, as became his office.

"The Serpent is above such petty considerations," said he. "You speak with too much levity of sacred things."

"A fault of my education. Forgive me for it. And the summons is to be issued on New Year's Day?"

"Or on the eve."

"I understand you. God and his counterfeit will help or hinder you. Good-night!"

Next morning, walking in the Park, he came on Rosalie walking with the frog. Quite unconscious of the impending trial, she stopped on meeting him.

"Good morning!" said she. "You look very thoughtful."

"Yes. I'm thinking of taking a very unusual step."

"What, pray?"

"Paying a visit to my mother," and he looked at her.

"That means your father, too, does it not?"

"No," he answered, still looking at her in the same thoughtful, absent way. "I frequently visit him. At present they are separated."

Now it was her turn to be thoughtful. "That's very sad, isn't it?"

"Sadder than you'd think of; for, but for the irony of Fate, they would be quite inseparable."

"And is it an unusual thing for you to visit her?"

"Yes; I do not care to burden her with my presence, unless there is some reason in it."

"That sounds unnatural. Does she love you?"

"As much as I love her."

"That conveys nothing to my mind. Your powers of love are very enigmatical."

"They're simple enough on a worthy object."

"And she is very worthy?"

He made no answer, but said presently, with sudden decision:

"Mariana has begun upon the dress. It will be finished on New Year's Eve."

"And I to wear it?"

"Yes."

"I went to see her. You guessed at it. But she seemed more dead than living."

"A little extra sleep. She said she needed it."

"What of the jewel that I lent you?"

"It is very safe. I have a request to make to you."

"What is it?"

"I wish to beg the jewel for my mother."

"What is she like?"

He smiled.

"Words cannot describe her; to my eyes, the perfection of beauty and loveliness. As innocent and simple and free from care or evil as the light."

"You don't resemble her, do you?" asked Rosalie, unconscious of the bitterness of her remark.

He laughed, perceiving it.

"You may rest safely assured there. I know no one who resembles her."

"Is she kind?"

"The essence of it."

"Then what of Mariana, and such as she?"

His brow clouded. "You ask questions I'm not disposed to answer."

"Ah! but I'm thinking of my jewel. I love it so. Your mother would not value it a tenth part as much as I. Nay, before to-day it, and others like it, have been reckoned rubbish. She might think so too."

"Give me leave to take it to her, and await her verdict. If she underrates it, I'll bring it back to you."

"I'm afraid I must give the dragon so strong a dose there'll be no life left in it."

"If it is what you told me, the more honour remains to you in killing it with such a potion."

And Rosalie laughed, but her eyes were wonderfully serious, and she said simply:

"I'll give it to you, Mr. Barringcourt, because it seems to me to love one's mother is the greatest and the simplest thing in the duty towards one's neighbour, if that mother is as she should be. And it is more than pleasant to me to know that somewhere in the wide universe there is someone who has broken through the natural hardness of your heart, and called forth a respect and love of which I never thought you capable."

The remaining days till New Year's Eve passed quickly. The weather was gloriously fine, the sunsets unequalled.

Early in the evening Mariana arrived, and brought with her a large box containing the dress and other things. She came in a carriage drawn by chestnut horses, not occupants of the stables at Marble House.

Rosalie came out into the hall to meet her, and kissed her with affection, which Mariana in her colder way returned.

Together they went upstairs, Rosalie suddenly finding herself very short of words to express her delight at meeting this old friend.

And it was Mariana who dressed her completely, from the arranging of her hair to the tying on of her clog-shaped, satin-jewelled slippers.

And oh! what a dress! With designs of lovers' knots worked in delicately-tinted jewels all over its shining surface, and a train that hung from the shoulders in showers of priceless lace. It was studded with jewels in the bodice, and on her hair was placed a tiara that stood high, and had the same design worked in diamonds. Clasps of gold and jewels were on her arms, and round her neck one fine chain of gold—no other ornament.

"I'm afraid, after all, Mariana," said she at length, "your great ambition has not come to pass."

"What thing was that?"

"You wished it for a wedding-dress."

"I am content to see it as it is, and you so beautiful."

"And when to-night is over you will want it back?"

But Mariana smiled, half dreamily.

"To-night is not yet over, and you will never wish to part with such a robe. You begged it from the Master, and you'll keep it I know none other who would care to bear so great a load, though in its beauty all forget to think of that."

"I do not find it very heavy."

"It's well."

Suddenly Rosalie laughed.

"I say, Mariana," said she, "suppose—suppose when I come to Marble House it should shine red all round about me. They'd take me for a veritable scarlet woman. I have misgivings. I remember once before."

But Mariana shook her head.

"I heard from the Master you had gained strength from weakness; and I heard from Everard you had jewels of your own that you have worn to counteract the fatal charm of these."

"Not of my own, Mariana; they were of God." "Ah, God! I had forgotten Him. The dream has passed so long ago."

"God is no dream, but a living reality, Mariana."

"I was once bitten by a snake, and here they call the Serpent God. I love not such an image, but live in the never-ending twilight. I think it is the shadowed light the idol throws, placing itself betwixt the world and God."

And suddenly Rosalie took her hands in hers, and drew her to her with a gentle force, and kissed her lips and forehead, saying:

"But soon the idol will vanish out of sight, and the true light come. You needn't live in the twilight, Mariana, any more than I. You only need to trust the Glorious Spirit working behind the leaden cloud, and struggle silently toward the healing light. And some day, even though the waiting time be long, the icy burden will be rolled away, and you all warm and bright again to love and honour God with strength unfettered."

And then Brightcoat said: "I should like to go with Mariana back to Marble House."

"Do you care for such a companion?" asked Rosalie of Mariana.

But the frog jumped across and settled on her shoulder.

"You need me no more now, Rosalie. I have done what work I could for you. But now to Mariana. She may need me as once you did. And though her heart is cold to-day, the New Year dawns, and with it in the distance I see a fairer prospect and a warmer light breaking upon the horizon of heaven."

And so with this new companion Mariana went away back to the Marble House. Into that gloomy dwelling, though now all brilliantly lit, the frog entered unafraid, and none thought to harm it, for the charm had worked, or perhaps was working.

CHAPTER XXXV
THE SUN RISES ON THE YEAR

A brilliant house again, a brilliant crowd, the eve of the New Year, the death-bed of the Old. Just three hours more to wait.

But as Rosalie drove along, it was as if depression and the highest spirits fought one another for the mastery.

"The effects of wearing fine clothing," said she, and laughed and sighed in a breath. "There is magic in these jewels, I feel certain. Oh! if I could but wear again my own precious moonstone talisman against all heaviness, instead of all this finery, that does its best to cramp my spirits, and half succeeds."

On entering, she was almost immediately joined by Mr. Barringcourt. Never had he looked to Rosalie as to-night, never perhaps she to him. With a scrutiny which had become habitual, they eyed each other, and at last Rosalie said:

"Do you not think I was right in being covetous of such a lovely gown?"

"And the jewels?"

"Oh, they were an extra thrown in. I'd much rather have been without them. You should be kind, not lavish, Mr. Barringcourt. After an hour's wearing they begin to assert their individuality and weight."

"And at first you felt them light?"

"Being alive to their beauty, I was dead to their encumbrance." And then again, this time seriously, she said: "But in truth I must acknowledge, perhaps, their weight cannot be very great, for I have the greatest wish to dance through every dance, and look to you to find me partners. I am not really altered because I stole behind the temple curtain; for one night it might be forgotten."

"The first dance is with me, and the last one."

"Oh, no! I am in a mood of ingratitude to-night. I cannot for the favour of this dress, and all its valuable accessories, even say 'Thank you.' Find me a partner for the dance that's just beginning. No one has come near me since I came."

"The first dance is with me."

"Indeed, no. I'm entering on a life of self-denial. As soon as I want to do a thing I shall cross myself and do the opposite. What chance shall I stand of heaven, do you think, at that rate?"

"You'll never get there. Be guided by me, and be less contrary."

"It goes very much against the grain for me to dance with you. Must I be consistent, or must I be contrary?"

"Become impersonal, and leave the decision with me."

"You are too selfish to be altogether trusted."

"I? Selfish?"

"Yes. I want to dance, and here you keep me talking. I want to study men and form comparisons."

"You can't in a place like this. On these occasions they're all more or less alike."

"And on all others. The similarity of humanity is nerve-destroying."

"A very pleasant state of things. None but a fool would wish it otherwise. But if you wish to dance you shall have partners in sufficiency. I'll say you're quite harmless to-night."

"Say no such thing. Mariana tells me she was once bitten by a snake, and so was I. Since then I've had the greatest inclination to bite everyone who comes near me. She took it badly; I, by God's help, was enabled to take it well."

"What particular snake was it that bit you?"

"I think it must have been the God of Lucifram."

Then he left her and went away, and through the evening Rosalie danced, seemingly happy, on to that hour when the Old Year and the New meet and part again.

Then she sought Mr. Barringcourt, and found him, not amongst his guests, but in that now deserted drawing-room where once Mariana had played for her. He was looking out on to the gas-lit streets, and the window being open, the cold night air blew into the room. The lights in it were shining fully, yet the city without was plainly visible.

"You have left the crowd?" said she.

"Yes," he answered. "They can amuse themselves. You look tired."

She laughed, an apology for deeper feeling, and looked at him with eyes whose tiredness was lost in a certain appeal and pathetic beauty, that characterised them long since in the days of silence.

"I think I overrated my powers of—of endurance. I—I should be very pleased to give the last dance to you. I left it empty."

But he shook his head.

"I have not danced all evening; I do not wish to make myself conspicuous now."

"We could sit it out."

"We might; but I am contrary."

Then Rosalie went up to him and put her hand very gently in his arm, and almost whispered:

"I have a feeling of insecurity that grows with almost every hour. It may be childish, but I never professed to be much different from a child. When I stay with you it leaves me more or less, and always has done from the very first I met you. And now Brightcoat has left me, and I feel quite alone, a thing hardly enviable in any sphere. And I've gone through the evening as best I could, and tried to get the better of my weakness." And then she laughed and drew her hand away, and said: "If such confessions are unusual, you only have this dress to thank for it. The jewels have magnetic power, and draw me to the owner."

At this he turned round from the window and looked at her, and a very curious smile curved on his lips.

"That's your solution, is it?" he said, and scratched his head thoughtfully with one finger. Then he added: "My mother said I was to thank you for the stone you sent her."

"Was she well?"

"Yes. At the first stroke after midnight I go again to her. These guests will then have all departed."

"I, too."

"You say that sadly."

"The magnetism of the stone I sent her draws me to your mother."

Just then Everard entered the room, carrying in his hand a large sealed envelope addressed to Rosalie. At the back it was sealed with the image of the Serpent.

"You, Everard?" said Mr. Barringcourt, with some surprise.

"I heard the door bell ring, and knew it was no ordinary guest of the evening."

She took and opened it. A summons to appear before the High Priest's court, and on the morrow morning, this first day of the New Year.

She read it through, half mystified, the truth with some difficulty dawning upon her. Then on a sudden she handed it to Mr. Barringcourt, her face as white as the background of her dress, and he in his turn read it. Then he turned to Everard and said:

"Who brought this?"

"A priest who, with his companion, waits outside. I did not let them in."

Master and man looked at one another, the same grim smile half visible upon each face. Then Mr. Barringcourt took out his watch and looked at it.

"It wants still twenty minutes till the dance is ended. It is barely twenty minutes after twelve. Are they impatient of delay?"

"I did not ask them."

"We'll go upon the supposition that they're patient." Then turning to Rosalie, he continued: "There was a time you told me that you scorned to run away, and never had done. Afterwards, upon much less occasion, you trusted to the fleetness of your feet. And now? Are you prepared to meet the enemy?"

"Indeed, no. Or perhaps I cannot tell. If you stood for council on my behalf I think I might enjoy it. For myself, I could never get much farther than the truth."

"A marvellous short journey, with a sudden ending, but little reckoned upon Lucifram. What think you of lifetime imprisonment, Rosalie?"

"Ah! It is that that frightens me. I never liked the thought of prison. Must I really go?"

"What plan of escape is there?"

Her brow knitted thoughtfully; then suddenly clearing, she said:

"Take me away with you. Take me to your mother?"

And she looked so very beautiful, with something so imperious in her manner, yet so sweet, that little wonder if the Master consented.

"It's a long journey, and a very final one, and, moreover, my horses are black."

"I'll trust to the rule of contrary where you're concerned, and trust you too. Take me where you will. I have sufficient power given me of my own to guard against a vital evil."

"You trust me to a certain point. No farther."

She laughed.

"I trust you altogether, but wish to show it is not quite from weakness I wish to come with you."

"Then we'll go. My mother is hospitable, and so are others round about her. Some are better known to you, no doubt, than she. A stranger is a rarity among them. You will be welcomed."

"Alas! But who can travel in a dress like this—at midnight, in the depth of winter? It is so conspicuous."

"No dress could be so suitable. Safe-guarded against wind or snow, and simple in comparison of those where we are going. Heat or cold, darkness or light cannot touch it. It was sewn in the inner darkness, and shines in the inner light. Come, Rosalie, the time is up. We must away to see the sun rise on the New Year."

Then he led her through those great empty rooms into the fuller ones, where general hilarity preceded the closing of the dance. But here they never waited. Across the palm-house to the doors of glass with the image of the toad and temple so finely and so clearly worked in them.

At one touch they both flew open, and there, flooded in a tide of light— red—red—and an accompanying silence. It travelled swiftly, yet without sound or violence into the rooms of feasting and of mirth, carrying silence and a vague alarm. And noting where it came from, the guests instinctively crowded out towards that curious garden, on which faced the real front of Marble House.

And there, below the terrace steps, upon the wide carriage drive, stood a chariot of gold, with seats of crimson velvet, and harnessed to it the six black steeds, with tossing heads and eyes of fire, strong, and sleek, and slim.

One youth alone stood at the foremost bridle. And in the midst of all this ruddy glamour shone the pure whiteness of Rosalie's robe, with all its flimsy showers of lace and jewels. And there beside the carriage step stood Mariana, the frog upon her shoulder, and with her Everard, who had preceded them.

Then Rosalie stepped in lightly and gracefully, and sat down. Mariana bent forward, and with the grace peculiar to her arranged the spreading train about her feet. Then looking up, with mutual feeling each drew an arm round the other's neck and kissed. Rosalie whispered:

"You will follow, Mariana, and we'll meet again, in no land of shadows, red or black, but in the sunlight. And you'll bring Everard. A little company along the road is most desirable. But for the present, good-bye!"

And then the Master, gathering the long reins in his hand as he sat down beside her, wrung Everard's hand, and seeing Mariana held her hand toward him too, bent over it and kissed it, by that one act undoing all the past in which she suffered through him.

The Master shook the reins. A thousand tingling stars shook from them upon and round about the coal-black steeds. One wild bound forward all in unison, not on a straight road, but up some climbing steep.

Rosalie turned round. And laughing, half in fear and half in happiness, kissed her hand to Brightcoat.

"Good-bye—till—till we meet again!"

Then the Master turned round also, a face very unlike to hers.

His face was dark and shadowy as it ever had been. The same contemptuous curl lay on his firm lips; a mocking laughter was in his eyes. His glance fell upon Marble House, and the guests all drawn towards the terraces.

With his free hand he felt in the pocket of the long coat he wore.

"I forgot to leave my New Year's presents, Rosalie," said he, and brought out a large handful of precious stones, flinging them down to Lucifram.

Then drawing out another, he handed these to Rosalie, and bade her throw them too.

They fell among the crowd, who gathered them and praised their beauty.

But the six black steeds with little apparent effort climbed up the steep mountain-side, or so it seemed to be. And gradually the red light disappeared, and Lucifram along with it, and darkness followed.

And now there was nothing but the wind and icy snow and loneliness—nothing but the path. Nothing was to be seen on either side.

The spirited steeds, wild as ocean foam, flew up and on the mountain track, the winds moaned after them with a song as wild, as full of sad complaint, as if they were embodied spirits of the sighs and tears of broken hearts.

But no feeling of cold came near Rosalie. The jewelled robes encased her, proof against everything. And gradually it seemed as if the darkness gave way to a glimmering of light. At first it was feeble, but grew in distinctness, steady, and still steadier.

Suddenly a ray of brilliant light—light that could never blind the eyes—shot straight across the path. Then came another, another, following thick and fast from every direction.

Swiftly the coal-black horses changed in the flooding light to purest white, visions of inexpressible and perfect beauty. Rosalie's heart beat faster with sudden, unexpected joy. She looked up at the Master, her own face transfigured by the light, as so was his. For all the weariness, all the contempt, all the dark shadows, had vanished from his features, and left nothing but what was full of life, of vigour, and of kindliness. His eyes, still dark and deep, looked into hers, the first time on the long and perilous journey, and he said, laughing, as sometimes of old:

"Do you prefer looking at me to the magnificence of all this scenery?"

But she clasped his arm in both her hands, and leaned her forehead against his shoulder.

And suddenly he brought the horses to a check, and drawing her still closer, bent his head and kissed her cheek. Then she looked up with eyes all wet with tears, and bright with happiness, and drawing back a little, said:

"I never thought that things would come out this way. I—I never imagined that black horses could come out white—nor you become so altered."

He laughed.

"It all depends upon the journey that I take. Sometimes I cross upon another rainbow, that leads us all down hill from Lucifram at almost break-neck speed. Then neither I nor these, my horses, alter much. But look, Rosalie, round about you. This is a scene worth seeing and remembering."

He stood up, and giving her his hand, helped her to her feet.

And then she saw that streams of light and rainbow garlands were flung from a thousand spheres to meet this central road, itself a giant rainbow crossing from Lucifram (a tiny speck of gleaming red in the far, far distance) towards a country quite unsurpassed for loveliness. And all around, from the different worlds of light, came scenes of fairyland.

And now she saw a towered city folded in night, the change from day; and here the bright sunshine of mid-day glinting upon a noble river, with sloping, tree-clad hills, and meadows smooth and green.

Again the sun was setting behind a sea of golden glory, on whose restless surface danced three round boats inlaid with pearl. And in the boats sat three maidens of exquisite beauty, attended by the gentle wind, their servant, who wafted them towards the distant shore. And as they went they sang a song that trembled sweetly on the air and reached in the soft silence to that golden car, ringing tones of happiness and joy.

So on around: a thousand scenes, and all delightful, delicate yet clear, country and city all in perfection spread out everywhere. And each sphere was linked to each with garlands of lights, so that the nimble spirit crossed on them, a perfect path of beauty.

Rosalie looked and breathed a sigh of admiration. Then her eyes travelled to the path which they were crossing. The steep part had been passed. There now remained only a lesser portion, and that sloped gently down. This remaining part was free from danger. Pillars of light garlanded with flowers guarded the sides.

The horses, unwearied with the night's long race, moved slowly towards this nearing country, over whose waking sky the bright dawn was spreading wings of glory, with silver flutings right east to west. The descent led to a regal city, where nothing mean or sordid, no toil and tribulation, no anxious care or killing sorrow, no oppression, no dark deeds, no foul disease, no hardened priests or creeds had ever come. But all was God, the essence of immortal greatness.

And to this city came Rosalie, led by him whom some had called on Lucifram the Master. And being all tired with the journey, Rosalie fell asleep just as they were entering the gates.

For no traveller from a darker sphere can enter there unweary. The soft air, too strong for them, wafts the frail form to tender sleep, that it undergo the great and immortal change.

The sound of laughter and welcome, Heaven's truest music of joy, and then for us a silence.

So ends a little chapter in the life of Lucifram. A chapter that bore indirectly upon the Serpent, and helped gradually to its undoing. But that's another tale.

ABOUT THE AUTHOR

Edward Payson Roe was an American novelist, Presbyterian clergyman, gardener, and historian. Edward Payson Roe was born in the settlement of Moodna, which is now part of New Windsor, New York. He attended Williams College and the Auburn Theological Seminary. In 1862, he was appointed chaplain of the Second New York Cavalry, United States Volunteers, and in 1864, chaplain of Hampton Hospital in Virginia. From 1866 to 1874, he was pastor of the First Presbyterian Church in Highland Falls, New York. In 1874, he moved to Cornwall-On-Hudson, where he focused on fiction writing and horticulture. During the American Civil War, he published weekly letters to the New York Evangelist and later lectured on the conflict and wrote for publications. He married Anna Paulina Sands in 1863 and had a number of children. Sarah married Olympic fencer Charles T. Tatham, while Pauline married landscape painter Henry Charles Lee. His writings were well-received in their day, particularly among middle-class readers in England and America, and were translated into other European languages. Their strong moral and theological aim helped to overcome America's Puritan prejudice toward works of fiction. One of his most common criticisms was that his writing resembled sermons.

CONTENTS

PREFACE

The following story has been taking form in my mind for several years, and at last I have been able to write it out. With a regret akin to sadness, I take my leave, this August day, of people who have become very real to me, whose joys and sorrows I have made my own. Although a Northern man, I think my Southern readers will feel that I have sought to do justice to their motives. At this distance from the late Civil War, it is time that passion and prejudice sank below the horizon, and among the surviving soldiers who were arrayed against each other I think they have practically disappeared. Stern and prolonged conflict taught mutual respect. The men of the Northern armies were convinced, beyond the shadow of a doubt, that they had fought men and Americans—men whose patriotism and devotion to a cause sacred to them was as pure and lofty as their own. It is time that sane men and women should be large-minded enough to recognize that, whatever may have been the original motives of political leaders, the people on both sides were sincere and honest; that around the camp-fires at their hearths and in their places of worship they looked for God's blessing on their efforts with equal freedom from hypocrisy.

I have endeavored to portray the battle of Bull Run as it could appear to a civilian spectator: to give a suggestive picture and not a general description. The following war-scenes are imaginary, and colored by personal reminiscence. I was in the service nearly four years, two of which were spent with the cavalry. Nevertheless, justly distrustful of my knowledge of military affairs, I have submitted my proofs to my friend Colonel H. C. Hasbrouck, Commandant of Cadets at West Point, and therefore have confidence that as mere sketches of battles and skirmishes they are not technically defective.

The title of the story will naturally lead the reader to expect that deep shadows rest upon many of its pages. I know it is scarcely the fashion of the present time to portray men and women who feel very deeply about anything, but there certainly was deep feeling at the time of which I write, as, in truth, there is to-day. The heart of humanity is like the ocean. There are depths to be stirred when the causes are adequate. E. P. R.

CORNWALL-ON-THE-HUDSON, *August* 21, 1883.

CHAPTER I
AN EMBODIMENT OF MAY

"Beyond that revolving light lies my home. And yet why should I use such a term when the best I can say is that a continent is my home? Home suggests a loved familiar nook in the great world. There is no such niche for me, nor can I recall any place around which my memory lingers with especial pleasure."

In a gloomy and somewhat bitter mood, Alford Graham thus soliloquized as he paced the deck of an in-coming steamer. In explanation it may be briefly said that he had been orphaned early in life, and that the residences of his guardians had never been made homelike to him. While scarcely more than a child he had been placed at boarding-schools where the system and routine made the youth's life little better than that of a soldier in his barrack. Many boys would have grown hardy, aggressive, callous, and very possibly vicious from being thrown out on the world so early. Young Graham became reticent and to superficial observers shy. Those who cared to observe him closely, however, discovered that it was not diffidence, but indifference toward others that characterized his manner. In the most impressible period of his life he had received instruction, advice and discipline in abundance, but love and sympathy had been denied. Unconsciously his heart had become chilled, benumbed and overshadowed by his intellect. The actual world gave him little and seemed to promise less, and, as a result not at all unnatural, he became something of a recluse and bookworm even before he had left behind him the years of boyhood.

Both comrades and teachers eventually learned that the retiring and solitary youth was not to be trifled with. He looked his instructor steadily in the eye when he recited, and while his manner was respectful, it was never deferential, nor could he be induced to yield a point, when believing himself in the right, to mere arbitrary assertion; and sometimes he brought confusion to his teacher by quoting in support of his own view some unimpeachable authority.

At the beginning of each school term there were usually rough fellows who thought the quiet boy could be made the subject of practical jokes and petty annoyances without much danger of retaliation. Graham would usually remain patient up to a certain point, and then, in dismay and astonishment, the offender would suddenly find himself receiving a punishment which he seemed powerless to resist. Blows would fall like hail, or if the combatants closed in the struggle, the aggressor appeared to find in Graham's slight form sinew and fury only. It seemed as if the lad's spirit broke forth in such a flame of indignation that no one could withstand him. It was also remembered that while he was not noted for prowess on the playground, few could surpass him in the gymnasium, and that he took long solitary rambles. Such of his classmates, therefore, as were inclined to quarrel with him because of his unpopular ways soon learned that he kept up his muscle with the best of them, and that, when at last roused, his anger struck like lightning from a cloud.

During the latter part of his college course he gradually formed a strong friendship for a young man of a different type, an ardent sunny-natured youth, who proved an antidote to his morbid tendencies. They went abroad together and studied for two years at a German university, and then Warren Hilland, Graham's friend, having inherited large wealth, returned to his home. Graham, left to himself, delved more and more deeply in certain phases of sceptical philosophy. It appeared to him that in the past men had believed almost everything, and that the heavier the drafts made on credulity the more largely had they been honored. The two friends had long since resolved that the actual and the proved should be the base from which they would advance into the unknown, and they discarded with equal indifference unsubstantiated theories of science and what they were pleased to term the illusions of faith. "From the verge of the known explore the unknown," was their motto, and it had been their hope to spend their lives in extending the outposts of accurate knowledge, in some one or two directions, a little beyond the points already reached. Since the scalpel and microscope revealed no soul in the human mechanism they regarded all theories and beliefs concerning a separate spiritual existence as mere assumption. They accepted the materialistic view. To them each generation was a link in an endless chain, and man himself wholly the product of an evolution which had no relations to a creative mind, for they had no belief in the existence of such a mind. They held that one had only to live wisely and well, and thus transmit the principle of life, not only unvitiated, but strengthened and enlarged. Sins against body and mind were sins against the race, and it was their creed that the stronger, fuller and more nearly complete they made their lives the richer and fuller would be the life that succeeded them. They scouted as utterly unproved and irrational the idea that they could live after death, excepting as the plant lives by adding to the material life and well-being of other plants. But at that time the spring and vigor of youth were in their heart and brain, and it seemed to them a glorious thing to live and do their part in the advancement of the race toward a stage of perfection not dreamed of by the unthinking masses.

Alas for their visions of future achievement! An avalanche of wealth had overwhelmed Hilland. His letters to his friend had grown more and more infrequent, and they contained many traces of the business cares and the distractions inseparable from his possessions and new relations. And now for causes just the reverse Graham also was forsaking his studies. His modest inheritance, invested chiefly in real estate, had so far depreciated that apparently it could not much longer provide for even his frugal life abroad.

"I must give up my chosen career for a life of bread-winning," he had concluded sadly, and he was ready to avail himself of any good opening that offered. Therefore he knew not where his lot would be cast on the broad continent beyond the revolving light that loomed every moment more distinctly in the west.

A few days later found him at the residence of Mrs. Mayburn, a pretty cottage in a suburb of an eastern city. This lady was his aunt by marriage, and had long been a widow. She had never manifested much interest in her nephew, but since she was his nearest relative he felt that he could not do less than call upon her. To his agreeable surprise he found that time had mellowed her spirit and softened her angularities. After the death of her husband she had developed unusual ability to take care of herself, and had shown little disposition to take care of any one else. Her thrift and economy had greatly enhanced her resources, and her investments had been profitable, while the sense of increasing abundance had had a happy effect on her character. Within the past year she had purchased the dwelling in which she now resided, and to which she welcomed Graham with unexpected warmth. So far from permitting him to make simply a formal call, she insisted on an extended visit, and he, divorced from his studies and therefore feeling his isolation more keenly than ever before, assented.

"My home is accessible," she said, "and from this point you can make inquiries and look around for business opportunities quite as well as from a city hotel."

She was so cordial, so perfectly sincere, that for the first time in his life he felt what it was to have kindred and a place in the world that was not purchased.

He had found his financial affairs in a much better condition than he had expected. Some improvements were on foot which promised to advance the value of his real estate so largely as to make him independent, and he was much inclined to return to Germany and resume his studies.

"I will rest and vegetate for a time," he concluded. "I will wait till my friend Hilland returns from the West, and then, when the impulse of work takes possession of me again, I will decide upon my course."

He had come over the ocean to meet his fate, and not the faintest shadow of a presentiment of this truth crossed his mind as he looked tranquilly from his aunt's parlor window at the beautiful May sunset. The cherry blossoms were on the wane, and the light puffs of wind brought the white petals down like flurries of snow; the plum-trees looked as if the snow had clung to every branch and spray, and they were as white as they could have been after some breathless, large-flaked December storm; but the great apple-tree that stood well down the path was the crowning product of May. A more exquisite bloom of pink and white against an emerald foil of tender young leaves could not have existed even in Eden, nor could the breath of Eve have been more sweet than the fragrance exhaled. The air was soft with summer-like mildness, and the breeze that fanned Graham's cheek brought no sense of chilliness. The sunset hour, with its spring beauty, the song of innumerable birds, and especially the strains of a wood-thrush, that, like a *prima donna*, trilled her melody, clear, sweet and distinct above the feathered chorus, penetrated his soul with subtle and delicious influences. A vague longing for something he had never known or felt, for something that books had never taught, or experimental science revealed, throbbed in his heart. He felt that his life was incomplete, and a deeper sense of isolation came over him than he had ever experienced in foreign cities where every face was strange. Unconsciously he was passing under the most subtle and powerful of all spells, that of spring, when the impulse to mate comes not to the birds alone.

It so happened that he was in just the condition to succumb to this influence. His mental tension was relaxed. He had sat down by the wayside of life to rest awhile. He had found that there was no need that he should bestir himself in money-getting, and his mind refused to return immediately to the deep abstractions of science. It pleaded weariness of the world and of the pros and cons of conflicting theories and questions. He admitted the plea and said:—

"My mind *shall* rest, and for a few days, possibly weeks, it shall be passively receptive of just such influences as nature and circumstances chance to bring to it. Who knows but that I may gain a deeper insight into the hidden mysteries than if I were delving among the dusty tomes of a university library? For some reason I feel to-night as if I could look at that radiant, fragrant apple-tree and listen to the lullaby of the birds forever. And yet their songs suggest a thought that awakens an odd pain and dissatisfaction. Each one is singing to his mate. Each one is giving expression to an overflowing fulness and completeness of life; and never before have I felt my life so incomplete and isolated.

"I wish Hilland was here. He is such a true friend that his silence is companionship, and his words never jar discordantly. It seems to me that I miss him more to-night than I did during the first days after his departure. It's odd that I should. I wonder if the friendship, the love of a woman could be more to me than that of Hilland. What was that paragraph from Emerson that once struck me so forcibly? My aunt is a woman of solid reading; she must have Emerson. Yes, here in her bookcase, meagre only in the number of volumes it contains, is what I want," and he turned the leaves rapidly until his eyes lighted on the following passage:—

"No man ever forgot the visitations of that power to his heart and brain which created all things new; which was the dawn in him of music, poetry, and art; which made the face of nature radiant with purple light, the morning and the night varied enchantments; when a single tone of one voice could make the heart bound, and the most trivial circumstance associated with one form was put in the amber of memory; when he became all eye when one was present, and all memory when one was gone."

"Emerson never learned that at a university, German or otherwise. He writes as if it were a common human experience, and yet I know no more about it than of the sensations of a man who has lost an arm. I suppose losing one's heart is much the same. As long as a man's limbs are intact he is scarcely conscious of them, but when one is gone it troubles him all the time, although it isn't there. Now when Hilland left me I felt guilty at the ease with which I could forget him in the library and laboratory. I did not become all memory. I knew he was my best, my only friend; he is still; but he is not essential to my life. Clearly, according to Emerson, I am as ignorant as a child of one of the deepest experiences of life, and very probably had better remain so, and yet the hour is playing strange tricks with my fancy."

Thus it may be perceived that Alford Graham was peculiarly open on this deceitful May evening, which promised peace and security, to the impending stroke of fate. Its harbinger first appeared in the form of a white Spitz dog, barking vivaciously under the apple-tree, where a path from a neighboring residence intersected the walk leading from Mrs. Mayburn's cottage to the street. Evidently some one was playing with the little creature, and was pretending to be kept at bay by its belligerent attitude. Suddenly there was a rush and a flutter of white draperies, and the dog retreated toward Graham, barking with still greater excitement. Then the young man saw coming up the path with quick, lithe tread, sudden pauses, and little impetuous dashes at her canine playmate, a being that might have been an emanation from the radiant apple-tree, or, rather, the human embodiment of the blossoming period of the year. Her low wide brow and her neck were snowy white, and no pink petal on the trees above her could surpass the bloom on her cheeks. Her large, dark, lustrous eyes were brimming over with fun, and unconscious of observation, she moved with the natural, unstudied grace of a child.

Graham thought, "No scene of nature is complete without the human element, and now the very genius of the hour and season has appeared;" and he hastily concealed himself behind the curtains, unwilling to lose one glimpse of a picture that made every nerve tingle with pleasure. His first glance had revealed that the fair vision was not a child, but a tall, graceful girl, who happily had not yet passed beyond the sportive impulses of childhood.

Every moment she came nearer, until at last she stood opposite the window. He could see the blue veins branching across her temples, the quick rise and fall of her bosom, caused by rather violent exertion, the wavy outlines of light brown hair that was gathered in a Greek coil at the back of the shapely head. She had the rare combination of dark eyes and light hair which made the lustre of her eyes all the more striking. He never forgot that moment as she stood panting before him on the gravel walk, her girlhood's grace blending so harmoniously with her budding womanhood. For a moment the thought crossed his mind that under the spell of the spring evening his own fancy had created her, and that if he looked away and turned again he would see nothing but the pink and white blossoms, and hear only the jubilant song of the birds.

The Spitz dog, however, could not possibly have any such unsubstantial origin, and this small Cerberus had now entered the room, and was barking furiously at him as an unrecognized stranger. A moment later his vision under the window stood in the doorway. The sportive girl was transformed at once into a well-bred young woman who remarked quietly, "I beg your pardon. I expected to find Mrs. Mayburn here;" and she departed to search for that lady through the house with a prompt freedom which suggested relations of the most friendly intimacy.

CHAPTER II
MERE FANCIES

Graham's disposition to make his aunt a visit was not at all chilled by the discovery that she had so fair a neighbor. He was conscious of little more than an impulse to form the acquaintance of one who might give a peculiar charm and piquancy to his May-day vacation, and enrich him with an experience that had been wholly wanting in his secluded and studious life. With a smile he permitted the fancy—for he was in a mood for all sorts of fancies on this evening—that if this girl could teach him to interpret Emerson's words, he would make no crabbed resistance. And yet the remote possibility of such an event gave him a sense of security, and prompted him all the more to yield himself for the first time to whatever impressions a young and pretty woman might be able to make upon him. His very disposition toward experiment and analysis inclined him to experiment with himself. Thus it would seem that even the perfect evening, and the vision that had emerged from under the apple-boughs, could not wholly banish a tendency to give a scientific cast to the mood and fancies of the hour.

His aunt now summoned him to the supper-room, where he was formally introduced to Miss Grace St. John, with whom his first meal under his relative's roof was destined to be taken.

As may naturally be supposed, Graham was not well furnished with small talk, and while he had not the proverbial shyness and awkwardness of the student, he was somewhat silent because he knew not what to say. The young guest was entirely at her ease, and her familiarity with the hostess enabled her to chat freely and naturally on topics of mutual interest, thus giving Graham time for those observations to which all are inclined when meeting one who has taken a sudden and strong hold upon the attention.

He speedily concluded that she could not be less than nineteen or twenty years of age, and that she was not what he would term a society girl—a type that he had learned to recognize from not a few representatives of his countrywomen whom he had seen abroad, rather than from much personal acquaintance. It should not be understood that he had shunned society altogether, and his position had ever entitled him to enter the best; but the young women whom it had been his fortune to meet had failed to interest him as completely as he had proved himself a bore to them. Their worlds were too widely separated for mutual sympathy; and after brief excursions among the drawing-rooms to which Hilland had usually dragged him, he returned to his books with a deeper satisfaction and content. Would his acquaintance with Miss St. John lead to a like result? He was watching and waiting to see, and she had the advantage—if it was an advantage—of making a good first impression.

Every moment increased this predisposition in her favor. She must have known that she was very attractive, for few girls reach her age without attaining such knowledge; but her observer, and in a certain sense her critic, could not detect the faintest trace of affectation or self-consciousness. Her manner, her words, and even their accent seemed unstudied, unpracticed, and unmodelled after any received type. Her glance was peculiarly open and direct, and from the first she gave Graham the feeling that she was one who might be trusted absolutely. That she had tact and kindliness also was evidenced by the fact that she did not misunderstand or resent his comparative silence. At first, after learning that he had lived much abroad, her manner toward him had been a little shy and wary, indicating that she may have surmised that his reticence was the result of a certain kind of superiority which travelled men—especially young men—often assume when meeting those whose lives are supposed to have a narrow horizon; but she quickly discovered that Graham had no foreign-bred pre-eminence to parade—that he wanted to talk with her if he could only find some common subject of interest. This she supplied by taking him to ground with which he was perfectly familiar, for she asked him to tell her something about university life in Germany. On such a theme he could converse well, and before long a fire of eager questions proved that he had not only a deeply interested listener but also a very intelligent one.

Mrs. Mayburn smiled complacently, for she had some natural desire that her nephew should make a favorable impression. In regard to Miss St. John she had long ceased to have any misgivings, and the approval that she saw in Graham's eyes was expected as a matter of course. This approval she soon developed into positive admiration by leading her favorite to speak of her own past.

"Grace, you must know, Alford, is the daughter of an army officer, and has seen some odd phases of life at the various military stations where her father has been on duty."

These words piqued Graham's curiosity at once, and he became the questioner. His own frank effort to entertain was now rewarded, and the young girl, possessing easy and natural powers of description, gave sketches of life at military posts which to Graham had more than the charm of novelty. Unconsciously she was accounting for herself. In the refined yet unconventional society of officers and their wives she had acquired the frank manner so peculiarly her own. But the characteristic which won Graham's interest most strongly was her abounding mirthfulness. It ran through all her words like a golden thread. The instinctive craving of every nature is for that which supplements itself, and Graham found something so genial in Miss St. John's ready smile and laughing eyes, which suggested an over-full fountain of joyousness within, that his heart, chilled and repressed from childhood, began to give signs of its existence, even during the first hour of their acquaintance. It is true, as we have seen, that he was in a very receptive condition, but then a smile, a glance that is like warm sunshine, is never devoid of power.

The long May twilight had faded, and they were still lingering over the supper-table, when a middle-aged colored woman in a flaming red turban appeared in the doorway and said, "Pardon, Mis' Mayburn; I'se a-hopin' you'll 'scuse me. I jes step over to tell Miss Grace dat de major's po'ful oneasy,—'spected you back afo'."

The girl arose with alacrity, saying, "Mr. Graham, you have brought me into danger, and must now extricate me. Papa is an inveterate whist-player, and you have put my errand here quite out of my mind. I didn't come for the sake of your delicious muffins altogether"—with a nod at her hostess; "our game has been broken up, you know, Mrs. Mayburn, by the departure of Mrs. Weeks and her daughter. You have often played a good hand with us, and papa thought you would come over this evening, and that you, from your better acquaintance with our neighbors, might know of some one who enjoyed the game sufficiently to join us quite often. Mr. Graham, you must be the one I am seeking. A gentleman versed in the lore of two continents certainly understands whist, or, at least, can penetrate its mysteries at a single sitting."

"Suppose I punish the irony of your concluding words," Graham replied, "by saying that I know just enough about the game to be aware how much skill is required to play with such a veteran as your father?"

"If you did you would punish papa also, who is innocent."

"That cannot be thought of, although, in truth, I play but an indifferent game. If you will make amends by teaching me I will try to perpetrate as few blunders as possible."

"Indeed, sir, you forget. You are to make amends for keeping me talking here, forgetful of filial duty, by giving me a chance to teach you. You are to be led meekly in as a trophy by which I am to propitiate my stern parent, who has military ideas of promptness and obedience."

"What if he should place me under arrest?"

"Then Mrs. Mayburn and I will become your jailers, and we shall keep you here until you are one of the most accomplished whist-players in the land."

"If you will promise to stand guard over me some of the time I will submit to any conditions."

"You are already making one condition, and may think of a dozen more. It will be better to parole you with the understanding that you are to put in an appearance at the hour for whist;" and with similar light talk they went down the walk under the apple-boughs, whence in Graham's fancy the fair girl had had her origin. As they passed under the shadow he saw the dusky outline of a rustic seat leaning against the bole of the tree, and he wondered if he should ever induce his present guide through the darkened paths to come there some moonlight evening, and listen to the fancies which her unexpected appearance had occasioned. The possibility of such an event in contrast with its far greater improbability caused him to sigh, and then he smiled broadly at himself in the darkness.

When they had passed a clump of evergreens, a lighted cottage presented itself, and Miss St. John sprang lightly up the steps, pushed open the hall door, and cried through the open entrance to a cosey apartment, "No occasion for hostilities, papa. I have made a capture that gives the promise of whist not only this evening but also for several more to come."

As Graham and Mrs. Mayburn entered, a tall, white-haired man lifted his foot from off a cushion, and rose with some little difficulty, but having gained his feet, his bearing was erect and soldier-like, and his courtesy perfect, although toward Mrs. Mayburn it was tinged with the gallantry of a former generation. Some brief explanations followed, and then Major St. John turned upon Graham the dark eyes which his daughter had inherited, and which seemed all the more brilliant in contrast with his frosty eyebrows, and said genially, "It is very kind of you to be willing to aid in beguiling an old man's tedium." Turning to his daughter he added a little querulously, "There must be a storm brewing, Grace," and he drew in his breath as if in pain.

"Does your wound trouble you to-night, papa?" she asked gently.

"Yes, just as it always does before a storm."

"It is perfectly clear without," she resumed. "Perhaps the room has become a little cold. The evenings are still damp and chilly;" and she threw two or three billets of wood on the open fire, kindling a blaze that sprang cheerily up the chimney.

The room seemed to be a combination of parlor and library, and it satisfied Graham's ideal of a living apartment. Easy-chairs of various patterns stood here and there and looked as if constructed by the very genius of comfort. A secretary in the corner near a window was open, suggesting absent friends and the pleasure of writing to them amid such agreeable surroundings. Again Graham queried, prompted by the peculiar influences that had gained the mastery on this tranquil but eventful evening, "Will Miss St. John ever sit there penning words straight from her heart to me?"

He was brought back to prose and reality by the major. Mrs. Mayburn had been condoling with him, and he now turned and said, "I hope, my dear sir, that you may never carry around such a barometer as I am afflicted with. A man with an infirmity grows a little egotistical, if not worse."

"You have much consolation, sir, in remembering how you came by your infirmity," Graham replied. "Men bearing such proofs of service to their country are not plentiful in our money-getting land."

His daughter's laugh rang out musically as she cried, "That was meant to be a fine stroke of diplomacy. Papa, you will now have to pardon a score of blunders."

"I have as yet no proof that any will be made," the major remarked, and in fact Graham had underrated his acquaintance with the game. He was quite equal to his aunt in proficiency, and with Miss St. John for his partner he was on his mettle. He found her skilful indeed, quick, penetrating, and possessed of an excellent memory. They held their own so well that the major's spirits rose hourly. He forgot his wound in the complete absorption of his favorite recreation.

As opportunity occurred Graham could not keep his eyes from wandering here and there about the apartment that had so taken his fancy, especially toward the large, well-filled bookcase and the pictures, which, if not very expensive, had evidently been the choice of a cultivated taste.

They were brought to a consciousness of the flight of time by a clock chiming out the hour of eleven, and the old soldier with a sigh of regret saw Mrs. Mayburn rise. Miss St. John touched a silver bell, and a moment later the same negress who had reminded her of her father's impatience early in the evening entered with a tray bearing a decanter of wine, glasses, and some wafer-like cakes.

"Have I earned the indulgence of a glance at your books?" Graham asked.

"Yes, indeed," Miss St. John replied; "your martyr-like submission shall be further rewarded by permission to borrow any of them while in town. I doubt, however, if you will find them profound enough for your taste."

"I shall take all point from your irony by asking if you think one can relish nothing but intellectual roast beef. I am enjoying one of your delicate cakes. You must have an excellent cook."

"Papa says he has, in the line of cake and pastry; but then he is partial."

"What! did you make them?"

"Why not?"

"Oh, I'm not objecting. Did my manners permit, I'd empty the plate. Still, I was under the impression that young ladies were not adepts in this sort of thing."

"You have been abroad so long that you may have to revise many of your impressions. Of course retired army officers are naturally in a condition to import *chefs de cuisine*, but then we like to keep up the idea of republican simplicity."

"Could you be so very kind as to induce your father to ask me to make one of your evening quartette as often as possible?"

"The relevancy of that request is striking. Was it suggested by the flavor of the cakes? I sometimes forget to make them."

"Their absence would not prevent my taste from being gratified if you will permit me to come. Here is a marked volume of Emerson's works. May I take it for a day or two?"

She blushed slightly, hesitated perceptibly, and then said, "Yes."

"Alford," broke in his aunt, "you students have the name of being great owls, but for an old woman of my regular habits it's getting late."

"My daughter informs me," the major remarked to Graham in parting, "that we may be able to induce you to take a hand with us quite often. If you should ever become as old and crippled as I am you will know how to appreciate such kindness.'"

"Indeed, sir, Miss St. John must testify that I asked to share your game as a privilege. I can scarcely remember to have passed so pleasant an evening."

"Mrs. Mayburn, do try to keep him in this amiable frame of mind," cried the girl.

"I think I shall need your aid," said that lady, with a smile. "Come, Alford, it is next to impossible to get you away."

"Papa's unfortunate barometer will prove correct, I fear," said Miss St. John, following them out on the piazza, for a thin scud was already veiling the stars, and there was an ominous moan of the wind.

"To-morrow will be a stormy day," remarked Mrs. Mayburn, who prided herself on her weather wisdom.

"I'm sorry," Miss St. John continued, "for it will spoil our fairy world of blossoms, and I am still more sorry for papa's sake."

"Should the day prove a long, dismal, rainy one," Graham ventured, "may
I not come over and help entertain your father?"

"Yes," said the girl, earnestly. "It cannot seem strange to you that time should often hang heavily on his hands, and I am grateful to any one who helps me to enliven his hours."

Before Graham repassed under the apple-tree boughs he had fully decided to win at least Miss St. John's gratitude.

CHAPTER III
THE VERDICT OF A SAGE

When Graham reached his room he was in no mood for sleep. At first he lapsed into a long revery over the events of the evening, trivial in themselves, and yet for some reason holding a controlling influence over his thoughts. Miss St. John was a new revelation of womanhood to him, and for the first time in his life his heart had been stirred by a woman's tones and glances. A deep chord in his nature vibrated when she spoke and smiled. What did it mean? He had followed his impulse to permit this stranger to make any impression within her power, and he found that she had decidedly interested him. As he tried to analyze her power he concluded that it lay chiefly in the mirthfulness, the joyousness of her spirit. She quickened his cool, deliberate pulse. Her smile was not an affair of facial muscles, but had a vivifying warmth. It made him suspect that his life was becoming cold and self-centred, that he was missing the deepest and best experiences of an existence that was brief indeed at best, and, as he believed, soon ceased forever. The love of study and ambition had sufficed thus far, but actuated by his own materialistic creed he was bound to make the most of life while it lasted. According to Emerson he was as yet but in the earlier stages of evolution, and his highest manhood wholly undeveloped. Had not "music, poetry, and art" dawned in his mind? Was nature but a mechanism after whose laws he had been groping like an anatomist who finds in the godlike form bone and tissue merely? As he had sat watching the sunset a few hours previous, the element of beauty had been present to him as never before. Could this sense of beauty become so enlarged that the world would be transfigured, "radiant with purple light"? Morning had often brought to him weariness from sleepless hours during which he had racked his brain over problems too deep for him, and evening had found him still baffled, disappointed, and disposed to ask in view of his toil, *Cui bono?* What ground had Emerson for saying that these same mornings and evenings might be filled with "varied enchantments"? The reason, the cause of these unknown conditions of life, was given unmistakably. The Concord sage had virtually asserted that he, Alford Graham, would never truly exist until his one-sided masculine nature had been supplemented by the feminine soul which alone could give to his being completeness and the power to attain his full development.

"Well," he soliloquized, laughing, "I have not been aware that hitherto I have been only a mollusk, a polyp of a man. I am inclined to think that Emerson's 'Pegasus' took the bit—got the better of him on one occasion; but if there is any truth in what he writes it might not be a bad idea to try a little of the kind of evolution that he suggests and see what comes of it. I am already confident that I could see infinitely more than I do if I could look at the world through Miss St. John's eyes as well as my own, but I run no slight risk in obtaining that vision. Her eyes are stars that must have drawn worshippers, not only from the east, but from every point of the compass. I should be in a sorry plight if I should become 'all memory,' and from my fair divinity receive as sole response, 'Please forget.' If the philosopher could guarantee that she also would be 'all eye and all memory,' one might indeed covet Miss St. John as the teacher of the higher mysteries. Life is not very exhilarating at best, but for a man to set his heart on such a woman as this girl promises to be, and then be denied—why, he had better remain a polyp. Come, come, Alford Graham, you have had your hour of sentiment—out of deference to Mr. Emerson I won't call it weakness—and it's time you remembered that you are a comparatively poor man, that Miss St. John has already been the choice of a score at least, and probably has made her own choice. I shall therefore permit no delusions and the growth of no false hopes."

Having reached this prudent conclusion, Graham yawned, smiled at the unwonted mood in which he had indulged, and with the philosophic purpose of finding an opiate in the pages that had contained one paragraph rather too exciting, he took up the copy of Emerson that he had borrowed. The book fell open, indicating that some one had often turned to the pages before him. One passage was strongly marked on either side and underscored. With a laugh he saw that it was the one he had been dwelling upon—"No man ever forgot," etc.

"Now I know why she blushed slightly and hesitated to lend me this volume," he thought. "I suppose I may read in this instance, 'No woman ever forgot.' Of course, it would be strange if she had not learned to understand these words. What else has she marked?"

Here and there were many delicate marginal lines indicating approval and interest, but they were so delicate as to suggest that the strong scoring of the significant passage was not the work of Miss St. John, but rather of some heavy masculine hand. This seemed to restore the original reading, "No *man* ever forgot," and some man had apparently tried to inform her by his emphatic lines that he did not intend to forget.

"Well, suppose he does not and cannot," Graham mused. "That fact places her under no obligations to be 'all eye and memory' for him. And yet her blush and hesitancy and the way the book falls open at this passage look favorable for him. I can win her gratitude by amusing the old major, and with that, no doubt, I shall have to be content."

This limitation of his chances caused Graham so little solicitude that he was soon sleeping soundly.

CHAPTER IV
WARNING OR INCENTIVE?

The next morning proved that the wound which Major St. John had received in the Mexican War was a correct barometer. From a leaden, lowering sky the rain fell steadily, and a chilly wind was fast dismantling the trees of their blossoms. The birds had suspended their nest-building, and but few had the heart to sing.

"You seem to take a very complacent view of the dreary prospect without," Mrs. Mayburn remarked, as Graham came smilingly into the breakfast-room and greeted her with a cheerful note in his tones. "Such a day as this means rheumatism for me and an aching leg for Major St. John."

"I am very sorry, aunt," he replied, "but I cannot help remembering also that it is not altogether an ill wind, for it will blow me over into a cosey parlor and very charming society—that is, if Miss St. John will give me a little aid in entertaining her father."

"So we old people don't count for anything."

"That doesn't follow at all. I would do anything in my power to banish your rheumatism and the major's twinges, but how was it with you both at my age? I can answer for the major. If at that time he knew another major with such a daughter as blesses his home, his devotion to the preceding veteran was a little mixed."

"Are you so taken by Miss St. John?"

"I have not the slightest hope of being taken by her."

"You know what I mean?"

"Yes, but I wished to suggest my modest hopes and expectations so that you may have no anxieties if I avail myself, during my visit, of the chance of seeing what I can of an unusually fine girl. Acquaintance with such society is the part of my education most sadly neglected. Nevertheless, you will find me devotedly at your service whenever you will express your wishes."

"Do not imagine that I am disposed to find fault. Grace is a great favorite of mine. She is a good old-fashioned girl, not one of your vain, heartless, selfish creatures with only a veneer of good breeding. I see her almost every day, either here or in her own home, and I know her well. You have seen that she is fitted to shine anywhere, but it is for her home qualities that I love and admire her most. Her father is crippled and querulous; indeed he is often exceedingly irritable. Everything must please him or else he is inclined to storm as he did in his regiment, and occasionally he emphasizes his words without much regard to the third commandment. But his gusts of anger are over quickly, and a kinder-hearted and more upright man never lived. Of course American servants won't stand harsh words. They want to do all the fault-finding, and the poor old gentleman would have a hard time of it were it not for Grace. She knows how to manage both him and them, and that colored woman you saw wouldn't leave him if he beat and swore at her every day. She was a slave in the family of Grace's mother, who was a Southern lady, and the major gave the poor creature her liberty when he brought his wife to the North. Grace is sunshine embodied. She makes her old, irritable, and sometimes gouty father happy in spite of himself. It was just like her to accept of your offer last evening, for to banish all dullness from her father's life seems her constant thought. So if you wish to grow in the young lady's favor don't be so attentive to her as to neglect the old gentleman."

Graham listened to this good-natured gossip with decided interest, feeling that it contained valuable suggestions. The response seemed scarcely relevant. "When is she to be married?" he asked.

"Married!"

"Yes. It is a wonder that such a paragon has escaped thus long."

"You have lived abroad too much," said his aunt satirically. "American girls are not married out of hand at a certain age. They marry when they please or not at all if they please. Grace easily escapes marriage."

"Not from want of suitors, I'm sure."

"You are right there."

"How then?"

"By saying, 'No, I thank you.' You can easily learn how very effectual such a quiet negative is, if you choose."

"Indeed! Am I such a very undesirable party?" said Graham, laughing, for he heartily enjoyed his aunt's brusque way of talking, having learned already the kindliness it masked.

"Not in my eyes. I can't speak for Grace. She'd marry you if she loved you, and were you the Czar of all the Russias you wouldn't have the ghost of a chance unless she did. I know that she has refused more than one fortune. She seems perfectly content to live with her father, until the one prince having the power to awaken her appears. When he comes rest assured she'll follow him, and also be assured that she'll take her father with her, and to a selfish, exacting Turk of a husband he might prove an old man of the sea. And yet I doubt it. Grace would manage any one. Not that she has much management either. She simply laughs, smiles, and talks every one into good humor. Her mirthfulness, her own happiness, is so genuine that it is contagious. Suppose you exchange duties and ask her to come over and enliven me while you entertain her father," concluded the old lady mischievously.

"I would not dare to face such a fiery veteran as you have described alone."

"I knew you would have some excuse. Well, be on your guard. Grace will make no effort to capture you, and therefore you will be in all the more danger of being captured. If you lose your heart in vain to her you will need more than German philosophy to sustain you."

"I have already made to myself in substance your last remark."

"I know you are not a lady's man, and perhaps for that very reason you are all the more liable to an acute attack."

Graham laughed as he rose from the table, and asked, "Should I ever venture to lay siege to Miss St. John, would I not have your blessing?"

"Yes, and more than my blessing."

"What do you mean by more than your blessing?"

"I shall not commit myself until you commit yourself, and I do not wish you to take even the first step without appreciating the risk of the venture."

"Why, bless you, aunt," said Graham, now laughing heartily, "how seriously you take it! I have spent but one evening with the girl."

The old lady nodded her head significantly as she replied, "I have not lived to my time of life without learning a thing or two. My memory also has not failed as yet. There were young men who looked at me once just as you looked at Grace last evening, and I know what came of it in more than one instance. You are safe now, and you may be invulnerable, although it does not look like it; but if you can see much of Grace St. John and remain untouched you are unlike most men."

"I have always had the name of being that, you know. But as the peril is so great had I not better fly at once?"

"Yes, I think we both have had the name of being a little peculiar, and my brusque, direct way of coming right to the point is one of my peculiarities. I am very intimate with the St. Johns, and am almost as fond of Grace as if she were my own child. So of course you can see a great deal of her if you wish, and this arrangement about whist will add to your opportunities. I know what young men are, and I know too what often happens when their faces express as much admiration and interest as yours did last night. What's more," continued the energetic old lady with an emphatic tap on the floor with her foot, and a decided nod of her head, "if I were a young man, Grace would have to marry some one else to get rid of me. Now I've had my say, and my conscience is clear, whatever happens. As to flight, why, you must settle that question, but I am sincere and cordial in my request that you make your home with me until you decide upon your future course."

Graham was touched, and he took his aunt's hand as he said, "I thank you for your kindness, and more than all for your downright sincerity. When I came here it was to make but a formal call. With the exception of one friend, I believed that I stood utterly alone in the world—that no one cared about what I did or what became of me. I was accustomed to isolation and thought I was content with it, but I find it more pleasant than I can make you understand to know there is one place in the world to which I can come, not as a stranger to an inn, but as one that is received for other than business considerations. Since you have been so frank with me I will be equally outspoken;" and he told her just how he was situated, and what were his plans and hopes. "Now that I know there is no necessity of earning my livelihood," he concluded, "I shall yield to my impulse to rest awhile, and then quite probably resume my studies here or abroad until I can obtain a position suited to my plans and taste. I thank you for your note of alarm in regard to Miss St. John, although I must say that to my mind there is more of incentive than of warning in your words. I think I can at least venture on a few reconnoissances, as the major might say, before I beat a retreat. Is it too early to make one now?"

Mrs. Mayburn smiled. "No," she said, laconically,

"I see that you think my reconnoissance will lead to a siege," Graham added. "Well, I can at least promise that there shall be no rash movements."

CHAPTER V
IMPRESSIONS

Graham, smiling at his aunt and still more amused at himself, started to pay his morning visit. "Yesterday afternoon," he thought, "I expected to make but a brief call on an aunt who was almost a stranger to me, and now I am domiciled under her roof indefinitely. She has introduced me to a charming girl, and in an ostensible warning shrewdly inserted the strongest incentives to venture everything, hinting at the same time that if I succeeded she would give me more than her blessing. What a vista of possibilities has opened since I crossed her threshold! A brief time since I was buried in German libraries, unaware of the existence of Miss St. John, and forgetting that of my aunt. Apparently I have crossed the ocean to meet them both, for had I remained abroad a few days longer, letters on the way would have prevented my returning. Of course it is all chance, but a curious chance. I don't wonder that people are often superstitious; and yet a moment's reasoning proves the absurdity of this sort of thing. Nothing truly strange often happens, and only our egotism invests events of personal interest with a trace of the marvellous. My business man neglected to advise me of my improved finances as soon as he might have done. My aunt receives me, not as I expected, but as one would naturally hope to be met by a relative. She has a fair young neighbor with whom she is intimate, and whom I meet as a matter of course, and as a matter of course I can continue to meet her as long as I choose without becoming 'all eye and all memory.' Surely a man can enjoy the society of any woman without the danger my aunt suggests and—as I half believe—would like to bring about. What signify my fancies of last evening? We often enjoy imagining what might be without ever intending it shall be. At any rate, I shall not sigh for Miss St. John or any other woman until satisfied that I should not sigh in vain. The probabilities are therefore that I shall never sigh at all."

As he approached Major St. John's dwelling he saw the object of his thoughts standing by the window and reading a letter. A syringa shrub partially concealed him and his umbrella, and he could not forbear pausing a moment to note what a pretty picture she made. A sprig of white flowers was in her light wavy hair, and another fastened by her breastpin drooped over her bosom. Her morning wrapper was of the hue of the sky that lay back of the leaden clouds. A heightened color mantled her cheeks, her lips were parted with a smile, and her whole face was full of delighted interest.

"By Jove!" muttered Graham. "Aunt Mayburn is half right, I believe. A man must have the pulse of an anchorite to look often at such a vision as that and remain untouched. One might easily create a divinity out of such a creature, and then find it difficult not to worship. I could go away now and make her my ideal, endowing her with all impossible attributes of perfection. Very probably fuller acquaintance will prove that she is made of clay not differing materially from that of other womankind. I envy her correspondent, however, and would be glad if I could write a letter that would bring such an expression to her face. Well, I am reconnoitring true enough, and had better not be detected in the act;" and he stepped rapidly forward.

She recognized him with a piquant little nod and smile. The letter was folded instantly, and a moment later she opened the door for him herself, saying, "Since I have seen you and you have come on so kind an errand I have dispensed with the formality of sending a servant to admit you."

"Won't you shake hands as a further reward?" he asked. "You will find me very mercenary."

"Oh, certainly. Pardon the oversight. I should have done so without prompting since it is so long since we have met."

"And having known each other so long also," he added in the same light vein, conscious meantime that he held a hand that was as full of vitality as it was shapely and white.

"Indeed," she replied; "did last evening seem an age to you?"

"I tried to prolong it, for you must remember that my aunt said that she could not get me away; and this morning I was indiscreet enough to welcome the rain, at which she reminded me of her rheumatism and your father's wound."

"And at which I also hope you had a twinge or two of conscience. Papa," she added, leading the way into the parlor, "here is Mr. Graham. It was his fascinating talk about life in Germany that so delayed me last evening."

The old gentleman started out of a doze, and his manner proved that he welcomed any break in the monotony of the day. "You will pardon my not rising," he said; "this confounded weather is playing the deuce with my leg."

Graham was observant as he joined in a general condemnation of the weather; and the manner in which Miss St. John rearranged the cushion on which her father's foot rested, coaxed the fire into a more cheerful blaze, and bestowed other little attentions, proved beyond a doubt that all effort in behalf of the suffering veteran would be appreciated. Nor was he so devoid of a kindly good-nature himself as to anticipate an irksome task, and he did his utmost to discover the best methods of entertaining his host. The effort soon became remunerative, for the major had seen much of life, and enjoyed reference to his experiences. Graham found that he could be induced to fight his battles over again, but always with very modest allusion to himself. In the course of their talk it also became evident that he was a man of somewhat extensive reading, and the daily paper must have been almost literally devoured to account for his acquaintance with contemporary affairs. The daughter was often not a little amused at Graham's blank looks as her father broached topics of American interest which to the student from abroad were as little known or understood as the questions which might have been agitating the inhabitants of Jupiter. Most ladies would have been politely oblivious of her guest's blunders and infelicitous remarks, but Miss St. John had a frank, merry way of recognizing them, and yet malice and ridicule were so entirely absent from her words and ways that Graham soon positively enjoyed being laughed at, and much preferred her delicate open raillery, which gave him a chance to defend himself, to a smiling mask that would leave him in uncertainty as to the fitness of his replies. There was a subtle flattery also in this course, for she treated him as one capable of holding his own, and not in need of social charity and protection. With pleasure he recognized that she was adopting toward him something of the same sportive manner which characterized her relations with his aunt, and which also indicated that as Mrs. Mayburn's nephew he had met with a reception which would not have been accorded to one less favorably introduced.

How vividly in after years Graham remembered that rainy May morning! He could always call up before him, like a vivid picture, the old major with his bushy white eyebrows and piercing black eyes, the smoke from his meerschaum creating a sort of halo around his gray head, the fine, venerable face often drawn by pain which led to half-muttered imprecations that courtesy to his guest and daughter could not wholly suppress. How often he saw again the fire curling softly from the hearth with a contented crackle, as if pleased to be once more an essential to the home from which the advancing summer would soon banish it! He could recall every article of the furniture with which he afterward became so familiar. But that which was engraven on his memory forever was a fair young girl sitting by the window with a background of early spring greenery swaying to and fro in the storm. Long afterward, when watching on the perilous picket line or standing in his place on the battlefield, he would close his eyes that he might recall more vividly the little white hands deftly crocheting on some feminine mystery, and the mirthful eyes that often glanced from it to him as the quiet flow of their talk rippled on. A rill, had it conscious life, would never forget the pebble that deflected its course from one ocean to another; human life as it flows onward cannot fail to recognize events, trivial in themselves, which nevertheless gave direction to all the future.

Graham admitted to himself that he had found a charm at this fireside which he had never enjoyed elsewhere in society—the pleasure of being perfectly at ease. There was a genial frankness and simplicity in his entertainers which banished restraint, and gave him a sense of security. He felt instinctively that there were no adverse currents of mental criticism and detraction, that they were loyal to him as their invited guest, notwithstanding jest, banter, and good-natured satire.

The hours had vanished so swiftly that he was at a loss to account for them. Miss St. John was a natural foe to dulness of all kinds, and this too without any apparent effort. Indeed, we are rarely entertained by evident and deliberate exertion. Pleasurable exhilaration in society is obtained from those who impart, like warmth, their own spontaneous vivacity. Miss St. John's smile was an antidote for a rainy day, and he was loath to pass from its genial power out under the dripping clouds. Following an impulse, he said to the girl, "You are more than a match for the weather."

These words were spoken in the hall after he had bidden adieu to the major.

"If you meant a compliment it is a very doubtful one," she replied, laughing. "Do you mean that I am worse than the weather which gives papa the horrors, and Mrs. Mayburn the rheumatism?"

"And me one of the most delightful mornings I ever enjoyed," he added, interrupting her. "You were in league with your wood fire. The garish sunshine of a warm day robs a house of all cosiness and snugness. Instead of being depressed by the storm and permitting others to be dull, you have the art of making the clouds your foil."

"Possibly I may appear to some advantage against such a dismal background," she admitted.

"My meaning is interpreted by my unconscionably long visit. I now must reluctantly retreat into the dismal background."

"A rather well-covered retreat, as papa might say, but you will need your umbrella all the same;" for he, in looking back at the archly smiling girl, had neglected to open it.

"I am glad it is not a final retreat," he called back. "I shall return this evening reinforced by my aunt."

"Well," exclaimed that lady when he appeared before her, "lunch has been waiting ten minutes or more."

"I feared as much," he replied, shaking his head ruefully.

"What kept you?"

"Miss St. John."

"Not the major? I thought you went to entertain him?"

"So I did, but man proposes—"

"Oh, not yet, I hope," cried the old lady with assumed dismay. "I thought you promised to do nothing rash."

"You are more precipitate than I have been. All that I propose is to enjoy my vacation and the society of your charming friend."

"The major?" she suggested.

"A natural error on your part, for I perceived he was very gallant to you. After your remarks, however, you cannot think it strange that I found the daughter more interesting—so interesting indeed that I have kept you waiting for lunch. I'll not repeat the offence any oftener than I can help. At the same time I find that I have not lost my appetite, or anything else that I am aware of."

"How did Grace appear?" his aunt asked as they sat down to lunch.

"Like myself."

"Then not like any one else you know?"

"We agree here perfectly."

"You have no fear?"

"No, nor any hopes that I am conscious of. Can I not admire your paragon to your heart's content without insisting that she bestow upon me the treasures of her life? Miss St. John has a frank, cordial manner all her own, and I think also that for your sake she has received me rather graciously, but I should be blind indeed did I not recognize that it would require a siege to win her; and that would be useless, as you said, unless her own heart prompted the surrender. I have heard and read that many women are capable of passing fancies of which adroit suitors can take advantage, and they are engaged or married before fully comprehending what it all means. Were Miss St. John of this class I should still hesitate to venture, for nothing in my training has fitted me to take an advantage of a lady's mood. I don't think your favorite is given to fancies. She is too well poised. Her serene, laughing confidence, her more than content, comes either from a heart already happily given, or else from a nature so sound and healthful that life in itself is an unalloyed joy. She impresses me as the happiest being I ever met, and as such it is a delight to be in her presence; but if I should approach her as a lover, something tells me that I should find her like a snowy peak, warm and rose-tinted in the sunlight, as seen in the distance, but growing cold as you draw near. There may be subterranean fires, but they would manifest themselves from some inward impulse. At least I do not feel conscious of any power to awaken them."

Mrs. Mayburn shook her head ominously.

"You are growing very fanciful," she said, "which is a sign, if not a bad one. Your metaphors, too, are so farfetched and extravagant as to indicate the earliest stages of the divine madness. Do you mean to suggest that Grace will break forth like a volcano on some fortuitous man? If that be your theory you would stand as good a chance as any one. She might break forth on you."

"I have indeed been unfortunate in my illustration, since you can so twist my words even in jest. Here's plain enough prose for you. No amount of wooing would make the slightest difference unless by some law or impulse of her own nature Miss St. John was compelled to respond."

"Isn't that true of every woman?"

"I don't think it is."

"How is it that you are so versed in the mysteries of the feminine soul?"

"I have not lived altogether the life of a monk, and the history of the world is the history of women as well as of men. I am merely giving the impression that has been made upon me."

CHAPTER VI
PHILOSOPHY AT FAULT

If Mrs. Mayburn had fears that her nephew's peace would be affected by his exposure to the fascinations of Miss St. John, they were quite allayed by his course for the next two or three weeks. If she had indulged the hope that he would speedily be carried away by the charms which seemed to her irresistible, and so give the chance of a closer relationship with her favorite, she saw little to encourage such a hope beyond Graham's evident enjoyment in the young girl's society, and his readiness to seek it on all fitting occasions. He played whist assiduously, and appeared to enjoy the game. He often spent two or three hours with the major during the day, and occasionally beguiled the time by reading aloud to him, but the element of gallantry toward the daughter seemed wanting, and the aunt concluded, "No woman can rival a book in Alford's heart—that is, if he has one—and he is simply studying Grace as if she were a book. There is one symptom, however, that needs explanation—he is not so ready to talk about her as at first, and I don't believe that indifference is the cause."

She was right: indifference was not the cause. Graham's interest in Miss St. John was growing deeper every day, but the stronger the hold she gained upon his thoughts, the less inclined was he to speak of her. He was the last man in the world to be carried away by a Romeo-like gust of passion, and no amount of beauty could hold his attention an hour, did not the mind ray through it with a sparkle and power essentially its own.

Miss St. John had soon convinced him that she could do more than look sweetly and chatter. She could not only talk to a university-bred man, but also tell him much that was new. He found his peer, not in his lines of thought, but in her own, and he was so little of an egotist that he admired her all the more because she knew what he did not, and could never become an echo of himself. In her world she had been an intelligent observer and thinker, and she interpreted that world to him as naturally and unassumingly as a flower blooms and exhales its fragrance. For the first time in his life he gave himself up to the charm of a cultivated woman's society, and to do this in his present leisure seemed the most sensible thing possible.

"One can see a rare flower," he had reasoned, "without wishing to pluck it, or hear a wood-thrush sing without straightway thinking of a cage. Miss St. John's affections may be already engaged, or I may be the last person in the world to secure them. Idle fancies of what she might become to me are harmless enough. Any man is prone to indulge in these when seeing a woman who pleases his taste and kindles his imagination. When it comes to practical action one may expect and desire nothing more than the brightening of one's wits and the securing of agreeable pastime. I do not see why I should not be entirely content with these motives, until my brief visit is over, notwithstanding my aunt's ominous warnings;" and so without any misgivings he had at first yielded himself to all the spells that Miss St. John might unconsciously weave.

As time passed, however, he began to doubt whether he could maintain his cool, philosophic attitude of enjoyment. He found himself growing more and more eager for the hours to return when he could seek her society, and the intervening time was becoming dull and heavy-paced. The impulse to go back to Germany and to resume his studies was slow in coming. Indeed, he was at last obliged to admit to himself that a game of whist with the old major had more attractions than the latest scientific treatise. Not that he doted on the irascible veteran, but because he thus secured a fair partner whose dark eyes were beaming with mirth and intelligence, whose ever-springing fountain of happiness was so full that even in the solemnity of the game it found expression in little piquant gestures, brief words, and smiles that were like glints of sunshine. Her very presence lifted him to a higher plane, and gave a greater capacity for enjoyment, and sometimes simply an arch smile or an unexpected tone set his nerves vibrating in a manner as delightful as it was unexplainable by any past experience that he could recall. She was a good walker and horsewoman, and as their acquaintance ripened he began to ask permission to join her in her rides and rambles. She assented without the slightest hesitancy, but he soon found that she gave him no exclusive monopoly of these excursions, and that he must share them with other young men. Her absences from home were always comparatively brief, however, and that which charmed him most was her sunny devotion to her invalid and often very irritable father. She was the antidote to his age and to his infirmities of body and temper. While she was away the world in general, and his own little sphere in particular, tended toward a hopeless snarl. Jinny, the colored servant, was subserviency itself, but her very obsequiousness irritated him, although her drollery was at times diverting. It was usually true, however, that but one touch and one voice could soothe the jangling nerves. As Graham saw this womanly magic, which apparently cost no more effort than the wood fire put forth in banishing chilliness and discomfort, the thought would come, "Blessed will be the man who can win her as the light and life of his home!"

When days passed, and no one seemed to have a greater place in her thoughts and interest than himself, was it unnatural that the hope should dawn that she might create a home for him? If she had a favored suitor his aunt would be apt to know of it. She did not seem ambitious, or disposed to invest her heart so that it might bring fortune and social eminence. Never by word or sign had she appeared to chafe at her father's modest competency, but with tact and skill, taught undoubtedly by army experience, she made their slender income yield the essentials of comfort and refinement, and seemed quite indifferent to non-essentials. Graham could never hope to possess wealth, but he found in Miss St. John a woman who could impart to his home the crowning grace of wealth—simple, unostentatious elegance. His aunt had said that the young girl had already refused more than one fortune, and the accompanying assurance that she would marry the man she loved, whatever might be his circumstances, seemed verified by his own observation. Therefore why might he not hope? Few men are so modest as not to indulge the hope to which their heart prompts them. Graham was slow to recognize the existence of this hope, and then he watched its growth warily. Not for the world would he lose control of himself, not for the world would he reveal it to any one, least of all to his aunt or to her who had inspired it, unless he had some reason to believe she would not disappoint it. He was prompted to concealment, not only by his pride, which was great, but more by a characteristic trait, an instinctive desire to hide his deeper feelings, his inner personality from all others. He would not admit that he had fallen in love. The very phrase was excessively distasteful. To his friend Hilland he might have given his confidence, and he would have accounted for himself in some such way as this:—

"I have found a child and a woman; a child in frankness and joyousness, a woman in beauty, strength, mental maturity, and unselfishness. She interested me from the first, and every day I know better the reason why—because she *is* interesting. My reason has kept pace with my fancy and my deeper feeling, and impels me to seek this girl quite as much as does my heart. I do not think a man meets such a woman or such a chance for happiness twice in a lifetime. I did not believe there was such a woman in the world. You may laugh and say that is the way all lovers talk. I answer emphatically, No. I have not yet lost my poise, and I never was a predestined lover. I might easily have gone through life and never given to these subjects an hour's thought. Even now I could quietly decide to go away and take up my old life as I left it. But why should I? Here is an opportunity to enrich existence immeasurably, and to add to all my chances of success and power. So far from being a drag upon one, a woman like Miss St. John would incite and inspire a man to his best efforts. She would sympathize with him because she could understand his aims and keep pace with his mental advance. Granted that my prospects of winning her are doubtful indeed, still as far as I can see there *is* a chance. I would not care a straw for a woman that I could have for the asking—who would take me as a *dernier ressort*. Any woman that I would marry, many others would gladly marry also, and I must take my chance of winning her from them. Such would be my lot under any circumstances, and if I give way to a faint heart now I may as well give up altogether and content myself with a library as a bride."

Since he felt that he might have taken Hilland into his confidence, he had, in terms substantially the same as those given, imagined his explanation, and he smiled as he portrayed to himself his friend's jocular response, which would have nevertheless its substratum of true sympathy. "Hilland would say," he thought, "'That is just like you, Graham. You can't smoke a cigar or make love to a girl without analyzing and philosophizing and arranging all the wisdom of Solomon in favor of your course. Now I would make love to a girl because I loved her, and that would be the end on't.'"

Graham was mistaken in this case. Not in laughing sympathy, but in pale dismay, would Hilland have received this revelation, for *he* was making love to Grace St. John because he loved her with all his heart and soul. There had been a time when Graham might have obtained a hint of this had circumstances been different, and it had occurred quite early in his acquaintance with Miss St. John. After a day that had been unusually delightful and satisfactory he was accompanying the young girl home from his aunt's cottage in the twilight. Out of the complacency of his heart he remarked, half to himself, "If Hilland were only here, my vacation would be complete."

In the obscurity he could not see her sudden burning flush, and since her hand was not on his arm he had no knowledge of her startled tremor. All that he knew was that she was silent for a moment or two, and then she asked quietly, "Is Mr. Warren Hilland an acquaintance of yours?"

"Indeed he is not," was the emphatic and hearty response. "He is the best friend I have in the world, and the best fellow in the world."

Oh, fatal obscurity of the deepening twilight! Miss St. John's face was crimson and radiant with pleasure, and could Graham have seen her at that moment he could not have failed to surmise the truth.

The young girl was as jealous of her secret as Graham soon became of his, and she only remarked demurely, "I have met Mr. Hilland in society," and then she changed the subject, for they were approaching the piazza steps, and she felt that if Hilland should continue the theme of conversation under the light of the chandelier, a telltale face and manner would betray her, in spite of all effort at control. A fragrant blossom from the shrubbery bordering the walk brushed against Graham's face, and he plucked it, saying, "Beyond that it is fragrant I don't know what this flower is. Will you take it from me?"

"Yes," she said, hesitatingly, for at that moment her absent lover had been brought so vividly to her consciousness that her heart recoiled from even the slightest hint of gallantry from another. A moment later the thought occurred, "Mr. Graham is *his* dearest friend; therefore he is my friend, although I cannot yet be as frank with him as I would like to be."

She paused a few moments on the piazza, to cool her hot face and quiet her fluttering nerves, and Graham saw with much pleasure that she fastened the flower to her breastpin. When at last she entered she puzzled him a little by leaving him rather abruptly at the parlor door and hastening up the stairs.

She found that his words had stirred such deep, full fountains that she could not yet trust herself under his observant eyes. It is a woman's delight to hear her lover praised by other men, and Graham's words had been so hearty that they had set her pulses bounding, for they assured her that she had not been deceived by love's partial eyes.

"It's true, it's true," she murmured, softly, standing with dewy eyes before her mirror. "He is the best fellow in the world, and I was blind that I did not see it from the first. But all will yet be well;" and she drew a letter from her bosom and kissed it.

Happy would Hilland have been had he seen the vision reflected by that mirror—beauty, rich and rare in itself, but enhanced, illumined, and made divine by the deepest, strongest, purest emotions of the soul.

CHAPTER VII
WARREN HILLAND

The closing scenes of the preceding chapter demand some explanation. Major St. John had spent part of the preceding summer at a seaside resort, and his daughter had inevitably attracted not a little attention. Among those that sought her favor was Warren Hilland, and in accordance with his nature he had been rather precipitate. He was ardent, impulsive, and, indulged from earliest childhood, he had been spoiled in only one respect— when he wanted anything he wanted it with all his heart and immediately. Miss St. John had seemed to him from the first a pearl among women. As with Graham, circumstances gave him the opportunity of seeing her daily, and he speedily succumbed to the "visitation of that power" to which the strongest must yield. Almost before the young girl suspected the existence of his passion, he declared it. She refused him, but he would take no refusal. Having won from her the admission that he had no favored rival, he lifted his handsome head with a resolution which she secretly admired, and declared that only when convinced that he had become hateful to her would he give up his suit.

He was not a man to become hateful to any woman. His frank nature was so in accord with hers that she responded in somewhat the same spirit, and said, half laughingly and half tearfully, "Well, if you will, you will, but I can offer no encouragement."

And yet his downright earnestness had agitated her deeply, disturbing her maiden serenity, and awaking for the first time the woman within her heart. Hitherto her girlhood's fancies had been like summer zephyrs, disturbing but briefly the still, clear waters of her soul; but now she became an enigma to herself as she slowly grew conscious of her own heart and the law of her woman's nature to love and give herself to another. But she had too much of the doughty old major's fire and spirit, and was too fond of her freedom, to surrender easily. Both Graham and Mrs. Mayburn were right in their estimate—she would never yield her heart unless compelled to by influences unexpected, at first unwelcomed, but in the end overmastering.

The first and chief effect of Hilland's impetuous wooing was, as we have seen, to destroy her sense of maidenly security, and to bring her face to face with her destiny. Then his openly avowed siege speedily compelled her to withdraw her thoughts from man in the abstract to himself. She could not brush him aside by a quiet negative, as she had already done in the case of several others. Clinging to her old life, however, and fearing to embark on this unknown sea of new experiences, she hesitated, and would not commit herself until the force that impelled was greater than that which restrained. He at last had the tact to understand her and to recognize that he had spoken to a girl, indeed almost a child, and that he must wait for the woman to develop. Hopeful, almost confident, for success and prosperity had seemingly made a league with him in all things, he was content to wait. The major had sanctioned his addresses from the first, and he sought to attain his object by careful and skilful approaches. He had shown himself such an impetuous wooer that she might well doubt his persistence; now he would prove himself so patient and considerate that she could not doubt him.

When they parted at the seaside Hilland was called to the far West by important business interests. In response to his earnest pleas, in which he movingly portrayed his loneliness in a rude mining village, she said he might write to her occasionally, and he had written so quietly and sensibly, so nearly as a friend might address a friend, that she felt there could be no harm in a correspondence of this character. During the winter season their letters had grown more frequent, and he with consummate skill had gradually tinged his words with a warmer hue. She smiled at his artifice. There was no longer any need of it, for by the wood fire, when all the house was still and wrapped in sleep, she had become fully revealed unto herself. She found that she had a woman's heart, and that she had given it irrevocably to Warren Hilland.

She did not tell him so—far from it. The secret seemed so strange, so wonderful, so exquisite in its blending of pain and pleasure, that she did not tell any one. Hers was not the nature that could babble of the heart's deepest mysteries to half a score of confidants. To him first she would make the supreme avowal that she had become his by a sweet compulsion that had at last proved irresistible, and even he must again seek that acknowledgment directly, earnestly. He was left to gather what hope he could from the fact that she did not resent his warmer expressions, and this leniency from a girl like Grace St. John meant so much to him that he did gather hope daily. Her letters were not nearly so frequent as his, but when they did come he fairly gloated over them. They were so fresh, crisp and inspiring that they reminded him of the seaside breezes that had quickened his pulses with health and pleasure during the past summer. She wrote in an easy, gossiping style of the books she was reading; of the good things in the art and literary journals, and of such questions of the day as would naturally interest her, and he so gratefully assured her that by this course she kept him within the pale of civilization, that she was induced to write oftener. In her effort to gather material that would interest him, life gained a new and richer zest, and she learned how the kindling flame within her heart could illumine even common things. Each day brought such a wealth of joy that it was like a new and glad surprise. The page she read had not only the interest imparted to it by the author, but also the far greater charm of suggesting thoughts of him or for him; and so began an interchange of books and periodicals, with pencillings, queries, marks of approval and disapproval. "I will show him," she had resolved, "that I am not a doll to be petted, but a woman who can be his friend and companion."

And she proved this quite as truly by her questions, her intelligent interest in his mining pursuits and the wild region of his sojourn, as by her words concerning that with which she was familiar.

It was hard for Hilland to maintain his reticence or submit to the necessity of his long absence. She had revealed the rich jewel of her mind so fully that his love had increased with time and separation, and he longed to obtain the complete assurance of his happiness. And yet not for the world would he again endanger his hopes by rashness. He ventured, however, to send the copy of Emerson with the quotation already given strongly underscored. Since she made no allusion to this in her subsequent letter, he again grew more wary, but as spring advanced the tide of feeling became too strong to be wholly repressed, and words indicating his passion would slip into his letters in spite of himself. She saw what was coming as truly as she saw all around her the increasing evidences of the approach of summer, and no bird sang with a fuller or more joyous note than did her heart at the prospect.

Graham witnessed this culminating happiness, and it would have been well for him had he known its source. Her joyousness had seemed to him a characteristic trait, and so it was, but he could not know how greatly it was enhanced by a cause that would have led to very different action on his part.

Hilland had decided that he would not write to his friend concerning his suit until his fate was decided in one way or the other. In fact, his letters had grown rather infrequent, not from waning friendship, but rather because their mutual interests had drifted apart. Their relations were too firmly established to need the aid of correspondence, and each knew that when they met again they would resume their old ways. In the sympathetic magnetism of personal presence confidences would be given that they would naturally hesitate to write out in cool blood.

Thus Graham was left to drift and philosophize at first. But his aunt was right: he could not daily see one who so fully satisfied the cravings of his nature and coolly consider the pros and cons. He was one who would kindle slowly, but it would be an anthracite flame that would burn on while life lasted.

He felt that he had no reason for discouragement, for she seemed to grow more kind and friendly every day. This was true of her manner, for, looking upon him as Hilland's best friend, she gave him a genuine regard, but it was an esteem which, like reflected light, was devoid of the warmth of affection that comes direct from the heart.

She did not suspect the feeling that at last began to deepen rapidly, nor had he any adequate idea of its strength. When a grain of corn is planted it is the hidden root that first develops, and the controlling influence of his life was taking root in Graham's heart. If he did not fully comprehend this at an early day it is not strange that she did not. She had no disposition to fall in love with every interesting man she met, and it seemed equally absurd to credit the gentlemen of her acquaintance with any such tendency. Her manner, therefore, toward the other sex was characterized by a frank, pleasant friendliness which could be mistaken for coquetry by only the most obtuse or the most conceited of men. With all his faults Graham was neither stupid nor vain. He understood her regard, and doubted whether he could ever change its character. He only hoped that he might, and until he saw a better chance for this he determined not to reveal himself, fearing that if he did so it might terminate their acquaintance.

"My best course," he reasoned, "is to see her as often as possible, and thus give her the opportunity to know me well. If I shall ever have any power to win her love, she, by something in her manner or tone, will unconsciously reveal the truth to me. Then I will not be slow to act. Why should I lose the pleasure of these golden hours by seeking openly that which as yet she has not the slightest disposition to give?"

This appeared to him a safe and judicious policy, and yet it may well be doubted whether it would ever have been successful with Grace St.

John, even had she been as fancy free as when Hilland first met her. She was a soldier's daughter, and could best be won by Hilland's soldier-like wooing. Not that she could have been won any more readily by direct and impetuous advances had not her heart been touched, but the probabilities are that her heart never would have been touched by Graham's army-of-observation tactics. It would scarcely have occurred to her to think seriously of a man who did not follow her with an eager quest.

On the other hand, as his aunt had suggested from the first, poor Graham was greatly endangering his peace by this close study of a woman lovely in herself, and, as he fully believed, peculiarly adapted to satisfy every requirement of his nature. A man who knows nothing of a hidden treasure goes unconcernedly on his way; if he discovers it and then loses it he feels impoverished.

CHAPTER VIII
SUPREME MOMENTS

Graham's visit was at last lengthened to a month, and yet the impulse of work or of departure had not seized him. Indeed, there seemed less prospect of anything of the kind than ever. A strong mutual attachment was growing between himself and his aunt. The brusque, quick-witted old lady interested him, while her genuine kindness and hearty welcome gave to him, for the first time in his life, the sense of being at home. She was a woman of strong likes and dislikes. She had taken a fancy to Graham from the first, and this interest fast deepened into affection. She did not know how lonely she was in her isolated life, and she found it so pleasant to have some one to look after and think about that she would have been glad to have kept him with her always.

Moreover, she had a lurking hope, daily gaining confirmation, that her nephew was not so indifferent to her favorite as he seemed. In her old age she was beginning to long for kindred and closer ties, and she felt that she could in effect adopt Grace, and could even endure the invalid major for the sake of one who was so congenial. She thought it politic however to let matters take their own course, for her strong good sense led her to believe that meddling rarely accomplishes anything except mischief. She was not averse to a little indirect diplomacy, however, and did all in her power to make it easy and natural for Graham to see the young girl as often as possible, and one lovely day, early in June, she planned a little excursion, which, according to the experience of her early days, promised well for her aims.

One breathless June morning that was warm, but not sultry, she went over to the St. Johns', and suggested a drive to the brow of a hill from which there was a superb view of the surrounding country. The plan struck the major pleasantly, and Grace was delighted. She had the craving for out-of-door life common to all healthful natures, but there was another reason why she longed for a day under the open sky with her thoughts partially and pleasantly distracted from one great truth to which she felt she must grow accustomed by degrees. It was arranged that they should take their lunch and spend the larger part of the afternoon, thus giving the affair something of the aspect of a quiet little picnic.

Although Graham tried to take the proposition quietly, he could not repress a flush of pleasure and a certain alacrity of movement eminently satisfactory to his aunt. Indeed, his spirits rose to a degree that made him a marvel to himself, and he wonderingly queried, "Can I be the same man who but a few weeks since watched the dark line of my native country loom up in the night, and with prospects as vague and dark as that outline?"

Miss St. John seemed perfectly radiant that morning, her eyes vying with the June sunlight, and her cheeks emulating the roses everywhere in bloom. What was the cause of her unaffected delight? Was it merely the prospect of a day of pleasure in the woods? Could he hope that his presence added to her zest for the occasion? Such were the questions with which Graham's mind was busy as he aided the ladies in their preparations. She certainly was more kind and friendly than usual—yes, more familiar. He was compelled to admit, however, that her manner was such as would be natural toward an old and trusted friend, but he hoped—never before had he realized how dear this hope was becoming—that some day she would awaken to the consciousness that he might be more than a friend. In the meantime he would be patient, and, with the best skill he could master, endeavor to win her favor, instead of putting her on the defensive by seeking her love.

"Two elements cannot pass into combination until there is mutual readiness," reasoned the scientist. "Contact is not combination. My province is to watch until in some unguarded moment she gives the hope that she would listen with her heart. To speak before that, either by word or action, would be pain to her and humiliation to me."

The gulf between them was wide indeed, although she smiled so genially upon him. In tying up a bundle their hands touched. He felt an electric thrill in all his nerves; she only noticed the circumstance by saying, "Who is it that is so awkward, you or I?"

"You are Grace," he replied. "It was I."

"I should be graceless indeed were I to find fault with anything to-day," she said impulsively, and raising her head she looked away into the west as if her thoughts had followed her eyes.

"It certainly is a very fine day," Graham remarked sententiously.

She turned suddenly, and saw that he was watching her keenly. Conscious of her secret she blushed under his detected scrutiny, but laughed lightly, saying, "You are a happy man, Mr. Graham, for you suggest that perfect weather leaves nothing else to be desired."

"Many have to be content with little else," he replied, "and days like this are few and far between."

"Not few and far between for me," she murmured to herself as she moved away.

She was kinder and more friendly to Graham than ever before, but the cause was a letter received that morning, against which her heart now throbbed. She had written to Hilland of Graham, and of her enjoyment of his society, dwelling slightly on his disposition to make himself agreeable without tendencies toward sentiment and gallantry.

Love is quick to take alarm, and although Graham was his nearest friend, Hilland could not endure the thought of leaving the field open to him or to any one a day longer. He knew that Graham was deliberate and by no means susceptible. And yet, to him, the fact conveyed by the letter, that his recluse friend had found the society of Grace so satisfactory that he had lingered on week after week, spoke volumes. It was not like his studious and solitary companion of old. Moreover, he understood Graham sufficiently well to know that Grace would have peculiar attractions for him, and that upon a girl of her mind he would make an impression very different from that which had led society butterflies to shun him as a bore. Her letter already indicated this truth. The natural uneasiness that he had felt all along lest some master spirit should appear was intensified. Although Graham was so quiet and undemonstrative, Hilland knew him to be possessed of an indomitable energy of will when once it was aroused and directed toward an object. Thus far from Grace's letter he believed that his friend was only interested in the girl of his heart, and he determined to forestall trouble, if possible, and secure the fruits of his patient waiting and wooing, if any were to be gathered. At the same time he resolved to be loyal to his friend, as far as he could admit his claims, and he wrote a glowing eulogy of Graham, unmarred by a phrase or word of detraction. Then, as frankly, he admitted his fears, in regard not only to Graham, but to others, and followed these words with a strong and impassioned plea in his own behalf, assuring her that time and absence, so far from diminishing her mastery over him, had rendered it complete. He entreated for permission to come to her, saying that his business interests, vast as they were, counted as less than nothing compared with the possession of her love—that he would have pressed his suit by personal presence long before had not obligations to others detained him. These obligations he now could and would delegate, for all the wealth of the mines on the continent would only be a burden unless she could share it with him. He also informed her that a ring made of gold, which he himself had mined deep in the mountain's heart, was on the way to her—that his own hands had helped to fashion the rude circlet-and that it was significant of the truth that he sought her not from the vantage ground of wealth, but because of a manly devotion that would lead him to delve in a mine or work in a shop for her, rather than live a life of luxury with any one else in the world.

For the loving girl what a treasure was such a letter! The joy it brought was so overwhelming that she was glad of the distractions which Mrs. Mayburn's little excursion promised. She wished to quiet the tumult at her heart, so that she could write as an earnest woman to an earnest man, which she could not do on this bright June morning, with her heart keeping tune with every bird that sang. Such a response as she then might have made would have been the one he would have welcomed most, but she did not think so. "I would not for the world have him know how my head is turned," she had laughingly assured herself, not dreaming that such an admission would disturb his equilibrium to a far greater degree.

"After a day," she thought, "out of doors with Mrs. Mayburn's genial common-sense and Mr. Graham's cool, half-cynical philosophy to steady me, I shall be sane enough to answer."

They were soon bowling away in a strong, three-seated rockaway, well suited to country roads, Graham driving, with the object of his thoughts and hopes beside him. Mrs. Mayburn and the major occupied the back seat, while Jinny, with a capacious hamper, was in the middle seat, and in the estimation of the diplomatic aunt made a good screen and division.

All seemed to promise well for her schemes, for the young people appeared to be getting on wonderfully together. There was a constant succession of jest and repartee. Grace was cordiality itself; and in Graham's eyes that morning there was coming an expression of which he may not have been fully aware, or which at last he would permit to be seen. Indeed, he was yielding rapidly to the spell of her beauty and the charm of her mind and manner. He was conscious of a strange, exquisite exhilaration. Every nerve in his body seemed alive to her presence, while the refined and delicate curves of her cheek and throat gave a pleasure which no statue in the galleries of Europe had ever imparted.

He wondered at all this, for to him it was indeed a new experience. His past with its hopes and ambitions seemed to have floated away to an indefinite distance, and he to have awakened to a new life—a new phase of existence. In the exaltation of the hour he felt that, whatever might be the result, he had received a revelation of capabilities in his nature of which he had not dreamed, and which at the time promised to compensate for any consequent reaction. He exulted in his human organism as a master in music might rejoice over the discovery of an instrument fitted to respond perfectly to his genius. Indeed, the thought crossed his mind more than once that day that the marvel of marvels was that mere clay could be so highly organized. It was not his thrilling nerves alone which suggested this thought, or the pure mobile face of the young girl, so far removed from any suggestion of earthliness, but a new feeling, developing in his heart, that seemed so deep and strong as to be deathless.

They reached their destination in safety. The June sunlight would have made any place attractive, but the brow of the swelling hill with its wide outlook, its background of grove and intervening vistas, left nothing to be desired. The horses were soon contentedly munching their oats, and yet their stamping feet and switching tails indicated that even for the brute creation there is ever some alloy. Graham, however, thought that fortune had at last given him one perfect day. There was no perceptible cloud. The present was so eminently satisfactory that it banished the past, or, if remembered, it served as a foil. The future promised a chance for happiness that seemed immeasurable, although the horizon of his brief existence was so near; for he felt that with her as his own, human life with all its limitations was a richer gift than he had ever imagined possible. And yet, like a slight and scarcely heard discord, the thought would come occasionally, "Since so much is possible, more ought to be possible. With such immense capability for life as I am conscious of to-day, how is it that this life is but a passing and perishing manifestation?"

Such impressions took no definite form, however, but merely passed through the dim background of his consciousness, while he gave his whole soul to the effort to make the day one that from its unalloyed pleasure could not fail to recall him to the memory of Miss St. John. He believed himself to be successful, for he felt as if inspired. He was ready with a quick reply to all her mirthful sallies, and he had the tact to veil his delicate flattery under a manner and mode of speech that suggested rather than revealed his admiration. She was honestly delighted with him and his regard, as she understood it, and she congratulated herself again and again that Hilland's friend was a man that she also would find unusually agreeable. His kindness to her father had warmed her heart toward him, and now his kindness and interest were genuine, although at first somewhat hollow and assumed.

Graham had become a decided favorite with the old gentleman, for he had proved the most efficient ally that Grace had ever gained in quickening the pace of heavy-footed Time. Even the veteran's chilled blood seemed to feel the influences of the day, and his gallantry toward Mrs. Mayburn was more pronounced than usual. "We, too, will be young people once more," he remarked, "for the opportunity may not come to us again."

They discussed their lunch with zest, they smiled into one another's face, and indulged in little pleasantries that were as light and passing as the zephyrs that occasionally fluttered the leaves above their heads; but deep in each heart were memories, tides of thought, hopes, fears, joys, that form the tragic background of all human life. The old major gave some reminiscences of his youthful campaigning. In his cheerful mood his presentation of them was in harmony with the sunny afternoon. The bright sides of his experiences were toward his auditors, but what dark shadows of wounds, agony, and death were on the further side! And of these he could never be quite unconscious, even while awakening laughter at the comic episodes of war.

Mrs. Mayburn seemed her plain-spoken, cheery self, intent only on making the most of this genial hour in the autumn of her life, and yet she was watching over a hope that she felt might make her last days her best days. She was almost praying that the fair girl whom she had so learned to love might become the solace of her age, and fill, in her childless heart, a place that had ever been an aching void. Miss St. John was too preoccupied to see any lover but one, and he was ever present, though thousands of miles away. But she saw in Graham his friend, and had already accepted him also as her most agreeable friend, liking him all the better for his apparent disposition to appeal only to her fancy and reason, instead of her heart. She saw well enough that he liked her exceedingly, but Hilland's impetuous wooing and impassioned words had made her feel that there was an infinite difference between liking and loving; and she pictured to herself the pleasure they would both enjoy when finding that their seemingly chance acquaintance was but preparation for the closer ties which their several relations to Hilland could not fail to occasion.

The object of this kindly but most temperate regard smiled into her eyes, chatted easily on any topic suggested, and appeared entirely satisfied; but was all the while conscious of a growing need which, denied, would impoverish his life, making it, brief even as he deemed it to be, an intolerable burden. But on this summer afternoon hope was in the ascendant, and he saw no reason why the craving of all that was best and noblest in his nature should not be met. When a supreme affection first masters the heart it often carries with it a certain assurance that there must be a response, that when so much is given by a subtle, irresistible, unexpected impulse, the one receiving should, sooner or later, by some law of correspondence, be inclined to return a similar regard. All living things in nature, when not interfered with, at the right time and in the right way, sought and found what was essential to the completion of their life, and he was a part of nature. According to the law of his own individuality he had yielded to Miss St. John's power. His reason had kept pace with his heart. He had advanced to his present attitude toward her like a man, and had not been driven to it by the passion of an animal. Therefore he was hopeful, self-complacent, and resolute. He not only proposed to win the girl he loved, cost what it might in time and effort, but in the exalted mood of the hour felt that he could and must win her.

She, all unconscious, smiled genially, and indeed seemed the very embodiment of mirth. Her talk was brilliant, yet interspersed with strange lapses that began to puzzle him. Meanwhile she scarcely saw him, gave him but the passing attention with which one looks up from an absorbing story, and all the time the letter against which her heart pressed seemed alive and endowed with the power to make each throb more glad and full of deep content.

How isolated and inscrutable is the mystery of each human life! Here were four people strongly interested in each other and most friendly, between whom was a constant interchange of word and glance, and yet their thought and feeling were flowing in strong diverse currents, unseen and unsuspected.

As the day declined they all grew more silent and abstracted. Deeper shadows crept into the vistas of memory with the old, and those who had become but memories were with them again as they had been on like June days half a century before. With the young the future, outlined by hope, took forms so absorbing that the present was forgotten. Ostensibly they were looking off at the wide and diversified landscape; in reality they were contemplating the more varied experiences, actual and possible, of life.

> At last the major complained querulously
> that he was growing chilly.
> The shadow in which he shivered was not
> caused by the sinking sun.

The hint was taken at once, and in a few moments they were on their way homeward. The old sportive humor of the morning did not return. The major was the aged invalid again. Mrs. Mayburn and Graham were perplexed, for Grace had seemingly become remote from them all. She was as kind as ever; indeed her manner was characterized by an unusual gentleness; but they could not but see that her thoughts were not with them. The first tumultuous torrent of her joy had passed, and with it her girlhood. Now, as an earnest woman, she was approaching the hour of her betrothal, when she would write words that would bind her to another and give direction to all her destiny. Her form was at Graham's side; the woman was not there. Whither and to whom had she gone? The question caused him to turn pale with fear.

"Miss Grace," he said at last, and there was a tinge of reproach in his voice, "where are you? You left us some time since," and he turned and tried to look searchingly into her eyes.

She met his without confusion or rise in color. Her feelings had become so deep and earnest, so truly those of a woman standing on the assured ground of fealty to another, that she was beyond her former girlish sensitiveness and its quick, involuntary manifestations. She said gently, "Pardon me, Mr. Graham, for my unsocial abstraction. You deserve better treatment for all your efforts for our enjoyment to-day."

"Please do not come back on compulsion," he said. "I do not think I am a natural Paul Pry, but I would like to know where you have been."

"I will tell you some day," she said, with a smile that was so friendly that his heart sprang up in renewed hope. Then, as if remembering what was due to him and the others, she buried her thoughts deep in her heart until she could be alone with them and their object. And yet her secret joy, like a hidden fire, tinged all her words with a kindly warmth. Graham and his aunt were not only pleased but also perplexed, for both were conscious of something in Grace's manner which they could not understand. Mrs. Mayburn was sanguine that her June-day strategy was bringing forth the much-desired results; her nephew only hoped. They all parted with cordial words, which gave slight hint of that which was supreme in each mind.

CHAPTER IX
THE REVELATION

Graham found letters which required his absence for a day or two, and it seemed to him eminently fitting that he should go over in the evening and say good-by to Miss St. John. Indeed he was disposed to say more, if the opportunity offered. His hopes sank as he saw that the first floor was darkened, and in answer to his summons Jinny informed him that the major and Miss Grace were "po'ful tired" and had withdrawn to their rooms. He trembled to find how deep was his disappointment, and understood as never before that his old self had ceased to exist. A month since no one was essential to him; now his being had become complex. Then he could have crossed the ocean with a few easily spoken farewells; now he could not go away for a few hours without feeling that he must see one who was then a stranger. The meaning of this was all too plain, and as he walked away in the June starlight he admitted it fully. Another life had become essential to his own. And still he clung to his old philosophy, muttering, "If this be true, why will not my life become as needful to her?" His theory, like many another, was a product of wishes rather than an induction from facts.

When he returned after a long ramble, the light still burning in Miss St. John's window did not harmonize with the story of the young girl's fatigue. The faint rays, however, could reveal nothing, although they had illumined page after page traced full of words of such vital import to him.

Mrs. Mayburn shared his early breakfast, and before he took his leave he tried to say in an easy, natural manner:

"Please make my adieus to Miss St. John, and say I called to present them in person, but it seemed she had retired with the birds. The colored divinity informed me that she was 'po'ful tired,' and I hope you will express my regret that the day proved so exceedingly wearisome." Mrs. Mayburn lifted her keen gray eyes to her nephew's face, and a slow rising flush appeared under her scrutiny. Then she said gently, "That's a long speech, Alford, but I don't think it expresses your meaning. If I give your cordial good-by to Grace and tell her that you hope soon to see her again, shall I not better carry out your wishes?"

"Yes," was the grave and candid reply.

"I believe you are in earnest now."

"I am, indeed," he replied, almost solemnly, and with these vague yet significant words they came to an understanding.

Three days elapsed, and still Graham's business was not completed. In his impatience he left it unfinished and returned. How his heart bounded as he saw the familiar cottage! With hasty steps he passed up the path from the street. It was just such another evening as that which had smiled upon his first coming to his aunt's residence, only now there was summer warmth in the air, and the richer, fuller promise of the year. The fragrance that filled the air, if less delicate, was more penetrating, and came from flowers that had absorbed the sun's strengthening rays. If there was less of spring's ecstasy in the song of the birds, there was now in their notes that which was in truer accord with Graham's mood.

At a turn of the path he stopped short, for on the rustic seat beneath the apple-tree he saw Miss St. John reading a letter; then he went forward to greet her, almost impetuously, with a glow in his face and a light in his eyes which no one had ever seen before. She rose to meet him, and there was an answering gladness in her face which made her seem divine to him.

"You are welcome," she said cordially. "We have all missed you more than we dare tell you;" and she gave his hand a warm, strong pressure.

The cool, even-pulsed man, who as a boy had learned to hide his feelings, was for a moment unable to speak. His own intense emotion, his all-absorbing hope, blinded him to the character of her greeting, and led him to give it a meaning it did not possess. She, equally preoccupied with her one thought, looked at him for a moment in surprise, and then cried, "He has told you—has written?"

"He! who?" Graham exclaimed with a blanching face.

"Why, Warren Hilland, your friend. I told you I would tell you, but I could not before I told him," she faltered.

He took an uncertain step or two to the tree, and leaned against it for support.

The young girl dropped the letter and clasped her hands in her distress. "It was on the drive—our return, you remember," she began incoherently. "You asked where my thoughts were, and I said I would tell you soon. Oh! we have both been blind. I am so—so sorry."

Graham's face and manner had indeed been an unmistakable revelation, and the frank, generous girl waited for no conventional acknowledgment before uttering what was uppermost in her heart.

By an effort which evidently taxed every atom of his manhood, Graham gained self-control, and said quietly, "Miss St. John, I think better of myself for having loved you. If I had known! But you are not to blame. It is I who have been blind, for you have never shown other than the kindly regard which was most natural, knowing that I was Hilland's friend. I have not been frank either, or I should have learned the truth long ago. I disguised the growing interest I felt in you from the first, fearing I should lose my chance if you understood me too early. I am Hilland's friend. No one living now knows him better than I do, and from the depths of my heart I congratulate you. He is the best and truest man that ever lived."

"Will you not be my friend, also?" she faltered.

He looked at her earnestly as he replied, "Yes, for life."

"You will feel differently soon," said the young girl, trying to smile reassuringly. "You will see that it has all been a mistake, a misunderstanding; and when your friend returns we will have the merriest, happiest times together."

"Could you soon feel differently?" he asked.

"Oh! why did you say that?" she moaned, burying her face in her hands. "If you will suffer even in a small degree as I should!"

Her distress was so evident and deep that he stood erect and stepped toward her. "Why are you so moved, Miss St. John?" he asked. "I have merely paid you the highest compliment within my power."

Her hands dropped from her face, and she turned away, but not so quickly as to hide the tears that dimmed her lustrous eyes. His lip quivered for a moment at the sight of them, but she did not see this.

"You have merely paid me a compliment," she repeated in a low tone.

The lines of his mouth were firm now, his face grave and composed, and in his gray eyes only a close observer might have seen that an indomitable will was resuming sway. "Certainly," he continued, "and such compliments you have received before and would often again were you free to receive them. I cannot help remembering that there is nothing unique in this episode."

She turned and looked at him doubtingly, as she said with hesitation, "You then regard your—your—"

"My vacation experience," he supplied.

Her eyes widened in what resembled indignant surprise, and her tones grew a little cold and constrained as she again repeated his words.

"You then regard your experience as a vacation episode."

"Do not for a moment think I have been insincere," he said, with strong emphasis, "or that I should not have esteemed it the chief honor of my life had I been successful—"

"As to that," she interrupted, "there are so many other honors that a man can win."

"Assuredly. Pardon me, Miss St. John, but I am sure you have had to inflict similar disappointments before. Did not the men survive?"

The girl broke out into a laugh in which there was a trace of bitterness. "Survive!" she cried. "Indeed they did. One is already married, and another I happen to know is engaged. I'm sure I'm glad, however. Your logic is plain and forcible, Mr. Graham, and you relieve my mind greatly. Men must be different from women."

"Undoubtedly."

"What did you mean by asking me, 'Could you soon feel differently?'"

He hesitated a moment and flushed slightly, then queried with a smile, "What did you mean by saying that I should soon learn to feel differently, and that when Hilland returned we should have the merriest times together?"

It was her turn now to be confused now; and she saw that her words were hollow, though spoken from a kindly impulse.

He relieved her by continuing: "You probably spoke from an instinctive estimate of me. You remembered what a cool and wary suitor I had been. Your father would say that I had adopted an-army-of-observation tactics, and I might have remembered that such armies rarely accomplish much. I waited for you to show some sign of weakness, and now you see that I am deservedly punished. It is ever best to face the facts as they are."

"You appear frank, Mr. Graham, and you certainly have not studied philosophy in vain."

"Why should I not take a philosophical view of the affair? In my policy, which I thought so safe and astute, I blundered. If from the first I had manifested the feeling"—the young girl smiled slightly at the word—"which you inspired, you would soon have taught me the wisdom of repressing its growth. Thus you see that you have not the slightest reason for self-censure; and I can go on my way, at least a wiser man."

She bowed gracefully, as she said with a laugh, "I am now beginning to understand that Mr. Graham can scarcely regret anything which adds to his stores of wisdom, and certainly not so slight an 'affair' as a 'vacation episode.' Now that we have talked over this little misunderstanding so frankly and rationally, will you not join us at whist to-night?"

"Certainly. My aunt and I will come over as usual."

Her brow contracted in perplexity as she looked searchingly at him for a moment; but his face was simply calm, grave, and kindly in its expression, and yet there was something about the man which impressed her and even awed her—something unseen, but felt by her woman's intuition. It must be admitted that it was felt but vaguely at the time; for Grace after all was a woman, and Graham's apparent philosophy was not altogether satisfactory. It had seemed to her as the interview progressed that she had been surprised into showing a distress and sympathy for which there was no occasion—that she had interpreted a cool, self-poised man by her own passionate heart and boundless love. In brief, she feared she had been sentimental over an occasion which Graham, as he had suggested, was able to view philosophically. She had put a higher estimate on his disappointment than he, apparently; and she had too much of her father's spirit, and too much womanly pride not to resent this, even though she was partially disarmed by this very disappointment, and still more so by his self-accusation and his tribute to Hilland. But that which impressed her most was something of which she saw no trace in the calm, self-controlled man before her. As a rule, the soul's life is hidden, except as it chooses to reveal itself; but there are times when the excess of joy or suffering cannot be wholly concealed, even though every muscle is rigid and the face marble. Therefore, although there were no outward signals of distress, Graham's agony was not without its influence on the woman before him, and it led her to say, gently and hesitatingly, "But you promised to be my friend, Mr. Graham."

His iron will almost failed him, for he saw how far removed she was from those women who see and know nothing save that which strikes their senses. He had meant to pique her pride as far as he could without offence, even though he sank low in her estimation; but such was the delicacy of her perceptions that she half divined the trouble he sedulously strove to hide. He felt as if he could sit down and cry like a child over his immeasurable loss, and for a second feared he would give way. There was in his eyes a flash of anger at his weakness, but it passed so quickly that she could scarcely note, much less interpret it.

Then he stepped forward in a friendly, hearty way, and took her hand as he said: "Yes, Miss St. John, and I will keep my promise. I will be your friend for life. If you knew my relations to Hilland, you could not think otherwise. I shall tell him when we meet of my first and characteristic siege of a woman's heart, of the extreme and prudent caution with which I opened my distant parallels, and how, at last, when I came within telescopic sight of the prize, I found that he had already captured it. My course has been so perfectly absurd that I must laugh in spite of myself;" and he did laugh so naturally and genially that Grace was constrained to join him, although the trouble and perplexity did not wholly vanish from her eyes.

"And now," he concluded, "that I have experienced my first natural surprise, I will do more than sensibly accept the situation. I congratulate you upon it as no one else can. Had I a sister I would rather that she married Hilland than any other man in the world. We thus start on the right basis for friendship, and there need be no awkward restraint on either side. I must now pay my respects to my aunt, or I shall lose not only her good graces but my supper also;" and with a smiling bow he turned and walked rapidly up the path, and disappeared within Mrs. Mayburn's open door.

Grace looked after him, and the perplexed contraction of her brow deepened. She picked up Hilland's letter, and slowly and musingly folded it. Suddenly she pressed a fervent kiss upon it, and murmured: "Thank God, the writer of this has blood in his veins; and yet—and yet—he looked at first as if he had received a mortal wound, and—and—all the time I felt that he suffered. But very possibly I am crediting him with that which would be inevitable were my case his."

With bowed head she returned slowly and thoughtfully through the twilight to her home.

CHAPTER X
THE KINSHIP OF SUFFERING

When Graham felt that he had reached the refuge of his aunt's cottage, his self-control failed him, and he almost staggered into the dusky parlor and sank into a chair. Burying his face in his hands, he muttered: "Fool, fool, fool!" and a long, shuddering sigh swept through his frame.

How long he remained in this attitude he did not know, so overwhelmed was he by his sense of loss. At last he felt a hand laid upon his shoulder; he looked up and saw that the lamp was lighted and that his aunt was standing beside him. His face was so altered and haggard that she uttered an exclamation of distress.

Graham hastily arose and turned down the light. "I cannot bear that you should look upon my weakness," he said, hoarsely.

"I should not be ashamed of having loved Grace St. John," said the old lady, quietly.

"Nor am I. As I told her, I think far better of myself for having done so. A man who has seen her as I have would be less than a man had he not loved her. But oh, the future, the future! How am I to support the truth that my love is useless, hopeless?"

"Alford, I scarcely need tell you that my disappointment is bitter also. I had set my heart on this thing."

"You know all, then?"

"Yes, I know she is engaged to your friend, Warren Hilland. She came over in the dusk of last evening, and, sitting just where you are, told me all. I kept up. It was not for me to reveal your secret. I let the happy girl talk on, kissed her, and wished her all the happiness she deserves. Grace is unlike other girls, or I should have known about it long ago. I don't think she even told her father until she had first written to him her full acknowledgment. Your friend, however, had gained her father's consent to his addresses long since. She told me that."

"Oh, my awful future!" he groaned. "Alford," Mrs. Mayburn said, gently but firmly, "think of *her* future. Grace is so good and kind that she would be very unhappy if she saw and heard you now. I hope you did not give way thus in her presence."

He sprang to his feet and paced the room rapidly at first, then more and more slowly. Soon he turned up the light, and Mrs. Mayburn was surprised at the change in his appearance.

"You are a strong, sensible woman," he began.

"Well, I will admit the premise for the sake of learning what is to follow."

"Miss St. John must never know of my sense of loss—my present despair," he said, in low, rapid speech. "Some zest in life may come back to me in time; but, be that as it may, I shall meet my trouble like a man. To make her suffer now—to cloud her well-merited happiness and that of my friend—would be to add a bitterness beyond that of death. Aunt, you first thought me cold and incapable of strong attachments, and a few weeks since I could not have said that your estimate was far astray, although I'm sure my friendship for Hilland was as strong as the love of most men. Until I met you and Grace it was the only evidence I possessed that I had a heart. Can you wonder? He was the first one that ever showed me any real kindness. I was orphaned in bitter truth, and from childhood my nature was chilled and benumbed by neglect and isolation. Growth and change are not so much questions of time as of conditions. From the first moment that I saw Grace St. John, she interested me deeply; and, self-complacent, self-confident fool that I was, I thought I could deal with the supreme question of life as I had dealt with those which half the world never think about at all. I remember your warning, aunt; and yet, as I said to myself at the time, there was more of incentive than warning in your words, flow self-confidently I smiled over them! How perfectly sure I was that I could enjoy this rare girl's society as I would look at a painting or listen to a symphony! Almost before I was aware, I found a craving in my heart which I now know all the world cannot satisfy. That June day which you arranged so kindly in my behalf made all as clear as the cloudless sun that shone upon us. That day I was revealed fully unto myself, but my hope was strong, for I felt that by the very law and correspondence of nature I could not have such an immeasurable need without having that need supplied. In my impatience I left my business unfinished and returned this evening, for I could not endure another hour of delay. She seemed to answer my glad looks when we met; she gave her hand in cordial welcome. I, blinded by feeling, and thinking that its very intensity must awaken a like return, stood speechless, almost overwhelmed by my transcendent hope. She interpreted my manner naturally by what was uppermost in her mind, and exclaimed: 'He has told you—he has written.' In a moment I knew the truth, and I scarcely think that a knife piercing my heart could inflict a deeper pang. I could not rally for a moment or two. When shall I forget the sympathy—the tears that dimmed her dear eyes! I have a religion at last, and I worship the divine nature of that complete woman. The thought that I made her suffer aroused my manhood; and from that moment I strove to make light of the affair—to give the impression that she was taking it more seriously than I did. I even tried to pique her pride—I could not wound her vanity, for she has none—and I partially succeeded. My task, however, was and will be a difficult one, for her organization is so delicate and fine that she feels what she cannot see. But I made her laugh in spite of herself at my prudent, wary wooing. I removed, I think, all constraint, and we can meet as if nothing had happened. Not that we can meet often—that would tax me beyond my strength—but often enough to banish solicitude from her mind and from Hilland's. Now you know the facts sufficiently to become a shrewd and efficient ally. By all your regard for me—what is far more, by all your love for her—I entreat you let me bring no cloud across her bright sky. We are going over to whist as usual to-night. Let all be as usual."

"Heaven bless you, Alford!" faltered his aunt, with tearful eyes.

"Heaven! what a mockery! Even the lichen, the insect, lives a complete life, while we, with all our reason, so often blunder, fail, and miss that which is essential to existence."

Mrs. Mayburn shook her head slowly and thoughtfully, and then said: "This very fact should teach us that our philosophy of life is false. We are both materialists—I from the habit of living for this world only; you, I suppose, from mistaken reasoning; but in hours like these the mist is swept aside, and I feel, I know, that this life cannot, must not, be all in all."

"Oh, hush!" cried Graham, desperately. "To cease to exist and therefore to suffer, may become the best one can hope for. Were it not cowardly, I would soon end it all "

"You may well use the word 'cowardly,'" said his aunt in strong emphasis; "and brave Grace St. John would revolt at and despise such cowardice by every law of her nature."

"Do not fear. I hope never to do anything to forfeit her respect, except it is for the sake of her own happiness, as when to-day I tried to make her think my veins were filled with ice-water instead of blood. Come, I have kept you far too long. Let us go through the formality of supper; and then I will prove to you that if I have been weak here I can be strong for her sake. I do not remember my mother; but nature is strong, and I suppose there comes a time in every one's life when he must speak to some one as he would to a mother. You have been very kind, dear aunt, and I shall never forget that you have wished and schemed for my happiness."

The old lady came and put her arm around the young man's neck and looked into his face with a strange wistfulness as she said, slowly: "There is no blood relationship between us, Alford, but we are nearer akin than such ties could make us. You do not remember your mother; I never had a child. But, as you say, nature is strong; and although I have tried to satisfy myself with a hundred things, the mother in my heart has never been content. I hoped, I prayed, that you and Grace might become my children. Alford, I have been learning of late that I am a lonely, unhappy old woman. Will you not be my boy? I would rather share your sorrow than be alone in the world again."

Graham was deeply touched. He bowed his head upon her shoulder as if he were her son, and a few hot tears fell from his eyes. "Yes, aunt," he said, in a low tone, "you have won the right to ask anything that I can give. Fate, in denying us both what our hearts most craved, has indeed made us near akin; and there can be an unspoken sympathy between us that may have a sustaining power that we cannot now know. You have already taken the bitterness, the despair out of my sorrow; and should I go to the ends of the earth I shall be the better for having you to think of and care for."

"And you feel that you cannot remain here, Alford?"

"No, aunt, that is now impossible; that is, for the present."

"Yes, I suppose it is," she admitted, sadly.

"Come, aunty dear, I promised Miss St. John that we would go over as usual to-night, and I would not for the world break my word."

"Then we shall go at once. We shall have a nice little supper on our return. Neither of us is in the mood for it now."

After a hasty toilet Graham joined his aunt. She looked at him, and had no fears.

CHAPTER XI
THE ORDEAL

Grace met them at the door. "It is very kind of you," she said, "to come over this evening after a fatiguing journey."

"Very," he replied, laughingly; "a ride of fifty miles in the cars should entitle one to a week's rest."

"I hope you are going to take it."

"Oh, no; my business man in New York has at last aroused me to heroic action. With only the respite of a few hours' sleep I shall venture upon the cars again and plunge into all the perils and excitements of a real estate speculation. My property is going up, and 'there's a tide,' you know, 'which, taken at its flood—'"

"Leads away from your friends. I see that it is useless for us to protest, for when did a man ever give up a chance for speculation?"

"Then it is not the fault of man: we merely obey a general law."

"That is the way with you scientists," she said with a piquant nod and smile. "You do just as you please, but you are always obeying some profound law that we poor mortals know nothing about. We don't fall back upon the arrangements of the universe for our motives, do we, Mrs. Mayburn?"

"Indeed we don't," was the brusque response. "'When she will, she will, and when she won't, she won't,' answers for us."

"Grace! Mrs. Mayburn!" called the major from the parlor; "if you don't come soon I'll order out the guard and have you brought in. Mr. Graham," he continued, as the young man hastened to greet him, "you are as welcome as a leave of absence. We have had no whist since you left us, and we are nearly an hour behind time to-night. Mrs. Mayburn, your humble servant. Excuse me for not rising. Why the deuce my gout should trouble me again just now I can't see. I've not seen you since that juvenile picnic which seemed to break up all our regular habits. I never thought that you would desert me. I suppose Mr. Graham carries a roving commission and can't be disciplined. I propose, however, that we set to at once and put the hour we've lost at the other end of the evening."

It was evident that the major was in high spirits, in spite of his catalogue of ills; and in fact his daughter's engagement had been extremely satisfactory to him. Conscious of increasing age and infirmity, he was delighted that Grace had chosen one so abundantly able to take care of her and of him also. For the last few days he had been in an amiable mood, for he felt that fortune had dealt kindly by him. His love for his only child was the supreme affection of his heart, and she by her choice had fulfilled his best hopes. Her future was provided for and safe. Then from the force of long habit he thought next of himself. If his tastes were not luxurious, he had at least a strong liking for certain luxuries, and to these he would gladly add a few more did his means permit. He was a connoisseur in wines and the pleasures of the table—not that he had any tendencies toward excess, but he delighted to sip the great wines of the world, to expatiate on their age, character, and origin. Sometimes he would laughingly say, "Never dilate on the treasures bequeathed to us by the old poets, sages, and artists, but for inspiration and consolation give me a bottle of old, old wine—wine made from grapes that ripened before I was born."

He was too upright a man, however, to gratify these tastes beyond his means; but Grace was an indulgent and skilful housekeeper, and made their slender income minister to her father's pleasure in a way that surprised even her practical friend, Mrs. Mayburn. In explanation she would laughingly say, "I regard housekeeping as a fine art. The more limited your materials the greater the genius required for producing certain results. Now, I'm a genius, Mrs. Mayburn. You wouldn't dream it, would you? Papa sometimes has a faint consciousness of the fact when he finds on his table wines and dishes of which he knows the usual cost. 'My dear,' he will say severely, 'is this paid for?' 'Yes,' I reply, meekly. 'How did you manage it?' Then I stand upon my dignity, and reply with offended majesty, 'Papa, I am housekeeper. You are too good a soldier to question the acts of your superior officer.' Then he makes me a most profound bow and apology, and rewards me amply by his almost childlike enjoyment of what after all has only cost me a little undetected economy and skill in cookery."

But the major was not so blind as he appeared to be. He knew more of her "undetected" economies, which usually came out of her allowance, than she supposed, and his conscience often reproached him for permitting them; but since they appeared to give her as much pleasure as they afforded him, he had let them pass. It is hard for a petted and weary invalid to grow in self-denial. While the old gentleman would have starved rather than angle for Hilland or plead his cause by a word—he had given his consent to the young man's addresses with the mien of a major-general—he nevertheless foresaw that wealth as the ally of his daughter's affection would make him one of the most discriminating and fastidious gourmands in the land.

In spite of his age and infirmity the old soldier was exceedingly fond of travel and of hotel life. He missed the varied associations of the army. Pain he had to endure much of the time, and from it there was no escape. Change of place, scene, and companionship diverted his mind, and he partially forgot his sufferings. As we have shown, he was a devourer of newspapers, but he enjoyed the world's gossip far more when he could talk it over with others, and maintain on the questions of the day half a dozen good-natured controversies. When at the seashore the previous summer he had fought scores of battles for his favorite measures with other ancient devotees of the newspaper. Grace had made Graham laugh many a time by her inimitable descriptions of the quaint tilts and chaffings of these graybeards, as each urged the views of his favorite journals; and then she would say, "You ought to see them sit down to whist. Such prolonged and solemn sittings upset my gravity more than all their *bric-a-brac* jokes." And then she had sighed and said, "I wish we could have remained longer, for papa improved so much and was so happy."

The time was coming when he could stay longer—as long as he pleased—for whatever pleased her father would please Grace, and would have to please her husband. Her mother when dying had committed the old man to her care, and a sacred obligation had been impressed upon her childish mind which every year had strengthened.

As we have seen, Grace had given her heart to Hilland by a compulsion which she scarcely understood herself. No thrifty calculations had had the slightest influence in bringing the mysterious change of feeling that had been a daily surprise to the young girl. She had turned to Hilland as the flower turns to the sun, with scarcely more than the difference that she was conscious that she was turning. When at last she ceased to wonder at the truth that her life had become blended with that of another—for, as her love developed, this union seemed the most natural and inevitable thing in the world—she began to think of Hilland more than of herself, and of the changes which her new relations would involve. It became one of the purest sources of her happiness that she would eventually have the means of gratifying every taste and whim of her father, and could surround him with all the comforts which his age and infirmities permitted him to enjoy.

Thus the engagement ring on Miss St. John's finger had its heights and depths of meaning to both father and daughter; and its bright golden hue pervaded all the prospects and possibilities—the least as well as the greatest—of the future. It was but a plain, heavy circlet of gold, and looked like a wedding-ring. Such to Graham it seemed to be, as its sheen flashed upon his eyes during their play, which continued for two hours or more, with scarcely a remark or an interruption beyond the requirements of the game. The old major loved this complete and scientific absorption, and Grace loved to humor him. Moreover, she smiled more than once at Graham's intentness. Never had he played so well, and her father had to put forth all his veteran skill and experience to hold his own. "To think that I shed tears over his disappointment, when a game of whist can console him!" she thought. "How different he is from his friend! I suppose that is the reason that they are such friends—they are so unlike. The idea of Warren playing with that quiet, steady hand and composed face under like circumstances! And yet, why is he so pale?"

Mrs. Mayburn understood this pallor too well, and she felt that the ordeal had lasted long enough. She, too, had acted her part admirably, but now she pleaded fatigue, saying that she had not been very well for the last day or two. She was inscrutable to Grace, and caused no misgivings. It is easier for a woman than for a man to hide emotions from a woman, and Mrs. Mayburn's gray eyes and strong features rarely revealed anything that she meant to conceal. The major acquiesced good-naturedly, saying, "You are quite right to stop, Mrs. Mayburn, and I surely have no cause to complain. We have had more play in two hours than most people have in two weeks. I congratulate you, Mr. Graham; you are becoming a foeman worthy of any man's steel."

Graham rose with the relief which a man would feel on leaving the rack, and said, smilingly, "Your enthusiasm is contagious. Any man would soon be on his mettle who played often with you."

"Is enthusiasm one of your traits?" Grace asked, with an arch smile over her shoulder, as she went to ring the bell.

"What! Have you not remarked it?"

"Grace has been too preoccupied to remark anything—sly puss!" said the major, laughing heartily. "My dear Mrs. Mayburn, I shall ask for your congratulations tonight. I know we shall have yours, Mr. Graham, for Grace has informed me that Hilland is your best and nearest friend. This little girl of mine has been playing blind-man's-buff with her old father. She thought she had the handkerchief tight over my eyes, but I always keep One corner raised a little. Well, Mr. Graham, this dashing friend of yours, who thinks he can carry all the world by storm, asked me last summer if he could lay siege to Grace. I felt like wringing his neck for his audacity and selfishness. The idea of any one taking Grace from me!"

"And no one shall, papa," said Grace, hiding her blushing face behind his white shock of hair. "But I scarcely think these details will interest—"

"What!" cried the bluff, frank old soldier—"not interest Mrs. Mayburn, the best and kindest of neighbors? not interest Hilland's alter ego?"

"I assure you," said Graham, laughing, "that I am deeply interested; and I promise you, Miss Grace, that I shall give Hilland a severer curtain lecture than he will ever receive from you, because he has left me in the dark so long."

"Stop pinching my arm," cried the major, who was in one of his jovial moods, and often immensely enjoyed teasing his daughter. "You may well hide behind me. Mrs. Mayburn, I'm going to expose a rank case of filial deception that was not in the least successful. This 'I came, I saw, I conquered' friend of yours, Mr. Graham, soon discovered that he was dealing with a race that was not in the habit of surrendering. But your friend, like Wellington, never knew when he was beaten. He wouldn't retreat an inch, but drawing his lines as close as he dared, sat down to a regular siege."

Graham again laughed outright, and with a comical glance at the young girl, asked, "Are you sure, sir, that Miss St. John was aware of these siege operations?"

"Indeed she was. Your friend raised his flag at once, and nailed it to the staff. And this little minx thought that she could deceive an old soldier like myself by playing the role of disinterested friend to a lonely young man condemned to the miseries of a mining town. I was often tempted to ask her why she did not extend her sympathy to scores of young fellows in the service who are in danger of being scalped every day. But the joke of it was that I knew she was undermined and must surrender long before Hilland did."

"Now, papa, it's too bad of you to expose me in this style. I appeal to Mrs. Mayburn if I did not keep my flag flying so defiantly to the last that even she did not suspect me."

"Yes," said the old lady, dryly; "I can testify to that."

"Which is only another proof of my penetration," chuckled the major. "Well, well, it is so seldom I can get ahead of Grace in anything that I like to make the most of my rare good fortune; and it seems, Mr. Graham, as if you and your aunt had already become a part of our present and prospective home circle. I have seen a letter in which Warren speaks of you in a way that reminds me of a friend who was shot almost at my side in a fight with the Indians. That was nearly half a century ago, and yet no one has taken his place. With men, friendships mean something, and last."

"Come, come," cried Mrs. Mayburn, bristling up, "neither Grace nor I will permit such an implied slur upon our sex."

"My friendship for Hilland will last," said Graham, with quiet emphasis. "Most young men are drawn together by a mutual liking—by something congenial in their natures. I owe him a debt of gratitude that can never be repaid, He found me a lonely, neglected boy, who had scarcely ever known kindness, much less affection, and his ardent, generous nature became an antidote to my gloomy tendencies. From the first he has been a constant and faithful friend. He has not one unworthy trait. But there is nothing negative about him, for he abounds in the best and most manly qualities; and I think," he concluded, speaking slowly and deliberately, as if he were making an inward vow, "that I shall prove worthy of his trust and regard."

Grace looked at him earnestly and gratefully, and the thought again asserted itself that she had not yet gauged his character or his feeling toward herself. To her surprise she also noted that Mrs. Mayburn's eyes were filled with tears, but the old lady was equal to the occasion, and misled her by saying, "I feel condemned, Alford, that you should have been so lonely and neglected in early life, but I know it was so."

"Oh, well, aunt, you know I was not an interesting boy, and had I been imposed upon you in my hobbledehoy period, our present relations might never have existed. I must ask your congratulations also," he continued, turning toward the major and his daughter. "My aunt and I have in a sense adopted each other. I came hither to pay her a formal call, and have made another very dear friend."

"Have you made only one friend since you became our neighbor?" asked Grace, with an accent of reproach in her voice.

"I would very gladly claim you and your father as such," he replied, smilingly.

The old major arose with an alacrity quite surprising in view of his lameness, and pouring out two glasses of the wine that Jinny had brought in answer to Grace's touch of the bell, he gave one of the glasses to Graham, and with the other in his left hand, he said, "And here I pledge you the word of a soldier that I acknowledge the claim in full, not only for Hilland's sake, but your own. You have generously sought to beguile the tedium of a crotchety and irritable old man; but such as he is he gives you his hand as a true, stanch friend; and Grace knows this means a great deal with me."

"Yes, indeed," she cried. "I declare, papa, you almost make me jealous. You treated Warren as if you were the Great Mogul, and he but a presuming subject. Mr. Graham, if so many new friends are not an embarrassment of riches, will you give me a little niche among them?" "I cannot give you that which is yours already," he replied; "nor have I a little niche for you. You have become identified with Hilland, you know, and therefore require a large space."

"Now, see here, my good friends, you are making too free with my own peculiar property. You are already rich in each other, not counting Mr. Hilland, who, according to Alford, seems to embody all human excellence. I have only this philosophical nephew, and even with him shall find a rival in every book he can lay hands upon. I shall therefore carry him off at once, especially as he is to be absent several days."

The major protested against his absence, and was cordiality itself in his parting words.

Grace followed them out on the moonlit piazza. "Mr. Graham," she said, hesitatingly, "you will not be absent very long, I trust."

"Oh, no," he replied, lightly; "only two or three weeks. In addition to my affairs in the city, I have some business in Vermont, and while there shall follow down some well-remembered trout-streams."

She turned slightly away, and buried her face in a spray of roses from the bush that festooned the porch. He saw that a tinge of color was in her cheeks, as she said in a low tone, "You should not be absent long; I think your friend will soon visit us, and you should be here to welcome him," and she glanced hastily toward him. Was it the moonlight that made him look so very pale? His eyes held hers. Mrs. Mayburn had walked slowly on, and seemingly he had forgotten her. The young girl's eyes soon fell before his fixed gaze, and her face grew troubled. He started, and said lightly, "I beg your pardon, Miss Grace, but you have no idea what a picture you make with the aid of those roses. The human face in clear moonlight reveals character, it is said, and I again congratulate my friend without a shadow of doubt. Unversed as I am in such matters, I am quite satisfied that Hilland will need no other welcome than yours, and that he will be wholly content with it for some time to come. Moreover, when I find myself among the trout, there's no telling when I shall get out of the woods."

"Is fishing, then, one of your ruling passions?" the young girl asked, with an attempt to resume her old piquant style of talk with him.

"Yes," he replied, laughing, so that his aunt might hear him; "but when one's passions are of so mild a type one may be excused for having a half-dozen. Good-by!"

She stepped forward and held out her hand. "You have promised to be my friend," she said, gently.

His hand trembled in her grasp as he said quietly and firmly, "I will keep my promise."

She looked after him wistfully, as she thought, "I'm not sure about him. I hope it's only a passing disappointment, for we should not like to think that our happiness had brought him wretchedness."

CHAPTER XII
FLIGHT TO NATURE

Graham found his aunt waiting for him on the rustic seat beneath the apple-tree. Here, a few hours before, his heart elate with hope, he had hastened forward to meet Grace St. John. Ages seemed to have passed since that moment of bitter disappointment, teaching him how relative a thing is time.

The old lady joined him without a word, and they passed on silently to the house. As they entered, she said, trying to infuse into the commonplace words something of her sympathy and affection, "Now we will have a cosey little supper."

Graham placed his hand upon her arm, and detained her, as he replied, "No, aunt; please get nothing for me. I must hide myself for a few hours from even your kind eyes. Do not think me weak or unmanly. I shall soon get the reins well in hand, and shall then be quiet enough."

"I think your self-control has been admirable this evening."

"It was the self-control of sheer, desperate force, and only partial at that. I know I must have been almost ghostly in my pallor. I have felt pale—as if I were bleeding to death. I did not mean to take her hand in parting, for I could not trust myself; but she held it out so kindly that I had to give mine, which, in spite of my whole will power, trembled. I troubled and perplexed her. I have infused an element of sorrow and bitterness into her happy love; for in the degree in which it gives her joy she will fear that it brings the heartache to me, and she is too good and kind not to care. I must go away and not return until my face is bronzed and my nerves are steel. Oh, aunt! you cannot understand me; I scarcely understand myself. It seems as if all the love that I might have given to many in the past, had my life been like that of others, had been accumulating for this hopeless, useless waste—this worse than waste, since it only wounds and pains its object."

"And do I count for so little, Alford?"

"You count for more now than all others save one; and if you knew how contrary this utter unreserve is to my nature and habit, you would understand how perfect is my confidence in you and how deep is my affection. But I am learning with a sort of dull, dreary astonishment that there are heights and depths of experience of which I once had not the faintest conception. This is a kind of battle that one must fight out alone. I must go away and accustom myself to a new condition of life. But do not worry about me. I shall come back a vertebrate;" and he tried to summon a reassuring smile, as he kissed her in parting.

That night Graham faced his trouble, and decided upon his future course.

After an early breakfast the next morning, the young man bade his aunt good-by. With moist eyes, she said, "Alford, I am losing you, just as I find how much you are and can be to me."

"No, aunty dear; my course will prove best for us both," he replied, gently. "You would not be happy if you saw me growing more sad and despairing every day through inaction, and—and—well, I could never become strong and calm with that cottage there just beyond the trees. You have not lost me, for I shall try to prove a good correspondent."

Graham kept his word. His "real estate speculation" did not detain him long in the city, for his business agent was better able to manage such interests than the inexperienced student; and soon a letter dated among the mountains and the trout streams of Vermont assured Mrs. Mayburn that he had carried out his intentions. Not long after, a box with a score of superb fish followed the letter, and Major St. John's name was pinned on some of the largest and finest. During the next fortnight these trophies of his sport continued to arrive at brief intervals, and they were accompanied by letters, giving in almost journal form graphic descriptions of the streams he had fished, their surrounding scenery, and the amusing peculiarities of the natives. There was not a word that suggested the cause that had driven him so suddenly into the wilderness, but on every page were evidences of tireless activity.

The major was delighted with the trout, and enjoyed a high feast almost every day. Mrs. Mayburn, imagining that she had divined Graham's wish, read from his letters glowing extracts which apparently revealed an enthusiastic sportsman.

After his departure Grace had resumed her frequent visits to her congenial old friend, and confidence having now been given in respect to her absent lover, the young girl spoke of him out of the abundance of her heart. Mrs. Mayburn tried to be all interest and sympathy, but Grace was puzzled by something in her manner—something not absent when she was reading Graham's letters. One afternoon she said: "Tell your father that he may soon expect something extraordinarily fine, for Alford has written me of a twenty-mile tramp through the mountains to a stream almost unknown and inaccessible."

"Won't you read the description to us this evening? You have no idea how much pleasure papa takes in Mr. Graham's letters. He says they increase the gamy flavor of the fish he enjoys so much; and I half believe that Mr. Graham in this indirect and delicate way is still seeking to amuse my father, and so compensate him for his absence. Warren will soon be here, however, and then we can resume our whist parties. Do you know that I am almost jealous? Papa talks more of Vermont woods than of Western mines. You ought to hear him expatiate upon the trout. He seems to follow Mr. Graham up and down every stream; and he explains to me with the utmost minuteness just how the flies are cast and just where they were probably thrown to snare the speckled beauties. By the way, Mr. Graham puzzles me. He seems to be the most indefatigable sportsman I ever heard of. But I should never have suspected it from the tranquil weeks he spent with us. He seemed above all things a student of the most quiet and intellectual tastes, one who could find more pleasure in a library and laboratory than in all the rest of the world together. Suddenly he develops into the most ardent disciple of Izaak Walton. Indeed, he is too ardent, too full of restless activity, to be a true follower of the gentle, placid Izaak. At his present rate he will soon overrun all Vermont;" and she looked searchingly at her friend.

A faint color stole into the old lady's cheeks, but she replied, quietly: "I have learned to know Alford well enough to love him dearly; and yet you must remember that but a few weeks ago he was a comparative stranger to me. He certainly is giving us ample proof of his sportsmanship, and now that I recall it, I remember hearing of his fondness for solitary rambles in the woods when a boy."

"His descriptions certainly prove that he is familiar with them," was the young girl's answer to Mrs. Mayburn's words. Her inward comment on the slight flush that accompanied them was: "She knows. He has told her; or she, less blind than I, has seen." But she felt that the admission of his love into which Graham had been surprised was not a topic for her to introduce, although she longed to be assured that she had not seriously disturbed the peace of her lover's friend. A day or two later Hilland arrived, and her happiness was too deep, too complete, to permit many thoughts of the sportsman in the Vermont forests. Nor did Hilland's brief but hearty expressions of regret at Graham's temporary absence impose upon her. She saw that the former was indeed more than content with her welcome; that while his friendship was a fixed star of the first magnitude, it paled and almost disappeared before the brightness and fulness of her presence.

"Nature," indeed, became "radiant" to both "with purple light, the morning and the night varied enchantments."

Grace waited for Graham to give his own confidence to his friend if he chose to do so, for she feared that if she spoke of it estrangement might ensue. The unsuspecting major was enthusiastic in his praises of the successful fisherman, and Hilland indorsed with emphasis all he said. Graham's absence and Grace's reception had banished even the thought that he might possibly find a rival in his friend, and his happiness was unalloyed.

One sultry summer evening in early July Graham returned to his aunt's residence, and was informed that she was, as usual, at her neighbor's. He went immediately to his room to remove the dust and stains of travel. On his table still lay the marked copy of Emerson that Grace had lent him, and he smiled bitterly as he recalled his complacent, careless surmises over the underscored passage, now so well understood and explained. Having finished his toilet, he gazed steadily at his reflection in the mirror, as a soldier might have done to see if his equipment was complete. It was evident he had not gone in vain to nature for help. His face was bronzed, and no telltale flush or pallor could now be easily recognized. His expression was calm and resolute, indicating nerves braced and firm. Then he turned away with the look of a man going into battle, and without a moment's hesitancy he sought the ordeal. The windows and doors of Major St. John's cottage were open, and as he mounted the piazza the group around the whist-table was in full view—the major contracting his bushy eyebrows over his hand as if not altogether satisfied, Mrs. Mayburn looking at hers with an interest so faint as to suggest that her thoughts were wandering, and Hilland with his laughing blue eyes glancing often from his cards to the fair face of his partner, as if he saw there a story that would deepen in its inthralling interest through life. There was no shadow, no doubt on his wide, white brow. It was the genial, frank, merry face of the boy who had thawed the reserve and banished the gathering gloom of a solitary youth at college, only now it was marked by the stronger lines of early manhood. His fine, short upper lip was clean shaven, and its tremulous curves indicated a nature quick, sensitive, and ready to respond to every passing influence, while a full, tawny beard and broad shoulders banished all suggestion of effeminacy. He appeared to be, what in truth he was, an unspoiled favorite of fortune, now supremely happy in her best and latest gift. "If I could but have known the truth at first," sighed Graham, "I would not have lingered here until my very soul was enslaved; for he is the man above all others to win and hold a woman's heart."

That he held the heart of the fair girl opposite him was revealed by every glance, and Graham's heart ached with a pain hard to endure, as he watched for a moment the exquisite outlines of her face, her wide, low brow with its halo of light-colored hair that was in such marked contrast with the dark and lustrous eyes, now veiled by silken lashes as she looked downward intent on the game, now beaming with the very spirit of mirth and mischief as she looked at her opponents, and again softening in obedience to the controlling law of her life as she glanced half shyly from time to time at the great bearded man on the other side of the table.

"Was not the world wide enough for me to escape seeing that face?" he groaned. "A few months since I was content with my life and lot. Why did I come thousands of miles to meet such a fate? I feared I should have to face poverty and privation for a time. Now they are my lot for life, an impoverishment that wealth would only enhance. I cannot stay here, I will not remain a day longer than is essential to make the impression I wish to leave;" and with a firm step he crossed the piazza, rapped lightly in announcement of his presence, and entered without ceremony.

Hilland sprang forward joyously to meet him, and gave him just such a greeting as accorded with his ardent spirit. "Why, Graham!" he cried, with a crushing grasp, and resting a hand on his shoulder at the same time, "you come unexpectedly, like all the best things in the world. We looked for a letter that would give us a chance to celebrate your arrival as that of the greatest fisherman of the age."

"Having taken so many unwary trout, it was quite in keeping to take us unawares," said Grace, pressing forward with outstretched hand, for she had determined to show in the most emphatic way that Hilland's friend was also hers.

Graham took the proffered hand and held it, while, with a humorous glance at his friend, he said: "See here, Hilland, I hold an indisputable proof that it's time you appeared on the confines of civilization and gave an account of yourself."

"I own up, old fellow. You have me on the hip. I have kept one secret from you. If we had been together the thing would have come out, but somehow I couldn't write, even to you, until I knew my fate."

"Mr. Graham," broke in the major, "if we were in the service, I should place you in charge of the commissary department, and give you a roving commission. I have lived like a lord for the past two weeks;" and he shook Graham's hand so cordially as to prove his heart had sympathized with an adjacent organ that had been highly gratified.

"I have missed you, Alford," was his aunt's quiet greeting, and she kissed him as if he were her son, causing a sudden pang as he remembered how soon he would bid her farewell again.

"Why, Graham, how you have improved! You have gained a splendid color in the woods. The only trouble is that you are as attenuated as some of the theories we used to discuss."

"And you, giddy boy, begin to look quite like a man. Miss Grace, you will never know how greatly you are indebted to me for my restraining influence. There never was a fellow who needed to be sat down upon so often as Hilland. I have curbed and pruned him; indeed, I have almost brought him up."

"He does you credit," was her reply, spoken with mirthful impressiveness, and with a very contented glance at the laughing subject of discussion.

"Yes, Graham," he remarked, "you were a trifle heavy at times, and were better at bringing a fellow down than up. It took all the leverage of my jolly good nature to bring you up occasionally. But I am glad to see and hear that you have changed so happily. Grace and the major say you have become the best of company, taking a human interest in other questions than those which keep the scientists by the ears."

"That is because I have broken my shell and come out into the world. One soon discovers that there are other questions, and some of them conundrums that the scientists may as well give up at the start. I say, Hilland, how young we were over there in Germany when we thought ourselves growing hourly into *savants!*"

"Indeed we were, and as sublimely complacent as we were young. Would you believe it, Mrs. Mayburn, your nephew and I at one time thought we were on the trail of some of the most elusive secrets of the universe, and that we should soon drag them from cover. I have learned since that this little girl could teach me more than all the universities."

Graham shot a swift glance at his aunt, which Grace thought she detected; but he turned to the latter, and said genially: "I congratulate you on excelling all the German doctors. I know he's right, and he'll remember the lore obtained from you long after he has forgotten the deep, guttural abstractions that droned on his ears abroad. It will do him more good, too."

"I fear I am becoming a subject of irony to you both," said Grace.

"They are both becoming too deep for us, are they not, Mrs. Mayburn?" put in the major. "You obtained your best knowledge, Mr. Graham, when you trampled the woods as a boy, and though you gathered so much of it by hook it's like the fish you killed, rare to find. If we were in the service and I had the power, I'd have you brevetted at once, and get some fellow knocked on the head to make a vacancy. You have been contributing royally to our mess, and now you must take a soldier's luck with us to-night. Grace, couldn't you improvise a nice little supper?"

"Please do not let me cause any such trouble this hot evening," Graham began; "I dined late in town, and—"

"No insubordination," interrupted Grace, rising with alacrity. "Certainly I can, papa," and as she paused near Graham, she murmured: "Don't object; it will please papa."

She showed what a provident housekeeper she was, for they all soon sat down to an inviting repast, of which fruit was the staple article, with cake so light and delicate that it would never disturb a man's conscience after he retired. Then with genial words and smiles that masked all heartache, Graham and his aunt said good-night and departed, Hilland accompanying his friend, that he might pour out the long-delayed confidence. Graham shivered as he thought of the ordeal, as a man might tremble who was on his way to the torture-chamber, but outwardly he was quietly cordial.

CHAPTER XIII
THE FRIENDS

After accompanying Mrs. Mayburn to her cottage door, the friends strolled away together, the sultry evening rendering them reluctant to enter the house. When they reached the rustic seat under the apple-tree, Hilland remarked: "Here's a good place for our—"

"Not here," interrupted Graham, in a tone that was almost sharp in its tension.

"Why not?" asked his friend, in the accent of surprise.

"Oh, well," was the confused answer, "some one may be passing— servants may be out in the grounds. Suppose we walk slowly."

"Graham, you seem possessed by the very demon of restlessness. The idea of walking this hot night!"

"Oh, well, it doesn't matter," Graham replied, carelessly, although his face was rigid with the effort; and he threw himself down on the rustic seat. "We are not conspirators that we need steal away in the darkness. Why should I not be restless after sitting in the hot cars all day, and with the habit of tramping fresh upon me?"

"What evil spirit drove you into the wilderness and made you the champion tramp of the country? It seems to me you must have some remarkable confidences also."

"No evil spirit, I assure you; far from it. My tramp has done me good; indeed, I never derived more benefit from an outing in the woods in my life. You will remember that when we were boys at college no fellow took longer walks than I. I am simply returning to the impulses of my youth. The fact is, I've been living too idly, and of course there would be a reaction in one of my temperament and habits. The vital force which had been accumulating under my aunt's high feeding and the inspiration resulting from the society of two such charming people as Major and Miss St. John had to be expended in some way. Somehow I've lost much of my old faith in books and laboratories. I've been thinking a great deal about it, and seeing you again has given a strong impulse to a forming purpose. I felt a sincere commiseration when you gave up your life of a student. I was a fool to do so. I have studied your face and manner this evening, and can see that you have developed more manhood out in those Western mines, in your contact with men and things and the large material interests of the world, than you could have acquired by delving a thousand years among dusty tomes."

"That little girl over there has done more for me than Western mines and material interests."

"That goes without saying; and yet she could have done little for you, had you been a dawdler. Indeed, in that case she would have had nothing to do with you. She recognized that you were like the gold you are mining—worth taking and fashioning; and I tell you she is not a girl to be imposed upon."

"Flatterer!"

"No; friend."

"You admire Grace very much."

"I do indeed, and I respect her still more. You know I never was a lady's man; indeed, the society of most young women was a weariness to me. Don't imagine I am asserting any superiority. You enjoyed their conversation, and you are as clever as I am."

"I understand," said Hilland, laughing; "you had nothing in common. You talked to a girl as if she were a mile off, and often broached topics that were cycles away. Now, a girl likes a fellow to come reasonably close—metaphorically, if not actually—when he chats with her. Moreover, many that you met, if they had brains, had never cultivated them. They were as shallow as a duck-pond, and with their small deceits, subterfuges, and affectations were about as transparent. Some might imagine them deep. They puzzled and nonplussed you, and you slunk away. Now I, while rating them at their worth, was able from previous associations to talk a little congenial nonsense, and pass on. They amused me, too. You know I have a sort of laughing philosophy, and everything and everybody amuses me. The fellows would call these creatures angels, and they would flap their little butterfly wings as if they thought they were. How happened it that you so soon were *en rapport* with Grace?"

"Ah, wily wretch!" Graham laughed gayly, while the night hid his lowering brows; "praise of your mistress is sweeter than flattery to yourself. Why, simply because she is Grace St. John. I imagine that it is her army life that has so blended unconventionality with perfect good breeding. She is her bluff, honest, high-spirited old father over again, only idealized, refined, and womanly. Then she must have inherited some rare qualities from her Southern mother: you see my aunt has told me all about them. I once met a Southern lady abroad, and although she was middle-aged, she fascinated me more than any girl I had ever met. In the first place, there was an indescribable accent that I never heard in Europe—slight, indeed, but very pleasing to the ear. I sometimes detect traces of it in Miss St. John's speech. Then this lady had a frankness and sincerity of manner which put you at your ease at once; and yet with it all there was a fine reserve. You no more feared that she would blurt out something unsanctioned by good taste than that she would dance a hornpipe. She was singularly gentle and retiring in her manner; and yet one instinctively felt he would rather insult a Southern fire-eater than offend her. She gave the impression that she had been accustomed to a chivalric deference from men, rather than mere society attentions; and one unconsciously infused a subtle homage in his very accent when speaking to her. Now, I imagine that Miss St. John's mother must have been closely akin to this woman in character. You know my weakness for analyzing everything. You used to say I couldn't smoke a cigar without going into the philosophy of it. I had not spent one evening in the society of Miss St. John before I saw that she was a *rara avis*. Then her devotion to her invalid father is superb. She enlisted me in his service the first day of my arrival. Although old, crippled, often racked with pain, and afflicted with a temper which arbitrary command has not improved, she beguiles him out of himself, smiles away his gloom—in brief, creates so genial an atmosphere about him that every breath is balm, and does it all, too, without apparent effort You see no machinery at work. Now, this was all a new and very interesting study of life to me, and I studied it. There, too, is my aunt, who is quite as interesting in her way. Such women make general or wholesale cynicism impossible, or else hypocritical;" and he was about to launch out into as extended an analysis of the old lady's peculiarities, when Hilland interrupted him with a slap on the shoulder and a ringing laugh.

"Graham, you haven't changed a mite. You discourse just as of old, when in our den at the university we befogged ourselves in the tobacco-smoke and the denser obscurities of German metaphysics, only your theme is infinitely more interesting. Now, when I met my paragon, Grace, whom you have limned with the feeling of an artist rather than of an analyst, although with a blending of both, I fell in love with her."

"Yes, Hilland, it's just like you to fall in love. My fear has ever been that you would fall in love with a face some day, and not with a woman. But I now congratulate you from the depths of my soul."

"How comes it that *you* did not fall in love with one whom you admire so much? You were not aware of my suit."

"I suppose it is not according to my nature to 'fall in love,' as you term it. The very phrase is repugnant to me. When a man is falling in any sense of the word, his reason is rather apt to be muddled and confused, and he cannot be very sure where he will land. If you had not appeared on the scene my reason would have approved of my marriage with Miss St. John—that is, if I had seen the slightest chance of acceptance, which, of course, I never have. I should be an egregious fool were it otherwise."

"How about your heart?"

"The heart often leads to the sheerest folly," was the sharp rejoinder.

Hilland laughed in his good-humored way. His friend's reply seemed the result of irritation at the thought that the heart should have much to say when reason demurred. "Well, Graham," he said, kindly and earnestly, "if I did not know you so well, I should say you were the most cold-blooded, frog-like fellow in existence. You certainly are an enigma to me on the woman question. I must admit that my heart went headlong from the first; but when at last reason caught up, and had time to get her breath and look the case over, she said it was 'all right'—far better than she had expected. To one of my temperament, however, it seems very droll that reason should lead the way to love, and the heart come limping after."

"Many a one has taken the amatory tumble who would be glad to reason his way up and back. But we need not discuss this matter in the abstract, for we have too much that is personal to say to each other. You are safe; your wonted good fortune has served you better than ever. All the wisdom of Solomon could not have enabled you to fall in love more judiciously. Indeed, when I come to think of it, the wisdom of Solomon, according to history, was rather at fault in these matters. Tell me how it all came about" (for he knew the story must come); "only outline the tale to-night. I've been speculating and analyzing so long that it is late; and the major, hearing voices in the grounds, may bring some of his old army ordnance to bear on us."

But Hilland, out of the abundance of his heart, found much to say; and his friend sat cold, shivering in the sultry night, his heart growing more despairing as he saw the heaven of successful wooing that he could never enter. At last Hilland closed with the words, "I say, Graham, are you asleep?"

"Oh, no," in a husky voice.

"You are taking cold."

"I believe I am."

"I'm a brute to keep you up in this style. As I live, I believe there is the tinge of dawn in the east."

"May every dawn bring a happy day to you, Warren," was said so gently and earnestly that Hilland rested his arm on his friend's shoulder as he replied, "You've a queer heart, Alford, but such as it is I would not exchange it for that of any man living." Then abruptly, "Do you hold to our old views that this life ends all?"

A thrill of something like exultation shot through Graham's frame as he replied, "Certainly."

Hilland sprang up and paced the walk a moment, then said, "Well, I don't know. A woman like Grace St. John shakes my faith in our old belief. It seems profanation to assert that she is mere clay."

The lurid gleam of light which the thought of ceasing to exist and to suffer had brought to Graham faded. It did seem like profanation. At any rate, at that moment it was a hideous truth that such a creature might by the chance of any accident resolve into mere dust. And yet it seemed a truth which must apply to her as well as to the grossest of her sisterhood. He could only falter, "She is very highly organized."

They both felt that it was a lame and impotent conclusion.

But the spring of happiness was in Hilland's heart. The present was too rich for him to permit such dreary speculations, and he remarked cordially and laughingly, "Well, Graham, we have made amends for our long separation and silence. We have talked all the summer night. I am rich, indeed, in such a friend and such a sweetheart; and the latter must truly approach perfection when my dear old philosopher of the stoic school could think it safe and wise to marry her, were all the conditions favorable. You don't wish that I was at the bottom of one of my mines, do you, Alford?"

Graham felt that the interview must end at once, so he rose and said, "No, I do not. My reason approves of your choice. If you wish more, my 'queer heart, such as it is,' approves of it also. If I had the power to change everything this moment I would not do so. You have fairly won your love, and may all the forces of nature conspire to prosper you both. But come," he added in a lighter vein, "Miss St. John may be watching and waiting for your return, and even imagining that I, with my purely intellectual bent, may regard you as a disturbing element in the problem, and so be led to eliminate you in a quiet, scientific manner."

"Well, then, good night, or morning, rather. Forgive a lover's garrulousness."

"I was more garrulous than you, without half your excuse. No, I'll see you safely home. I wish to walk a little to get up a circulation. With your divine flame burning so brightly, I suppose you could sit through a zero night; but you must remember that such a modicum of philosophy as I possess will not keep me warm. There, good-by, old fellow. Sleep the sleep of the just, and, what is better in this chance-medley world, of the happy. Don't be imagining that you have any occasion to worry about me."

Hilland went to his room in a complacent mood, and more in love than ever. Had not his keen-eyed, analytical friend, after weeks of careful observation, testified to the exceeding worth of the girl of his heart? He had been in love, and he had ever heard that love is blind. It seemed to him that his friend could never love as he understood the word; and yet the peerless maiden had so satisfied the exactions of Graham's taste and reason, and had proved herself so generally admirable, that he felt it would be wise and advantageous to marry her.

"It's a queer way of looking at these things," he concluded, with a shrug, "but then it is Graham's way."

Soon he was smiling in his repose, for the great joy of his waking hours threw its light far down into the obscurity of sleep.

Graham turned slowly away, and walked with downcast face to the rustic seat. He stood by it a moment, and then sank into it like a man who has reached the final limit of human endurance. He uttered no sound, but at brief intervals a shiver ran through his frame. His head sank into his hands, and he looked and felt like one utterly crushed by a fate from which there was no escape. His ever-recurring thought was, "I have but one life, and it's lost, worse than lost. Why should I stagger on beneath the burden of an intolerable existence, which will only grow heavier as the forces of life fail?"

At last in his agony he uttered the words aloud. A hand was laid upon his shoulder, and a husky, broken voice said, "Here is one reason."

He started up, and saw that his aunt stood beside him.

The dawn was gray, but the face of the aged woman was grayer and more pallid. She did not entreat—her feeling seemed too deep for words— but with clasped hands she lifted her tear-dimmed eyes to his. Her withered bosom rose and fell in short, convulsive sobs, and it was evident that she could scarcely stand.

His eyes sank, and a sudden sense of guilt and shame at his forgetfulness of her overcame him. Then yielding to an impulse, all the stronger because mastering one who had few impulses, he took her in his arms, kissed her repeatedly, and supported her tenderly to the cottage. When at last they reached the quaint little parlor he placed her tenderly in her chair, and, taking her hand, he kissed it, and said solemnly, "No, aunty, I will not die. I will live out my days for your sake, and do my best."

"Thank God!" she murmured—"thank God!" and for a moment she leaned her head upon his breast as he knelt beside her. Suddenly she lifted herself, with a return of her old energy; and he rose and stood beside her. She looked at him intently as if she would read his thoughts, and then shook her finger impressively as she said, "Mark my words, Alford, mark my words: good will come of that promise."

"It has come already," he gently replied, "in that you, my best friend, are comforted. Now go and rest and sleep. Have no fear, for your touch of love has broken all evil spells."

Graham went to his room, calmed by an inflexible resolution. It was no longer a question of happiness or unhappiness, or even of despair; it was simply a question of honor, of keeping his word. He sat down and read once more the paragraph in the marked copy of Emerson, "No man ever forgot—" He gave the words a long, wistful look, and then closed the volume as if he were closing a chapter of his life.

"Well," he sighed, "I did my best last night not to dispel their enchantment, for of course Hilland will tell her the substance of our talk. Now, it must be my task for a brief time to maintain and deepen the impression that I have made."

Having no desire for sleep, he softly paced his room, but it was not in nervous excitement. His pulse was quiet and regular, and his mind reverted easily to a plan of extended travel upon which he had been dwelling while in the woods. At last he threw himself upon his couch, and slept for an hour or two. On awaking he found that it was past the usual breakfast hour, and after a hasty toilet he went in search of his aunt, but was informed that she was still sleeping.

"Do not disturb her," he said to the servant. "Let her sleep as long as she will."

He then wrote a note, saying that he had decided to go to town to attend to some business which had been neglected in his absence, and was soon on his way to the train.

CHAPTER XIV
NOBLE DECEPTION

In the course of the forenoon Hilland called on his friend, and was informed that Graham had gone to the city on business, but would return in the evening. He also learned that Mrs. Mayburn was indisposed, and had not yet risen. At these tidings Grace ran over to see her old friend, hoping to do something for her comfort, and the young girl was almost shocked when she saw Mrs. Mayburn's pinched and pallid face upon her pillow. She seemed to have aged in a night.

"You are seriously ill!" she exclaimed, "and you did not let me know. Mr. Graham should not have left you."

"He did not know," said the old lady, sharply, for the slightest imputation against Graham touched her keenly. "He is kindness itself to me. He only heard this morning that I was sleeping, and he left word that I should not be disturbed. He also wrote a note explaining the business which had been neglected in his absence. Oh, I assure you, no one could be more considerate."

"Dear, loyal Mrs. Mayburn, you won't hear a word against those you love. I think Mr. Graham wonderfully considerate for a man. You know we should not expect much of men. I have to manage two, and it keeps me busy, but never so busy that I cannot do all in my power for my dear old friend. I'll get your breakfast myself, and bring it to you with my own hands, and force it upon you with the inexorable firmness of Sairy Gamp;" and she vanished to the kitchen.

The old lady turned her face to the wall and moaned, "Oh, if it could only have been! Why is it that we so often set our hearts on that which is denied? After a long, dull sleep of years it seemed as if my heart had wakened in my old age only to find how poor and lonely I am. Alford cannot stay with me—I could not expect it—neither can Grace; and so I must go on alone to the end. I'm punished, punished that years ago I did not make some one love me; but I was self-sufficient then."

Her regret was deepened when Grace returned with a dainty breakfast, and waited on her with a daughter's gentleness and tenderness, making her smile in spite of herself at her funny speeches, and beguiling her into enjoyment of the present moment with a witchery that none could resist.

Presently Mrs. May burn sighed, "It's a fearfully hot day for Alford to be in town."

"For a student," cried Grace, "he is the most indefatigable man I ever heard of. Warren told me that they sat out there under the apple-tree and poured out their hearts till dawn. Talk about schoolgirls babbling all night. My comment on Warren's folly was a dose of quinine. It's astonishing how these *savants*, these intellectual giants, need taking care of like babies. Woman's mission will never cease as long as there are learned men in the world. They will sit in a draught and discuss some obscure law concerning the moons of Jupiter; but when the law resulting in influenza manifests itself, then they learn our worth."

"Oh, dear!" groaned Mrs. Mayburn, "I didn't give Alford any quinine. You were more provident than I."

"How could you, when you were asleep?"

"Ah, true!" was the confused reply. "But then I should have been awake. I should have remembered that he did not come in when I did last night."

The faint color that stole into the face that had been so pale gave some surprise to the young girl. When once her mind was directed to a subject her intuitions were exceedingly keen.

From the time the secret of his regard for her had been, surprised from him, Graham had been a puzzle to her. Was he the cool, philosophical lover that he would have her think? Hilland was so frank in nature and so wholly under her influence that it was next to impossible for him not to share with her his every thought. She had, therefore, learned substantially the particulars of last night's interview, and she could not fully accept his belief that Graham's intellect alone had been captivated. She remembered how he had leaned against the tree for support; how pale he had been during the evening that followed; and how his hand had trembled in parting. She remembered his sudden flight to the mountains, his tireless energy there, as if driven on by an aching wound that permitted no rest. True, he had borne himself strongly and well in her presence the evening before; and he had given the friend who knew him so well the impression that it was merely an instance of the quiet weighing of the pros and cons, in which, after much deliberation, the pros had won. There had been much in his course, too, to give color to this view of the case; but her woman's instinct suggested that there was something more—something she did not know about; and she would have been less or more than woman had she not wished to learn the whole truth in a matter of this nature. She hoped that her lover was right, and that Graham's heart, in accordance with his development theory, was so inchoate as to be incapable of much suffering. She was not sure, however. There was something she surmised rather than detected. She felt it now in Mrs. Mayburn's presence, and caught a glimpse of it in the flush that was fading from her cheeks. Had the nephew given his aunt his confidence? or had she with her ripe experience and keen insight discovered the ultimate truth?

It was evident that while Mrs. Mayburn still loved her dearly, and probably was much disappointed that things had turned out as they had, she had given her loyalty to Graham, and would voluntarily neither do nor say anything that would compromise him. The slight flush suggested to Grace that the aunt had awaited the nephew's return in the early dawn, and that they had spoken freely together before separating; but she was the last one in the world to attempt to surprise a secret from another.

Still she wished to know the truth, for she felt a little guilty over her reticence in regard to her relations with Hilland. She, perhaps, had made too much of the luxury of keeping her secret until it could shine forth as the sun of her life; and Graham had been left in an ignorance that had not been fair to him. With a growing perception of his character, now that she had given thought to the subject, she saw that if he had learned to love her at all, it must have been in accordance with his nature, quietly, deliberately, even analytically. He was the last man to fall tumultuously in love. But when he had given it in his own way, could she be sure it was a cool, easily managed preference that he might at his leisure transfer to another who satisfied his reason and taste even more fully than herself? If this were true, her mind would be at rest; and she could like Hilland's friend heartily, as one of the most agreeable human oddities it had been her fortune to meet. She had serious misgivings, however, which Mrs. Mayburn's sudden indisposition, and the marks of suffering upon her face, did not tend to banish.

Whatever the truth might be, she felt that he had shown much thoughtfulness for her in his frankness with Hilland. He had rendered it unnecessary for her to conceal her knowledge of his regard. She need have no secrets, so far as he was concerned. The only question was as to the nature of this regard. If the impression he sought to give her lover was correct, neither of them had cause for much solicitude. If to save them pain he was seeking to hide a deeper wound, it was a noble deception, and dictated by a noble, unselfish nature. If the latter supposition should prove true, she felt that she would discover it without any direct effort. But she also felt that her lover should be left, if possible, under the impression his friend had sought to make, and that Graham should have the solace of thinking he had concealed his feelings from them both.

As the long evening shadows stretched eastward across the sloping lawn in front of the St. John cottage, the family gathered on the piazza to enjoy the welcome respite from the scorching heat of the day.

The old major looked weary and overcome. A July sun was the only fire before which he had ever flinched. Hilland still appeared a little heavy from his long hot afternoon nap, his amends for the vigils of the previous night. Grace was enchanting in her light clinging draperies, which made her lovely form tenfold more beautiful, because clothed in perfect taste. The heat had deepened the flush upon her cheeks, and brought a soft languor into her eyes, and as she stood under an arch of the American woodbine, that mantled the supports of the piazza roof, she might easily have fulfilled an artist's dream of summer. Hilland's eyes kindled as he looked upon her, as she stood with averted face, conscious meanwhile of his admiration, and exulting in it. What sweeter incense is ever offered to a woman?

"Grace," he whispered, "you would create a pulse in a marble statue to-night. You never looked more lovely."

"There is a glamour on your eyes, Warren," she replied; and yet the quick flash of joy that came into her face proved the power of his words, which still had all the exquisite charm of novelty.

"It's the glamour that will last while I do," he responded, earnestly. "Are not this scene and hour perfect? and you are the gem of it all. I don't see how a man could ask or wish for more than I have to-night, except that it might last forever." A shadow passed over his face, and he added, presently, "To think that after a few weeks I must return to those blasted mines! One thing is settled, however. I shall close out my interests there as speedily as possible; and were it not for my obligations to others, I'd never go near them again. I have money enough twice over, and am a fool to miss one hour with you."

"You will be all the happier, Warren, if you close up your interests in the West in a manly, business-like way. I always wish to be as proud of you as I am now. What's more, I don't believe in idle men, no matter how rich they are. I should be worried at once if you had nothing to do but sit around and make fine speeches. You'd soon weary of the sugar-plum business, and so should I. I have read somewhere that the true way to keep a man a lover is to give him plenty of work."

"Will you choose my work for me?"

"No; anything you like, so it is not speculation."

"I think I'll come and be your father's gardener."

"If you do," she replied, with a decisive little nod, "you will have to rake and hoe so many hours a day before you can have any dinner."

"But you, fair Eve, would bring your fancy-work, and sit with me in the shade."

"The idea of a gardener sitting in the shade, with weeds growing on every side."

"But you would, my Eve."

"Possibly, after I had seen that you had earned your bread by the 'perspiration of your brow,' as a very nice maiden lady, a neighbor of ours, always phrases it."

"That shall be my calling as soon as I can get East again. Major, I apply for the situation of gardener as soon as I can sell out my interests in the mines."

"I have nothing to do with it," was the reply. "Grace commands this post, and while here you are under her orders."

"And you'll find out, too, what a martinet I am," she added. "There's no telling how often I'll put you under arrest and mount guard over you myself. So!"

"What numberless breaches of discipline there will be!"

Lovers' converse consists largely in tone and glance, and these cannot be written; and were this possible, it could have but the slenderest interest to the reader.

After a transient pause Hilland remarked: "Think of poor Graham in the fiery furnace of New York to-day. I can imagine what a wilted and dilapidated-looking specimen he will be if he escapes alive—By Jove, there he is!" and the subject of his speech came as briskly up the walk as if the thermometer had been in the seventies instead of the nineties. His dress was quiet and elegant, and his form erect and step elastic.

As he approached the piazza and doffed his hat, Hilland cried: "Graham, you are the coolest fellow I ever saw. I was just commiserating you, and expecting you to look like a cabbage—no, rose-leaf that had been out in the sun; and you appear just as if you had stepped from a refrigerator."

"All a matter of temperament and will, my dear fellow. I decided I would not be hot to-day; and I've been very comfortable."

"Why did you not decide not to be cold last night?"

"I was so occupied with your interminable yarns that I forgot to think about it. Miss Grace, for your sake and on this evening, I might wish that there was a coolness between us, but from your kind greeting I see there is not. Good-evening, major; I have brought with me a slight proof that I do not forget my friends;" and he handed him a large package of newspapers, several of them being finely illustrated foreign prints.

"I promote you on the spot," cried the delighted veteran. "I felt that fate owed me some amends for this long, horrid day. My paper did not come this morning, and I had too much regard for the lives of my household to send any one up the hot streets after one."

"Oh, papa!" cried Grace, "forgive me that I did not discover the fact. I'm sure I saw you reading a paper."

"It was an old one. I read it through again, advertisements and all. Oh, I know you. You'd have turned out the whole garrison at twelve M., had you found it out."

Graham dropped carelessly into an easy-chair, and they all noted the pleasure with which the old gentleman adjusted his glasses, and scanned the pictures of the world's current history. Like many whose sight is failing, and to whom the tastes and memories of childhood are returning, the poor old man found increasing delight in a picture which suggested a great deal, and aided him to imagine more; and he would often beguile his tedium by the hour with the illustrated journals.

"Mr. Graham," said Grace, after a pause in their talk, "have you seen your aunt since your return?"

"No," he replied, turning hastily toward her.

"She is not very well; I've been to see her twice."

He gave her a momentary but searching glance, rose instantly, and said: "Please excuse me, then. I feel guilty that I have delayed a moment, but this piazza was so inviting!" and he hastened away.

"Does he look and act like a man who 'hid a secret sorrow'?" whispered Hilland, confidently. "I never saw him appear so well before."

Grace smiled, but kept her thoughts to herself. To her also Graham had never appeared so well. There was decision in his step and slightest movement. The old easy saunter of leisure was gone; the old half-dreamy and slightly cynical eyes of the student showed a purpose which was neither slight nor indefinite; and that brief, searching glance—what else could it be than a query as to the confidences his aunt may have bestowed during the day? Moreover, why did he avoid looking at her unless there was distinct occasion for his glance?

She would have known too well had she heard poor Graham mutter: "My will must be made of Bessemer steel if I can see her often as she looked to-night and live."

In the evening Hilland walked over to call on his friend and make inquiries. Through the parlor windows he saw Graham reading to his aunt, who reclined on a lounge; and he stole away again without disturbing them.

The next few days passed uneventfully away, and Graham's armor was almost proof against even the penetration of Grace. He did not assume any mask of gayety. He seemed to be merely his old self, with a subtle difference, and a very unobtrusive air of decision in all his movements. He was with his friend a great deal; and she heard them talking over their old life with much apparent zest. He was as good company for the major as ever, and when a whist played so good a game as to show that he was giving it careful attention. There was a gentleness toward his aunt that rather belied his character of stoic philosopher. Indeed, he seemed to have dropped this phase also, and was simply a well-bred man of the world, avoiding reference to himself, and his past or present views, as far as possible.

To a question of Hilland's one day he replied: "No; I shall not go back to my studies at present. As I told you the other night, my excursion into the world has shown me the advantage of studying it more fully. While I shall never be a Croesus like yourself, I am modestly independent; and I mean to see the world we live in, and then shall know better what I am studying about."

When Hilland told Grace of this purpose, she felt it was in keeping with all the rest. It might mean what was on the surface; it might mean more. It might be a part of the possible impulse that had driven him into the Vermont woods, or the natural and rational step he would have taken had he never seen her. At any rate, she felt that he was daily growing more remote, and that by a nice gradation of effort he was consciously withdrawing himself. And yet she could scarcely dwell on a single word or act, and say: "This proves it." His manner toward her was most cordial. When they conversed he looked at her steadily and directly, and would respond in kind to her mirthful words and Hilland's broad raillery; but she never detected one of the furtive, lingering glances that she now remembered with compunction were once frequent. It was quite proper that this should be so, but it was unnatural. If hitherto she had only pleased his taste and satisfied his reason, it would be a safe and harmless pastime for him to linger near her still in thought and reality. If he was struggling with a passion that had struck its root deep, then there was good reason for that steady withdrawal from her society which he managed so naturally that no one observed it but herself. Hilland had no misgivings, and she suggested none; but whenever she was in the presence of Graham or Mrs. Mayburn, although their courtesy and kind manner were unexceptionable, she felt there was "something in the air."

CHAPTER XV
"I WISH HE HAD KNOWN"

The heat continued so oppressive that the major gave signs of prostration, and Grace decided to take him to his old haunt by the seashore. The seclusion of their cottage was, of course, more agreeable to Hilland and herself under the circumstances; but Grace never hesitated when her father was concerned. Shortly after the decision was reached, Hilland met his friend, and promptly urged that he and Mrs. Mayburn should accompany them.

"Certainly," was the quiet reply, "if my aunt wishes to go."

But for some cause, if not for the reasons given, the old lady was inexorable that evening, even though the major with much gallantry urged her compliance. She did not like the seashore. It did not agree with her; and, what was worse, she detested hotels. She was better in her own quiet nook, etc. Alford might go, if he chose.

But Graham when appealed to said it was both his duty and his pleasure to remain with his aunt, especially as he was going abroad as soon as he could arrange his affairs. "Don't put on that injured air," he added, laughingly, to Hilland. "As if you needed me at present! You two are sufficient for yourselves; and why should I tramp after you like the multitude I should be?

"What do you know about our being sufficient for our-selves, I'd like to ask?" was the bantering response.

"I have the best authority for saying what I do—written authority, and that of a sage, too. Here it is, heavily under-scored by a hand that I imagine is as heavy as your own. Ah! Miss Grace's conscious looks prove that I am right," he added, as he laid the open volume of Emerson, which he had returned, before her. "I remember reading that paragraph the first evening I came to my aunt's house; and I thought it a very curious statement. It made me feel as if I were a sort of polyp or mollusk, instead of a man."

"Let me see the book," cried Hilland. "Oh, yes," he continued, laughing; "I remember it all well—the hopes, the misgivings with which I sent the volume eastward on its mission—the hopes and fears that rose when the book was acknowledged with no chidings or coldness, and also with no allusions to the marked passage—the endless surmises as to what this gentle reader would think of the sentiments within these black lines. Ha! ha! Graham. No doubt but this is Sanscrit; and all the professors of all the universities could not interpret it to you."

"That's what I said in substance on the evening referred to—that Emerson never learned this at a university. I confess that it's an experience that is and ever will be beyond me. But it's surely good authority for remaining here with my aunt, who needs me more than you do."

"How is it, then, Mr. Graham, that you can leave your aunt for months of travel?" Grace asked.

"Why, Grace," spoke up Mrs. Mayburn, quickly, "you cannot expect Alford to transform himself into an old lady's life-long attendant. He will enjoy his travel and come back to me."

The young girl made no answer, but thought: "Their defensive alliance is a strong one."

"Besides," continued the old lady, after a moment, "I think it's very kind of him to remain with me, instead of going to the beach for his own pleasure and the marring of yours."

"Now, that's putting it much too strong," cried Hilland. "Graham never marred our pleasure."

"And I hope he never will," was the low, earnest response. To Grace's ear it sounded more like a vow or the expression of a controlling purpose than like a mere friendly remark.

The next day the St. John cottage was alive with the bustle of preparation for departure. Graham made no officious offers of assistance, which, of course, would be futile, but quietly devoted himself to the major. Whenever Grace appeared from the upper regions, she found her father amused or interested, and she smiled her gratitude. In the evening she found a chance to say in a low aside: "Mr. Graham, you are keeping your word to be my friend. If the sea-breezes prove as beneficial to papa as your society to-day, I shall be glad indeed. You don't know how much you have aided me by entertaining him so kindly."

Both her tone and glance were very gentle as she spoke these words, and for a moment his silence and manner perplexed her. Then he replied lightly: "You are mistaken, Miss Grace. Your father has been entertaining me."

They were interrupted at this point, and Graham seemed to grow more remote than ever.

Hilland was parting from his friend with evident and sincere regret. He had made himself very useful in packing, strapping trunks, and in a general eagerness to save his betrothed from all fatigue; but whenever occasion offered he would sally forth upon Graham, who, with the major, followed the shade on the piazza. Some jocular speech usually accompanied his appearance, and he always received the same in kind with such liberal interest that he remarked to Grace more than once, "You are the only being in the world for whom I'd leave Graham during his brief stay in this land."

"Oh, return to him by all means," she had said archly upon one occasion. "We did very well alone last year before we were aware of your existence."

"YOU may not care," was his merry response, "but it is written in one of the oldest books of the world, 'It is not good for MAN to be alone.' Oh, Grace, what an infinite difference there is between love for a woman like you and the strongest friendship between man and man! Graham just suits me as a friend. After a separation of years I find him just the same even-pulsed, half-cynical, yet genial good fellow he always was. It's hard to get within his shell; but when you do, you find the kernel sweet and sound to the core, even if it is rather dry. From the time we struck hands as boys there has never been an unpleasant jar in our relations. We supplement each other marvellously; but how infinitely more and beyond all this is your love! How it absorbs and swallows up every other consideration, so that one hour with you is more to me than an age with all the men of wit and wisdom that ever lived! No; I'm not a false friend when I say that I am more than content to go and remain with you; and if Graham had a hundredth part as much heart as brains he would understand me. Indeed, his very intellect serves in the place of a heart after a fashion; for he took Emerson on trust so intelligently as to comprehend that I should not be inconsolable."

"Mr. Graham puzzles me," Grace had remarked, as she absently inspected the buttons on one of her father's vests. "I never met just such a man before."

"And probably never will again. He has been isolated and peculiar from childhood. I know him well, and he has changed but little in essentials since I left him over two years ago."

"I wish I had your complacent belief about him," was her mental conclusion. "I sometimes think you are right, and again I feel as if some one in almost mortal pain is near me, and that I am to blame in part."

Whist was dispensed with the last night they were together, for the evening was close, and all were weary. Grace thought Graham looked positively haggard; but, whether by design or chance, he kept in the shadows of the piazza most of the time. Still she had to admit that he was the life of the party. Mrs. Mayburn was apparently so overcome by the heat as to be comparatively silent; and Hilland openly admitted that the July day and his exertions had used him up. Therefore the last gathering at the St. Johns' cottage came to a speedy end; and Graham not only said good-night, but also good-by; for, as he explained, business called him to town early the following morning. He parted fraternally with Hilland, giving a promise to spend a day with him before he sailed for Europe. Then he broke away, giving Grace as a farewell only a strong, warm pressure of the hand, and hastened after his aunt, who had walked on slowly before. The major, after many friendly expressions, had retired quite early in the evening.

Grace saw the dark outline of Graham's form disappear like a shadow, and every day thereafter he grew more shadowy to her. To a degree she did not imagine possible he had baffled her scrutiny and left her in doubt. Either he had quietly and philosophically accepted the situation, or he wished her to think so. In either case there was nothing to be done. Once away with father and lover she had HER world with her; and life grew richer and more full of content every day.

Lassitude and almost desperate weariness were in Graham's step as he came up the path the following evening, for there was no further reason to keep up the part he was acting. When he greeted his aunt he tried to appear cheerful, but she said gently, "Put on no mask before me, Alford. Make no further effort. You have baffled even Grace, and thoroughly satisfied your friend that all is well. Let the strain cease now; and let my home be a refuge while you remain. Your wound is one that time only can heal. You have made an heroic struggle not to mar their happiness, and I am proud of you for it. But don't try to deceive me or put the spur any longer to your jaded spirit. Reaction into new hopes and a new life will come all the sooner if you give way for the present to your mood."

The wise old woman would have been right in dealing with most natures. But Graham would not give way to his bitter disappointment, and for him there would come no reaction. He quietly read to her the evening papers, and after she had retired stole out and gazed for hours on the St. John cottage, the casket that had contained for him the jewel of the world. Then, compressing his lips, he returned to his room with the final decision, "I will be her friend for life; but it must be an absent friend. I think my will is strong; but half the width of the world must be between us."

For the next two weeks he sought to prepare his aunt for a long separation. He did not hide his feeling; indeed, he spoke of it with a calmness which, while it surprised, also convinced her that it would dominate his life. She was made to see clearly the necessity of his departure, if he would keep his promise to live and do his best. He promised to be a faithful and voluminous correspondent, and she knew she would live upon his letters. After the lapse of three weeks he had arranged his affairs so as to permit a long absence, and then parted with his aunt as if he had been her son.

"Alford," she said, "all that I have is yours, as you will find in my will."

"Dear aunty," was his reply, "in giving me your love you have given me all that I crave. I have more than enough for my wants. Forgive me that I cannot stay; but I cannot. I have learned the limit of my power of endurance. I know that I cannot escape myself or my memories, but new scenes divert my thoughts. Here, I believe, I should go mad, or else do something wild and desperate. Forgive me, and do not judge me harshly because I leave you. Perhaps some day this fever of unrest will pass away, When it does, rest assured you shall see me again."

He then went to the seaside resort where Hilland with the major and his daughter was sojourning, and never had they seen a man who appeared so far removed from the lackadaisical, disconsolate lover. His dress was elegant, although very quiet, his step firm and prompt, and his manner that of a man who is thoroughly master of the situation. The major was ill from an indiscretion at the table during the preceding day, and Grace could not leave him very long. He sent to his favorite companion and antagonist at whist many feeling messages and sincere good wishes, and they lost nothing in hearty warmth as they came from Grace's lips; and for some reason, which she could scarcely explain to herself, tears came into her eyes as she gave him her hand in parting.

He had been laughing and jesting vivaciously a moment before; but as he looked into her face, so full of kindly feeling which she could not wholly repress, his own seemed to grow rigid, and the hand she held was so cold and tense as to remind her of a steel gauntlet. In the supreme effort of his spiritual nature he belied his creed. His physical being was powerless in the grasp of the dominant soul. No martyr at the stake ever suffered more than he at that moment, but he merely said with quiet emphasis, "Good-by, Grace St. John. I shall not forget my promise, nor can there come a day on which I shall not wish you all the happiness you deserve."

He then bowed gravely and turned away. She hastily sought her room, and then burst into an irrepressible passion of tears. "It's all in vain," she sobbed. "I felt it. I know it. He suffers as I should suffer, and his iron will cannot disguise the truth."

The friends strolled away up the beach for their final talk, and at length Hilland came back in a somewhat pensive but very complacent mood. Grace looked at him anxiously, but his first sentences reassured her.

"Well," he exclaimed, "if Graham is odd, he's certainly the best and most sensible fellow that ever lived, and the most steadfast of friends. Here we've been separated for years, and yet, for any change in his attitude toward me, we might have parted overnight at the university. He was as badly smitten by the girl I love as a man of his temperament could be; but on learning the facts he recognizes the situation with a quiet good taste which leaves nothing to be desired. He made it perfectly clear to me that travel for the present was only a broader and more effective way of continuing his career as a student, and that when tired of wandering he can go back to books with a larger knowledge of how to use them. One thing he has made clearer still—if we do not see each other for ten years, he will come back the same stanch friend."

"I think you are right, Warren. He certainly has won my entire respect."

"I'm glad he didn't win anything more, sweetheart."

"That ceased to be possible long before he came, but I—I wish he had known it," was her hesitating response, as she pushed Hilland's hair back from his heated brow.

"Nonsense, you romantic little woman! You imagine he has gone away with a great gaping wound in his heart. Graham is the last man in the world for that kind of thing, and no one would smile more broadly than he, did he know of your gentle solicitude."

Grace was silent a moment, and then stole away to her father's side.

The next tidings they had of Graham was a letter dated among the fiords and mountains of Norway.

At times no snowy peak in that wintry land seemed more shadowy or remote to Grace than he. Again, while passing to and fro between their own and Mrs. Mayburn's cottage in the autumn, she would see him, with almost the vividness of life, deathly pale as when he leaned against the apple-tree at their well-remembered interview.

CHAPTER XVI
THE CLOUD IN THE SOUTH

The summer heat passed speedily, and the major returned to his cottage invigorated and very complacent over his daughter's prospects. Hilland had proved himself as manly and devoted a lover as he had been an ardent and eventually patient suitor. The bubbling, overflowing stream of happiness in Grace's heart deepened into a wide current, bearing her on from day to day toward a future that promised to satisfy every longing of her woman's heart. There was, of course, natural regret that Hilland was constrained to spend several months in the West in order to settle up his large interests with a due regard to the rights of others, and yet she would not have it otherwise. She was happy in his almost unbounded devotion; she would have been less happy had this devotion kept him at her side when his man's part in the world required his presence elsewhere. Therefore she bade him farewell with a heart that was not so very heavy, even though tears gemmed her eyes.

The autumn and early winter months lapsed quietly and uneventfully, and the inmates of the two cottages ever remembered that period of their lives as the era of letters—Graham's from over the sea abounding in vivid descriptions of scenes that to Mrs. Mayburn's interested eyes were like glimpses of another world, and Hilland's, even more voluminous and infinitely more interesting to one fair reader, to whom they were sacred except as she doled out occasional paragraphs which related sufficiently to the general order of things to be read aloud.

Graham's letters, however, had a deep interest to Grace, who sought to trace in them the working of his mind in regard to herself. She found it difficult, for his letters were exceedingly impersonal, while the men and things he saw often stood out upon his page with vivid realism. It seemed to her that he grew more shadowy, and that he was wandering rather than travelling, drifting whithersoever his fancy or circumstances pointed the way. It was certain he avoided the beaten paths, and freely indulged his taste for regions remote and comparatively unknown. His excuse was that life was far more picturesque and unhackneyed, with a chance for an occasional adventure, in lands where one was not jostled by people with guide-books—that he saw men and women as the influences of the ages had been fashioning them, and not conventionalized by the mode of the hour. "Chief of all," he concluded, jestingly, "I can send to my dear aunt descriptions of people and scenery that she will not find better set forth in half a dozen books within her reach."

After a month in Norway, he crossed the mountains into Sweden, and as winter approached drifted rapidly to the south and east. One of his letters was dated at the entrance of the Himalayas in India, and expressed his purpose to explore one of the grandest mountain systems in the world.

Mrs. Mayburn gloated over the letters, and Grace laughingly told her she had learned more about geography since her nephew had gone abroad than in all her life before. The major, also, was deeply interested in them, especially as Graham took pains in his behalf to give some account of the military organizations with which he came in contact. They had little of the nature of a scientific report. The soldier, his life and weapons, were sketched with a free hand merely, and so became even to the ladies a picturesque figure rather than a military abstraction. From time to time a letter appeared in Mrs. Mayburn's favorite journal signed by the initials of the traveller; and these epistles she cut out and pasted most carefully in a book which Grace jestingly called her "family Bible."

But as time passed, Graham occupied less and less space in the thoughts of all except his aunt. The major's newspaper became more absorbing than ever, for the clouds gathering in the political skies threatened evils that seemed to him without remedy. Strongly Southern and conservative in feeling, he was deeply incensed at what he termed "Northern fanaticism." Only less hateful to him was a class in the South known in the parlance of the times as "fire-eaters."

All through the winter and spring of 1860 he had his "daily growl," as Grace termed it; and she assured him it was growing steadily deeper and louder. Yet it was evidently a source of so much comfort to him that she always smiled in secret over his invective—noting, also, that while he deplored much that was said and done by the leaders of the day, the prelude of the great drama interested him so deeply that he half forgot his infirmities. In fact, she had more trouble with Hilland, who had returned, and was urging an early date for their marriage. Her lover was an ardent Republican, and hated slavery with New England enthusiasm. The arrogance and blindness of the South had their counterpart at the North, and Hilland had not escaped the infection. He was much inclined to belittle the resources of the former section, to scoff at its threats, and to demand that the North should peremptorily and imperiously check all further aggressions of slavery. At first it required not a little tact on the part of Grace to preserve political harmony between father and lover; but the latter speedily recognized that the major's age and infirmities, together with his early associations, gave him almost unlimited privilege to think and say what he pleased. Hilland soon came to hear with good-natured nonchalance his Northern allies berated, and considered himself well repaid by one mirthful, grateful glance from Grace.

After all, what was any political squabble compared with the fact that Grace had promised to marry him in June? The settlement of the difference between the North and South was only a question of time, and that, too, in his belief, not far remote.

"Why should I worry about it?" he said to Grace. "When the North gets angry enough to put its foot down, all this bluster about State-rights, and these efforts to foist slavery on a people who are disgusted with it, will cease."

"Take care," she replied, archly. "I'm a Southern girl. Think what might happen if I put my foot down."

"Oh, when it comes to you," was his quick response, "I'm the Democratic party. I will get down on my knees at any time; I'll yield anything and stand everything."

"I hope you will be in just such a frame of mind ten years hence."

It was well that the future was hidden from her.

Hilland wrote to his friend, asking, indeed almost insisting, that he should return in time for the wedding. Graham did not come, and intimated that he was gathering materials which might result in a book. He sent a letter, however, addressed to them both, and full of a spirit of such loyal good-will that Hilland said it was like a brother's grip. "Well, well," he concluded, "if Graham has the book-making fever upon him, we shall have to give him up indefinitely."

Grace was at first inclined to take the same view, feeling that, even if he had been sorely wounded, his present life and the prospects it gave of authorship had gained so great a fascination that he would come back eventually with only a memory of what he had suffered. Her misgivings, however, returned when, on seeing the letter, Mrs. Mayburn's eyes became suddenly dimmed with tears. She turned away abruptly and seemed vexed with herself for having shown the emotion, but only said quietly, "I once thought Alford had no heart; but that letter was not written 'out of his head,' as we used to say when children."

She gave Grace no reason to complain of any lack of affectionate interest in her preparations; and when the wedding day came she assured the blushing girl that "no one had ever looked upon a lovelier bride."

Ever mindful of her father, Grace would take no wedding journey, although her old friend offered to come and care for him. She knew well how essential her voice and hand were to his comfort; and she would not permit him to entertain, even for a moment, the thought that in any sense he had lost her. So they merely returned to his favorite haunt by the sea, and Hilland was loyal to the only condition in their engagement—that she should be permitted to keep her promise to her dying mother, and never leave her father to the care of others, unless under circumstances entirely beyond her control.

Later in the season Mrs. Mayburn joined them at the beach, for she found her life at the cottage too lonely to be endured.

It was a summer of unalloyed happiness to Hilland and his wife, and the major promised to renew his youth in the warm sunlight of his prosperity. The exciting presidential canvass afforded abundant theme for the daily discussions in his favorite corner of the piazza, where, surrounded by some veteran cronies whom he had known in former years, he joined them in predictions and ominous head-shakings over the monstrous evils that would follow the election of Mr. Lincoln. Hilland, sitting in the background with Grace, would listen and stroke his tawny beard as he glanced humorously at his wife, who knew that he was working, quietly out of deference to his father-in-law, but most effectively, in the Republican campaign. Although Southern born she had the sense to grant to men full liberty of personal opinion—a quality that it would be well for many of her sisterhood to imitate. Indeed, she would have despised a man who had not sufficient force to think for himself; and she loved her husband all the more because in some of his views he differed radically with her father and herself.

Meantime the cloud gathering in the South grew darker and more portentous; and after the election of President Lincoln the lightning of hate and passion began to strike from it directly at the nation's life. The old major was both wrong and right in regard to the most prominent leaders of the day. Many whom he deemed the worst fanatics in the land were merely exponents of a public opinion that was rising like an irresistible tide from causes beyond human control—from the God-created conscience illumined by His own truth. In regard to the instigators of the Rebellion, he was right. Instead of representing their people, they deceived and misled them; and, with an astute understanding of the chivalrous, hasty Southern temper, they so wrought upon their pride of section by the false presentation of fancied and prospective wrongs, that loyalty to the old flag, which at heart they loved, was swept away by the madness which precedes destruction. Above all and directing all was the God of nations; and He had decreed that slavery, the gangrene in the body politic, must be cut out, even though it should be with the sword. The surgery was heroic, indeed; but as its result the slave, and especially the master and his posterity, will grow into a large, healthful, and prosperous life; and the evidences of such life are increasing daily.

At the time of which I am writing, however, the future was not dreamed of by the sagacious Lincoln even, or his cabinet, much less was it foreseen by the humbler characters of my story. Hilland after reading his daily journal would sit silent for a long time with contracted brow. The white heat of anger was slowly kindling in his heart and in that of the loyal North; and the cloud in the South began to throw its shadow over the hearth of the happy wife.

Although Hilland hated slavery it incensed him beyond measure that the South could be made to believe that the North would break through or infringe upon the constitutional safeguards thrown around the institution. At the same time he knew, and it seemed to him every intelligent man should understand, that if a sufficient majority should decide to forbid the extension of the slave system to new territory, that should end the question, or else the Constitution was not worth the paper on which it was written. "Law and order," was his motto; and "All changes and reforms under the sanction of law, and at the command of the majority," his political creed.

The major held the Southern view. "Slaves are property," he said; "and the government is bound to permit a man to take his property where he pleases, and protect him in all his rights." The point where the veteran drew the line was in disloyalty to the flag which he had sworn to defend, and for which he had become a cripple for life. As the Secession spirit became more rampant and open in South Carolina, the weight of his invective fell more heavily upon the leaders there than upon the hitherto more detested abolitionists.

When he read the address of Alexander H. Stephens, delivered to the same people on the following evening, wherein that remarkable man said, "My object is not to stir up strife, but to allay it; not to appeal to your passions, but to your reason. Shall the people of the South secede from the Union in consequence of the election of Mr. Lincoln? My countrymen, I tell you frankly, candidly, and earnestly, that I do not think they ought. In my judgment the election of no man, constitutionally chosen, is sufficient cause for any State to separate from the Union. It ought to stand by and aid still in maintaining the Constitution of the country. We are pledged to maintain the Constitution. Many of us are sworn to support it"—when the veteran came to these words, he sprang to his feet without a thought of his crutch, and cried in a tone with which he would order a charge, "There is the man who ought to be President. Read that speech."

Hilland did read it aloud, and then said thoughtfully, "Yes; if the leaders on both sides were of the stamp of Mr. Stephens and would stand firm all questions at issue could be settled amicably under the Constitution. But I fear the passion of the South, fired by the unscrupulous misrepresentations of a few ambitious men, will carry the Cotton States into such violent disloyalty that the North in its indignation will give them a lesson never to be forgotten."

"Well!" shouted the major, "if they ever fire on the old flag, I'll shoulder my crutch and march against them myself—I would, by heaven! though my own brother fired the gun." Grace's merry laugh rang out—for she never lost a chance to throw oil on the troubled waters—and she cried, "Warren, if this thing goes on, you and papa will stand shoulder to shoulder."

But the time for that had not yet come. Indeed, there would ever remain wide differences of opinion between the two men. The major believed that if Congress conceded promptly all that the slave power demanded, "the demagogues of the South would soon be without occupation;" while Hilland asserted that the whole thing originated in bluster to frighten the North into submission, and that the danger was that the unceasing inflammatory talk might so kindle the masses that they would believe the lies, daily iterated, and pass beyond the control of their leaders.

When at last South Carolina seceded, and it became evident that other States would follow, the major often said with bitter emphasis that the North would have to pay dearly for its sentiment in regard to the negro. In Hilland's case strong exultation became a growing element in his anger, for he believed that slavery was destined to receive heavier blows from the mad zeal of its friends than Northern abolitionists could have inflicted in a century.

"If the South casts aside constitutional protection," he reasoned, "she must take the consequences. After a certain point is passed, the North will make sharp, quick work with anything that interferes with her peace and prosperity."

"The work will be sharp enough, young man," replied the major testily; "but don't be sure about its being quick. If the South once gets to fighting, I know her people well enough to assure you that the Republican party can reach its ends only through seas of blood, if they are ever attained."

Hilland made no reply—he never contradicted the old gentleman—but he wrote Graham a rather strong letter intimating that it was time for Americans to come home.

Graham would not have come, however, had not Grace, who had just returned from Mrs. Mayburn's cottage, caused a postscript to be added, giving the information that his aunt was seriously ill, and that her physician thought it might be a long time before she recovered, even if life was spared.

This decided him at once; and as he thought he might never see his kind old friend again, he bitterly regretted that he had remained away so long. And yet he felt he could scarcely have done otherwise; for in bitter disappointment he found that his passion, so far from being conquered, had, by some uncontrollable law of his nature, simply grown with time and become interwoven with every fibre of his nature. Hitherto he had acted on the principle that he must and would conquer it; but now that duty called him to the presence of the one whose love and kindness formed an indisputable claim upon him, he began to reason that further absence was futile, that he might as well go back, and—as he promised his aunt—"do the best he could."

It must be admitted that Hilland's broad hint, that in the coming emergency Americans should be at home, had little weight with him. From natural bent he had ever been averse to politics. In accordance with his theory of evolution, he believed the negro was better off in his present condition than he could be in any other. He was the last man to cherish an enthusiasm for an inferior race Indeed, he would have much preferred it should die out altogether and make room for better material. The truth was that his prolonged residence abroad had made the questions of American politics exceedingly vague and inconsequential. He believed them to be ephemeral to the last degree—in the main, mere struggles of parties and partisans for power and spoils; and for their hopes, schemes, and stratagems to gain temporary success, he cared nothing.

He had not been an idler in his prolonged absence. In the first place, he had striven with the whole force of a powerful will to subdue a useless passion, and had striven in vain. He had not, however, yielded for a day to a dreamy melancholy, but, in accordance with his promise "to do his best," had been tireless in mental and physical activity. The tendency to wander somewhat aimlessly had ceased, and he had adopted the plan of studying modern life at the old centres of civilization and power.

Hilland's letter found him in Egypt, and only a few weeks had elapsed after its reception when, with deep anxiety, he rang the bell at his aunt's cottage door. He had not stopped to ask for letters in London, for he had learned that by pushing right on he could catch a fast outgoing steamer and save some days.

The servant who admitted him uttered a cry of joy; and a moment later his aunt rose feebly from the lounge in her sitting-room, and greeted him as her son.

CHAPTER XVII
PREPARATION

Graham learned with deep satisfaction that the dangerous symptoms of his aunt's illness had passed away, and that she was now well advanced in convalescence. They gave to each other an hour or two of unreserved confidence; and the old lady's eyes filled with tears more than once as she saw how vain had been her nephew's struggle. It was equally clear, however, that he had gained strength and a nobler manhood in the effort; and so she told him.

"If supper is ready," he replied, "I'll prove to you that I am in very fair condition."

An hour later he left her, cheerful and comparatively happy, for the St. Johns' cottage. From the piazza he saw through the lighted windows a home-scene that he had once dreamed might bless his life. Hilland, evidently, was reading the evening paper aloud, and his back was toward his friend. The major was nervously drumming on the table with his fingers, and contracting his frosty eyebrows, as if perturbed by the news. But it was on the young wife that Graham's eyes dwelt longest. She sat with some sewing on the further side of the open fire, and her face was toward him. Had she changed? Yes; but for the better. The slight matronly air and fuller form that had come with wifehood became her better than even her girlish grace. As she glanced up to her husband from time to time, Graham saw serene loving trust and content.

"It is all well with them," he thought; "and so may it ever be."

A servant who was passing out opened the door, and thus he was admitted without being announced, for he cautioned the maid to say nothing. Then pushing open the parlor door, which was ajar, he entered, and said quietly: "I've come over for a game of whist."

But the quietness of his greeting was not reciprocated. All rose hastily, even to the major, and stared at him. Then Hilland half crushed the proffered hand, and the major grasped the other, and there came a fire of exclamations and questions that for a moment or two left no space for answer.

Grace cried: "Come, Warren, give Mr. Graham a chance to get his breath and shake hands with me. I propose to count for something in this welcome."

"Give him a kiss, sweetheart," said her delighted husband.

Grace hesitated, and a slight flush suffused her face. Graham quickly bent over her hand, which he now held, and kissed it, saying: "I've been among the Orientals so long that I've learned some of their customs of paying homage. I know that you are queen here as of old, and that Hilland is by this time the meekest of men."

"Indeed, was I so imperious in old times?" she asked, as he threw himself, quite at home, into one of the easy-chairs.

"You are of those who are born to rule. You have a way of your own, however, which some other rulers might imitate to advantage."

"Well, my first command is that you give an account of yourself. So extensive a traveller never sat down at our quiet fireside before. Open your budget of wonders. Only remember we have some slight acquaintance with Baron Munchausen."

"The real wonders of the world are more wonderful than his inventions. Beyond that I hastened home by the shortest possible route after receiving Hilland's letter, I have little to say."

"I thought my letter would stir you up."

"In sincerity, I must say it did not. The postscript did, however."

"Then, in a certain sense, it was I who brought you home, Mr. Graham," said Grace. "I had just returned from a call on Mrs. Mayburn, and I made Warren open the letter and add the postscript. I assure you we were exceedingly anxious about her for weeks."

"And from what she has told me I am almost convinced that she owes her life more to you than to her physician. Drugs go but a little way, especially at her time of life; but the delicacies and nourishing food you saw she was provided with so regularly rallied her strength. Yes; it was your postscript that led to my immediate return, and not Hilland's political blast."

"Why, Graham! Don't you realize what's going on here?"

"Not very seriously."

"You may have to fight, old fellow."

"I've no objections after I have decided which side to take."

"Good heavens, Graham! you will be mobbed if you talk that way here in New England. This comes of a man's living abroad so much that he loses all love for his native land."

"Squabbling politicians are not one's native land. I am not a hater of slavery as you are; and if it produces types of men and women like that Southern lady of whom I told you, it must be an excellent institution."

"Oh, yes," cried Hilland laughing. "By the way, Grace, my cool, cynical friend was once madly in love—at first sight, too—and with a lady old enough to be his mother. I never heard a woman's character sketched more tenderly; and his climax was that your mother must have closely resembled her."

"Mr. Graham is right," said the major impressively. "The South produces the finest women in the world; and when the North comes to meet its men, as I fear it must, it will find they are their mothers' sons."

"Poor Warren!" cried Grace; "here are all three of us against you—all pro-slavery and Southern in our sympathies."

"I admit at once that the South has produced THE finest woman in the world," said Hilland, taking his wife's hand. "But I must add that many of her present productions are not at all to my taste; nor will they be to yours, Graham, after you have been here long enough to understand what is going on—that is, if anything at home can enlist your interest."

"I assure you I am deeply interested. It's exhilarating to breathe American air now, especially so after just coming from regions where everything has been dead for centuries; for the people living there now are scarcely alive. Of course I obtained from the papers in Egypt very vague ideas of what was going on; and after receiving your letter my mind was too preoccupied with my aunt's illness to dwell on much besides. If the flag which gave me protection abroad, and under which I was born, is assailed, I shall certainly fight for it, even though I may not be in sympathy with the causes which led to the quarrel. What I said about being undecided as to which side I would take was a half-jocular way of admitting that I need a great deal of information; and between you and the major I am in a fair way to hear both sides. I cannot believe, however, that a civil war will break out in this land of all others. The very idea seems preposterous, and I am not beyond the belief that the whole thing is political excitement. I have learned this much, that the old teachings of Calhoun have borne their legitimate fruit, and that the Cotton States by some hocus-pocus legislation declare themselves out of the Union. But then the rational, and to my mind inevitable, course will be, that the representative men of both sides will realize at last to what straits their partisanship is bringing them, and so come together and adjust their real or fancied grievances. Meanwhile, the excitement will die out; and a good many will have a dim consciousness that they have made fools of themselves, and go quietly about their own business the rest of their days."

"Graham, you don't know anything about the true state of affairs," said Hilland; and before the evening was over he proved his words true to his friend, who listened attentively to the history of his native land for the past few months. In conclusion, Hilland said, "At one time—not very long ago, either—I held your opinion that it was the old game of bluster and threatening on the part of Southern politicians. But they are going too far; they have already gone too far. In seizing the United States forts and other property, they have practically waged war against the government. My opinions have changed from week to week under the stern logic of events, and I now believe that the leading spirits in the South mean actual and final separation. I've no doubt that they hope to effect their purpose peaceably, and that the whole thing will soon be a matter of diplomacy between two distinct governments. But they are preparing for war, and they will have it, too, to their hearts' content. President Buchanan is a muff. He sits and wrings his hands like an old woman, and declares he can do nothing. But the new administration will soon be in power, and it will voice the demand of the North that this nonsense be stopped; and if no heed is given, it will stop it briefly, decisively."

"My son Warren," said the major, "you told your friend some time since that he knew nothing about this affair. You must permit me to say the same to you. I feat that both sides have gone too far, much too far; and what the end will be, and when it will come, God only knows."

Before many weeks passed Graham shared the same view.

Events crowded upon each other; pages of history were made daily, and often hourly. In every home, as well as in the cottages wherein dwelt the people of my story, the daily journals were snatched and read at the earliest possible moment. Many were stern and exultant like Hilland; more were dazed and perplexed, feeling that something ought to be done to stem the torrent, and at the same time were astonished and troubled to find that perhaps a next-door neighbor sympathized with the rebellion and predicted its entire success. The social atmosphere was thick with doubt, heavy with despondency, and often lurid with anger.

Graham became a curious study to both Grace and his aunt; and sometimes his friend and the major were inclined to get out of patience with him. He grew reticent on the subject concerning which all were talking, but he read with avidity, not only the history of the day, but of the past as it related to the questions at issue.

One of his earliest acts had been the purchase of a horse noted in town as being so powerful, spirited, and even vicious, that few dared to drive or ride him. He had finally brought his ill-repute to a climax by running away, wrecking the carriage, and breaking his owner's ribs. He had since stood fuming in idleness; and when Graham wished him brought to the unused stable behind his aunt's cottage, no one would risk the danger. Then the young man went after the horse himself.

"I've only one man in my employ who dares clean and take care of him," remarked the proprietor of the livery stable where he was kept; "and he declares that he won't risk his life much longer unless the brute is used and tamed down somewhat. There's your property and I'd like to have it removed as soon as possible."

"I'll remove it at once," said Graham, quietly; and paying no heed to the crowd that began to gather when it was bruited that "Firebrand"—for such was the horse's name—was to be brought out, he took a bridle and went into the stall, first speaking gently, then stroking the animal with an assured touch. The horse permitted himself to be bridled and led out; but there was an evil fire in his eye, and he gave more than one ominous snort of defiance. The proprietor, smitten by a sudden compunction, rushed forward and cried, "Look here, sir; you are taking your life in your hand."

"I say, Graham," cried Hilland's voice, "what scrape are you in, that you have drawn such a crowd?"

"No scrape at all," said Graham, looking around and recognizing his friend and Grace mounted and passing homeward from their ride. "I've had the presumption to think that you would permit me to join you occasionally, and so have bought a good horse. Isn't he a beauty?"

"What, Firebrand?"

"That's his present name. I shall re-christen him."

"Oh, come, Graham! if you don't value your neck, others do. You've been imposed upon."

"I've warned him—" began the keeper of the livery stable; but here the horse reared and tried to break from Graham's grasp.

"Clear the way," the young man cried; and as the brute came down he seized his mane and vaulted upon his bare back. The action was so sudden and evidently so unexpected that the horse stood still and quivered for a moment, then gave a few prodigious bounds; but the rider kept his seat so perfectly that he seemed a part of the horse. The beast next began to rear, and at one time it seemed as if he would fall over backward, and his master sprang lightly to the ground. But the horse was scarcely on all fours before Graham was on his back again. The brute had the bit in his teeth, and paid no attention to it. Graham now drew a flexible rawhide from his pocket, and gave his steed a severe cut across the flanks. The result was another bound into the air, such as experts present declared was never seen before; and then the enraged animal sped away at a tremendous pace There was a shout of applause; and Hilland and Grace galloped after, but soon lost sight of Graham. Two hours later he trotted quietly up to their door, his coal-black horse white with foam, quivering in every muscle, but perfectly subdued.

"I merely wished to assure you that my neck was safe, and that I have a horse fit to go to the war that you predict so confidently," he said to Hilland, who with Grace rushed out on the piazza.

"I say, Graham, where did you learn to ride?" asked his friend.

"Oh, the horses were nobler animals than the men in some of the lands where I have been, and I studied them. This creature will be a faithful friend in a short time. You have no idea how much intelligence such a horse as this has if he is treated intelligently. I don't believe he has ever known genuine kindness. I'll guarantee that I can fire a pistol between his ears within two weeks, and that he won't flinch. Good-by. I shall be my own hostler for a short time, and must work an hour over him after the run he's had."

"Well," exclaimed Hilland, as he passed into the house with his wife, "I admit that Graham has changed. He was always great on tramps, but I never knew him to care for a horse before."

Grace felt that he had changed ever since he had leaned for support against the apple-tree by which he was now passing down the frozen walk, but she only said, "I never saw such superb horsemanship."

She had not thought Graham exactly fine-looking in former days; but in his absence his slight figure had filled out, and his every movement was instinct with reserved force. The experiences through which he had passed removed him, as she was conscious, beyond the sphere of ordinary men.

Even his marked reticence about himself and his views was stimulating to the imagination. Whether he had conquered his old regard for her she could not tell. He certainly no longer avoided her, and he treated her with the frank courtesy he would naturally extend to his friend's wife. But he spent far more time with his aunt than with them; and it became daily more and more evident that he accepted the major's view, and was preparing for what he believed would be a long and doubtful conflict. Since it must come, he welcomed the inevitable, for in his condition of mind it was essential that he should be intensely occupied. Although his aunt had to admit that he was a little peculiar, his manner was simple and quiet; and when he joined his friends on their drives or at their fireside, he was usually as genial as they could desire, and his tenderness for his aunt daily increased the respect which he had already won from Grace.

CHAPTER XVIII
THE CALL TO ARMS

On the 4th of March, 1861, was inaugurated as President the best friend the South ever had. He would never have deceived or misled her. In all the bloody struggle that followed, although hated, scoffed at, and maligned as the vilest monster of earth, he never by word or act manifested a vindictive spirit toward her. Firm and sagacious, Lincoln would have protected the South in her constitutional rights, though every man at the North had become an abolitionist. Slavery, however, had long been doomed, like other relics of barbarism, by the spirit of the age; and his wisdom and that of men like him, with the logic of events and the irresistible force of the world's opinion, would have found some peaceful, gradual remedy for an evil which wrought even more injury to the master than to the bondman. In his inaugural address he repeated that he had "no purpose, directly or indirectly, to interfere with slavery in the States where it existed."

An unanswerable argument against disunion, and an earnest appeal to reason and lawful remedy, he followed by a most impressive declaration of peace and good-will: "In your hands, my dissatisfied fellow-countrymen, and not mine, is the momentous issue of civil war. The government will not assail you. You can have no conflict without being yourselves the aggressors. You have no oath registered in heaven to destroy the government; while I shall have the most solemn one to preserve, protect, and defend it."

These were noble words, and to all minds not confused by the turmoil, passion, and prejudices of the hour, they presented the issue squarely. If the leaders of the South desired peaceful negotiation, the way was opened, the opportunity offered; if they were resolved on the destruction of the Union, Lincoln's oath meant countless men and countless treasure to defend it.

Men almost held their breath in suspense. The air became thick with rumors of compromise and peace. Even late in March, Mr. Seward, the President's chief adviser, "believed and argued that the revolution throughout the South had spent its force and was on the wane; and that the evacuation of Sumter and the manifestation of kindness and confidence to the Rebel and Border States would undermine the conspiracy, strengthen the Union sentiment and Union majorities, and restore allegiance and healthy political action without resort to civil war."

To Graham, who, in common with millions in their homes, was studying the problem, this course seemed so rational and so advantageous to all concerned, that he accepted it as the outline of the future. The old major shook his head and growled, "You don't know the South; it's too late; their blood is up."

Hilland added exultantly, "Neither do you know the North, Graham. There will come a tidal wave soon that will carry Mr. Seward and the hesitating President to the boundaries of Mexico."

The President was not hesitating, in the weak sense of the word. Equally removed from Mr. Buchanan's timidity and Mr. Seward's optimistic confidence, he was feeling his way, gathering the reins into his hands, and seeking to comprehend an issue then too obscure and vast for mortal mind to grasp. What is plain to-day was not plain then.

It speedily became evident, however, that all talk of compromise on the part of the Southern leaders was deceptive—that they were relentlessly pursuing the course marked out from the first, hoping, undoubtedly, that the government would be paralyzed by their allies at the North, and that their purposes would be effected by negotiation and foreign intervention.

And so the skies grew darker and the political and social atmosphere so thick with doubt and discordant counsels that the horizon narrowed about even those on the mountain-top of power. All breathed heavily and felt the oppression that precedes some convulsion of nature

At length, on the morning of the 12th of April, as the darkness which foreruns the dawn was lifting from Charleston Harbor, and Sumter lay like a shadow on the waves, a gun was fired whose echoes repeated themselves around the world. They were heard in every home North and South, and their meaning was unmistakable. The flash of that mortar gun and of the others that followed was as the lightning burning its way across the vault of heaven, revealing everything with intense vividness, and rending and consuming all noxious vapors. The clouds rolled speedily away, and from the North came the sound of "a rushing, mighty wind."

The crisis and the leader came together. The news reached Washington on Saturday. On Sunday Mr. Lincoln drafted his memorable call to arms, and on Monday it was telegraphed throughout the land. The response to that call forms one of the sublimest chapters of history.

In the St. John cottage, as in nearly all other homes, differences of opinion on minor questions melted into nothingness.

Graham read the electric words aloud, and his friend's only excited comment was:

"Graham, you will go."

"Not yet," was the quiet response "and I sincerely hope you will not."

"How can a man do otherwise?"

"Because he is a man, and not an infuriated animal. I've been very chary in giving my opinion on this subject, as you know. You also know that I have read and thought about it almost constantly since my return. I share fully in Major St. John's views that this affair is not to be settled by a mad rush southward of undisciplined Northern men. I have traced the history of Southern regiments and officers in the Revolution and in our later wars, and I assure you that we are on the eve of a gigantic conflict. In that degree that we believe the government right, we, as rational men, should seek to render it effective service. The government does not need a mob: it needs soldiers, and such are neither you nor I. I have informed myself somewhat on the militia system of the country, and there are plenty of organized regiments of somewhat disciplined men who can go at an hour's notice. If you went now, you—a millionaire—would not count for as much as an Irishman who had spent a few months in a drill-room. The time may come when you can equip a regiment if you choose. Moreover, you have a controlling voice in large business interests; and this struggle is doomed from the start if not sustained financially."

"Mr. Graham is right," said Grace, emphatically. "Even my woman's reason makes so much clear to me."

"Your woman's reason would serve most men better than their own," was his smiling reply. Then, as he looked into her lovely face, pale at the bare thought that her husband was going into danger, he placed his hand on Hilland's shoulder and continued, "Warren, there are other sacred claims besides those of patriotism. The cause should grow desperate indeed before you leave that wife."

"Mr. Graham," Grace began, with an indignant flush mantling the face that had been so pale, "I am a soldier's daughter; and if Warren believed it to be his duty—" Then she faltered, and burst into a passion of tears, as she moaned, "O God! it's—it's true. The bullet that struck him would inflict a deadlier wound on me;" and she hid her face on Hilland's breast and sobbed piteously.

"It is also true," said Graham, in tones that were as grave and solemn as they were gentle, "that your father's spirit—nay, your own—would control you. Under its influence you might not only permit but urge your husband's departure, though your heart broke a thousand times, Therefore, Hilland, I appeal to your manhood. You would be unworthy of yourself and of this true woman were you guided by passion or excitement. As a loyal man you are bound to render your country your best service. To rush to the fray now would be the poorest aid you could give."

"Graham talks sense," said the major, speaking with the authority of a veteran. "If I had to meet the enemy at once, I'd rather have a regiment of *canaille*, and cowards at that, who could obey orders like a machine, than one of hot-headed millionaires who might not understand the command 'Halt!' Mr. Graham is right again when he says that Grace will not prevent a man from doing his duty any more than her mother did."

"What do *you* propose to do?" asked Hilland, breathing heavily. It was evident that a tremendous struggle was going on in his breast, for it had been his daily and nightly dream to join the grand onset that should sweep slavery and rebellion out of existence.

"Simply what I advise—watch, wait, and act when I can be of the most service."

"I yield," said Hilland, slowly, "for I suppose you are right. You all know well, and you best of all, sweetheart"—taking his wife's face in his hands and looking down into her tearful eyes—"that here is the treasure of my life. But you also know that in all the past there have come times when a man must give up everything at the need of his country."

"And when that time comes," sobbed his wife, "I—I—will not—" But she could not finish the sentence.

Graham stole away, awed, and yet with a peace in his heart that he had not known for years. He had saved his friend from the first wild melee of the war—the war that promised rest and nothingness to him, even while he kept his promise to "live and do his best."

CHAPTER XIX
THE BLOOD-RED SKY

Days and weeks of intense excitement followed the terrific Union reverses which at one time threatened the loss of the national capital; and the North began to put forth the power of which it was only half conscious, like a giant taken unawares; for to all, except men of Hilland's hopeful confidence, it soon became evident that the opponent was a giant also. It is not my purpose to dwell upon this, however, except as it influenced the actors of my story.

Hilland, having given up his plans, was contentedly carrying out the line of action suggested by his friend. By all the means within his power he was furthering the Union cause, and learned from experience how much more he could accomplish as a business man than by shouldering a musket, or misleading a regiment in his ignorance. He made frequent trips to New York, and occasionally went to Washington. Graham often accompanied him, and also came and went on affairs of his own. Ostensibly he was acting as correspondent for the journal to which he had written when abroad. In reality, he was studying the great drama with an interest that was not wholly patriotic or scientific. He had found an antidote. The war, dreaded so unspeakably by many, was a boon to him; and the fierce excitement of the hour a counter-irritant to the pain at heart which he believed had become his life-long heritage.

He had feared the sorrowful reproaches of his aunt, as he gave himself almost wholly up to its influences, and became an actor in the great struggle. In this he was agreeably mistaken, for the spirited old lady, while averse to politics as such, had become scarcely less belligerent than the major since the fall of Sumter. She cheerfully let him come and go at his will; and in his loving gratitude it must be admitted that his letters to her were more frequent and interesting than those to the journal whose badge was his passport to all parts of our lines. He spent every hour he could with her, also; and she saw with pleasure that his activity did him good. Grace thought he found few opportunities to pass an evening with them. She was exceedingly grateful—first, that he had interpreted her so nobly, but chiefly because it was his influence and reasoning that had led her husband into his present large, useful, happy action; and she could not help showing it.

Graham's position of correspondent gave him far better opportunities for observation than he could have had in any arm of the service. Of late he was following the command of General Patterson, believing from his sanguinary vaporing that in his army would be seen the first real work of the war.[Footnote: Patterson wrote to the Secretary of War: "You have the means; place them at my disposal, and shoot me if I do not use them to advantage."] He soon became convinced, however, that the veteran of the Mexican War, like the renowned King of France, would march his "twenty thousand men" up the hill only to march them down again. Hearing that McDowell proposed to move against the enemy at Manassas, he hastily repaired to Washington, hoping to find a general that dared to come within cannon-range of the foe.

A sultry day late in the month of July was drawing to a close. Hilland and his wife, with Mrs. Mayburn, were seated under the apple-tree, at which point the walk intersected with the main one leading to the street. The young man, with a heavy frown, was reading from an "extra" a lurid outline of General McDowell's overwhelming defeat and the mad panic that ensued. Grace was listening with deep solicitude, her work lying idle in her lap. It had been a long, hard day for her. Of late her father had been deeply excited, and now was sleeping from sheer reaction. Mrs. Mayburn, looking as grim as fate, sat bolt upright and knitted furiously. One felt instinctively that in no emergency of life could she give way to a panic.

"Well," cried Hilland, springing to his feet and dashing the paper to the ground with something like an oath, "one battle has been fought in America at which I thank the immortal gods I was not present. Why did not McDowell drive a flock of sheep against the enemy, and furnish his division commanders with shepherds' crooks? Oh, the burning, indelible disgrace of it all! And yet—and the possibility of it makes me feel that I would destroy myself had it happened—I might have run like the blackest sheep of them all. I once read up a little on the subject of panics; and there's a mysterious, awful contagion about them impossible to comprehend. These men were Americans; they had been fighting bravely; what the devil got into them that they had to destroy themselves and everything in an insane rush for life?"

"Oh, Warren, see the sky!" cried his wife, the deep solicitude of her expression giving place to a look of awe.

They all turned to the west, and saw a sunset that from the excitable condition of their minds seemed to reflect the scenes recently enacted, and to portend those in prospect now for years to come. Lines of light and broken columns of cloud had ranged themselves across the western arch of the sky, and almost from the horizon to the zenith they were blood-red. So deep, uniform, and ensanguined was the crimson, that the sense of beauty was subordinated to the thought of the national tragedy reflected in the heavens. Hilland's face grew stern as he looked, and Grace hid hers on his breast.

After a moment, he said, lightly, "What superstitious fools we are! It's all an accidental effect of light and cloud."

A cry from Mrs. Mayburn caused them to turn hastily, and they saw her rushing down the path to the street entrance. Two men were helping some one from a carriage. As their obscuring forms stood aside, Graham was seen balancing himself on crutches.

Hilland placed his wife hastily but tenderly on the seat, and was at the gateway in almost a single bound.

"You had better let us carry you," Grace heard one of the men say in gruff kindness.

"Nonsense!" was the hearty reply. "I have not retreated thus far so masterfully only to give my aunt the hysterics at last."

"Alford," said his aunt, sternly, "if it's wise for you to be carried, be carried. Any man here is as liable to hysterics as I am."

"Graham, what does this mean?" cried his friend, in deep excitement. "You look as if half cut to pieces."

"It's chiefly my clothes; I am a fitter subject for a tailor than for a surgeon. Come, good people, there is no occasion for melodrama. With aunty's care I shall soon be as sound as ever. Very well, carry me, then. Perhaps I ought not to use my arm yet;" for Hilland, taking in his friend's disabled condition more fully, was about to lift him in his arms without permission or apology. It ended in his making what is termed a "chair" with one of the men, and Graham was borne speedily up the path.

Grace stood at the intersection with hands clasped in the deepest anxiety; but Graham smiled reassuringly, as he said, "Isn't this an heroic style of returning from the wars? Not quite like Walter Scott's knights; but we've fallen on prosaic times. Don't look so worried. I assure you I'm not seriously hurt."

"Mrs. Mayburn," said Hilland, excitedly, "let us take him to our cottage. We can all take better care of him there."

"Oh, do! please do!" echoed Grace. "You are alone; and Warren and I could do so much—"

"No," said the old lady quietly and decisively; for the moment the proposition was broached Graham's eyes had sought hers in imperative warning. "You both can help me as far as it is needful."

Grace detected the glance and noted the result, but Hilland began impetuously: "Oh, come, dear Mrs. Mayburn, I insist upon it. Graham is making light of it; but I'm sure he'll need more care than you realize—"

"Hilland, I know the friendship that prompts your wish," interrupted Graham, "but my aunt is right. I shall do better in my own room. I need rest more than anything else. You and your wife can do all you wish for me. Indeed, I shall visit you to-morrow and fight the battle over again with the major. Please take me to my room at once," he added in a low tone. "I'm awfully tired."

"Come, Mr. Hilland," said Mrs. Mayburn, in a tone almost authoritative; and she led the way decisively.

Hilland yielded, and in a few moments Graham was in his own room, and after taking a little stimulant, explained.

"My horse was shot and fell on me. I am more bruised, scratched and used up, than hurt;" and so it proved, though his escape had evidently been almost miraculous. One leg and foot had been badly crushed. There were two flesh wounds in his arm; and several bullets had cut his clothing, in some places drawing blood. All over his clothes, from head to foot, were traces of Virginia soil; and he had the general appearance of a man who had passed through a desperate melee.

"I tried to repair damages in Washington," he said, "but the confusion was so dire I had to choose between a hospital and home; and as I had some symptoms of fever last night, I determined to push on till under the wing of my good old aunty and your fraternal care. Indeed, I think I was half delirious when I took the train last evening; but it was only from fatigue, lack of sleep, and perhaps loss of blood. Now, please leave me to aunty's care to-night, and I will tell you all about it to-morrow."

Hilland was accordingly constrained to yield to his friend's wishes. He brought the best surgeon in town, however, and gave directions that, after he had dressed Graham's wounds, he should spend the night in Mrs. Mayburn's parlor, and report to him if there was any change for the worse. Fortunately, there was no occasion for his solicitude. Graham slept with scarcely a break till late the next morning; and his pulse became so quiet that when he waked with a good appetite the physician pronounced all danger passed.

In the evening he was bent on visiting the major. He knew they were all eager for his story, and, calculating upon the veteran's influence in restraining Hilland from hasty action, he resolved that his old and invalid friend should hear it with the first. From the character of Hilland he knew the danger to be apprehended was that he would throw himself into the struggle in some way that would paralyze, or at the least curtail, his efficiency. Both his aunt and the physician, who underrated the recuperative power of Graham's fine physical condition, urged quiet until the following day; but he assured them he would suffer more from restlessness than from a moderate degree of effort. He also explained to his aunt that he wished to talk with Hilland, and, if possible, in the presence of his wife and the major.

"Then they must come here," said the old lady, resolutely.

With this compromise he had to be content; and Hilland, who had been coming and going, readily agreed to fetch the major.

CHAPTER XX
TWO BATTLES

In less than an hour Graham was in the parlor, looking, it is true, somewhat battered, but cheerful and resolute. His friends found him installed in a great armchair, with his bruised foot on a cushion, his arm in a sling, and a few pieces of court-plaster distributed rather promiscuously over his face and head. He greeted Hilland and his wife so heartily, and assured the major so genially that he should now divide with him his honors as a veteran, that they were reassured, and the rather tragic mood in which they had started on the visit was dispelled.

"I must admit, though," he added to his old friend, who was also made comfortable in his chair, which Hilland had brought over, "that in my fall on the field of glory I made a sorry figure. I was held down by my horse and trampled on as if I had been a part of the 'sacred soil.'"

"'Field of glory,' indeed!" exclaimed Hilland, contemptuously.

"I did not know that you had become a soldier," said Grace, with surprise.

"I was about as much of a soldier as the majority, from the generals down," was the laughing reply.

"I don't see how you could have been a worse one, if you had tried," was his friend's rejoinder. "I may do no better; but I should be less than a man if I did not make an effort to wipe out the disgrace as soon as possible. No reflection on you, Graham. Your wounds exonerate you; and I know you did not get them in running away."

"Yes, I did—two of them, at least—these in my arm. As to 'wiping out this disgrace as soon as possible,' I think that is a very secondary matter."

"Well! I don't understand it at all," was Hilland's almost savage answer. "But I can tell you from the start you need not enter on your old prudent counsels that I should serve the government as a stay-at-home quartermaster and general supply agent. In my opinion, what the government needs is men—men who at least won't run away. I now have Grace's permission to go—dear, brave girl!—and go I shall. To stay at home because I am rich seems to me the very snobbishness of wealth; and the kind of work I have been doing graybeards can do just as well, and better."

Graham turned a grave look of inquiry upon the wife. She answered it by saying with a pallid face: "I had better perish a thousand times than destroy Warren's self-respect."

"What right have you to preach caution," continued Hilland, "when you went far enough to be struck by half a dozen bullets?"

"The right of a retreat which scarcely slackened until I was under my aunt's roof."

"Come, Graham, you are tantalizing us," said Hilland, impatiently. "There, forgive me, old fellow. I fear you are still a little out of your head," he added, with a slight return of his old good-humor. "Do give us, then, if you can, some account of your impetuous advance on Washington, instead of Richmond."

"Yes, Mr. Graham," added the major, "if you are able to give me some reason for not blushing that I am a Northern man, I shall be glad to hear it."

"Mrs. Hilland," said Graham, with a smiling glance at the young wife's troubled face, "you have the advantage of us all. You can proudly say, 'I'm a Southerner.' Hilland and I are nothing but 'low-down Yankees.' Come, good friends, I have seen enough tragedy of late; and if, I have to describe a little to-night, let us look at matters philosophically. If I received some hard knocks from your kin, Mrs. Hilland—"

"Don't say 'Mrs. Hilland,'" interrupted his friend. "As I've told you before, my wife is 'Grace' to you."

"So be it then. The hard knocks from your kin have materially added to my small stock of sense; and I think the entire North will be wiser as well as sadder before many days pass. We have been taught that taking Richmond and marching through the South will be no holiday picnic. Major St. John has been right from the start. We must encounter brave, determined men; and, whatever may be true of the leaders, the people are as sincere in their patriotism as we are. They don't even dream that they are fighting in a bad cause. The majority will stand up for it as stoutly and conscientiously as your husband for ours. Have I not done justice to your kin, Grace?"

"Yes," she replied, with a faint smile.

"Then forgive me if I say that until four o'clock last Sunday afternoon, and in a fair, stand-up fight between a Northern mob and a Southern mob, we whipped them."

"But I thought the men of the North prided themselves on their 'staying power.'"

"They had no 'staying power' when they found fresh regiments and batteries pouring in on their flank and rear. I believe that retreat was then the proper thing. The wild panic that ensued resulted naturally from the condition of the men and officers, and especially from the presence of a lot of nondescript people that came to see the thing as a spectacle, a sort of gladiatorial combat, upon which they could look at a safe distance. Two most excellent results have been attained: I don't believe we shall ever send out another mob of soldiers; and I am sure that a mob of men and women from Washington will never follow it to see the fun."

"I wish Beauregard had corralled them all—the mob of sight-seers, I mean," growled the major. "I must say, Mr. Graham, that the hard knocks you and others have received may result in infinite good. I think I take your meaning, and that we shall agree very nearly before you are through. You know that I was ever bitterly opposed to the mad 'On to Richmond' cry; and now the cursed insanity of the thing is clearly proved."

"I agree with you that it was all wrong—that it involved risks that never should have been taken at this stage of the war; and I am told that General Scott and other veteran officers disapproved of the measure. Nevertheless, it came wonderfully near being successful. We should have gained the battle if the attack had been made earlier, or if that old muff, Patterson, had done his duty."

"If you are not too tired, give us the whole movement, just as you saw it," said Hilland, his eyes glowing with excitement.

"Oh, I feel well enough for another retreat tonight. My trouble was chiefly fatigue and lack of sleep."

"Because you make light of wounds, we do not," said Grace.

"Hilland knows that the loss of a little blood as pale and watery as mine would be of small account," was Graham's laughing response.

"Well, to begin at the beginning, I followed Patterson till convinced that his chief impulse was to get away from the enemy. I then hastened to Washington only to learn that McDowell had already had a heavy skirmish which was not particularly to our advantage. This was Saturday morning, and the impression was that a general engagement would be fought almost immediately. The fact that our army had met little opposition thus far created a false confidence. I did not care to risk my pet horse, Mayburn. You must know, aunty, I've rechristened Firebrand in your honor," said Graham. "I tried to get another mount, but could not obtain one for love or money. Every beast and conveyance in the city seemed already engaged for the coming spectacle. The majority of these civilians did not leave till early on Sunday morning, but I had plenty of company on Saturday, when with my good horse I went in a rather leisurely way to Centerville; for as a correspondent I had fairly accurate information of what was taking place, and had heard that there would be no battle that day.

"I reached Centerville in the evening, and soon learned that the forward movement would take place in the night. Having put my horse in thorough condition for the morrow, and made an enormous supper through the hospitality of some staff-officers, I sought a quiet knoll on which to sleep in soldier fashion under the sky, but found the scene too novel and beautiful for such prosaic oblivion. I was on the highest ground I could find, and beneath and on either side of me were the camp-fires of an army. Around the nearest of these could be seen the forms of the soldiers in every picturesque attitude; some still cooking and making their rude suppers, others executing double-shuffles like war-dances, more discussing earnestly and excitedly the prospects of the coming day, and not a few looking pensively into the flames as if they saw pictures of the homes and friends they might never see again. In the main, however, animation and jollity prevailed; and from far and near came the sound of song, and laughter, and chaffing. Far down the long slope toward the dark, wooded valley of Bull Run, the light of the fires shaded off into such obscurity as the full moon permitted, while beyond the stream in the far distance a long, irregular line of luminous haze marked the encampments of the enemy.

"As the night advanced the army grew quiet; near and distant sounds died away; the canvas tents were like mounds of snow; and by the flickering, dying flames were multitudes of quiet forms. At midnight few scenes could be more calm and beautiful, so tenderly did the light of the moon soften and etherealize everything. Even the parked artillery lost much of its grim aspect, and all nature seemed to breathe peace and rest.

"It was rumored that McDowell wished to make part of the march in the evening, and it would have been well if he had done so. A little past midnight a general stir and bustle ran through the sleeping army. Figures were seen moving hurriedly, men forming into lines, and there was a general commotion. But there was no promptness of action. The soldiers stood around, sat down, and at last lay on their arms and slept again. Mounting my horse, with saddle-bags well stuffed with such rations as I could obtain, I sought the centres of information. It appeared that the division under General Tyler was slow in starting, and blocked the march of the Second and the Third Division. As I picked my way around, only a horse's sagacity kept me from crushing some sleeping fellow's leg or arm, for a horse won't step on a man unless excited.

"Well, Tyler's men got out of the way at last in a haphazard fashion, and the Second and Third Divisions were also steadily moving, but hours behind time. Such marching! It reminded one of countrymen streaming along a road to a Fourth of July celebration.

"My main policy was to keep near the commander-in-chief, for thus I hoped to obtain from the staff some idea of the plan of battle and where its brunt would fall. I confess that I was disgusted at first, for the general was said to be ill, and he followed his columns in a carriage. It seemed an odd way of leading an army. But he came out all right; and he did his duty as a soldier and a general, although every one is cursing him to-day. He was the first man on the real battlefield, and by no means the first to leave it.

"Of course I came and went along the line of march, or of straggling rather, as I pleased; but I kept my eye on the general and his staff. I soon observed that he decided to make his headquarters at the point where a road leading from the great Warrenton Turnpike passed to the north through what is known as the 'Big Woods.' Tyler's command continued westward down the turnpike to what is known as the Stone Bridge, a single substantial arch at which the enemy were said to be in force. It now became clear that the first fighting would be there, and that it was McDowell's plan to send his main force under Hunter and Heintzelman further north through the woods to cross at some point above. I therefore followed Tyler's column, as that must soon become engaged.

"The movements had all been so mortally slow that any chance for surprise was lost. As we approached the bridge it was as lovely a summer morning as you would wish to see. I had ridden ahead with the scouts. Thrushes, robins, and other birds were singing in the trees. Startled rabbits, and a mother-bird with a brood of quails, scurried across the road, and all seemed as still and peaceful as any Sunday that had ever dawned on the scene. It was hard to persuade one's self that in front and rear were the forces of deadly war.

"We soon reached an eminence from which we saw what dispelled at once the illusion of sylvan solitude. The sun had been shining an hour or two, and the bridge before us and the road beyond were defended by *abatis* and other obstructions. On the further bank a line of infantry was in full view with batteries in position prepared to receive us. I confess it sent a thrill through every nerve when I first saw the ranks of the foe we must encounter in no mere pageant of war.

"In a few moments our forces came up, and at first one brigade deployed on the left and another on the right of the pike. At last I witnessed a scene that had the aspect of war. A great thirty-pound Parrot gun unlimbered in the centre of the pike, and looked like a surly mastiff. In a moment an officer, who understood his business, sighted it. There was a flash, bright even in the July sunlight, a grand report awakening the first echoes of a battle whose thunder was heard even in Washington; and a second later we saw the shell explode directly over the line of Confederate infantry. Their ranks broke and melted away as if by magic."

"Good shot, well aimed. Oh heavens! what would I not give to be thirty years younger! Go on, Graham, go on;" for the young man had stopped to take a sip of wine.

"Yes, Graham," cried Hilland, springing to his feet; "what next?"

"I fear we are doing Mr. Graham much wrong," Grace interrupted. "He must be going far beyond his strength."

The young man had addressed his words almost solely to the major, not only out of courtesy, but also for a reason that Grace partially surmised. He now turned and smiled into her flushed, troubled face, and said, "I fear you find these details of war dull and wearisome."

"On the contrary, you are so vivid a *raconteur* that I fear Warren will start for the front before you are through."

"When I am through you will think differently."

"But you *are* going beyond your strength."

"I assure you I am not; though I thank you for your thoughtfulness. I never felt better in my life; and it gives me a kind of pleasure to make you all realize things as I saw them."

"And it gives us great pleasure to listen," cried Hilland. "Even Mrs. Mayburn there is knitting as if her needles were bayonets; and Grace has the flush of a soldier's daughter on her cheeks."

"Oh, stop your chatter, and let Graham go on," said the major—"that is, if it's prudent for him," he added from a severe sense of duty. "What followed that blessed shell?"

"A lame and impotent conclusion in the form of many other shells that evoked no reply; and beyond his feeble demonstration Tyler did nothing. It seemed to me that a determined dash at the bridge would have carried it. I was fretting and fuming about when a staff-officer gave me a hint that nothing was to be done at present—that it was all only a feint, and that the columns that had gone northward through the woods would begin the real work. His words were scarcely spoken before I was making my way to the rear. I soon reached McDowell's carriage at the intersection of the roads, and found it empty. Learning that the general, in his impatience, had taken horse and galloped off to see what had become of his tardy commanders, I followed at full speed.

"It was a wild, rough road, scarcely more than a lane through the woods; but Mayburn was equal to it, and like a bird carried me through its gloomy shades, where I observed not a few skulkers cowering in the brush as I sped by. I overtook Heintzelman's command as it was crossing the run at Sudley's Ford; and such a scene of confusion I hope never to witness again. The men were emptying their canteens and refilling them, laving their hands and faces, and refreshing themselves generally. It was really quite a picnic. Officers were storming and ordering 'the boys'—and boys they seemed, indeed—to move on; and by dint of much profanity, and the pressure of those following, regiment after regiment at last straggled up the further bank, went into brigade formation, and shambled forward."

"The cursed mob!" muttered the major.

"Well, poor fellows! they soon won my respect; and yet, as I saw them then, stopping to pick blackberries along the road, I did feel like riding them down. I suppose my horse and I lowered the stream somewhat as we drank, for the day had grown sultry and the sun's rays intensely hot. Then I hastened on to find the general. It seemed as if we should never get out of the woods, as if the army had lost itself in an interminable forest. Wild birds and game fled before us; and I heard one soldier call out to another that it was 'a regular Virginia coon-hunt.' As I reached the head of the column the timber grew thinner, and I was told that McDowell was reconnoitring in advance. Galloping out into the open fields, I saw him far beyond me, already the target of Rebel bullets. His staff and a company of cavalry were with him; and as I approached he seemed rapidly taking in the topographical features of the field. Having apparently satisfied himself, he galloped to the rear; and at the same time Hunter's troops came pouring out of the woods.

"There was now a prospect of warm work and plenty of it. For the life of me I can't tell you how the battle began. Our men came forward in an irregular manner, rushing onward impetuously, halting unnecessarily, with no master mind directing. It seemed at first as if the mere momentum of the march carried us under the enemy's fire; and then there was foolish delay. By the aid of my powerful glass I was convinced that we might have walked right over the first thin Rebel line on the ridge nearest us.

"The artillery exchanged shots awhile. Regiments under the command of General Burnside deployed in the fields to the left of the road down which we had come; skirmishers were thrown out rapidly and began their irregular firing at an absurd distance from the enemy. There was hesitancy, delay; and the awkwardness of troops unaccustomed to act together in large bodies was enhanced by the excitement inseparable from their first experience of real war.

"In spite of all this the battlefield began to present grand and inspiring effects. The troops were debouching rapidly from the woods, their bayonets gleaming here and there through the dust raised by their hurrying feet, and burning in serried lines when they were ranged under the cloudless sun. In every movement made by every soldier the metal points in his accoutrements flashed and scintillated. Again there was something very spirited in the appearance of a battery rushed into position at a gallop—the almost instantaneous unlimbering, the caissons moving to the rear, and the guns at the same moment thundering their defiance, while the smoke, lifting slowly on the heavy air, rises and blends with that of the other side, and hangs like a pall to leeward of the field. The grandest thing of all, however, was the change in the men. The uncouth, coarsely jesting, blackberry-picking fellows that lagged and straggled to the battle became soldiers in their instincts and rising excitement and courage, if not in machine-like discipline and coolness. As I rode here and there I could see that they were erect, eager, and that their eyes began to glow like coals from their dusty, sunburned visages. If there were occasional evidences of fear, there were more of resolution and desire for the fray.

"The aspect of affairs on the ridge, where the enemy awaited us, did not grow encouraging. With my glass I could see re-inforcements coming up rapidly during our delay. New guns were seeking position, which was scarcely taken before there was a puff of smoke and their iron message. Heavens! what a vicious sound those shells had! something between a whiz and a shriek. Even the horses would cringe and shudder when one passed over them, and the men would duck their heads, though the missile was thirty feet in the air. I suppose there was some awfully wild firing on both sides; but I saw several of our men carried to the rear. But all this detail is an old, old story to you, Major."

"Yes, an old story, but one that can never lose its fierce charm. I see it all as you describe it. Go on, and omit nothing you can remember of the scene. Mrs. Mayburn looks as grim as one of your cannon; and Grace, my child, you won't flinch, will you?"

"No, papa."

"That's my brave wife's child. She often said, 'Tell me all. I wish to know just what you have passed through.'"

A brief glance assured Graham that her father's spirit was then supreme, and that she looked with woman's admiration on a scene replete with the manhood woman most admires.

"I cannot describe to you the battle, as such," continued Graham. "I can only outline faintly the picture I saw dimly through dust and smoke from my own standpoint. Being under no one's orders, I could go where I pleased, and I tried to find the vital points. Of course, there was much heavy fighting that I saw nothing of, movements unknown to me or caught but imperfectly. During the preliminary conflict I remained on the right of Burnside's command near the Sudley Road by which our army had reached the field.

"When at last his troops began to press forward, their advance was decided and courageous; but the enemy held their own stubbornly. The fighting was severe and deadly, for we were now within easy musket range. At one time I trembled for Burnside's lines, and I saw one of his aides gallop furiously to the rear for help. It came almost immediately in the form of a fine body of regulars under Major Sykes; and our wavering lines were rendered firm and more aggressive than ever. At the same time it was evident that our forces were going into action off to the right of the Sudley Road, and that another battery had opened on the enemy. I afterward learned that they were Rickett's guns. Under this increasing and relentless pressure the enemy's lines were seen to waver. Wild cheers went up from our ranks; and such is the power of the human voice—the echo direct from the heart—that these shouts rose above the roar of the cannon, the crash of musketry, and thrilled every nerve and fibre. Onward pressed our men; the Rebel lines yielded, broke, and our foes retreated down the hill, but at a dogged, stubborn pace, fighting as they went. Seeing the direction they were taking, I dashed into the Sudley Road near which I had kept as the centre of operations. At the intersection of this road with the Warrenton Turnpike was a stone house, and behind this the enemy rallied as if determined to retreat no further. I had scarcely observed this fact when I saw a body of men forming in the road just above me. In a few moments they were in motion. On they came, a resistless human torrent with a roar of hoarse shouts and cries. I was carried along with them; but before we reached the stone house the enemy broke and fled, and the whole Rebel line was swept back half a mile or more.

"Thus you see that in the first severe conflict of the day, and when pitted against numbers comparatively equal, we won a decided victory."

Both the major and Hilland drew a long breath of relief; and the former said: "I have been hasty and unjust in my censure. If that raw militia could be made to fight at all, it can in time be made to fight well. Mr. Graham, you have deeply gratified an old soldier to-night by describing scenes that carry me back to the grand era of my life. I believe I was born to be a soldier; and my old campaigns stand out in memory like sun-lighted mountain-tops. Forgive such high-flown talk—I know it's not like me—but I've had to-night some of my old battle excitement. I never thought to feel it again. We'll hear the rest of your story to-morrow. I outrank you all, by age at least; and I now order 'taps.'"

Graham was not sorry, for in strong reaction a sudden sense of almost mortal weakness overcame him. Even the presence of Grace, for whose sake, after all, he had unconsciously told his story, could not sustain him any longer, and he sank back looking very white.

"You *have* overexerted yourself," she said gently, coming, to his side. "You should have stopped when I cautioned you; or rather, we should have been more thoughtful."

"Perhaps I have overrated my strength—it's a fault of mine," was his smiling reply, "I shall be perfectly well after a night's rest."

He had looked up at her as he spoke; and in that moment of weakness there was a wistful, hungry look in his eyes that smote her heart.

A shallow, silly woman, or an intensely selfish one, would have exulted. Here was a man, cool, strong, and masterful among other men—a man who had gone to the other side of the globe to escape her power—one who within the last few days had witnessed a battle with thes quiet poise that enabled him to study it as an artist or a tactician; and yet he could not keep his eyes from betraying the truth that there was something within his heart stronger than himself.

Did Grace Hilland lay this flattering unction to her soul? No. She went away inexpressibly sad. She felt that two battle scenes had been presented to her mind; and the conflict that had been waged silently, patiently, and unceasingly in a strong man's soul had to her the higher elements of heroism. It was another of those wretched problems offered by this imperfect world for which there seems no remedy.

When Hilland hastened over to see his friend and add a few hearty words to those he had already spoken, he was told that he was sleeping.

CHAPTER XXI
THE LOGIC OF EVENTS

Graham was right in his prediction that another night's rest would carry him far on the road to recovery; and he insisted, when Hilland called in the morning, that the major should remain in his accustomed chair at home, and listen to the remainder of the story. "My habit of life is so active," he said, "that a little change will do me good;" and so it was arranged. By leaning on Hilland's shoulder he was able to limp the short distance between the cottages; and he found that Grace had made every arrangement for his comfort on the piazza, where the major welcomed him with almost the eagerness of a child for whom an absorbing story is to be continued.

"You can't know how you interested us all last night," Grace began. "I never knew papa to be more gratified; and as for Warren, he could not sleep for excitement. Where did you learn to tell stories?"

"I was said to be very good at fiction when a boy, especially when I got into scrapes. But you can't expect in this garish light any such effects as I may have created last evening. It requires the mysterious power of night and other conditions to secure a glamour; and so you must look for the baldest prose to-day."

"Indeed, Graham, we scarcely know what to expect from you any more," Hilland remarked. "From being a quiet cynic philosopher, content to delve in old libraries like the typical bookworm, you become an indefatigable sportsman, horse-tamer, explorer of the remote parts of the earth, and last, and strangest, a newspaper correspondent who doesn't know that the place to see and write about battles is several miles in the rear. What will you do next?"

"My future will be redeemed from the faintest trace of eccentricity. I shall do what about a million other Americans will do eventually—go into the army."

"Ah! now you talk sense, and I am with you. I shall be ready to go as soon as you are well enough."

"I doubt it."

"I don't."

"Grace, what do you say to all this?" turning a troubled look upon the wife.

"I foresee that, like my mother, I am to be the wife of a soldier," she replied with a smile, while tears stood in her eyes. "I did not marry Warren to destroy his sense of manhood."

"You see, Graham, how it is. You also perceive what a knight I must be to be worthy of the lady I leave in bower."

"Yes; I see it all too well. But I must misquote Shakespeare to you, and 'charge you to stand on the *order* of your going;' and I think the rest of my story will prove that I have good reason for the charge."

"I should have been sorry," said the major, "to have had Grace marry a man who would consult only ease and safety in times like these. It will be awfully hard to have him go. But the time may soon come when it would be harder for Grace to have him stay; that is, if she is like her mother. But what's the use of looking at the gloomy side? I've been through a dozen battles; and here I am to plague the world yet. But now for the story. You left off, Mr. Graham, at the rout of the first Rebel line of battle."

"And this had not been attained," resumed Graham, "without serious loss to our side. Colonel Hunter, who commanded the Second Division, you remember, was so severely wounded by a shell that he had to leave the field early in the action. Colonel Slocum of one of the Rhode Island regiments was mortally wounded; and his major had his leg crushed by a cannon ball which at the same time killed his horse. Many others were wounded and must have had a hard time of it, poor fellows, that hot day. As for the dead that strewed the ground—their troubles were over."

"But not the troubles of those that loved them," said Grace, bitterly.

Graham turned hastily away. When a moment later he resumed his narrative, she noticed that his eyes were moist and his tones husky.

"Our heaviest loss was in the demoralization of some of the regiments engaged. They appeared to have so little cohesion that one feared all the time that they might crumble away into mere human atoms.

"The affair continually took on a larger aspect, as more troops became engaged. We had driven the Confederates down a gentle slope, across a small stream called Young's Branch, and up a hill beyond and to the south. This position was higher and stronger than any they had yet occupied. On the crest of the hill were two houses; and the enemy could be seen forming a line extending from one to the other. They were evidently receiving re-enforcements rapidly. I could see gray columns hastening forward and deploying; and I've no doubt that many of the fugitives were rallied beyond this line. Meanwhile, I was informed that Tyler's Division, left in the morning at Stone Bridge, had crossed the Run, in obedience to McDowell's orders, and were on the field at the left of our line. Such, as far as I could judge, was the position of affairs between twelve and one, although I can give you only my impressions. It appeared to me that our men were fighting well, gradually and steadily advancing, and closing in upon the enemy. Still, I cannot help feeling that if we had followed up our success by the determined charge of one brigade that would hold together, the hill might have been swept, and victory made certain.

"I had taken my position near Rickett's and Griffin's batteries on the right of our line, and decided to follow them up, not only because they were doing splendid work, but also for the reason that they would naturally be given commanding positions at vital points. By about two o'clock we had occupied the Warrenton Turnpike; and we justly felt that much had been gained. The Confederate lines between the two houses on the hill had given way; and from the sounds we heard, they must have been driven back also by a charge on our extreme left. Indeed, there was scarcely anything to be seen of the foe that thus far had been not only seen but felt.

"From a height near the batteries where I stood, the problem appeared somewhat clear to me. We had driven the enemy up and over a hill of considerable altitude, and across an uneven plateau, and they were undoubtedly in the woods beyond, a splendid position which commanded the entire open space over which we must advance to reach them. They were in cover; we should be in full view in all efforts to dislodge them. Their very reverses had secured for them a position worth half a dozen regiments; and I trembled as I thought of our raw militia advancing under conditions that would try the courage of veterans. You remember that if Washington, in the Revolution, could get his new recruits behind a rail-fence, they thought they were safe.

"Well, there was no help for it. The hill and plateau must be crossed under a pointblank fire, in order to reach the enemy, and that, too, by men who had been under arms since midnight, and the majority wearied by a long march under a blazing sun.

"About half-past two, when the assault began, a strange and ominous quiet rested on the field. As I have said, the enemy had disappeared. The men scarcely knew what to think of it; and in some a false confidence, speedily dispelled, was begotten. Rickett's battery was moved down across the valley to the top of a hill just beyond the residence owned and occupied by a Mrs. Henry. I followed and entered the house, already shattered by shot and shell, curious to know whether it was occupied, and by whom. Pitiful to relate, I found that Mrs. Henry was a widow and a helpless invalid. The poor woman was in mortal terror; and it was my hope to return and carry her to some place of safety, but the swift and deadly tide of war gave me no chance. [Footnote: Mrs. Henry, although confined to her bed, was wounded two or three times, and died soon afterward.]

"Ricketts' battery had scarcely unlimbered before death was busy among his cannoneers and even his horses. The enemy had the cover not only of the woods, but of a second growth of pines, which fringed them and completely concealed the Rebel sharpshooters. When a man fell, nothing could be seen but a puff of smoke. These little jets and wreaths of smoke half encircled us, and made but a phantom-like target for our people; and I think it speaks well for officers and men that they not only did their duty, but that Griffin's battery also came up, and that both batteries held their own against a terrific pointblank fire from the Rebel cannon, which certainly exceeded ours in number. The range was exceedingly short, and a more terrific artillery duel it would be hard to imagine. At the same time the more deadly little puffs of smoke continued; and men in every attitude of duty would suddenly throw up their hands and fall. The batteries had no business to be so exposed, and their supports were of no real service.

"I can give you an idea of what occurred at this point only; but, from the sounds I heard, there was very heavy fighting elsewhere, which I fear, however, was too spasmodic and ill-directed to accomplish the required ends. A heavy, persistent, concentrated attack, a swift push with the bayonet through the low pines and woods, would have saved the day. Perhaps our troops were not equal to it; and yet, poor fellows, they did braver things that were utterly useless.

"I still believe, however, all might have gone well, had it not been for a horrible mistake. I was not very far from Captain Griffin, and was watching his cool, effective superintendence of his guns, when suddenly I noticed a regiment in full view on our right advancing toward us. Griffin caught sight of it at the same moment, and seemed amazed. Were they Confederates or National? was the question to be decided instantly. They might be his own support. Doubtful and yet exceedingly apprehensive, he ordered his guns to be loaded with canister and trained upon this dubious force that had come into view like an apparition; but he still hesitated, restrained, doubtless, by the fearful thought of annihilating a Union regiment.

"'Captain,' said Major Barry, chief of artillery, 'they are your battery support.'

"'They are Confederates.' Griffin replied, intensely excited. 'As certain as the world, they are Confederates.'

"'No,' was the answer, 'I know they are your battery support.'

"I had ridden up within ear-shot, and levelled my glass upon them. 'Don't fire,' cried Griffin, and he spurred forward to satisfy himself.

"At the same moment the regiment, now within short range, by a sudden instantaneous act levelled their muskets at us. I saw we were doomed, and yet by some instinct tightened my rein while I dug my spurs into my horse. He reared instantly. I saw a line of fire, and then poor Mayburn fell upon me, quivered, and was dead. The body of a man broke my fall in such a way that I was not hurt. Indeed, at the moment I was chiefly conscious of intense anger and disgust. If Griffin had followed his instinct and destroyed that regiment, as he could have done by one discharge, the result of the whole battle might have been different. As it was, both his and Rickett's batteries were practically annihilated."

[Footnote: Since the above was written Colonel Hasbrouck has given me an account of this crisis in the battle. He was sufficiently near to hear the conversation found in the text, and to enable me to supplement it by fuller details. Captain Griffin emphatically declared that no Union regiment could possibly come from that quarter, adding, "They are dressed in gray."

Major Barry with equal emphasis asserted that they were National troops, and unfortunately we had regiments in gray uniforms. Seeing that Captain Griffin was not convinced, he said peremptorily, "I command you not to fire on that regiment."

Of course this direct order ended the controversy, and Captain Griffin directed that his guns be shifted again toward the main body of the enemy, while he rode forward a little space to reconnoitre.

During all this fatal delay the Confederate regiment was approaching, marching by the flank, and so passed at one time within pointblank range of the guns that would scarcely have left a man upon his feet. The nature of their advance was foolhardy in the extreme, and at the time that Captain Griffin wished to fire they were practically helpless. A Virginia worm-fence was in their path, and so frightened, nervous, and excited were they that, instead of tearing it down, they began clambering over it until by weight and numbers it was trampled under foot.

They approached so near that the order to "fire low" was distinctly heard by our men as the Confederates went into battle-line formation.

The scene following their volley almost defies description. The horses attached to caissons not only tore down and through the ascending

National battle-line, but Colonel—then Lieutenant—Hasbrouck saw several teams dash over the knoll toward the Confederate regiment, that opened ranks to let them pass. So novel were the scenes of war at that time that the Confederates were as much astonished as the members of the batteries left alive, and at first did not advance, although it was evident that there were, at the moment, none to oppose them. The storm of Rebel bullets had ranged so low that Lieutenant Hasbrouck and Captain Griffin owed their safety to the fact that they were mounted. The horses of both officers were wounded. On the way down the northern slope of the hill, with the few Union survivors, Captain Griffin met Major Barry, and in his intense anger and grief reproached him bitterly. The latter gloomily admitted that he had been mistaken.

Captain Ricketts was wounded, and the battle subsequently surged back and forth over his prostrate form, but eventually he was sent as a captive to Richmond.]

The major uttered an imprecation.

"I was pinned to the ground by the weight of my horse, but not so closely but that I could look around. The carnage had been frightful. But few were on their feet, and they in rapid motion to the rear. The horses left alive rushed down the hill with the caissons, spreading dismay, confusion, and disorder through the ascending line of battle. Our supporting regiment in the rear, that had been lying on their arms, sprang to their feet and stood like men paralyzed with horror; meanwhile, the Rebel regiment, reenforced, was advancing rapidly on the disabled guns—their defenders lay beneath and around them—firing as they came. Our support gave them one ineffectual volley, then turned and fled."

Again the major relieved his mind in his characteristic way.

"But you, Alford?" cried Grace, leaning forward with clasped hands, while his aunt came and buried her face upon his shoulder. "Are you keeping your promise to live?" she whispered.

"Am I not here safe and sound?" he replied, cheerily. "Nothing much happened to me, Grace. When I saw the enemy was near, I merely doubled myself up under my horse, and was nothing to them but a dead Yankee. I was only somewhat trodden upon, as I told you, when the Confederates tried to turn the guns against our forces.

"I fear I am doing a wrong to the ladies by going into these sanguinary details."

"No," said the major, emphatically; "Mrs. Mayburn would have been a general had she been a man; and Grace has heard about battles all her life. It's a great deal better to understand from the start what this war means."

"I especially wished Hilland to hear the details of this battle as far as I saw them, for I think they contain lessons that may be of great service to him. That he would engage in the war was a foregone conclusion from the first; and with his means and ability he may take a very important part in it. But of this later.

"As I told you, I made the rather close acquaintance of your kin, Grace, and can testify that the 'fa' of their feet' was not 'fairy-like.' Before they could accomplish their purpose of turning the guns on our lines, I heard the rushing tramp of a multitude, with defiant shouts and yells. Rebels fell around me. The living left the guns, sought to form a line, but suddenly gave way in dire confusion, and fled to the cover from which they came. A moment later a body of our men surged like an advancing wave over the spot they had occupied.

"Now was my chance; and I reached up and seized the hand of a tall, burly Irishman. "What the divil du ye want?" he cried, and in his mad excitement was about to thrust me through for a Confederate.

"'Halt!' I thundered. The familiar word of command restrained him long enough for me to secure his attention. 'Would you kill a Union man?'"

"'Is it Union ye are? What yez doin' here, thin, widut a uniform?'

"I showed him my badge of correspondent, and explained briefly.

"Strange as it may seem to you, he uttered a loud, jolly laugh. 'Faix, an' it's a writer ye are. Ye'll be apt to git some memmyrandums the day that ye'll carry about wid ye till ye die, and that may be in about a minnit. I'll shtop long enough to give yez a lift, or yez hoss, rather;' and he seized poor Mayburn by the head. His excitement seemed to give him the strength of a giant, for in a moment I was released and stood erect.

"'Give me a musket,' I cried, 'and I'll stand by you.'

"'Bedad, hilp yersilf,' he replied, pushing forward. 'There's plenty o' fellers lyin' aroun' that has no use for them;' and he was lost in the confused advance.

"All this took place in less time than it takes to describe it, for events at that juncture were almost as swift as bullets. Lame as I was, I hobbled around briskly, and soon secured a good musket with a supply of cartridges. As with the rest, my blood was up—don't smile, Hilland: I had been pretty cool until the murderous discharge that killed my horse—and I was soon in the front line, firing with the rest.

"Excited as I was, I saw that our position was desperate, for a heavy force of Confederates was swarming toward us. I looked around and saw that part of our men were trying to drag off the guns. This seemed the more important work; and discretion also whispered that with my bruised foot I should be captured in five minutes unless I was further to the rear. So I took a pull at a gun; but we had made little progress before there was another great surging wave from the other direction, and our forces were swept down the hill again, I along with the rest. The confusion was fearful; the regiments with which I had been acting went all to pieces, and had no more organization than if they had been mixed up by a whirlwind.

"I was becoming too lame to walk, and found myself in a serious dilemma." "Ha! ha! ha!" laughed Hilland. "It was just becoming serious, eh?"

"Well, I didn't realize my lameness before; and as retreat was soon to be order of the day, there was little prospect of my doing my share. As I was trying to extricate myself from the shattered regiments, I saw a riderless horse plunging toward me. To seize his bridle and climb into the saddle was the work of a moment; and I felt that, unlike McDowell, I was still master of the situation. Working my out of the press and to our right, I saw that another charge for the guns by fresh troops was in progress. It seemed successful at first. The guns were retaken, but soon the same old story was repeated, and a corresponding rush from the other side swept our men back.

"Would you believe it, this capture and recapture occurred several times. A single regiment even would dash forward, and actually drive the Rebels back, only to lose a few moments later what they had gained. Never was there braver fighting, never worse tactics. The repeated successes of small bodies of troops proved that a compact battle line could have swept the ridge, and not only retaken the guns, but made them effective in the conflict. As it was, the two sides worried and tore each other like great dogs, governed merely by the impulse and instinct of fight. The batteries were the bone between them.

"This senseless, wasteful struggle could not go on forever. That it lasted as long as it did speaks volumes in favor of the material of which our future soldiers are to be made. As I rode slowly from the line and scene of actual battle, of which I had had enough, I became disheartened. We had men in plenty—there were thousands on every side—but in what condition! There was no appearance of fear among the men I saw at about four P.M. (I can only guess the time, for my watch had stopped), but abundant evidence of false confidence and still more of the indifference of men who feel they have done all that should be required of them and are utterly fagged out. Multitudes, both officers and privates, were lying and lounging around waiting for their comrades to finish the ball.

"For instance, I would ask a man to what regiment he belonged, and he would tell me.

"'Where is it?'

"'Hanged if I know. Saw a lot of the boys awhile ago.'

"Said an officer in answer to my inquiries, 'No; I don't know where the colonel is, and I don't care. After one of our charges we all adjourned like a town meeting. I'm played out; have been on my feet since one o'clock last night.'

"These instances were characteristic of the state of affairs in certain parts of the field that I visited. Plucky or conscientious fellows would join their comrades in the fight without caring what regiment they acted with; but the majority of the great disorganized mass did what they pleased, after the manner of a country fair, crowding in all instances around places where water could be obtained. Great numbers had thrown away their canteens and provisions, as too heavy to carry in the heat, or as impediments in action. Officers and men were mixed up promiscuously, hobnobbing and chaffing in a languid way, and talking over their experiences, as if they were neighbors at home. The most wonderful part of it all was that they had no sense of their danger and of the destruction they were inviting by their unsoldierly course.

"I tried to impress these dangers on one or two, but the reply was, 'Oh, hang it! The Rebs are as badly used up as we are. Don't you see things are growing more quiet? Give us a rest!'

"By this time I had worked my way well to my right, and was on a little eminence watching our line advance, wondering at the spirit with which the fight was still maintained. Indeed, I grew hopeful once more as I saw the good work that the regiments still intact were doing. There was much truth in the remark that the Rebels were used up also, unless they had reserves of which we knew nothing. At that time we had no idea that we had been fighting, not only Beauregard, but also Johnson from the Shenandoah.

"My hope was exceedingly intensified by the appearance of a long line of troops emerging from the woods on our flank and rear, for I never dreamed that they could be other than our own re-enforcements. Suddenly

I caught sight of a flag which I had learned to know too well. The line halted a moment, muskets were levelled, and I found myself in a perfect storm of bullets. I assure you I made a rapid change of base, for when our line turned I should be between two fires. As it was, I was cut twice in this arm while galloping away. In a few moments a battery also opened upon our flank; and it became as certain as day that a large Confederate force from some quarter had been hurled upon the flank and rear of our exhausted forces. The belief that Johnson's army had arrived spread like wildfire. How absurd and crude it all seems now! We had been fighting Johnson from the first.

"All aggressive action on our part now ceased; and as if governed by one common impulse, the army began its retreat.

"Try to realize it. Our retirement was not ordered. There were thousands to whom no order could be given unless with a voice like a thunder peal. Indeed, one may say, the order was given by the thunder of that battery on our flank. It was heard throughout the field; and the army, acting as individuals or in detachments, decided to leave. To show how utterly bereft of guidance, control, and judgment were our forces, I have merely to say that each man started back by exactly the same route he had come, just as a horse would do, while right before them was the Warrenton Pike, a good, straight road direct to Centerville, which was distant but little over four miles.

"This disorganized, exhausted mob was as truly in just the fatal condition for the awful contagion we call 'panic' as it would have been from improper food and other causes, for some other epidemic. The Greeks, who always had a reason for everything, ascribed the nameless dread, the sudden and unaccountable fear, which bereaves men of manhood and reason, to the presence of a god. It is simply a latent human weakness, which certain conditions rarely fail to develop. They were all present at the close of that fatal day. I tell you frankly that I felt something of it myself, and at a time, too, when I knew I was not in the least immediate danger. To counteract it I turned and rode deliberately toward the enemy, and the emotion passed. I half believe, however, that if I had yielded, it would have carried me away like an attack of the plague. The moral of it all is, that the conditions of the disease should be guarded against.

"When it became evident that the army was uncontrollable and was leaving the field, I pressed my way to the vicinity of McDowell to see what he would do. What could he do? I never saw a man so overwhelmed with astonishment and anger. Almost to the last I believe he expected to win the day. He and his officers commanded, stormed, entreated. He might as well have tried to stop Niagara above the falls as that human tide. He sent orders in all directions for a general concentration at Centerville, and then with certain of his staff galloped away. I tried to follow, but was prevented by the interposing crowd.

"I then joined a detachment of regulars and marines, who marched quietly in prompt obedience of orders; and we made our way through the disorder like a steamer through the surging waves. All the treatises on discipline that were ever written would not have been so convincing as that little oasis of organization. They marched very slowly, and often halted to cover the retreat.

"I had now seen enough on the further bank of Bull Run, and resolved to push ahead as fast as my horse would walk to the eastern side. Moreover, my leg and wounds were becoming painful, and I was exceedingly weary. I naturally followed the route taken by Tyler's command in coming upon and returning from the field, and crossed Bull Run some distance above the Stone Bridge. The way was so impeded by fugitives that my progress was slow, but when I at last reached the Warrenton Turnpike and proceeded toward a wretched little stream called Cub Run, I witnessed a scene that beggars description.

"Throughout the entire day, and especially in the afternoon, vehicles of every description—supply wagons, ambulances, and the carriages of civilians—had been congregating in the Pike vicinity of Stone Bridge. When the news of the defeat reached this point, and the roar of cannon and musketry began to approach instead of recede, a general movement toward Centerville began. This soon degenerated into the wildest panic, and the road was speedily choked by storming, cursing, terror-stricken men, who in their furious haste, defeated their own efforts to escape. It was pitiful, it was shameful, to see ambulances full of the wounded shoved to one side and left by the cowardly thieves who had galloped away on the horses. It was one long scene of wreck and ruin, through which pressed a struggling, sweating, cursing throng. Horses with their traces cut, and carrying two and even three men, were urged on and over everybody that could not get out of the way. Everything was abandoned that would impede progress, and arms and property of all kinds were left as a rich harvest for the pursuing Confederates. Their cavalry, hovering near, like hawks eager for the prey, made dashes here and there, as opportunity offered.

"I picked my way through the woods rather than take my chances in the road, and so my progress was slow. To make matters tenfold worse, I found when I reached the road leading to the north through the 'Big Woods' that the head of the column that had come all the way around by Sudley's Ford, the route of the morning march, was mingling with the masses already thronging the Pike. The confusion, the selfish, remorseless scramble to get ahead, seemed as horrible as it could be; but imagine the condition of affairs when on reaching the vicinity of Cub Run we found that a Rebel battery had opened upon the bridge, our only visible means of crossing. A few moments later, from a little eminence, I saw a shot take effect on a team of horses; and a heavy caisson was overturned directly in the centre of the bridge, barring all advance, while the mass of soldiers, civilians, and nondescript army followers, thus detained under fire, became perfectly wild with terror. The caisson was soon removed, and the throng rushed on.

"I had become so heart-sick, disgusted, and weary of the whole thing, that my one impulse was to reach Centerville, where I supposed we should make a stand. As I was on the north side of the Pike, I skirted up the stream with a number of others until we found a place where we could scramble across, and soon after we passed within a brigade of our troops that were thrown across the road to check the probable pursuit of the enemy.

"On reaching Centerville, we found everything in the direst confusion. Colonel Miles, who commanded the reserves at that point, was unfit for the position, and had given orders that had imperilled the entire army. It was said that the troops which had come around by Sudley's ford had lost all their guns at Cub Run; and the fugitives arriving were demoralized to the last degree. Indeed, a large part of the army, without waiting for orders or paying heed to any one, continued their flight toward Washington. Holding the bridle of my horse, I lay down near headquarters to rest and to learn what would be done. A council of war was held, and as the result we were soon on the retreat again. The retreat, or panic-stricken flight rather, had, in fact, never ceased on the part of most of those who had been in the main battle. That they could keep up this desperate tramp was a remarkable example of human endurance when sustained by excitement, fear, or any strong emotion. The men who marched or fled on Sunday night had already been on their feet twenty-four hours, and the greater part of them had experienced the terrific strain of actual battle.

"My story has already been much too long. From the daily journals you have learned pretty accurately what occurred after we reached Centerville. Richardson's and Blenker's brigades made a quiet and orderly retreat when all danger to the main body was over. The sick and wounded were left behind with spoils enough to equip a good-sized Confederate army. I followed the headquarters escort, and eventually made my way into Washington in the drenching rain of Monday, and found the city crowded with fugitives to whom the loyal people were extending unbounded hospitality. I felt ill and feverish, and yielded to the impulse to reach home; and I never acted more wisely.

"Now you have the history of my first battle; and may I never see one like it again. And yet I believe the battle of Bull Run will become one of the most interesting studies of American history and character. On our side it was not directed by generals, according to the rules of war. It was fought by Northern men after their own fashion and according to their native genius; and I shall ever maintain that it was fought far better than could have been expected of militia who knew less of the practical science of war than of the philosophy of Plato.

"The moral of my story, Hilland, scarcely needs pointing; and it applies to us both. When we go, let us go as soldiers; and if we have only a corporal's command, let us lead soldiers. The grand Northern onset of which you have dreamed so long has been made. You have seen the result. You have the means and ability to equip and command a regiment. Infuse into it your own spirit; and at the same time make it a machine that will hold together as long as you have a man left."

"Graham," said Hilland, slowly and deliberately, "there is no resisting the logic of events. You have convinced me of my error, and I shall follow your advice."

"And, Grace," concluded Graham, "believe me, by so doing he adds tenfold to his chances of living to a good old age."

"Yes," she said, looking at him gratefully through tear-dimmed eyes. "You have convinced me of that also."

"Instead of rushing off to some out-of-the-way place or camp, he must spend months in recruiting and drilling his men; and you can be with him."

"Oh, Alford!" she exclaimed, "is that the heavenly logic of your long, terrible story?"

"It's the rational logic; you could not expect any other kind from me."

"Well, Graham," ejaculated the major, with a long sigh of relief, "I wouldn't have missed your account of the battle for a year's pay. And mark my words, young men, you may not live to see it, or I either, but the North will win in this fight. That's the fact that I'm convinced of in spite of the panic."

"The fact that I'm convinced of," said Mrs. Mayburn brusquely, mopping her eyes meanwhile, "is that Alford needs rest. I'm going to take him home at once." And the young man seconded her in spite of all protestations.

"Dear, vigilant old aunty," said Graham, when they were alone, "you know when I have reached the limit of endurance."

"Ah! Alford, Alford," moaned the poor woman, "I fear you are seeking death in this war."

He looked at her tenderly for a moment, and then said, "Hereafter I will try to take no greater risks than a soldier's duties require."

CHAPTER XXII
SELF-SENTENCED

Days, weeks, and months with their changes came and went. Hilland, with characteristic promptness, carried out his friend's suggestion; and through his own means and personal efforts, in great measure, recruited and equipped a regiment of cavalry. He was eager that his friend should take a command in it; but Graham firmly refused.

"Our relations are too intimate for discipline," he said. "We might be placed in situations wherein our friendship would embarrass us."

Grace surmised that he had another reason; for, as time passed, she saw less and less of him. He had promptly obtained a lieutenancy in a regiment that was being recruited at Washington; and by the time her husband's regiment reached that city, the more disciplined organization to which Graham was attached was ordered out on the Virginia picket line beyond Arlington Heights.

Hilland, with characteristic modesty, would not take the colonelcy of the regiment that he chiefly had raised; but secured for the place a fine officer of the regular army, and contented himself with a captaincy. "Efficiency of the service is what I am aiming at," he said. "I would much rather rise by merit from the ranks than command a brigade by favor."

Unlike many men of wealth, he had a noble repugnance to taking any public advantage of it; and the numerous officers of the time that had obtained their positions by influence were his detestation.

Graham's predictions in regard to Grace were fulfilled. For long months she saw her husband almost daily, and, had it not been for the cloud that hung over the future, it would have been one of the happiest periods of her life. She saw Hilland engaged in tasks that brought him a deep and growing satisfaction. She saw her father in his very element. There were no more days of dulness and weariness for him. The daily journals teemed with subjects of interest, and with their aid he planned innumerable campaigns. Military men were coming and going, and with these young officers the veteran was an oracle. He gave Hilland much shrewd advice; and even when it was not good, it was listened to with deference, and so the result was just as agreeable to the major.

What sweeter joy is there for the aged than to sit in the seat of judgment and counsel, and feel that the world would go awry were it not for the guidance and aid of their experience! Alas for the poor old major, and those like him! The world does not grow old as they do. It only changes and becomes more vast and complicated. What was wisest and best in their day becomes often as antiquated as the culverin that once defended castellated ramparts.

Happily the major had as yet no suspicion of this; and when he and Grace accompanied Hilland and his regiment to Washington, the measure of his content was full. There he could daily meet other veterans of the regular service; and in listening to their talk, one might imagine that McClellan had only to attend their sittings to learn how to subdue the rebellion within a few months. These veterans were not bitter partisans. General Robert E. Lee was "Bob Lee" to them; and the other chiefs of the Confederacy were spoken of by some familiar *sobriquet*, acquired in many instances when boys at West Point. They would have fought these old friends and acquaintances to the bitter end, according to the tactics of the old school; but after the battle, those that survived would have hobnobbed together over a bottle of wine as sociably as if they had been companions in arms.

Mrs. Mayburn accompanied the major's party to Washington, for, as she said, she was "hungry for a sight of her boy." As often as his duties permitted, Graham rode in from the front to see her. But it began to be noticed that after these visits he ever sought some perilous duty on the picket line, or engaged in some dash at the enemy or guerillas in the vicinity. He could not visit his aunt without seeing Grace, whose tones were now so gentle when she spoke to him, and so full of her heart's deep gratitude, that a renewal of his old fierce fever of unrest was the result. He was already gaining a reputation for extreme daring, combined with unusual coolness and vigilance; and before the campaign of '62 opened he had been promoted to a first lieutenancy.

Time passed; the angry torrent of the war broadened and deepened. Men and measures that had stood out like landmarks were engulfed and forgotten.

It goes without saying that the friends did their duty in camp and field. There were no more panics. The great organizer, McClellan, had made soldiers of the vast army; and had he been retained in the service as the creator of armies for other men to lead, his labors would have been invaluable.

At last, to the deep satisfaction of Graham and Hilland, their regiments were brigaded together, and they frequently met. It was then near the close of the active operations of '62, and the friends now ranked as Captain Graham and Major Hilland. Notwithstanding the reverses suffered by the Union arms, the young men's confidence was unabated as to the final issue. Hilland had passed through several severe conflicts, and his name had been mentioned by reason of his gallantry. Grace began to feel that fate could never be so cruel as to destroy her very life in his life. She saw that her father exulted more over her husband's soldierly qualities than in all his wealth; and although they spent the summer season as usual at the seaside with Mrs. Mayburn, the hearts of all three were following two regiments through the forests and fields of Virginia. Half a score of journals were daily searched for items concerning them, and the arrival of the mails was the event of the day.

There came a letter in the autumn which filled the heart of Grace with immeasurable joy and very, very deep sadness. Mrs. Mayburn was stricken to the heart, and would not be comforted, while the old major swore and blessed God by turns.

The cause was this. The brigade with which the friends were connected was sent on a *reconnaissance*, and they felt the enemy strongly before retiring, which at last they were compelled to do precipitately. It so happened that Hilland commanded the rear-guard. In an advance he ever led; on a retreat he was apt to keep well to the rear. In the present instance the pursuit had been prompt and determined, and he had been compelled to make more than one repelling charge to prevent the retiring column from being pressed too hard. His command had thus lost heavily, and at last overwhelming numbers drove them back at a gallop.

Graham, in the rear of the main column, which had just crossed a small wooden bridge over a wide ditch or little run through the fields, saw the headlong retreat of Hilland's men, and he instantly deployed his company that he might check the close pursuit by a volley. As the Union troopers neared the bridge it was evidently a race for life and liberty, for they were outnumbered ten to one. In a few moments they began to pour over, but Hilland did not lead. They were nearly all across, but their commander was not among them; and Graham was wild with anxiety as he sat on his horse at the right of his line waiting to give the order to fire. Suddenly, in the failing light of the evening, he saw Hilland with his right arm hanging helpless, spurring a horse badly blown; while gaining fast upon him were four savage-looking Confederates, their sabres emitting a steely, deadly sheen, and uplifted to strike the moment they could reach him.

With the rapidity of light, Graham's eye measured the distance between his friend and the bridge, and his instantaneous conviction was that Hilland was doomed, for he could not order a volley without killing him almost to a certainty. At that supreme crisis, the suggestion passed through his mind like a lurid flash, "In a few moments Hilland will be dead, and Grace may yet be mine."

Then, like an avenging demon, the thought confronted him. He saw it in its true aspect, and in an outburst of self-accusing fury he passed the death sentence on himself. Snatching out the long, straight sword he carried, he struck with the spur the noble horse he bestrode, gave him the rein, and made straight for the deep, wide ditch. There was no time to go around by the bridge, which was still impeded by the last of the fugitives.

His men held their breath as they saw his purpose. The feat seemed impossible; but as his steed cleared the chasm by a magnificent bound, a loud cheer rang down the line. The next moment Hilland, who had mentally said farewell to his wife, saw Graham passing him like a thunderbolt. There was an immediate clash of steel, and then the foremost pursuer was down, cleft to the jaw. The next shared the same fate; for Graham, in what he deemed his death struggle, had almost ceased to be human. His spirit, stung to a fury that it had never known and would never know again, blazed in his eyes and flashed in the lightning play of his sword. The two others pursuers reined up their steeds and sought to attack him on either side. He threw his own horse back almost upon his haunches, and was on his guard, meaning to strike home the moment the fence of his opponents permitted. At this instant, however, there were a dozen shots from the swarming Rebels, that were almost upon him, and he and his horse were seen to fall to the ground. Meantime Hilland had instinctively tried to rein in his horse, that he might return to the help of his friend, although from his wound he could render no aid. Some of his own men who had crossed the bridge, and in a sense of safety had regained their wits, saw his purpose, and dashing back, they formed a body-guard around him, and dragged his horse swiftly beyond the line of battle.

A yell of anger accompanied by a volley came from Graham's men that he had left in line, and a dozen Confederate saddles were emptied; but their return fire was so deadly, and their numbers were so overwhelming, that the officer next in command ordered retreat at a gallop. Hilland, in his anguish, would not have left his friend had not his men grasped his rein and carried him off almost by force. Meanwhile the darkness set in so rapidly that the pursuit soon slackened and ceased.

During the remainder of the ride back to their camp, which was reached late at night, the ardent-natured Hilland was almost demented. He wept, raved, and swore. He called himself an accursed coward, that he had left the friend who had saved his life. His broken arm was as nothing to him, and eventually the regimental surgeon had to administer strong opiates to quiet him.

When late the next day he awoke, it all came back to him with a dully heavy ache at heart. Nothing could be done. His mind, now restored to its balance, recognized the fact. The brigade was under orders to move to another point, and he was disabled and compelled to take a leave of absence until fit for duty. The inexorable mechanism of military life moves on, without the slightest regard for the individual; and Graham's act was only one of the many heroic deeds of the war, some seen and more unnoted.

CHAPTER XXIII
AN EARLY DREAM FULFILLED

A few days later Grace welcomed her husband with a long, close embrace, but with streaming eyes; while he bowed his head upon her shoulder and groaned in the bitterness of his spirit.

"Next to losing you, Grace," he said, "this is the heaviest blow I could receive; and to think that he gave his life for me! How can I ever face Mrs. Mayburn?"

But his wife comforted him as only she knew how to soothe and bless; and Mrs. Mayburn saw that he was as sincere a mourner as herself. Moreover they would not despair of Graham, for although he had been seen to fall, he might only have been wounded and made a prisoner. Thus the bitterness of their grief was mitigated by hope.

This hope was fulfilled in a most unexpected way, by a cheerful letter from Graham himself; and the explanation of this fact requires that the story should return to him.

He thought that the sentence of death which he had passed upon himself had been carried into effect. He had felt himself falling, and then there had been sudden darkness. Like a dim taper flickering in the night, the spark of life began to kindle again. At first he was conscious of but one truth-that he was not dead. Where he now was, in this world or some other, what he now was, he did not know; but the essential *ego*, Alford Graham, had not ceased to exist. The fact filled him with a dull, wondering awe. Memory slowly revived, and its last impression was that he was to die and had died, and yet he was not dead.

As a man's characteristic traits will first assert themselves, he lay still and feebly tried to comprehend it all. Suddenly a strange, horrid sound smote upon his senses and froze his blood with dread. It must be life after death, for only his mind appeared to have any existence. He could not move. Again the unearthly sound, which could not be a human shriek, was repeated; and by half-involuntary and desperate effort he started up and looked around. The scene at first was obscure, confused, and awful. His eye could not explain it, and he instinctively stretched out his hands;

and through the sense of touch all that had happened came back to his confused brain. He first felt of himself, passed his hand over his forehead, his body, his limbs: he certainly was in the flesh, and that to his awakening intelligence meant much, since it accorded with his belief that life and the body were inseparable. Then he felt around him in the darkness, and his hands touched the grassy field. This fact righted him speedily. As in the old fable, when he touched the earth he was strong. He next noted that his head rested on a smooth rock that rose but little above the plain, and that he must have fallen upon it. He sat up and looked around; and as the brain gradually resumed its action after its terrible shock, the situation became intelligible. The awful sounds that he had heard came from a wounded horse that was struggling feebly in the light of the rising moon, now in her last quarter. He was upon the scene of last evening's conflict, and the obscure objects that lay about him were the bodies of the dead. Yes, there before him were the two men he had killed; and their presence brought such a strong sense of repugnance and horror that he sprang to his feet and recoiled away.

He looked around. There was not a living object in sight except the dying horse. The night wind moaned about him, and soughed and sighed as if it were a living creature mourning over the scene.

It became clear to him that he had been left as dead. Yes, and he had been robbed, too; for he shivered, and found that his coat and vest were gone, also his hat, his money, his watch, and his boots. He walked unsteadily to the little bridge, and where he had left his line of faithful men, all was dark and silent. With a great throb of joy he remembered that Hilland must have sped across that bridge to safety, while he had expiated his evil thought.

He then returned and circled around the place. He was evidently alone; but the surmise occurred to him that the Confederates would return in the morning to bury their dead, and if he would escape he must act promptly. And yet he could not travel in his present condition. He must at least have hat, coat, and boots. His only resource was to take them from the dead; but the thought of doing so was horrible to him. Reason about it as he might, he drew near their silent forms with an uncontrollable repugnance. He almost gave up his purpose, and took a few hasty steps away, but a thorn pierced his foot and taught him his folly. Then his imperious will asserted itself, and with an imprecation on his weakness he returned to the nearest silent form, and took from it a limp felt hat, a coat, and a pair of boots, all much the worse for wear; and having arrayed himself in these, started on the trail of the Union force.

He had not gone over a mile when, on surmounting an eminence, he saw by dying fires in a grove beneath him that he was near the bivouac of a body of soldiers. He hardly hoped they could be a detachment of Union men; and yet the thought that it was possible led him to approach stealthily within earshot. At last he heard one patrol speak to another in unmistakable Southern accent, and he found that the enemy was in his path.

Silently as a ghost he stole away, and sought to make a wide detour to the left, but soon lost himself hopelessly in a thick wood. At last, wearied beyond mortal endurance, he crawled into what seemed the obscurest place he could find, and lay down and slept.

The sun was above the horizon when he awoke, stiff, sore, and hungry, but refreshed, rested. A red squirrel was barking at him derisively from a bough near, but no other evidences of life were to be seen. Sitting up, he tried to collect his thoughts and decide upon his course. It at once occurred to him that he would be missed, and that pursuit might be made with hounds. At once he sprang to his feet and made his way toward a valley, which he hoped would be drained by a running stream. The welcome sound of water soon guided him, and pushing through the underbrush he drank long and deeply, bathed the ugly bruise on his head, and then waded up the current.

He had not gone much over half a mile before he saw through an opening a negro gazing wonderingly at him. "Come here, my good fellow," he cried.

The man approached slowly, cautiously.

"I won't hurt you," Graham resumed; "indeed you can see that I'm in your power. Won't you help me?"

"Dunno, mas'r," was the non-committal reply.

"Are you in favor of Lincoln's men or the Confederates?" "Dunno, mas'r. It 'pends."

"It depends upon what?"

"On whedder you'se a Linkum man or 'Federate."

"Well, then, here's the truth. The Lincoln men are your best friends, if you've sense enough to know it; and I'm one of them. I was in the fight off there yesterday, and am trying to escape."

"Oh golly! I'se sense enough;" and the genial gleam of the man's ivory was an omen of good to Graham. "But," queried the negro, "how you wear 'Federate coat and hat?"

"Because I was left for dead, and mine were stolen. I had to wear something. The Confederates don't wear blue trousers like these."

"Dat's so; an' I knows yer by yer talk and look. I knows a 'Federate well as I does a coon. But dese yere's mighty ticklish times; an' a nigger hab no show ef he's foun' meddlin'. What's yer gwine ter do?"

"Perhaps you can advise me. I'm afraid they'll put hounds on my trail"

"Dat dey will, if dey misses yer."

"Well, that's the reason I'm here in the stream. But I can't keep this up long. I'm tired and hungry. I've heard that you people befriended Lincoln's men. We are going to win, and now's the time for you to make friends with those who will soon own this country."

"Ob corse, you'se a-gwine ter win. Linkum is de Moses we're all a-lookin' ter. At all our meetin's we'se a-prayin' for him and to him. He's de Lord's right han' to lead we alls out ob bondage."

"Well, I swear to you I'm one of his men."

"I knows you is, and I'se a-gwine to help you, houn's or no houn's. Keep up de run a right smart ways, and you'se'll come ter a big flat stun'. Stan' dar in de water, an I'll be dar wid help." And the man disappeared in a long swinging run.

Graham did as he was directed, and finally reached a flat rock, from which through the thick bordering growth something like a path led away. He waited until his patience was wellnigh exhausted, and then heard far back upon his trail the faint bay of a hound. He was about to push his way on up the stream, when there was a sound of hasty steps, and his late acquaintance with another stalwart fellow appeared.

"Dere's no time ter lose, mas'r. Stan' whar you is," and in a moment he splashed in beside him. "Now get on my back. Jake dar will spell me when I wants him; fer yer feet mustn't touch de groun';" and away they went up the obscure path.

This was a familiar mode of locomotion to Graham, for he had been carried thus by the hour over the mountain passes of Asia. They had not gone far before they met two or three colored women with a basket of clothes.

"Dat's right," said Graham's conveyance; "wash away right smart, and dunno nothin'. Yer see," he continued, "dis yer is Sunday, and we'se not in de fields, an de women folks can help us;" and Graham though that the old superstition of a Sabbath has served him well for once.

They soon left the path and entered some very heavy timber, through an opening of which he saw the negro quarters and plantation dwellings in the distance.

At last they stopped before an immense tree. Some brush was pushed aside, revealing an aperture through which Graham was directed to crawl, and he found himself within a heart of oak.

"Dar's room enough in dar ter sit down," said his sable friend. "An' you'se 'll find a jug ob milk an' a pone ob corn meal. Luck ter yer. Don't git lonesome like and come out. We'se a-gwine ter look ater yer;" and the opening was hidden by brush again, and Graham was left alone.

From a small aperture above his head a pencil of sunlight traversed the gloom, to which his eyes soon grew accustomed, and he saw a rude seat and the food mentioned. By extending his feet slightly through the opening by which he had entered, he found the seat really comfortable; and the coarse fare was ambrosial to his ravenous appetite. Indeed, he began to enjoy the adventure. His place of concealment was so unexpected and ingenious that it gave him a sense of security. He had ever had a great love for trees, and now it seemed as if one had opened its very heart to hide him.

Then his hosts and defenders interested him exceedingly. By reason of residence in New England and his life abroad, he was not familiar with the negro, especially his Southern type. Their innocent guile and preposterous religious belief amused him. He both smiled and wondered at their faith in "Linkum," whom at that time he regarded as a long headed, uncouth Western politician, who had done not a little mischief of interfering with the army.

"It is ever so with all kinds of superstition and sentimental belief," he soliloquized. "Some conception of the mind is embodied, or some object is idealized and magnified until the original is lost sight of, and men come to worship a mere fancy of their own. Then some mind, stronger and more imaginative than the average, gives shape and form to this confused image; and so there grows in time a belief, a theology, or rather a mythology. To think that this Lincoln, whom I've seen in attitudes anything but divine, and telling broad, coarse stories—to think that he should be a demigod, antitype of the venerated Hebrew! In truth it leads one to suspect, according to analogy, that Moses was a money-making Jew, and his effort to lead his people to Palestine an extensive land speculation."

Graham lived to see the day when he acknowledged that the poor negroes of the most remote plantations had a truer conception of the grand proportions of Lincoln's character at that time than the majority of his most cultivated countrymen.

His abstract speculations were speedily brought to a close by the nearer baying of hounds as they surmounted an eminence over which lay his trail. On came the hunt, with its echoes rising and falling with the wind or the inequalities of the ground, until it burst deep-mouthed and hoarse over the brow of the hill that sloped to the stream. Then there were confused sounds, both of the dogs and of men's voices, which gradually approached until there was a pause, caused undoubtedly by a colloquy with Aunt Sheba and her associate washerwomen. It did not last very long; and then, to Graham's dismay, the threatening sounds were renewed, and seemed coming directly toward him. He soon gave up all hope, and felt that he had merely to congratulate himself that, from the nature of his hiding-place, he could not be torn by the dogs, when he perceived that the hunt was coming no nearer—in brief, that it was passing. He then understood that his refuge must be near the bed of the stream, from which his pursuers were seeking on either side his diverging trail. This fact relieved him at once, and quietly he listened to the sounds, dying away as they had come.

As the sun rose higher the ray of light sloped downward until it disappeared; and in the profound gloom and quiet he fell asleep. He was awaked by hearing a voice call, "Mas'r."

Looking down, he saw that the brush had been removed, and that the opening was partially obstructed by a goblin-like head with little horns rising all over it.

"Mas'r," said the apparition, "Aunt Sheba sends you dis, and sez de Lord be wid you."

"Thanks for Aunt Sheba, and you, too, whatever you are," cried Graham; and to gratify his curiosity he sprang down on his knees and peered out in time to see a little negro girl replacing the brush, while what he had mistaken for horns was evidently the child's manner of wearing her hair. He then gave his attention to the material portion of Aunt Sheba's offering, and found a rude sort of platter, or low basket, made of corn husks, and in this another jug of milk, corn bread, and a delicious broiled chicken done to that turn of perfection of which only the colored aunties of the South are capable.

"Well!" ejaculated Graham. "From this day I'm an abolitionist, a Republican of the blackest dye." A little later he added, "Any race that can produce a woman capable of such cookery as this has a future before it."

Indeed, the whole affair was taking such an agreeable turn that he was inclined to be jocular.

After another long sleep in the afternoon, he was much refreshed, and eager to rejoin his command. But Issachar, or Iss, as his associates called him, the negro who had befriended him in the first instance, came and explained that the whole country was full of Confederates; and that it might be several days before it would be safe to seek the Union lines.

"We'se all lookin' out fer yer, mas'r," he continued; "you won't want for nothin'. An' we won't kep yer in dis woodchuck hole arter nine ob de ev'nin'. Don't try ter come out. I'm lookin' t'oder way while I'se a-talkin. Mean niggers an' 'Federates may be spyin' aroun'. But I reckon not; I'se laid in de woods all day, a-watchin'.

"Now I tell yer what 'tis, mas'r, I'se made up my mine to put out ob heah. I'se gwine ter jine de Linkum men fust chance I gits. An' if yer'll wait an' trus' me, I'll take yer slick and clean; fer I know dis yer country and ebery hole whar ter hide well as a fox. If I gits safe ter de Linkum folks, yer'll say a good word fer Iss, I reckon."

"Indeed, I will. If you wish, I'll take you into my own service, and pay you good wages."

"Done, by golly; and when dey cotch us, dey'll cotch a weasel asleep."

"But haven't you a wife and children?"

"Oh, yah. I'se got a wife, an' I'se got a lot ob chillen somewhar in de 'Fed'racy; but I'll come wid you uns bime by, an' gedder up all I can fine. I'se 'll come 'long in de shank ob de ev'nin', mas'r, and guv yer a shakedown in my cabin, an' I'll watch while yer sleeps. Den I'll bring yer back heah befo' light in de mawnin'."

The presence of Confederate forces required these precautions for several days, and Iss won Graham's whole heart by his unwearied patience and vigilance. But the young man soon prevailed on the faithful fellow to sleep nights while he watched; for after the long inaction of the day he was almost wild for exercise. Cautious Iss would have been nearly crazed with anxiety had he known of the *reconnaissances* in which his charge indulged while he slept. Graham succeeded in making himself fully master of the disposition of the Rebel forces in the vicinity, and eventually learned that the greater part of them had been withdrawn. When he had communicated this intelligence to Iss, they prepared to start for the Union lines on the following night, which proved dark and stormy.

Iss, prudent man, kept the secret of his flight from even his wife, and satisfied his marital compunctions by chucking her under the chin and calling her "honey" once or twice while she got supper for him. At eight in the evening he summoned Graham from his hiding-place, and led him, with almost the unerring instinct of some wild creature of the night, due northeast, the direction in which the Union forces were said to be at that time. It was a long, desolate tramp, and the dawn found them drenched and weary. But the glorious sun rose warm and bright, and in a hidden glade of the forest they dried their clothes, rested, and refreshed themselves. After a long sleep in a dense thicket they were ready to resume their journey at nightfall. Iss proved an invaluable guide, for, concealing Graham, he would steal away, communicate with the negroes, and bring fresh provisions.

On the second night he learned that there was a Union force not very far distant to the north of their line of march. Graham had good cause to wonder at the sort of freemasonry that existed among the negroes, and the facility with which they obtained and transmitted secret intelligence. Still more had he reason to bless their almost universal fidelity to the Union cause.

Another negro joined them as guide, and in the gray of the morning they approached the Union pickets. Graham deemed it wise to wait till they could advance openly and boldly; and by nine o'clock he was received with acclamations by his own regiment as one risen from the dead.

After congratulations and brief explanations were over, his first task was to despatch the two brief letters mentioned, to his aunt and Hilland, in time to catch the daily mail that left their advanced position. Then he saw his brigade commander, and made it clear to him that with a force of about two regiments he could strike a heavy blow against the Confederates whom he had been reconnoitring; and he offered to act as guide. His proposition was accepted, and the attacking force started that very night. By forced marches they succeeded in surprising the Confederate encampment and in capturing a large number of prisoners. Iss also surprised his wife and Aunt Sheba even more profoundly, and before their exclamations ceased he had bundled them and their meagre belongings into a mule cart, with such of the "chillen" as had been left to him, and was following triumphantly in the wake of the victorious Union column; and not a few of their sable companions kept them company.

The whole affair was regarded as one of the most brilliant episodes of the campaign and Graham received much credit, not only in the official reports, but in the press. Indeed, the latter, although with no aid from the chief actor, obtained an outline of the whole story, from the rescue of his friend to his guidance of the successful expedition, and it was repeated with many variations and exaggerations. He cared little for these brief echoes of fame; but the letters of his aunt, Hilland, and even the old major, were valued indeed, while a note from the grateful wife became his treasure of treasures.

They had returned some time before to the St. John cottage, and she had at last written him a letter "straight from her heart," on the quaint secretary in the library, as he had dreamed possible on the first evening of their acquaintance.

CHAPTER XXIV
UNCHRONICLED CONFLICTS

Graham's friends were eager that he should obtain leave of absence, but he said, "No, not until some time in the winter."

His aunt understood him sufficiently well not to urge the matter, and it may be added that Grace did also.

Hilland's arm healed rapidly, and happy as he was in his home life at the cottage he soon began to chafe under inaction. Before very long it became evident that the major had not wholly outlived his influence at Washington, for there came an order assigning Major Hilland to duty in that city; and thither, accompanied by Grace and her father, he soon repaired. The arrangement proved very agreeable to Hilland during the period when his regiment could engage in little service beyond that of dreary picket duty. He could make his labors far more useful to the government in the city, and could also enjoy domestic life with his idolized wife. Mrs. Mayburn promised to join them after the holidays, and the reason for her delay was soon made evident.

One chilly, stormy evening, when nature was in a most uncomfortable mood, a card was brought to the door of Hilland's rooms at their inn just as he, with his wife and the major, was sitting down to one of those exquisite little dinners which only Grace knew how to order. Hilland glanced at the card, and gave such a shout that the waiter nearly fell over backward.

"Where is the gentleman? Take me to him on the double-quick. It's Graham. Hurrah! I'll order another dinner!" and he vanished, chasing the man downstairs and into the waiting-room, as if he were a detachment of Confederate cavalry. The decorous people in the hotel parlor were astounded as Hilland nearly ran over the breathless waiter at the door, dashed in like a whirlwind, and carried off his friend, laughing, chaffing, and embracing him all the way up the stairs. It was the old, wild exuberancy of his college days, only intensified by the deepest and most grateful emotion.

Grace stood within her door blushing, smiling, and with tears of feeling in her lovely eyes.

"Here he is," cried Hilland—"the very god of war. Give him his reward, Grace—a kiss that he will feel to the soles of his boots."

But she needed no prompting, for instead of taking Graham's proffered hand, she put her hands on his shoulders and kissed him again and again, exclaiming, "You saved Warren's life; you virtually gave yours for his; and in saving him you saved me. May God bless you every hour you live!"

"Grace," he said, gravely and gently, looking down into her swimming eyes and retaining her hands in a strong, warm clasp, "I am repaid a thousand-fold. I think this is the happiest moment of my life;" and then he turned to the major, who was scarcely less demonstrative in his way than Hilland had been.

"By Jove!" cried the veteran, "the war is going to be the making of you young fellows. Why, Graham, you no more look like the young man that played whist with me years since than I do. You have grown broad-shouldered and *distingue*, and you have the true military air in spite of that quiet civilian's dress."

"Oh, I shall always be comparatively insignificant," replied Graham, laughing. "Wait till Hilland wears the stars, as he surely will, and then you'll see a soldier."

"We see far more than a soldier in you, Alford," said Grace, earnestly. "Your men told Warren of your almost miraculous leap across the ditch; and Warren has again and again described your appearance as you rushed by him on his pursuers. Oh, I've seen the whole thing in my dreams so often!"

"Yes, Graham; you looked like one possessed. You reminded me of the few occasions when, in old college days, you got into a fury."

A frown as black as night lowered on Graham's brow, for they were recalling the most hateful memory of his life—a thought for which he felt he ought to die; but it passed almost instantly, and in the most prosaic tones he said, "Good friends, I'm hungry. I've splashed through Virginia mud twelve mortal hours to-day. Grace, be prepared for such havoc as only a cavalryman can make. We don't get such fare as this at the front."

She, with the pretty housewifely bustle which he had admired years ago, rang the bell and made preparations for a feast.

"Every fatted calf in Washington should be killed for you," she cried—"prodigal that you are, but only in brave deeds. Where's Iss? I want to see and feast him also."

"I left him well provided for in the lower regions, and astounding the 'cullud bredren' with stories which only the African can swallow. He shall come up by and by, for I have my final orders to give. He leads my horse back to the regiment in the morning, and takes care of him in my absence. I hope to spend a month with aunt."

"And how much time with us?" asked Hilland, eagerly.

"This evening."

"Now, Graham, I protest—"

"Now, Hilland, I'm ravenous, and here's a dinner fit for the Great Mogul."

"Oh, I know you of old. When you employ a certain tone you intend to have your own way; but it isn't fair."

"Don't take it to heart. I'll make another raid on you when I return, and then we shall soon be at the front together again. Aunty's lonely, you know."

"Grace and I don't count, I suppose," said the major.

"I had a thousand questions to ask you;" and he looked so aggrieved that Graham compromised and promised to spend the next day with him.

Then he gave an almost hilarious turn to the rest of the evening, and one would have thought that he was in the high spirits natural to any young officer with a month's leave of absence. He described the "woodchuck hole" which had been his hiding-place, sketched humorously the portraits of Iss, Aunt Sheba, who was now his aunt's cook, and gave funny episodes of his midnight prowlings while waiting for a chance to reach the Union lines. Grace noted how skilfully he kept his own personality in the background unless he appeared in some absurd or comical light; and she also noted that his eyes rested upon her less and less often, until at last, after Iss had had his most flattering reception, he said good-night rather abruptly.

The next day he entertained the major in a way that was exceedingly gratifying and flattering to the veteran. He brought some excellent maps, pointed out the various lines of march, the positions of the opposing armies, and showed clearly what had been done and what might have been. He next became the most patient and absorbed listener, as the old gentleman, by the aid of the same maps, planned a campaign which during the coming year would have annihilated the Confederacy. Grace, sitting near the window, might have imagined herself almost ignored. But she interpreted him differently. She now had the key which explained his conduct, and more than once tears came into her eyes.

Hilland returned early, having hastened through his duties, and was in superb spirits. They spent an afternoon together which stood out in memory like a broad gleam of sunshine in after years; and then Graham took his leave with messages from all to Mrs. Mayburn, who was to return with him.

As they were parting, Grace hesitated a moment, and then stepping forward impulsively she took Graham's hand in both of hers, and said impetuously: "You have seen how very, very happy we all are. Do you think that I forget for a moment that I owe it to you?"

Graham's iron nerves gave way. His hand trembled. "Don't speak to me in that way," he murmured. "Come, Hilland, or I shall miss the train;" and in a moment he was gone.

Mrs. Mayburn never forgot the weeks he spent with her. Sometimes she would look at him wonderingly, and once she said: "Alford, it is hard for me to believe that you have passed through all that you have. Day after day passes, and you seem perfectly content with my quiet, monotonous life. You read to me my old favorite authors. You chaff me and Aunt Sheba about our little domestic economies. Beyond a hasty run through the morning paper you scarcely look at the daily journals. You are content with one vigorous walk each day. Indeed you seem to have settled down and adapted yourself to my old woman's life for the rest of time. I thought you would be restless, urging my earlier return to Washington, or seeking to abridge your leave, so that you might return to the excitement of the camp "

"No, aunty dear, I am not restless. I have outlived and outgrown that phase of my life. You will find that my pulse is as even as yours. Indeed I have a deep enjoyment of this profound quiet of our house. I have fully accepted my lot, and now expect only those changes that come from without and not from within. To be perfectly sincere with you, the feeling is growing that this profound quietude that has fallen upon me may be the prelude to final rest. It's right that I should accustom your mind to the possibilities of every day in our coming campaign, which I well foresee will be terribly severe. At first our generals did not know how to use cavalry, and beyond escort and picket duty little was asked of it. Now all this is changed. Cavalry has its part in every pitched battle, and in the intervals it has many severe conflicts of its own. Daring, ambitious leaders are coming to the front, and the year will be one of great and hazardous activity. My chief regret is that Hilland's wound did not disable him wholly from further service in the field. Still he will come out all right. He always has and ever will. There are hidden laws that control and shape our lives. It seems to me that you were predestined to be just what you are. Your life is rounded out and symmetrical according to its own law. The same is true of Hilland and of myself thus far. The rudiments of what we are to-day were clearly apparent when we were boys. He is the same ardent, jolly, whole-souled fellow that clapped me on the back after leaving the class-room. Everybody liked him then, everything favored him. Often when he had not looked at a lesson he would make a superb recitation. I was moody and introspective; so I am to-day. Even the unforeseen events of life league together to develop one's characteristics. The conditions of his life today are in harmony with all that has been; the same is true of mine, with the strange exception that I have found a home and a dear staunch friend in one who I supposed would ever be a stranger. See how true my theory is of Grace and her father. Her blithesome girlhood has developed into the happiest wifehood. Her brow is as smooth as ever, and her eyes as bright. They have only gained in depth and tenderness as the woman has taken the place of the girl. Her form has only developed into lovelier proportions, and her character into a more exquisite symmetry. She has been one continuous growth according to the laws of her being; and so it will be to the end. She will be just as beautiful and lovable in old age as now; for nature, in a genial mood, infused into her no discordant, disfiguring elements. The major also is completing his life in consonance with all that has gone before."

"Alford, you are more of a fatalist than a materialist. In my heart I feel, I know, you are wrong. What you say seems so plausible as to be true; but my very soul revolts at it all. There is a deep undertone of sadness in your words, and they point to a possibility that would imbitter every moment of the remnant of my life. Suppose you should fall, what remedy would there be for me? Oh, in anguish I have learned what life would become then. I am a materialist like yourself, although all the clergymen in town would say I was orthodox. From earliest recollection mere things and certain people have been everything to me; and now you are everything, and yet at this hour the bullet may be molded which will strike you down. Grace, with her rich, beautiful life, is in equal danger. Hilland will go into the field and will expose himself as recklessly as yourself. I have no faith in your obscure laws. Thousands were killed in the last campaign, thousands are dying in hospitals this moment, and all this means thousands of broken hearts, unless they are sustained by something I have not. This world is all very well when all is well, but it can so easily become an accursed world!" The old lady spoke with a strange bitterness, revealing the profound disquietude that existed under the serene amenities of her age and her methodical life.

Graham sought to give a lighter tone to their talk and said: "Oh, well, aunty, perhaps we are darkening the sun with our own shadows. We must take life as we find it. There is no help for that. You have done so practically.

With your strong good sense you could not do otherwise. The trouble is that you are haunted by old-time New England beliefs that, from your ancestry, have become infused into your very blood. You can't help them any more than other inherited infirmities which may have afflicted your grandfather. Let us speak of something else. Ah, here is a welcome diversion—the daily paper—and I'll read it through to you, and we'll gain another hint as to the drift of this great tide of events."

The old lady shook her head sadly; and the fact that she watched the young man with hungry, wistful eyes, often blinded with tears, proved that neither state nor military policy was uppermost in her mind.

CHAPTER XXV
A PRESENTIMENT

On Christmas morning Graham found his breakfast-plate pushed back, and in its place lay a superb sword and belt, fashioned much like the one he had lost in the rescue of his friend. With it was a genial letter from Hilland, and a little note from Grace, which only said:

"You will find my name engraved upon the sword with Warren's. We have added nothing else, for the good reason that our names mean everything—more than could be expressed, were the whole blade covered with symbols, each meaning a volume. You have taught us how you will use the weapon, my truest and best of friends. GRACE HILLAND."

His eyes lingered on the name so long that his aunt asked: "Why don't you look at your gift?"

He slowly drew the long, keen, shining blade, and saw again the name "Grace Hilland," and for a time he saw nothing else. Suddenly he turned the sword and on the opposite side was "Warren Hilland," and he shook his head sadly.

"Alford, what *is* the matter?" his aunt asked impatiently.

"Why didn't they have their names engraved together?" he muttered slowly, "It's a bad omen. See, a sword is between their names. I wish they had been together. Oh, I wish Hilland could be kept out of the field!"

"There it is, Alford," began his aunt, irritably; "you men who don't believe anything are always the victims of superstition. Bad omen, indeed!"

"Well, I suppose I am a fool; but a strange chill at heart struck me for which I can't account;" and he sprang up and paced the floor uneasily. "Well," he continued, "I would bury it in my own heart rather than cause her one hour's sorrow, but I wish their names had been together." Then he took it up again and said: "Beautiful as it is, it may have to do some stern work, Grace—work far remote from your nature. All I ask is that it may come between Hilland and danger again. I wish I had not had that strange, cursed presentiment."

"Oh, Alford! I never saw you in such a mood, and on Christmas morning, too!"

"That is just what I don't like about it—it's not my habit to indulge such fancies, to say the least. Come what may, however, I dedicate the sword to her service without counting any cost;" and he kissed her name, and laid the weapon reverently aside.

"You are morbid this morning. Go to the door and see my present to you. You will find no bad omens on his shining coat."

Graham felt that it was weak to entertain such impressions as had mastered him, and hastened out. There, pawing the frozen ground, was a horse that satisfied even his fastidious eye. There was not a white hair in the coal-black coat. In his enthusiasm he forgot his hat, and led the beautiful creature up and down, observing with exultation his perfect action, clean-cut limbs, and deep, broad chest.

"Bring me a bridle," he said to the man in attendance, "and my hat."

A moment later he had mounted.

"Breakfast is getting cold," cried his aunt from the window, delighted, nevertheless, at the appreciation of her gift.

"This horse is breakfast and dinner both," he shouted, as he galloped down the path.

Then, to the old lady's horror, he dashed through the trees and shrubbery, took a picket-fence in a flying leap, and circled round the house till Mrs. Mayburn's head was dizzy. Then she saw him coming toward the door as if he would ride through the house; but the horse stopped almost instantly, and Graham was on his feet, handing the bridle to the gaping groom.

"Take good care of him," he said to the man, "for he is a jewel."

"Alford," exclaimed his aunt, "could you make no better return for my gift than to frighten me out of my wits?"

"Dear aunty, you are too well supplied ever to lose them for so slight a cause. I wanted to show the perfection of your gift, and how well it may serve me. You don't imagine that our cavalry evolutions are all performed on straight turnpike roads, do you? Now you know that you have given me an animal that can carry me wherever a horse can go, and so have added much to my chances of safety. I can skim out of a melee like a bird with Mayburn—for that shall be his name—where a blundering, stupid horse would break my neck, if I wasn't shot. I saw at once from his action what he could do. Where on earth did you get such a creature?"

"Well," said the old lady, beaming with triumphant happiness, "I have had agents on the lookout a long time. The man of whom you had your first horse, then called Firebrand, found him; and he knew well that he could not impose any inferior animal upon you. Are you really sincere in saying that such a horse as this adds to your chances of safety?"

"Certainly. That's what I was trying to show you. Did you not see how he would wind in and out among the trees and shrubbery—how he would take a fence lightly without any floundering? There is just as much difference among horses as among men. Some are simply awkward, heavy, and stupid; others are vicious; more are good at times and under ordinary circumstances, but fail you at a pinch. This horse is thoroughbred and well broken. You must have paid a small fortune for him."

"I never invested money that satisfied me better."

"It's like you to say so. Well, take the full comfort of thinking how much you have added to my comfort and prospective well-being. That gallop has already done me a world of good, and given me an appetite. I'll have another turn across the country after breakfast, and throw all evil presentiments to the winds."

"Why, now you talk sense. When you are in any more such moods as this morning I shall prescribe horse."

Before New Year's day Graham had installed his aunt comfortably in rooms adjoining the Hillands', and had thanked his friends for their gift in a way that proved it to be appreciated. Mrs. Mayburn had been cautioned never to speak of what he now regarded as a foolish and unaccountable presentiment, arising, perhaps, from a certain degree of morbidness of mind in all that related to Grace. Iss was on hand to act as groom, and Graham rode out with Hilland and Grace several times before his leave expired. Even at that day, when the city was full of gallant men and fair women, many turned to look as the three passed down the avenue.

Never had Grace looked so radiantly beautiful as when in the brilliant sunshine of a Washington winter and in the frosty air she galloped over the smooth, hard roads. Hilland was proud of the almost wondering looks of admiration that everywhere greeted her, and too much in love to note that the ladies they met looked at him in much the same way. The best that was said of Graham was that he looked a soldier, every inch of him, and that he rode the finest horse in the city as if he had been brought up in a saddle. He was regarded by society as reserved, unsocial, and proud; and at two or three receptions, to which he went because of the solicitation of his friends, he piqued the vanity of more than one handsome woman by his courteous indifference.

"What is the matter with your husband's friend?" a reigning belle asked Grace. "One might as well try to make an impression on a paving-stone."

"I think your illustration unhappy," was her quiet reply. "I cannot imagine Mr. Graham at any one's feet."

"Not even your own?" was the malicious retort.

"Not even my own," and a flash of anger from her dark eyes accompanied her answer.

Still, wherever he went he awakened interest in all natures not dull or sodden. He was felt to be a presence. There was a consciousness of power in his very attitudes; and one felt instinctively that he was far removed from the commonplace—that he had had a history which made him different from other men.

But before this slight curiosity was kindled to any extent, much less satisfied, his leave of absence expired; and with a sense of deep relief he prepared to say farewell. His friends expected to see him often in the city; he knew they would see him but seldom, if at all. He bad made his visit with his aunt, and she understood him. His quiet poise was departing, and he longed for the stern, fierce excitement of active service.

Before he joined his regiment he spent the day with his friends, and took occasion once, when alone with Hilland, to make an appeal that was solemn and almost passionate in its earnestness, adjuring him to remain employed in duties like those which now occupied him. But he saw that his efforts were vain.

"No, Graham," was Hilland's emphatic reply; "just as soon as there is danger at the front I shall be with my regiment Now I can do more here."

With Grace he took a short ride in the morning while Hilland was engaged in his duties, and he looked at the fair woman by his side with the thought that he might never see her again. It almost seemed as if Grace understood him, for although the rich color mantled in her cheeks and she abounded in smile and repartee, a look of deep sadness rarely left her eyes.

Once she said abruptly, "Alford, you will come and see us often before the campaign opens? Oh, I dread this coming campaign. You will come often?"

"I fear not, Grace," he said, gravely and gently, "I will try to come, but not often." Then he added, with a short, abrupt laugh, "I wish I could break Hilland's leg." In answer to a look of surprise he continued, "Could not your father procure an order that would keep him in the city? He would have to obey orders."

"Ah, I understand you," and there was a quick rush of tears to her eyes. "It's of no use. I have thought of everything, but Warren's heart is set on joining his regiment in the spring."

"I know it. I have said all that I could say to a brother on the subject."

"From the first, Alford, you have tried to make the ordeal of this war less painful to me, and how well you have succeeded! You have been our good genius. Warren, in his impetuous, chivalrous feeling, would have gone into it unadvisedly, hastily; and before this might—Oh, I can't even think of it," she said with a shudder. "But years have passed since your influence guided him into a wiser and more useful course, and think how much of the time I have been able to be with him! And it has all been due to you, Alford. But the war seems no nearer its end. It rather assumes a larger and more threatening aspect Why do not men think of us poor women before they go to war?"

"You think, then, that even your influence cannot keep him from the field?"

"No, it could not. Indeed, beyond a certain point I dare not exert it. I should be dumb before questions already asked, 'Why should I shrink when other husbands do not? What would be said of me here? what by my comrades in the regiment? What would your brave father think, though he might acquiesce? Nay, more, what would my wife think in her secret heart?' Alas! I find I am not made of such stern stuff as are some women. Pride and military fame could not sustain me if—if—"

"Do not look on the gloomy side, Grace. Hilland will come out of it all a major-general."

"Oh, I don't know, I don't know. I do know that he will often be in desperate danger; what a dread certainty that is for me! Oh, I wish you could be always near him; and yet 'tis a selfish wish, for you would not count the cost to yourself."

"No, Grace; I've sworn that on the sword you gave me."

"I might have known as much." Then she added earnestly, "Believe me, if you should fall it would also imbitter my life."

"Yes, you would grieve sincerely; but there would be an infinite difference, an infinite difference. One question, however, is settled beyond recall. If my life can serve you or Hilland, no power shall prevent my giving it. There is nothing more to be said: let us speak of something else."

"Yes, Alford, one thing more. Once I misjudged you. Forgive me;" and she caused her horse to spring into a gallop, resolving that no commonplace words should follow closely upon a conversation that had touched the most sacred feelings and impulses of each heart.

For some reason there was a shadow over their parting early in the evening, for Graham was to ride toward the front with the dawn. Even Hilland's genial spirits could not wholly dissipate it. Graham made heroic efforts, but he was oppressed with a despondency which was wellnigh overwhelming. He felt that he was becoming unmanned, and in bitter self-censure resolved to remain with his regiment until the end came, as he believed would be the case with him before the year closed.

"Alford, remember your promise. We all may need you yet," were his aunt's last words in the gray of the morning.

CHAPTER XXVI
AN IMPROVISED PICTURE GALLERY

Much to Graham's satisfaction, his regiment, soon after he joined it, was ordered into the Shenandoah Valley, and given some rough, dangerous picket duty that fully accorded with his mood. Even Hilland could not expect a visit from him now; and he explained to his friend that the other officers were taking their leaves of absence, and he, in turn, must perform their duties. And so the winter passed uneventfully away in a cheerful interchange of letters. Graham found that the front agreed with him better than Washington, and that his pulse resumed its former even beat A dash at a Confederate picket post on a stormy night was far more tranquilizing than an evening in Hilland's luxurious rooms.

With the opening of the spring campaign Hilland joined his regiment, and was eager to remove by his courage and activity the slightest impression, if any existed, that he was disposed to shun dangerous service. There was no such impression, however; and he was most cordially welcomed, for he was a great favorite with both officers and men.

During the weeks that followed, the cavalry was called upon to do heavy work and severe fighting; and the two friends became more conspicuous than ever for their gallantry. They seemed, however, to bear charmed lives, for, while many fell or were wounded, they escaped unharmed.

At last the terrific and decisive campaign of Gettysburg opened; and from the war-wasted and guerilla-infested regions of Virginia the Northern troops found themselves marching through the friendly and populous North. As the cavalry brigade entered a thriving village in Pennsylvania the people turned out almost *en masse* and gave them more than an ovation. The troopers were tired, hungry, and thirsty; and, since from every doorway was offered a boundless hospitality, the column came to a halt. The scene soon developed into a picturesque military picnic. Young maids and venerable matrons, gray-bearded fathers, shy, blushing girls, and eager-eyed children, all vied with each other in pressing upon their defenders every delicacy and substantial viand that their town could furnish at the moment. A pretty miss of sixteen, with a peach-like bloom in her cheeks, might be seen flitting here and there among the bearded troopers with a tray bearing goblets of milk. When they were emptied she would fly back and lift up white arms to her mother for more, and the almost equally blooming matron, smiling from the window, would fill the glasses again to the brim. The magnates of the village with their wives were foremost in the work, and were passing to and fro with great baskets of sandwiches, while stalwart men and boys were bringing from neighboring wells and pumps cool, delicious water for the horses. How immensely the troopers enjoyed it all! No scowling faces and cold looks here. All up and down the street, holding bridle-reins over their arms or leaning against the flanks of their horses, they feasted as they had not done since their last Thanksgiving Day at home. Such generous cups of coffee, enriched with cream almost too thick to flow from the capacious pitchers, and sweetened not only with snow-white sugar, but also with the smiles of some gracious woman, perhaps motherly in appearance, perhaps so fair and young that hearts beat faster under the weather-stained cavalry jackets.

"How pretty it all is!" said a familiar voice to Graham, as he was dividing a huge piece of cake with his pet Mayburn; and Hilland laid his hand on his friend's shoulder.

"Ah, Hilland, seeing you is the best part of this banquet *a la militaire*. Yes, it is a heavenly change after the dreary land we've been marching and fighting in. It makes me feel that I have a country, and that it's worth all it may cost."

"Look, Graham—look at that little fairy creature in white muslin, talking to that great bearded pard of a sergeant. Isn't that a picture? Oh, I wish Grace, with her eye for picturesque effects, could look upon this scene."

"Nonsense, Hilland! as if she would look at anybody or anything but you! See that white-haired old woman leading that exquisite little girl to yonder group of soldiers. See how they duff their hats to her. There's another picture for you."

Hilland's magnificent appearance soon attracted half a dozen village belles about him, each offering some dainty; and one—a black-eyed witch a little bolder than the others—offered to fasten a rose from her hair in his button-hole.

He entered into the spirit of the occasion with all the zest of his old student days, professed to be delighted with the favor as she stood on tiptoe to reach the lappet of his coat; and then he stooped down and pressed his lips to the fragrant petals, assuring the blushing little coquette, meanwhile, that it was the next best thing to her own red lips.

How vividly in after years Graham would recall him, as he stood there, his handsome head thrown back, looking the ideal of an old Norse viking, laughing and chatting with the merry, innocent girls around him, his deep-blue eyes emitting mirthful gleams on every side! According to his nature, Graham drew off to one side and watched the scene with a smile, as he had viewed similar ones far back in the years, and far away in Germany. He saw the ripples of laughter that his friend's words provoked, and recognized the old, easy grace, the light, French-like wit, that was wholly free from the French *double entendre*, and he thought: "Would that Grace could see him now, and she would fall in love with him anew, for her nature is too large for petty jealousy at a scene like that Oh, Hilland! you and the group around you make the finest picture of this long improvised gallery of pictures."

Suddenly there was a loud report of a cannon from a hill above the village, and a shell shrieked over their heads. Hilland's laughing aspect changed instantly. He seemed almost to gather the young girls in his arms as he hurried them into the nearest doorway, and then with a bound reached Graham, who held his horse, vaulted into the saddle, and dashed up the street to his men who were standing in line.

Graham sprang lightly on his horse, for in the scenes resulting from the kaleidoscopic change that had taken place he would be more at home.

"Mount!" he shouted; and the order, repeated up and down the street, changed the jolly, feasting troopers of a moment since into veterans who would sit like equestrian statues, if so commanded, though a hundred guns thundered against them.

From the further end of the village came the wild yell characteristic of the cavalry charges of the Confederates, while shell after shell shrieked and exploded where had just been unaffected gayety and hospitality.

The first shot had cleared the street of all except the Union soldiers; and those who dared to peep from window or door saw, with dismay, that the defenders whom they had so honored and welcomed were retreating at a gallop from the Rebel charge.

They were soon undeceived, however, for at a gallop the national cavalry dashed into an open field near by, formed with the precision of machinery, and by the time that the Rebel charge had wellnigh spent itself in the sabring or capture of a few tardy troopers, Hilland with platoon after platoon was emerging upon the street again at a sharp trot, which soon developed into a furious gallop as he dashed against their assailants; and the pretty little coquette, bold not only in love but in war, saw from a window her ideal knight with her red rose upon his breast leading a charge whose thunder caused the very earth to tremble; and she clapped her hands and cheered so loudly as he approached that he looked up, saw her, and for an instant a sunny smile passed over the visage that had become so stern. Then came the shock of battle.

Graham's company was held in reserve, but for some reason his horse seemed to grow unmanageable; and sabres had scarcely clashed before he, with the blade on which was engraved "Grace Hilland," was at her husband's side, striking blows which none could resist. The enemy could not stand the furious onset, and gave way slowly, sullenly, and at last precipitately. The tide of battle swept beyond and away from the village; and its street became quiet again, except for the groans of the wounded.

Mangled horses, mangled men, some dead, some dying, and others almost rejoicing in wounds that would secure for them such gentle nurses, strewed the streets that had been the scene of merry festivity.

The pretty little belle never saw her tawny, bearded knight again. She undoubtedly married and tormented some well-to-do dry-goods clerk; but a vision of a man of heroic mold, with a red rose upon his breast, smiling up to her just as he was about to face what might be death, will thrill her feminine soul until she is old and gray.

That night Graham and Hilland talked and laughed over the whole affair as they sat by a camp-fire.

"It has all turned out as usual," said Graham, ruefully. "You won a victory and no end of glory; I a reprimand from my colonel."

"If you have received nothing worse than a reprimand you are fortunate," was Hilland's response. "The idea of any horse becoming unmanageable in your hands! The colonel understands the case as well as I do, and knows that it was your own ravenous appetite for a fight that became unmanageable. But I told him of the good service you rendered, and gave him the wink to wink also. You were fearfully rash to-day, Graham. You were not content to fight at my side, but more than once were between me and the enemy. What the devil makes you so headlong in a fight—you that are usually so cool and self-controlled?"

Graham's hand rested on a fair woman's name engraved upon his sword, but he replied lightly: "When you teach me caution in a fight I'll learn."

"Well, excuse me, old fellow, I'm going to write to Grace. May not have a chance very soon again. I say, Graham, we'll have *the* battle of the war in a day or two."

"I know it," was the quiet response.

"And we must win, too," Hilland continued, "or the Johnnies will help themselves to Washington, Baltimore, Philadelphia, and perhaps New York. Every man should nerve himself to do the work of two. As I was saying, I shall write to Grace that your horse ran away with you and became uncontrollable until you were directly in front of me, when you seemed to manage him admirably, and struck blows worthy of the old French duellist who killed a man every morning before breakfast. I think she'll understand your sudden and amazingly poor horsemanship as well as I do."

She did, and far better.

Hilland's prediction proved true. The decisive battle of Gettysburg was fought, and its bloody field marked the highest point reached by the crimson tide of the Rebellion. From Cemetery Ridge it ebbed slowly and sullenly away to the south.

The brigade in which were the friends passed through another fearful baptism of fire in the main conflict and the pursuit which followed, and were in Virginia again, but with ranks almost decimated. Graham and Hilland still seemed to bear charmed lives, and in the brief pause in operations that followed, wrote cheerful letters to those so dear, now again at their seaside resort. Grace, who for days had been so pale, and in whose dark eyes lurked an ever-present dread of which she could not speak, smiled again. Her husband wrote in exuberant spirits over the victory, and signed himself "Lieutenant-Colonel." Graham in his letter said jestingly to his aunt that he had at last attained his "majority," and that she might therefore look for a little more discretion on his part.

"How the boys are coming on!" exulted the old major. "They will both wear the stars yet. But confound it all, why did Meade let Lee escape? He might have finished the whole thing up."

Alas! the immeasurable price of liberty was not yet paid.

One morning Hilland's and Graham's regiments were ordered out on what was deemed but a minor *reconnoissance*; and the friends, rested and strong, started in high spirits with their sadly shrunken forces. But they knew that the remaining handfuls were worth more than full ranks of untrained, unseasoned men. All grow callous, if not indifferent, to the vicissitudes of war; and while they missed regretfully many familiar faces, the thought that they had rendered the enemy's lines more meagre was consoling.

Graham and Hilland rode much of the long day together. They went over all the past, and dwelt upon the fact that their lives had been so different from what they had planned.

"By the way, Graham," said Hilland, abruptly, "it seems strange to me that you are so indifferent to women. Don't you expect ever to marry?"

Graham burst into a laugh as he replied: "I thought we had that subject out years ago, under the apple-tree—that night, you remember, when you talked like a schoolgirl till morning—"

"And you analyzed and philosophized till long after midnight—"

"Well, you knew then that Grace had spoiled me for every one else; and she's been improving ever since. When I find her equal I'll marry her, if I can."

"Poor, forlorn old bachelor that you are, and ever will be!" cried Hilland. "You'll never find the equal of Grace Hilland."

"I think I shall survive, Hilland. My appetite is good. As I live, there are some Confederates in yonder clump of trees;" and he put spurs to his horse on a little private *reconnoissance*. The few horsemen vanished, in the thick woods beyond, the moment they saw that they were perceived; and they were regarded as prowling guerillas only.

That night they bivouacked in a grove where two roads intersected, threw out pickets and patrols, and kindled their fires, for they did not expect to strike the enemy in force till some time on the following day.

CHAPTER XXVII
A DREAM

Graham and his friend had bidden each other an early and cordial good-night, for the entire force under the command of Hilland's colonel was to resume its march with the dawn. Although no immediate danger was apprehended, caution had been learned by long experience. The detachment was comparatively small, and it was far removed from any support; and while no hints of the presence of the enemy in formidable numbers had been obtained during the day, what was beyond them could not be known with any certainty. Therefore the horses had been carefully rubbed down, and the saddles replaced. In many instances the bridles also had been put on again, with the bit merely slipped from the mouth. In all cases they lay or hung within reach of the tired troopers, who, one after another, were dropping off into the catlike slumber of a cavalry outpost.

As the fires died down, the shadows in the grove grew deeper and more obscure, and all was quiet, except when the hours came round for the relief of pickets and the men who were patrolling the roads. Graham remembered the evanescent group of Confederates toward whom he had spurred during the day. He knew that they were in a hostile region, and that their movements must be already well known to the enemy if strong in their vicinity. Therefore all his instincts as a soldier were on the alert. It so happened that he was second in command of his regiment on this occasion, and he felt the responsibility. He had been his own groom on their arrival at the grove, and his faithful charger, Mayburn, now stood saddled and bridled by his side, as he reclined, half dozing, again thinking deeply, by the low, flickering blaze of his fire. He had almost wholly lost the gloomy presentiments that had oppressed him at the beginning of the year. Both he and Hilland had passed through so many dangers that a sense of security was begotten. Still more potent had been the influence of his active out-of-door life. His nerves were braced, while his soldier's routine and the strong excitement of the campaign had become a preoccupying habit.

Only those who brood in idleness over the misfortunes and disappointments of life are destroyed by them.

He had not seen Grace for over half a year; and while she was and ever would be his fair ideal, he could now think of her with the quietude akin to that of the devout Catholic who worships a saint removed from him at a heavenly distance. The wisdom of this remoteness became more and more clear to him; for despite every power that he could put forth as a man, there was a deeper, stronger manhood within him which acknowledged this woman as sovereign. He foresaw that his lot would be one of comparative exile, and he accepted it with a calm and inflexible resolution.

Hearing a step he started up hastily, and saw Hilland approaching from the opposite side of his fire.

"Ah, Graham, glad you are not asleep," said his friend, throwing himself down on the leaves, with his head resting on his hands. "Put a little wood on the fire, please; I'm chilly in the night air, and the dews are so confoundedly heavy."

"Why, Hilland, what's the matter?" Graham asked, as he complied. "You are an ideal cavalryman at a nap, and can sleep soundly with one eye open. It has seemed to me that you never lost a wink when there was a chance for it, even under fire."

"Why are you not sleeping?"

"Oh, I have been, after my fashion, dozing and thinking by turns I always was an owl, you know. Moreover, I think it behooves us to be on the alert. We are a good way from support if hard pressed; and the enemy must be in force somewhere to the west of us."

"I've thought as much myself. My horse is ready, as yours is, and I left an orderly holding him. I suppose you will laugh at me, but I've had a cursed dream; and it has shaken me in spite of my reason. After all, how often our reason fails us at a pinch! I wish it was morning and we were on the road. I've half a mind to go out with the patrols and get my blood in circulation. I would were it not that I feel I should be with my men."

"Where's your colonel?"

"The old war-dog is sleeping like a top. Nothing ever disturbs him, much less a dream. I say, Graham, I made a good selection in him, didn't I?"

"Yes, but he'll be promoted soon, and you will be in command. What's more, I expect to see a star on *your* shoulder in less than six months."

"As I feel to-night, I don't care a picayune for stars or anything else relating to the cursed war. I'd give my fortune to be able to kiss Grace and tell her I'm well."

"You are morbid, Hilland. You will feel differently to-morrow, especially if there's a chance for a charge."

"No doubt, no doubt. The shadow of this confounded grove seems as black as death, and it oppresses me. Why should I, without apparent cause, have had such a dream?"

"Your supper and fatigue may have been the cause. If you don't mind, tell me this grisly vision."

"While you laugh at me as an old woman—you, in whom reason ever sits serene and dispassionate on her throne, except when you get into a fight."

"My reason's throne is often as rickety as a two-legged stool. No, I won't laugh at you. There's not a braver man in the service than you. If you feel as you say, there's some cause for it; and yet so complex is our organism that both cause and effect may not be worthy of very grave consideration, as I have hinted."

"Think what you please, this was my dream. I had made my dispositions for the night, and went to sleep as a matter of course. I had not slept an hour by my watch—I looked at it afterward—when I seemed to hear some one moaning and crying, and I thought I started up wide awake, and I saw the old library at home—the room you know so well. Every article of furniture was before me more distinctly than I can see any object now, and on the rug before the open fire Grace was crouching, while she moaned and wrung her hands and cried as if her heart was breaking. She was dressed in black—Oh, how white her hands and neck and face appeared against that mournful black—and, strangest of all, her hair fell around her snowy white, like a silver veil. I started forward to clasp her in my arms, and then truly awoke, for there was nothing before me but my drooping horse, a few red coals of my expiring fire, and over all the black, black shadow of this accursed grove. Oh, for sunlight! Oh, for a gale of wind, that I might breathe freely again!" and the powerful man sprang to his feet and threw open his coat at his breast.

As he ceased speaking, the silence and darkness of the grove did seem ominous and oppressive, and Graham's old wretched presentiment of Christmas morning returned, but he strove with all the ingenuity in his power to reason his friend out of his morbid mood, as he termed it. He kindled his fire into a cheerful blaze, and Hilland cowered and shivered over it; then looking up abruptly, he said, "Graham, you and I accepted the belief long ago that man was only highly organized matter. I must admit to you that my mind has often revolted at this belief; and the thought that Grace was merely of the earth has always seemed to me sacrilegious. She never was what you would call a religious girl; but she once had a quiet, simple faith in a God and a hereafter, and she expected to see her mother again. I fear that our views have troubled her exceedingly; although with that rare reserve in a woman, she never interfered with one's strong personal convictions. The shallow woman tries to set everybody right with the weighty reason, 'Oh, because it IS so; all good people say it is so.' I fear our views have unsettled hers also. I wish they had not; indeed I wish I could believe somewhat as she did.

"Once, only once, she spoke to me with a strange bitterness, but it revealed the workings of her mind. I, perhaps, was showing a little too much eagerness in my spirit and preparation for active service, and she broke out abruptly, 'Oh, yes, you and Alford can rush into scenes of carnage very complacently. You believe that if the bullet is only sure enough, your troubles are over forever, as Alford once said. I suppose you are right, for you learned men have studied into things as we poor women never can. If it's true, those who love as we do should die together.' It has often seemed that her very love—nay, that mine—was an argument against our belief. That a feeling so pure, vivid, and unselfish, so devoid of mere earthiness—a feeling that apparently contains within itself the very essence of immortality—can be instantly blotted out as a flame is extinguished, has become a terrible thought. Grace Hilland is worthy of an immortal life, and she has all the capacity for it. It's not her lovely form and face that I love so much as the lovely something—call it soul, spirit, or what you choose—that will maintain her charm through all the changes from youth to feeble and withered age. How can I be sure that the same gentle, womanly spirit may not exist after the final change we call death, and that to those worthy of immortal life the boon is not given? Reason is a grand thing, and I know we once thought we settled this question; but reason fails me to-night, or else love and the intense longings of the heart teach a truer and deeper philosophy—

"You are silent, Graham. You think me morbid—that wishes are fathers of my thoughts. Well, I'm not. I honestly don't know what the truth is. I only wish to-night that I had the simple belief in a reunion with Grace which she had with regard to her mother. I fear we have unsettled her faith; not that we ever urged our views—indeed we have scarcely ever spoken of them— but there has been before her the ever-present and silent force of example. It was natural for her to believe that those were right in whom she most believed; and I'm not sure we are right—I'm not *sure*. I've not been sure for a long time."

"My dear Warren, you are not well. Exposure to all sorts of weather in this malarial country is telling on you; and I fear your feelings to-night are the prelude of a fever. You shall stay and sleep by my fire, and if I hear the slightest suspicious sound I will waken you. You need not hesitate, for I intend to watch till morning, whether you stay or not."

"Well, Graham, I will. I wish to get through this horrible night in the quickest way possible. But I'll first go and bring my horse here, so the poor orderly can have a nap."

He soon returned and lay down close to the genial fire, and Graham threw over him his own blankets.

"What a good, honest friend you are, Graham!—too honest even to say some hollow words favoring my doubts of my doubt and unbelief. If it hadn't been for you, I should have been dead long ago. In my blind confidence, I should have rushed into the war, and probably should have been knocked on the head at Bull Run. How many happy months I've passed with Grace since then!—how many since you virtually gave your life for me last autumn! You made sure that I took a man's, not a fool's, part in the war. Oh, Grace and I know it all and appreciate it; and—and—Alford, if I should fall, I commend Grace to your care."

"Hilland, stop, or you will unman me. This accursed grove *is* haunted, I half believe; and were I in command I would order 'Boots and Saddles' to be sounded at once. There, sleep, Warren, and in the morning you will be your own grand self. Why speak of anything I could do for you and Grace? How could I serve myself in any surer way? As schoolgirls say, 'I won't speak to you again.' I'm going to prowl around a little, and see that all is right;" and he disappeared among the shadowy boles of the trees.

When he returned from his rounds his friend was sleeping, but uneasily, with sudden fits and starts.

"He is surely going to have a fever," Graham muttered. "I'd give a year's pay if we were safe back in camp." He stood before the fire with folded arms, watching his boyhood's friend, his gigantic shadow stretching away into the obscurity as unwaveringly as those of the tree-trunks around him. His lips were compressed. He sought to make his will as inflexible as his form. He would not think of Grace, of danger to her and Hilland; and yet, by some horrible necromancy of the hour and place, the scene in Hilland's dream would rise before him with a vividness that was overawing. In the sighing of the wind through the foliage, he seemed to hear the poor wife's moans.

"Oh," he muttered, "would that I could die a thousand deaths to prevent a scene like that!"

When would the interminable night pass? At last he looked at his watch and saw that the dawn could not be far distant. How still everything had become! The men were in their deepest slumber. Even the wind had died out, and the silence was to his overwrought mind like the hush of expectancy.

This silence was at last broken by a shot on the road leading to the west. Other shots followed in quick succession.

Hilland was on his feet instantly. "We're attacked," he shouted, and was about to spring upon his horse when Graham grasped his hand in both of his as he said, "In the name of Grace, Hilland, be prudent."

Then both the men were in the saddle, Hilland dashing toward his own command, and each shouting, "Awake! Mount!"

At the same instant the bugle from headquarters rang through the grove, giving the well-known order of "Boots and Saddles."

In place of the profound stillness of a moment before, there were a thousand discordant sounds—the trampling of feet, the jingling of sabres, the champing of bits by aroused, restless horses that understood the bugle call as well as the men, hoarse, rapid orders of officers, above all which in the distance could be heard Hilland's clarion voice.

Again and again from headquarters the brief, musical strains of the bugle echoed through the gloom, each one giving to the veterans a definite command. Within four minutes there was a line of battle on the western edge of the grove, and a charging column was in the road leading to the west, down which the patrols were galloping at a headlong pace. Pickets were rushing in, firing as they came. To the uninitiated it might have seemed a scene of dire confusion. In fact, it was one of perfect order and discipline. Even in the darkness each man knew just what to do and where to go, as he heard the bugle calls and the stern, brief, supplementary orders of the officers.

Graham found himself on the line of battle at the right of the road, and the sound that followed close upon the sharp gallop of the patrol was ominous indeed. It was the rushing, thunderous sound of a heavy body of cavalry—too heavy, his ear soon foretold him, to promise equal battle.

The experienced colonel recognized the fact at the same moment, and would not leave his men in the road to meet the furious onset. Again, sharp, quick, and decisive as the vocal order had been, the bugle rang out the command for a change of position. Its strains had not ceased when the officers were repeating the order all down the column that had been formed in the road for a charge, and scarcely a moment elapsed before the western pike was clear, and faced by a line of battle a little back among the trees.

The Union force would now ask nothing better than that the enemy should charge down that road within pointblank range.

If the Nationals were veterans they were also dealing with veterans who were masters of the situation in their overwhelming force and their knowledge of the comparative insignificance of their opponents, whose numbers had been quite accurately estimated the day before.

The patrols were already within the Union lines and at their proper places when the Confederate column emerged into the narrow open space before the grove. Its advance had subsided into a sharp trot; but, instead of charging by column or platoon, the enemy deployed to right and left with incredible swiftness. Men dismounted and formed into line almost instantly, their gray forms looking phantom-like in the gray dawn that tinged the east.

The vigilant colonel was as prompt as they, and at the first evidence of their tactics the bugle resounded, and the line of battle facing the road which led westward wheeled at a gallop through the open trees and formed at right angles with the road behind the first line of battle. Again there was a bugle call. The men in both lines dismounted instantly, and as their horses were being led to the rear by those designated for the duty, a Union volley was poured into the Confederate line that had scarcely formed, causing many a gap. Then the first Union line retired behind the second, loading as they went, and, with the ready instinct of old fighters, putting trees between themselves and the swiftly advancing foe while forming a third line of battle. From the second Union line a deadly volley blazed in the dim obscurity of the woods. It had no perceptible effect in checking the impetuous onset of the enemy, who merely returned the fire as they advanced.

The veteran colonel, with cool alertness, saw that he was far outnumbered, and that his assailants' tactics were to drive him through the grove into the open fields, where his command would be speedily dispersed and captured. His only chance was to run for it and get the start. Indeed the object of his reconnoissance seemed already accomplished, for the enemy was found to be in force in that direction. Therefore, as he galloped to the rear his bugler sounded "Retreat" long and shrilly.

The dim Union lines under the trees melted away as by magic, and a moment later there was a rush of horses through the underbrush that fringed the eastern side of the grove. But some men were shot, some sabred, and others captured before they could mount and extricate themselves. The majority, however, of the Union forces were galloping swiftly away, scattering at first rather than keeping together, in order to distract the pursuit which for a time was sharp and deadly. Not a few succumbed; others would turn on their nearest pursuer in mortal combat, which was soon decided in one way or the other. Graham more than once wheeled and confronted an isolated foe, and the sword bearing the name of the gentle Grace Hilland was bloody indeed.

All the while his eye was ranging the field for Hilland, and with his fleet steed, that could soon have carried him beyond all danger, he diverged to right and left, as far as their headlong retreat permitted, in his vain search for his friend.

Suddenly the bugle from the Confederate side sounded a recall. The enemy halted, fired parting shots, and retired briskly over the field, gathering up the wounded and the prisoners. The Union forces drew together on a distant eminence, from which the bugler of the colonel in command was blowing a lively call to rendezvous.

"Where, Hilland?" cried Graham, dashing up.

The colonel removed a cigar from his mouth and said, "Haven't seen him since I ordered the retreat. Don't worry. He'll be here soon. Hilland is sure to come out all right. It's a way he has. 'Twas a rather rapid change of base, Major Graham. That the enemy should have ceased their pursuit so abruptly puzzles me. Ah, here comes your colonel, and when Hilland puts in an appearance we must hold a brief council, although I suppose there is nothing left for us but to make our way back to camp and report as speedily as possible. I'd like to come back with a division, and turn the tables on those fellows I believe we fought a divis—"

"Hilland!" shouted Graham, in a voice that drowned the colonel's words, and echoed far and wide.

There was no answer, and the fugitives were nearly all in.

Graham galloped out beyond the last lagging trooper, and with a cry that smote the hearts of those that heard it he shouted, "Hilland!" and strained his eyes in every direction. There was no response—no form in view that resembled his friend.

At wild speed he returned and rode among Hilland's command. His manner was so desperate that he drew all eyes upon him, and none seemed able or willing to answer. At last a man said, "I heard his voice just as we were breaking from that cursed grove, and I've seen or heard nothing of him since. I supposed he was on ahead with the colonel;" and that was all the information that could be obtained.

The men looked very downcast, for Hilland was almost idolized by them. Graham saw that there was an eager quest of information among themselves, and he waited with feverish impatience for further light; but nothing could be elicited from officers or privates beyond the fact that Hilland had been bravely doing his duty up to the moment when, as one of the captains said, "It was a scramble, 'each man for himself, and the devil take the hindmost.'"

As long as there had been a gleam of hope that Hilland had escaped with the rest, Graham had been almost beside himself in his feverish impatience.

He now rode to where the two colonels were standing, and the senior began rapidly, "Major Graham, we sympathize with you deeply. We all, and indeed the army, have sustained a severe loss in even the temporary absence of Lieutenant-Colonel Hilland; for I will not believe that worse has happened than a wound and brief captivity. The enemy has acted peculiarly. I have fears that they may be flanking us and trying to intercept us on some parallel road. Therefore I shall order that we return to camp in the quickest possible time. Good God, Graham! don't take it so to heart. You've no proof that Hilland is dead. You look desperate, man. Come, remember that you are a soldier and that Hilland was one too. We've had to discount such experiences from the start."

"Gentlemen," said Graham, in a low, concentrated voice, and touching his hat to the two colonels, "I am under the command of you both—one as my superior officer, the other as leader of the expedition. I ask permission to return in search of my friend."

"I forbid it," they both cried simultaneously, while the senior officer continued, "Graham, you are beside yourself. It would be almost suicide to go back. It would certainly result in your capture, while there is not one chance in a thousand that you could do Hilland any good."

Graham made no immediate reply, but was studying the ill-omened grove with his glass. After a moment he said, "I do not think there will be any further pursuit. The enemy are retiring from the grove. My explanation of their conduct is this: There is some large decisive movement in progress, and we were merely brushed out of the way that we might learn nothing of it. My advice is that we retain this commanding position, throw out scouts on every side, and I doubt whether we find anything beyond a small rearguard in ten miles of us within a few hours."

"Your anxiety for your friend warps your judgment, and it is contrary to my instructions, which were simply to learn if there was any considerable force of the enemy in this region. Your explanation of the enemy's conduct is plausible, and has already occurred to me as a possibility. If it be the true explanation, all the more reason that we should return promptly and report what we know and what we surmise. I shall therefore order 'Retreat' to be sounded at once."

"And I, Major Graham," said his own colonel, "must add, that while you have my sympathy, I nevertheless order you to your place in the march. Rather than permit you to carry out your mad project, I would place you under arrest."

"Gentlemen, I cannot complain of your course, or criticise your military action. You are in a better condition of mind to judge what is wise than I; and under ordinary circumstances I would submit without a word. But the circumstances are extraordinary. Hilland has been my friend since boyhood. I will not remain in suspense as to his fate; much less will I leave his wife and friends in suspense. I know that disobedience of orders in the face of the enemy is one of the gravest offences, but I must disobey them, be the consequences what they may."

As he wheeled his horse, his colonel cried, "Stop him. He's under arrest!" But Mayburn, feeling the touch of the spur, sprang into his fleet gallop, and they might as well have pursued a bird.

They saw this at once, and the colonel in command only growled, "—- this reconnoissance. Here we've lost two of the finest officers in the brigade, as well as some of our best men. Sound 'Retreat.'"

There was a hesitancy, and a wild impulse among Hilland's men to follow Graham to the rescue, but it was sternly repressed by their officers, and the whole command was within a few moments on a sharp trot toward camp.

CHAPTER XXVIII
ITS FULFILMENT

Graham soon slackened his pace when he found that he was not pursued, and as his friends disappeared he returned warily to the brow of the eminence and watched their rapid march away from the ill-fated locality. He rode over the brow of the hill as if he was following, for he had little doubt that the movements of the Union force were watched. Having tied his horse where he could not be seen from the grove, he crept back behind a sheltering bush, and with his glass scanned the scene of conflict. In the road leading through the grove there were ambulances removing the wounded. At last these disappeared, and there was not a living object in sight. He watched a little longer, and buzzards began to wheel over and settle upon the battleground—sure evidence that for the time it was deserted.

He hesitated no longer. Mounting his horse he continued down the hill so as to be screened from any possible observers, then struck off to his left to a belt of woods that extended well up to the vicinity of the grove. Making his way through this bit of forest, he soon came to an old wood-road partially grown up with bushes, and pushed his way rapidly back toward the point he wished to attain. Having approached the limits of the belt of woods, he tied his horse in a thicket, listened, then stole to the edge nearest the grove. It appeared deserted. Crouching along a rail fence with revolver in hand, he at last reached its fatal shade, and pushing through its fringe of lower growth, peered cautiously around. Here and there he saw a lifeless body or a struggling, wounded horse, over which the buzzards hovered, or on which they had already settled. Disgusting as was their presence, they reassured him, and he boldly and yet with an awful dread at heart began his search, scanning with rapid eye each prostrate form along the entire back edge of the grove through which the Union forces had burst in their swift retreat.

He soon passed beyond all traces of conflict, and then retraced his steps, uttering half-unconsciously and in a tone of anguish his friend's name. As he approached what had been the extreme right of the Union line in their retreat, and their left in the advance, he beheld a dead horse that looked familiar. He sprang forward and saw that it was Hilland's.

"Hilland! Warren!" he shouted, wild with awful foreboding.

From a dense thicket near he heard a feeble groan. Rushing into it, he stumbled against the immense mossy trunk of a prostrate, decaying tree. Concealed beyond it lay his friend, apparently dying.

"Oh, Warren!" he cried, "my friend, my brother, don't you know me? Oh, live, live! I can rescue you."

There was no response from the slowly gasping man.

Graham snatched a flask from his pocket and wet the pallid lips with brandy, and then caused Hilland to swallow a little. The stimulant kindled for a few moments the flame of life, and the dying man slowly became conscious.

"Graham," he murmured feebly—"Graham, is that you?"

"Yes, yes, and I'll save you yet. Oh, in the name of Grace, I adjure you to live."

"Alas for Grace! My dream—will come true."

"Oh, Hilland, no, no! Oh, that I could die in your place! What is my life to yours! Rally, Warren, rally. My fleet horse is tied near, or if you are too badly wounded I will stay and nurse you. I'll fire a pistol shot through my arm, and then we can be sent to the hospital together. Here, take more brandy. That's right. With your physique you should not think of death I et me lift you up and stanch your wound."

"Don't move me, Graham, or I'll bleed to death instantly, and—and—I want to look in your face—once more, and send my—true love to Grace. More brandy, please. It's getting light again. Before it was dark—oh, so dark! How is it you are here?"

"I came back for you. Could I ride away and you not with me? Oh, Warren! I must save your life. I must, I must!"

"Leave me, Graham; leave me at once. You will be captured, if not killed," and Hilland spoke with energy.

"I will never leave you. There, your voice proves that your strength is coming back. Warren, Warren, can't you live for Grace's sake?"

"Graham," said Hilland, solemnly, "even my moments are numbered. One more gush of blood from my side and I'm gone. Oh, shall I become nothing? Shall I be no more than the decaying tree behind which I crawled when struck down? Shall I never see my peerless bride again? She would always have been a bride to me. I can't believe it. There must be amends somewhere for the agony of mind, not body, that I've endured as I lay here, and for the anguish that Grace will suffer. Oh, Graham, my philosophy fails me in this strait, my whole nature revolts at it. Mere corruption, chemical change, ought not to be the end of a *man*."

"Do not waste your strength in words. Live, and in a few short weeks Grace may be your nurse. Take more brandy, and then I'll go for assistance."

"No, Graham, no. Don't leave me. Life is ebbing again. Ah, ah! farewell— true friend. Un—bounded love—Grace. Commit—her—your care!"

There was a convulsive shudder and the noble form was still.

Graham knelt over him for a few moments in silent horror. Then he tore open Hilland's vest and placed his hand over his heart. It was motionless. His hand, as he withdrew it, was bathed in blood. He poured brandy into the open lips, but the powerful stimulant was without effect. The awful truth overwhelmed him.

Hilland was dead.

He sat down, lifted his friend up against his breast, and hung over him with short, dry sobs—with a grief far beyond tears, careless, reckless of his own safety.

The bushes near him were parted, and a sweet girlish face, full of fear, wonder, and pity, looked upon him. The interpretation of the scene was but too evident, and tears gushed from the young girl's eyes.

"Oh, sir," she began in a low, faltering voice.

The mourner paid no heed.

"Please, sir," she cried, "do not grieve so. I never saw a man grieve like that. Oh, papa, papa, come, come here."

The quick pride of manhood was touched, and Graham laid his friend reverently down, and stood erect, quiet, but with heaving breast. Hasty steps approached, and a gray-haired man stood beside the young girl.

"I am your prisoner, sir," said Graham, "but in the name of humanity I ask you to let me bury my dead."

"My dear young sir, in the name of humanity and a more sacred Name, I will do all for you in my power. I am a clergyman, and am here with a party from a neighboring village, charged with the office of burying the dead with appropriate rites. I have no desire to take you prisoner, but will be glad to entertain you as my guest if the authorities will permit. Will you not give me some brief explanation of this scene while they are gathering up the dead?"

Graham did so in a few sad words. The daughter sat crying on the mossy log meanwhile, and the old man wiped his eyes again and again.

"Was there ever a nobler-looking man?" sobbed the girl; "and to think of his poor wife! Papa, he must not be buried here. He must be taken to our little cemetery by the church, and I will often put flowers on his grave."

"If you will carry out this plan, sweet child" said Graham, "one broken-hearted woman will bless you while she lives."

"Think, papa," resumed the girl—"think if it was our Henry what we would wish."

"I'm glad you feel as you do, my child. It proves that this horrible war is not hardening your heart or making you less gentle or compassionate. I will carry out your wishes and yours, sir, and will use my whole influence to prevent your noble fidelity to your friend from becoming the cause of your captivity. I will now summon assistance to carry your friend to the road, where a wagon can take him to the village."

In a few moments two negro slaves, part of the force sent to bury the dead, with their tattered hats doffed out of respect, slowly bore the body of Hilland to the roadside. Graham, with his bare head bowed under a weight of grief that seemed wellnigh crushing, followed closely, and then the old clergyman and his daughter. They laid the princely form down on the grass beside a dark-haired young Confederate officer, who was also to be taken to the cemetery.

The sad rites of burial which the good old man now performed over both friend and foe of subordinate rank need not be dwelt upon. While they were taking place Graham stood beside his friend as motionless as if he had become a statue, heedless of the crowd of villagers and country people that had gathered to the scene.

At last a sweet voice said: "Please, sir, it's time to go. You ride with papa. I am young and strong and can walk."

His only response was to take her hand and kiss it fervently. Then he turned to her father and told him of his horse that was hidden in the nearest edge of the belt of woods, and asked that it might be sent for by some one who was trustworthy.

"Here is Sampson, one of my own people; I'd trust him with all I have;" and one of the negroes who had borne the body of Hilland hastened away as directed, and soon returned with the beautiful horse that awakened the admiration of all and the cupidity of a few of the nondescript characters that had been drawn to the place.

A rude wagon was drawn to the roadside, its rough boards covered with leafy boughs, and the Union and the Confederate officer were placed in it side by side. Then the minister climbed into his old-fashioned gig, his daughter sprang lightly in by his side, took the reins and slowly led the way, followed by the extemporized hearse, while Graham on his horse rode at the feet of his friend, chief mourner in bitter truth. The negroes who had buried the dead walked on either side of the wagon bareheaded and oblivious of the summer sun, and the country people and villagers streamed along the road after the simple procession.

The bodies were first taken to the parsonage, and the stains of battle removed by an old colored aunty, a slave of the clergyman. Graham gave into the care of the clergyman's daughter Hilland's sword and some other articles that he did not wish to carry on his return to the Union lines. Among these was an exquisite likeness of Grace smiling in her happy loveliness.

Tears again rushed into the young girl's eyes as she asked in accents of deepest commiseration: "And will you have to break the news to her?"

"No," said Graham hoarsely; "I could not do that. I'd rather face a thousand guns than that poor wife."

"Why do you not keep the likeness?"

"I could not look upon it and think of the change which this fatal day will bring to those features. I shall leave it with you until she comes for his sword and to visit his grave. No one has a better right to it than you, and in this lovely face you see the promise of your own womanhood reflected. You have not told me your name. I wish to know it, for I shall love and cherish it as one of my most sacred memories."

"Margarita Anderson," was the blushing reply. "Papa and my friends call me Rita."

"Let me call you what your name signifies, and what you have proved yourself to be—Pearl. Who is Henry?"

"My only brother. He is a captain in our army."

"You are a true Southern girl?"

"Yes, in body and soul I'm a Southern girl;" and her dark eyes flashed through her tears.

"So was the original of this likeness. She is kin to you in blood and feeling as well as in her noble qualities; but she loved her Northern husband more than the whole world, and all in it was nothing compared with him. She will come and see you some day, and words will fail her in thanks."

"And will you come with her?"

"I don't know. I may be dead long before that time."

The young girl turned away, and for some reason her tears flowed faster than ever before.

"Pearl, my tender-hearted child, don't grieve over what would be so small a grief to me. This evil day has clouded your young life with the sadness of others. But at your age it will soon pass;" and he returned to his friend and took from him the little mementoes that he knew would be so dear to Grace.

Soon after, the two bodies were borne to the quaint old church and placed before the altar. Both were dressed in their full uniforms, and there was a noble calmness on the face of each as they slumbered side by side in the place sacred to the God of peace, and at peace with each other for evermore.

For an hour the bell tolled slowly, and the people passed in at one door, looked upon the manly forms, and with awed faces crept out at the other.

It was indeed a memorable day for the villagers. They had been awakened in the dawn by sounds of distant conflict. They had exulted over a brilliant victory as the Confederate forces came marching rapidly through their streets.

They had been put on the *qui vive* to know what the rapid movement of their troops meant. Some of the most severely wounded had been left in their care. The battlefield with its horrors had been visited, and there was to be a funeral service over two actors in the bloody drama, whose untimely fate excited not only sympathy, but the deep interest and curiosity which ever attend upon those around whom rumor has woven a romantic history. The story of Graham's return in search of his friend, of the circumstances of their discovery by Rita, of the likeness of the lovely wife who would soon be heart broken from the knowledge of what was known to them, had got abroad among the people, and their warm Southern hearts were more touched by the fate of their Northern foe than by that of the officer wearing the livery of their own service, but of whom little was known.

Graham's profound grief also impressed them deeply; and the presence of a Union officer, sitting among them, forgetful of his danger, of all except that his friend was dead, formed a theme which would be dwelt upon for months to come.

Near the close of the day, after some appropriate words in the church, the venerable clergyman, with his white locks uncovered, led the way through the cemetery to its further side, where, under the shade of an immense juniper-tree, were two open graves. As before, Graham followed his friend, and after him came Rita with a number of her young companions, dressed in white and carrying baskets of flowers. After an impressive burial service had been read, the young girls passed to and fro between the graves, throwing flowers in each and singing as they went a hymn breathing the certainty of the immortality that had been the object of poor Hilland's longing aspiration. Graham's heart thrilled as he heard the words, for they seemed the answer to his friend's questions. But, though his feelings might be touched deeply, he was the last man to be moved by sentiment or emotion from a position to which his inexorable reason had conducted him.

The sun threw its level rays over a scene that he never forgot—the white-haired clergyman standing between the open graves; the young maidens, led by the dark-eyed Rita, weaving in and out, their white hands and arms glowing like ivory as they strewed the flowers, meanwhile singing with an unconscious grace and pathos that touched the rudest hearts; the concourse of people, chiefly women, old men, and children, for the young and strong were either mouldering on battlefields or marching to others; the awed sable faces of the negroes in the further background; the exquisite evening sky; the songs of unheeding birds, so near to man in their choice of habitation, so remote from his sorrows and anxieties—all combined to form a picture and a memory which would be vivid and real to his latest day.

The graves were at last filled and piled up with flowers. Then Graham, standing uncovered before them all, spoke slowly and earnestly:

"People of the South, you see before you a Northern man, an officer in the Union army; but as I live I cherish no thought of enmity toward one of you. On the contrary, my heart is overwhelmed with gratitude. You have placed here side by side two brave men. You have rendered to their dust equal reverence and honor. I am in accord with you. I believe that the patriotism of one was as sincere as that of the other, the courage of one as high as that of the other, that the impulses which led them to offer up their lives were equally noble. In your generous sympathy for a fallen foe you have proved yourselves Americans in the best sense of the word. May the day come when that name shall suffice for us all. Believe me, I would defend your homes and my own with equal zeal;" and with a bow of profound respect he turned to the grave of his friend.

With a delicate appreciation of his wish, the people, casting backward lingering, sympathetic glances, ebbed away and he was soon left alone.

CHAPTER XXIX
A SOUTHERN GIRL

When Graham was left alone he knelt and bowed his head in the flowers that Rita had placed on Hilland's grave, and the whole horrible truth seemed to grow, to broaden and deepen, like a gulf that had opened at his feet. Hilland, who had become a part of his own life and seemed inseparable from all its interests, had disappeared forever. But yesterday he was the centre of vast interests and boundless love; now he had ceased to be. The love would remain, but oh, the torture of a boundless love when its object has passed beyond its reach!

The thought of Grace brought to the mourner an indescribable anguish. Once his profound love for her had asserted itself in a way that had stung him to madness, and the evil thought had never returned. Now she seemed to belong to the dead husband even more than when he was living. The thought that tortured him most was that Grace would not long survive Hilland. The union between the two had been so close and vital that the separation might mean death. The possibility overwhelmed him, and he grew faint and sick. Indeed it would seem that he partially lost consciousness, for at last he became aware that some one was standing near and pleading with him. Then he saw it was Rita.

"Oh, sir," she entreated, "do not grieve so. It breaks my heart to see a man so overcome. It seems terrible. It makes me feel that there are depths of sorrow that frighten me. Oh, come with me—do, please. I fear you've eaten nothing to-day, and we have supper all ready for you."

Graham tottered to his feet and passed his hand across his brow, as if to brush away an evil dream.

"Indeed, sir, you look sick and faint. Take my arm and lean on me. I assure you I am very strong."

"Yes, Pearl, you are strong. Many live to old age and never become as true a woman as you are to-day. This awful event has wellnigh crushed me, and, now I think of it, I have scarcely tasted food since last evening. Thank you, my child, I will take your arm. In an hour or two I shall gain self-control."

"My heart aches for you, sir," she said, as they passed slowly through the twilight.

"May it be long before it aches from any sorrow of your own, Pearl."

The parsonage adjoined the church. The old clergyman abounded in almost paternal kindness, and pressed upon Graham a glass of home-made wine. After he had taken this and eaten a little, his strength and poise returned, and he gave his entertainers a fuller account of Hilland and his relations, and in that Southern home there was as genuine sympathy for the inmates of the Northern home as if they all had been devoted to the same cause.

"There are many subjects on which we differ," said his host. "You perceive that I have slaves, but they are so attached to me that I do not think they would leave me if I offered them their freedom. I have been brought up to think slavery right. My father and grandfather before me held slaves and always treated them well. I truly think they did better by them than the bondmen could have done for themselves. To give them liberty and send them adrift would be almost like throwing little children out into the world. I know that there are evils and abuses connected with our system, but I feel sure that liberty given to a people unfitted for it would be followed by far greater evils."

"It's a subject to which I have given very little attention," Graham replied. "I have spent much of my life abroad, and certainly your servants are better off than the peasantry and very poor in many lands that I have visited."

With a kind of wonder, he thought of the truth that Hilland, who so hated slavery, had been lifted from the battlefield by slaves, and that his remains had been treated with reverent honor by a slave-holder.

The old clergyman's words also proved that, while he deprecated the war unspeakably, his whole sympathy was with the South. His only son, of whom neither he nor Rita could speak without looks of pride and affection kindling in their faces, was in the Confederate service, and the old man prayed as fervently for success to the cause to which he had devoted the treasure of his life as any Northern father could petition the God of nations for his boy and the restoration of the Union. At the same time his nature was too large, too highly ennobled by Christianity, for a narrow vindictive bitterness. He could love the enemy that he was willing his son should oppose in deadly battle.

"We hope to secure our independence," he added, "and to work out our national development according to the genius of our own people. I pray and hope for the time when the North and South may exist side by side as two friendly nations. Your noble words this afternoon found their echo in my heart. Even though my son should be slain by a Northern hand, as your friend has been by a Southern, I wish to cherish no vindictive bitterness and enmity. The question must now be settled by the stern arbitrament of battle; but when the war is over let it not be followed by an era of hate."

He then told Graham how he had lost his beloved wife years before, and how lonely and desolate he had been until Rita had learned to care for him and provide for his comfort with almost hourly vigilance.

"Yes," said Graham, "I have seen it; she is to you what my friend's wife is to her invalid father, the immeasurable blessing of his life. How it will be now I hardly know, for I fear that her grief will destroy her, and the old major, her father, could not long survive."

A note was now handed to the old gentleman, who, having read it, appeared greatly distressed. After a moment's hesitancy he gave it to Graham, who read as follows:

"I heard the North'ner speak this arternoon, an' I can't be one to take and rob him of his horse and send him to prison. But it'll be done to-night if you can't manage his escape. Every rode is watched, an' your house will be searched to-night. ONE OF THE BAND.

"You'll burn this an' keep mum or my neck will be stretched."

"Who brought the note?" Mr. Anderson asked, going to the door and questioning a colored woman.

"Dunno, mas'r. De do' open a little, and de ting flew in on de flo'."

"Well," said Graham, "I must mount and go at once;" and he was about to resume his arms.

"Wait, wait; I must think!" cried his host. "For you to go alone would be to rush into the very evils we are warned against. I am pained and humiliated beyond measure by this communication. Mr. Graham, do not judge us harshly. There is, I suppose, a vile sediment in every community, and there is here a class that won't enlist in open, honorable warfare, but prowl around, chiefly at night, intent on deeds like this."

"Papa," said Rita, who had read the warning, "I know what to do;" and her brave spirit flashed in her eyes.

"You, my child?"

"Yes. I'll prove to Mr. Graham what a Southern girl will do for a guest — for one who has trusted her. The deep, deep disgrace of his capture and robbery shall not come on our heads. I will guide him at once through the woods to old Uncle Jehu's cabin. No one will think of looking for him there; for there is little more than a bridle-path leading to it; but I know the way, every inch of it."

"But, Rita, I could send one of the servants with Mr. Graham."

"No, papa; he would be missed and afterward questioned, and some awful revenge taken on him. You must say that I have retired when the villains come. You must keep all our servants in. Mr. Graham and I will slip out. He can saddle his horse, and I, you know well, can saddle mine. Now we must apparently go to our rooms and within half an hour slip out unperceived and start. No one will ever dare touch me, even if it is found out."

"Pearl, priceless Pearl, I'll fight my way through all the guerillas in the land, rather than subject you to peril."

"You could not fight your way through them, the cowardly skulkers. What chance would you have in darkness? My plan brings me no peril, for if they met us they would not dare to touch me. But if it costs me my life I *will* go," she concluded passionately. "This disgrace must not fall on our people."

"Rita is right," said the old clergyman, solemnly. "I could scarcely survive the disgrace of having a guest taken from my home, and they would have to walk over my prostrate form before it could be done; and to send you out alone would be even more shameful. The plan does not involve much peril to Rita. Although, in a sense, you are my enemy, I will trust this pearl beyond price to your protection, and old Jehu will return with her until within a short distance of the house. As she says, I think no one in this region would harm her. I will co-operate with you, Rita, and entreat the Heavenly Father until I clasp you in my arms again. Act, act at once."

Graham was about to protest again, but she silenced him by a gesture that was almost imperious. "Don't you see that for papa's sake, for my own, as well as yours, I must go? Now let us say good-night as if we were parting unsuspicious of trouble. When I tap at your door, Mr. Graham, you will follow me; and you, papa, try to keep our people in ignorance."

Graham wrung the clergyman's hand in parting, and said, "You will always be to me a type of the noblest development of humanity."

"God bless you, sir," was the reply, "and sustain you through the dangers and trying scenes before you. I am but a simple old man, trying to do right with God's help. And, believe me, sir, the South is full of men as sincere as I am."

Within half an hour Graham followed his fair guide down a back stairway and out into the darkness. Rita's pony was at pasture in a field adjoining the stable, but he came instantly at her soft call.

"I shall not put on my saddle," she whispered. "If I leave it hanging in the stable it will be good evidence that I am in my room. There will be no need of our riding fast, and, indeed, I have often ridden without a saddle for fun. I will guide you to your horse and saddle in the dark stable, for we must take him out of a back door, so that there will be no sound of his feet on the boards."

Within a few moments they were passing like shadows down a shaded lane that led from the house to the forest, and then entered what was a mere bridle-path, the starlight barely enabling the keen-eyed Rita to make it out at times. The thick woods on either side prevented all danger of flank attacks. After riding some little time they stopped and listened. The absolute silence, broken only by the cries of the wild creatures of the night, convinced them that they were not followed. Then Rita said, "Old Jehu has a bright boy of sixteen or thereabout, and he'll guide you north through the woods as far as he can, and then God will protect and guide you until you are safe. I know He will help you to escape, that you may say words of comfort to the poor, broken-hearted wife."

"Yes, Pearl, I think I shall escape. I take your guidance as a good omen. If I could only be sure that no harm came to you and your noble father!"

"The worst of harm would have come to us had we permitted the evil that was threatened."

"You seem very young, Pearl, and yet you are in many ways very mature and womanly."

"I am young—only sixteen-but mamma's death and the responsibility it brought me made my childhood brief. Then Henry is five years older than I, and I always played with him, and, of course, you know I tried to reach up to those things that he thought about and did. I've never been to school. Papa is educating me, and oh, he knows so much, and he makes knowledge so interesting, that I can't help learning a little. And then Henry's going into the war, and all that is happening, makes me feel so very, very old and sad at times;" and so she continued in low tones to tell about herself and Henry and her father, of their hopes of final victory, and all that made up her life. This she did with a guileless frankness, and yet with a refined reserve that was indescribable in its simple pathos and beauty. In spite of himself Graham was charmed and soothed, while he wondered at the exquisite blending of girlhood and womanhood in his guide. She also questioned him about the North and the lands he had visited, about his aunt and Grace and her father; and Graham's tremulous tones as he spoke of Grace led her to say sorrowfully, "Ah, she is very, very dear to you also."

"Yes," he said, imitating her frankness, "she is dearer to me than my life. I would gladly have died in Hilland's place to have saved her this sorrow. Were it not for the hope of serving her in some way, death would have few terrors to me. There, my child, I have spoken to you as I have to only one other, my dear old aunty, who is like a mother. Your noble trust begets trust."

Then he became aware that she was crying bitterly.

"Pearl, Pearl," he said, "don't cry. I have become accustomed to a sad heart, and it's an old, old story."

"Oh, Mr. Graham, I remember hearing mamma say once that women learn more through their hearts than their heads. I have often thought of her words, and I think they must be true. Almost from the first my heart told me that there was something about you which made you different from other people. Why is the world so full of trouble of every kind? Ah, well, papa has taught me that heaven will make amends for everything."

They had now reached a little clearing, and Rita said that they were near Jehu's cabin, and that their final words had better be said before awakening the old man. "I must bathe my face, too," she added, "for he would not understand my tears," and went to a clear little spring but a few paces away.

Graham also dismounted. When she returned he took her hand and raised it reverently to his lips as he said, "Pearl, this is not a case for ordinary thanks. I no doubt owe my life, certainly my liberty, to you. On that I will not dwell. I owe to you and your father far more, and so does poor Grace Hilland. You insured a burial for my friend that will bring a world of comfort to those who loved him. The thought of your going to his grave and placing upon it fresh flowers from time to time will contain more balm than a thousand words of well-meant condolence. Pearl, my sweet, pure, noble child, is there nothing I can do for you?"

"Yes," she faltered; "it may be that you can return all that we have done a hundred-fold. It may be that you will meet Henry in battle. In the memory of his little sister you will spare him, will you not? If he should be captured I will tell him to write to you, and I feel sure that you will remember our lonely ride and the gray old father who is praying for you now, and will not leave him to suffer."

Graham drew a seal ring from his finger and said: "Dear Pearl, take this as a pledge that I will serve him in any way in my power and at any cost to myself. I hope the day will come when he will honor me with his friendship, and I would as soon strike the friend I have lost as your brother."

"Now I am content," she said. "I believe every word you say."

"And Grace Hilland will come some day and claim you as a sister dearly beloved. And I, sweet Pearl, will honor your memory in my heart of hearts. The man who wins you as his bride may well be prouder than an emperor."

"Oh, no, Mr. Graham, I'm just a simple Southern girl."

"There are few like you, I fear, South or North. You are a girl to kindle every manly instinct and power, and I shall be better for having known you. The hope of serving you and yours in some way and at some time will give a new zest and value to my life."

"Do not speak so kindly or I shall cry again. I've been afraid you would think me silly, I cry so easily. I do not think we Southern girls are like those at the North. They are colder, I imagine, or at least more able to control their feelings. Papa says I am a child of the South. I can't decide just how much or how little I ought to feel on all occasions, and ever since I saw you mourning over your friend with just such passionate grief as I should feel, my whole heart has ached for you. You will come and see us again if you have a chance?"

"I will make chances, Pearl, even though they involve no little risk."

"No, no; don't do that. You ought to care too much for us to do that. Nothing would give me pleasure that brought danger to you. If I could only know that you reached your friends in safety!"

"I'll find a way of letting you know if I can."

"Well, then, good-by. It's strange, but you seem like an old, old friend. Oh, I know Henry will like you, and that you will like him. Next to mamma's, your ring shall be my dearest treasure. I shall look at it every night and think I have added one more chance of Henry's safety. Oh, I could worship the man who saved his life."

"And any man might worship you. Good-by, Pearl;" and he kissed her hand again and again, then lifted her on her pony with a tenderness that was almost an embrace, and she rode slowly to the door of a little log cabin, while Graham remained concealed in the shadow of the woods until it was made certain that no one was in the vicinity except Jehu and his family.

The old man was soon aroused, and his ejaculations and exclamations were innumerable.

"No, missy, dars no un been roun' heah for right smart days. It's all safe, an' Jehu an' his ole ooman knows how ter keep mum when Mas'r

Anderson says mum; an' so does my peart boy Huey"—who, named for his father, was thus distinguished from him. "An' de hossifer is a Linkum man? Sho, sho! who'd a tink it, and his own son a 'Federate! Well, well, Mas'r Anderson isn't low-down white trash. If he thought a ting was right I reckon de hull worl' couldn't make him cut up any white-trash didoes."

When Rita explained further the old negro replied with alacrity: "Ob cose Jehu will took you home safe, an' proud he'll be ter go wid you, honey. You'se a mighty peart little gal, an' does youse blood an' broughten up jestice. Mighty few would dar' ride five mile troo de lonesome woods wid a strange hossifer, if he be a Linkum man. He mus' be sumpen like Linkum hisself. Yes, if you bain't afeared ter show him de way, Huey needn't be;" and the boy, who was now wide awake, said he'd "like notten better dan showin' a Linkum man troo de woods."

Graham was summoned, and in a few moments all was arranged.

He then drew the old man aside and said, "You good, faithful old soul, take care of that girl as the apple of your eye, for she has only one equal in the world. Here is one hundred dollars. That will pay for a good many chickens and vegetables, won't it?"

"Lor' bless you, mas'r, dey ain't chickens nuff in Ole Virginny to brought hundred dollars."

"Well, I'll tell you what I'm afraid of. This region may be wasted by war, like so many others. You may not be troubled in this out-of-the-way place. If Mr. Anderson's family is ever in need, you are now paid to supply them with all that you can furnish."

"'Deed I is, mas'r, double paid."

"Be faithful to them and you shall have more 'Linkum money,' as you call it. Keep it, for your money down here won't be worth much soon."

"Dat's shoah. De cullud people bain't all prayin' for Linkum for notten."

"Good-by. Do as I say and you shall be taken care of some day. Say nothing about this."

"Mum's de word all roun' ter-night, mas'r."

"Huey, are you ready?"

"I is, mas'r."

"Lead the way, then;" and again approaching Rita, Graham took off his hat and bowed low as he said, "Give my grateful greeting to your honored father, and may every hope of his heart be fulfilled in return for his good deeds today. As for you, Miss Anderson, no words can express my profound respect and unbounded gratitude. We shall meet again in happier times;" and backing his horse, while he still remained uncovered, he soon turned and followed Huey.

"Well, now," ejaculated Jehu. "'Clar ter you ef dat ar Linkum hossifer bain't nigh onter bein' as fine a gemman as Mas'r Henry hisself. Won't you take some 'freshment, missy? No? Den I'se go right 'long wid you."

Rita enjoined silence, ostensibly for the reason that it was prudent, but chiefly that she might have a respite from the old man's garrulousness. Her thoughts were very busy. The first romance of her young life had come, and she still felt on her hands the kisses that had been so warm and sincere, although she knew they were given by one who cherished a hopeless love. After all, it was but her vivid Southern imagination that had been kindled by the swift, strange events of the past twenty-four hours. With the fine sense of the best type of dawning womanhood, she had been deeply moved by Graham's strong nature. She had seen in him a love for another man that was as tender and passionate as that of a woman, and yet it was bestowed upon the husband of the woman whom he had loved for years. That he had not hesitated to risk captivity and death in returning for his friend proved his bravery to be unlimited, and a Southern girl adores courage. For a time Graham would be the ideal of her girlish heart. His words of admiration and respect were dwelt upon, and her cheeks flushed up seen in the deep shadow of the forest. Again her tears would fall fast as she thought of his peril and of all the sad scenes of the day and the sadder ones still to come. Grace Hilland, a Southern girl like herself, became a glorified image to her fancy, and it would now be her chief ambition to be like her. She would keep her lovely portrait on her bureau beside her Bible, and it should be almost equally sacred.

In the edge of the forest she parted from Jehu with many and warm thanks, for she thought it wise that there should not be the slightest chance of his being seen. She also handed him a Confederate bill out of her slender allowance, patted him on the shoulder as she would some faithful animal, and rode away. He crept along after her till he saw her let down some bars and turn her pony into the fields. He then crept on till he saw her enter a door, and then stole back to the forest and shambled homeward as dusky as the shadows in which he walked, chuckling, "Missy Rita, sweet honey, guv me one of dern 'Federate rags. Oh, golly! I'se got more money—live Linkum money—dan Mas'r Anderson hisself, and I'se got notten ter do but raise chickens an' garden sass all my born days. Missy Rita's red cheeks never grow pale long as Jehu or Huey can tote chickens and sass."

CHAPTER XXX
GUERILLAS

Graham, beyond a few low, encouraging words, held his peace and also enjoined silence on his youthful guide. His plan was to make a wide circuit around the battlefield of the previous day, and then strike the trail of the Union forces, which he believed he could follow at night. Huey thought that this could be done and that they could keep in the shelter of the woods most of the distance, and this they accomplished, reconnoitring the roads most carefully before crossing them. Huey was an inveterate trapper; and as his pursuit was quite as profitable as raising "sass," old Jehu gave the boy his own way. Therefore he knew every path through the woods for miles around.

The dawn was in the east before Graham reached the Union trail, and he decided to spend the day in a dense piece of woods not very far distant. Huey soon settled the question of Mayburn's provender by purloining a few sheaves of late oats from a field that they passed; but when they reached their hiding-place Graham was conscious that he was in need of food himself, and he also remembered that a boy is always ravenous.

"Well, Huey," he said, "in providing for the horse you have attended to the main business, but what are we going to do?"

"We'se gwine ter do better'n de hoss. If mas'r'll 'zamine his saddle-bags, reckon he'll fine dat Missy Rita hain't de leddy to sen' us off on a hunt widout a bite of suthin' good. She sez, sez she to me, in kind o' whisper like, 'Mas'r Graham'll fine suthin' you'll like, Huey;'" and the boy eyed the saddle-bags like a young wolf.

"Was there ever such a blessed girl!" cried Graham, as he pulled out a flask of wine, a fowl cut into nice portions, bread, butter, and relishes—indeed, the best that her simple housekeeping afforded in the emergency. In the other bag there was also a piece of cake of such portentous size that Huey clasped his hands and rolled up his eyes as he had seen his parents do when the glories of heaven were expatiated upon in the negro prayer-meetings.

"That's all for you, Huey, and here's some bread and cold ham to go with it. When could she have provided these things so thoughtfully? It must have been before she called me last night. Now, Huey, if you ever catch anything extra nice in the woods you take it to Miss Rita. There is ten dollars to pay you; and when the Lincoln men get possession here I'll look after you and give you a fine chance, if you have been faithful. You must not tell Miss Rita what I say, but seem to do all of your own accord. I wish I had more money with me, but you will see me again, and I will make it all right with you."

"It's all right now, mas'r. What wouldn't I do for Missy Rita? When my ole mammy was sick she bro't med'cin, and a right smart lot ob tings, and brung her troo de weariness. Golly! Wonder Missy Rita don't go straight up ter heben like dem rackets dey shoots when de 'Federates say dey hab a vict'ry;" and then the boy's mouth became so full that he was speechless for a long time.

The sense of danger, and the necessity for the utmost vigilance, had diverted Graham's thoughts during his long night ride; and with a soldier's habit he had concentrated his faculties on the immediate problem of finding the trail, verifying Huey's local knowledge by observation of the stars. Now, in the cool summer morning, with Rita's delicious repast before him, life did not seem so desperate a thing as on the day before. Although exceedingly wearied, the strength of mind which would enable him to face his sad tasks was returning. He thought little about the consequences of his disobedience to orders, and cared less. If he lost his rank he would enlist as a private soldier after he had done all in his power for Grace, who had been committed to his care by Hilland's last words. He felt that she had the most sacred claims upon him, and yet he queried, "What can I do for her beyond communicating every detail of her husband's last hours and his burial? What remedy is there for a sorrow like hers?"

At the same time he felt that a lifelong and devoted friendship might bring solace and help at times, and this hope gave a new value to his life. He also thought it very possible that the strange vicissitudes of war might put it in his power to serve the Andersons, in whom he felt a grateful interest that only such scenes as had just occurred could have awakened. It would ever be to him a source of unalloyed joy to add anything to Rita Anderson's happiness.

His kind old aunt, too, had her full share of his thoughts as he reclined on the dun-colored leaves of the previous year and reviewed the past and planned for the future. He recalled her words, "that good would come of it," when he had promised to "live and do his best." Although in his own life he had missed happiness, there was still a prospect of his adding much to the well-being of others.

But how could he meet Grace again? He trembled at the very thought. Her grief would unman him. It was agony even to imagine it; and she might, in her ignorance of an officer's duties in battle, think that if he had kept near Hilland the awful event might have been averted.

After all, he could reach but one conclusion—to keep his old promise "to do his best," as circumstances indicated.

Asking Huey, who had the trained ear of a hunter, to watch and listen, he took some sleep in preparation for the coming night, and then gave the boy a chance to rest.

The day passed quietly, and in the evening he dismissed Huey, with assurances to Rita and her father that a night's ride would bring him within the Union lines, and that he now knew the way well. The boy departed in high spirits, feeling that he would like "showin' Linkum men troo de woods" even better than trapping.

Then looking well to his arms, and seeing that they were ready for instant use, Graham started on his perilous ride, walking his horse and stopping to listen from time to time. Once in the earlier part of the night he heard the sound of horses' feet, and drawing back into the deep shadow of the woods he saw three or four men gallop by. They were undoubtedly guerillas looking for him, or on some prowl with other objects in view. At last he knew he must be near his friends, and he determined to push on, even though the dawn was growing bright; but he had hardly reached this conclusion when but a short distance in advance a dozen horsemen dashed out of a grove and started toward him.

They were part of "The Band," who, with the instincts of their class, conjectured too truly that, since he had eluded them thus far, their best chance to intercept him would be at his natural approach to the Union lines; and now, with the kind of joy peculiar to themselves, they felt that their prey was in their power, beyond all hope of escape, for Graham was in plain sight upon a road inclosed on either side by a high rail fence. There were so many guerillas that there was not a ghost of a chance in fighting or riding through them, and for a moment his position seemed desperate.

"It's Mayburn to the rescue now," he muttered, and he turned and sped away, and every leap of his noble horse increased the distance between him and his pursuers. His confidence soon returned, for he felt that unless something unforeseen occurred he could ride all around them. His pursuers fired two shots, which were harmless enough, but to his dismay Graham soon learned that they were signals, for from a farmhouse near other horsemen entered the road, and he was between two parties.

There was not a moment to lose. Glancing ahead, he saw a place where the fence had lost a rail or two. He spurred toward it, and the gallant horse flew over like a bird into a wide field fringed on the further side by a thick growth of timber. Bullets from the intercepting party whizzed around him; but he sped on unharmed, while his pursuers only stopped long enough to throw off a few rails, and then both of the guerilla squads rode straight for the woods, with the plan of keeping the fugitive between them, knowing that in its tangle he must be caught.

Graham resolved to risk another volley in order to ride around the pursuers nearest the Union lines, thus throwing them in the rear, with no better chance than a stern chase would give them. In order to accomplish this, however, he had to circle very near the woods, and in doing so saw a promising wood-road leading into them. The yelling guerillas were so close as to make his first plan of escape extremely hazardous; therefore, following some happy instinct he plunged into the shade of the forest. The road proved narrow, but it was open and unimpeded by overhanging boughs. Indeed, the trees were the straight, slender pines in which the region abounded, and he gained on all of his pursuers except two, who, like himself, were superbly mounted. The thud of their horses' hoofs kept near, and he feared that he might soon come to some obstruction which would bring them to close quarters. Mayburn was giving signs of weariness, for his mettle had been sorely tried of late, and Graham resolved to ambush his pursuers if possible. An opportunity occurred speedily, for the road made a sharp turn, and there was a small clearing where the timber had been cut. The dawn had as yet created but a twilight in the woods, and the obscurity aided his purpose. He drew up by the roadside at the beginning of the clearing, and in a position where he could not readily be seen until the guerillas were nearly abreast, and waited, with his heavy revolver in hand and his drawn sword lying across the pommel of his saddle.

On they came at a headlong pace, and passed into the clearing but a few feet away. There were two sharp reports, with the slightest possible interval. The first man dropped instantly; the other rode wildly for a few moments and then fell headlong, while the riderless horses galloped on for a time.

Graham, however, soon overtook them, and with far more compunction than he had felt in shooting their riders, he struck them such a blow with his sword on their necks, a little back of their ears, that they reeled and fell by the roadside. He feared those horses more than all "The Band"; for if mounted again they might tire Mayburn out in a prolonged chase.

To his great joy the wood lane soon emerged into another large open field, and he now felt comparatively safe.

The guerillas, on hearing the shots, spurred on exultantly, feeling sure of their prey, but only to stumble over their fallen comrades. One was still able to explain the mode of their discomfiture; and the dusky road beyond at once acquired wholesome terrors for the survivors, who rode on more slowly and warily, hoping now for little more than the recapture of the horses, which were the envy of all their lawless hearts. Your genuine guerilla will always incur a heavy risk for a fine horse. They soon discovered the poor brutes, and saw at a glance that they would be of no more service in irregular prowlings. Infuriated more at the loss of the beasts than at that of the men, they again rushed forward only to see Graham galloping easily away in the distance.

Even in their fury they recognized that further pursuit was useless, and with bitter curses on their luck, they took the saddles from the fallen horses, and carried their associates, one dead and the other dying, to the farmhouse in which dwelt a sympathizer, who had given them refreshment during the night.

A few hours later—for he travelled the rest of the way very warily— Graham reported to his colonel, and found the brigade under orders to move on the following morning, provided with ten days' rations.

The officer was both delighted and perplexed. "It's a hard case," he said. "You acted from the noblest impulses; but it was flat disobedience to orders."

"I know it. I shall probably be dismissed from the service. If so, colonel, I will enlist as a private in your regiment. Then you can shoot me if I disobey again."

"Well, you are the coolest fellow that ever wore the blue. Come with me to headquarters."

The fact of his arrival, and an imperfect story of what had occurred, soon got abroad among the men; and they were wild in their approval, cheering him with the utmost enthusiasm as he passed to the brigadier's tent. The general was a genuine cavalryman; and was too wise in his day and generation to alienate his whole brigade by any martinetism. He knew

Graham's reputation well, and he was about starting on a dangerous service. The cheers of the men crowding to his tent spoke volumes. Hilland's regiment seemed half beside themselves when they learned that Graham had found their lieutenant-colonel dying on the field, and that he had been given an honorable burial. The general, therefore, gave Graham a most cordial welcome; and said that the question was not within his jurisdiction, and that he would forward full particulars at once through the proper channels to the Secretary of War, adding, "We'll be on the march before orders can reach you. Meanwhile take your old command."

Then the story had to be repeated in detail to the chief officers of the brigade. Graham told it in as few words as possible, and they all saw that his grief was so profound that the question of his future position in the army was scarcely thought of. "I am not a sentimental recruit," he said in conclusion. "I know the nature of my offence, and will make no plea beyond that I believed that all danger to our command had passed, and that it would ride quietly into camp, as it did. I also thought that my superiors in giving the order were more concerned for my safety than, for anything else. What the consequences are to myself personally, I don't care a straw. There are some misfortunes which dwarf all others." The conference broke up with the most hearty expressions of sympathy, and the regret for Hilland's death was both deep and genuine.

"I have a favor to ask my colonel, with your approval, General," said Graham. "I would like to take a small detachment and capture the owner of the farmhouse at which was harbored part of the guerilla band from which I escaped. I would like to make him confess the names of his associates, and send word to them that if harm comes to any who showed kindness or respect to officers of our brigade, severe punishment will be meted out on every one whenever the region is occupied by Union forces."

"I order the thing to be done at once," cried the general. "Colonel, give Major Graham as many men as he needs; and, Graham, send word we'll hang every mother's son of 'em and burn their ranches if they indulge in any more of their devilish outrages. Bring the farmer into camp, and I will send him to Washington as a hostage."

On this occasion Graham obeyed orders literally. The farmer and two of the guerillas were captured; and when threatened with a noosed rope confessed the names of the others. A nearly grown son of the farmer was intrusted with the general's message to their associates; and Graham added emphatically that he intended to come himself some day and see that it was obeyed. "Tell them to go into the army and become straightforward soldiers if they wish, but if I ever hear of another outrage I'll never rest till the general's threat is carried out."

Graham's deadly pistol shots and the reputation he had gained in the vicinity gave weight to his words; and "The Band" subsided into the most humdrum farmers of the region. Rita had ample information of his safety, for it soon became known that he had killed two of the most active and daring of the guerillas and captured three others; and she worshipped the hero of her girlish fancy all the more devoutly.

CHAPTER XXXI
JUST IN TIME

Graham returned to camp early in the afternoon, and was again greeted with acclamations, for the events that had occurred had become better known. The men soon saw, however, from his sad, stern visage that he was in no mood for ovations, and that noisy approval of his course was very distasteful. After reporting, he went directly to his tent; its flaps were closed, and Iss was instructed to permit no one to approach unless bearing orders. The faithful negro, overjoyed at his master's safe return, marched to and fro like a belligerent watch-dog.

Graham wrote the whole story to his aunt, and besought her to make known to Grace with all the gentleness and tact that she possessed the awful certainty of her husband's death. A telegram announcing him among the missing had already been sent. "Say to her," he said, in conclusion, "that during every waking moment I am grieving for her and with her. Oh, I tremble at the effect of her grief: I dread its consequences beyond all words. You know that every power I possess is wholly at her service. Write me daily and direct me what to do—if, alas! it is within my power to do anything in regard to a grief that is without remedy."

He then explained that the command was under orders to move the following day, and that he would write again when he could.

During the next two weeks he saw some active service, taking part in several skirmishes and one severe engagement. In the last it was his fortune to receive on the shoulder a sabre-cut which promised to be a painful though not a dangerous wound, his epaulet having broken the force of the blow.

On the evening of the battle a telegram was forwarded to him containing the words:

> "Have written fully. Come home if you can for a short
> time. All need you. CHARLOTTE MAYBURN."

In the rapid movements of his brigade his aunt's letters had failed to reach him, and now he esteemed his wound most fortunate since it secured him a leave of absence.

His journey home was painful in every sense of the word. He was oppressed by the saddest of memories. He both longed and dreaded unspeakably to see Grace, and the lack of definite tidings from her left his mind a prey to the dreariest forebodings, which were enhanced by his aunt's telegram. The physical pain from which he was never free was almost welcomed as a diversion from his distress of mind. He stopped in Washington only long enough to have his wound re-dressed, and pushed northward. A fatality of delays irritated him beyond measure; and it was late at night when he left the cars and was driven to his aunt's residence.

A yearning and uncontrollable interest impelled him to approach first the cottage which contained the woman, dearer to him than all the world, who had been so strangely committed to his care. To his surprise there was a faint light in the library; and Hilland's ill-omened dream flashed across his mind. With a prophetic dread at heart, he stepped lightly up the piazza to a window. As he turned the blinds he witnessed a scene that so smote his heart that he had to lean against the house for support. Before him was the reality of poor Hilland's vision.

On the rug before the flickering fire the stricken wife crouched, wringing her hands, which looked ghostly in their whiteness. A candle burning dimly on a table increased the light of the fire; and by their united rays he saw, with a thrill of horror, that her loosened hair, which covered her bowed face and shoulders, was, in truth, silver white; and its contrast with her black wrapper made the whole scene, linked as it was with a dead man's dream, so ghostly that he shuddered, and was inclined to believe it to be the creation of his overwrought senses. In self-distrust he looked around. Other objects were clear in the faint moonlight. He was perfectly conscious of the dull ache of his wound. Had the phantom crouched before the fire vanished? No; but now the silver hair was thrown back, and Grace Hilland's white, agonized face was lifted heavenward. Oh, how white it was!

She slowly took a dark-colored vial from her bosom.

Thrilled with unspeakable horror, "Grace!" he shouted, and by a desperate effort threw the blind upward and off from its hinges, and it fell with a crash on the veranda. Springing into the apartment, he had not reached her side before the door opened, and his aunt's frightened face appeared.

"Great God! what does this mean, Alford?"

"What *does* it mean, indeed!" he echoed in agonized tones, as he knelt beside Grace, who had fallen on the floor utterly unconscious. "Bring the candle here," he added hoarsely.

She mechanically obeyed and seemed almost paralyzed. After a moment's search he snatched up something and cried: "She's safe, she's safe! The cork is not removed." Then he thrust the vial into his pocket, and lifted Grace gently on the lounge, saying meanwhile: "She has only fainted; surely 'tis no more. Oh, as you value my life and hers, act. You should know what to do. I will send the coachman for a physician instantly, and will come when you need me."

Rushing to the man's room, he dragged him from his bed, shook him awake, and gave him instructions and offers of reward that stirred the fellow's blood as it had never been stirred before; and yet when he reached the stable he found that Graham had broken the lock and had a horse saddled and ready.

"Now ride," he was commanded, "as if the devil you believe in was after you."

Then Graham rushed back into the house, for he was almost beside himself. But when he heard the poor old major calling piteously, and asking what was the matter, he was taught his need of self-control. Going up to the veteran's room, he soothed him by saying that he had returned late in the night in response to his aunt's telegram, and that he had found Grace fainting on the floor, that Mrs. Mayburn and the servants were with her, and that a physician had been sent for.

"Oh, Graham, Graham," moaned the old man, "I fear my peerless girl is losing her mind, she has acted so strangely of late. It's time you came. It's time something was done, or the worst may happen."

With an almost overwhelming sense of horror, Graham remembered how nearly the worst had happened, but he only said: "Let us hope the worst has passed. I will bring you word from Mrs. Mayburn from time to time."

His terrible anxiety was only partially relieved, for his aunt said that Grace's swoon was obstinate, and would not yield to the remedies she was using. "Come in," she cried. "This is no time for ceremony. Take brandy and chafe her wrists."

> What a mortal chill her cold hands gave him! It was worse
> than when Hilland's hands were cold in his.

"Oh, aunt, she will live?"

"Certainly," was the brusque reply. "A fainting turn is nothing. Come, you are cool in a battle: be cool now. It won't do for us all to lose our wits, although Heaven knows there's cause enough."

"How white her face and neck are!" — for Mrs. Mayburn had opened her wrapper at the throat, that she might breathe more easily — "just as Hilland saw her in his dream."

"Have done with your dreams, and omens, and all your weird nonsense. It's time for a little more *common*-sense. Rub her wrists gently but strongly; and if she shows signs of consciousness, disappear."

At last she said hastily, "Go"

Listening at the door, he heard Grace ask, a few moments later, in a faint voice, "What has happened?'"

"You only fainted, deary."

"Why — why — I'm in the library."

"Yes, you got up in your sleep, and I followed you; and the doctor will soon be here, although little need we have of him."

"Oh, I've had a fearful dream. I thought I saw Warren or Alford. I surely heard Alford's voice."

"Yes, dear, I've no doubt you had a bad dream; and it may be that Alford's voice caused it, for he arrived late last night and has been talking with your father."

"That must be it," she sighed; "but my head is so confused. Oh, I am so glad he's come! When can I see him?"

"Not till after the doctor comes and you are much stronger."

"I wish to thank him; I can't wait to thank him."

"He doesn't want thanks, deary; he wants you to get well. You owe it to him and your father to get well — as well as your great and lifelong sorrow permits. Now, deary, take a little more stimulant, and then don't talk. I've explained everything, and shown you your duty; and I know that my brave Grace will do it."

"I'll try," she said, with a pathetic weariness in her voice that brought a rush of tears to Graham's eyes.

Returning to Major St. John, he assured him that Grace had revived, and that he believed she would be herself hereafter.

"Oh, this cursed war!" groaned the old man; "and how I have exulted in it and Warren's career! I had a blind confidence that he would come out of it a veteran general while yet little more than a boy. My ambition has been punished, punished; and I may lose both the children of whom I was so proud. Oh, Graham, the whole world is turning as black as Grace's mourning robes."

"I have felt that way myself. But, Major, as soldiers we must face this thing like men. The doctor has come; and I will bring him here before he goes, to give his report."

"Well, Graham, a father's blessing on you for going back for Warren. If Grace had been left in suspense as to his fate she would have gone mad in very truth. God only knows how it will be now; but she has a better chance in meeting and overcoming the sharp agony of certainty."

Under the physician's remedies Grace rallied more rapidly; and he said that if carried to her room she would soon sleep quietly.

"I wish to see Mr. Graham first," she said, decisively.

To Mrs. Mayburn's questioning glance, he added, "Gratify her. I have quieting remedies at hand."

"He will prove more quieting than all remedies. He saved my husband's life once, and tried to do so again; and I wish to tell him I never forget it night or day. He is brave, and strong, and tranquil; and I feel that to take his hand will allay the fever in my brain."

"Grace, I am here," he said, pushing open the door and bending his knee at her side while taking her hand. "Waste no strength in thanks. School your broken heart into patience; and remember how dear, beyond all words, your life is to others. Your father's life depends on yours."

"I'll try," she again said; "I think I feel better, differently. An oppression that seemed stifling, crushing me, is passing away. Alford, was there no chance—no chance at all of saving him?"

"Alas! no; and yet it is all so much better than it might have been! His grave is in a quiet, beautiful spot, which you can visit; and fresh flowers are placed upon it every day. Dear Grace, compare your lot with that of so many others whose loved ones are left on the field."

"As he would have been were it not for you, my true, true friend," and she carried his hand to her lips in passionate gratitude. Then tears gushed from her eyes, and she sobbed like a child.

"Thank the good God!" ejaculated Mrs. Mayburn. "These are the first tears she has shed. She will be better now. Come, deary, you have seen Alford. He is to stop with us a long time, and will tell you everything over and over. You must sleep now."

Graham kissed her hand and left the room, and the servants carried her to her apartment. Mrs. Mayburn and the physician soon joined him in the library, which was haunted by a memory that would shake his soul to his dying day.

The physician in a cheerful mood said, "I now predict a decided change for the better. It would almost seem that she had had some shock which has broken the evil spell; and this natural flow of tears is better than all the medicine in the world;" and then he and Mrs. Mayburn explained how Grace's manner had been growing so strange and unnatural that they feared her mind was giving way.

"I fear you were right," Graham replied sadly; and he told them of the scene he had witnessed, and produced the vial of laudanum.

The physician was much shocked, but Mrs. Mayburn had already guessed the truth from her nephew's words and manner when she first discovered him.

"Neither Grace nor her father must ever know of this," she said, with a shudder.

"Certainly not; but Dr. Markham should know. As her physician, he should know the whole truth."

"I think that phase of her trouble has passed," said the doctor, thoughtfully; "but, as you say, I must be on my guard. Pardon me, you do not look well yourself. Indeed, you look faint;" for Graham had sunk into a chair.

"I fear I have been losing considerable blood," said Graham, carelessly; "and now that this strong excitement is passing, it begins to tell. I owe my leave of absence to a wound."

"A wound!" cried his aunt, coming to his side. "Why did you not speak of it?"

"Indeed, there has been enough to speak of beyond this trifle. Take a look at my shoulder, doctor, and do what you think best."

"And here is enough to do," was his reply as soon as Graham's shoulder was bared: "an ugly cut, and all broken loose by your exertions this evening. You must keep very quiet and have good care, or this reopened wound will make you serious trouble."

"Well, doctor, we have so much serious trouble on hand that a little more won't matter much."

His aunt inspected the wound with grim satisfaction, and then said, sententiously: "I'm glad you have got it, Alford, for it will keep you home and divert Grace's thoughts. In these times a wound that leaves the heart untouched may be useful; and nothing cures a woman's trouble better than having to take up the troubles of others. I predict a deal of healing for Grace in your wound."

"All which goes to prove," added the busy physician, "that woman's nature is different from man's."

When he was gone, having first assured the major over and over again that all danger was past, Graham said, "Aunt, Grace's hair is as white as yours."

"Yes; it turned white within a week after she learned the certainty of her husband's death."

"Would that I could have died in Hilland's place!"

"Yes," said the old lady, bitterly; "you were always too ready to die."

He drew her down to him as he lay on the lounge, and kissed her tenderly, as he said, "But I have kept my promise 'to live and do my best.'"

"You have kept your promise *to live* after a fashion. My words have also proved true, 'Good has come of it, and more good will come of it.'"

CHAPTER XXXII
A WOUNDED SPIRIT

Grace's chief symptom when she awoke on the following morning was an extreme lassitude. She was almost as weak as a violent fever would have left her, but her former unnatural and fitful manner was gone. Mrs. Mayburn told Graham that she had had long moods of deep abstraction, during which her eyes would be fixed on vacancy, with a stare terrible to witness, and then would follow uncontrollable paroxysms of grief.

"This morning," said her anxious nurse, "she is more like a broken lily that has not strength to raise its head. But the weakness will pass; she'll rally. Not many die of grief, especially when young."

"Save her life, aunty, and I can still do a man's part in the world."

"Well, Alford, you must help me. She has been committed to your care; and it's a sacred trust."

Graham was now installed in his old quarters, and placed under Aunt Sheba's care. His energetic aunt, however, promised to look in upon him often, and kept her word. The doctor predicted a tedious time with his wound, and insisted on absolute quiet for a few days. He was mistaken, however. Time would not be tedious, with frequent tidings of Grace's convalescence and her many proofs of deep solicitude about his wound.

Grace did rally faster than had been expected. Her system had received a terrible shock, but it had not been enfeebled by disease. With returning strength came an insatiate craving for action—an almost desperate effort to occupy her hands and mind. Before it was prudent for Graham to go out or exert himself—for his wound had developed some bad symptoms—she came to see him, bringing delicacies made with her own hands.

Never had her appearance so appealed to his heart. Her face had grown thin, but its lovely outlines remained; and her dark eyes seemed tenfold more lustrous in contrast with her white hair. She had now a presence that the most stolid would turn and look after with a wondering pity and admiration, while those gifted with a fine perception could scarcely see her without tears. Graham often thought that if she could be turned into marble she would make the ideal statue representing the women of both the contending sections whose hearts the war had broken.

As she came and went, and as he eventually spent long hours with her and her father, she became to him a study of absorbing interest, in which his old analytical bent was not wholly wanting. "What," he asked himself every hour in the day, "will be the effect of an experience like this on such a woman? what the final outcome?" There was in this interest no curiosity, in the vulgar sense of the word. It was rather the almost sleepless suspense of a man who has everything at stake, and who, in watching the struggle of another mind to cope with misfortune, must learn at the same time his own fate. It was far more than this—it was the vigilance of one who would offer help at all times and at any cost, Still, so strong are natural or acquired characteristics that he could not do this without manifesting some of the traits of the Alford Graham who years before had studied the mirthful Grace St. John with the hope of analyzing her power and influence. And had he been wholly indifferent to her, and as philosophical and cynical as once it was his pride to think he was, she would still have remained an absorbing study. Her sudden and awful bereavement had struck her strong and exceptional spiritual nature with the shattering force of the ball that crashes through muscle, bone, and nerves. In the latter case the wound may be mortal, or it may cause weakness and deformity. The wounded spirit must survive, although the effects of the wound may be even more serious and far-reaching—changing, developing, or warping character to a degree that even the most experienced cannot predict. Next to God, time is the great healer; and human love, guided by tact, can often achieve signal success.

But for Graham there was no God; and it must be said that this was becoming true of Grace also. As Hilland had feared, the influence of those she loved and trusted most had gradually sapped her faith, which in her case had been more a cherished tradition, received from her mother, than a vital experience.

Hilland's longings for a life hereafter, and his words of regret that she had lost the faith of her girlhood, were neutralized by the bitter revolt of her spirit against her immeasurable misfortune. Her own experience was to her a type of all the desolating evil and sorrow of the world; and in her agony she could not turn to a God who permitted such evil and suffering. It seemed to her that there could be no merciful, overruling Providence—that her husband's view, when his mind was in its most vigorous and normal state, was more rational than a religion which taught that a God who loved good left evil to make such general havoc.

"It's the same blind contention of forces in men as in nature," she said to herself; "and only the strong or the fortunate survive."

One day she asked Graham abruptly, "Do you believe that the human spirit lives on after death?"

He was sorely troubled to know how to answer her, but after a little hesitation said, "I feel, as your husband did, that I should be glad if you had the faith of your girlhood. I think it would be a comfort to you."

"That's truly the continental view, that superstition is useful to women. Will you not honestly treat me as your equal, and tell me what you, as an educated man, believe?"

"No," he replied, gravely and sadly, "I will only recall with emphasis your husband's last words."

"You are loyal to him, at least; and I respect you for it. But I know what you believe, and what Warren believed when his faculties were normal and unbiased by the intense longing of his heart. I am only a woman, Alford, but I must use such little reason as I have; and no being except one created by man's ruthless imagination could permit the suffering which this war daily entails. It's all of the earth, earthy. Alford," she added, in low, passionate utterance, "I could believe in a devil more easily than in a God; and yet my unbelief sinks me into the very depths of a hopeless desolation. What am I? A mere little atom among these mighty forces and passions which rock the world with their violence. Oh, I was so happy! and now I am crushed by some haphazard bullet shot in the darkness."

He looked at her wonderingly, and was silent.

"Alford," she continued, her eyes glowing in the excitement of her strong, passionate spirit, "I will not succumb to all this monstrous evil. If I am but a transient emanation of the earth, and must soon return to my kindred dust, still I can do a little to diminish the awful aggregate of suffering. My nature, earth-born as it is, revolts at a selfish indifference to it all. Oh, if there is a God, why does He not rend the heavens in His haste to stay the black torrents of evil? Why does He not send the angels of whom my mother told me when a child, and bid them stand between the armies that are desolating thousands of hearts like mine? Or if He chooses to work by silent, gentle influences like those of spring, why does He not bring human hearts together that are akin, and enhance the content and happiness which our brief life permits? But no. Unhappy mistakes are made. Alas, my friend, we both know it to our sorrow! Why should I feign ignorance of that which your unbounded and unselfish devotion has proved so often? Why should you not know that before this deadly stroke fell my one grief was that you suffered; and that as long as I could pray I prayed for your happiness? Now I can see only merciless force or blind chance, that in nature smites with the tornado the lonely forest or the thriving village, the desolate waves or some ship upon them. Men, with all their boasted reason, are even worse. What could be more mad and useless than this war? Alford, I alone have suffered enough to make the thing accursed; and I must suffer to the end: and I am only one of countless women. What is there for me, what for them, but to grow lonelier and sadder every day? But I won't submit to the evil. I won't be a mere bit of helpless drift. While I live there shall be a little less suffering in the world. Ah, Alford! you see how far removed I am from the sportive girl you saw on that May evening years ago. I am an old, white-haired, broken-hearted woman; and yet," with a grand look in her eyes, she concluded, "I have spirit enough left to take up arms against all the evil and suffering within my reach. I know how puny my efforts will be; but I would rather try to push back an avalanche than cower before it."

Thus she revealed to him the workings of her mind; and he worshipped her anew as one of the gentlest and most loving of women, and yet possessed of a nature so strong that under the guidance of reason it could throw off the shackles of superstition and defy even fate. Under the spell of her words the evil of the world did seem an avalanche, not of snow, but of black molten lava; while she, too brave and noble to cower and cringe, stood before it, her little hand outstretched to stay its deadly onset.

CHAPTER XXXIII
THE WHITE-HAIRED NURSE

Life at the two cottages was extremely secluded. All who felt entitled to do so made calls, partly of condolence and partly from curiosity. The occupants of the two unpretending dwellings had the respect of the community; but from their rather unsocial ways could not be popular. The old major had ever detested society in one of its phases — that is, the claims of mere vicinage, the duty to call and be called upon by people who live near, when there is scarcely a thought or taste in common. With his Southern and army associations he had drifted to a New England city; but he ignored the city except as it furnished friends and things that pleased him. His attitude was not contemptuous or unneighborly, but simply indifferent.

"I don't thrust my life on any one," he once said to Mrs. Mayburn, "except you and Grace. Why should other people thrust their lives on me?"

His limited income had required economy, and his infirmities a life free from annoyance. As has been shown, Grace had practiced the one with heart as light as her purse; and had interposed her own sweet self between the irritable veteran and everything that could vex him. The calling world had had its revenge. The major was profane, they had said; Grace was proud, or led a slavish life. The most heinous sin of all was, they were poor. There were several families, however, whom Grace and the major had found congenial, with various shades of difference; and the young girl had never lacked all the society she cared for. Books had been her chief pleasure; the acquaintance of good whist-players had been cultivated; army and Southern friends had appeared occasionally; and when Mrs. Mayburn had become a neighbor, she had been speedily adopted into the closest intimacy. When Hilland had risen above their horizon he soon glorified the world to Grace. To the astonishment of society, she had married a millionaire, and they had all continued to live as quietly and unostentatiously as before. There had been another slight effort to "know the people at the St. John cottage," but it had speedily died out. The war had brought chiefly military associations and absence. Now again there was an influx of callers largely from the church that Grace had once attended. Mrs. Mayburn received the majority with a grim politeness, but discriminated very favorably in case of those who came solely from honest sympathy. All were made to feel, however, that, like a mourning veil, sorrow should shield its victims from uninvited observation.

Hilland's mother had long been dead, and his father died at the time when he was summoned from his studies in Germany. While on good terms with his surviving relatives, there had been no very close relationship or intimacy remaining. Grace had declared that she wished no other funeral service than the one conducted by the good old Confederate pastor; and the relatives, learning that they had no interest in the will, speedily discovered that they had no further interest whatever. Thus the inmates of the two cottages were left to pursue their own shadowed paths, with little interference from the outside world. The major treasured a few cordial eulogies of Hilland cut from the journals at the time; and except in the hearts wherein he was enshrined a living image, the brave, genial, high-souled man passed from men's thoughts and memories, like thousands of others in that long harvest of death.

Graham's wound at last was wellnigh healed, and the time was drawing near for his return to the army. His general had given such a very favorable account of the circumstances attending his offence, and of his career as a soldier both before and after the affair, that the matter was quietly ignored. Moreover, Hilland, as a soldier and by reason of the loyal use of his wealth, stood very high in the estimation of the war authorities; and the veteran major was not without his surviving circle of influential friends. Graham, therefore, not only retained his rank, but was marked for promotion.

Of all this, however, he thought and cared little. If he had loved Grace before, he idolized her now. And yet with all her deep affection for him and her absolute trust, she seemed more remote than ever. In the new phase of her grief she was ever seeking to do little things which she thought would please him. But this was also true of her course toward Mrs. Mayburn, especially so toward her father, and also, to a certain extent, toward the poor and sick in the vicinity. Her one effort seemed to be to escape from her thoughts, herself, in a ceaseless ministry to others. And the effort sometimes degenerated into restlessness. There was such a lack of repose in her manner that even those who loved her most were pained and troubled. There was not enough to keep her busy all the time, and yet she was ever impelled to do something.

One day she said to Graham, "I wish I could go back with you to the war; not that I wish to shed another drop of blood, but I would like to march, march forever."

Shrewd Mrs. Mayburn, who had been watching Grace closely for the last week or two, said quietly: "Take her back with you, Alford. Let her become a nurse in some hospital. It will do both her and a lot of poor fellows a world of good."

"Mrs. Mayburn, you have thought of just the thing," cried Grace. "In a hospital full of sick and wounded men I could make my life amount to something; I should never need to be idle then."

"Yes, you would. You would be under orders like Alford, and would have to rest when off duty. But, as you say, you could be of great service, instead of wasting your energy in coddling two old people. You might save many a poor fellow's life."

"Oh," she exclaimed, clasping her hands, "the bare thought of saving one poor woman from such suffering as mine is almost overwhelming. But how can I leave papa?"

"I'll take care of the major and insure his consent. If men are so possessed to make wounds, it's time women did more to cure them. It's all settled: you are to go. I'll see the major about it now, if he *has* just begun his newspaper;" and the old lady took her knitting and departed with her wonted prompt energy.

At first Graham was almost speechless from surprise, mingled doubt and pleasure; but the more he thought of it, the more he was convinced that the plan was an inspiration.

"Alford, you will take me?" she said, appealingly.

"Yes," he replied, smilingly, "if you will promise to obey my orders in part, as well as those of your superiors."

"I'll promise anything if you will only take me. Am I not under your care?"

"Oh, Grace, Grace, I can do so little for you!"

"No one living can do more. In providing this chance of relieving a little pain, of preventing a little suffering, you help me, you serve me, you comfort me, as no one else could. And, Alford, if you are wounded, come to the hospital where I am; I will never leave you till you are well. Take me to some exposed place in the field, where there is danger, where men are brought in desperately wounded, where you would be apt to be."

"I don't know where I shall be, but I would covet any wound that would bring you to my side as nurse."

She thought a few moments, and then said, resolutely: "I will keep as near to you as I can. I ask no pay for my services. On the contrary, I will employ my useless wealth in providing for exposed hospitals. When I attempt to take care of the sick or wounded, I will act scrupulously under the orders of the surgeon in charge; but I do not see why, if I pay my own way, I cannot come and go as I think I can be the most useful."

"Perhaps you could, to a certain extent, if you had a permit," said Graham, thoughtfully; "but I think you would accomplish more by remaining in one hospital and acquiring skill by regular work. It would be a source of indescribable anxiety to me to think of your going about alone. If I know just where you are, I can find you and write to you."

"I will do just what you wish," she said, gently.

"I wish for only what is best for you."

"I know that. It would be strange if I did not."

Mrs. Mayburn was not long in convincing the major that her plan might be the means of incalculable benefit to Grace as well as to others. He, as well as herself and Graham, had seen with deep anxiety that Grace was giving way to a fever of unrest; and he acquiesced in the view that it might better run its course in wholesome and useful activity, amid scenes of suffering that might tend to reconcile her to her own sorrow.

Graham, however, took the precaution of calling on Dr. Markham, who, to his relief, heartily approved of the measure. On one point Graham was firm. He would not permit her to go to a hospital in the field, liable to vicissitudes from sudden movements of the contending armies. He found one for her, however, in which she would have ample scope for all her efforts; and before he left he interested those in charge so deeply in the white-haired nurse that he felt she would always be under watchful, friendly eyes.

"Grace," he said, as he was taking leave, "I have tried to be a true friend to you."

"Oh, Alford!" she exclaimed, and she seized his hand and held it in both of hers.

His face grew stern rather than tender as he added: "You will not be a true friend to me—you will wrong me deeply—if you are reckless of your health and strength. Remember that, like myself, you have entered the service, and that you are pledged to do your duty, and not to work with feverish zeal until your strength fails. You are just as much under obligation to take essential rest as to care for the most sorely wounded in your ward. I shall take the advice I give. Believing that I am somewhat essential to your welfare and the happiness of those whom we have left at home, I shall incur no risks beyond those which properly fall to my lot. I ask you to be equally conscientious and considerate of those whose lives are bound up in you."

"I'll try," she said, with that same pathetic look and utterance which had so moved him on the fearful night of his return from the army. "But, Alford, do not speak to me so gravely, I had almost said sternly, just as we are saying good-by."

He raised her hand to his lips, and smiled into her pleading face as he replied, "I only meant to impress you with the truth that you have a patient who is not in your ward—one who will often be sleeping under the open sky, I know not where. Care a little for him, as well as for the unknown men in your charge. This you can do only by taking care of yourself. You, of all others, should know that there are wounds besides those which will bring men to this hospital."

Tears rushed into her eyes as she faltered, "You could not have made a stronger appeal."

"You will write to me often?"

"Yes, and you cannot write too often. Oh, Alford, I cannot wish you had never seen me; but it would have been far, far better for you if you had not."

"No, no," he said, in low, strong emphasis. "Grace Hilland, I would rather be your friend than have the love of any woman that ever lived."

"You do yourself great wrong (pardon me for saying it, but your happiness is so dear to me), you do yourself great wrong. A girl like Pearl Anderson could make you truly happy; and you could make her happy."

"Sweet little Pearl will be happy some day; and I may be one of the causes, but not in the way you suggest. It is hard to say good-by and leave you here alone, and every moment I stay only makes it harder."

He raised her hand once more to his lips, then almost rushed away.

Days lapsed into weeks, and weeks into months. The tireless nurse alleviated suffering of every kind; and her silvery hair was like a halo around a saintly head to many a poor fellow. She had the deep solace of knowing that not a few wives and mothers would have mourned had it not been for her faithfulness.

But her own wound would not heal. She sometimes felt that she was slowly bleeding to death. The deep, dark tide of suffering, in spite of all she could do, grew deeper and darker; and she was growing weary and discouraged.

Graham saw her at rare intervals; and although she brightened greatly at his presence, and made heroic efforts to satisfy him that she was doing well, he grew anxious and depressed. But there was nothing tangible, nothing definite. She was only a little paler, a little thinner; and when he spoke of it she smilingly told him that he was growing gaunt himself with his hard campaigning.

"But you, Grace," he complained, "are beginning to look like a wraith that may vanish some moonlight night."

Her letters were frequent, sometimes even cheerful, but brief. He wrote at great length, filling his pages with descriptions of nature, with scenes that were often humorous but not trivial, with genuine life, but none of its froth. Life for both had become too deep a tragedy for any nonsense. He passed through many dangers, but these, as far as possible, he kept in the background; and fate, pitying his one deep wound, spared him any others.

At last there came the terrible battle of the Wilderness, and the wards were filled with desperately wounded men. The poor nurse gathered up her failing powers for one more effort; and Confederate and Union men looked after her wonderingly and reverently, even in their mortal weakness. To many she seemed like a ministering spirit rather than a woman of flesh and blood; and lips of dying men blessed her again and again. But they brought no blessing. She only shuddered and grew more faint of heart as the scenes of agony and death increased. Each wound was a type of Hilland's wound, and in every expiring man she saw her husband die. Her poor little hands trembled now as she sought to stem the black, black tide that deepened and broadened and foamed around her.

Late one night, after a new influx of the wounded, she was greatly startled while passing down her ward by hearing a voice exclaim, "Grace— Grace Brentford!"

It was her mother's name.

The call was repeated; and she tremblingly approached a cot on which was lying a gray-haired man.

"Great God!" he exclaimed, "am I dreaming? am I delirious? How is it that I see before me the woman I loved forty-odd years ago? You cannot be Grace Brentford, for she died long years since."

"No, but I am her daughter."

"Her daughter!" said the man, struggling to rise upon his elbow—"her daughter! She should not look older than you."

"Alas, sir, my age is not the work of time, but of grief. I grew old in a day. But if you knew and loved my mother, you have sacred claims upon me. I am a nurse in this ward, and will devote myself to you."

The man sank back exhausted. "This is strange, strange indeed," he said. "It is God's own providence. Yes, my child, I loved your mother, and I love her still. Harry St. John won her fairly; but he could not have loved her better than I. I am now a lonely old man, dying, I believe, in my enemy's hands, but I thank God that I've seen Grace Brentford's child, and that she can soothe my last hours."

"Do not feel so discouraged about yourself," said Grace, her tears falling fast. "Think rather that yon have been brought here that I might nurse you back to life. Believe me, I will do so with tender, loving care."

"How strange it all is!" the man said again. "You have her very voice, her manner. But it was by your eyes that I recognized you. Your eyes are young and beautiful like hers, and full of tears, as hers were when she sent me away with an ache to my heart that has never ceased. It will soon be cured now. Your father will remember a wild young planter down in Georgia by the name of Phil Harkness."

"Indeed, sir, I've heard both of my parents speak of you, and it was ever with respect and esteem."

"Give my greeting to your father, and say I never bore him any ill-will. In the saddest life there is always some compensation. I have had wealth and honors; I am a colonel in our army, and have been able to serve the cause I loved; but, chief of all, the child of Grace Brentford is by my side at the end. Is your name Grace also?"

"Yes. Oh, why is the world so full of hopeless trouble?"

"Not hopeless trouble, my child. I am not hopeless. For long years I have had peace, if not happiness—a deep inward calm which the confusion and roar of the bloodiest battles could not disturb. I can close my eyes now in my final sleep as quietly as a child. In a few hours, my dear, I may see your mother; and I shall tell her that I left her child assuaging her own sorrow by ministering to others."

"Oh, oh!" sobbed Grace, "pray cease, or I shall not be fit for my duties; your words pierce my very soul. Let me nurse you back to health. Let me take you to my home until you are exchanged, for I must return. I must, must. My strength is going fast; and you bring before me my dear old father whom I have left too long."

"My poor child! God comfort and sustain you. Do not let me keep you longer from your duties, and from those who need you more than I. Come and say a word to me when you can. That's all I ask. My wound was dressed before your watch began, and I am doing as well as I could expect. When you feel like it, you can tell me more about yourself."

Their conversation had been in a low tone as she sat beside him, the patients near either sleeping or too preoccupied by their own sufferings to give much heed.

Weary and oppressed by bitter despondency, she went from cot to cot, attending to the wants of those in her charge. To her the old colonel's sad history seemed a mockery of his faith, and but another proof of a godless or God-forgotten world. She envied his belief, with its hope and peace; but he had only increased her unbelief. But all through the long night she watched over him, coming often to his side with delicacies and wine, and with gentle words that were far more grateful.

Once, as she was smoothing back his gray locks from his damp forehead, he smiled, and murmured, "God bless you, my child. This is a foretaste of heaven."

In the gray dawn she came to him and said, "My watch is over, and I must leave you for a little while; but as soon as I have rested I will come again."

"Grace," he faltered, hesitatingly, "would you mind kissing an old, old man? I never had a child of my own to kiss me."

She stooped down and kissed him again and again, and he felt her hot tears upon his face.

"You have a tender heart, my dear," he said, gently. "Good-by, Grace— Grace Brentford's child. Dear Grace, when we meet again perhaps all tears will be wiped from your eyes forever."

She stole away exhausted and almost despairing. On reaching her little room she sank on her couch, moaning; "Oh, Warren, Warren, would that I were sleeping your dreamless sleep beside you!"

Long before it was time for her to go on duty again she returned to the ward to visit her aged friend. His cot was empty. In reply to her eager question she was told that he had died suddenly from internal hemorrhage soon after she had left him.

She looked dazed for a moment, as if she had received a blow, then fell fainting on the cot from which her mother's friend had been taken. The limit of her endurance was passed.

Before the day closed, the surgeon in charge of the hospital told her gently and firmly that she must take an indefinite leave of absence. She departed at once in the care of an attendant; but stories of the white-haired nurse lingered so long in the ward and hospital that at last they began to grow vague and marvellous, like the legends of a saint.

CHAPTER XXXIV
RITA'S BROTHER

All through the campaign of '64 the crimson tide of war deepened and broadened. Even Graham's cool and veteran spirit was appalled at the awful slaughter on either side. The Army of the Potomac—the grandest army ever organized, and always made more sublime and heroic by defeat—was led by a man as remorseless as fate. He was fate to thousands of loyal men, whom he placed at will as coolly as if they had been the pieces on a chessboard. He was fate to the Confederacy, upon whose throat he placed his iron grasp, never relaxed until life was extinct. In May, 1864, he quietly crossed the Rapidan for the death-grapple. He took the most direct route for Richmond, ignoring all obstacles and the fate of his predecessors. To think that General Grant wished to fight the battle of the Wilderness is pure idiocy. One would almost as soon choose the Dismal Swamp for a battleground. It was undoubtedly his hope to pass beyond that gloomy tangle, over which the shadow of death had brooded ever since fatal Chancellorsville. But Lee, his brilliant and vigilant opponent, rarely lost an advantage; and Graham's experienced eye, as with the cavalry he was in the extreme advance, clearly saw that their position would give their foes enormous advantages. Lee's movements would be completely masked by the almost impervious growth, He and his lieutenants could approach within striking distance, whenever they chose, without being seen, and had little to fear from the Union artillery, which the past had given them much cause to dread. It was a region also to disgust the very soul of a cavalryman; for the low, scrubby growth lined the narrow roads almost as effectually as the most scientifically prepared *abatis*.

Graham's surmise was correct. Lee would not wait till his antagonist had reached open and favorable ground, but he made an attack at once, where, owing to peculiarities of position, one of his thin regiments had often the strength of a brigade.

On the morning of the 5th of May began one of the most awful and bloody battles in the annals of warfare. Indeed it was the beginning of one long and almost continuous struggle which ended only at Appomattox.

With a hundred thousand more, Graham was swept into the bloody vortex, and through summer heat, autumn rains, and winter cold, he marched and fought with little rest. He was eventually given the colonelcy of his regiment, and at times commanded a brigade. He passed through unnumbered dangers unscathed; and his invulnerability became a proverb among his associates. Indeed he was a mystery to them, for his face grew sadder and sterner every day, and his reticence about himself and all his affairs was often remarked upon. His men and officers had unbounded respect for him, that was not wholly unmixed with fear; for while he was considerate, and asked for no exposure to danger in which he did not share, his steady discipline was never relaxed, and he kept himself almost wholly aloof, except as their military relations required contact. He could not, therefore, be popular among the hard-swearing, rollicking, and convivial cavalrymen. In a long period of inaction he might have become very unpopular, but the admirable manner in which he led them in action, and his sagacious care of them and their horses on the march and in camp, led them to trust him implicitly. Chief of all, he had acquired that which with the stern veterans of that day went further than anything else—a reputation for dauntless courage. What they objected to were his "glum looks and unsocial ways," as they termed them.

They little knew that his cold, stern face hid suffering that was growing almost desperate in its intensity. They little knew that he was chained to his military duty as to a rock, while a vulture of anxiety was eating out his very heart. What was a pale, thin, white-haired woman to them? But what to him? How true it is that often the heaviest burdens of life are those at which the world would laugh, and of which the overweighted heart cannot and will not speak!

For a long time after his plunge into the dreary depths of the Wilderness he had received no letters. Then he had learned of Grace's return home; and at first he was glad indeed. His aunt had written nothing more alarming than that Grace had overtaxed her strength in caring for the throngs of wounded men sent from the Wilderness, that she needed rest and good tonic treatment. Then came word that she was "better"; then they "hoped she was gaining"; then they were about to go to "the seashore, and Grace had always improved in salt air." It was then intimated that she had found "the summer heat very enervating, and now that fall winds were blowing she would grow stronger." At last, at the beginning of winter, it was admitted that she had not improved as they had hoped; but they thought she was holding her own very well—that the continued and terrific character of the war oppressed her—and that every day she dreaded to hear that he had been stricken among other thousands.

Thus, little by little, ever softened by some excuse or some hope, the bitter truth grew plain: Grace was failing, fading, threatening to vanish. He wrote as often as he could, and sought with all his skill to cheer, sustain, and reconcile her to life. At first she wrote to him not infrequently, but her letters grew further and further apart, and at last she wrote, in the early spring of '65.

"I wish I could see you, Alford; but I know it is impossible. You are strong, you are doing much to end this awful war, and it's your duty to remain at your post. You must not sully your perfect image in my mind, or add to my unhappiness by leaving the service now for my sake. I have learned the one bitter lesson of the times. No matter how much *personal* agony, physical or mental, is involved, the war must go on; and each one must keep his place in the ranks till he falls or is disabled. I have fallen. I am disabled. My wound will not close, and drop by drop life and strength are ebbing. I know I disappoint you, my true, true friend; but I cannot help it. Do not reproach me. Do not blame me too harshly. Think me weak, as I truly am. Indeed, when I am gone your chances will be far better. It costs me a great effort to write this. There is a weight on my hand and brain as well as on my heart. Hereafter I will send my messages through dear, kind Mrs. Mayburn, who has been a mother to me in all my sorrow. Do not fear: I will wait till you can come with honor; for I must see you once more."

For a long time after receiving this letter a despair fell on Graham. He was so mechanical in the performance of his duties that his associates wondered at him, and he grew more gaunt and haggard than ever. Then in sharp reaction came a feverish eagerness to see the war ended.

Indeed all saw that the end was near, and none, probably, more clearly than the gallant and indomitable Lee himself. At last the Confederate army was outflanked, the lines around Petersburg were broken through, and the final pursuit began. It was noted that Graham fought and charged with an almost tiger-like fierceness; and for once his men said with reason that he had no mercy on them. He was almost counting the hours until the time when he could sheathe his sword and say with honor, "I resign."

One morning they struck a large force of the enemy, and he led a headlong charge. For a time the fortunes of the battle wavered, for the Confederates fought with the courage of desperation. Graham on his powerful horse soon became a conspicuous object, and all gave way before him as if he were a messenger of death, at the same time wondering at his invulnerability.

The battle surged on and forward until the enemy were driven into a thick piece of woods. Graham on the right of his line directed his bugler to give the order to dismount, and a moment later his line of battle plunged into the forest. In the desperate *melee* that followed in the underbrush, he was lost to sight except to a few of his men. It was here that he found himself confronted by a Confederate officer, from whose eyes flashed the determination either to slay or to be slain. Graham had crossed swords with him but a moment when he recognized that he had no ordinary antagonist; and with his instinct of fight aroused to its highest pitch he gave himself up wholly to a personal and mortal combat, shouting meantime to those near, "Leave this man to me."

Looking his opponent steadily in the eye, like a true swordsman, he remained first on the defensive; and such was his skill that his long, straight blade was a shield as well as a weapon. Suddenly the dark eyes and features of his opponent raised before him the image of Rita Anderson; and he was so overcome for a second that the Confederate touched his breast with his sabre and drew blood. That sharp prick and the thought that Rita's brother might be before him aroused every faculty and power of his mind and body. His sword was a shield again, and he shouted, "Is not your name Henry Anderson?"

"My name is our cause," was the defiant answer; "with it I will live or die."

Then came upon Graham one of those rare moments in his life when no mortal man could stand before him. Ceasing his wary, rapid fence, his sword played like lightning; and in less than a moment the Confederate's sabre flew from his hand, and he stood helpless.

"Strike," he said, sullenly; "I won't surrender."

"I'd sooner cut off my right hand," replied Graham, smiling upon him, "than strike the brother of Rita Anderson."

"Is your name Graham?" asked his opponent, his aspect changing instantly.

"Yes; and you are Henry. I saw your sister's eyes in yours. Take up your sword, and go quietly to the rear as my friend, not prisoner. I adjure you, by the name of your old and honored father and your noble-hearted sister, to let me keep my promise to them to save your life, were it ever in my power."

"I yield," said the young man, in deep despondency. "Our cause *is* lost, and you are the only man in the North to whom I should be willing to surrender. Colonel, I will obey your orders."

Summoning his orderly and another soldier, he said to them, "Escort this gentleman to the rear. Let him keep his arms. I have too much confidence in you, Colonel Anderson, even to ask that you promise not to escape. Treat him with respect. He will share my quarters to-night." And then he turned and rushed onward to overtake the extreme advance of his line, wondering at the strange scene which had passed with almost the rapidity of thought.

That night by Graham's camp-fire began a friendship between himself and Henry Anderson which would be lifelong. The latter asked, "Have you heard from my father and sister since you parted with them?"

"No. My duties have carried me far away from that region. But it is a source of unspeakable gratification that we have met, and that you can tell me of their welfare."

"It does seem as if destiny, or, as father would say, Providence, had linked my fortunes and those of my family with you. He and Rita would actually have suffered with hunger but for you. Since you were there the region has been tramped and fought over by the forces of both sides, and swept bare. My father mentioned your name and that of Colonel Hilland; and a guard was placed over his house, and he and Rita were saved from any personal annoyance. But all of his slaves, except the old woman you remember, were either run off or enticed away, and his means of livelihood practically destroyed. Old Uncle Jehu and his son Huey have almost supported them. They, simple souls, could not keep your secret, though they tried to after their clumsy fashion. My pay, you know, was almost worthless; and indeed there was little left for them to buy. Colonel Graham, I am indebted to you for far more than life, which has become wellnigh a burden to me."

"Life has brought far heavier burdens to others than to you, Colonel Anderson. Those you love are living; and to provide for and protect such a father and sister as you possess might well give zest to any life. Your cause is lost; and the time may come sooner than you expect when you will be right glad of it. I know you cannot think so now, and we will not dwell on this topic. I can testify from four years' experience that no cause was ever defended with higher courage or more heroic self-sacrifice. But your South is not lost; and it will be the fault of its own people if it does not work out a grander destiny within the Union than it could ever achieve alone. But don't let us discuss politics. You have the same right to your views that I have to mine. I will tell you how much I owe to your father and sister, and then you will see that the burden of obligation rests upon me;" and he gave his own version of that memorable day whose consequences threatened to culminate in Grace Hilland's death.

Under the dominion of this thought he could not hide the anguish of his mind; and Rita had hinted enough in her letters to enable Anderson to comprehend his new-found friend. He took Graham's hand, and as he wrung it he said, "Yes, life has brought to others heavier burdens than to me."

"You may have thought," resumed Graham, "that I fought savagely to-day; but I felt that it is best for all to end this useless, bloody struggle as soon as possible. As for myself, I'm just crazed with anxiety to get away and return home. Of course we cannot be together after tonight, for with the dawn I must be in the saddle. Tonight you shall share my blankets. You must let me treat you as your father and Rita treated me. I will divide my money with you: don't grieve me by objecting. Call it a loan if you will. Your currency is now worthless. You must go with the other prisoners; but I can soon obtain your release on parole, and then, in the name of all that is sacred, return home to those who idolize you. Do this, Colonel Anderson, and you will lift a heavy burden from one already overweighted."

"As you put the case I cannot do otherwise," was the sad reply. "Indeed I have no heart for any more useless fighting. My duty now is clearly to my father and sister."

That night the two men slumbered side by side, and in the dawn parted more like brothers than like foes.

As Graham had predicted, but a brief time elapsed before Lee surrendered, and Colonel Anderson's liberty on parole was soon secured. They parted with the assurance that they would meet again as soon as circumstances would permit.

At the earliest hour in which he could depart with honor, Graham's urgent entreaty secured him a leave of absence; and he lost not a moment in his return, sending to his aunt in advance a telegram to announce his coming.

CHAPTER XXXV
HIS SOMBRE RIVALS

Never had his noble horse Mayburn seemed to fail him until the hour that severed the military chain which had so long bound him to inexorable duty, and yet the faithful beast was carrying him like the wind. Iss, his servant, soon fell so far behind that Graham paused and told him to come on more leisurely, that Mayburn would be at the terminus of the military railroad. And there Iss found him, with drooping head and white with foam. The steam-engine was driven to City Point with the reckless speed characteristic of military railroads; but to Graham the train seemed to crawl. He caught a steamer bound for Washington, and paced the deck, while in the moonlight the dark shores of the James looked stationary. From Washington the lightning express was in his view more dilatory than the most lumbering stage of the old regime.

When at last he reached the gate to his aunt's cottage and walked swiftly up the path, the hour and the scene were almost the same as when he had first come, an indifferent stranger, long years before. The fruit-trees were as snowy white with blossoms, the air as fragrant, the birds singing as jubilantly, as when he had stood at the window and gazed with critical admiration on a sportive girl, a child-woman, playing with her little Spitz dog. As he passed the spot where she had stood, beneath his ambush behind the curtains, his exalted mind brought back her image with lifelike realism—the breeze in her light hair, her dark eyes brimming with mirth, her bosom panting from her swift advance, and the color of the red rose in her cheeks.

He groaned as he thought of her now.

His aunt saw him from the window, and a moment later was sobbing on his breast.

"Aunt," he gasped, "I'm not too late?"

"Oh, no," she said, wearily; "Grace is alive; but one can scarcely say much more. Alford, you must be prepared for a sad change."

He placed her in her chair, and stood before her with heaving breast. "Now tell me all," he said, hoarsely.

"Oh, Alford, you frighten me. You must be more composed. You cannot see Grace, looking and feeling as you do. She is weakness itself;" and she told him how the idol of his heart was slowly, gradually, but inevitably sinking into the grave.

"Alford, Alford," she cried, entreatingly, "why do you look so stern? You could not look more terrible in the most desperate battle."

In low, deep utterance, he said, "This is my most desperate battle; and in it are the issues of life and death."

"You terrify *me*, and can you think that a weak, dying woman can look upon you as you now appear?"

"She shall not die," he continued, in the same low, stern utterance, "and she must look upon me, and listen, too. Aunt, you have been faithful to me all these years. You have been my mother. I must entreat one more service. You must second me, sustain me, co-work with me. You must ally all your experienced womanhood with my manhood, and with my will, which may be broken, but which shall not yield to my cruel fate."

"What do you propose to do?"

"That will soon be manifest. Go and prepare Grace for my visit. I wish to see her alone. You will please be near, however;" and he abruptly turned and went to his room to remove his military suit and the dust of travel.

He had given his directions as if in the field, and she wonderingly and tremblingly obeyed, feeling that some crisis was near.

Grace was greatly agitated when she heard of Graham's arrival; and two or three hours elapsed before she was able to be carried down and placed on the sofa in the library. He, out in the darkness on the piazza, watched with eyes that glowed like coals—watched as he had done in the most desperate emergency of all the bloody years of battle. He saw her again, and in her wasted, helpless form, her hollow cheeks, her bloodless face, with its weary, hopeless look, her mortal weakness, he clearly recognized his *sombre rivals*, *Grief and Death*; and with a look of indomitable resolution he raised his hand and vowed that he would enter the lists against them. If it were within the scope of human will he would drive them from their prey.

His aunt met him in the hall and whispered, "Be gentle."

"Remain here," was his low reply. "I have also sent for Dr. Markham;" and he entered.

Grace reached out to him both her hands as she said, "Oh, Alford, you are barely in time. It is a comfort beyond all words to see you before— before—" She could not finish the sinister sentence.

He gravely and silently took her hands, and sat down beside her.

"I know I disappoint you," she continued. "I've been your evil genius, I've saddened your whole life; and you have been so true and faithful! Promise me, Alford, that after I'm gone you will not let my blighted life cast its shadow over your future years. How strangely stern you look!"

"So you intend to die, Grace?" were his first, low words.

"Intend to die?"

"Yes. Do you think you are doing right by your father in dying?"

"Dear, dear papa! I have long ceased to be a comfort to him. He, too, will be better when I am gone. I am now a hopeless grief to him. Alford, dear Alford, do not look at me in that way."

"How else can I look? Do you not comprehend what your death means to *me*, if not to others?"

"Alford, can I help it?"

"Certainly you can. It will be sheer, downright selfishness for you to die. It will be your one unworthy act. You have no disease: you have only to comply with the conditions of life in order to live."

"You are mistaken," she said, the faintest possible color coming into her face. "The bullet that caused Warren's death has been equally fatal to me. Have I not tried to live?"

"I do not ask you to *try* to live, but to *live*. Nay, more, I demand it; and I have the right. I ask for nothing more. Although I have loved you, idolized you, all these years, I ask only that you comply with the conditions of life and live." The color deepened perceptibly under his emphatic words, and she said, "Can a woman live whose heart, and hope, and soul, if she has one, are dead and buried?"

"Yes, as surely as a man whose heart and hope were buried long years before. There was a time when I weakly purposed to throw off the burden of life; but I promised to live and do my best, and I am here to-day. You must make me the same promise. In the name of all the past, I demand it. Do you imagine that I am going to sit down tamely and shed a few helpless tears if you do me this immeasurable wrong?"

"Oh, Alford!" she gasped, "what do you mean?"

"I am not here, Grace, to make threats," he said gravely; "but I fear you have made a merely superficial estimate of my nature. Hilland is not. You know that I would have died a hundred times in his place. He committed you to my care with his last breath, and that trust gave value to my life. What right have you to die and bring to me the blackness of despair? I am willing to bear my burden patiently to the end. You should be willing to bear yours."

"I admit your claim," she cried, wringing her hands. "You have made death, that I welcome, a terror. How can I live? What is there left of me but a shadow? What am I but a mere semblance of a woman? The snow is not whiter than my hair, or colder than my heart. Oh, Alford, you have grown morbid in all these years. You cannot know what is best. Your true chance is to let me go. I am virtually dead now, and when my flickering breath ceases, the change will be slight indeed."

"It will be a fatal change for me," he replied, with such calm emphasis that she shuddered. "You ask how you can live. Again I repeat, by complying with the conditions of life. You have been complying with the conditions of death; and I will not yield you to him. Grief has been a far closer and more cherished friend than I; and you have permitted it, like a shadow, to stand between us. The time has now come when you must choose between this fatal shadow, this useless, selfish grief, and a loyal friend, who only asks that he may see you at times, that he may know where to find the one life that is essential to his life. Can you not understand from your own experience that a word from you is sweeter to me than all the music of the world?—that smiles from you will give me courage to fight the battle of life to the last? Had Hilland come back wounded, would you have listened if he had reasoned, 'I am weak and maimed—not like my old self: you will be better off without me'?"

"Say no more," she faltered. "If a shadow can live, I will. If a poor, heartless, hopeless creature can continue to breathe, I will. If I die, as I believe I must, I will die doing just what you ask. If it is possible for me to live, I shall disappoint you more bitterly than ever. Alford, believe me, the woman is dead within me. If I live I shall become I know not what—a sort of unnatural creature, having little more than physical life."

"Grace, our mutual belief forbids such a thought. If a plant is deeply shadowed, and moisture is withdrawn, it begins to die. Bring to it again light and moisture, the conditions of its life, and it gradually revives and resumes its normal state. This principle applies equally to you in your higher order of existence. Will you promise me that, at the utmost exertion of your will and intelligence, you will try to live?"

"Yes, Alford; but again I warn you. You will be disappointed."

He kissed both her hands with a manner that evinced profound gratitude and respect, but nothing more; and then summoned his aunt and Dr. Markham.

Grace lay back on the sofa, white and faint, with closed eyes.

"Oh, Alford, what have you done?" exclaimed Mrs. Mayburn.

"What is right and rational. Dr. Markham, Mrs. Hilland has promised to use the utmost exertion of her will and intelligence to live. I ask that you and my aunt employ your utmost skill and intelligence in co-operation with her effort. We here—all four of us—enter upon a battle; and, like all battles, it should be fought with skill and indomitable courage, not sentimental impulse. I know that Mrs. Hilland will honestly make the effort, for she is one to keep her word. Am I not right, Grace?"

"Yes," was the faint reply.

"Why, now I can go to work with hope," said the physician briskly, as he gave his patient a little stimulant.

"And I also," cried the old lady, tears streaming down her face. "Oh, darling Grace, you will live and keep all our hearts from breaking."

"I'll try," she said, in almost mortal weariness.

When she had been revived somewhat by his restoratives, Dr. Markham said, "I now advise that she be carried back to her room, and I promise to be unwearied in my care."

"No," said Graham to his aunt. "Do not call the servants; I shall carry her to her room myself;" and he lifted her as gently as he would take up a child, and bore her strongly and easily to her room.

"Poor, poor Alford!" she whispered—"wasting your rich, full heart on a shadow."

CHAPTER XXXVI
ALL MATERIALISTS

When Graham returned to the library he found that the major had tottered in, and was awaiting him with a look of intense anxiety.

"Graham, Graham!" he cried, "do you think there is any hope?"

"I do, sir. I think there is almost a certainty that your daughter will live."

"Now God be praised! although I have little right to say it, for I've put His name to a bad use all my life."

"I don't think any harm has been done," said Graham, smiling.

"Oh, I know, I know how wise you German students are. You can't find God with a microscope or a telescope, and therefore there is none. But I'm the last man to criticise. Grace has been my divinity since her mother died; and if you can give a reasonable hope that she'll live to close my eyes, I'll thank the God that my wife worshipped, in spite of all your new-fangled philosophies."

"And I hope I shall never be so wanting in courtesy, to say the least, as to show anything but respect for your convictions. You shall know the whole truth about Grace; and I shall look to you also for aid in a combined effort to rally and strengthen her forces of life. You know, Major, that I have seen some service."

"Yes, yes; boy that you are, you are a hundred-fold more of a veteran than I am. At the beginning of the war I felt very superior and experienced. But the war that I saw was mere child's-play."

"Well, sir, the war that I've been through was child's play to me compared with the battle begun to-night. I never feared death, except as it might bring trouble to others, and for long years I coveted it; but I fear the death of Grace Hilland beyond anything in this world or any other. As her father, you now shall learn the whole truth;" and he told his story from the evening of their first game of whist together.

"Strange, strange!" muttered the old man. "It's the story of Philip Harkness over again. But, by the God who made me, she shall reward you if she lives."

"No, Major St. John, no. She shall devote herself to you, and live the life that her own feelings dictate. She understands this, and I *will* it. I assure you that whatever else I lack it's not a will."

"You've proved that, Graham, if ever a man did. Well, well, well, your coming has brought a strange and most welcome state of affairs. Somehow you've given me a new lease of life and courage. Of late we've all felt like hauling down the flag, and letting grim death do his worst. I couldn't have survived Grace, and didn't want to. Only plucky Mrs. Mayburn held on to your coming as a forlorn hope. You now make me feel like nailing the flag to the staff, and opening again with every gun. Grace is like her mother, if I do say it. Grace Brentford never lacked for suitors, and she had the faculty of waking up *men*. Forgive an old man's vanity. Phil Harkness was a little wild as a young fellow, but he had grand mettle in him. He made more of a figure in the world than I—was sent to Congress, owned a big plantation, and all that—but sweet Grace Brentford always looked at me reproachfully when I rallied her on the mistake she had made, and was contentment itself in my rough soldier's quarters," and the old man took off his spectacles to wipe his tear-dimmed eyes. "Grace is just like her. She, too, has waked up men. Hilland was a grand fellow; and, Graham, you are a soldier every inch of you, and that's the highest praise I can bestow. You are in command in this battle, and God be with you. Your unbelief doesn't affect *Him* any more than a mole's."

Graham laughed—he could laugh in his present hopefulness—as he replied, "I agree with you fully. If there is a personal Creator of the universe, I certainly am a small object in it." "That's not what I've been taught to believe either; nor is it according to my reason. An infinite God could give as much attention to you as to the solar system."

"From the present aspect of the world, a great deal would appear neglected," Graham replied, with a shrug.

"Come, Colonel Graham," said the major, a little sharply, "you and I have both heard the rank and file grumble over the tactics of their general. It often turned out that the general knew more than the men. But it's nice business for me to be talking religion to you or any one else;" and the idea struck him as so comical that he laughed outright.

Mrs. Mayburn, who entered at that moment, said: "That's a welcome sound. I can't remember, Major, when I've heard you laugh. Alford, you are a magician. Grace is sleeping quietly."

"Little wonder! What have I had to laugh about?" said the major. "But melancholy itself would laugh at my joke to-night. Would you believe it, I've been talking religion to the colonel,—if I haven't!"

"I think it's time religion was talked to all of us."

"Oh, now, Mrs. Mayburn, don't you begin. You haven't any God any more than Graham has. You have a jumble of old-fashioned theological attributes, that are of no more practical use to you than the doctrines of Aristotle. Please ring for Jinny, and tell her to bring us a bottle of wine and some cake. I want to drink to Grace's health. If I could see her smile again I'd fire a *feu de joie* if I could find any ordnance larger than a popgun. Don't laugh at me, friends," he added, wiping the tears from his dim old eyes; "but the bare thought that Grace will live to bless my last few days almost turns my head. Where is Dr. Markham?"

"He had other patients to see, and said he would return by and by," Mrs. Mayburn replied.

"It's time we had a little relief," she continued, "whatever the future may be. The slow, steady pressure of anxiety and fear was becoming unendurable. I could scarcely have suffered more if Grace had been my own child; and I feared for you, Alford, quite as much."

"And with good reason," he said, quietly.

She gave him a keen look, and then did as the major had requested.

"Come, friends," cried he, "let us give up this evening to hope and cheer. Let what will come on the morrow, we'll have at least one more gleam of wintry sunshine to-day."

Filling the glasses of all with his trembling hand, he added, when they were alone: "Here's to my darling's health. May the good God spare her, and spare us all, to see brighter days. Because I'm not good, is no reason why He isn't."

"Amen!" cried the old lady, with Methodistic fervor.

"What are you saying amen to?—that I'm not good?"

"Oh, I imagine we all average about alike," was her grim reply—"the more shame to us all!"

"Dear, conscience-stricken old aunty!" said Graham, smiling at her. "Will nothing ever lay your theological ghosts?"

"No, Alford," she said, gravely. "Let us change the subject."

"I've told Major St. John everything from the day I first came here," Graham explained; "and now before we separate let it be understood that he joins us as a powerful ally. His influence over Grace, after all, is more potent than that of all the rest of us united. My words to-night have acted more like a shock than anything else. I have placed before her clearly and sharply the consequences of yielding passively, and of drifting further toward darkness. We must possess ourselves with an almost infinite patience and vigilance. She, after all, must bear the brunt of this fight with death; but we must be ever on hand to give her support, and it must be given also unobtrusively, with all the tact we possess. We can let her see that we are more cheerful in our renewed hope, but we must be profoundly sympathetic and considerate."

"Well, Graham, as I said before, you are captain. I learned to obey orders long ago as well as to give them;" and the major summoned his valet and bade them goodnight.

Graham, weary in the reaction from his intense feeling and excitement, threw himself on the sofa, and his aunt came and sat beside him.

"Alford," she said, "what an immense change your coming has made!"

"The beginning of a change, I hope."

"It was time—it was time. A drearier household could scarcely be imagined. Oh, how dreary life can become! Grace was dying. Every day I expected tidings of your death. It's a miracle that you are alive after all these bloody years. All zest in living had departed from the major. We are all materialists, after our own fashion, wholly dependent on earthly things, and earthly things were failing us. In losing Grace, you and the major would have lost everything; so would I in losing you. Alford, you have become a son to me. Would you break a mother's heart? Can you not still promise to live and do your best?"

"Dear aunt, we shall all live and do our best."

"Is that the best you can say, Alford?"

"Aunty, there are limitations to the strength of every man. I have reached the boundary of mine. From the time I began the struggle in the Vermont woods, and all through my exile, I fought this passion. I hesitated at no danger, and the wilder and more desolate the region, the greater were its attractions to me. I sought to occupy my mind with all that was new and strange; but such was my nature that this love became an inseparable part of my being. I might just as well have said I would forget my sad childhood, the studies that have interested me, your kindness. I might as well have decreed that I should not look the same and be the same—that all my habits of thought and traits of character should not be my own. Imagine that a tree in your garden had will and intelligence. Could it ignore the law of its being, all the long years which had made it what it is, and decide to be some other kind of tree, totally different? A man who from childhood has had many interests, many affections, loses, no doubt, a sort of concentration when the one supreme love of his life takes possession of him. If Grace lives, and I can see that she has at last tranquilly and patiently accepted her lot, you will find that I can be tranquil and patient. If she dies, I feel that I shall break utterly. I can't look into the abyss that her grave would open. Do not think that I would consciously and deliberately become a vulgar suicide—I hope I long since passed that point, and love and respect for you forbid the thought—but the long strain that I have been under, and the dominating influence of my life, would culminate. I should give way like a man before a cold, deadly avalanche. I have been frank with you, for in my profound gratitude for your love and kindness I would not have you misunderstand me, or think for a moment that I proposed deliberately to forget you in my own trouble. The truth is just this, aunt: I have not strength enough to endure Grace Hilland's death. It would be such a lame, dreary, impotent conclusion that I should sink under it, as truly as a man who found himself in the sea weighted by a ton of lead. But don't let us dwell on this thought. I truly believe that Grace will live, if we give her all the aid she requires. If she honestly makes the effort to live—as she will, I feel sure—she can scarcely help living when the conditions of life are supplied."

"I think I understand you, Alford," said the old lady, musingly; "and yet your attitude seems a strange one."

"It's not an unnatural one. I am what I have been growing to be all these years. I can trace the sequence of cause and effect until this moment."

"Well, then," said the old lady, grimly, "Grace must live, if it be in the power of human will and effort to save her. Would that I had the faith in God that I ought to have! But He is afar off, and He acts in accordance with an infinite wisdom that I can't understand. The happiness of His creatures seems a very secondary affair."

"Now, aunty, we are on ground where we differ theoretically, to say the least; but I accord to you full right to think what you please, because I know you will employ all the natural and rational expedients of a skilful nurse."

"Yes, Alford; you and Grace only make me unhappy when you talk in that way. I know you are wrong, just as certainly as the people who believed the sun moved round the earth. The trouble is that I know it only with the same cold mental conviction, and therefore can be of no help to either of you. Pardon me for my bluntness: do you expect to marry Grace, should she become strong and well?"

"No, I can scarcely say I have any such hope. It is a thought I do not even entertain at present, nor does she. I am content to be her friend through life, and am convinced that she could not think of marriage again for years, if ever. That is a matter of secondary importance. All that I ask is that she shall live."

"Well, compared with most men, a very little contents you," said his aunt dryly. "We shall see, we shall see. But you have given me such an incentive that, were it possible, I'd open my withered veins and give her half of my poor blood."

"Dear aunty, how true and stanch your love is! I cannot believe it will be disappointed."

"I must go back to my post now, nor shall I leave it very often."

"Here is Dr. Markham. He will see that you have it often enough to maintain your own health, and I will too. I've been a soldier too long to permit my chief of staff to be disabled. Pardon me, doctor, but it seems to me that this is more of a case for nursing and nourishment than for drugs."

"You are right, and yet a drug can also become a useful ally. In my opinion, it is more a case for change than anything else. When Mrs. Hilland is strong enough, you must take her from this atmosphere and these associations. In a certain sense she must begin life over again, and take root elsewhere."

"There may be truth in what you say;" and Graham was merged in deep thought when he was left alone. The doctor, in passing out a few moments later, assured him that all promised well.

CHAPTER XXXVII
THE EFFORT TO LIVE

As Graham had said, it did seem that infinite patience and courage would be required to defeat the dark adversaries now threatening the life upon which he felt that his own depended. He had full assurance that Grace made her promised effort, but it was little more than an effort of will, dictated by a sense of duty. She had lost her hold on life, which to her enfeebled mind and body promised little beyond renewed weariness and disappointment. How she could live again in any proper sense of the word was beyond her comprehension; and what was bare existence? It would be burdensome to herself and become wearisome to others. The mind acts through its own natural medium, and all the light that came to her was colored by almost despairing memories.

Too little allowance is often made for those in her condition. The strong man smiles half contemptuously at the efforts of one who is feeble to lift a trifling weight. Still, he is charitable. He knows that if the man has not the muscle, all is explained. So material are the conceptions of many that they have no patience with those who have been enfeebled in mind, will, and courage. Such persons would say, "Of course Mrs. Hilland cannot attend to her household as before; but she ought to have faith, resignation; she ought to make up her mind cheerfully to submit, and she would soon be well. Great heavens! haven't other women lost their husbands? Yes, indeed, and they worried along quite comfortably."

Graham took no such superficial view. "Other women" were not Grace. He was philosophical, and tried to estimate the effect of her own peculiar experience on her own nature, and was not guilty of the absurdity of generalizing. It was his problem to save Grace as she was, and not as some good people said she ought to be. Still, his firm belief remained, that she could live if she would comply with what he believed to be the conditions of life; indeed, that she could scarcely help living. If the time could come when her brain would be nourished by an abundance of healthful blood, he might hope for almost anything. She would then be able to view the past dispassionately, to recognize that what *was past* was gone forever, and to see the folly of a grief which wasted the present and the future. If she never became strong enough for that—and the prospect was only a faint, half-acknowledged hope—then he would reverently worship a patient, gentle, white-haired woman, who should choose her own secluded path, he being content to make it as smooth and thornless as possible.

Beyond a brief absence at the time his regiment was mustered out of the service, he was always at home, and the allies against death—with their several hopes, wishes, and interests—worked faithfully. At last there was a more decided response in the patient. Her sleep became prolonged, as if she were making amends for the weariness of years. Skilful tonic treatment told on the wasted form. New blood was made, and that, in Graham's creed, was new life.

His materialistic theory, however, was far removed from any gross conception of the problem. He did not propose to feed a woman into a new and healthful existence, except as he fed what he deemed to be her whole nature. In his idea, flowers, beauty in as many forms as he could command and she enjoy at the time, were essential. He ransacked nature in his walks for things to interest her. He brought her out into the sunshine, and taught her to distinguish the different birds by their notes. He had Mrs. Mayburn talk to her and consult with her over the homely and wholesome details of housekeeping. Much of the news of the day was brought to her attention as that which should naturally interest her, especially the reconstruction of the South, as represented and made definite by the experience of Henry Anderson and his sister. He told her that he had bought at a nominal sum a large plantation in the vicinity of the parsonage, and that Colonel Anderson should be his agent, with the privilege of buying at no more of an advance than would satisfy the proud young Southerner's self respect.

Thus from every side he sought to bring natural and healthful influences to bear upon her mind, to interest her in life at every point where it touched her, and to reconnect the broken threads which had bound her to the world.

He was aided earnestly and skilfully on all sides. Their success, however, was discouragingly slow. In her weakness Grace made pathetic attempts to respond, but not from much genuine interest. As she grew stronger her manner toward her father was more like that of her former self than was the rest of her conduct. Almost as if from the force of habit, she resumed her thoughtful care for his comfort; but beyond that there seemed to be an apathy, an indifference, a dreary preoccupation hard to combat.

In Graham's presence she would make visible effort to do all he wished, but it was painfully visible, and sometimes she would recognize his unobtrusive attentions with a smile that was sadder than any words could be. One day she seemed almost wholly free from the deep apathy that was becoming characteristic, and she said to him, "Alas, my friend! as I said to you at first, the woman *is* dead within me. My body grows stronger, as the result of the skill and help you all are bringing to bear on my sad problem, but my heart is dead, and my hope takes no hold on life. I cannot overcome the feeling that I am a mere shadow, and have no right to be here among the living. You are so brave, patient, and faithful that I am ever conscious of a sort of dull remorse; but there is a weight on my brain and a despairing numbness at my heart, making everything seem vain and unreal. Please do not blame me. Asking me to feel is like requiring sight of the blind. I've lost the faculty. I have suffered so much that I have become numb, if not dead. The shadows of the past mingle with the shadows of to-day. Only you seem real in your strong, vain effort, and as far as I can suffer any more it pains me to see you thus waste yourself on a hopeless shadow of a woman. I told you I should disappoint you."

"I am not wasting myself, Grace. Remain a shadow till you can be more. I will bear my part of the burden, if you will be patient with yours. Won't you believe that I am infinitely happier in caring for you as you are than I should be if I could not thus take your hand and express to you my thought, my sympathy? Dear Grace, the causes which led to your depression were strong and terrible. Should we expect them to be counteracted in a few short weeks?"

"Alas, Alford! is there any adequate remedy? Forgive me for saying this to you, and yet you, of all people, can understand me best. You cling to me who should be nothing to a man of your power and force. You say you cannot go on in life without me, even as a weak, dependent friend—that you would lose all zest, incentive, and interest; for I cannot think you mean more. If you feel in this way toward me, who in the eyes of other men would be a dismal burden, think how Warren dwells in my memory, what he was to me, how his strong sunny nature was the sun of my life. Do you not see you are asking of me what you say you could not do yourself, although you would, after your own brave, manly fashion? But your own belief should teach you the nature of my task when you ask me to go on and take up life again, from which I was torn more completely than the vine which falls with the tree to which it clung."

"Dear Grace, do not think for a moment that I am not always gratefully conscious of the immense self-sacrifice you are making for me and others. You long for rest and forgetfulness, and yet you know well that your absence would leave an abyss of despair. You now add so much to the comfort of your father! Mrs. Mayburn clings to you with all the love of a mother. And I, Grace—what else can I do? Even your frail, sad presence is more to me than the sun in the sky. Is it pure selfishness on my part to wish to keep you?

Time, the healer, will gradually bring to you rest from pain, and serenity to us all. When you are stronger I will take you to Hilland's grave—"

"No, no, no!" she cried, almost passionately. "Why should I go there? Oh, this is the awful part of it! What I so loved has become nothing, worse than nothing—that from which I shrink as something horrible. Oh, Alford! why are we endowed with such natures if corruption is to be the end? It is this thought that paralyzes me. It seems as if pure, unselfish love is singled out for the most diabolical punishment. To think that a form which has become sacred to you may be put away at any moment as a horrible and unsightly thing! and that such should be the end of the noblest devotion of which man is capable! My whole being revolts at it; and yet how can I escape from its truth? I am beset by despairing thoughts on every side when able to think at all, and my best remedy seems a sort of dreary apathy, in which I do little more than breathe. I have read that there comes a time when the tortured cease to feel much pain. There was a time, especially at the hospital, when I suffered constantly—when almost everything but you suggested torturing thoughts. I suffered with you and for you, but there was always something sustaining in your presence. There is still. I should not live a month in your absence, but it seems as if it were your strong will that holds me, not my own. You have given me the power, the incentive, to make such poor effort as I am putting forth. Moreover, in intent, you gave your life for Warren again and again, and as long as I have any volition left I will try and do all you wish, since you so wish it. But my hope is dead. I do not see how any more good can come to me or through me."

"You are still willing, however, to permit me to think for you, to guide you? You will still use your utmost effort to live?"

"Yes. I can refuse to the man who went back to my dying husband nothing within my power to grant. It is indeed little. Besides, I am in your care, but I fear I shall prove a sad, if not a fatal legacy."

"Of that, dear Grace, you must permit me to be the judge. All that you have said only adds strength to my purpose. Does not the thought that you are doing so very much for me and for all who love you bring some solace?"

"It should. But what have I brought you but pain and deep anxiety? Oh, Alford, Alford! you will waken some bitter day to the truth that you love but the wraith of the girl who unconsciously won your heart. You have idealized her, and the being you now love does not exist. How can I let you go on thus wronging yourself?"

"Grace," replied he, gravely and almost sternly, "I learned in the northern woods, among the fiords of Norway, under the shadow of the Himalayas, and in my long, lonely hours in the war, whom I loved, and why I loved her. I made every effort at forgetfulness that I, at least, was capable of exerting, and never forgot for an hour. Am I a sentimental boy, that you should talk to me in this way? Let us leave that question as settled for all time. Moreover, never entertain the thought that I am planning and hoping for the future. I see in your affection for me only a pale reflection of your love for Hilland."

"No, Alford, I love you for your own sake. How tenderly you have ever spoken of little Rita Anderson, and yet—"

"And yet, as I have told you more than once, the thought of loving her never entered my mind. I could plan for her happiness as I would for a sister, had I one."

"Therefore you can interpret me."

"Therefore I have interpreted you, and, from the first, have asked for nothing more than that you still make one of our little circle, each member of which would be sadly missed, you most of all."

"I ought to be able to do so little as that for you. Indeed, I am trying."

"I know you are, and, as you succeed, you will see that I am content. Do not feel that when I am present you must struggle and make unwonted effort. The tide is setting toward life; float gently on with it. Do not try to force nature. Let time and rest daily bring their imperceptible healing. The war is over. I now have but one object in life, and if you improve I shall come and go and do some man's work in the world. My plantation in Virginia will soon give me plenty of wholesome out-of-door thoughts."

She gave him one of her sad smiles as she replied wearily, "You set me a good example."

This frank interchange of thought appeared at first to have a good effect on Grace, and brought something of the rest which comes from submission to the inevitable. She found that Graham's purpose was as immovable as the hills, and at the same time was more absolutely convinced that he was not looking forward to what seemed an impossible future. Nor did he ask that her effort should be one of feeble struggles to manifest an interest before him which she did not feel. She yielded to her listlessness and apathy to a degree that alarmed her father and Mrs. Mayburn, but Graham said: "It's the course of nature. After such prolonged suffering, both body and mind need this lethargy. Reaction from one extreme to another might be expected."

Dr. Markham agreed in the main with this view, and yet there was a slight contraction of perplexity on his brows as he added: "I should not like to see this tendency increase beyond a certain point, or continue too long.

From the first shock of her bereavement Mrs. Hilland's mind has not been exactly in a normal condition. There are phases of her trouble difficult to account for and difficult to treat. The very fineness of her organization made the terrible shock more serious in its injury. I do not say this to discourage you—far from it—but in sincerity I must call your attention to the fact that every new phase of her grief has tended to some extreme manifestation, showing a disposition toward, not exactly mental weakness, but certainly an abnormal mental condition. I speak of this that you may intelligently guard against it. If due precaution is used, the happy mean between these reactions may be reached, and both mind and body recover a healthful tone. I advise that you all seek some resort by the sea, a new one, without any associations with the past."

Within a few days they were at a seaside inn, a large one whose very size offered seclusion. From their wide and lofty balconies they could watch the world come and go on the sea and on the land; and the world was too large and too distant for close scrutiny or petty gossip. They could have their meals in their rooms, or in the immense dining-hall, as they chose; and in the latter place the quiet party would scarcely attract a second glance from the young, gay, and sensation-loving. Their transient gaze would see two old ladies, one an invalid, an old and crippled man, and one much younger, who evidently would never take part in a german.

It was thought and hoped that this nearness to the complex world, with the consciousness that it could not approach her to annoy and pry, might tend to awaken in Grace a passing interest in its many phases. She could see without feeling that she was scanned and surmised about, as is too often the case in smaller houses wherein the guests are not content until they have investigated all newcomers.

But Grace disappointed her friends. She was as indifferent to the world about her as the world was to her. At first she was regarded as a quiet invalid, and scarcely noticed. The sea seemed to interest her more than all things else, and, if uninterrupted, she would sit and gaze at its varying aspects for hours.

According to Graham's plan, she was permitted, with little interference, to follow her mood. Mrs. Mayburn was like a watchful mother, the major much his former self, for his habits were too fixed for radical changes. Grace would quietly do anything he asked, but she grew more forgetful and inattentive, coming out of her deep abstraction—if such it could be termed— with increasing effort. With Graham she seemed more content than with any one else. With him she took lengthening walks on the beach. He sat quietly beside her while she watched the billows chasing one another to the shore. Their swift onset, their defeat, over which they appeared to foam in wrath, their backward and disheartened retreat, ever seemed to tell her in some dim way a story of which she never wearied. Often she would turn and look at him with a vague trouble in her face, as if faintly remembering something that was a sorrow to them both; but his reassuring smile quieted her, and she would take his hand as a little child might have done, and sit for an hour without removing her eyes from the waves. He waited patiently day after day, week after week, reiterating to himself, "She will waken, she will remember all, and then will have strength and calmness to meet it. This is nature's long repose."

It was growing strangely long and deep.

Meanwhile Grace, in her outward appearance, was undergoing a subtle change. Graham was the first to observe it, and at last it was apparent to all. As her mind became inert, sleeping on a downy couch of forgetfulness, closely curtained, the silent forces of physical life, in her deep tranquillity, were doing an artist's work. The hollow cheeks were gradually rounded and given the faintest possible bloom. Her form was gaining a contour that might satisfy a sculptor's dream.

The major had met old friends, and it was whispered about who they were—the widow of a millionaire; Colonel Graham, one of the most dashing cavalry officers in the war which was still in all minds; Major St. John, a veteran soldier of the regular service, who had been wounded in the Mexican War and who was well and honorably known to the chief dignitaries of the former generation. Knowing all this, the quidnuncs complacently felt at first that they knew all. The next thing was to know the people. This proved to be difficult indeed. The major soon found a few veteran cronies at whist, but to others was more unapproachable than a major-general of the old school. Graham was far worse, and belles tossed their heads at the idea that he had ever been a "dashing cavalry officer" or dashing anything else. Before the summer was over the men began to discover that Mrs. Hilland was the most beautiful woman in the house—strangely, marvellously, supernaturally beautiful.

An artist, who had found opportunity to watch the poor unconscious woman furtively—not so furtively either but that any belle in the hostelry would know all about it in half a minute—raved about the combination of charms he had discovered.

"Just imagine," he said, "what a picture she made as she sat alone on the beach! She was so remarkable in her appearance that one might think she had arisen from the sea, and was not a creature of the earth. Her black, close-fitting dress suggested the form of Aphrodite as she rose from the waves. Her profile was almost faultless in its exquisite lines. Her complexion, with just a slight warm tinge imparted by the breeze, had not the cold, dead white of snow, but the clear transparency which good aristocratic blood imparts. But her eyes and hair were her crowning features. How shall I describe the deep, dreamy languor of her large, dark eyes, made a hundred-fold more effective by the silvery whiteness of her hair, which had partly escaped from her comb, and fell upon her neck! And then her sublime, tranquil indifference! That I was near, spellbound with admiration, did not interest her so much as a sail, no larger than a gull's wing, far out at sea."

"Strange, strange!" said one of his friends, laughing; "her unconsciousness of your presence was the strangest part of it all. Why did you not make a sketch?"

"I did, but that infernal Colonel Graham, who is said to be her shadow — after her million, you know — suddenly appeared and asked sternly: 'Have you the lady's permission for this sketch?' I stammered about being 'so impressed, that in the interests of art,' etc. He then snatched my sketch and threw it into the waves. Of course I was angry, and I suppose my words and manner became threatening. He took a step toward me, looking as I never saw a man look. 'Hush,' he said, in a low voice. 'Say or do a thing to annoy that lady, and I'll wring your neck and toss you after your sketch. Do you think I've been through a hundred battles to fear your insignificance?' By Jove! he looked as if he could do it as easily as say it. Of course I was not going to brawl before a lady."

"No; it wouldn't have been prudent — I mean gentlemanly," remarked his bantering friend.

"Well, laugh at me," replied the young fellow, who was as honest as light-hearted and vain. 'I'd risk the chance of having my neck wrung for another glimpse at such marvellous beauty. Would you believe it? the superb creature never so much as once turned to glance at us. She left me to her attendant as completely as if he were removing an annoying insect. Heavens! but it was the perfection of high breeding. But I shall have my revenge: "I'll paint her yet."

"Right, my friend, right you are; and your revenge will be terrible. Her supernatural and high-bred nonchalance will be lost forever should she see her portrait;" and with mutual chaffing, spiced with good-natured satire, as good-naturedly received, the little party in a smoking-room separated.

But furtive eyes soon relieved the artist from the charge of exaggeration. Thus far Grace's manner had been ascribed to high-bred reserve and the natural desire for seclusion in her widowhood. Now, however, that attention was concentrated upon her, Graham feared that more than her beauty would be discovered.

He himself also longed inexpressibly to hide his new phase of trouble from the chattering throng of people who were curious to know about them. To know? As if they could know! They might better sit down to gossip over the secrets of the differential and the integral calculus.

But he saw increasing evidences that they were becoming objects of "interest," and the beautiful millionaire widow "very interesting," as it was phrased; and he knew that there is no curiosity so penetrating as that of the fashionable world when once it is aroused, and the game deemed worthy of pursuit.

People appeared from Washington who had known Lieutenant-Colonel Hilland and heard something of Graham, and the past was being ferreted out. "Her hair had turned white from grief in a night," it was confidently affirmed.

Poor Jones shrugged his shoulders as he thought: "I shall never be the cause of my wife's hair turning white, unless I may, in the future, prevent her from dyeing it."

After all, sympathy was not very deep. It was generally concluded that Colonel Graham would console her, and one lady of elegant leisure, proud of her superior research, declared that she had seen the colonel "holding Mrs. Hilland's hand," as they sat in a secluded angle of the rocks.

Up to a certain time it was comparatively easy to shield Grace; but now, except as she would turn her large, dreamy eyes and unresponsive lips upon those who sought her acquaintance, she was as helpless as a child. The major and Mrs. Mayburn at once acquiesced in Graham's wish to depart. Within a day or two the gossips found that their prey had escaped, and Grace was once more in her cottage home.

At first she recognized familiar surroundings with a sigh of content. Then a deeply troubled look flitted across her face and she looked at Graham inquiringly.

"What is it, Grace?" he asked, gently.

She pressed her hand to her brow, glanced around once more, shook her head sadly, and went to her room to throw off her wraps.

They all looked at one another with consternation. Hitherto they had tried to be dumb and blind, each hiding the growing and awful conviction that Grace was drifting away from them almost as surely as if she had died.

"Something must be done at once," said practical Mrs. Mayburn.

"I have telegraphed for Dr. Markham," replied Graham, gloomily. "Nothing can be done till he returns. He is away on a distant trip."

"Oh!" groaned the old major, "there will be an end of me before there is to all this trouble."

CHAPTER XXXVIII
GRAHAM'S LAST SACRIFICE

A terrible foreboding oppressed Graham. Would Grace fulfil her prediction and disappoint him, after all? Would she elude him, escape, *die*, and yet remain at his side, beautiful as a dream? Oh, the agony of possessing this perfect casket, remembering the jewel that had vanished! He had vowed to defeat his gloomy rivals, Grief and Death, and they were mocking him, giving the semblance of what he craved beyond even imagined perfection, but carrying away into their own inscrutable darkness the woman herself.

What was Grace?—what becoming? As he looked he thought of her as a sculptor's ideal embodied, a dream of beauty only, not a woman—as the legend of Eve, who might, before becoming a living soul, have harmonized with the loveliness of her garden without seeing or feeling it.

He could not think of her mind as blotted out or perverted; he could not conceive of it otherwise than as corresponding with her outward symmetry. To his thought it slumbered, as her form might repose upon her couch, in a death-like trance. She went and came among them like a somnambulist, guided by unconscious instincts, memories, and habits.

She knew their voices, did, within limitations, as they requested; but when she waited on her father there was a sad, mechanical repetition of what she had done since childhood. Mrs. Mayburn found her docile and easily controlled, and the heart-stricken old lady was vigilance itself.

Toward Graham, however, her manner had a marked characteristic. He was her master, and she a dumb, lovely, unreasoning creature, that looked into his eyes for guidance, and gathered more from his tones than from his words. Some faint consciousness of the past had grown into an instinct that to him she must look for care and direction; and she never thought of resisting his will. If he read to her, she turned to him her lovely face, across which not a gleam of interest or intelligence would pass. If he brought her flowers, she would hold them until they were taken from her. She would pace the garden walks by his side, with her hand upon his arm, by the hour if he wished it, sometimes smiling faintly at his gentle tones, but giving no proof that she understood the import of his words. At Hilland's name only she would start and tremble as if some deep chord were struck, which could merely vibrate until its sounds were faint and meaningless.

It was deeply touching also to observe in her sad eclipse how her ingrained refinement asserted itself. In all her half-conscious action there was never a coarse look or word. She was a rose without its perfume. She was a woman without a woman's mind and heart. These had been subtracted, with all the differences they made; otherwise she was Grace Hilland.

Graham was profoundly perplexed and distressed. The problem had become too deep for him. The brain, nourished by good blood, had not brought life. All his skill and that of those allied with him had failed. The materialist had matter in the perfection of breathing outline, but where was the woman he loved? How could he reach her, how make himself understood by her, except as some timid, docile creature responds to a caress or a tone? His very power over her was terrifying. It was built upon the instinct, the allegiance that cannot reason but is unquestioning. Nothing could so have daunted his hope, courage, and will as the exquisite being Grace had become, as she looked up to him with her large, mild, trusting eyes, from which thought, intelligence, and volition had departed.

At last Dr. Markham came, and for several days watched his patient closely, she giving little heed to his presence. They all hung on his perturbed looks with a painful anxiety. For a time he was very reticent, but one day he followed Graham to his quarters in Mrs. Mayburn's cottage, where he was now much alone. Grace seemed to miss him but slightly, although she always gave some sign of welcome on his return. The mocking semblance of all that he could desire often so tantalized him that her presence became unendurable. The doctor found him pacing his room in a manner betokening his half-despairing perplexity.

"Colonel Graham," he said, "shall I surprise you when I say physicians are very fallible? I know that it is not the habit of the profession to admit this, but I have not come here to talk nonsense to you. You have trusted me in this matter, and admitted me largely into your confidence, and I shall speak to you in honest, plain English. Mrs. Hilland's symptoms are very serious. What I feared has taken place. From her acute and prolonged mental distress and depression, of which she would have died had you not come, she reacted first into mental lethargy, and now into almost complete mental inactivity. I cannot discover that any disturbed physical functions have been an element in her mental aberration, for more perfect physical life and loveliness I have never seen. Her white hair, which might have made her look old, is a foil to a beauty which seems to defy age.

"Pardon me for saying it, but I fear our treatment has been superficial. We men of the world may believe what we please, but to many natures, especially to an organization like Mrs. Hilland's, hope and faith are essential. She has practically been without these from the first, and, as you know, she was sinking under the struggle maintained by her own brave, womanly spirit. She was contending with more than actual bereavement. It was the hopelessness of the struggle that crushed her, for she is not one of that large class of women who can find consolation in crape and becoming mourning.

"In response to your appeal, she did make the effort you required, but it was the effort of a mind still without hope or faith—one that saw no remedy for the evils that had already overwhelmed her—and I must bear witness that her efforts were as sincere as they were pathetic. We all watched to give every assistance in our power. I've lain awake nights, Colonel Graham, to think of remedies that would meet her needs; and good Mrs. Mayburn and your old black cook, Aunt Sheba, prepared food fit for the gods. You were more untiring and effective than any of us, and the major's very infirmities were among her strongest allies. Well, we have the result—a woman who might be a model for a goddess, even to her tranquil face, in which there is no trace of varying human feeling. Explanation of the evil that crushed her, hope, and faith were not given—who can give them?—but they were essential to her from the first. Unbelief, which is a refuge to some, was an abyss to her. In it she struggled and groped until her mind, appalled and discouraged and overwhelmed, refused to act at all. In one sense it is a merciful oblivion, in another a fatal one, from which she must be aroused if possible. But it's a hard, hard case."

"You make it hard indeed," said Graham, desperately. "What faith can I instil except the one I have? I can't lie, even for Grace Hilland. She knew well once that I could easily die for her."

"Well, then," said the physician, "permit a plain, direct question. Will you marry her?"

"Marry her—as she now is?" cried Graham, in unfeigned astonishment.

"You said you could die for her. This may be going much further. Indeed I should call it the triumph of human affection, for in honesty I must tell you that she may never be better, she may become worse. But I regard it as her only chance. At any rate, she needs a vigilant caretaker. Old Mrs. Mayburn will not be equal to the task much longer, and her place will have to be filled by hired service. I know it is like suggesting an almost impossible sacrifice to broach even the thought, remembering her condition, but—"

"Dr. Markham," said Graham, pacing the floor in great agitation, "you wholly misunderstand me. I was thinking of her, not of myself. What right have I to marry Grace Hilland without her consent? She could give no intelligent assent at present."

"The right of your love; the right her husband gave when he committed her to your care; the right of your desire to prevent her from drifting into hopeless, lifelong imbecility, wherein she would be almost at the mercy of hired attendants, helpless to shield herself from any and every wrong; the right of a man to sacrifice himself absolutely for another if he chooses."

"But she might waken from this mental trance and feel that I had taken a most dishonorable advantage of her helplessness."

"Yes, you run that risk; but here is one man who will assure her to the contrary, and you would be sustained by the consciousness of the purest motives. It is that she may waken that I suggest the step; mark, I do not advise it. As I said at first, I am simply treating you with absolute confidence and sincerity. If matters go on as they are, I have little or no hope. Mrs. Mayburn is giving way under the strain, and symptoms of her old disorder are returning. She cannot watch Mrs. Hilland much longer as she has been doing. Whom will you put in her place? Will you send Mrs. Hilland to an asylum, with its rules and systems and its unknown attendants? Moreover, her present tranquil condition may not last. She may become as violent as she now is gentle. She may gradually regain her intelligence, or it may be restored to her by some sudden shock. If the mysteries of the physical nature so baffle us, who can predict the future of a disordered intellect? I have presented the darkest side of the picture; I still think it has its bright side. She has no hereditary mental weakness to contend with. As it developed somewhat gradually, it may pass in the same manner. If you should marry her and take her at once to Europe, change of scene, of life, with your vigilant presence ever near, might become important factors in the problem. The memory that she was committed to your care has degenerated into a controlling instinct; but that is far better than nothing. The only real question in my mind is, Are you willing to make the sacrifice and take the risks? You know the world will say you married her for her money, and that will be hard on a man like you."

Graham made a gesture of contempt: "That for the world," he said. "Have you broached this subject to her father and my aunt?"

"Certainly not before speaking to you."

"You then give me your assurance, as a man, that you believe this right, and that it is Grace Hilland's best chance—indeed, almost her only chance— for recovery?"

"I do most unhesitatingly, and I shall do more. I shall bring from New York an eminent physician who has made mental disease a study all his life, and he shall either confirm my opinion or advise you better."

"Do so, Dr. Markham," said Graham, very gravely. "I have incurred risks before in my life, but none like this. If from any cause Mrs. Hilland should recover memory and full intelligence, and reproach me for having taken advantage of a condition which, even among savage tribes, renders the afflicted one sacred, all the fiendish tortures of the Inquisition would be nothing to what I should suffer. Still, prove to me, prove to her father, that it is her best chance, and for Grace Hilland I will take even this risk. Please remember there must be no professional generalities. I must have your solemn written statement that it is for Mrs. Hilland's sake I adopt the measure."

"So be it," was the reply. "I shall telegraph to Dr. Armand immediately to expect me, and shall say that I wish him to be prepared to come at once."

"Do so, and consider no question of expense. I am no longer poor, and if I were, I would mortgage my blood at this juncture."

On the following evening Dr. Armand was almost startled by the vision on the veranda of the St. John cottage. A silvery-haired woman sat looking placidly at the glowing sunset, with its light and its rose-hues reflected in her face.

"If ever there was a picture of a glorified saint, there is one," he muttered, as he advanced and bowed.

She gave him no attention, but with dark eyes, made brilliant by the level rays, she gazed steadily on the closing day. The physician stole a step or two nearer, and looked as steadily at her, while his experienced eye detected in all her illuminated beauty the absence of the higher, more subtle light of reason. Dr. Markham had told him next to nothing about the case, and had asked him to go and see for himself, impressing him only with the fact that it was a question of vital importance that he was to aid in deciding; that he must give it his whole professional skill, and all the necessary time, regardless of expense. The moment he saw Grace, however, the business aspect of the affair passed from his mind. His ruling passion was aroused, and he was more than physician—a student—as the great in any calling ever are.

Graham came to the door and recognized instinctively the intent, eagle-eyed man, who merely nodded and motioned him to approach his patient. Graham did so, and Grace turned her eyes to him with a timid, questioning glance. He offered her his arm; she rose instantly and took it, and began walking with him.

"Were you looking at the sunset, Grace?"

She turned upon him the same inquiring eyes, but did not answer.

"Do you not think it very beautiful? Does it not remind you of the sunset you saw on the evening when I returned from my first battle?"

She shook her head, and only looked perplexed,

"Why, Grace," he continued, as if provoked, "you *must* remember. I was carried, you know, and you and Mrs. Mayburn acted as if my scratches were mortal wounds."

She looked frightened at his angry tones, clasped her hands, and with tears in her eyes looked pleadingly up to him.

"Dear Grace, don't be worried." He now spoke in the gentlest tones, and lifted her hand to his lips. A quick, evanescent smile illumined her face. She fawned against his shoulder a moment, placed his hand against her cheek, and then leaned upon his arm as they resumed their walk, Dr. Armand keeping near them without in the least attracting her attention.

"Grace," resumed Graham, "you must remember. Hilland, Warren, you know."

She dropped his arm, looked wildly around, covered her face with her hands, and shuddered convulsively.

After a moment he said, kindly but firmly, "Grace, dear Grace."

She sprang to him, seized his hand, and casting a look of suspicion at Dr. Armand, drew him away.

A few moments later she was again looking tranquilly at the west, but the light had departed from the sky and from her face. It had the look of one who saw not, thought and felt not. It was breathing, living death.

Graham looked at her mournfully for a few moments, and then, with a gesture that was almost despairing, turned to the physician, who had not lost a single expression.

"Thank you," was that gentleman's first laconic remark; and he dropped into a chair, still with his eyes on the motionless figure of Grace.

At last he asked, "How long would she maintain that position?"

"I scarcely know," was the sad response; "many hours certainly."

"Please let her retain it till I request you to interfere. The moon is rising almost full, the evening is warm, and she can take no harm."

The major tottered out on his crutches, and was given his chair, the physician meanwhile being introduced. Brief and courteous was Dr.

Armand's acknowledgment, but he never took his eyes from his patient. The same was true of his greeting to Mrs. Mayburn; but that good lady's hospitable instincts soon asserted themselves, and she announced that dinner was ready.

"Take Mrs. Hilland to dinner," said the physician to Graham; "but first introduce me."

The young man approached and said, "Grace." She rose instantly and took his arm. "This is Dr. Armand, Grace. He has called to see you." She made him a courteous inclination, and then turned to Graham to see what next was expected of her, but he only led her to the dining-room.

"Gracie, darling, bring me my cushion," said her father, speaking as he had been used to do when she was a little girl.

She brought it mechanically and arranged it, then stood in expectancy. "That will do, dear;" and she returned to her seat in silence. Throughout the meal she maintained this silence, although Dr. Armand broached many topics, avoiding only the name of her husband. Her manner was that of a little, quiet, well-bred child, who did not understand what was said, and had no interest in it. The physician's scrutiny did not embarrass her; she had never remembered, much less forgotten him.

When the meal was over they all returned to the piazza. At the physician's request she was placed in her old seat, and they all sat down to watch. The moon rose higher and higher, made her hair more silvery, touched her still face with a strange, ethereal beauty, and threw the swaying shadow of a spray of woodbine across her motionless figure—so motionless that she seemed a sculptured rather than a breathing woman.

After a while the old major rose and groaned as he tottered away. Mrs. Mayburn, in uncontrollable nervous restlessness, soon followed, that she might find relief in household cares. The two men watched on till hours had passed, and still the lovely image had not stirred. At last Dr. Armand approached her and said, "Mrs. Hilland."

She rose, and stood coldly aloof. The name, with her prefix, did not trouble her. She had long been accustomed to that "Hilland," as Graham uttered the word, alone affected her, touching some last deep chord of memory.

"Mrs. Hilland," the doctor continued, "it is getting late. Do you not think you had better retire?"

She looked at him blankly, and glanced around as if in search of some one.

"I am here, Grace," said Graham, emerging from the doorway.

She came to him at once, and he led her to Mrs. Mayburn, kissing her hand, and receiving, in return, her strange, brief, fawning caress.

"I would like to know the history of Mrs. Hilland's malady from the beginning," said Dr. Armand, when Graham returned.

"I cannot go over it again," replied Graham, hoarsely. "Dr. Markham can tell you about all, and I will answer any questions. Your room is ready for you here, where Dr. Markham will join you presently. I must bid you good-night;" and he strode away.

But as he passed under the apple-tree and recalled all that had occurred there, he was so overcome that once more he leaned against it for support.

CHAPTER XXXIX
MARRIED UNCONSCIOUSLY

There was no sleep for Graham that night, for he knew that two skilful men were consulting on a question beyond any that had agitated his heart before. As he paced the little parlor with restless steps, Aunt Sheba's ample form filled the doorway, and in her hands was a tray bearing such coffee as only she knew how to brew.

"Thanks, Aunt Sheba," he said, motioning to a table, without pausing in his distracted walk.

She put down the tray, retreated hesitatingly, and then began: "Dear Mas'r Graham, my ole heart jes aches for yer. But don't yer be so cast down, mas'r; de good Lord knows it all, and I'se a-prayin' for yer and de lubly Miss Grace night and day."

He was so utterly miserable that he was grateful for even this homely sympathy, and he took the old woman's hand in his as he said kindly, "Pray on, then, good old aunty, if it's any comfort to you. It certainly can do no harm."

"Oh, Mas'r Graham, you dunno, you dunno. Wid all yer wise knowin' yer dunno. You'se all—good Mis' Mayburn, de ole major, an' all—are in de dark land ob unbelievin', like poor Missy Grace. She doesn't know how you'se all tink about her an' lub her; needer does you know how de good Lord tinks about you and lubs you. You guv me my liberty; you guv what I tinks a sight more on; you'se been kind to de poor old slave dat los' all her chillen in de weary days dat's gone. I'se a 'memberin' yer all de time. You hab no faith, Mas'r Graham, and poor ole Aunt Sheba mus' hab faith for yer. An' so I will. I'se a wrastlin' wid de Lord for yer all de time, an' I'se a-gwine to wrastle on till I sees yer an' Missy Grace an' all comin' inter de light;" and she threw her apron over her head, and went sobbing away.

He paused for a moment when she left him, touched deeply by the strong, homely, human sympathy and gratitude of the kind old soul who fed him—as he never forgot—when he was a fugitive in a hostile land. That she had manifested her feeling after what he deemed her own ignorant, superstitious fashion was nothing. It was the genuine manifestation of the best human traits that touched him—pure gems illumining a nature otherwise so clouded and crude.

Late at night footsteps approached, and the two physicians entered. "I first permitted Dr. Armand to form his own impressions, and since have told him everything," said Dr. Markham, "and he strongly inclines to my view. Realizing the gravity of the case, however, he has consented to remain a day or two longer. We will give you no hasty opinion, and you shall have time on your part to exercise the most deliberate judgment."

Dr. Armand confirmed his associate's words, and added, "We will leave you now to the rest you must need sorely. Let me assure you, however, that I do not by any means consider Mrs. Hilland's case hopeless, and that I am strongly impressed with the belief that her recovery must come through you. A long train of circumstances has given you almost unbounded influence over her, as you enabled me to see this evening. It would be sad to place such a glorious creature in the care of strangers, for it might involve serious risk should she regain her memory and intelligence with no strong, sympathetic friend, acquainted with her past, near her. I am inclined to think that what is now little more than an instinct will again develop into a memory, and that the fact that she was committed to your care will fully reconcile her to the marriage—indeed, render her most grateful for it, if capable of understanding the reasons which led to it. If further observation confirms my present impressions, I and Dr. Markham will plainly state our opinions to her father and Mrs. Mayburn. As my colleague has said, you must comprehend the step in all its bearings. It is one that I would not ask any man to take. I now think that the probabilities are that it would restore Mrs. Hilland to health eventually. A year of foreign travel might bring about a gradual and happy change."

"Take time to satisfy yourselves, gentlemen, and give me your decision as requested. Then you have my permission to give your opinions to Major St. John."

Within a week this was done, and the poor old man bowed his head on Graham's shoulder and wept aloud in his gratitude. Mrs. Mayburn also, wiping away her tears, faltered, "You know, Alford, how I schemed for this marriage years ago; you remember my poor blind strategy on that June day, do you not? How little I thought it would take place under circumstances like these! And yet, I've thought of it of late often, very often. I could not go on much longer, for I am old and feeble, and it just broke my heart to think of Grace, our Grace, passing into the hands of some hired and indifferent stranger or strangers. I believe she will recover and reward your sacrifice."

"It is no sacrifice on my part, aunt, except she wakens only to reproach me."

"Well, devotion, then; and little sense she'd ever have," concluded the old lady, after her own brusque fashion, "if she does not fall on her knees and bless you. You could now take better care of her than I, for she trusts and obeys you implicitly. She is docile and gentle with me, but often strangely inattentive. She would be still more so with a stranger; and the idea of some strong, unfeeling hands forcing her into the routine of her life!" Thus almost completely was removed from his mind the unspeakable dread lest he was taking an unfair advantage of helplessness. He fully recognized also that the ordeal for himself would be a terrible one—that it would be the fable of Tantalus repeated for weeks, months, perhaps for years, or for life. The unfulfilled promise of happiness would ever be before him. His dark-visaged rivals, Grief and Death, would jeer and mock at him from a face of perfect beauty. In a blind, vindictive way he felt that his experience was the very irony of fate. He could clasp the perfect material form of a woman to his heart, and at the same time his heart be breaking for what could not be seen or touched.

The question, however, was decided irrevocably. He knew that he could not leave helpless Grace Hilland to the care of strangers, and that there was no place for him in the world but at her side; and yet it was with something of the timidity and hesitation of a lover that he asked her, as they paced a shady garden-walk, "Grace, dear Grace, will you marry me?"

His voice was very low and gentle, and yet she turned upon him a startled, inquiring look. "Marry you?" she repeated slowly.

"Yes, let me take care of you always," he replied, smilingly, and yet as pale almost as herself.

The word "care" reassured her, and she gave him her wonted smile of content, as she replied, very slowly, "Yes. I want you to take care of me always. Who else can?"

"That's what I mean by marrying you—taking care of you always," he said, raising her hand to his lips.

"You are always to take care of me," she replied, leaning her head on his shoulder for a moment.

"Mrs. Mayburn is not strong enough to take care of you any longer. She will take care of your father. Will you let me take care of you as she does?"

She smiled contentedly, for the word "care" appeared to make all natural and right.

It was arranged that they should be married in the presence of Dr. Markham, Aunt Sheba, and Jinny, in addition to those so deeply interested. The physician prepared the clergyman for the ceremony, which was exceedingly brief and simple, Grace smiling into Graham's face when he promised to take care of her always, and she signifying her consent and pleasure in the manner that was so mute and sad. Then he told her that he was going to take her away, that she might get perfectly strong and well; and she went at his request without hesitancy, although seeming to wonder slightly at the strong emotion of her father and Mrs. Mayburn when parting from her. Jinny, who had been her nurse in childhood, accompanied her. Dr. Markham also went with them as far as the steamer, and they sailed away into a future as vague and unknown to them as the ocean they were crossing.

The waves seen from the deck of the steamer produced in Grace the same content with which she had gazed at them from the shore during the previous summer; only now there were faint signs of wonder in her expression, and sometimes of perplexity. Her eyes also wandered around the great vessel with something of the interest of a child, but she asked no questions. That Graham was with her and smiled reassuringly seemed sufficient, while the presence of her old colored nurse, who in some dim way was connected with her past, gave also an additional sense of security.

As time elapsed and they began their wanderings abroad, it seemed to Graham that his wife was beginning life over again, as a very little quiet child would observe the strange and unaccountable phenomena about it. Instead of her fixed vacancy of gaze, her eyes began to turn from object to object with a dawning yet uncomprehending interest. He in simplest words sought to explain and she to listen, though it was evident that their impression was slight indeed. Still there was perceptible progress, and when in his tireless experimenting he began to bring before her those things which would naturally interest a child, he was encouraged to note that they won a larger and more pleased attention. A garden full of flowers, a farmyard with its sleek, quiet cattle, a band of music, a broad, funny pantomime, were far more to her than Westminster Abbey or St. Paul's. Later, the variety, color, and movement of a Paris boulevard quite absorbed her attention, and she followed one object after another with much the same expression that might be seen on the face of a little girl scarcely three years old. This infantile expression, in contrast with her silver hair and upon her mature and perfect features, was pathetic to the last degree, and yet Graham rejoiced with exceeding joy. With every conscious glance and inquiring look the dawn of hope brightened. He was no longer left alone in the awful solitude of living death. The beautiful form was no longer like a deserted home. It now had a tenant, even though it seemed but the mind of a little child. The rays of intelligence sent out were feeble indeed, but how much better than the blank darkness that had preceded! Something like happiness began to soften and brighten the husband's face as he took his child-wife here and there. He made the long galleries of the Louvre and of Italy her picture-books, and while recognizing that she was pleased with little more than color, form, and action—that the sublime, equally with the vicious and superstitious meanings of the great masters, were hidden—he was nevertheless cheered and made more hopeful by the fact that she *was* pleased and observant— that she began to single out favorites; and before these he would let her stand as long as she chose, and return to them when so inclined.

She had lost the power of reading a line. She did not know even her letters; and these he began to teach her with unflagging zeal and patience. How the mysterious problem would end he could not tell. It might be that by kindling a little light the whole past would become illumined; it might be that he would have to educate her over again; but be the future what it would, the steadfast principle of devotion to her became more fixed, and to care for her the supreme law of his being.

From the time of his first message to them he had rarely lost an opportunity to send a letter to the anxious ones at home, and their replies abounded in solicitous, grateful words. Dr. Markham often called, and rubbed his hands with increasing self-gratulation over the success of his bold measure, especially as encomiums on his sagacity had been passed by the great Dr. Armand.

Nearly a year had passed, and Graham and his wife, after their saunterings over the Continent, were spending the summer in the Scottish Highlands. They sailed on the lochs, fished from their banks, and climbed the mountain passes on little shaggy ponies that were Scotch in their stubbornness and unflinching endurance. Grace had become even companionable in her growing intelligence, and in the place of her silent, inquiring glances there were sometimes eager, childlike questionings.

Of late, however, Graham noted the beginnings of another change. With growing frequency she passed her hand over her brow, that was contracted in perplexity. Sometimes she would look at him curiously, at Jinny, and at the unfamiliar scenes of her environment, then shake her head as if she could not comprehend it all. Speedily, however, she would return with the zest of a quiet little girl to the pleasures and tasks that he unweariedly provided. But Graham grew haggard and sleepless in his vigilance, for he believed that the time of her awakening was near.

One day, while sailing on a loch, they were overtaken by a heavy storm and compelled to run before it, and thus to land at no little distance from their inn. Grace showed much alarm at the dashing waves and howling tempest. Nor was her fright at the storm wholly that of an unreasoning child. Its fury seemed to arouse and shock her, and while she clung to Graham's hand, she persisted in sitting upright and looking about, as if trying to comprehend it all. After landing they had a long, fatiguing ride in the darkness, and she was unusually silent. On reaching her room she glanced around as if all was unfamiliar and incomprehensible. Graham had a presentiment that the hour was near, and he left her wholly to the care of her old colored nurse, but almost immediately, from excessive weariness, she sank into a deep slumber.

Her lethargy lasted so late in the following day that he was alarmed, fearing lest her old symptoms were returning. With anxious, hollow eyes, he watched and waited, and at last she awoke and looked at him with an expression that he had longed for through many weary months, and yet now it terrified him.

"Alford—Mr. Graham," she began, in deep surprise.

"Hush, dear Grace. You have been very ill."

"Yes, but where am I? What has happened?"

"Very much; but you are better now. Here is Jinny, your old nurse, who took care of you as a child."

The old colored woman came in, and, as instructed, said: "Yes, honey, I'se tooken care ob you since you was a baby, and I'se nebber lef' you."

"Everything looks very strange. Why, Alford, I had a long, sad talk with you but a short time since in the library, and you were so kind and unselfish!"

"Yes, Grace; we spoke frankly to each other, but you have been very ill since then, worse than ever before. At your father's request and Dr. Markham's urgent counsel, I brought you to Europe. It was said to be your only chance."

"But where is Mrs. Mayburn?"

"She is at home taking care of your father. Her old sickness threatened to return. She could take care of you no longer, and you needed constant care."

A slow, deep flush overspread her face and even her neck as she faltered: "And—and—has no one else been with me but Jinny?"

"No one else except myself. Grace, dear Grace, I am your husband. I was married to you in the presence of your father, Mrs. Mayburn, and your family physician."

"Now long since?" she asked, in a constrained voice.

"About a year ago."

"Have we been abroad ever since?"

"Yes, and you have been steadily improving. You were intrusted to my care, and there came a time when I must either be faithful to that trust, or place you in the hands of strangers. You were helpless, dear Grace."

"Evidently," in the same low, constrained tone. "Could—could you not have fulfilled your trust in some other way?"

"Your father, your second mother, and your physician thought not."

"Still—" she began, hesitated, and again came that deep, deep flush.

"For your sake, Grace, I incurred the risk of this awful moment."

She turned, and saw an expression which brought tears to her eyes. "I cannot misjudge you," she said slowly; "the past forbids that. But I cannot understand it, I cannot understand it at all."

"Perhaps you never will, dear Grace; I took that risk also to save your life and mind."

"My mind?"

"Yes, your mind. If, in recalling the past, the memory of which has returned, you can preserve sufficient confidence in me to wait till all is clear and explained, I shall be profoundly grateful. I foresaw the possibility of this hour; I foresaw it as the chief danger and trial of my life; and I took the risk of its consequences for your sake because assured by the highest authority that it was your one chance for escape, not from death, but from a fate worse than death, which also would have removed you from my care—indeed the care of all who loved you. I have prepared myself for this emergency as well as I could. Here are letters from your father, Mrs. Mayburn, Dr. Markham, and Dr. Armand, one of the most eminent authorities in the world on brain diseases. But after all I must be judged by your woman's heart, and so stand or fall. I now have but one request, or entreaty rather, to make—that you do not let all the efforts we have made in your behalf be in vain. Can you not calmly and gradually receive the whole truth? There must be no more relapses, or they will end in black ruin to us all. Now that you can think for yourself, your slightest wish shall be my law. Jinny, remain with your mistress."

He lifted her passive hand to his lips, passed into their little parlor, and closed the door. Grace turned to her nurse, and in low, almost passionate utterance, said: "Now tell me all."

"Lor' bress you, Missy Grace, it 'ud take a right smart time to tell yer all. When de big doctors an' all de folks say you'se got to hab strangers take care ob you or go ter a'sylum, and arter all you'd git wuss, Mas'r Graham he guv in, and said he'd take care ob you, and dey all bress 'im and tank 'im, and couldn't say 'nuff. Den he took you 'cross de big ocean—golly I how big it be—jes' as de doctor said; an' nebber hab I seed sich lub, sich 'votion in a moder as Mas'r Graham hab had fer you. He had to take care ob you like a little chile, an' he was teachin' you how to read like a little chile when, all on a suddint, you wakes up an' knows ebryting you'se forgotten. But de part you doesn't know is de part mos' wuth knowin'. No woman eber had sich a husban' as Mas'r Graham, an' no chile sich a moder. 'Clar' ter grashus ef I b'lieve he's ebber slep' a wink wid his watchin' an' a-tinkin' what he could do fer you."

"But, Jinny, I'm not ill; I never felt stronger in my life."

"Laws, Missy Grace, dar's been a mirackle. You'se strong 'nuff 'cept your mine's been off wisitin' somewhar. Golly! you jes' git up an' let me dress you, an' I'll show yer de han'somest woman in de worl'. All yer's got ter do now is jes' be sensible like, an' yer won't have yer match."

Grace cast an apprehensive look toward the door of the parlor in which was her husband, and then said hurriedly: "Yes, dress me quick. Oh, heavens! how much I have to think about, to realize!"

"Now, honey dear, you jes' keep cool. Don't go an' fly right off de handle agin, or Mas'r Graham'll blow his brains out. Good Lor', how dat man do look sometimes! An' yet often, when he was pintin' out yer letters ter yer, or showin' yer pearty tings, like as you was a chile, he look so happy and gontle like, dat I say he jes' like a moder."

Grace was touched, and yet deep, deep in her soul she felt that a wrong had been done her, no matter what had been the motives. Jinny had no such fine perceptions, but with a feminine tact which runs down through the lowliest natures, she chose one of Grace's quietest, yet most becoming costumes, and would not let her go to the glass till arrayed to the dusky woman's intense satisfaction. Then she led her mistress to the mirror and said: "Look dar, honey! All de picters you'se eber seen can't beat dat!" and Grace gazed long and fixedly at the lovely creature that gazed back with troubled and bewildered eyes.

"Was—was I like that when—when he married me?"

"Yes, an' no, honey. You only look like a picter of a woman den—a berry pearty picter, but nothin' but a picter arter all. Mas'r Graham hab brought yer ter life."

With another lingering, wondering glance at herself, she turned away and said: "Leave me, now, Jinny; I wish to be alone."

The woman hesitated, and was about to speak, but Grace waved her away imperiously, and sat down to the letters Graham had given her. She read and re-read them. They confirmed his words. She was a wife: her husband awaited her but a few feet away—her *husband*, and she had never dreamed of marrying again. The past now stood out luminous to her, and Warren Hilland was its centre. But another husband awaited her—one whom she had never consciously promised "to love, honor, and obey." As a friend she could worship him, obey him, die for him; but as her *husband*— how could she sustain that mysterious bond which merges one life in another? She was drawn toward him by every impulse of gratitude. She saw that, whether misled or not, he had been governed by the best of motives— nay, more, by the spirit of self-sacrifice in its extreme manifestation—that he had been made to believe that it was her only chance for health and life. Still, in her deepest consciousness he was but Alford Graham, the friend most loved and trusted, whom she had known in her far distant home, yet not her husband. How could she go to him, what could she say to him, in their new relations that seemed so unreal?

She trembled to leave him longer in the agony of suspense; but her limbs refused to support her, and her woman's heart shrank with a strange and hitherto unknown fear.

There was a timid knock at the door.

"Come in, Alford," she said, tremblingly.

He stood before her haggard, pale, and expectant.

"Alford," she said, sadly, "why did you not let me die?"

"I could not," he replied, desperately. "As I told you, there is a limit to every man's strength. I see it all in your face and manner—what I feared, what I warned Dr. Markham against. Listen to me. I shall take you home at once. You are well. You will not require my further care, and you need never see my face again."

"And you, Alford?" she faltered.

"Do not ask about me. Beyond the hour when I place you in your father's arms I know nothing. I have reached my limit. I have made the last sacrifice of which I am capable. If you go back as you are now, you are saved from a fate which it seemed to me you would most shrink from could you know it—the coarse, unfeeling touch and care of strangers who could have treated you in your helplessness as they chose. You might have regained your reason years hence, only to find that those who loved you were broken-hearted, lost, gone. They are now well and waiting for you. Here are their letters, written from week to week and breathing hope and cheer. Here is the last one from your father, written in immediate response to mine. In it he says, 'My hand trembles, but it is more from joy than age.' You were gaining steadily, although only as a child's intelligence develops. He writes, 'I shall have my little Grace once more, and see her mind grow up into her beautiful form.'"

She bent her head low to hide the tears that were falling fast as she faltered: "Was it wholly self-sacrifice when you married me?"

"Yes—in the fear of this hour, the bitterest of my life—yes. It has followed me like a spectre through every waking and sleeping hour. Please make the wide distinction. My care for you, the giving up of my life for you, is nothing. That I should have done in any case, as far as I could. But with my knowledge of your nature and your past, I could not seem to take advantage of your helplessness without an unspeakable dread. When shown by the best human skill that I could thus save you, or at least ensure that you would ever have gentle, sympathetic care, I resolved to risk the last extremity of evil to myself for your sake. Now you have the whole truth "

She rose and came swiftly to him—for he had scarcely entered the room in his wish to show her respect—and putting her arm around his neck, while she laid her head upon his breast, said gently and firmly: "The sacrifice shall not be all on your side. I have never consciously promised to be your wife, but now, as far as my poor broken spirit will permit, I do promise it. But be patient with me, Alford. Do not expect what I have not the power to give. I can only promise that all there is left of poor Grace Hilland's heart—it aught—shall be yours."

Then for the first time in his life the strong man gave way. He disengaged her so hastily as to seem almost rough, and fell forward on the couch unconscious. The long strain of years had culminated in the hour he so dreaded, and in the sudden revulsion caused by her words nature gave way.

Almost frantic with terror, Grace summoned her servant, and help from the people of the inn. Fortunately an excellent English physician was stopping at the same house, and he was speedily at work. Graham recovered, only to pass into muttering delirium, and the burden of his one sad refrain was: "If she should never forgive me!"

"Great heavens, madam! what *has* he done?" asked the matter-of-fact Englishman.

What a keen probe that question was to the wife as she sat watching through the long, weary night! In an agony of self-reproach she recalled all that he had done for her and hers in all the years, and now in her turn she entreated *him* to live; but he was as unconscious as she had been in the blank past. No wooing, no pleading, could have been so potent as his unconscious form, his strength broken at last in her service.

"O God!" she cried—forgetting in her anguish that she had no God—"have I been more cruel than all the war? Have I given him the wound that shall prove fatal—him who saved Warren's life, my own, my reason, and everything that a woman holds dear?"

Graham's powerful and unvitiated nature soon rallied, however, and under the skilful treatment the fever within a few days gave place to the first deep happiness he had ever known. Grace was tender, considerate, her own former self, and with something sweeter to him than self-sacrifice in her eyes; and he gave himself up to an unspeakable content.

It was she who wrote the home letters that week, and a wondrous tale they told to the two old people, who subsisted on foreign news even more than on Aunt Sheba's delicate cookery.

Graham was soon out again, but he looked older and more broken than his wife, who seemingly had passed by age into a bloom that could not fade. She decided that for his sake they would pass the winter in Italy, and that he should show her again as a woman what he had tried to interest her in as a child. Her happiness, although often deeply shadowed, grew in its quiet depths. Graham had too much tact to be an ardent lover. He was rather her stanch friend, her genial but most considerate companion. His powerful human love at last kindled a quiet flame on the hearth of her own heart that had so long been cold, and her life was warmed and revived by it. He also proved in picture galleries and cathedrals that he had seen much when he was abroad beyond wild mountain regions and wilder people, and her mind, seemingly strengthened by its long sleep, followed his vigorous criticism with daily increasing zest.

The soft, sun-lighted air of Italy appeared to have a healing balm for both, and even to poor Grace there came a serenity which she had not known since the "cloud in the South" first cast its shadow over her distant hearth.

To Graham at last there had come a respite from pain and fear, a deep content. His inner life had been too impoverished, and his nature too chastened by stern and bitter experience, for him to crave gayety and exuberant sentiment in his wife. Her quiet face, in which now was the serenity of rest, and not the tranquillity of death in life, grew daily more lovely to him; and he was not without his human pride as he saw the beauty-loving Italians look wonderingly at her. She in turn was pleased to observe how he impressed cultivated people with his quiet power, with a presence that such varied experiences had combined to create. Among fine minds, men and women are more truly felt than seen. We meet people of the plainest appearance and most unostentatious manner, and yet without effort they compel us to recognize their superiority, while those who seek to impress others with their importance are known at once to be weak and insignificant.

It was also a source of deep gratification to Grace that now, since her husband had obtained rest of mind, he turned naturally to healthful business interests. Her own affairs, of which he had charge in connection with Hilland's lawyer, were looked after and explained fully to her; and his solicitude for Henry Anderson's success led to an exchange of letters with increasing frequency. Much business relating to the Virginia plantation was transacted on the shores of the Mediterranean.

Grace sought to quiet her compunctions at leaving her father and Mrs. Mayburn so long by frequent letters written in her dear old style, by cases of Italian wines, delicate and rare; exquisite fabrics of the loom, and articles of *vertu*; and between the letters and the gifts the old people held high carnival after their quaint fashion all that winter.

The soft Italian days lapsed one after another, like bright smiles on the face of nature; but at last there came one on which Grace leaned her head upon her husband's shoulder and whispered, "Alford, take me home, please."

Had he cared for her before, when she was as helpless as a little child? Jinny, in recalling that journey and in dilating on the wonders of her experience abroad, by which she invariably struck awe into the souls of Aunt Sheba and Iss, would roll up her eyes, and turn outward the palms of her hands, as she exclaimed, "Good Lor', you niggers, how I make you 'prehen' Mas'r Graham's goin's on from de night he sez, sez he ter me, 'Pack up, Jinny; we'se a-gwine straight home.' Iss 'clares dat Mas'r Graham's a ter'ble soger wid his long, straight sword and pistol, an' dat he's laid out more 'Federates dan he can shake a stick at. Well, you'd nebber b'lieve he'd a done wuss dan say, 'How d'ye' to a 'Federate ef yer'd seen how he 'volved roun' Missy Grace. He wouldn't let de sun shine on her, nor de win' blow near her, and eberybody had ter git right up an' git ef she eben wanted ter sneeze. On de ship he had eberybody, from de cap'n to de cabin-boys, a waitin' on her. Dey all said we hab a mighty quiet v'yage, but Lor' bress yer! it was all 'long ob Mas'r Graham. He wouldn't let no wabes run ter pitch his darlin' roun'. Missy Grace, she used ter sit an' larf an' larf at 'im—bress her dear heart, how much good it do me to hear de honey larf like her ole dear self! Her moder used ter be mighty keerful on her, but 'twan't nothin' 'pared ter Mas'r Graham's goin's on."

Jinny had never heard of Baron Munchausen, but her accounts of foreign experiences and scenes were much after the type of that famous *raconteur*; and by each repetition her stories seemed to make a portentous growth. There was, however, a residuum of truth in all her marvels. The event which she so vaguely foreshadowed by ever-increasing clouds of words took place. In June, when the nests around the cottage were full of little birds, there was also, in a downy, nest-like cradle, a miniature of sweet Grace Graham; and Jinny thenceforth was the oracle of the kitchen.

CHAPTER XL
RITA ANDERSON

The belief of children that babies are brought from heaven seems often verified by the experiences that follow their advent. And truly the baby at the St. John cottage was a heavenly gift, even to the crotchety old major, whom it kept awake at night by its unseasonable complaints of the evils which it encountered in spite of Grandma Mayburn, faithful old Aunt Sheba, who pleaded to be its nurse, and the gentle mother, who bent over it with a tenderness new and strange even to her heart.

She could laugh now, and laugh she would, when Graham, with a trepidation never felt in battle, took the tiny morsel of humanity, and paraded up and down the library. Lying back on the sofa in one of her dainty wrappers, she would cry, "Look at him, papa; look at that grim cavalryman, and think of his leading a charge!"

"Well, Gracie, dear," the old major would reply, chuckling at his well-worn joke, "the colonel was *only* a cavalryman, you know. He's not up in infantry tactics."

One morning Grandma Mayburn opened a high conclave in regard to the baby's name, and sought to settle the question in advance by saying, "Of course it should be Grace."

"Indeed, madam," differed the major, gallantly, "I think it should be named after its grandmother."

Grace lifted her eyes inquiringly to her husband, who stood regarding what to him was the Madonna and child.

"I have already named her," he said, quietly.

"You, you!" cried his aunt, brusquely. "I'd have you know that this is an affair for grave and general deliberation."

"Alford shall have his way," said the mother, with quiet emphasis, looking down at the child, while pride and tenderness blended sweetly in her face.

"Her name is Hilda, in memory of the noblest man and dearest friend I have ever known."

Instantly she raised her eyes, brimming with tears, to his, and faltered, "Thank you, Alford"; and she clasped the child almost convulsively to her breast, proving that there was one love which no other could obliterate.

"That's right, dear Grace. Link her name with the memory of Warren. She will thus make you happier, and it's my wish."

The conclave ended at once. The old major took off his spectacles to wipe his eyes, and Mrs. Mayburn stole away.

From that hour little Hilda pushed sorrow from Grace's heart with her baby hands, as nothing had ever done before, and the memory of the lost husband ceased to be a shadow in the background. The innocent young life was associated with his, and loved the more intensely.

Graham had spoken from the impulse of a generous nature, too large to feel the miserable jealousies that infest some minds; but he had spoken more wisely than he knew. Thereafter there was a tenderness in Grace's manner toward him which he had never recognized before. He tasted a happiness of which he had never dreamed, alloyed only by the thought that his treasures were mortal and frail. But as the little one thrived, and his wife bloomed into the most exquisite beauty seen in this world, that of young and happy motherhood, he gave himself up to his deep content, believing that fate at last was appeased. The major grew even hilarious, and had his morning and evening parades, as he called them, when the baby, in its laces and soft draperies, was brought for his inspection. Mrs. Mayburn, with all the accumulated maternal yearnings of her heart satisfied, would preside at the ceremony. Grace, happy and proud, would nod and smile over her shoulder at her husband, who made a poor pretence of reading his paper, while the old veteran deliberately adjusted his spectacles and made comments that in their solemn drollery and military jargon were irresistible to the household that could now laugh so easily. The young life that had come had brought a new life to them all, and the dark shadows of the past shrank further and further into the background.

But they were there—all the sad mysteries of evil that had crushed the mother's heart. Once they seemed to rush forward and close around her. Little Hilda was ill and Grace in terror. But Dr. Markham speedily satisfied her that it was a trivial matter, and proved it to be so by his remedies. The impression of danger remained, however, and she clung to her little idol more closely than ever; and this was true of all.

Time sped tranquilly on. Hilda grew in endearing ways, and began to have knowing looks and smiles for each. Her preference for her grandfather with his great frosty eyebrows pleased the old gentleman immensely. It was both droll and touching to observe how one often so irascible would patiently let her take off his spectacles, toy with and often pull his gray locks, and rumple his old-fashioned ruffles, which he persisted in wearing on state occasions. It was also silently noted that the veteran never even verged toward profanity in the presence of the child.

Each new token of intelligence was hailed with a delight of which natures coarse or blunted never know. The Wise Men of old worshipped the Babe in the manger, and sadly defective or perverted in their organizations are those who do not see something divine in a little innocent child.

Henry and Rita Anderson, at the urgent solicitation of Graham and his wife, came on in the autumn to make a visit, and, by a very strange coincidence, Graham's favorite captain, a manly, prosperous fellow, happened to be visiting him at the time. By a still more remarkable conjunction of events, he at once shared in his former colonel's admiration of the dark-eyed Southern girl. She was very shy, distant, and observant at first, for this fortuitous captain was a Northerner. But the atmosphere of the two cottages was not in the least conducive to coolness and reserve. The wood fires that crackled on the hearth, or something else, thawed perceptibly the spirited girl. Moreover, there were walks, drives, horseback excursions, daily; and Iss shone forth in a glory of which he had never dreamed as a plantation hand. There were light steps passing to and fro, light laughter, cheery, hearty voices—in which the baby's crowing and cooing were heard as a low, sweet chord—music and whist to the major's infinite consent. The shadows shrank further into the background than ever before. No one thought of or heeded them now; but they were there, cowering and waiting.

Only Aunt Sheba was ill at ease. Crooning her quaint lullabies to the baby, she would often lift her eyes to heaven and sigh, "De good Lord hab marcy on dem! Dey's all a drinkin' at de little shaller pools dat may dry up any minit. It's all ob de earth; it's all ob tings, nothin' but tings which de eyes can see and de han's can touch. De good Lord lift dar eyes from de earth widout takin' dat mos' dear!"

But no one thought of old Aunt Sheba except as a faithful creature born to serve them in her humble way.

The Northern captain soon proved that he had not a little Southern dash and ardor, and he had already discovered that his accidental visit to Graham was quite providential, as he had been taught to regard events that promised favorably. He very significantly asked Colonel Anderson to take a gallop with him one morning, but they had not galloped far before he halted and plumply asked the brother's permission, as the present representative of her father, to pay his addresses to Rita. Now Captain Windom had made a good impression on the colonel, which Graham, in a very casual way, had been at pains to strengthen; and he came back radiant over one point gained. But he was more afraid of that little Virginian girl than he had ever been of all her Southern compatriots. He felt that he must forego his cavalry tactics and open a regular siege; but she, with one flash of her mirthful eyes, saw through it all, laughed over it with Grace, whom from worshipping as a saint she now loved as a sister. Amid the pauses in their mutual worship of the baby, they talked the captain over in a way that would have made his ears tingle could he have heard them; but Grace, underneath all her good-natured criticism, seconded her husband's efforts with a mature woman's tact. Rita should be made happy in spite of all her little perversities and Southern prejudices, and yet the hands that guided and helped her should not be seen.

The captain soon abandoned his siege tactics, in which he was ill at ease, and resumed his old habit of impetuous advances in which Graham had trained him. Time was growing short. His visit and hers would soon be over. He became so downright and desperately in earnest that the little girl began to be frightened. It was no laughing matter now, and Grace looked grave over the affair. Then Rita began to be very sorry for him, and at last, through Graham's unwonted awkwardness and inattention to his guests, the captain and Rita were permitted to take a different road from the others on an equestrian party. When they appeared the captain looked as if he were returning from a successful charge, and Rita was as shy and blushing as one of the wild roses of her native hills. She fled to Grace's room, as if it were the only refuge left in the world, and her first breathless words were: "I haven't promised anything—that is, nothing definite. I said he might come and see me in Virginia and talk to papa about it, and I'd think it over, and—and—Well, he was so impetuous and earnest! Good heavens! I thought the Northern people were cold, but that captain fairly took away my breath. You never heard a man talk so."

Grace had put down the baby, and now stood with her arm around her friend, smiling the sweetest encouragement.

"I'll explain it all to you, Miss Rita," began Graham's deep voice, as he advanced from a recess.

"Oh, the powers! are you here?" and she started back and looked at him with dismay.

"Yes," said he, "and I merely wished to explain that my friend Windom was in the cavalry, and from much fighting with your brave, impetuous hard-riders we gradually fell into their habits."

"I half believe that you are laughing at me—that you are in league with him, and have been all along."

"Yes, Rita, noble little woman, truest friend at the time of my bitter need, I am in league with any man worthy of you—that is, as far as a man can be who seeks to make you happy;" and he took her hand and held it warmly.

"Here come my silly tears again," and she dashed them to right and left. Then, looking up at him shyly, she faltered, "I must admit that I'm a little bit happy."

"I vowed you should be, all through that dark ride on which you led me away from cruel enemies; and every flower you have placed on the grave of that noble man that Grace and I both loved has added strength to my vow."

"Oh, Rita, Rita, darling!" cried Grace, clasping her in close embrace; "do you think we ever forget it?"

"Can you think, Rita, that in memory of that never-to-be-forgotten day I would give Captain Windom the opportunities he has enjoyed if I did not think he would make you happy? One cannot live and fight side by side with a man for years and not know his mettle. He was lion-like in battle, but he will ever be gentleness itself toward you. Best of all, he will appreciate you, and I should feel like choking any fellow who didn't."

"But indeed, indeed, I haven't promised anything; I only said—"

"No matter what you said, my dear, so long as the captain knows. We are well assured that your every word and thought and act were true and maidenly. Let Windom visit you and become acquainted with your father. The more you all see of him the more you will respect him."

"You are wonderfully reassuring," said the young girl, "and I learned to trust you long ago. Indeed, after your course toward Henry, I believe I'd marry any one you told me to. But to tell the truth, I have felt, for the last few hours, as if caught up by a whirlwind and landed I don't know where. No one ever need talk to me any more about cold-blooded Northerners. Well, I must land at the dinner-table before long, and so must go and dress. It's proper to eat under the circumstances, isn't it?"

"I expect to," said Graham, laughing, "and I'm more in love than you are."

"Little wonder!" with a glance of ardent admiration toward Grace, and she whisked out. In a moment she returned and said, "Now, Colonel, I must be honest, especially as I think of your vow in the dark woods. I am very, *very* happy;" and then in a meteoric brilliancy of smiles, tears, and excitement, she vanished.

On the day following Captain Windom marched triumphantly away, and his absence proved to Rita that the question was settled, no matter what she had said when having little breath left to say anything.

She and her brother followed speedily, and Graham accompanied them, to superintend in person the setting up of a beautiful marble column which he and Grace had designed for Hilland's grave.

It was a time of sad, yet chastened, memories to both. In their consciousness Hilland had ceased to exist. He was but a memory, cherished indeed with an indescribable honor and love—still only a memory. There was an immense difference, however, in the thoughts of each as they reverted to his distant grave. Graham felt that he had there *closed* a chapter of his life—a chapter that he would ever recall with the deep melancholy that often broods in the hearts of the happiest of men whose natures are large enough to be truly impressed by life's vicissitudes. Grace knew that her girlhood, her former self, was buried in that grave, and with her early lover had vanished forever. Graham had, in a sense, raised her from the dead. His boundless love and self-sacrifice, his indomitable will, had created for her new life, different from the old, yet full of tranquil joys, new hopes and interests. He had not rent the new from the old, but had bridged with generous acts the existing chasm. He was doing all within his power, not jealously to withdraw her thoughts from that terrible past, but to veil its more cruel and repulsive features with flowers, laurel wreaths, and sculptured marble; and in her heart, which had been dead, but into which his love had breathed a new life, she daily blessed him with a deeper affection.

He soon returned to her from Virginia, and by his vivid descriptions made real to her the scenes he had visited. He told her how Rita and her brother had changed the plot in which slept the National and the Confederate officer into a little garden of blossoming greenery; how he had arranged with Colonel Anderson to place a fitting monument over the young Confederate officer, whose friends had been impoverished by the war; and he kissed away the tears, no longer bitter and despairing, evoked by the memories his words recalled. Then, in lighter vein, he described the sudden advent of the impetuous captain; the consternation of the little housekeeper, who was not expecting him so soon; her efforts to improvise a feast for the man who would blissfully swallow half-baked "pones" if served by her; her shy presentation of her lover to the venerable clergyman, which he and Henry had witnessed on the veranda through the half-closed blinds, and the fond old man's immense surprise that his little Rita should have a lover at all.

"My dear sir," he said, "this is all very premature. You must wait for the child to grow up before imbuing her mind with thoughts beyond her years."

"'My dear Dr. Anderson,' had pleaded the adroit Windom, 'I will wait indefinitely, and submit to any conditions that you and Miss Rita impose. If already she has impressed me so deeply, time can only increase my respect, admiration, and affection, if that were possible. Before making a single effort to win your daughter's regard, I asked permission of her brother, since you were so far away. I have not sought to bind her, but have only revealed the deep feeling which she has inspired, and I now come to ask your sanction also to my addresses.'

"'Your conduct,' replied the old gentleman, unbending urbanely toward the young man, 'is both honorable and considerate. Of course you know that my child's happiness is my chief solicitude. If, after several years, when Rita's mind has grown more mature, her judgment confirms—'

"Here Rita made a little *moue* which only her red lips could form, and Henry and I took refuge in a silent and precipitate retreat, lest our irreverent mirth should offend the blind old father, to whom Rita is his little Rita still. You know well how many years, months rather, Windom will wait.

"Well, I left the little girl happier than the day was long, for I believe her eyes sparkle all through the night under their long lashes. As for Windom, he is in the seventh heaven. 'My latest campaign in Virginia,' he whispered to me as I was about to ride away; 'good prospects of the best capture yet won from the Confederacy.'"

And so he made the place familiar to her, with its high lights and deep shadows, and its characters real, even down to old Jehu and his son Huey.

CHAPTER XLI
A LITTLE CHILD SHALL LEAD THEM

Autumn merged imperceptibly into winter, and the days sped tranquilly on. With the exception of brief absences on business, Graham was mostly at home, for there was no place like his own hearth. His heart, so long denied happiness, was content only at the side of his wife and child. The shadows of the past crouched further away than ever, but even their own health and prosperity, their happiness, and the reflected happiness of others could not banish them wholly. The lights which burned so brightly around them, like the fire on their hearth, had been kindled and were fed by human hands only, and were ever liable to die out. The fuel that kept them burning was the best that earth afforded, but the supply had its inherent limitations. Each new tranquil day increased the habitual sense of security. Graham was busy with plans of a large agricultural enterprise in Virginia. The more he saw of Henry Anderson the more he appreciated his sterling integrity and fine business capabilities, and from being an agent he had become a partner. Grace's writing-desk, at which Graham had cast a wistful glance the first time he had seen it, was often covered with maps of the Virginia plantation, which he proposed to develop into its best capabilities. Grace had a cradle by the library fire as well as in her room. Beside this the adopted grandmother knitted placidly, and the major rustled his paper softly lest he should waken the little sleeper. Grace, who persisted in making all of her little one's dainty plumage herself, would lift her eyes from time to time, full of genuine interest in his projects and in his plans for a dwelling on the plantation, which should be built according to her taste and constructed for her convenience.

The shadows had never been further away. Even old Aunt Sheba was lulled into security. Into her bereaved heart, as into the hearts of all the others, the baby crept; and she grew so bewitching with her winsome ways, so absorbing in her many little wants and her need of watching, as with the dawning spirit of curiosity she sought to explore for herself what was beyond the cradle and the door, that Aunt Sheba, with the doting mother, thought of Hilda during all waking hours and dreamed of her in sleep.

At last the inconstant New England spring passed away, and June came with its ever-new heritage of beauty. The baby's birthday was to be the grand fete of the year, and the little creature seemed to enter into the spirit of the occasion. She could now call her parents and grandparents by name, and talk to them in her pretty though senseless jargon, which was to them more precious than the wisdom of Solomon.

It was a day of roses and rose-colors. Roses banked the mantelpieces, wreathed the cradle, crowned the table at which Hilda sat in state in her high chair, a fairy form in gossamer laces, with dark eyes—Grace's eyes—that danced with the unrestrained delight of a child.

"She looks just like my little Grace of long, long years ago," said the major, with wistful eyes; "and yet, Colonel, it seems but yesterday that your wife was the image of that laughing little witch yonder."

"Well, I can believe," admitted Grandma Mayburn, "that Grace was as pretty—a tremendous compliment to you, Grace—but there never was and never will be another baby as pretty and cunning as our Hilda."

The good old lady never spoke of the child as Grace's baby. It was always "ours." In Graham, Grace, and especially Hilda, she had her children about her, and the mother-need in her heart was satisfied.

"Yes, Hilda darling," said the colonel, with fond eyes, "you have begun well. You could not please me more than by looking like your mother; the next thing is to grow like her."

"Poor blind papa, with the perpetual glamour on his eyes! He will never see his old white-haired wife as she is."

He looked at her almost perfect features with the bloom of health upon them, into her dark eyes with their depths of motherly pride and joy, at her snowy neck and ivory arms bare to the summer heat, and longest at the wavy silver of her hair, that crowned her beauty with an almost supernatural charm.

"Don't I see you as you are, Grace?" he said. "Well, I am often spellbound by what I do see. If Hilda becomes like you, excepting your sorrows, my dearest wish in her behalf will be fulfilled."

Old Aunt Sheba, standing behind the baby's chair, felt a chill at heart as she thought: "Dey'se all a-worshippin' de chile and each oder. I sees it so plain dat I'se all ob a-tremble."

Surely the dark shadows of the past have no place near that birthday feast, but they are coming nearer, closing in, remorseless, relentless as ever, and among them are the gloomy rivals against whom Graham struggled so long. He thought he had vanquished them, but they are stealing upon him again like vindictive, unforgiving savages.

There was a jar of thunder upon the still air, but it was not heeded. The room began to darken, but they thought only of a shower that would banish the sultriness of the day. Darker shadows than those of thunder-clouds were falling upon them, had they known it.

The wine was brought, and the health of the baby drank. Then Graham, ordering all glasses to be filled, said reverently: "To the memory of Warren Hilland! May the child who is named for him ever remind us of his noble life and heroic death."

They drank in silence, then put down the glasses and sat for moments with bowed heads, Grace's tears falling softly. Without, nature seemed equally hushed. Not a breath stirred the sultry air, until at last a heavier and nearer jar of thunder vibrated in the distance.

The unseen shadows are closing around the little Hilda, whose eyelids are heavy with satiety. Aunt Sheba is about to take her from her chair, when a swift gust, cold and spray-laden, rushes through the house, crushing to the doors and whirling all light articles into a carnival of disorder.

The little gossamer-clad girl shivered, and, while others hastily closed windows, Grace ran for a shawl in which to wrap her darling.

The shower passed, bringing welcome coolness. Hilda slept quietly through its turmoil and swishing torrents—slept on into the twilight, until Aunt Sheba seemed a shadow herself. But there were darker shadows brooding over her.

Suddenly, in her sleep, the child gave an ominous barking cough.

"Oh, de good Lor'!" cried Aunt Sheba, springing to her feet. Then with a swiftness in which there was no sign of age, she went to the landing and called, "Mas'r Graham."

Grace was in the room before him. "What is it?" she asked breathlessly.

"Well, Missy Grace, don't be 'larmed, but I tinks Mas'r Graham 'ud better sen' for de doctor, jes' for caution like."

Again came that peculiar cough, terror-inspiring to all mothers.

"Alford, Alford, lose not a moment!" she cried. "It's the croup."

The soldier acted as if his camp were attacked at midnight. There were swift feet, the trampling of a horse; and soon the skill of science, the experience of age, and motherly tenderness confronted the black shadows, but they remained immovable.

The child gasped and struggled for life. Grace, half frantic, followed the doctor's directions with trembling hands, seeking to do everything for her idol herself as far as possible. Mrs. Mayburn, gray, grim, with face of ashen hue, hovered near and assisted. Aunt Sheba, praying often audibly, proved by her deft hands that the experience of her long-past motherhood was of service now. The servants gathered at the door, eager and impatient to do something for "de bressed chile." The poor old major thumped restlessly back and forth on his crutches in the hall below, half swearing, half praying. Dr. Markham, pale with anxiety, but cool and collected as a veteran general in battle, put forth his whole skill to baffle the destroyer. Graham, standing in the background with clenched hands, more excited, more desperate than he had ever been when sitting on his horse waiting for the bugle to sound the charge, watched his wife and child with eyes that burned in the intensity of his feeling.

Time, of which no notice was taken, passed, although moments seemed like hours. The child still struggled and gasped, but more and more feebly. At last, in the dawn, the little Hilda lay still, looked up and smiled. Was it at her mother's face, or something beyond?

"She is better," cried Grace, turning her imploring eyes to the physician, who held the little hand.

Alas! it was growing cold in his. He turned quickly to Graham and whispered: "Support your wife. The end is near."

He came mechanically and put his arm around her.

"Grace, dear Grace," he faltered, hoarsely, "can you not bear this sorrow also for my sake?"

"Alford!" she panted with horror in her tones—"Alford! why, why, her hand is growing cold!"

There was a long low sigh from the little one, and then she was still.

"Take your wife away," said Dr. Markham, in a low, authoritative tone.

Graham sought to obey in the same mechanical manner. She sprang from him and stood aloof. There was a terrible light in her eyes, before which he quailed.

"Take me away!" she cried, in a voice that was hoarse, strained, and unnatural. "Never! Tell me the belief of your heart. Have I lost my child forever? Is that sweet image of my Hilda nothing but clay? Is there nothing further for this idol of my heart but horrible corruption? If this is true, no more learned jargon to me about law and force! If this is true, I am the creation of a fiend who, with all the cruel ingenuity of a fiend, has so made me that he can inflict the utmost degree of torture. If this is true, my motherhood is a lie, and good is punished, not evil. If this is true, there is neither God nor law, but only a devil. But let me have the truth: have I lost that child forever?"

He was dumb, and an awful silence fell upon the chamber of death.

Graham's philosophy failed him at last. His own father-heart could not accept of corruption as the final end of his child. Indeed, it revolted at it with a resistless rebound as something horrible, monstrous, and, as his wife had said, devilish. His old laborious reasoning was scorched away as by lightning in that moment of intense consciousness when *his* soul told him that, if this were true, his nature also was a lie and a cheat. He knew not what he believed, or what was true. He was stunned and speechless.

Despair was turning his wife's face into stone, when old Aunt Sheba, who had been crouching, sobbing and praying at the foot of the little couch, rose with streaming eyes and stretched out her hands toward the desperate mother.

"No, Missy Grace," she cried, in tones that rang through the house; "no, no, no. Your chile am not lost to you; your chile am not dead. She on'y sleeps. Did not de good Lord say: 'Suffer de little chillen ter come unter Me'? An' Hilda, de dear little lamb, hab gone ter Him, an' is in de Good Shepherd's arms. Your little chile am not lost to you, she's safe at home, de dear bressed home ob heben, whar your moder is Missy Grace. De Hebenly Father say, 'Little Hilda, you needn't walk de long flinty, thorny path and suffer like you'se dear moder. You kin come home now, and I'se 'll take keer ob ye till moder comes.' Bress de little lamb, she smile when de angels come fer her, an' she's safe, safe for ebermore. No tears fer little Hilda, no heartbreak in all her 'ternal life. Dear Missy Grace, my little baby die, too, but I hain't los' it. No, no. De Good Shepherd is a keepin' it safe fer me, an' I shall hab my baby again."

It is impossible to describe the effect of this passionate utterance of faith as it came warm and direct from the heart of another bereaved mother, whose lowliness only emphasized the universal human need of something more than negations and theories of law and force. The major heard it in the hall below, and was awed. Mrs. Mayburn and the servants sobbed audibly. The stony look went out of Grace's face; tears welled up into her hot, dry eyes, and she drew near and bent over her child with an indescribable yearning in her face. Aunt Sheba ceased, sank down on the floor, and throwing her apron over her face she rocked back and forth and prayed as before.

Suddenly Grace threw herself on the unconscious little form, and cried with a voice that pierced every heart: "O God, I turn to Thee, then. Is my child lost to me forever, or is she in Thy keeping? Was my mother's faith true? Shall I have my baby once more? Jesus, art Thou a Shepherd of the little ones? Hast Thou suffered my Hilda to come unto Thee? Oh, if Thou art, Thou canst reveal Thyself unto me and save a broken-hearted mother from despair. This child *was* mine. Is it mine still?" and she clasped her baby convulsively to her bosom.

"Suffer de little chillen ter come unter me, and forbid dem not,'" repeated Aunt Sheba in low tones.

Again a deep, awed silence fell upon them all. Grace knelt so long with her own face pressed against her child's that they thought she had fainted. The physician motioned Graham to lift her up, but he shook his head. He was crushed and despairing, feeling that in one little hour he had lost the belief of his manhood, the child that had brought into his home a heaven that he at least could understand, and as he heard his wife's bitter cry he felt that her life and reason might soon go also. He recognized again the presence of his bitter rivals, Grief and Death, and felt that at last they had vanquished him. He had not the courage or the will to make another effort.

"Mrs. Graham, for your husband's sake—" began Dr. Markham.

"Ah! forgive me, Alford," she said, rising weakly; "I should not have forgotten you for a moment."

She took an uncertain step toward him, and he caught her in his arms.

Laying her head upon his breast, she said gently, "Alford, our baby is not dead."

"Oh, Grace, darling!" he cried in agony, "don't give way, or we are both lost. I have no strength left. I cannot save you again. Oh! if the awful past should come back!"

"It now can never come back. Alford, we have not lost our child. Aunt Sheba has had a better wisdom than you or I, and from this hour forth my mother's faith is mine. Do not think me wild or wandering. In my very soul has come the answer to my cry. Horrible corruption is not the end of that lovely life. You can't believe it, any more than I. Dear little sleeper, you are still *my* baby. I shall go to you, and you will never suffer as I have suffered. God bless you, Aunt Sheba! your heaven-inspired words have saved me from despair. Alford, dear Alford, do not give way so; I'll live and be your true and faithful wife. I'll teach you the faith that God has taught me."

He drew long, deep breaths. He was like a great ship trying to right itself in a storm. At last he said, in broken tones:

"Grace, you are right. It's not law or force. It's either God, who in some way that I can't understand, will bring good out of all this evil, or else it's all devilish, fiendish. If after this night you can be resigned, patient, hopeful, your faith shall be mine."

The shadows, affrighted, shrank further away than ever before. "I take you at your word," she replied, as she drew him gently away. "Come, let us go and comfort papa."

One after another stole out after them until Mrs. Mayburn was alone with the dead. Long and motionless she stood, with her eyes fixed on the quiet, lovely face.

"Hilda," at last she moaned, "little Hilda, shall poor old grandma ever see our baby again?"

At that moment the sun rose high enough to send a ray through the lattice, and it lighted the baby's face with what seemed a smile of unearthly sweetness.

A few moments later Aunt Sheba found the aged woman with her head upon little Hilda's bosom, and there she received a faith that brought peace.

A few evenings later there was a grassy mound, covered with roses, under the apple-tree by the rustic seat; and at the head of the little grave there was placed a block of marble bearing the simple inscription:

"Here sleeps our Baby Hilda."

Years have passed. The little monument is now near another and a stately one in a Virginia cemetery. Fresh flowers are on it, showing that "Our Baby Hilda" is never forgotten. Fresh flowers are beneath the stately column, proving that the gallant soldier sleeping under it is never forgotten. Fresh flowers are on the young Confederate's grave, commemorating a manly and heroic devotion to a cause that was sacred to him. The cause was lost; and had he lived to green old age he would have thanked God for it. Not least among the reasons for thankfulness is the truth that to men and peoples that which their hearts craved is often denied.

Not far away is a home as unostentatious as the Northern cottage, but larger, and endowed with every homelike attribute. Sweet Grace Graham is its mistress. Her lovely features are somewhat marked by time and her deep experiences, but they have gained a beauty and serenity that will defy time. Sounds of joyous young life again fill the house, and in a cradle by her side "little Grace" is sleeping. Grandma Mayburn still knits slowly by the hearth, but when the days are dry and warm it is her custom to steal away to the cemetery and remain for hours with "Our Baby." The major has grown very feeble, but his irritable protest against age and infirmity has given place to a serene, quiet waiting till he can rest beside the brave soldiers who have forgotten their laurels.

Colonel Anderson, now a prosperous planter, has his own happy home life, and his aged father shares the best there is in it. He still preaches in the quaint old church, repaired but not modernized, and his appearance and life give eloquence to his faltering words. The event of the quiet year is the annual visit of Rita and Captain Windom with their little brood. Then truly the homes abound in breezy life; but sturdy, blue-eyed Warren Graham is the natural leader of all the little people's sport. The gallant black horse Mayburn is still Iss's pride, but he lets no one mount him except his master. Aunt Sheba presides at the preparation of state dinners, and sits by the cradle of baby Grace. She is left, however, most of the time, to her own devices, and often finds her way also to the cemetery to "wisit dat dear little lamb, Hilda," murmuring as she creeps slowly with her cane, "We'se all a-followin' her now, bress de Lord."

Jinny's stories of what she saw and of her experiences abroad have become so marvellous that they might be true of some other planet, but not of ours. Dusky faces gather round her by the kitchen fire, and absolute faith is expressed by their awed looks. Old Jehu has all the chickens and "sass" he wants without working for them, and his son Huey has settled down into a steady "hand," who satisfies his former ruling passion with an occasional coon-hunt. Both of the colonels have the tastes of sportsmen, and do all in their power to preserve the game in their vicinity. They have become closer friends with the lapsing years, and from crossing swords they look forward to the time when they can cross their family escutcheons by the marriage of the sturdy Warren with another little Rita, who now romps with him in a child's happy unconsciousness.

There are flecks of gray in Graham's hair and beard, and deep lines on his resolute face, but he maintains his erect, soldierly bearing even when superintending the homely details of the plantation. Every one respects him; the majority are a little afraid of him, for where his will has sway there is law and order, but to the poor and sorrowful he gives increasing reason to bless his name. His wife's faith has become his. She has proved it true by the sweet logic of her life. In their belief, the baby Hilda is only at home before them, and the soldier without fear and without reproach has found the immortality that he longed for in his dying moments. He is no longer a cherished, honored memory only; he is the man they loved, grown more manly, more noble in the perfect conditions of a higher plane of life. The dark mysteries of evil are still dark to them—problems that cannot be solved by human reason. But in the Divine Man, toward whose compassionate face the sorrowful and sinful of all the centuries have turned, they have found One who has mastered the evil that threatened their lives. They are content to leave the mystery of evil to Him who has become in their deepest consciousness Friend and Guide. He stands between them and the shadows of the past and the future.